VIRTUAL IMMORTALITY

MATTHEW S. COX

DIVISION ZERO PRESS

ISBN (ebook): 978-1-949174-56-4

ISBN (print): 978-1-949174-57-1

CONTENTS

RESTLESS

Ephemeral rectangles of light drifted across the ceiling in a silent ballet. The sporadic whine of passing hovercars drowned the faint whisper of Nina's breath. Along the north wall, floor-to-ceiling glass allowed the glow of the city in. The intruding light imparted a spectral radiance to her white bedclothes and left the far reaches of the room darker by contrast, detail lost in a mass of indistinct shadows. Tiny, flickering spots winked from various unseen devices.

Time drew to an agonizing stall. No distraction she tried to force into her mind kept her from worrying about her meeting with Lieutenant Oliver in a few short hours. Nothing good ever came of Division 0, and she couldn't understand why they wanted to meet. Nix, the old stuffed pink rabbit on her pillow, had more psionic ability than she did. They couldn't intend to recruit her, which left only one possibility—someone wanted them to go rooting around in her mind. Her growing anxiety kept sleep at bay.

She teased at the smooth fabric of her pajamas while the Comforgel pad beneath her cycled among subdued blues and violets. To her right, two silver bars atop the nightstand detected her gaze upon them and came to life. The smaller one made a faint noise as a panel of holographic light opened like a window shade above it. The sound lurked just beyond the reach of the human ear, a presence one couldn't claim to hear as much as feel. Flecks of dust glinted from inside the spectral image of Nina's parents. Her weary smile came as a reflex, but fell flat as the other bar shimmered with green light.

Floating numbers taunted her with 03:03.

Desperate to find sleep, Nina tried to convince herself that the interview was an opportunity. It might be the first step of her transfer to Division 2. It had been more than two years since she graduated University and joined the force. Everyone knew she disliked Division 1. She hated street patrol.

With a growl of frustration, she threw the covers off and sat on the edge of the bed. The Comforgel shifted to a soft red as it tried to compensate for lost warmth. For several minutes, she teased a clump of carpet lint with her toe before trudging over to the windows. Her reflection focused a restless gaze back from under jet-black hair that hung to her shoulders. It had been down to her waist in school, another in a long list of things she had given up for the job she wanted. Her pajamas draped loose on her frame, as though she had raided an older sister's wardrobe.

Nina stared through her ghost at the city beyond, watching hovercars dart around each other three floors below like a swarm of mice in a maze. Watching the city often helped her relax. Millions of people, all with their own problems, made hers seem trivial by comparison. The never-quite-dark of West City offered no solace tonight, the world rendered a meaningless blur by her sleepless haze.

She gave up on the window and flopped across the bed. Within seconds, the pad adjusted to her shape and she snuggled into the bedding with a half-contented moan. Her father's voice whispered in the back of her mind, chiding her for throwing away her status for a 'job.' His plan would have been less stressful. The Duchenne family wealth could keep her comfortable, but oh so bored. A call to Vincent would cheer her up, though she didn't want to wake him. With each agonizing minute, her regret at passing on his offer to spend the night increased.

Solitude felt like a bad idea in retrospect. It left her with nothing but her thoughts and the squares of light that slid across the grey above her.

A pale waif wrapped in rose-pink cloth, she sprawled on the bed like a rag doll. Her hair fanned out across the silk while her gaze chased random lights across the ceiling. Not since finals week had so much anxiety shared her bed. She pictured Vincent's tan skin, and the wry smile he always made, as if privy to humor no one else knew about.

Unlike the rest of her unit, he didn't make a habit of teasing her about her size or desire to be a tech. She had been the victim of several pranks during her first weeks, some silly and some cruel. He volunteered as her partner after Officer Alvin locked her in a trash processing unit and went on patrol alone.

She got his message—he would rather have no partner at all than ride with her.

Vincent treated her well, if not overprotectively, and he always seemed to showboat to impress her. Whatever it was that he did, it worked. Nina had been paired with him for a month shy of two years, and their relationship had gone far beyond a working one. She hadn't yet been able to break the news to her father that she wanted to marry someone 'below her station,' as he would say. That could wait until after Vincent popped the question. Nina almost looked forward to the argument. Her eyes closed as she rolled into the sheets, thinking about Vincent.

A digitized cacophony jogged her awake—her NetMini announcing an incoming call. Nina's mind floated, absent any sense of the passage of time. One eye popped open, staring at the palm-sized slab of technology on her nightstand. Vibration accompanied the ringer, causing the NetMini to creep toward the edge. Heaviness permeated her limbs, making movement arduous. She rolled away from the pestering electronic device and curled into a ball. A fleeting moment of comfort passed before the beeping turned to banging and pulled her brain back from the precipice of sleep yet again. After a futile attempt to ignore it, she realized the banging wasn't in her head, but at her door. Anger shoved her into a seated position. She glared out from under a curtain of hair, already composing what she would scream at whoever dared bother her.

Sunlight flooded the apartment. Morning had snuck in during her fleeting nap. She lifted her arm to block the sun and cast a pleading look to her nightstand. The holographic clock again mocked her: 06:45. Now wide-awake, she ran to the door. It slid to the side with a faint squeak as she slapped the panel. Vincent waved. After planting a hasty kiss on the faceplate of his helmet, she ran to the rear of the apartment without a word.

"Good"—He blinked as she ran right out of her pajamas and disappeared down the hall —"morning."

The garments hadn't even floated to the carpet when a distant door slammed. Vincent removed his helmet and set it on the table, stretching his arms while wandering about. Scratches and scuffs across the otherwise shiny blue armor gave away the five-year tenure of his assignment. He often told Nina he liked patrol division because it kept him close to the people he wanted to help. The sound of the shower unit starting up rumbled through the wall, and he paced. His boots thunked as he moved, despite the indigo carpet and his attempt to be considerate to the downstairs neighbor.

"You ok?" he yelled.

"Crap, what time is it?"

"If anyone else was driving, you'd be late." He laughed and grabbed his helmet. "I'll be out front."

Despite living here his entire life, Vincent still found the expanse of West City an impressive sight to behold from a high-up perch within a glass bubble elevator. Hurtling without sound along a magnetic track on the outside of the building, it carried him down into the rising grasp of the city. Shimmering towers of steel and glass devoured the horizon, until the sounds of the street-level flooded the compartment, mixing with the life-sucking noise that tried to pass itself off as music. By the time he reached the street, the sky had vanished behind nearby buildings, floating advert bots, and a steady stream of pedestrian traffic. Even unoccupied, Vincent's patrol craft seemed to scare civilians into giving it a wide berth.

Dark blue and white, the vehicle was half again the length and width of an average car. Armor shrouded its four ground wheels and numerous pods bulged from here and there with sensor and communication equipment. The gull-wing door opened upward with a pneumatic hiss as it sensed Vincent's transponder approaching. He dropped into the driver's position but left the door up and one leg hanging out, watching people go by.

NINA STOOD IN THE CLEAR TUBE OF THE SHOWER UNIT, TAPPING HER FINGER ON THE plastic shield in an impatient beat as a mixture of cleaning agent and warm water sprayed from the orbiting jets. She held her arms over her head and turned to allow the machine to clean her. When the water stopped, she grabbed the handrail. Someone had mistuned the dry cycle, and she didn't fancy being blown off her feet again as the dry cycle was stuck on a setting too powerful for someone her size. Cringing, she struggled to keep her toes in contact with the floor against the gale.

Her weight settled back onto her feet as the fans died down, and she sprinted from the bathroom.

She ignored the frigid air and slapped the button to open the cabinet. In less than a minute, she was dressed and armored. Nina checked her UCF MP21 on the elevator down, flipping the switch to the ready position. Blue LEDs lit up above the trigger in sequence before it chirped and clicked as a caseless round moved into the firing chamber. Every morning she hoped she would make it through another day without needing it. After flicking the safety on, she slipped the gun into its holster and tapped her foot until the door let her sprint out across the courtyard.

He started driving before the door closed. Nina sagged in the seat and stared at Vincent's smirk with the accusatory glare of someone left out of a joke. He pulled back on the control sticks and the road fell out of view below the hood. Nina was thankful at having overslept and not eaten anything yet—the maneuver would have left her breakfast all over her boots. Vincent drove recklessly enough when he wasn't rushing. The car pivoted up at a sharp angle, and the acceleration crushed her into the seat with enough force to make breathing difficult for several seconds.

She stared at his stupid grin. "What?"

"I'm just happy to see you."

They edged past three hundred miles per hour, and the civilian traffic below them changed from individual objects into a stream of color.

"Bullshit."

She narrowed her eyes, smiling, finding it difficult to sound menacing with a two-handed grip on the "oh shit" handle. He allowed the patrol craft to settle in at a beyond-casual 275 mph and flipped the bar lights on, but left the siren off.

"You'll get pissed."

"It'll piss me off more if I have to find out on my own." She cringed through a hard sweeping left turn.

"It was the way you came running down the steps with your helmet in your hands." He winked. "You looked like a kid dressed up as a cop for Halloween."

Even after two years, short jokes still got a rise out of her.

"How—"

The remaining "could you" changed into an unladylike combination of noises as a sudden loss of altitude and speed caused her stomach to upend itself.

"You really should keep your mouth closed for those kinds of maneuvers, hon."

As soon as she felt safe enough to let go, she punched him twice in the shoulder. He laughed harder, and she hit him a third time before pouting out the window. Every so often, a line of static appeared in the "glass." The car had seen its share of rough and tumble, and the system that turned inch-thick armor plates into windows had the occasional glitch. From him, she took it as the friendly poke it was meant to be, but no one else took her seriously as a police officer.

Even Nina didn't take Nina seriously as a cop.

The past two years had been an uneventful drudgery of patrols in quiet sectors. Everyone knew the captain gave them a cushy route. Nina landed in Division 1 only because the regulations demanded it. She didn't want to be a patrol officer. Vincent knew it, too, and she loved him more for not complaining about the easy ride.

She grabbed the 'oh shit' handle hard enough to numb her hand. "Vince! Vince! Vince!"

The parking deck of the police complex came in fast—too fast. She would have pointed if she could have let go.

He rolled the car upside down and slammed on the lateral thrusters, sending it into a sliding sideways arc across the parking garage. They careened along the ceiling before a spiral roll around a column dropped them into an open parking space amid a sea of ionized fog and coolant fumes.

He leaned over and kissed her sweaty forehead. "Two minutes to spare."

Embedded in the seat, she had stopped breathing, and her lips curled into a creepy grin. Her darkening eyes tried to burn the side of his head.

For a minute, the car remained silent, save the sound of her gasping breath.

"Was it going from 250 to stop in four seconds or the sideways spinning across the ceiling that bothered you?" He sounded as calm as if he were discussing which wrapping paper to use. "If you don't get moving you'll be late for your meeting."

The bubbling mixture of fear and anger exploded into panic as the dread of Division 0 wiped away the thought of their almost-crash. She kicked the door open and tore off through the parking garage. Vincent put his feet up and laced his fingers behind his head, grinning as the echoing footfalls of her boots grew faint.

2

ZERO HOPE

Nina hurried past the bustling Division 1 command area, ignoring a handful of patronizing comments from her squad. The din continued in the central hub of the police complex, but subsided to quiet once she reached the Division 0 wing. The clear, sliding doors closed behind her, and the onset of an eerie silence distracted her from her worries.

At the end of the hall, a pleasant looking red-haired woman in a neat black uniform sat behind a desk. Nina approached, feeling as if she had strayed into the wrong part of the building and braced for a scolding. Before she could open her mouth, the woman spoke.

"Good morning, Officer Duchenne. Lieutenant Oliver is down the hall to the left, fifth door."

Nina's eyes widened with fright as she wondered if her mind had just been read. She tried to say something but managed only a weak gasp.

The redhead lifted her gaze to look Nina in the eye.

"There is only one appointment today with a patrol officer, and your name is on your armor. We don't always have to read minds." She flashed a wry smile glancing once more at her terminal.

Nina composed herself and soon arrived in front of one of many jet-black doors set into a featureless grey hallway. *Great start; offend their front-desk person.* A series of clear triangular panels extended from the walls every fifteen feet, their edges glowing with intense light that sprayed onto the ceiling. A little further down, a few plain black chairs stood silent guard over a fake plant nestled among them.

Tall, silver letters on a black tile next to the door spelled out 'Lieutenant N. Oliver'. She knocked with two soft taps.

"Lieutenant Oliver?"

She closed her eyes after she spoke, hoping she hadn't sounded too squeaky.

"Come in."

The door slid open, revealing a room smaller than she expected. A gloss black desk dominated the area in the center, flanked by shelves on both sides that held an array of data pads, small faux plants, and other decorative objects. Lieutenant Oliver appeared to be in his late thirties with short close-cropped black hair and tanned skin. Thick eyebrows hung above his dark brown eyes, and his entire presence conveyed calm encouragement.

"Officer Nina Duchenne reporting, Sir."

"Lieutenant Nathaniel Oliver. Pleased to meet you." He stood, extending a hand. Her arm moved out of numb reflex, offering a limp version of a shake. He gestured at a chair. "Please, have a seat."

Nina settled into the chair and stared at the little bonsai tree on the edge of the desk. She couldn't help but feel like a schoolgirl sent to the principal's office. Oliver looked at her for a moment with an expression that radiated a peculiar combination of calm and intensity.

"First, please relax. I want you to know that this meeting is not any form of disciplinary action." Lt. Oliver smiled his most reassuring smile, speaking in a relaxing tone Nina hadn't expected.

"What? I mean, why did you..." Her nervousness peaked one last time, stealing her voice.

He shifted and leaned forward.

"Your commanding officer, Captain Farris, had some concerns regarding your well-being. He asked me to meet with you—unofficially—as a favor."

"Okay..." Nina's anxiety took flight on a strong exhale as she settled in to the cushions.

"It seems you are under an unusual amount of stress. Captain Farris and I are concerned about it. These past few weeks, you've been increasingly terse and confrontational. I have done some poking around, and it seems that there are issues within your squad. Yet I find no record of disciplinary action or complaints from you. Is there anything you would like to get off your chest?"

Nina picked at the helmet in her lap. "It was only supposed to be two years..."

"What was?" Oliver sat back and propped his chin up on his fingertips.

She sighed. "Div 1. The whole unit knows that I'm only over there because of the man-two."

"I see." Oliver nodded. "You feel the policy requiring all rookies to pull a two-year tour in Division 1 is unfair?"

"Yes." Nina nodded. "Look at me...I'm five-four, maybe a hundred pounds soaking wet... I have a BS in forensic science... second in my class!" Her face flushed. "It's a waste of resources to put someone like me out in a patrol craft."

Oliver opened his mind, sensing her emotion. "You feel it's beneath you?"

Indignation.

"No... I don't, I'm not like my father. I'm..."

Sadness.

"...not built for this kind of work, my education is not being used, and..." She looked off to the side at the floor.

Fear.

"Go on. What is frightening you?"

Anger.

"It's bad enough that I could get killed at any time by some ganger or criminal, but I'm just as worried the other cops are going to let me die or lock me in some cabinet again."

Loneliness.

"I feel isolated out there, like I have no backup. They'd leave me to die. Everyone but Vincent."

Love.

Nina paused. "Wait... scared? I'm not..." Nina's eyes locked onto his rank insignia—a matte black strip with a thick 0 next to a lieutenant's bar.

They're all psionic. Is he in my brain?

Terror.

Oliver held up his hands. "Ms. Duchenne, please relax. You have nothing to fear from me. Please, tell me about... Officer Montoya is it?"

Devotion.

Nina relaxed, thinking about him. "He doesn't treat me like an unwanted kid hanging out at her father's job." She hung her head. "Even other female officers have it in for me. In the locker room..."

Shame.

"I have a feeling I know what is going on, Ms. Duchenne. Their attitudes are driven primarily by fear."

One didn't have to be an empath like Lt. Oliver to read the emotion from Nina's face at that comment. "Fear? Of me? Are you serious?"

He chuckled. "Not fear *of* you, Nina. Is it okay if I call you Nina?"

She frowned at the wall. "Sure... umm, sir."

"It's fear of how you will react in a dangerous situation. With all due respect, your goal is to be reassigned to Division 2, forensics specifically. That is a rear echelon position that does not encounter hostile situations. I believe that the other officers have not come to trust you in the field."

Nina glanced at the rug. She didn't trust *herself* in the field, and she knew full well how the other cops felt. "Yeah..." was all she could muster.

The rear wall glowed with different colors as he perused her file on his holo-terminal. "Your aptitude tests were astounding. Your physical was okay... agility and coordination scores were impressive, strength and endurance well..."

"Yeah, I know. I was meant to be a decoration on the arm of a wealthy idiot."

"Your family is quite comfortable."

Nina glared. "That has nothing to do with..." Her mouth outran her brain. "My father didn't pay anyone off. If he did, I would have gone right to Div 2 without this bullshit."

He made a fanning motion. "Whoa, whoa, slow down."

The sudden spike of anger caused him to make a note in her file. "We can talk about your father later if you would like to."

"It's a month and a week past two years. My application for Division 2 is just sitting in cyberspace. Does it usually take this long? Does the brass think I'm a joke too?" She hissed air past clenched teeth, trying not to cry in front of him. Tears worked on Daddy. Here, they would mark her as weak.

Oliver rubbed his chin with a lone finger as his eyes fixed upon the little woman who sat across from him. She seemed eager to get out of Division 1 and was quite miserable there, but not miserable enough to quit. At the thought of passing the two-year mark, she broke out in a cold sweat. He sensed more to it than a desire to climb the career ladder. She was terrified of getting hurt. Fear seeped from her like fog from dry ice.

"Well, I am not personally involved in that process. Zero does things a little differently than the rest of the force." He flashed an offbeat smile, which seemed to unsettle her more. "Nina, no one is going to mess with your mind. I am an empath, not a telepath."

"An empath?" She clung to the helmet in her lap.

"Most people don't care to understand the subtle differences in psionic talents. Those who specialize in reading the minds of others are telepaths. My gift is based on emotion rather than thought. I can feel what other people feel and understand what their emotional state is. Like most of us, I have a degree of telepathic talent, but it is not my strongest ability."

NINA SHIFTED IN HER SEAT. MANY CITIZENS, HERSELF INCLUDED, FEARED PSIONICS regardless of what they could do.

"I can tell you are frightened right now." He tried his most relaxing voice. "I could make you feel calm and at ease if I wanted to, but that would be unethical." He paused to smile. "Division 0 was formed to deal with psionic criminals. Fight fire with fire, you know. We are the good guys."

Nina tried to relax. In a way, Lieutenant Nathaniel Oliver was a fellow officer, just in a unit that everyone spoke about in whispers and avoided whenever possible.

"I heard that Div 0 only got acknowledged after they got exposed, that they'd been around for a long time before that, but no one knew."

She cringed inside for daring to say that, but his unexpected laughter stunned her.

"I wasn't around back then, so I cannot say for sure. Anything is possible I suppose, considering we still try to keep a low profile to avoid creating panic. There really isn't a need for the entire citizenry to become experts on psionic matters." He leaned forward, smiling. "Tell me, what do you think about the other officers' opinion of you?"

"I don't hold it against them. I know I'm not soldier material. I want to use my education, not run around the city with a gun." She felt a lump climbing her throat. "It's just so hard to go out there when you wonder if that backup you call for will actually show up." She paused before her emotion showed in her voice, but after a minute let out a defeated whisper. "I just want to move on before I get someone hurt."

Is he doing something to me? I never even admitted that to Mom.

He listened, typing and nodding.

"If it's true that they don't like me because they think I'm just here for the paycheck and I don't care about being a cop, they're wrong. I do care about being a cop, just not *this* kind of cop."

Awkward silence lingered for a moment while he finished entering a thought.

"The two-year policy was put in place years ago when the roster was very thin. They had everyone rushing for spots with 5 and 6. It may be time to reconsider that policy, but a decision like that would have to come from way above my pay grade." He laughed. "I do think that there is an issue of trust here on both sides… and you are correct in that it could get someone hurt. My opinion, and it's one that I will share with Captain Farris, is that you should fly a desk for a while until your transition goes through."

She nodded. "That's okay. I can deal with a desk. I'm no glory hound. Wait, did you say there were *too many* volunteers for Division 5?"

"Yes, if you can believe it." He whistled. "Most were high-testosterone adrenaline junkies looking to get their hands on large weapons."

"But they send D5 after *cyborgs*." She shivered.

He stood up and extended a hand to her. "I think we're about done for now. You may have to deal with another day or two of patrol detail until Farris can get the proverbial paperwork in motion. Can you handle that?"

Nina grinned. The thought of an imminent move to Division 2 turned on a light at the end of a lengthy, exhausting tunnel. She all but bounced out of her chair to shake hands with the man whom, moments ago, she feared would melt her mind.

"No problem, sir." She didn't know whether to shake hands or salute him.

Oliver laughed. "You are the first person I have ever seen happy about being put on desk duty."

3

TWO MORE DAYS

Officer Eddie Alvin was a big guy. Six and a half feet tall and broad-shouldered, he had won the Division 1 regional weightlifting competition four years running in the un-augmented class. He sauntered out from behind a desk into Nina's path, disturbing her good mood.

"Well, well, what's got Princess Nina so happy?"

Nina's usual reaction would have been to go back the way she came. Today, she felt an upwelling of courage borne on the wings of her imminent transfer. She stopped in front of him, sighed, and looked up into his condescending glare. The last time she rolled up on him like that, she wound up locked in an armor cabinet for three hours, unable to move in the person-shaped space.

"Morning, Eddie." Nina folded her arms. "The way I see it, there's one of two things going on here. One, either you've got about an inch and a half of dick left after all the Synroids you've taken and you need to give a little woman like me a hard time to impress yourself, or you are a truly dedicated cop who thinks I'm a liability who'll get someone hurt."

Alvin blinked in disbelief at the sudden bravado. The liability bit had been on everyone's mind for months, but no one had ever had the balls to say it to her. Hearing Nina say it stunned the whole squad into silence. He glared. He hadn't heard anything after the dick joke, failing to notice the backhanded compliment.

"I won't be in your way much longer. My transfer is about to finalize, so I'll be elbow-deep in maggots soon enough. Of course, if you're still blocking me because of the penis-size issue, just stuff me in an armor cabinet already and let's both get on with the rest of our day."

Alvin's face reddened as both his hands clenched into fists. "You..."

Nina stood her ground, squinting.

"What are you gonna do Eddie, punch me? Too bad. I guess the problem really is dick size."

Alvin lurched backward as his partner Don prevented an imminent demotion for assaulting a fellow officer. Nina took advantage of the brewing argument to slip past them and cut across the ops center.

She jogged past rows of gleaming desks awash with a sea of azure light and ethereal holograms. A floor-to-ceiling curtain of blue light divided the room in half, displaying a map of the city where blue dots ghosted the position of every patrol craft and officer in the area. The hologram shimmered into sparkles around her silhouette for as long as it took her to walk through it. Out the far end of the control room, she ducked into a hallway into a common area.

She found Vincent by the assignment board, engrossed by the floating text, and wrapped her arms around him from behind.

He patted her hand. "Not here. You know how cops are."

Nina smirked. "If they haven't figured it out by now, they shouldn't be wearing the uniform."

"Are we that obvious?"

Her answering smile fell flat as she saw what he was reading.

"Why did our patrol route change?" Her voice faltered.

Vincent turned and put his hands on her shoulders. "Calm down. What's got you so worked up? Did you forget Senator Garr's media interview this afternoon?"

"Oh…" Nina slouched. "Right. I forgot." Downcast eyes caught the time on her forearm panel. "Shit! We should have been out there ten minutes ago."

She ran past rows of weapon lockers and armor storage bays, smiling. Not only was Vincent a dedicated cop, marksman, and a stunt pilot, he was quite handsome. The polar opposite of Eddie Alvin, he had a quirky irreverent sense of humor and cared more about other people than himself. Alvin, on the other hand, was the first person to tell you how great Alvin was.

The cold air outside chased away her daydreams about what they would be doing when their shift ended. As Vincent brought the patrol craft up to cruising altitude, Nina checked her sidearm again. She usually didn't fuss with her weapon, but, today, she had checked it twice already.

"Expecting trouble?" Vincent lifted an eyebrow.

"I hope not. It's just superstition. Something always goes pear-shaped when you've only got a few days left."

"Few days? Guess it didn't go well with the spook?"

She beamed. "It did! He said he doesn't think I should be out on the streets. They're gonna give me a desk for a while 'til the transfer becomes official."

"Nonsense, you're a fine cop."

She stared at the lines of green light that drifted across his face. "You know it's what I've wanted since I took this job. Lieutenant Oliver thinks he can hurry it along."

"I know. I'm just worried about what I'm going to get stuck with for a new partner."

"It's not like we won't see each other anymore. We should have dinner with my parents before they decide to hire a private investigator to find my mystery man."

The forced smile that accompanied any talk of long-term commitment appeared. He had a cute kind of uncomfortable, and she enjoyed watching him squirm in his seat. He'd let her know she went beyond simple girlfriend, but he wanted to take it slow. A few cheap shots from the guys about her family's money left him gun shy about giving her the wrong impression. He admired her spirit, the way she had jumped headfirst into an untenable situation and had the resilience to keep at it despite all the abuse.

Hours passed as they cruised the patrol route. Nina occupied herself monitoring various systems that scanned for distress signals from the citizenry. Anything from burglar alarms to stolen cars and even tracking implants meant to foil abductions could beacon at any moment.

She dutifully cycled through the holographic displays, and Vincent chuckled at her intensity. If she remained focused, she wouldn't think about the danger lurking in every dark alley.

A pack of augmented thugs hung out against the side of a blown-out apartment building, their bodies gleaming with random bits of metal. A few waved, one blew a kiss, and several gave them the finger. Any of them would just as readily shoot at them than obey an order to disperse. After two months on the job, she had come to understand how and why the police changed after the corporate war.

Almost three hundred years ago, while trying to protect their interests around the world from all manner of uncertainty from terrorists to unstable regimes, corporations had begun to grow private security forces into military ones. By 2092, the American corporations decided they no longer needed to pay taxes to a government they had no use for.

That was when the shooting started. The government had been slow to react, not taking the threat seriously at first. Between biopharma companies' gene-altered killing machines and robotics companies' killer androids, the government hadn't stood a chance. A few ill-planned military strikes with nuclear weapons left much of the interior uninhabitable. People flooded to the coasts, overpopulating cities that grew until the entire seaboard had become one vast expanse of panic-riddled society.

As the government scrambled for order, the corporations armed the disaffected and the unemployed. Bombs, guns, and gangs left most people trapped in their homes. The government had been left with few options to restore order.

Miranda rights, search warrants, all of that went away. Now, the color of the uniforms represented the only real difference between the police and the military, that and the size of their weapons. At first, no one noticed the slow erosion of civil liberties. The corporate burn squads offered a greater threat that sent people into the arms of a protector government.

When the war ended, the government conveniently forgot to put things back.

The control sticks creaked in Vincent's grip as he worked his tension out. For almost two years, he had formed a nice, predictable routine around her. A new partner would change things, but at least Nina would be safer.

On a straightaway, he turned with a loving stare, smiling at her focused look as she flicked through scanning modes and tried not to think about only having a day or two left. When he first met her, he figured she would have quit in a month, but she surprised him. Despite all the torment, here she still was. He grinned as reminiscence coincided with an immediate need.

"Hey, hon, remember that time that we found you wrapped up in tape in the autoshower room?"

Nina shuddered at the memory of tape on her skin. "They left me there all goddamn night. How could I forget. I think I *still* have tile marks on my ass."

"Want to grab some burritos?"

Six minutes later, the ionic downblast vaporized dry spots on the traction-coated plastisteel road as they landed in front of "The Burrito Baron." The wet ground glimmered in the glow of innumerable holographic signs and passing ad-bots. Vincent jumped out of the door, evading her sudden itch to punch him one more time.

He, laughing, to pick up the order. She folded her arms and fumed. Being trapped on the floor of the shower room wearing only a roll and a half of tape for eleven hours didn't make for a pleasant memory, even everyone called it one of those 'rite of passage' things they all had to endure. She sulked, certain she got it worse because they saw her as a weak link. She forced it out of her head and smiled. Soon Div 1 would be a memory, and none of what any of them had done to her would matter.

A take-out burrito in the patrol car wasn't exactly her dream celebration dinner, but at least she had a half hour with Vincent. She wanted to lean across the seat and hold him as he pulled the car into the air. Instead, she pouted and looked down at crowds of press, protestors, and spectators milling about in the restricted area around the West City Municipal Center.

Ahead of them, a massive advert bot hung at the same altitude as their patrol craft. Billboard-sized holograms on either side of it bombarded the crowd with employment opportunities on Mars, the latest in cosmetic cyberware, an ad for implanted skill chips, the obligatory military recruitment spot, and of course—a litany of erotic entertainment products.

"What's that?" Nina pointed.

An orange blur flickered at the edge of the grey sphere on the scanner, representing the huge ad-bot, resembling a solar eclipse.

Vincent edged the patrol craft closer. A civilian hovercar darted out and zoomed down a side street, diving for the ground. The shimmer grew into an orange dot that remained solid, text filled in beside it with tags, specs, and current speed. Because the patrol craft's sensors lost track of it as a separate object from the bot, Vincent knew the driver had to have been within inches of it.

He hit the emergency lights and turned to chase. She eyed the control stick for the laser cannon and clenched her jaw at the worry of having to use it. To her relief, the rogue vehicle flipped on hazard flashers and angled into a slow descent.

"Relax, I don't think you'll need that."

"I..." She sighed. "Something doesn't feel right. It just came out from behind that billboard like it wanted us to see him. If he didn't move, we would have gone right past him."

Vincent smirked. "It's also possible the driver is drunk, stupid, or has a poor sense of his surroundings. I bet he saw us coming and got spooked. Breathe. It's just two more hours."

"I know." She spoke in a whisper. "That's what I'm afraid of." The thought of using some sick time tomorrow sounded more like a good idea.

The grey car drifted away from crowded streets, gliding several blocks west into a deserted area. It pitched nose up as side panels split open, allowing ground wheels to slide out into position. It eased its weight into the tires and came to a halt in an area devoid of people. Vincent watched for the telltale flash that let him know the hover system powered down. As soon as he saw it, he landed behind the other car and covered it with floodlights. For some reason, the driver had made a run into in a grey zone: a lawless patch of blight occupied by those with too many legal problems or too little sense.

The street was extra-wide with a strip of brick running down the middle where benches and lampposts sat among the gravesites of five trees. Trash spiraled around, caught in a breeze, and a stray dog scratched at a toppled vendomat two blocks away. Vincent watched the car for a moment before appraising the area as Nina combed through screens to evaluate the vehicle they had just stopped.

Six blocks from here, the façade of a skyscraper was dying a slow death, crumbling into the street below month after month. The sight of it hinted at the edge of a black zone—an area so far lost to urban blight and unchecked cyber junkies that the government blacked it out of the city navigation system—not even the military wanted to go there.

"Let's get this over with." Vincent's uncharacteristic seriousness made Nina shiver.

"We got a single occupant. Male, probably in his late forties." She glanced at the panel. "Trunk is empty, no cyberware, pistol under his left arm, looks like a standard class 2 ballistic. Minimal threat."

A wireframe model of the other car appeared in the windscreen indicating the position and movements of its driver and his weapon. The civilian fidgeted and tapped at the controls.

Vincent and Nina sealed their helmets and got out. The routine of a garden-variety traffic stop soon chased away her fears. They approached on different sides, and the driver lowered all the windows and kept his hands in clear sight. The man looked as worried as they felt. The sensors impressed her yet again with their accuracy in regard to his age. Traces of grey brushed the sides of his dense curly hair, and he wore a suit that looked to be on the low end of overpriced. Nina pegged him for middle management. Before Vincent could say a word, the man broke the silence.

"I forgot about that damned conference. The traffic is backed up all the way to Sector 193. I'd been sitting on the same block for almost an hour. All of a sudden, the car took off, driving itself. Couple blocks later, it tucked up on that damn ad-bot and just sat there."

Nina waved her tactical light around the interior of the car, but found nothing out of the ordinary.

"Self-driving car?" Nina lifted an eyebrow.

The driver's dark skin glistened with sweat. "I thought the cops took it over."

Vincent studied the holo-pane over his left forearm. His armor's signal processor had already linked to the man's NetMini, displaying all the critical info and no criminal record.

"We don't have that capability, sir." Vincent had heard a lot of excuses before, this one included. "Guess you figured we wouldn't see you on the other side of that adbot?"

"I told you. It drove on its own." He let out a nervous laugh.

"You know it's illegal to fly within forty yards of those things, right, Mister, um, Benton?"

The driver's expression sank. "I'm sorry, officer. Please believe me. I understand how dangerous it is. The damn car did it on its own. I'm surprised you didn't hear me screamin' at it."

Vincent glanced at his arm again. Mr. Benton had an impeccable driving record.

"I'm not as concerned with you accidentally straying into the edge of the exclusion zone as you're clearly not a threat to the senator. Those bots are unpredictable, and, if you had hit it, there are hundreds of people on the street below that could have been injured or killed."

"Young man, please understand that I am not trying to make an excu—"

He stopped in mid-word as a scream followed a series of gunshots out of a distant alley. "Oh my!" Mr. Benton turned and looked as blue flashes lit up the face of a building at a corner two blocks distant.

Vincent sighed. "That doesn't sound good."

AN UNEXPECTED PROMOTION

The sight of the fog on the inside of Nina's visor stalled Vincent in his tracks. She stared at where the shots came from, her gun slid into trembling hands.

Damn.

He wanted to tell her to radio for backup and stay in the car, but she would never forgive him if he treated her like that.

"Mr. Benton. Please consider the bots a danger to you and to everyone around you as you continue to operate a hovercar in the city. Have a pleasant evening." Vincent gave him a wave off.

With an incredulous stare, the driver nodded and pulled away offering several assurances that he wouldn't even share the same hover lane as a bot again.

The screams carried a type of raw terror that neither of them had ever heard, more than some prostitute getting caught up in a gang shootout. Nina hit the panic button to call for backup. The same woman's voice cried out, repeating the word "no" as fast as she could yell.

Vincent whirled around the corner, sighting over his weapon at what he expected to be a rapist. What he saw made his heart skip a beat. A woman lay on the street, cowering next to a smear of hamburger that used to be a pimp. Her bright pink hair, luminous flashing fingernails, and outfit of iridescent fiberoptic tape gave away her occupation. The glowing garment left little to the imagination, and made her skin glow soft blue, purple where blood covered her.

She crawled backward away from a huge and grimy man that towered over her. Blood dripped from his arms and he made a slow unsettling laugh just loud enough to be audible. More than seven feet tall, he looked thinner than one would expect for his height. A huge square chin framed crumbly yellow teeth and a pair of bright orange street-grade cybernetic eyes whirred as they widened to focus at

Vincent. Sticking out of his head like old-style camera lenses, they offered no hint of emotion.

A ten-inch lime green Mohawk was the cherry on top of a murder sundae.

Steel plating covered parts of his body, and at least one of his legs appeared to be all metal. Oversized boots with metal spikes on the sides lent a disturbing emphasis to how far away from normal this man had gone.

Segmented hoses descended like dreadlocks from the back of his head, curving around and into the center of his back. He turned toward Vincent and they twitched as if whatever substance within them surged.

He raised his left arm straight up in the air and grinned at him. The curved blade that jutted from where his hand should have been shimmered in a coating of heat blur. Vincent stared at the vibro-blade that could slice his duty armor like sushi. The augmented crazy pivoted his arm, ready to kill the woman. If not for wanting to make a show of it, he easily could have done it already.

He shouted at the man to freeze. Fully expecting Nina to just stand next to him and aim at the ogre, her forward rush shocked him mute. She fired at the man while sprinting for a metal bench about fifteen yards ahead.

"Run! Get out of here," Nina screamed, clicking shot after shot at the monster.

With each blue flash of burning propellant, another slug sailed over his head. One nipped the mohawk, causing a burst of hair particles. After seven misses, she put three into his chest. His body twitched backward. The slugs glinted blue in the old streetlights, embedded in his chest without penetrating.

Subdermal armor...

Nina stared at her worst nightmare come to fruition—an augmented ganger and her only weapon a pistol so small other cops called it a toy.

The mammoth head swiveled away from Vincent, he picked at the bullets in his chest as though they itched. The glowing woman crawled forward into a run. The castoff light from her costume created a migrating glow along the walls of a distant alley. He plucked a single bullet out, licked his blood from it, and then dropped it. With a grunt, he pulled a boxy submachine gun out from under a tattered, black trenchcoat. Nina tucked herself against the metal bench when the gun came out, peering through the slats at him. Her happiness at having saved a life died as the ganger grinned at her in the same way he had the prostitute.

"Nina, what the hell are you doing?" Vincent sounded near panic.

Diving behind the fender of the patrol craft, he fired, hoping to draw attention away from her. His sidearm, bigger and louder, made Nina cringe with each shot. She heard every slug land, though they failed to do much beyond annoy him. The truth of her predicament crashed into her mind. She shrieked as the ganger opened fire in her direction. Projectiles ricocheted around her, clanking off the bench and clicking off the road. A few glanced off her back, hitting like punches but failing to pierce her armor.

"Stay down, backup is on the way." Vincent called out over the tactical broadcast channel. "We have an aug nut job in Sector 188, require *immediate* assistance from Division 5. This guy's boosted to fuck and back!"

Vincent kept shooting while shouting. One or two hits caused small spurts of blood on impact. Except for a tiny flinch, the man ignored it. Vincent's mind chased an elusive calm as he tried to tell himself that this ganger's weapon shouldn't be able to pierce Nina's armor. The blade, however, worried him.

"Come on... over here... over here..." Vincent muttered to himself, still shooting.

The aug ignored him, lost in a euphoric haze of consumed fear. He leaned back as if savoring a beautiful aroma in the air—a woman screaming. Nina shrank tighter as bullets sparked around her. Strips of aluminum bench liquefied into twisting spirals in the wake of passing projectiles. Her cover wouldn't last much longer.

Giving up on his sidearm, Vincent dove into the patrol craft and grabbed the control for the laser cannon. In the time the system took to deploy from its roof bulge, Nina reached a point of panic where she could no longer remain still.

Vincent pushed himself up, staring at the flickering orange targeting circle that appeared in the windscreen. His breath stopped as Nina bolted from cover. In a full on tear, she weaved around a light post and jumped over a tree fence ahead of automatic fire striking the ground. About twenty feet from the car, indirium projectiles bored into Nina's left leg, chest and right arm. The high-density asteroid metal hit like an onslaught of sledgehammers. She fell forward and skidded to a halt face down on the pavement.

Fuck! Armor-piercing rounds. Vincent pounded on the dashboard, trying to make the cannon deploy faster.

The aug's magazine ran dry. Nina dragged herself behind a damaged vendomat. Luminous green fog leaked from her armor's joints as the stimsuit lining activated, filling her blood with a cool rush of synthetic adrenaline, nutrient gel, and flesh-repairing nanobots.

He strolled after her with a lackadaisical gait, whistling a vaguely classical tune as he slid another magazine into his weapon. The eerie grin on his face reminded Vincent of a child that just got what he wanted for his birthday. A brief flash of orange traced a pin straight line from the patrol craft's cannon through his thigh and into the alley behind him, ending his revelry.

Mechanical irises whirred closed as the hole caught fire at the edges. The pavement behind him glowed into molten rock for several seconds before dimming. He swatted with his right hand to tamp out the flames as he careened to the ground, growling curses.

Vincent yelled over the comm. "Nina? Are you okay?"

He tried to take another shot but the cannon couldn't reach an angle low enough to hit a prone target at such a short distance. It was designed for shooting down hovercars from two hundred meters or more, not nailing a psycho aug at twenty feet.

"I don't know why I ran..." Her delirious voice creaked over the comm, a touch above a whisper. "That was stupid."

She coughed. Blood spattered the inside of her visor. Nina had never even had a bullet bounce off her armor—tonight she had three penetrate it.

"Vincent? Is that you?"

Shock.

Hoping that her disorientation was just a short-term response to the adrenals in her stimsuit, Vincent tried to calm himself, knowing she would be okay. Medical technology in 2417 could easily correct a pierced lung. As long as her heart remained intact, she would be fine. Still, the panic in her voice drew him toward her. His emotions got the better of him and he didn't consider the status of their assailant. No one could get back up from a weapon that could slice a hovercar in half. He ran toward her, all the while telling her to be calm.

Nina lay on her side, covering a hole in her armor that leaked blood. No pain registered from her wounds. She stared at the shimmering fog, wondering where their backup was and why she couldn't stand up. Sensing a change in light, she turned. Vincent skidded into view, rolling to a marionette halt a few feet away. A thunderous crash followed as the vendomat that hit him struck and bent a lamppost before coming to rest upon the island in the road, embedded in displaced bricks. A gouge yawned open along its side from where the psycho's blade had hauled it aloft.

The shockwave in the ground brought Nina back to the moment.

Vincent stared at her over bloody fragments of crushed helmet. He reached toward her, trying to speak—but only managed a weak gurgle. Driven by fear and guilt, she forced herself up, ignoring the pain that lanced her side. She struggled with the now ponderous weight of her sidearm, using both hands in order to lift it. 'Punctured lung detected—please remain immobile' flashed across her field of vision. Blood seeped from her mouth as she turned to face the monstrosity that had hurt Vincent.

He was only an arm's length away.

Her determined glower melted into the vacant stare of a deer in the face of oncoming traffic. The skin on either side of his mohawk wrinkled into a stack of ridges, lifted by a demon's grin. His metal irises made a sharp whirr, widening as he soaked in her fear. The sound of banded metal cables rubbing over each other drowned out her pounding heartbeat, and his sinister phlegmatic laughter snapped her out of her paralysis.

She fired the rest of her magazine, all six shots, into his abdomen at point-blank range. The slugs stalled in bloody puffs as frayed strands of Myofiber-reinforced muscles burst out of the skin around where they struck. He continued the smile of someone watching a stupid person repeat a task that had no chance of success, pleased that his assumption of failure had proven correct.

Her need to protect Vincent destroyed reason and she lunged at the aug with her stun rod. He caught her with his still-natural arm and lifted her into the air. His fingers closed around her neck. The slow crunch of her armor failing flooded the helmet. Myofiber strength enhancements embedded in his arms swelled beneath his skin.

A wash of sourness choked her breath away once her helmet's seal broke, allowing the diseased air of the grey zone to reach her. Metal, rot, urine, booze, chemicals, and sweat all battled for prominence. Gagging, she thrashed around in his grip like a caught fish. Nina's kicks to his chest amused him more than shooting him did. He didn't react aside from that same evil laugh.

He pulled her close. The unblinking lenses peered into her eyes while a distorted twist of a smile curled his lips like a cat toward a mouse. The sight of her face reflected in the cold glass paralyzed her, even as he caressed her cheek with his thumb. The irises narrowed. He savored the helpless dread in her voice and tilted his head back, adoring a beautiful symphony that existed only to him.

Her faculties returned long enough to take advantage of the distraction her looks caused. Hadn't she been terrified, the expression he made as her stun rod touched his crotch would have made her laugh. The dark blue sparks crawling up the sides of his head only added to the humorous effect, though Nina was far from appreciative. To her horror, the shock didn't weaken his grip but rather caused him to slam her into the pavement once a wave of involuntary convulsions passed.

H-he's still moving after taking a stunrod to the nuts. H-how?

A distinct *crunch* accompanied her landing, her left arm breaking at the shoulder. With her right, she clawed at the road and dragged herself toward Vincent. Blood leaked from his twitching body. His eyes no longer focused on her —they stared into nowhere. Nina cried and screamed his name as everything around her ceased existing except for him. She no longer cared about the monster behind her.

She just wanted to touch him before she died.

She jerked as something hit her. The smell of seared flesh added to the awfulness in the air but she didn't look back to see what the vibroblade had done to her. Vincent was only inches away when another impact shook her body and stopped her forward motion. The blade went all the way through her into the metal road. If she had the mental faculties to consider it, she would have been grateful that shock spared her feeling the searing hot edge. The street blurred into a patch of grey, and then flashed without warning into white blindness. The sound of a heavy vehicle was followed by loud rapports of weapon fire, men shouting, an explosion, and the faint sensation of hot flecks of something brushing across her cheek. A bestial roar of pain boomed above her, and the blade lurched out of her, burning this time. The gunfire faded to silence and numbness. Her fingers closed around his arm.

Together forever.

"MISS DUCHENNE?" AN UNFAMILIAR MAN'S VOICE ECHOED LIKE A GHOST IN THE whiteness. It carried a tone of authority, sounding intelligent and refined like someone her father might have known. "Officer Duchenne, can you hear me?" It changed, low and muttering. "Does this thing even work?"

She wanted to say something. No sound came when she tried to talk. No air moved inside her, and she couldn't tell if she was even breathing.

"...interested in our offer..." Fragments of words danced within the amorphous world in which she floated. "...need your agreement..."

Nina wondered if this was the afterlife. The blinding light existed in her thoughts simultaneously as the headlights of an armored crew car, the overhead lights of an operating room, and a the mysterious sublime presence of an otherworld she never cared to believe in before. She wanted to live, and tried to scream.

Yes! Yes, I want to live!

Her voice hid and refused to come out.

"It went green. We have a yes. Do it." The man's voice again.

The light dimmed. The rush of a strong exhale preceded the smell of a cigar.

Utter silence.

She drifted in a sea of numbness for a time that eluded perception. Days, hours, weeks—it could have been that or a few seconds before she broke from the mental fog. The light dimmed to black. The perfection of the infinite void filled with thousands of tiny specks that grew and took on detail. Traction coating, black and cold, hovered in her view—the feeling of the spray-on roadway caressed her cheek for the most fleeting of instants.

She tasted her own blood.

As her unconscious mind gave way to the waking world, the gore soaked surface rose up and away and flattened. The peaks of the magnified road shrank and became tiny dots, holes in the charcoal colored ceiling tiles of her apartment. She lay in bed with the sound of her own voice crying out to Vincent, a pale arm extended upward, clawing at empty air. That night had been almost ten months ago.

How cruel to dream you cannot sleep.

THE COWBOY

Distant gunfire cracked Joey Dillon's right eye open, a bloodshot portal into his foggy mind. The past twenty-four hours were as indistinct in his memory as the particles of dust that shimmered within a strip of sunlight above him. Dozens of bullet holes in the walls created crisscrossing streaks in the darkness, invading his inner sanctum.

His body stretched a lanky path of flesh beneath a layer of trash, embedded in the dull olive fabric of an object that, ten years ago, would have been considered a sofa.

Closing the eye, he released a groan of dread that scattered the luminescent particles into a flurry. Last night's frivolity had an iron fingered grip on the back of his neck, squeezing its way into a full-on occipital lobe throbber. He tensed his legs, pulling his body so that his head came to rest on the cushion rather than the arm. His choice of sleeping position was as complicit as the tequila in the war that raged within his cranium. The couch offered no comfort. He was too hungry, too tall, and too hung over.

With his attempts to find a posture that didn't hurt, falling bits of detritus created a clattering disharmonic assault of sound, a symphony borne of concrete floor and metal cans. With a grunt, he forced himself up and leaned forward, balancing his head in his hands. His long hair slid off his shoulders and hung in a raven curtain over his face, caressing the tops of his feet with each breath. Pain descended from his neck, filling out the rest of his existence in an even shade of discomfort.

A vehicle rumbled by outside, with shouted obscenities trailing in its wake. The last barrage of insults ended with the period of a gunshot. Joey didn't react, his disinterested gaze returning after a moment to the blurry wall. He tried without success to will the grip of phantom fingers from his neck. A clear plastic box shifted, catching his eye as it moved on the table in front of him. A four-inch roach investigated what remained of an instant pizza meal.

"Dammit, Howard." Joey flicked it away and swiped the box with his other hand. "I told you already, the pizza nibbles are mine... anything on the floor is yours."

Stunned from its landing, it seemed to glare at him for an instant before darting off like a shark through an ocean of debris.

The space in which he slept was a two-room affair that had once belonged to the superintendent of this dead apartment building. The back end split in half with one side an enclosed bathroom and the other a kitchen so small it could barely be considered a separate room. A lovely shade of bare concrete decorated the entire apartment, specked with blotches of colored mold that accentuated the ambiance of the city. It smelled of booze, sweat, rotting food, and a mysterious cloying chemical that left a sooty flavor in the back of the throat before he had finally gotten used to it.

A lone window on the north wall looked out from the sunken apartment, right along the level of the sidewalk. The same four rusting hulks of cars had been there since long before Joey found this place. To the west, a reinforced metal door hung half open to the outside. Its constant battle with the floor often saw it wedged immobile for weeks at a time. Despite its obvious flaws, the place exceeded the hopes of any reasonable person wanting to dwell within a grey zone.

Granted, reasonable people seldom wanted such things.

Joey plodded to the bathroom, coveting his discovered meal. The cold pastry exploded as his teeth closed around it, flooding his mouth with artificial sauce and something attempting to pass itself off as mozzarella cheese. Food made from OmniSoy, molecularly reassembled into other things, often devolved into the basic slime from whence it came after several hours.

This must be the third stage. Joey maneuvered it on his tongue as if tasting fine wine. "Early 2413. Excellent body, firm texture, possibly penicillium candidum."

The chemicals used to heat the instant food had little effect on the flavor initially, but after two days, they lent a piquant essence that he had come to savor.

Howard the roach slid out of sight.

"What?" Joey swallowed. "It's stage three... it has the consistency of cheese again."

He thought he saw the roach shudder.

Tossing the empty carton on the pile of trash that buried the bathroom wastebasket, Joey glanced around the cowboy hat that hung at the corner of the mirror. The emaciated form looking back at him was a stranger. Each rib was distinct in its protrusion from his chest and his body tapered inward like a cartoon until his jeans covered the rest.

"Yeah..." he muttered. "Probably 'bout time I get some damn food."

At some point during his childhood, he had developed a fondness for the Old West. The frontier life on Mars resembled that era. Perhaps that explained it. People on Earth considered it anachronistic, and that made it even more appealing. He spun the hat over his hand and put it on. Despite knowing the cabinet offered no painkillers, he looked anyway. Three empty bottles were crusted to a shelf, their tenure in this place far beyond his. Another roach waved its antennae at him from the bottom shelf. He pictured it gaping at him as if he had opened the bathroom door while it sat on the bowl.

Done in the bathroom, he stumbled over to a table against the far wall. Take-out food containers, synth beer cans, and an uncountable number of silver OmniSoy packets were stacked four feet high upon it. With one sweep of his arm, Joey cleared off his cyberspace deck and took a seat. Twenty-four inches long, eight deep, and three thick, the boxy device responded to his touch and filled the air above it with an array of holographic displays. The Teradyne Silver series was still an entry-level deck, even if it was grade 3, but his happiness at finding it for next to nothing at a pawnshop had long since faded away to annoyance at being stuck with a newbie's toy.

He stared into the expanding black squares that formed between him and the wall, grumbling at the lack of new messages. Bands of reflected light scrolled over his face as he pondered the paradox of needing a better deck to make real money —but needing money to get a better deck.

"I'm sure you'll figure it out soon." His father's singsong voice floated into the room.

"Yeah… yeah…" Joey had already prepared himself for the inevitable back and forth when it occurred to him that the old man had been dead for more than a year.

For the first time that day, Joey's eyes opened all the way. He swung around to look behind him, finding the room still quite dim, save for the dust particles dancing in the sunlight from the cluster of bullet holes. He was alone except for the scratching of an unseen roach.

"Fuck me…" He sank back into the seat, turning to face the deck. "I gotta make some creds before I lose it."

He pulled the link cable out of the side panel, fingers securing a grip on the plastic housing at the end of the wire. With a squeeze, a half inch metal prong snapped out with a click. He turned it over in his fingers, searching for dirt on the razor edged fins glinting in the holograms.

That plug, and his hat, represented the only two things about which Joey gave a damn.

He felt around behind his ear for the receiver and lined it up with the prong. It slid in with a soft *click* that resonated over his skull. Joey expected the world around him to dissolve into the constructed reality of cyberspace.

He didn't expect the burning electrical current that came over his skull like an army of crawling needle-legged spiders, wrapping around his arms until flickering arcs of blue lightning connected his fingertips to the metal table. He thrashed like a fish on a line for several seconds before a shower of orange sparks spewed from the deck and it went dark. His face bounced off the chair on its way to the floor, where he lay twitching for several minutes. Smoke fumed out from his hair in silence. The scent of burnt Joey filled the air.

"You *bitch*," he shouted as he sat bolt upright.

Removing the hot wire from the side of his head, he pulled his protesting body back into the chair and surveyed the damage. The deck survived with minimal damage, just a blown fuse. The shock elevated his hangover headache into an Armageddon-class event, but posed no risk to his life.

Cleopatra. Four months of this never-ending bullshit…

The few times he had managed to find her in cyberspace, her skills felt far from impressive, making it more vexing how slippery she was. One chance meeting left him enough time to mount an attack and her defense was one shade removed from nonexistent.

Makes no damn sense.

She could be a beginner with an expensive deck. A high grade unit with ghost mods could make it hard for his pitiful board to find her. That would be his revenge. Once he found her, he would take her amazing deck.

Hours later, he brought the Teradyne Silver back to life in a cloud of solder fumes. The reassuring glow of holographic displays flickered on one after the next and made him smile. A few chips around the power uplink had blown out as well, an easy but tedious fix. He held the wire up, but paused. Squinting at the plug, he put it down and ran a diagnostic.

Ugh, this bitch is making me type with my hands.

He pawed at the menus, tossing shimmering images and icons aside one after the next. A poke at a cartoon dog triggered a Watchdog program that leapt about, scanning memory constructs. Gravity pulled him down in the chair as thousands of alphanumeric addresses scrolled by in text too fast to read.

So damn boring.

This line of work, if you could call it work, appealed to his need for the thrill of going into secret and well-protected places. His stuck up bitch of a sister didn't share his enthusiasm for what he did with his degree in electrical engineering.

Growling snapped him out of his fantasy of embarrassing her in front of her lawyer friends. The watchdog sat back with a data tile in its mouth, thrashing it back and forth after having hunted down a concealed joybuzzer soft. Visions filled his head of strangling some faceless woman with an interface wire. He wanted to beat Cleopatra until she begged. No longer propped upright on coursing anger, he slumped. With more than three seconds of thought, he decided he would still feel guilty about hitting a girl that didn't try to kill him. Vengeance would have to take some other form, once he knew what she most feared. Unfortunately, before he could do a damn thing, he had to overcome the little issue of being unable to find her.

Joey fantasized the various tortures he could visit upon her as he checked the business end of the M3 plug. After a long hesitant stare, he stuck it into his head and cringed. The wall in front of him liquefied and melted away into nothingness. A momentary sensation of floating passed and random flashing lights danced about as his brain adjusted to receiving its input from the Neural Interface Unit instead of his normal senses. Billions of electrons swarmed from the deck, over the wire and into his mind courtesy of the NIU. In less than the span of a single breath, he stood in the center of a well-kept ranch house with a view of rolling plains. Deer heads and ancient rifles lined the walls around a room warmed by a virtual fireplace.

Within the realm of cyberspace he took on the appearance of an older man every bit as gaunt and pale as Joey, but taller. Coarse grey hair hung to the shoulders of a long black coat. The visage of an aging gunslinger radiated a paranormal otherness to anyone in the same node. Mood manipulation was tricky. A bit of software he borrowed from an entertainment sim could manipulate the amygdala, the deep brain region responsible for emotion, of other plugged-in users in a way that caused inexplicable dread at the sight of him—just enough to keep the kiddies and noobs from bothering him.

He had hoped it would scare Cleopatra off, but she didn't even notice it. In retrospect, it seemed to have made her come after him more.

He strode toward the exit, followed by the echo of his boots. Outside waited a sea of blackness, a sight far removed from the vibrant meadows in the window. A virtual representation of the real world, constructed of gloss black shapes highlighted in glowing azure, stretched into the digital sky. The backbone systems responsible for cyberspace filled in this basic grid wherever no one had customized it. People appeared in a given area of the GlobeNet either because they logged in from its real world counterpart, or they traveled there after login.

This deep in the grey, no one bothered coming here except to use the area for shooting games. In the real world, few risked abandoning their body to such a deep sleep in a dangerous place.

Time to make some creds.

Civilization waited several blocks west. The amber gleam of sundown beckoned from where drawn-in city covered the skeleton. A four-foot wide pane opened beside him: his contact management interface. The low profile he kept among the cyberspace crowd protected him from the police and corporate heavies, but it also kept jobs from coming to him. He plucked the face of a contact from the list and threw it into space in front of him, starting a call.

Alex Hunter was a product of a wealthy family and had the appearance of a man fond of the finer things in life. His shimmering blue suit glimmered in the cyberlight, its design somehow contemporary and antiquated at the same time. Dense brown hair framed a boyish face with an air of playful sophistication. Joey knew he was in his late twenties, but the man looked eighteen.

Must be nice to have creds to waste on cosmetic work.

"Bonjour, monsieur Dillon."

Joey rolled his eyes. "Again with the Frenchie crap?"

"Despite my best efforts to educate you in the ways of a civilized language, you continue to speak in the peasant's tongue." Alex chuckled with an air of haughtiness.

"Hunter... You were born in Sector 87. You're about as French as my scrotum." The dark cowboy's voice flowed thick with gravel and a supernatural echo. "Spare me the bullshit. I'm looking for work, you have anything?"

Alex's face reddened. He reached to hang up, but hesitated as displeasure shifted to amusement on a whim. The mischievous smirk caused Joey to narrow his eyes.

"I do..." Alex touched his fingertips in front of his face. "It just so happens that I have a small data acquisition request sitting around that fits you perfectly."

"Really, now?"

"Oh yes. It's simple, cheap, and dirty." Alex's smile broadened.

Joey growled low in his throat, too soft to go out over the comm signal. "How cheap is cheap?"

Alex swirled an unknown dark liquid in a glass. "A distrustful wife wants some proof that her husband is having an affair. The man has been patronizing a club in Sector 113 called 'Anonymous Notoriety'. There is a rumor that it may be a front for more than just social pleasantries."

As he spoke, a few data points popped up below the video feed, containing network information about the club's presence in cyberspace, as well as a picture of a man named David Stone.

The club's network looked weak in terms of security. It should be an easy in and out job, but that also meant it would be dull.

"That sounds like a job from you... boring and pretentious."

Alex smiled, reaching for the console in slow motion. "Oh well, then, if it's beneath you, I'll find someone else. I'm sure you don't really need five thousand credits that much."

"Fine... Fine..." He glanced into the distance at the glowing cityscape. "I'll call you when it's done."

MINOR NUISANCE

Gathering his bearings, Joey plotted a route to Anonymous Notoriety. As data nabs went, five grand was a crummy payoff, but the job was too easy to turn down. Added to that, he knew his credit statement couldn't afford one take out entree and it was a done deal.

Up ahead, the glow of populated areas came into view. Along a defined line that crept from one edge of the horizon to the other, the city went from black glass to full color as if someone had poured liquid reality over the digital models. Almost-human-shaped clouds of darkness drifted by, indicating the presence of people in the real world as detected by citywide surveillance cameras. Joey walked among the oblivious shadows, keeping a careful eye on a handful of other avatars.

A pink haired pixie complete with filament wings and a star capped wand chatted with a man in a suit. Across the street, a flaming skull with bat wings argued with an anthropomorphic bear in a blue ball cap. Something about Gee-ball scores from a game last Saturday.

He reached a series of glowing directional arrows that hovered an inch above the ground, a public I/O channel that provided high-speed connectivity between major sections of the GlobeNet. He rode the accelerated connection across several regions until he reached the network segment that contained the club. As soon as he stepped on it, the I/O link slammed to a halt. Glint sparkled from the teeth of a cartoony woman watching him from the corner of a nearby junction.

She had skin the color of creamed coffee and her hair was a thick fluffy mass that hung down to her thighs. The white and gold dress fell somewhere between cute and alluring. Atop her head, a gold tiara bore the image of a comical cross-eyed cobra, with blue bands in the hood. Her oversized brown eyes glowed with happiness at seeing him.

Cleopatra.

His mind racing, Joey assembled pieces of corrupt code intent on frying her connection. He yanked his silver revolvers off his belt and took aim as she blew a kiss at him. Her hand flipped over to wave goodbye. Undeterred, Joey ran the command to send the attack and his fingers squeezed the triggers. The shot went off to the right due to sudden violent acceleration. The guns spat smoky bullets, gouging virtual holes in the street a few feet shy of her bare foot. The moving sidewalk lurched forward at four times its normal speed, turning the city and all the avatars on both sides of him into smears of color.

A split second later, he found himself embedded headfirst in the now crumbling side of a building. Cleopatra had hacked the uplink path, adding a physics process. This, in turn, added inertia, which prevented him from following a ninety-degree turn at that speed. The illusion of stonework broke open to reveal blue and black digital debris inside the hole. Joey slid down from the crater in a river of pain to the pavement below. Chattering laughter drifted into his ears from a bright green cartoon snake and several stars circling around his head. With a dour frown, he seized the serpent and squeezed it until its eyes burst. The little creature, a 'pet' construct of Cleopatra's, was trivial to delete. He turned to stare in the direction it had come from, but a lingering throb in his head was the only trace of her presence.

Chunks of building fell out of his coat and clattered to the ground as he stood. Pieces of debris slid along the ground, drawn up the wall and into the crater where they stacked back into place. The damaged area rippled like the surface of a pond before it became as smooth and hard as the steel it purported to be.

None of the other avatars in the area hadn'ticed his crash, or reacted if they did, providing a small degree of comfort. Cleopatra had made it her mission in life to embarrass him, but this time she failed. Anger pounded the headache deeper into his brain.

His troubles on Mars scared him, but this bitch was just irritating—the kind of irritating that pushed men to action outside their character. Joey balled his hands into fists.

What the hell does this skank want? Why me? If she wants something, why does she always just giggle instead of speak?

None of it made sense.

Probably some lonely/ugly/old/fat chick strung out on Flowerbasket with a deck and nothing better to do.

His train of thought derailed with the sound of screeching tires and automatic weapon fire behind him. The screams of children echoed. He whirled, seeing nothing but the street behind him. Sounds floated off into the distance, gone as fast as they had manifested. So loud, so tangible, like a busload of screaming kids bearing down on him, yet no one else noticed. Other avatars walked past him like pedestrians in the real world, a few sending confused looks at his reaction to something they didn't hear.

Compulsion to know where the sound had come from gripped him. The old gunslinger opened his coat, letting a pack of ferrets fall to the ground. They chittered off at supernatural speed. A series of Traceweasel softs went in search of the source. After a cyberspace minute, a report came back that told him an audio-only transmission had entered his deck from sixteen separate sources, as if multiple entities conspired in a distributed bombardment of information. He dismissed Cleo, doubting she had the skill to multiplex a signal that well. Joey could do it, but it would take days to set up and leave a window of use of only minutes. The wonder of who would go to all that trouble just to send him some creepy sound effects was one more log on the bonfire of WTF that Cleo continued to feed.

A pang of hunger got him moving again. The sooner he did the job, the sooner he could eat. The dark cowboy rushed down a street that seemed alien by virtue of what it lacked. It looked real in every way, but the absence of trash, vagrants, ad-bots, and traffic made him feel like he was walking the streets of a city never touched by humans.

When he saw the club, he knew why Alex had that evil smile.

Men came here to encounter other men.

After a few mental acrobatics, his avatar shrank back to normal height and took on the appearance of a nondescript man in a business suit with a randomized face. Joey didn't care what he looked like as long as it looked nothing like him.

The virtual three-story building had a white arc trimmed in chrome spanning from the left side up and over the door, connecting the first and third floors. Shadows moving along the white panels hinted at a walkway inside.

The interior network had a public flag, enabling him to walk right in to the simulated lobby. Inside, his eyes watered from the powerful presence of incense. A phantom tickle on his cheek hinted that the virtual stink was intense enough for his body to cry in its sleep. Going from the scent-neutral realm of open cyberspace to a place running custom fragrance software made him cough. A fair number of men mingled around the place accompanied by simulated drinks and a steady stream of music that thrummed in time with the lights.

Joey rubbed his neck while he walked around the room, looking for the object that concealed the access path to the private part of the network. His mind wandered back to Mars, back to the time he had tangled with an MDF security construct that treated him like it was his first night in prison. The violent disconnect caused by a blown-out deck left him feeling as though his left eye was stuck open, accompanied by a ringing in his ears and the smell of burning silicon that lingered for two weeks. The thought of playing Gee-ball with a hangover and a heavy flu felt more appealing than experiencing that again. He had no idea how he had made it out of the cube motel before they came for him. His trip to the starport remained merely a nauseating blur of memory.

Alex thought he would be uncomfortable here, but Joey didn't care that much about it. He often teased Alex about that sort of thing, but he was such a dandy that he offered an easy target and his reactions made it worth it. Joey scowled at the thought of Alex. He was such a poser, or would Alex insist that it be *poseur?* The debate made him laugh aloud.

His search took him into the gaming area where several people killed time with various diversions. Dark carpeting filled the place, while wood paneled walls covered in the kind of kitsch usually reserved for trendy bistros ran behind several terminals where men gambled and spent time with their companions. A lone man focused on a video game in the back corner, raising Joey's eyebrow. The thought of a game that simulated a virtual reality inside an already false world could keep philosophers up at night. At the rear of the section of game consoles, a dull metal door glinted—the access point to the private network. A six-foot-five stack of unrealistic handsomeness with long blonde hair and an expensive black suit leaned against the wall by the door. He smiled and nodded at everyone that walked within a certain distance, repeating the same cycle of movements every few seconds.

A troll.

With a twitch of a synapse, Joey triggered a scan that confirmed his suspicion. Trolls, standard combat constructs, had little intelligence and tended to attack mindlessly when activated. This one scanned as weak. He could delete it with ease, but he needed to be subtle. The entire network, and anyone on it, would know. Starting a fight here could spill into a brawl with every other user in the club's network trying to score points with the owners for stopping a hacker. Grinning at the unexpected challenge, Joey approached the door and took up a position at the closest game panel. The digital Adonis turned its head to glance at him and winked.

He returned a pleasant smile and focused his attention on the virtual terminal. Some manner of generic hallway shooter with zombies, albeit uninspiring in design, surprised him with its entertainment value. It absorbed him enough that the troll paid him no attention. By the time a zombie burst from the floor and ended his game, the troll had disregarded him. Joey sent a string of spoofed responses to the GlobeNet geolocator pulse. A technique known as ghosting, it caused the network to lose track of him and made him invisible to anyone in the same segment not searching deliberately for intruders.

Creeping to within an arm's length from the oblivious virtual man, Joey turned his attention to the door, and got through the pathetic security on the first try. Beyond it, a plain white hallway stretched off into green-tiled infinity. Dozens of brown office doors lined both sides. Figuring the network to be a lot smaller than it appeared, he triggered a Lantern soft. The search process manifested as a pulse of light that shot down the hall, turning many of the doors transparent, before it returned and orbited him.

After checking several doors, he found a room with a floor drawn in the harsh lines of black and white checkerboard tiles. A row of filing cabinets, zeroes and ones folded into an artifact from offices of centuries past, stretched to a distant point where everything swirled together into a grey mass. The dark cowboy pulled an old-west style lamp out from under his coat, holding the burnished brass box aloft as he walked among the rows. Light from the digital lamp rendered the file cabinets transparent, revealing data tiles within the first twenty only. The rest represented unused storage space.

A pattern search for the name David Stone came up dry. An onyx panel scrolling with amber text appeared. Automated security had detected his intrusion, but couldn't locate him.

With a growl, he set about enduring the tedium of an in-depth file scan that took about thirty seconds per drawer. The job reached a level of agonizing boredom that made him question the payoff.

When he found the security vids, he dragged the drawer open, ten meters out into the room. Above it, a neat string of featureless chrome tiles rotated. One by one, they stopped spinning as the deck read their contents. The silver surfaces melted away to images of what they contained. Joey wallowed in the drudgery of it until a digitized voice startled him eighteen tiles in.

"Unauthorized presence detected, initiating combat protocol."

The twin brother of the door guard spoke with a voice that conjured up an image of the most boring bodybuilder to ever live.

Running into a monster like this in reality would have made him run without a second thought, but not here. Here, Joey smiled. The big man leapt, flying across the filing cabinets and landing in the space where Joey had been an instant before. A barrage of harmful data took the form of a massive fist that detonated one of the cabinets into thin digitizing strands shifting from metal to pure light, then to evaporating sparks of energy.

The guard turned on him, answering his impish grin with a frown. It lunged again but Joey disappeared. When the troll recovered, the dark cowboy stood across the room with a revolver leveled off. After a pause long enough to grin, he fired. The gun spat a small skull made of smoke, wailing its way in a straight line to the oaf's chest.

Spreading from the impact point, waves of force expanded over the white tuxedo shirt like ripples in the surface of a pond. The center rebounded and spat a geyser of virtual blood that changed from red to white, melting into pixilated debris in midair.

The guard staggered and pounded his fist into the tiles, sending a tsunami of data along a floor and ceiling that moved like syrup. Hanging fluorescent lights swayed from its passing and several of the cabinets fell askew. Joey levitated over the attack, firing both guns as he rose.

The troll staggered as its head burst into a geyser of black data fragments. With a scream that drowned in a digitized roar, the large figure fell into a slush of black, white, and blonde shards, skittering like broken glass across the floor. The image map of cloth and skin flickered away to plain silver, and the chunks dissolved.

He was once more alone with his search routine.

Joey flipped his guns over his fingers and slid them back into their holsters. "Well that was almost interesting."

After an intolerable wait, one of the data tiles grew larger than the rest, lighting up with a yellow border. He took the tile from the drawer. His caress caused a series of display panels to render above it. The object held hundreds of hours of holo-cam recordings.

One such video showed David Stone at a table with another man. They smiled and shared a drink, seeming far more interested in each other than a pair of buddies out for a drink. When they kissed, Joey nodded to himself at the five thousand credits in his hands.

"You might say I'm a bastard." He spoke to the object. "But he'll be happier when the dust settles."

7

PAYDAY

Halfway through the club, a minute movement caught Joey's eye from the direction of the door. An object rocketed toward him, a cartoony green snake flying at him like an arrow—another hacker trying to backdoor some code onto his system. His defensive cringe caused his deck to react, trapping the incoming file in a quarantined memory address.

He caught the snake out of the air before it hit him. A frown spread across his face as he recognized it as Cleopatra's work. His glare deepened at the realization that she tried to load a Depantser soft onto his deck to degrade its performance. If a cyberspace avatar had pants, which his current avatar did, the animation lived up to its name. Given his current surroundings, his face darkened with rage.

The amateurish attack had Cleopatra's stench all over it, and didn't speak well of her skills. The serpent salted the wound of his failure to locate her.

After I send this file to Alex, I'm coming for you, bitch. He bristled with indignation that she would dare use a newbie's technique on him. *You're way out of your league.*

He had had enough. Joey closed his eyes and let the disconnection command pull him out of the GlobeNet. The dizziness of the transition came over him and the comfortable neutral temperature of cyberspace gave way to a chilly apartment awash with the sour smell of decay. With a teary-eyed gasp, he pulled the M3 plug out of his head.

He tried to walk around the room to get his blood moving, but ended up in a clumsy spiral ballet that resembled a doll with a stuck knee joint. Only an hour of real time had passed, though his body objected to spending a night in a contortionist's sleep before being draped over a chair in the near death of cyberspace. Cold tendrils of numbness possessed his right leg, which refused to do anything but bombard him with pins and needles. Screaming past gritted teeth, he pulled himself over to a pile of clothes and sniff-tested a series of shirts. After a few horrendous failures, he settled on a black one with a dull grey ankh covered with circuit lines. He couldn't tell if it lacked stink or just had less than the surrounding area.

Crawling past the couch, he snagged his NetMini from the heap and hit 'repeat last connection' before tossing the device to his other hand. A moment later, Alex Hunter's head floated before him above the rainbow glow of the device's holo-emitter.

"That was quick, Joseph. Shall I assume that you didn't linger for a drink after you finished?" Alex's voice dripped with patronizing insincerity.

"Here's your damn file." With a flick of Joey's thumb, a nugget of information sailed a hundred miles in less than a second.

The glimmering head turned to the side with a nod of approval. "My my. What's got you so testy? You may be a cretin, but you do good work." Ephemeral chimes sounded as Alex poked at his terminal out of sight. "Your payment is in your account. Oh, by the way... I have another job if you are interested."

Joey wanted a decent meal, not the rattle of Alex's voice between his ears. "I'll think about it."

The illusory head spiraled around the NetMini as Joey tossed it back into the pile of debris on the couch. The spinning voice faded into a protesting chipmunk as the head shrank away to nothing. Something metal hit the floor and rolled, displaced by the impact. He rubbed the bridge of his nose as the loud noise aggravated his headache. The clamor mutated into whirring as a metal lid spun around, wobbling with increasing speed upon his brain until it settled still upon the concrete.

"I gotta get out of here."

As much as he didn't want to admit it, Alex was his best ticket away from this hole that passed for an apartment. It took him a few minutes to hunt around for his black duster coat, a garment that looked more like it belonged in the Old West than in the modern age. After fixing his hat, he collected his deck and tossed it in a practiced maneuver over his shoulder. It hit his back just as the retracting cable snapped closed into the case.

It took Joey heaving all of his hundred-and-sixty-five pound body into the door to get it to release its grip on the floor, and he squeezed himself through the narrow gap it afforded. Outside, the air blew crisp, offering only a mild improvement in smell over the stagnant interior. Like everyone else in this part of town, the sun kept itself out of sight. It would be dark soon, but Joey didn't mind. The denizens of this forgotten place ignored him. He didn't have tits, didn't look like he had anything worth taking, and most important of all—he kept to himself.

Some of the locals had even become friendly with him, especially after he had invited them to partake of the fifty gallons of synthetic tequila that appeared mysteriously at his apartment last month. He later discovered that Cleo ordered it as a prank, and of course put his name on the bill. It proved easier to erase the bill than get rid of the booze. Even with the help of the dozen or so people that hung out on the corner, more than half of it remained a month later. The mere thought of it churned his gut.

The bike was a chimera of disparate parts, naked steel held together by a handful of screws and a lot of hope. The superconducting battery and in-wheel motors worked, even if the frame felt like it was two speed bumps away from complete disintegration. It sat just outside the door, a dam in the river of passing detritus, catching the odd paper scrap or rolling can against its wheels. Picking a plastic bag off the seat, he kicked an aluminum canister out from under the wheel before throwing his leg over it and settling down.

The behemoth didn't notice his weight. He brushed a few scraps of paper from the featureless black glass between the handlebars. At his touch, the control elements lit up with the comforting glow of neon green. A thumbprint brought the drive system online and the entire machine vibrated. With a grunt, he heaved the bike off its kickstand and got it rolling. Electric motors in both wheel cores pulled solid strips of rubber around, propelling the machine forward.

Driving with one hand, he fished out his NetMini. The iridescent blue holographic panel faltered and dipped in the passing air as bits of debris and ash flew through it. The number on his cred statement brought a smile—5003.

To the average citizen, it was a decent bit of cash—most of one month's rent. It wouldn't take Joey out of the slum, but it would put something hot in his gut. Dodging dead car hulks, fallen lampposts, trash, and the occasional sleeping junkie —he crawled his way forward until the moldering ruin of the grey zone gave way to an ocean of glowing advertising bots, bright street lamps and other people.

A lean on the accelerator brought the machine up to around eighty miles per hour, though the speed was a guess. The speedometer had quit months ago and he hadn't bothered to replace it. Dodging several cars moving slower than he wanted to go, he made his way two miles into civilization to his favorite restaurant, the Fu Sheng House.

8

THE FU SHENG HOUSE

The tiny parking lot had six perpetually occupied spaces, even when the place was empty. The aftereffect of hours-old rain glistened on decaying grey bricks in the feeble vibrating glow of his headlamp. He parked the bike in a narrow gap between the trash compactor and the wall. Even the putrescent odor leaking from the dumpster couldn't tarnish his appetite. His boots splashed in puddles, shattering the reflections of a dozen glowing signs from the street.

Upon the front of the building, a seven-foot tall hologram of Chinese characters greeted him at the door. Bright enough to sear their image into any retina that looked directly at them, they threw off so much light it was impossible to tell if the two nearest streetlamps even worked.

He ducked past double doors covered in cracking bright red paint with gold inlay, into the wonderful fragrance of his dreams. The dark interior wrapped guests with a private coziness. A long gold dragon hung at the back of a room lined with red and gold wallpaper. The intensity of the sign out front made the heavy red curtains glow, bathing everything in burgundy and orange with the sense of an autumnal dream.

A woman behind a tiny counter covered in mints, lotto machines, and an army of tiny ceramic cats greeted him with a smile and said something in Chinese. Joey tipped his hat at her, offered a mute nod, and continued into the dining hall without waiting. She followed, still talking, while he ducked the arm of a huge painted-gold Buddha perched atop a wall of false stone. Once, a mechanical waterfall, but it had broken long before he set foot here. As he seated himself, she waved her arms, muttered, and returned to the counter.

Joey removed his hat and set it on the table before leaning back and spreading his arms over the bench seat. The maroon cushions bore the well-worn ass marks of many a patron, threadbare to pale grey fabric in several spots.

Old man Lao appeared like a phantom and placed an electric kettle on the table next to a small porcelain cup. His cologne soon overpowered the fragrance of the tea. Frail, Lao was bald save for a wispy white moustache that hung down to his chest. His neat white shirt hid beneath a black vest, itself covered by an apron. A white towel dangled from the pocket of his charcoal hued trousers, stained with a kaleidoscope of sauces. Joey had grown used to his strong accent, respecting him for learning the language rather than just using a chip.

"Good evening, Mistah Dillon. You must have found work if you here. I hope everything well for you." With a smile, Lao's eyes collapsed into thin lines, swallowed by the wrinkles on his face.

Pouring some of the tea, Joey grinned. "Could be worse, could be better."

"Good to hear, good to hear..." Lao gave an emphatic nod before his eyes widened with anticipation. "What you having tonight?"

"The usual, and please tell the cook I don't want it gaijin style."

"Gaijin Japanese, we are Chinese." Lao held up a finger to make his point, leaning in as he raised his voice in mock offense. "General's chicken. You want kill white man hot?" Thin lips curled and uncurled around yellow teeth as if he couldn't decide if he wanted to smile or laugh aloud.

Joey contemplated taking a chance, but decided to play it safe. "I'll settle for wounded, not killed."

Lao gave a quick nod and flew off toward the kitchen, hurling Mandarin at a closed door. A voice from behind answered—their back and forth went for a few lines before Lao took up his typical position behind the restaurant's bar.

Joey had been coming to this little restaurant built into the bottom corner of a residential building for months. The apartments here, tiny and jammed together, offered housing to the lowest end of middle class. He briefly considered getting one, but his current squat was about triple the size. In addition, if anything from cyberspace came back to haunt him in reality, he didn't want the Fu Sheng House to get caught up in the shitstorm.

A gold snake on the wall brought his mind back to Cleopatra.

Her pestering pranks had become so incessant that for the past two weeks, he expected to start seeing little cartoon snakes come out of nowhere in the real world. Not since his sister had gone all sanctimonious on him had Joey had such an urge to inflict pain on a woman. He wanted to do something that would make her never want to log into the GlobeNet again, but had yet to even figure out her identity.

Everywhere he went, his eyes darted around, searching for a strange woman following him. Maybe she worked for some company that he had hacked? No, that made little sense. What she did was more irritating and annoying than dangerous. Her pranks had a strange sense of humor that defied his attempts to ascribe motive. It could be his friend Kenny's ex-wife, a bit of a psycho, especially since the divorce. *Naah, she has issues speaking and walking at the same time now. Hitting the GlobeNet is right out.* Joey shook his head as he thought about that whole mess. He found some humor in the irony of Kenny's wife having the same name as his sister —they had the common bond of a Kathy as a pain in the ass.

Lao returned and placed four steaming dumplings in front of him. These were the primary reason that Joey came here. In all of West City, perhaps six or seven places still hand made their food and the Fu Sheng House was one of them. The burst of flavor filled his senses and wiped away all thoughts of Cleopatra, Alex, or even his immediate surroundings. Despite his best effort to savor them, the fourth one vanished before Lao made it back to his post at the bar.

The General Tso's would be a few minutes. Joey figured he might as well see what Alex wanted, and called him. The direct manner with which he mentioned a new job was rather unlike him, and piqued Joey's interest. Alex's sophisticated smirk hovered in its six-inch holographic glory, changed somewhat purple by the peach-hued glow that permeated the room.

"Did you have a change of heart?" Alex looked about ready for his usual games.

"Since when does "I need to think" translate to "no"? Must be some of that French bullshit you keep telling me about."

Alex frowned. "Your attempt at humor falls woefully short of the mark."

"Kind of like your attempt at passing as straight?" The corner of Joey's mouth curled into a wry grin.

"Why…" Alex turned red. "Do you insist on associating the affect of someone of superior lineage with homosexuality?"

"Because I find it amusing to watch your face change color." Joey slathered duck sauce on a strip of fried wonton, speaking through crunches. "And you do seem a little fancy."

Alex's eyes flared.

"As much as I love tormenting you, my food is about to come out and when it does, I am going to hang up. So what's this job?"

Alex failed to hide simmering rage. "You have the fortunate luck of being in the right place at the right time. Your unique combination of desperation and skill is something that I need. A client is offering fifty thousand credits for a piece of data hidden in the secure information vault at the Imperial Hotel."

He chewed in Alex's ear. "Combination of what?"

"Among the electronic infiltrators at my disposal of a given degree of competency, you are willing to… desperate to… accept this level of payment for a job like this."

No secret Joey was an adrenaline junkie. Even with such a low payoff, he would be loath to pass up a dodgy run like this. Most capable of pulling off an intrusion on the Imperial Hotel's network would ask for double that amount just to be told the job existed. Joey's financial situation didn't hurt either.

"I'm listening." Joey's tone lost its playfulness.

"My client has his heart set on a particular file that is being stored at the hotel. I do not know what guest owns the data, or what's in it, nor do I really care. We do know that it will only exist for two to three days at most. You will need to move with haste. I would prefer tomorrow if you can find time in your busy schedule of sitting around in your underwear flicking roaches from your scavenged food."

Joey filed that one away for later. There would be retribution for that comment soon enough, but now he drifted in the anticipatory elation of fifty thousand credits. "Send the data tag so I know what I'm looking for. I'll take it."

Alex's terminal chirped. "There. The particulars are on their way to you now. Call me when you have the file."

The holographic head shimmered as the food arrived. Joey grimaced at the sight of Alex's head attached to Lao's body and killed the connection.

"Here we are Mistah Dillon, General Chicken, extra spicy." He bowed with a polite nod as he slid the plate onto the table.

Strips of white meat with a light breading spread with artistic flair, fanned out amidst an arrangement of vegetables and hot peppers, all of it basted in a glistening dark orange sauce. They used vat-grown chicken, not reconstructed OmniSoy. The spicy steam watered his eyes in seconds. The cook had hit the perfect spice point.

By the time he finished, sweat and a euphoric smile were spread over his face. Eating such a large meal after a week of almost starving hurt, but it was worth it.

"Anything else today?" asked Lao, having sidled up to the table unnoticed.

In most cases that would have made Joey jump, but he was too full for sudden motion. Instead, he turned with an idiotic grin of total sublime contentment at the elderly proprietor.

"That was… awesome. I'm done."

With a nod, Lao cleared the dishes and left a small electronic device behind that displayed a receipt for the meal upon its touchscreen surface. Joey pulled out his NetMini and waved it past the device to pay the tab, 57 credits well spent.

He walked out into the night, not that he noticed. Between the oppressive radiance of the Fu Sheng sign and the ant army of advert bots overhead, the city never truly became dark, merely cycled among various degrees of dim.

Much to Joey's surprise, the bike turned on without protest. He did his best not to look like he struggled with a weight beyond his strength as he eased it out of the tiny space in which he had left it. Enjoying the obstruction-free roads, he cruised at a pedestrian-blurring pace until he found himself jamming on the brakes as a traffic signal switched without warning.

He glared at the traffic panel—the damn things acted as if they sensed the approach of a vehicle and went red to spite them, even when nothing came on the other side. His paranoid side told him that the government programmed them to be a pain in the ass. Somewhere, a bored cop made it turn red just to see if he'd run it. He let his head roll around on his neck to stretch, but froze at the sight to his left.

A shop on the corner had an arrangement of holo-bars in the window. Metal strips, oval in cross section and about as big around as a woman's arm. They created holographic panels that ranged in size from as small as 24 inches to over 150 if your living space allowed for it. Even with the store closed, a number of them remained on, tuned to the NewsNet. The middle-aged blonde-haired woman on the screen, droning on about the tragic disappearance of an up and coming new reporter, didn't catch his eye. The nondescript older man walking past her in the background did. He gazed around as if a tourist here for the first time, overwhelmed by the sights. Struggling, he fought his way upstream through the onrush of city dwellers like an overly polite country soul out of his element.

Dad? What the fuck?

Joey's fingers grew cold as his brain soaked up the surreal vision. His father died a little more than a year ago on Mars, not Earth. Now he was in the background of a live, street level news feed broadcast from about forty miles north of where Joey sat stopped at an impertinent traffic light. As far as he knew, the old man had never been on Earth at all. Supernatural eeriness faded at the realization Cleopatra was likely hacking the video stream and dicking with him. He fumed, gripping the handlebars of his bike and swearing an oath to inflict some kind of lingering pain, mental or physical, on her. Dredging up the image of his father went below the belt, and surpassed a simple prank.

Joey's weight pressed into the seat from hard acceleration. He ignored traffic laws for the twenty minutes it took him to get back home. An unusual number of gangers loitered across the street from his apartment, their numbers causing him to turn toward them. He stopped in front of an emaciated man lost in a blue coat two sizes too large. His knee-length fuchsia hair danced in the wind of Joey's arrival.

"Hey Pinky… What's up with the convention?" Joey sat back on the bike.

Eyes, dilated and bloodshot, snapped toward him. The pungent aroma of Flowerbasket permeated everything about Pinky. "Duuuuuuuuuude."

Joey waited. Someone on that chem moved at about a quarter of the mental speed of a sober individual.

His hand lifted and pointed. "There's a giant squid down in Sector 12… eatin' the buildings." Pinky fidgeted. "'cep the wood ones. It don't eat wood."

Joey couldn't help but laugh. "Wood buildings?"

"No… Wait." Pinky rubbed his head. "Stupid… It was a squid… It ate too much CyberBurger and now it's a fuckin' vampire werewolf with laser eyes." He showed off a broken piece of wood he had stashed in his belt. "Got this… just in case."

"A vampire werewolf?" Joey sighed at the clouds. "There's no C-Burgers in Sector 12, and shouldn't you use a silver stake for a vampiric werewolf?"

"Oh shit." Pinky gaped in horror at the scrap wood in his hand. "Whoa, I woulda died. Thanks, man."

A mass of blue spiked hair inserted himself into the conversation. His shiny lime colored coat failed to hide the pair of submachine guns hung on his belt. A strip of blue with metallic flecks crossed his face over both eyes, though Joey couldn't tell if it was paint or a subderm job.

"Yo Dillon." The guy raised a hand. "Something's out there. Bunch of SRaz got themselves dead. One got ripped in half." The guy shifted and wiped his nose with the back of his hand. "Somethin' done fucked them dudes up bad."

"Sasquatch!" Pinky blurted out in a triumphant tone as if he had just unlocked the deepest mystery of the universe. "Vampiric sasquatch maybe…" He hid the stake behind his back. "That would kill Steel Razors."

"Right…" Joey shook his head. "I still got a shitload of tequila if you guys feel like helping me get rid of it."

"Pff." Pinky made a dismissive wave about three feet to the left of Joey. "I don't drink, man, it rots your brains." He wobbled in an apparent attempt to avoid some hallucinatory object.

"Nice." The blue hair nodded to Joey, swaying like an anemone. "I'll check that out."

Joey turned the bike and crossed the street, guiding it down the ramp into its usual resting place. He thumbed through his contacts, tagging Masaru and Katya, and opened a call.

Masaru's face appeared first, a Japanese man in his early twenties. His stark white hair was down to his collar and had a green highlight over his right temple. A friend he made quite by accident a few months ago, his dark brown eyes radiated a "this better be worth it" glance. Masaru Kurotai was the heir to the

Kurotai Empire, arguably a contender for the most prominent electronics company in the world.

Katya, on the other hand, was an enigma. Of Russian descent and indeterminate age, she had the body of a fashion model wrapped around a wicked temper. Her hologram appeared, a smear of jet-black hair framing a porcelain face and ruby red lips. Ever since she paid him to sneak a false identity into the UCF census files, he battled the itch to dig into a past she refused to discuss. Something about her reminded him of the e-thrashing he'd received on Mars. The specter of government intrigue had thus far stalled his curiosity. That, and the expectation any thrashing from Katya would be of a far more physical nature.

With them both online, Joey smiled.

"Just got off the vid with Alex. You two feel like getting shot at with me?"

ANOTHER LONG NIGHT

C risp air traced across her naked body from the vent above. A lily-white outline of humanity, stark against the black satin bedclothes, stretched into her field of view. A year ago, the thought of going out in public in a skimpy bathing suit would have crippled Nina with embarrassment. Now, she sprawled on the bed without regard to what a passing hovercar may see. This was something altogether different from what her mother had brought into the world.

Detecting the orientation of her head pointing at it, the small chrome bar on the nightstand bathed the room in lime holographic radiance. The numbers announced the time as 4:40 AM. With a sigh, she rolled onto her back, eyes tracking panels of light in their silent ballet across the ceiling. Her mind conjured up images of a herd of square zebra at a run, superimposing them over the soundless rectangles that slid over each other in the dark.

They reminded her of before.

Unwelcome consciousness chased away the less welcome dream, and with it, the lingering shouts of the men that had found her on the street ten months ago. For weeks, the events of that day had repainted themselves upon the canvas of her nightmares. Again and again the scene unfolded before her sleeping eyes, leaving her a helpless spectator to Vincent's death. In time, the dream had faded. It hadn't come to visit for four months. The similarity between that night and this one became impossible to ignore. Her present night of restless anxiety brought her back to that one.

Tomorrow's operation seemed routine, though. Perhaps the sound of Vincent's voice emanating from her VidPhone that afternoon was what had brought the nightmare back. After an initial rush of hope, fear, and confusion faded, she realized it for what it was—a recorded vid call he placed to her the day before her last birthday. Some glitch in the system, or a hacker, tried to play games with her mind.

Her fingers traced across her stomach as she stared at this body. Perfect in every detail like a Greek goddess sculpted from flesh-colored marble. They let her keep her sylph's frame, but now the musculature held subtle definition. Gone were the soft curves of a spoiled porcelain doll. The engineers had outdone themselves in their effort to make her look as close as they could to the Nina that had been made of flesh. Even her own mother hadn't noticed until she stood up.

She searched the blank ceiling for answers, the subconscious habit of an anxious mind. Her touch felt normal, so ordinary she could close her eyes and forget the plastisteel coffin in which her brain lay trapped. Her hand slid from her hip, down between her legs. Her back arched. Even *that* sensation felt the same. The touch brought Vincent to her mind, and her fingers retreated in joyless shame.

She had never realized how loud the ventilation fan was before.

As much as her body appeared the same, her personality had changed. In some way, she felt that she *did* die that night. Only once had levity crept into her thoughts since. Her mother, Camille, had been pivotal in keeping her sane since the attack. Nina felt like a black balloon, detached and floating above the rest of humanity. Her mother could pull on the string, bringing her closer.

She made a suggestion that what had happened, albeit horrible, enabled Nina to become a true force for change in the world. Nina shot back that the only good thing to happen was that she no longer needed to shave her legs—or anywhere else. Her mother's mortified reaction made Nina laugh for the first time in half a year.

Father, on the other hand, didn't take it well.

He had been cold with her ever since she rejected his decree that she become a useless socialite, a flower dangled on the arm of a boring man. Despite her central nervous system being very much alive inside a doll body, he treated her like an impostor to his already dead daughter. She regretted telling him the truth. She could have faked it for years without him noticing. Unfortunately, she couldn't lie to him, even if he was a pompous ass.

Her internal loathing twisted the knife, reminding her that the creature upon her bed was a product of her own choice. If she accepted a life spent smiling at people she couldn't care less about while pretending to be interested in conversations about nothing, she would still be whole.

A fate better in whose eyes?

Nina abandoned that life to do something meaningful, but all she accomplished was what everyone feared she would do. Her recklessness caused the death of a cop, a cop she loved. If it would save Vincent's life, she would have wound back the clock so she never met him. Doubt about her decision to join the police had been rattling around her head since the night she spent naked and duct taped in the shower room.

With Vincent gone, she found guilt a far worse companion than regret.

She got out of bed and sulked at the window. The pale ghost in the glass resembled her former self in all respects except standing five foot eight. She had gained four inches. The primary contrast between a cyborg and a doll was that they engineered the latter to look as human as possible. Cheap class 1 models, AIs used for menial jobs, had human-like features but visibly mechanical joints and patches of exposed machinery. Even mid-grade Class 2 units were obvious in their artificiality. Division 9 gave her a class 3 military body that even mimicked the act of breathing and blushing, though she didn't think the crying function worked. It was supposed to, but ever since that first day of knowing, nothing happened when she tried.

Maybe it's me *that's broken.*

She could eat, and she still had to use the bathroom. All her parts seemed intact, albeit made from synthetic tissue. Fingertips traced over her stomach. It felt so real, but the skin didn't *live* in the truest sense. While artificial, and many times more resilient than genuine human skin, blood still flowed through it—the same blood that kept her brain alive. She felt pain when it was injured and pleasure when it was touched just right.

Nina smirked at her reflection over the city. This body didn't feel like hers, it was just a tool given to her like a badge or a gun. Her sense of modesty left with the tears that had fallen from her artificial eyes when they told her that Vincent didn't make it.

The mysterious voice from the light never had a face put to it, though she came to know him as Colonel Harper. He existed somewhere up the food chain where the line between Division 9 and C-Branch blurred. They had been interested in her since she took the entrance exam. Idealistic, motivated, stubborn, and she scored high on ethics. Not to mention, her family's money made her close to immune to bribes. Her lackluster physicality and disinterest in front line work kept them from approaching sooner.

The night of the attack, Harper arrived at the medical facility before she did. The augmented monster had done so much damage to her that her body was a lost cause. They hooked her brain to life support even before she arrived in the operating suite. A computer connected her conscious mind to a holographic terminal. Had she declined his offer, she would be as dead as Vincent. At the time, she thought they asked if she wanted to live. Now that she knew the truth of their question, she couldn't say if she would make the same choice.

She stood motionless for the better part of an hour, staring out over the vast cityscape as she pondered inhabiting a body that cost in excess of 14 million credits. They say sometimes one's job owns people, but in her case, it went beyond metaphor. She could always quit, but they would keep the body. If she got lucky, they would give her a civilian model that wasn't too obvious in its artificiality. Her eyes changed focus, reflection sharpening as the city blurred. This perfect porcelain face staring back wasn't her body, and yet she thought death preferable to appearing fake. A little bit of Duchenne vanity peeked out from behind the curtain of sorrow.

Tears welled in her eyes as she folded her arms and sank to the floor, curling against the cold glass window. It went beyond vanity. As long as she *looked* real, she could lie to herself and pretend she was.

Sparse traffic passed at that hour, one or two every thirty seconds, then a burst of six, and nothing for two minutes. Distant cars and ad-bots reduced to shimmering specks of light moving about in silence. The city stretched off, a massive glowing carpet of contiguous metal. Urban sprawl completely covered the land from the ocean to a little bit eastward of the old California border—straight up into what used to be Canada. The great wall in the east protected everyone from the horrors of the Badlands in the interior of the continent.

Officially, Division 9 existed to monitor foreign nationals and protect visiting dignitaries. Off the books, they dealt with individuals too powerful for normal legal channels to handle. The change came with a promotion to the rank of Lieutenant and a few months of training. For two weeks after she woke up in this thing, she couldn't get Vincent's blood-soaked stare out of her mind. The absence of anger in his eyes hurt most. He didn't scold her for being stupid and running like everyone said she would.

The last expression his face would ever make was one of concern for her.

Warm tears ran down her legs at the thought. She gasped, swiping her hand on her leg to capture one. On her fingertip, it caught a gleam of a passing set of headlights. It was her that had broken, not this simulacra of a spoiled rich girl doing what she wanted to spite Daddy.

Vincent, I'm sorry.

Nina crushed the tear into her fist, before pressing both hands to her face. She wanted to burst, let it all out in a soul-crushing rain of tears, but all she could do was stare at the one line of wetness leading down her leg to her toes.

Her mother had said that he would want her to be happy and alive. He had given his life trying to buy time for her to survive—and her mother begged her not to waste the sacrifice. After two weeks of not leaving her bed, the brass came close to pulling the plug. Her mother had convinced her. Nina lost herself in the training. Without Vincent, and with a father who considered her dead, she hadn't anything left to care about other than the job.

Her first solo ops exceeded command's expectations, and they gave her control of a small team for the operation that would start tomorrow. Her perfectionist nature earned her a reputation as a bit of a hardass, something she had never before imagined anyone accusing her of. That man had in fact killed a part of her, fear and weakness replaced with ambivalence about death. If any truth resided in the strange things Division 0 dealt with, her death would mean she could be with him again.

Tomorrow's operation sounded like an evaluation to see how she handled leading an event force. Someone must think she had potential, to give a new operative like her command, even of a small team on a 'bullshit op' as her new partner Dale Abrams called it.

Two quick beeps preceded a neon blue box appearing in the corner of her vision. Dale's face floated within, trying to smile past a veil of fatigue. At twenty-eight, he was older, but only by three years. Her father expected her to be a mother twice over by this age, but that was now something she could never be. The impassive virtual Nina glaring at Dale over the comm represented a vast departure from the body that shuddered as she held her hands against her gut, mourning the children she couldn't have.

Dale's forced grin did little to dispel the bags under his eyes. His dirty blond hair caught the azure luminescence of the hologram's frame and took on a hue closer to green. She wondered if he would be able to grow facial hair by the time he hit forty. He was easy enough on the eyes, but rather than Vincent's calm, assured, and self-deprecating grin, his face had the look of a dog that wanted to please its master.

As always, she steeled herself against her regrets and hugged her knees to her chest. Her head turned, tracking a hovercar thirty feet below as it drifted out of its lane.

TC88-12, failure to maintain hover lane. Seventeen hundred credit fine.

Even dead, she couldn't get away from Division 1.

Dale's head hung static as the world moved wherever she turned her head. The novelty of getting vid calls right into her mind had worn off in a few days.

"Guess you're awake." His dreary chuckle sounded like more of a grunt.

Nina's tone came flat, almost bored. "Did they hire you for how perceptive you are?"

"Umm…" Dale hesitated, wondering if he got off on the wrong foot with his new boss. "I… Er… Sorry to bother you at this hour—"

"What's on your mind?" Her fingers still teased at her belly. "I hope it's something worth calling over."

"Just can't sleep." He scratched the back of his head as he tried to smile at her.

"I'm not asleep either now."

"Uhh, sorry." He winced. "I keep reading over the dossier for this op and there's some stuff that's bothering me."

"*Some* stuff? The whole thing stinks." She tried to tell her brain to stop expecting Vincent's voice to reply. "Did you see this damn layout?"

"Yes. I'm not sure why they are being so public about it." Dale frowned. "Isn't standard procedure to get a room or two in an inconspicuous place?"

"For some reason, they created a cover operation at the Imperial hotel as a basket weaving convention. Amateurish."

"I guess that will work if they want us to have a lot of personnel—we are supposed to have a dozen Marines and an electronics team. Maybe they thought twenty trucks from Floyd's bakery parked around the hotel would be too obvious?"

"Did you catch the name of the presenter? Ira M. Boring." Hologram Nina scowled.

He lofted a nervous chuckle.

"Initials, Dale. I.M. Boring. Who came up with this shit, are they *trying* to get us killed? Any professional will see it." Nina continued, scowling and yelling from Dale's NetMini, though in the real world she sat in zombie silence.

Dale cringed under the verbal barrage. "Maybe they'll think a hacker was horsing around. I can change it to something that will attract less attention. One minute."

Returning to the bed, she sat on the edge, marveling at how smooth the satin felt.

The sound of Dale working on the mission data blurred away as her mind wandered. Her apartment hadn't changed much since the night before the attack, the only real difference being the black bedclothes. The white ones had Vincent's scent on them, and she couldn't bring herself to wash them. Black seemed appropriate enough. Nix, the stuffed rabbit, got consigned to a box in the closet. She didn't want her childhood companion to see her like this.

For a time, she wondered about any of a thousand subtle ways she could have done something different. She couldn't help but dwell on the question of whether Vincent would have proposed to her by now had that day not taken such an unbearable turn. After these ten months, numbness settled in. The thought of his face only triggered resigned silence now. She pulled her heels up to the bed, running her hands up and down her shins while wondering if her father had been right about her personality. Had she become the walking dead or had she dammed a tsunami of grief behind a wall of indifference so she could function?

The thought to seek out Lieutenant Oliver proved tempting, though she worried it could go too far. With her promotion came unrestricted access to cyberspace. She had found word some Division 0 operatives reported seeing ghosts. Command hadn't placed them on administrative duty after that claim, which meant that someone high up believed it. She could ask Oliver to have one of them look for Vincent so she could talk to him one last time, fearing and wanting that in equal parts. The desire to hear his voice again, to know that he still existed in some form, warred with the emotional crash that would follow once his spirit departed. Seeing him, even if only for a moment, would be like watching him die all over again.

A touch of cold struck her thigh, spreading into a tickle that ran down her leg. Silent tears fell over her stoic face at the thought of watching Vincent's ghost wave farewell. Almost as bad as wanting him back, she wanted to let it all out and cry him gone. Neither wish came at the asking.

Ghosts? Ugh. She rubbed her forehead, fingers through her hair. *I'm losing it.*

Dale's voice startled her. "That should do it. How does Robert Farmington sound?"

"A little on the generic side, but an improvement nonetheless." The voice Dale heard had no trace of her mood. "Try to get some sleep."

"Okay. See you in a few hours. I'll be there at six."

"Oh, Dale?"

"Yeah?"

"You didn't wake me up…"

The floating window collapsed as she ended the call. Now alone with her thoughts, she pushed the idea of ghosts out of her head. Regardless of what Division 0 could or couldn't do, a part of her was happier not knowing.

Nina sighed at the shifting glow of the Comforgel in the crumpled hollows of her satin sheets. Between thoughts of Vincent as a ghost and worry about the operation, sleep seemed a futile endeavor. The old standby of her treadmill offered little help—not like this body got tired.

It could still enjoy a hot shower, but she hadn't allowed herself to take pleasure in anything since that night. Why should she be happy when her mistake got him killed? Her mother said he made the choice to go after her, and he made a tactical failure with his assumption that one shot to the leg put the monster down. He should have controlled the situation before letting his guard relax. She found that stone a bit too heavy to heave at the memory. If she hadn't charged ahead like an idiot, Vincent never would have been in that position.

She found some comfort in having saved a life, even if she had all but given up her own to do it. The prostitute, his intended victim, turned out to only be seventeen. At least that night had scared her into finding a new line of work. A confused mix of emotion swirled as she paced.

Too many questions still lingered without an answer. If Captain Farris wanted her on a safe route, who altered it the night of the senator's speech, and why not say anything in person?

She fell into a chair by her terminal. The coldness of the simulated leather made her gasp and tense up. The Division 5 report had a disappointing lack of detail. The aug ganger sustained heavy weapons fire from the arriving A3V. From the looks of it, he lost his still-normal arm in a spray of blood and ran away singing Beethoven, in German. A month after the attack, Division 2 Investigations Department got the case, but the detective working on it had no luck finding him either.

Her nakedness glowed blue and green from the terminal panel as she batted at it, swatting files aside like a bored cat. A gleaming white and silver building appeared, bathing her in ivory light, and she paused.

That same night, the now-famous hack of the Silver Building went down, a supposedly impregnable cyberspace fortress that sold secure data storage for any client that could afford it. Law enforcement failed to notice it as all eyes had been on an abandoned section of grey zone, where two police officers died. Someone had managed to sneak in and steal data that belonged to StarPoint Industries, a manufacturer of military vehicles, but they never found out who did it or what they took. The stolen data had been important enough for StarPoint to spend millions trying to track down who had done it, but they failed.

Nina leaned back in the chair, and pulled her right heel up to the seat. She stared at the terminal, cheek resting on the side of her knee, and tried to find sense in it. Hackers love to brag about their exploits—but to claim to be the one that pulled off the Silver would be dangerous. Even in the UCF, corporations hold grudges for a long time. She found it too convenient that her route change happened on the same night. It looked so much like a deliberate distraction. Alas, all her poking around had so far failed to turn up any credible proof.

She rotated away from the screen and stretched out. There had been a series of prostitute murders in the past few months but Division 1 hadn't paid them much attention. She wondered if the same beast was responsible. At least two victims had been mutilated beyond recognition. Few within the police command cared if the street filth ate itself. Gangs killing gangers only meant one less drug-crazed fringer to worry about later down the line. Division 9 only became involved when foreign nationals, corporate fat cats, or dirty cops came into play.

With a flick of her foot against the rug, she spun in the chair and sighed. The thing that had killed Vincent vanished without a trace, and only one man bothered looking for him. She could pick it up in her spare time. If anyone asked, she merely followed up on an old case. Technically, it wasn't a lie.

Maybe if I dangle myself as bait, he'll find me.

After staring at her wardrobe, she slammed the cabinet closed. Not one bit of clothing in there looked anything like what a prostitute would wear. Living Nina had been a demure creature, and had issues even using the showers at the station. She let the door slide closed, feeling surprised relief. A little piece of her still clung to some dignity.

I have to get out of this apartment. I need some air.

Her ballistic stealth armor lay draped over the back of her chair where she had left it some hours ago. A full body suit infused with a layer of nanobot enhanced non-Newtonian gel that could harden almost instantly when exposed to high stress. The microscopic machines stitched plastisteel threads together as it hardened, adding strength to the impromptu plate in much the same way as steel rods in poured concrete.

The cold rubbery material made her gasp as she slipped her legs in. She stiffened out of reflex, her subconscious reaction unaware of her new body. A moment later, she shrugged it up and over her shoulders. The suit stretched to fit. Within seconds, it had become a form-fitting layer of gloss black with only her face, hands, and feet uncovered. Black socks, combat boots, a shoulder holster, and a long sand colored coat finished her gear.

A glint ran down the housing of her MCP 50 as she checked the feed. It was a much larger sidearm than she had that night, chambered for 15mm slugs instead of 8mm, but she still doubted its effectiveness against that monster. Considered a class 6 weapon, the largest handguns available, they were usually the purview of huge men.

She took it because of protocol. She didn't intend to use it if she found him. Her nightmare often dwelled on the sight of bullets stalling on his chest, feeble and useless. She had more faith in her new body and months of training in Wushu, a combat style that lent itself to her superhuman agility. Nina had only to learn the mechanics of the technique since her new body didn't need to be conditioned. She relished the thought of a distinct advantage. As one sided as their last meeting went, the next would be the opposite. The thought of avenging Vincent got her blood moving.

She imagined him in front of her as a pair of Nano blades shot out the back of her fist and locked in place. Most times, she forgot they were even there, and hadn't yet used them in a real situation. Such things inside her felt alien, breaking her fantasy of being human.

Nina stared at the clear synthetic diamond blades, wondering if they would meet the same futile fate as the bullets. Their edge, sharpened to the width of a single molecule, could cut anything their user had enough strength to handle. Deadly in the hands of normal people, on a doll they approached unstoppable.

She would dismantle him piece by piece, saving the claws for the coup de grace. Nina closed her eyes and pictured the face he would make once he knew death was imminent. She opened them and frowned. Would she go this far off the deep end of sanity? The fantasies felt like those of an addled mind, even to herself.

The claws retracted, sliding noiseless into her arm.

No, I'm not sinking to his level.

Nina traced a finger over the back of her hand, the slit through which the blades emerged already sealed to the point of invisibility. She only wanted him to know who she was before he died, only wanted him to realize her revenge. Her mother's voice haunted her as she left her apartment, asking if she would feel any sense of closure by taking another life.

He's not alive, Mother. He's a creature. Someone has to stop him... greater good, and all that.

Who knew how many more women he had killed since that night, and no one seemed to care.

She was already damaged. It didn't matter if she killed again.

10

FISHING EXPEDITION

Drifting in a silent descent on the outside face of the building, the glass bubble elevator vibrated in the glow of a loose lamp. The orange-yellow light of the endless city swallowed the black, starless sky as she sank toward the ground. Vincent's voice wafted over her mind, cracking a joke about the angel of death descending to Earth. A lump grew in her throat as she stared at the empty courtyard where he always parked to wait for her. She remembered how she looked like a kid dressed up as a cop for Halloween, and a single tear ran down her face.

A flicker of static shimmered on the barren grey. Vincent stepped out from behind the fountain, smiling at her. She stared at him until the elevator sank into the enclosed chamber at the bottom.

She sprinted across the lobby, racing out into an empty courtyard. In silence, she stared at the spot of ground where she had seen him, turning to look up at the rising silver blister on the side of the building. It was solid plastisteel. Cameras and a curved video display created the illusion of it being a bubble of glass—just like the windows of police hovercars. Nina squatted, tracing her fingers over the cold ground where she had seen him for a moment before storming back inside.

The lobby was still empty save for a red-haired Class 1 doll behind the information desk. Its uniform made her look like a flight attendant. The mouth and joints had small gaps through which underlying mechanisms peeked out. Nina didn't bother to waste a pleasant greeting on her. She, rather it, had no living brain and a rudimentary artificial intelligence—just a data terminal that could talk.

Helping herself to the terminal, she ignored the receptionist's protests and drew an M3 cable from the back of her neck, plugging in. The building's system logs had no recorded traces of anyone interacting with the video display on elevator 6.

Could Vincent be trying to reach her?

Frigid wind embraced her outside. At this time of night, the city had long ago given up any stored warmth from the day before. Shivering, she savored the feeling of feeling. In this state somewhere between alive and not, the most banal things could cause her to stop and appreciate normality. She tried to ignore the fact her body was immune to the effects of temperature, instead embracing the concept of being a twenty-five year old woman walking down a street at four in the morning—and feeling cold.

Her training included how to assume other identities. Learning languages became as simple as a trip to the tech lab and the addition of a data chip filled with a mimic of cortical imprints. Her French was almost as good as her English, and for her current assignment, she had requisitioned a language chip for German.

She walked the deserted streets, thinking about acting like a lost German tourist to give the chip a test drive. She changed her mind, not trusting herself to pull it off just yet. The desolation reminded her of the place she spent her last night as a normal person. Melancholy set in and she tucked her hands into her coat pockets.

What if we weren't cops?

Under the glow of a corner streetlamp, she concocted an alter ego based on that concept. An innocent young wife who just emigrated to the UCF from France witnessed a horrible assault as she left a show with her husband. She had only been in the country for a month and her valiant beau tried to help a poor woman under attack. The augmented monstrosity became a group of common thugs to fit the scene, and she had run away in fright—escaping rape but leaving her husband to die at their hands.

A loud hiss startled her as a PubTran came to a halt at the traffic signal. She had the green, but paused to look at the side of the vehicle. A smiling Indian woman wearing a white doctor's coat over a dark business suit greeted her from an ad panel. As soon as she looked at it, it projected audio at her. Dr. Preeti Khan, a psychologist who specialized in grief counseling, spoke about her cyberspace friendly practice that went by the name "The New Hope Center."

Her concocted identity could accomplish two things. She would visit this doctor and see if she could fool a professional. With a story so close to reality, she might find some benefit if the therapist was any good. It seemed logical that her dainty French doppelganger would look into something like that, and in cyberspace, she could be anyone she wanted to be. Her mother always said things happen for a reason. The timing of that bus seemed almost too convenient.

Walking around at random felt futile. A terminal window painted itself into her vision as she connected to the police net petty crimes database. A parser line below a graphic overlay map flashed with the computer's translation of her mental commands. Search parameters reduced a chaotic mass of color to distinct dots that appeared like a buildup of spray paint wherever prostitution arrests had occurred over the past two years. Cops rarely charged anyone with solicitation, having better things to worry about. Typically, they arrested prostitutes only as a legal technicality to bring underage runaways off the street.

Targeting the thickest concentration of dots, she tried to think like her old self, before the police training. She took on the walk of a frightened girl that just wanted to get inside as soon as possible. Her gaze fell to the street, and she shrank into a decent mimic of someone going out of her way to be victimized.

Passing cars sent mist into the air as they whooshed along. Perpetual wetness blanketed this part of the city, as if it had stopped raining an hour ago despite none having fallen for at least a week. Damp chilly air swirled around as she crossed another street and went down an alley. The smell of decay, urine, and sour trash hung in her throat. A few prostitutes, three women and two men, took shelter under the awning of a closed market, lit by glowing signs advertising cosmetic cyberware and replacement eyes.

An animated hologram woman danced around in the window with disappearing and reappearing cat ears, chirping "Aha!" each time they came back. Nina felt bad for whoever had to hear that all day long.

She disregarded the prostitutes, walking past them without an obvious glance. The five of them seemed at ease, and unconcerned with what might lurk in the night. If her nightmare still walked the streets, he wasn't in this part of the city. She grumbled, feeling stupid for entertaining the thought of finding him within blocks of her apartment building. Fate was cruel but irony wasn't that indelicate. She paused at the next curb, as an idea hit her. The grieving widow had a name:

Avril Boudreau.

11

ANOTHER SLICE

Nina's mental back and forth came to an abrupt halt when a tactical overlay jumped into her field of view. Two dots approached from behind at a threatening speed. Her gaze shifted left, catching a reflection in the window of a shop, magnifying it until she saw the two men moving up on her.

Both wore tattered pants and heavy boots. The one on the left had a black tank top and a red mesh jacket, the other a simulated leather coat with gold skull-shaped buttons. Both had outlandish hair. Skull Buttons had a bald stripe down the center of his head with neon blue hair on either side. Mesh's hair gathered into four thick spikes. Both carried, but neither had pulled a gun out yet. Glimmering green text identified their firearms—small Class 2 pistols that couldn't pierce her armor.

I go fishing for a shark and find a pair of mackerel.

She whirled. Her sudden movement spooked them to a halt. Nina kept her forlorn stare at the street as she spoke.

"You boys need something?" she asked, her tone taciturn, menacing.

The men exchanged a glance before blue hair grinned. "Ya got a pretty face."

Spikey nodded. "Yeah… no tits tho."

"I'll take what I can get." The other ganger chuckled. "Take it easy honey, play nice and this won't hurt at all. Just 'ave a little fun."

Nina didn't move. "Oh, I'm sure it will hurt. Just not me."

A full strength strike to either of these two unaugmented idiots would tear them in half. She didn't want to kill them. Spiky frowned. Holding his hands apart, he took a step back. The faintest hint of a tremble settled into his fingers.

Blue pointed, as if to say something, and made a grimace but couldn't form the words.

Nina's head snapped up, making them both jump. "You two fine young men wouldn't be looking to assault me, would you?"

Her intent look set Spiky's entire body shivering. His hand drifted to his gun and his eyes darted between her and the alley behind him. Blue stepped closer, oblivious to the warning in her gaze. Even at her new height, he stood a head taller and already touched her in dirty ways with his eyes. Statue-like, she left her hands in her pockets as he approached and pulled at the belt of her coat. Nina held her stare on Spiky as his friend put his arm around her waist.

A hand slid up her chest, cupping a breast through her ballistic suit, as the other did the same to her ass. Nina smiled faintly at the thought of how good a job the engineers did if this idiot hadn't sensed anything unusual. Even squeezing her, he didn't act as if anything were amiss. She smiled at passing for normal during such close contact. Blue let go of her breast. The impression of his fingers remained for a few seconds in the pliable armor.

Spiky broke out in a sweat watching her just stand there being pawed without so much as a whimper or even the slightest attempt to avoid it. His eyes widened with anticipation as his fear mutated into arousal and wonder at what kind of psycho they found.

"Yo, Buzzard... This one's fucked up." He laughed. "I think she likes it."

"Uh huh." The hand left her ass and rode up her left side. "What the...?"

The ridge of his hand had grazed the tip of her sidearm, and he pulled her coat away to expose it. The massive thing seemed out of place next to her waifish frame. The men exchanged a glance before breaking into cackling laughter.

"The only thing you'll do with that fucker is break your goddamn hand," said Buzzard.

Spiky patted her gun. "It's bigger than you are."

Something in his tone flipped a switch in her mind. He sounded a little too much like Eddie Alvin. With Buzzard chuckling back at his friend, Nina grabbed his wrist and yanked. Two hundred pounds of ganger flipped over in midair before crashing face-first into the street. Spiky's eyes widened, he babbled, and his hand swiped at his belt three times before it managed to find his gun.

Her perception of time slowed to a crawl. Enhanced reflexes moved her body and mind beyond human limitations. Spiky's gun slid from its holster, not quite half-way aimed by the time she had taken two steps. Her left arm swung to the side, swatting the weapon away at the same time as her right elbow smashed into his chest.

His arm bent around hers as if made of rubber—bones shattered on impact, throwing the gun into the air. The strike to his chest lifted him off his feet amid the cracking of ribs and sent a fine spray of blood from his mouth, misting her face. The flying weapon smashed the window of a parked car, landing on the seat in a rain of glass fragments. Spiky hit the ground on his back almost ten feet away, wheezing and gasping. Disregarding him, she turned back to watch Buzzard stagger to his feet. He charged at her, howling a guttural war cry.

Nina considered a spin kick, but didn't want to liquefy him. She waited for him to get closer, watching the skin of his face distort like a latex mask in his slow motion run. His arms circled about her chest. Nina sank away from the closing bear hug and, with a palm on his chest, shoved him backward and up. His feet left the ground as his momentum held him in midair against her hand and carried his legs forward. As soon as his body went horizontal, she drove him into the pavement flat on his back. The punk hit the ground hard, but broke no bones. He stared up at her with stunned disbelief, breathless.

She squatted beside him, removed the gun from his belt, and thumbed the release. The magazine bounced onto the pavement sending several blocks of loose ammo skittering off along the sidewalk. Holding the weapon over his face so he could see it, she closed her hand and crushed it into a useless hunk of metal and plastic.

"You're not too hurt right now. Let's keep it that way. If I see you move I'll do that to your other gun."

He babbled something unintelligible between gasping breaths. She stood, tossing the ruined gun on his chest and dividing her attention between the two men motionless on the sidewalk. Once certain no fight remained in them, she opened a comm.

"Ops, this is Lieutenant Nina Duchenne, Division 9 ID 804332C3."

"Proceed, Lieutenant," said a pleasant female voice. The face of one of the dispatch dolls, a class 1 AI unit, appeared in midair.

"I need a pickup in Sector 108, City Road 17. Two white males, approximate age late 20s, assault and attempted rape."

"Acknowledged, victim status?"

"Unhurt."

"Acknowledged, suspect status?"

"One suspect is injured. I think it's a broken rib with a pierced lung. Send a medical unit. The area is secure, I'll wait for them."

"Acknowledged. Units are on the way Lieutenant. Have a pleasant morning."

Nina glanced at Spiky as the virtual face collapsed out of her vision. Blood leaked from the corner of his mouth. His arms curved into his chest in a pantomime of a chicken hit by a car. Her cybereyes created a wireframe of his skeleton over reality, revealing two broken ribs as well as where the bones in his right arm were reduced to a smear of splinters from wrist to midpoint.

"You're not going to die." Nina turned off the medical scan and put a hand on his shoulder.

Spiky tried to lean away, trembling, as she got closer. She wondered if this feeling—eyes staring at her like that—was what drove her attacker to insanity. He didn't try to hide his augmentation—he screamed it from the rooftops.

No, that creature was at ease with what he was. He enjoyed it.

"Calm down. You're a pair of rapists. You should be damn happy I didn't kill you. A blue and white is on the way to scrape you morons off the sidewalk."

Spiky gurgled and tried to sit up. Nina's hand convinced him otherwise.

"Your ribs are broken and your lung's been torn. Stay still."

His eyes lost focus as he slipped into shock from the pain. She smiled at that, now he wouldn't do anything stupid. Buzzard took the hint and remained motionless. She stood between them, watching the sparse traffic drift overhead until two Division 1 patrol craft approached from the south, bar lights on but no sirens. They came in low and glided overhead at a crawl, flooding the area with a halogen glow. Nina smirked, unimpressed at their cautious approach to a pair of gang thugs. As the cars turned around and came back, she wondered if maybe she was the cause of their wariness.

She held up her ID. Her vision zoomed in on the passenger in the lead car. The patterns of light on his face said he checked her out on scanners, the usual routine. She remembered every key press in the procedure. The image magnified until she made out the terminal reflected on his eyes, inverted by her image processor so the words were not backward. Their tension faded as the ID checked out and the four patrol officers got out of their vehicles and walked over.

"Nice night for a walk?" The driver of the left car looked at the two men on the ground.

"Apparently. These two were looking for some tail and didn't give a damn if the tail was interested."

The two from the right car approached Buzzard. One secured what remained of his gun, holding it in two fingers. He looked up at Nina, who just smiled. The partner pointed at his datapad, at her ID. His whisper of explanation that the C3 at the end indicated a class 3 doll didn't elude her ears.

"I didn't want him to hurt himself." She overacted a demure tone.

"Where's the vic?" The driver of the other car walked up while his partner checked on Spiky.

Nina just smiled a wry little smile without saying a word.

"Oh you have to be kidding me... wow." He looked at her sideways and paused for a moment. "Really?"

"Yeah. These two geniuses figured my early morning stroll could use a fuck break."

"Of all the women..." He laughed. "I love it when the idiots do us favors."

"Got it from here, then?"

His face shone green in the castoff light from a datapad. "No problem, Lieutenant. Just need the usual statement."

Nina reached for the device. "I can just give you my log if you want."

He handed it over. She pulled the wire from the underside, and connected it to a socket in the back of her neck, hidden beneath her hair. Her onboard systems kept a running recording of everything she saw and heard, buffering the most recent hours' worth of information unless she recorded more on purpose. Rather than give a tedious verbal statement, she uploaded video of the entire event as her eyes recorded it. Nina ejected the plug with a thought and handed it back to him as the wire reeled itself in.

He reviewed the contents while she waited, having little reaction but curt nods until the point where she crushed the pistol. The others crowded around like spectators at a Gee-ball game, grinning at the time-slow point of view.

"You must be havin' a good day Lieutenant, you went easy on them. Holy shit..." He shook of his head.

I haven't had a good day in almost a year. Nina sighed. "There's not a whole lot left of my soul, and these two morons aren't worth losing another slice."

"I hear that. Have a good morning Lieutenant."

ACCEPTANCE

Nina walked away, heading in the same direction she had been going before the interruption. A MedVan nosed around a corner and flew over her on its way to the scene. She looked up, dragging her perception of time to a near standstill. She squinted at the boxy craft, aglow with a bevy of emergency lights and ground illuminating lamps. Four ion focusers at its corners created five-meter wide starbursts. She cut the reflex booster and it zoomed off, a fly freed from honey.

Head down, she trudged along wondering why a MedVan came this fast for a piece of street trash but when Vincent needed one, it arrived late. Her attempt to wallow in misery dried up as her rational side countered with an appraisal of elapsed time. If Spiky suffered the same kind of full body crushing injuries that Vincent had, the MedVan would have been too late for him as well.

Well, this was a total waste of time.

Nina turned, heading home at a brisk walk. The folly of expecting to stumble across that *thing* so close to her apartment mixed with her memory of charging at him that night, a nagging reminder that haunted her with the pointlessness of rash decisions.

Maybe I just wanted some air. It's not like I'm losing sleep.

Some comfort came with the thought that she spared some innocent woman a life-ruining night.

Maybe mom was right about destiny.

Hair fluttering in the wind, she glanced up at the sky and searched for any break in the endless pattern of indigo. Mother said that some higher power had chosen her for this change, that her new body with all its abilities came as a blessing. Nina didn't put any stock in the concept of a supreme being and only recently even accepted the truth about psionics. Ten months ago, she thought it little more than a pile of warm horseshit cooked up over an open fire of fear and sprinkled with paranoia by conspiracy theorists.

A gap in the smog opened for a fleeting moment, offering a clear view of a patch of starry sky—quite a rare sight in the city. The ever-present layer of vapor and pollution seldom yielded a view of anything but grey that sometimes turned purple during twilight. In the south, where Nina lived, the smog was at its thickest, forty miles north of what people called Los Angeles four hundred years ago.

She walked in the door a few minutes shy of 5:30 a.m., thinking Dale would be there in about a half an hour. Blood remained on her face from the fight and she wondered if a shower might relax her. Even if it didn't, it could make thirty minutes pass.

Her bathroom felt cramped despite the place being considered at the high end of middle class. A clear tube in the corner stretched from floor to ceiling between metal platforms. She stepped up into the device and the tube door slid closed behind her with a faint squeak. Along a metal ring at the center above the handrail, the autoshower's control terminal painted her with pink light. She once liked the girly theme she set on it, and still didn't care enough to expend the effort necessary to change it. With a jab of her finger, it came to life and water jets spun around, soaking her in soothing warmth. She let her head sag forward as she stood in the spray, lost in her thoughts. Nina stared at the droplets beading on the screen, distorting the pink into individual pixels.

They mocked her inability to have an honest cry since Vincent died.

She peered down a short tunnel of hanging hair as the water ran over her stomach and down her legs, swirling into the oblivion of the drain between her toes. She wanted to fall in a heap and sob it all out—but for a reason she couldn't fathom, she just stood there in stone-faced silence. A deep breath filled her synthetic lungs, inflating her chest like any ordinary person. The ghost of her former life, plus four inches, haunted her from the blurry reflection on the tube wall amid thousands of droplets.

She touched her fingertips to her reflected face. The idea that her life may not be ruined teased at the edges of her mind. If she could stop feeling sorry for herself, she could embrace the illusion. This body did most of the work. All she had to do was accept that Vincent would want her to be happy, and work for Division 9. It wasn't her dream, but at least she no longer feared death.

The sudden intrusion of an incoming phone call interrupted her with Dale's face.

"Morning Lieutenant. I just pulled up outside." Dale smiled.

I knew it. "Fifteen minutes early." Nina closed her eyes out of reflex as the shower sprayed her with foam, not that soap would sting mechanical eyes.

"You know… that whole can't sleep thing. I brought coffee." A cup slid into view on the image, waving as if teasing a dog with a treat.

"I need a few minutes, come on up. No need to sit there in the truck."

"Right. Okay, which apartment is it?" Dale fidgeted with his hair.

"Floor 62, room 407."

Dale blushed. "Understood, Lieutenant. I'm on my way."

The image collapsed into a point and the shower mechanism wrapped her in a warm rinse. Whirling around her in spirals, the streams soon freed her of the soapy shroud. She tried to hurry the process along with her hands. The water stopped as the shower kicked into its drying cycle. Jets of hot air came up from the floor as well as the rotating side sprayer.

The overpowered airstream no longer blew her about. She lifted her arms over her head and basked in the hot air. With the machine winding down, the sound of a ringing doorbell drowned out the fans. She opened it with a wireless command to her apartment's control system, patching her voice through to a panel on the wall out front.

"I'm almost done. Come in, I'll be right out."

It took a moment for the autoshower to shut down and release the safety interlock on the door. She slipped out into the chill of normal temperature air and combed at her hair with her fingers in the mirror before wandering without a word into the hall, padding down the short corridor to the main room. A shadow of a man shifted on the wall. She paused at the door, amused by his muttering about how the place looked unlived in, clean and perfect like a model apartment—except for the pile of clothing on the Comforgel pad.

Dale glanced around the place, fidgeting and picking at self-warming coffee cups. Nina kept walking, right past him as casually as if clothed.

He all but dropped the coffee, managing to steer the fumbled cup onto the table, then turned his back on her as fast as he could without causing further damage.

"Lieutenant! You're—"

"Naked. Yes, Dale, I am aware of that. I've tried showering in my armor and it doesn't work as well." She leaned past him and grabbed a cup.

He shied away. "But aren't you—"

"Embarrassed?" She took a sip. "No. This is just a machine, it's not me." *I'm just a brain in a jar now.*

Her shower rumination left her wondering if she still felt that way, but it seemed like the perfect thing to say to keep Dale at arm's length.

He risked a look, stammering for a second. "Sir... Lieutenant... ma'am... You look... um... You... you should be embarrassed."

Nina turned to face him full on. He flinched away as if she slapped him.

"Dale?"

"Yeah?"

"Speaking as a man, purely in a clinical sense, what do you think?" Nina put a hand on her hip and twisted a bit to the side as she modeled for him.

Dale didn't look. "You're my superior. This is just not right, why do I feel like I'm about to get an email from HR?"

Nina chuckled. "I'm sorry. I don't want to make you uncomfortable. I"—her voice softened, she stopped smiling—"you're right. I shouldn't have put you in that position. I needed to know if I'm still a person, or something... else."

With a hesitant turn, he looked at her feet. His eyes met hers, and then slid back down before he spun away.

"If no one told me you were a doll, I couldn't to tell. Isn't that the whole point of the Division 9 mods on the Class 3 body? All the military power crammed into a Maya 6?" He picked at the valve on his coffee. "You're supposed to be able to infiltrate places undetected. It wouldn't do any good if you thumped around like a combat cyborg."

A giant swig of coffee reddened his face from the heat.

Nina smiled despite Dale not seeing it. Hearing that made her feel a little more human, and the extreme awkwardness that drenched him amused her.

"Thanks Dale. You can look now." She chuckled, not remembering the last time she had done so.

He hazarded a peek, relaxing when he saw her dressed.

"Wow they even gave you a um…" His speech stalled with the thought that his attempt at an icebreaker might have just been the most incorrect thing he could have said at that moment.

Nina laughed with a genuine escape of levity. "Yes Dale, they did, and that's as far as we are going with that topic." *Vincent would have asked for a closer look.*

Now crimson, he couldn't look at her. "Yes ma'am."

The awkwardness of the preceding moment kept a pall of silence over them until they exited the lobby and strode across the courtyard in front of the building. A bronze statue ringed with curved benches occupied the center of a sunken square in the open expanse of metal, a human figure approximated by a series of elongated pyramids, rectangles, and spheres welded together. Several thin sweeping arcs jutted out in the artist's attempt to suggest motion. A little boy no older than eight sat upon the bench, bouncing and catching a flashing green ball. He smiled at her as they walked by, unafraid. She waved.

They passed on either side of the abstract man. Nina looked at the pattern of corrosion, green over dark bronze. It traced a path to the ground, driven by rainfall, where it stained the marble base green.

In her imagination, the statue changed into her body, devoid of skin as well as clothes. A deteriorating plastisteel skeleton posed like an athlete, staring out from its own oblivion. A metal husk propped up on display that no one even glanced at twice.

Is that what awaits me when my time runs out?

13

BASKET WEAVING

D ale's voice distracted from her gloomy stare. He had rounded to the front of the statue and looked back at her with an expectant raised brow.

"All postings and references to the seminar are updated to the new presenter name, everything looks squared away."

She turned away from the bronze, catching up. "Good. What kind of idiot came up with I.M. Boring? They might as well have labeled it a seminar on clandestine government operations."

"I figure it's one of two possibilities." His blush receded. "One, an idiot was trying to make people not want to go. I don't think anyone in their right mind would enjoy a seminar on basket weaving..." His chuckle died at her lack of response. "Second thought is that command wanted to see how you would react. If this is a low importance job, they may have done some things wrong on purpose to see if you'd catch it."

Nina scowled at the white van with the logo of Floyd's Bakery on it. "My credits are on the second option, and that's just me hoping against hope that we don't employ anyone that stupid." She shook her head at the slogan on the side of the vehicle. "The most mediocre bagels you've ever had? The moron theory is picking up credibility."

"Yeah." Dale slid open the driver side door and climbed in. "We've been using Floyd's for a while now, they didn't want a lot of foot traffic at the store, so they tried to make an unappealing slogan."

"The average idiot probably won't think about it—but operatives would see that stick out like a red flag. Who would ever advertise in a way that would *reduce* business? That will need to be changed too."

"It might not be worth it, the Floyd's cover is going to be retired after this op anyway. We've had it for six months and it was due to end in two more. Warner's been the most interesting thing to happen in a little over a year."

"We should still conceal that slogan. I don't want our cover blown at the wrong moment by something so foolish."

She came through the armored door from the back, and sat in the passenger seat. "At least the electronics suite works."

"Have surveillance teams one or two reported any unusual activity?" Nina glanced over the files.

"Nothing. Karl Warner is still at his residence, no sign of any outside contact. No sign of Nemsky or Korin."

"It's German," corrected Nina. "Pronounce the W like a V. *Var*-ner, not *War*-ner. Anyway, it looks like the network team came up empty handed too. Neither one of them have left much of a trace in the net since their shuttle passes cleared at Edmondson Memorial Starport."

"It's sad that it's easier to get into the UCF by going to Mars than simply crossing the ocean."

He eased the van around a corner, turning north toward Sector 86 and the Imperial Hotel. "There's something that's just not making sense about this."

"There you go again, stating the obvious." Nina looked over.

"Well, think about it. You have two foreign nationals, Itai Korin and Anatoly Nemsky, who are at best mercenaries and at worst clandestine operatives. Both of them turn into ghosts as soon as they land. The files don't say anything about either one of them being skilled hackers. Hell, Nemsky looks like he'd just as likely *eat* a deck than plug into it."

"Yeah…" She wanted to punch the dashboard but held back.

The pair had been almost impossible to trace save for a fleeting glimpse of a credit transaction here and there. The most credible evidence came from a few surveillance camera recordings that put them near Karl Warner's diplomatic residence. Of two possibilities, both of them smelled like rotten potatoes.

"Either they're both exceptional spies that are masters at covering their tracks in the real world or they have a hacker working with them that's good enough for us not to know about him… or her." She grumbled. "Either way, it points to something larger here than a playboy diplomat from Germany."

"Command thinks that Warner has hired them for something."

He grimaced as the distraction of their conversation almost caused him to miss a red light. Nina lifted a foot to keep her in the seat during the hard deceleration.

"I'm aware of that theory, it's the whole reason we're watching Warner. Let's go over what we *do* know."

"Karl Warner, age 47, diplomatic envoy from the ACC, specifically, Germany. He has been in-country for three months as an ambassador. He has a small personal guard team and favors fine food, expensive clothing, women, cars… looks like every other millionaire playboy in the ACC. If I remember the file correctly, he wasn't content harassing common women and the wrong man's daughter wound up on the business end of his attitude. All signs point to him being sent here as a dumping ground post. They're probably hoping one of us puts a bullet in him."

Dale looked at her for a moment before returning his eyes to the road. "He's conspicuous in his normality. Too normal?"

"Maybe," Nina mused. "Is it possible to be too normal? There is always a crack somewhere. He will eventually screw up. Have the net team check his background again and look for any traces of modification in the files. Verify all the log dates so we know that they didn't invent him four months ago."

"Check. Next we have Itai Korin, 36, former agent for the Mossad, our sources say he parted ways with them 4 years ago. His operational qualifications consist primarily of demolitions work, counterterrorism, and sniper training. They redacted his file to the point of being almost blank. We cannot tell the official nature of his separation with the Israeli military. There's no categorization here… dishonorable, honorable, AWOL… not a damn thing."

"That's suspicious. Usually there would be *some* kind of falsified record if he was going into a cover operation or assigned to a covert unit. The lack of it creates questions they wouldn't want asked."

Dale slammed on the brakes, again, to avoid hitting a malfunctioning delivery bot sputtering too low to the road. "He freelances with no allegiance to any sovereign nation or ideology, just to credits. We connected him to four assassinations, each in different corners of the ACC. Two kidnappings, again both in the ACC, and one attempted bombing at one of our military bases on Mars."

"Mr. Korin is quite the globetrotter, and it's not uncommon for their intelligence community to wipe out mistakes. Chances are, Mossad would have tried to burn him once it got out he went rogue. Hardin's friends in C-Branch said they couldn't find any records of that either, but the Israelis have never been very open with our intelligence community. Even if they know where he is, they wouldn't tell us. Have we gotten anything from our contacts at the UN?"

"Hardin doesn't want to risk mentioning him right now. If there is a connection to a sanctioned operation, we don't want to tip them off that we're on to him."

"They think he's still active Mossad?" Nina's face failed to hide her frustration. "What the hell for? Trying to cozy up to Warner for some reason while posing as a merc?" She pinched the bridge of her nose. "It doesn't add up, four years of mercenary activity that is clearly not on the same page as the rest of his country doesn't strike me as a deep cover operation."

"It's as much of a mystery as how Israel has managed to stay independent this long." Dale laughed. "Falsified?"

Her hands balled into fists. "Please don't tell me this wasn't checked, and checked again."

"No… We did, five times, and verified it with some of our contacts in Moscow. I'm just saying it could be a *very* good fake."

Dale raised a scary implication that made her question her readiness for this operation. "That would require a lot of resources, time, and effort… but for what? Warner is a mole on the ass of their system. He's a flea." She punched the armored wall behind her.

The *whump* startled nearby pedestrians.

While paging over the electronic document, she stopped to stare at a still from the starport surveillance system where it captured Itai. Close cropped hair, so short it was more like a dark stain on his skull. His thick brown eyebrows angled in a suspicious backward glance over his shoulder. His attire was plain and unassuming, like a working class guy just going about his uneventful life.

"He's been in the UCF for eight months and we have one still image? How is that possible? If he is really as good as the lack of our information implies, we're in for a hell of a ride."

"It gets better." Dale stretched. "General Anatoly Nemsky, age 42, dishonorably discharged three years ago for excessive brutality."

"I didn't think the ACC gave a rat's ass about the Geneva Accords, excessive brutality?" Nina looked up from the file with a doubtful glance at him.

"I guess even they have their limits, though I don't even want to think about what they are." He whistled, easing the van into a left turn. "He is doing the mercenary thing now too, but he made his name as the Butcher of Saint Petersburg, The Butcher of Rostov-na-Donu, The Reaper of Odessa... It goes on, name a town in Europe and you can put 'The butcher of' in front of it and it's in here. He claimed responsibility for the Revolution Day bombing of a supposed resistance cell in Petrozavodsk that killed thirty-eight members of the resistance and almost three hundred civilians. This guy loves turning automatic weapons on streets full of unarmed people."

"This isn't making any sense." Nina looked out the window, staring at the reflection of their van in passing buildings. "Nemsky is a general with a small personal army at his disposal. His exploits have all involved large-scale assaults or squad level maneuvers, largely against civilian populations. His history shows that he retained loyalty to the ACC after his dismissal..."

"Probably staged," interrupted Dale.

"...and works for them as a private contractor. There's nothing in his background that suggests even the smallest bit of training in spycraft or intelligence."

Dale leaned into a right turn. "Itai could be handling that. Maybe Nemsky is just extra muscle?"

"The best way to get his mercenary army in here would be through the Badlands up from Mexico. I checked the border logs and found nothing unusual. The alternative is one or two men at a time posing as civilians, entering the city spread out over many months. The net rats have been comparing flight records and photos for days now and have come up empty handed."

"That would suggest he's here alone then." Dale frowned. "That doesn't fit his background."

"Exactly. Karl Warner is the only common link. We know they are here, we just don't know *why*. A German diplomat, an ex-pat Israeli intelligence agent, and an insane Russian despot with dreams of grandeur don't seem like the kind of guys who would go out for drinks on a Thursday night."

"No, but it makes one hell of an opener to a joke." Dale laughed.

Still grinning five minutes later, he pulled into a spot in front of a large building sculpted out of maroon stone. Tall metal letters over the archway spelled out "Imperial" in steel that reflected the pale dusty reds of the building to which it was mounted. One-hundred and fourteen stories of opulence, the Imperial Hotel was one of the more prestigious places to stay in the city.

A holographic sign in the window announced a several day seminar on basket weaving complete with dates and times. Nina covered her face with her hand.

"On the damn sign right out front?" She hopped out, slamming the door so hard the van rocked, and took a step toward the building. "Get this thing set up and ready, I'll be right back... I need to go rip someone's head off."

"That was a euphemism, I hope."

Nina stormed across the expanse of sidewalk in front of the hotel and made her way into the conference center. Many shades of burgundy and maroon with gold touches here and there decorated the lobby, and a polished grey marble reception desk stood in front of two smiling women and a man, all in white uniforms. Red barrier cords sectioned off space into common feeder lines in front of several separate rooms. Her anger increased more when she saw the only line in the room that had anyone waiting in it was the basket weaving line.

One frumpy older woman stood amid an ocean of shopping bags containing craft supplies. A blond man in a tuxedo blocked her at the door to the hall, assuring her that they would begin seating at the appointed time, and he couldn't let anyone in early.

Nina waved at agent Perrin as she ducked past him and jogged down the aisle past dark blue seats that faced a small stage. Every ten yards, three steps down accommodated the descending grade.

"Young man, why did that woman just go inside? I thought you said it wasn't time to go in?"

"I'm sorry ma'am, she's an employee."

Nina leapt onto the stage and rushed past the curtain into the staff room. A dozen Division 9 personnel worked at holo-terminals or conferred in groups. Some brought up surveillance links to cameras facing the diplomatic building across the street while others handled communications between the various operations agents in the field. They had janitors in the Diplomatic Tower, a man on the security team, three other vans nearby, and a pair of phony HVAC technicians on the roof.

Samantha Cole, the senior member of the technical staff, conducted events from the center of the room. A fast riser among the ranks, only a year older than Nina, she had degrees in electronics and communications. An attractive black woman, she always dressed two pay grades higher. The scent of her berry-inspired perfume permeated the entire area. Samantha hovered over a tech agent who appeared to be having difficulty receiving a clean signal from a holo-cam module aimed at Warner's window.

"Looks like some kind of interference, there's probably a refractive overlay on the glass causing the laser to break up." Samantha folded her arms. "Does anyone have any intel about possible passive detection Warner has in there, how close can we get with listening devices without triggering the alarms?"

One man in at the end of the row of desks spoke up but didn't turn. "On it."

Nina looked at the display, at the pattern of static on the monitor that warped into a nimbus of color pulsing over the image. Sub-windows floated in her eyes, cycling among sample patterns from various diffusion overlays, clear adhesive film with millions of tiny mirror like flecks intended to break up laser listening devices. The static looked different. Variance in the pattern became noticeable only by superimposing the images. Interference patterns from active ACC jamming electronics was even further off. She ran through a number of other possible causes before she saw one that came close.

"It does look a lot like an overlay, but it isn't. Someone or something is interfering with the signal directly from cyberspace. The static pattern is characteristic of a data sequencing routine trying to emulate a diffusion overlay."

Samantha turned with a glare as if ready to yell at one of her underlings for questioning her diagnosis. Seeing Nina, all the vitriol drained from her voice. "Of course, ma'am." She turned to another man at a desk a few feet away. "Double check the network interlinks, make sure that we haven't been compromised. I want that signal cleaned up."

He nodded and took on a vacant stare as his mind dove into cyberspace. Samantha faced Nina and paused in her train of thought as she noticed the obvious look of displeasure.

"Someone tried to make us think there was a diffuser on that window. Very subtle, I only spotted it because I superimposed the patterns." She managed a brief smile to Cole despite her mood. "Who exactly is responsible for the sign in the lobby?" Just a hint of shout rode her voice.

"Sign in the lobby?" Samantha glanced around the room.

Nina pointed in the general direction. "There's a damned advert in the front window of the hotel about the seminar. What part of *low key* did people miss?"

"I… That shouldn't have been up there, we *told* the hotel not to do it."

"There's a woman waiting in line. We'll need to get someone in here to do a damn speech about basket weaving now. What is the contingency plan if people actually show up for it?" Nina folded her arms as she calmed the tone of her voice.

"We have a speaker ready. We anticipated that." A man's voice echoed from the far end of the room by the entrance.

Nina relaxed. "Good. Someone please kill that sign, and make sure the guy uses the right name."

Samantha ran over the specifics of the setup for the operation. One could see how she had made a name for herself in such a short amount of time. She had a reputation for being thorough and professional. The only doubt Nina had was wondering how Samantha would react if something went off plan. According to her file, that was an eventuality she hadn't yet encountered.

Aside from a few blips: the sign, the speaker's name, and a sleepless night, Nina felt a little more confident that the day would wind up being okay. Having Samantha at the nerve center lent an air of competence to everything.

Now it became a waiting game until Korin, Nemsky, or some intermediary made contact with Warner—and when they did, they would get the evidence they needed to act.

14

ROAD TRIP

Kenny James Marlon loved the Badlands. An artifact hunter by trade, he was one of the damaged individuals that risked leaving the safety of civilization in search of junk that fools with more money than sense would pay for. The trade yielded a surprising profit for things considered by practical people to be scrap, but regarded by the wealthy or eccentric as historical treasures. Unlike most of his forays into the untamed areas, this time, a dart thrown at a map hadn't chosen his destination. His friend Joey stumbled across some credible information and passed it along.

He gazed out at the passing beige blur of the land, interrupted every so often by a streak of green. The huge truck could seat six in the cabin and its cargo bed held supplies as well as room for whatever he found. Thickened body panels offered the reassurance of armor, and it rode high up on solid tires with deep grooved treads capable of paddling in thick mud. The reinforced doors muted sound and let the cabin fill with the low whine of the electric motors. Two shotguns and a combat rifle rattled in the rack behind him each time the wheels ate a piece of scrub brush or a small rock.

The glare of the fading sunlight set the rim of his cowboy style hat aglow and cast a strong shadow over his green eyes. A few days' worth of stubble spread across his face below a thin nose, dark chestnut hair to his shoulders. A brown duster coat added to the western affect, along with a pistol on each hip and the obligatory synthetic snakeskin boots.

The truck wound its way down a rough passage along the eastern side of the Rocky Mountains, into the area once called Colorado. He had some reservations about this trip, considering the final destination—the southwest corner of former Kansas, near the territory of the Steel Reavers.

Eldon Church tried without much success to get some sleep in the passenger seat. A former Recon soldier, he declined to re-up after serving nine years. He may have been out of the military, but the military wasn't out of him. A thin layer of sweat coated his chocolate skin, beading upon his shaved head. Neatly trimmed facial hair circled his mouth as if it had been drawn on with a marker.

Eldon opened his eyes and glanced at the window to his right, then at Kenny, then to the temperature display showing 89 degrees. He grasped his fatigue shirt and flapped it, glaring at the readout. With a flick of his finger over the console, the window whined into the door. A blast of cold air carried the scent of pine and burnt flesh. Seeing Kenny without a drop of sweat on him only seemed to anger him more.

"Dammit man... I'm sweatin' my balls off in here."

Kenny thumbed the steering wheel. "Spend enough time out here you get used to the heat."

"Maybe that's why Alyssa is bein' such a pain in your ass. You should try turning on the A/C."

Kenny frowned as his knuckles creaked.

Eldon sighed, softening his tone. "How you holdin' up?"

He wrung the wheel, scowling at the rearview mirror. His hesitant sigh became words, as he knew Eldon wouldn't let it go. "She's just acting out since the divorce, normal crap for a fourteen year-old."

"My sister's boy was quite a handful when they broke up, course he was only nine back then."

"Yeah, I'm sure she'll be okay." Kenny tried to distract himself from the thought by fussing with the navigation panel again. "Alyssa ain't too happy about me taking this trip, short notice and all."

"It's Katherine, isn't it?" Eldon wiped his forehead with his white tank top. "You ain't over her."

"You know it wasn't my idea." Kenny met Eldon's gaze for the first time. "Is it that obvious?"

"The last time we came out here, you was like a kid goin' to the toy store." Eldon waved his arms around in an exaggeration of the way he remembered Kenny. "Now you're all quiet and brooding and shit."

Kenny faced front, staring into the onrush of terrain.

"Yeah." He flinched as though pulling the details of his personal life out caused physical pain. "It's just how sudden it was. One day she's her normal self, and the next she's a psychotic bitch. I still love the woman she used to be."

"That E-14 is some nasty venomous shit." Eldon shook his head. "What I don't get is how she got hooked on it. The MI guys would use that crap and they didn't get addicted. Shit, they couldn't stand it."

"Yeah but military intelligence might have been given something to counteract it." Kenny's face fell at the thought. "I went back and forth with the doctor, he couldn't explain it either. He said it had to be some kind of genetic predisposal or something."

"Predisposition?" Eldon asked with a hint of a smile.

Kenny nodded. "Yeah, that. We tried a bunch of things to get her off it but it just made her more erratic and wacky. The cops would have taken Alyssa out of the house if Katherine didn't leave. How the fuck can they make you choose between your wife and daughter?"

Eldon grasped Kenny's shoulder. "Don't guilt on it any more man. You did what you had to do. You didn't put that knife in her hand."

"There's gotta be something I can do for her." He pounded the wheel.

"Maybe there is. Maybe there isn't. Who knows? What I do know is that I don't want to get my ass shot up because you've got that crazy ex-wife of yours in your head." Eldon let go of his shoulder. "If there is a way to get her back straight, you'll find it."

Kenny made a halfhearted chuckle. "Yeah."

The mountain trail ended at a pile of crumbled concrete, the only remnants of a small bridge. He slowed down, pulled to the right, and eased down the bank of a dead waterway. The truck rocked as the tires struggled for purchase on the irregular ground, and the in-wheel motors whined, tossing head sized stones to the rear while he feathered the accelerator. Kenny's stare hardened with determination as he fought with the controls to keep from flipping over. Eldon, despite the jostling, sat back and tried to nap. As rough as this was, it had nothing on a DS2 plummeting through the atmosphere of another planet.

As the tires bit into the ascending bank, Kenny spoke without taking his eyes off what he was doing. "Hey, Eldon?"

"Yeah?" He looked up from another failed attempt to nap.

"Speakin' of unwanted divorces, I've been wondering. Why did you leave the Marines?" Kenny shot him a questioning glance before his head snapped back forward. "You still act like you're in."

"Ain't nothin against them, it's the guys pulling the strings I got a beef with." Eldon drew a deep breath. "Two years ago, my team got picked to hit this ACC site in South America. Intelligence pegged it as a bio/chem weapons facility. We went in at night to scope the place out." He gestured with his hands to add emphasis. "So there we were, all twelve of us moving in on this collection of buildings in the jungle. They had guard towers, laser sentries, sensors... the whole nine. Anyway, we took the place easy. Our armor let us walk right up on 'em. They were scrubs, hardly even knew which end of the gun to point at us. The site turned out to be a manufacturing facility for drugs, both recreational and military."

"Okay, that sounds pretty basic... I'm guessing there's more to it?"

"They had about fifty locals there as unpaid labor. The only pay waitin' for 'em was death if their explosive collars went off if they ran."

"You rescued them, right?"

"That's what I was expecting..." Eldon shook his head. "'Cept a whispercraft came in on us once brass got word that the site was secure. Couple of suits from C-Branch showed up and took over, with other ideas. They kept that facility going with the locals working. They fed 'em better and didn't beat em, but left the bombs on. They wanted to taint the military drugs with some kind of experimental thing supposed to make soldiers want to desert or go AWOL. Some real heavy mind fuck shit." Eldon tapped two fingers on the side of his head.

"Whoa." Kenny exhaled.

"Worst part was that they kept making the rec drugs just to keep up appearances. They even gave orders to kill anyone that tried to escape to keep a lid on it." Eldon pounded his fist into the door's armrest. "Shit just ain't right. That's not what I signed on for."

"No shit. Maybe that's why I ignore the government. I like it better out here. *This* is freedom."

"Don't get me wrong, people in the military aren't about that weird shady underhanded crap. But C-Branch does whatever it wants. It's like a separate government inside the government. Whatever they think is in the UCF's best interest, and they don't give a shit who gets hurt."

"At least they're patriotic." Kenny shot Eldon a grin.

"Say what?" Eldon glared for a moment before recognizing the sarcasm, and they shared a laugh.

Something about the mystique of the Badlands had gotten into Kenny's blood from a young age, and he hadn't been able to get it out of his head. Katherine hated it whenever he would go there. Scars of the Corporate War were everywhere. Any number of hazards could kill you without warning, from genetic combat mutants to cyber-enhanced wildlife, to nuclear impact points. The Badlands had no laws, no MedVan would come scrape your ass off the pavement, and you had only what backup you brought with you.

The descending slope of the eastern mountains was day two of their trip. The old Nevada region's desert consumed most of the first.

"What's the farthest east you've been?" Eldon took his combat rifle out of the bag he left in the back seat.

"I got within scope range of the Mississippi last year. Thought about checking it out but there were some Fourth Reich jackasses in the area."

"You didn't shoot them, why?" Eldon's tone sounded almost serious.

"Not when it was one versus forty, no." Kenny chuckled. "Besides, those idiots will get themselves killed. If they're that far east they probably cross the river and go into the Scattered Lands after convoys."

"Scattered Lands?"

"Didn't they teach you about that in Marine school?"

Eldon glared, drew in a breath, and prepared to launch into a detailed explanation of all the different "schools" one could partake of in the military. He grumbled it into futility rather than words. "No..."

"Well... Most of the crap that lives in The Badlands won't cross the river. 'Tween the water and East City you got a patch of little independent towns trying to take back the land. No mutants, but tons of raiders."

"So it's like the Badlands without the fallout and the freaky genetic experiments?" Eldon lifted an eyebrow.

"Sort of. The people that live there ain't like the Scrags. Way less tribal, they live sort of like pre-war era, without a lot of the amena... amina... fancy shit of modern day." Kenny grumbled under his breath as Eldon laughed at his battle with the language.

"Amenities. You ever go there?"

Kenny raised his middle finger at the English lesson. "Naa. It's too well scavenged. Most of the good shit's been taken by the locals and the place doesn't have the same... feeling."

"Why hasn't the city just spread over it?"

"Mostly they didn't want to pay to expand it more. They would rather build *up* than west. Y'also got the fear of the creatures being close. No one with any money wants to be near the Badlands. West City has that big ass wall. East City has a few hundred miles of cities and militias and... oh never mind."

"What?" Eldon raised an eyebrow.

"Neither one of us is drunk enough to mention it."

Eldon nudged him in the arm. "Spit it out, man."

"You're going to think I'm shit nuts."

"You go out into the goddamn Badlands willingly, and you've done it more than once. You *are* shit nuts." Eldon laughed.

It only took two days, but Kenny's mood had returned to normal. He settled into his seat, grinning and adjusting the lay of his hat. "Well, some people talk. They say that all the death, all the pain—the emotional energy released by the war..."

"Drunk? You should have said high."

"Yeah, yeah... If you stay out here long enough you'll start to wonder too. Anyway, they say that the Badlands has an intelligence of its own. Like the land is aware and wants to keep people from leaving or changing it. It feeds off the suffering of the poor bastards that live out there."

"Now that is some seriously fucked up campfire bullshit." Eldon shook his head. "You don't really believe all that?"

Kenny pointed at the dashboard. Along with the modern control systems, a small section contained the starter for a diesel combustion engine. "In case the electric goes out."

"God damn, I didn't think they made those anymore."

"They don't. I did." He altered course a few degrees to the right. "Modern things sometimes crap out without warning or cause."

"Like it doesn't want you to leave." Eldon tried his best to sound serious.

"Exactly." Kenny's reaction left Eldon unsure if he noticed the sarcasm. "The drive train ain't hooked up, I'd have to crawl up underneath and swap shit around, but it's there if I need it."

"You really do believe that?" Eldon flipped his rifle over and checked it.

"Rather be a live superstitious fool than a dead realist." Kenny grinned. "I'm not sure to be honest. I have seen some stuff that makes me unsure enough not to dismiss it."

Eldon shifted in his seat, angling toward the passenger side to make room for his rifle. Despite the lightweight plastic and bullpup design, the M2402 combat rifle was a little long to maneuver inside the cab. Kenny grinned watching Eldon prep it.

He much preferred his pistols. They felt more appropriate out here.

15

NIBBLES

Kenny sighed under his breath, thinking about how his daughter had changed. All of a sudden, she found the western thing to be "lame." It used to give her a bit of a thrill, and she had even asked for her own hat and some boots while learning how to handle a firearm. He hoped it was just an effect of the divorce and not an attempt to pull away from him. Her screaming about this trip echoed in his mind.

How much like Katherine she sounded... She doesn't want me to get hurt.

He smiled.

The thought of her, six years old and running around in her underwear, cowboy boots, and the little pink cowgirl hat, brought a tear to his eye. In the daydream, she ran past her mother, leaning on the doorway with a big grin aimed right at him. He couldn't even look the memory of his ex-wife in the eye.

The men rode for a few hours, chatting as they passed the time. Eldon watched their right side while Kenny glanced left as often as the terrain would allow. By late afternoon, a gleam in the distance caught his eye and he steered for it. The shimmer grew into the outer wall of a building plated with metal. Long and narrow, the one story structure had an entryway that jutted out from the center as if an afterthought. A dusty grime-obscured window wrapped around the front face. Enough visibility remained for them to tell that it used to be some kind of restaurant.

"Just an old wrecked diner." Eldon waved it off.

Kenny's usual grin was back. "Might be something good in there. Place has just enough of an undisturbed look to it."

He brought the truck to a halt near the entrance and shut the drive system down.

"Just gonna poke around a bit, never know what you can find. Most of the Scrags out here leave the good stuff behind thinkin' it's junk."

Eldon shook his head. "It *is* junk, Ken."

"Yeah, but it's junk people buy."

Kenny lingered on the running board long enough to grab his rifle from the gun rack before they walked to the building. Eldon approached the door as if making entry to a hostile area. He cleared the attached entryway and edged up to an interior door. Kenny slung the rifle over his shoulder and strolled in as if the place still operated.

Eldon pressed his back into the wall by the door and gave him a hard stare. "We don't know what's here, get your ass down."

"Cover me." Kenny spat something out of his teeth as he strolled past the double doors into the main room. He couldn't help but give them the saloon shove.

Eldon rolled his eyes. "At least you're a skinny motherfucker. I'll be able to carry your body back to your kid."

Kenny chuckled. He hadn't seen any of the telltale signs that anything or anyone used the building.

"Not gonna be here long, just a quick walkabout."

Eldon rolled through door behind him, sweeping his rifle in both directions. Kenny went left, past rows of booth seating, kicking trash out of his way. He disturbed a crimson centipede as big around as a stick of butter that slithered deeper into the refuse on undulating black legs.

Nothing in the main seating area was worth selling.

Eldon went right, past a row of empty tables, all the way to the end where a bathroom door had a few bullet holes in it and a perceptible breeze blew in from two large broken windows. Dead grass and debris swirled about in the wind. Eldon used his boot to give the door a silent nudge. It creaked away to the side, revealing a skeleton perched on the toilet as if still in the process of using it. Shrouded in the decaying fibers of a grey jumpsuit, it looked like someone shot him in the face at close range. The bowl was stained black with the remnants of decomposition. An old style Kevlar helmet lay on the tile floor in a heap of dead plant matter and other windblown debris that had accumulated in here over the past few hundred years.

Meanwhile, Kenny had gone behind the counter and entered the kitchen. Most everything in here looked useless, though one item stood out. An old milkshake machine on a counter top covered in a plating of petrified dust. The device seemed intact. Hell, it might even work if the place had power. A shove confirmed bolts holding it to the counter, a minor nuisance, but still... a back and forth trip to the truck to grab tools. He could find a buyer for a vintage machine like this, and he figured he could get upward of a hundred thousand credits for it if it worked, maybe a quarter of that if it didn't.

In the bathroom, the dead man's uniform had patches showing he had been with the corporate security force of an old phone company that had fielded one of the better-equipped armies before the ones hostile to the government merged into the ACC.

"Shit man, you been dead a long time," Eldon said.

Traces of red still stood out against the drab grey where the company logo had once been. The irony that phone companies were as dead as this man wasn't lost on Eldon.

Eldon relaxed. Whatever happened here was done and over with long ago. The helmet might be worth something, he would have to ask Kenny. The instant he reached to take it, the debris pile moved. Leaves exploded with a hissing noise louder than an upset cougar. He leapt backward in shock as a skateboard-sized roach lurched toward him. A spray of pale yellow liquid shot out of its mouth, striking the wall just shy of Eldon's leg. Within seconds, the congealing mass bubbled and smoked.

Eldon shouted, backpedaling. "What the hell!"

He moved with well-trained reflexes, triggering a burst. Cinder blocks caved in at the back of the bathroom as the projectiles bounced off the bug's chitinous body. It wobbled from the force of the impact but seemed more annoyed than injured. Adrenaline coursed through Eldon as he weighed two options in an instant. He went with the first, not wanting to get close to this thing with a vibro knife.

He crouched and sighted at the bug's head. The massive insect swayed for a moment before recovering and hissing.

The mandibles snapped open.

Eldon's finger squeezed.

The minute click of the electronic trigger drowned in the report of a single shot. Six inches of blue flame appeared in a flash behind the projectile as it sailed straight into the open mouth of the bug, stopping up its venom spray with an 8mm indirium cork. It jerked backward, shaking with the rattle of a bullet bouncing around inside. Slime spewed from its front end as it wobbled and fell in place. One leg twitched twice and went still.

Eldon stared over his rifle, just in case it was faking. He had seen these projectiles shred inch-thick plastisteel plating as well as modern body armor. Wind jostled the bug's antennae, and he shot it again.

Kenny turned at the gunfire and started out of the kitchen, but stopped when he heard motion and voices beneath him. People in the basement had also heard the shots. He backed out the door, keeping it open, and glanced at Eldon out of the corner of his eye. Seeing him okay, he shifted his gaze to an opening hatch in the floor and the sound of boots on wooden steps.

Kenny raised a hand in greeting at the figure that appeared, but froze when he noticed his distinctive attire. Dust-covered brown leather crisscrossed with stitching cobbled together from scrap encased the body like a sausage skin. Two skeletal thin men emerged from the trapdoor. Both shaved bald, faces covered by tight leather straps leaving just their mouths and eyes exposed. Filed down into points, blood stained their teeth dark. Small metal bits protruded here and there, items taken from kills worn as trophies.

"Nibblers!" Kenny shouted.

"What the shit is a nibbler?"

"Cannibals… probably on military stims."

"Had to stop here… just *had* to stop here, didn't you?" Eldon moved toward the kitchen.

Kenny wanted none of it. The hand he raised in greeting flew down, and he yanked his pistols from their holsters. The first of the two nibblers hadn't made it all the way out of the hole in the floor when Kenny opened fire. He shot twice from each gun, alternating sides in rapid succession. The anemic man tried to twist out of the way but two landed in his chest, one winged him in the shoulder, and the last crowned him across the curve of his skull just above his left eye, splitting the top of his head open. The leather-wrapped body folded over itself with all the grace of a discarded puppet and hit the ground twitching. The other nibbler, still on the stairs, cut loose with a shrieking wail.

Eldon's rush stalled at motion outside. Another nibbler rounded the corner, sprinting to the front of the building. He carried a three-foot long pipe tipped with a nugget of concrete studded with bits of rebar. The sight of that—combined with what Kenny had said about cannibalism—provided all the motivation he needed.

Eldon crouched low among the booths, aiming at the main door. The nibbler raced in and headed right for the kitchen, raising his club with both hands as his screech grew louder and higher.

Kenny glanced backward just as Eldon aerated the lunatic's chest from behind. The slugs went through the leather armor, the nibbler, and the far wall without hesitating. The cannibal's excited run fell into a somber walk for a few paces. He stared at Kenny with a look of disappointment, like a little boy denied his ice cream, and crumpled to the floor.

Eldon waved at the window. "We got a clear shot at the truck, let's move."

"I got somethin' here worth a bit. If we can take them out, let's take them out." Kenny kept his back against the doorjamb with his left arm covering the kitchen and his right aiming into the main room.

Eldon grumbled. "Crazy mother…"

"Got one in the basement here." Kenny shifted his attention back to the kitchen.

Eldon spun at the sound of crunching glass. Two more nibblers climbed in the broken window by the bathroom. Eldon fired at the one on the left, sending him flying back out the window in a spray of blood and brain matter. The other surged forward, his body driven beyond human limits by old combat drugs. He came in with an erratic jerky sprint too fast for Eldon to retrain and fire.

The nibbler loped in with a right-handed *whomp*, hand covered by a glove bearing six-inch blades on each finger. Eldon blocked with his rifle, throwing his weight forward into the thing's chest. The stick man sailed into the air and onto his back. A hasty three round burst chased him to the ground, but he made a quick roll to the left and sprang back to his feet.

Kenny sighted over his pistol, weighing the odds of winging Eldon. Before he could decide, the squeak of the trapdoor made him turn. Another one crept up, using the hatch as a shield. It shifted its weight up onto the floor from below, hiding behind the panel of metal for cover.

In the front room, the other nibbler wailed, charging at Eldon with his arms flailing to the sides and body fully exposed. He almost managed a shocked look when Eldon lunged and walloped him across the face with the butt of his rifle. The hit sent the nibbler into a backflip that became a six-foot slide along the floor, ending with a crash into the post of a table. Eldon followed with a rapid tactical walk, painting the floor red with a series of shots to the chest. The nibbler convulsed, arching his back and gurgling as blood seeped from between his jagged teeth. One final round in the forehead finished him.

Kenny fired into the trapdoor and succeeded only in shattering tile off the top of a metal plate. The nibbler peeked around the side with a crossbow, but another shot past the corner made him duck a shower of tile fragments.

He fired twice more with his left to keep the nibbler down as he stowed the other pistol and shrugged the rifle off his shoulder. Once he brought it to bear, he unloaded into the trapdoor. Blue fire roared as the heavier weapon reduced the hatch to a work of modern art and flying shrapnel. Riddled with stretched holes, it thudded closed, pushing the dead nibbler under it down the stairs. For a moment, all was silent save for the sound of the cannibal's body thumping over wooden steps.

Eldon shouldered into the doorway behind him. "This better be fuckin' worth it man."

"Gotta grab my tools to unbolt it." Kenny pointed at the machine. "I'll be right back."

Eldon grabbed Kenny's arm. "I got a better idea."

He took a vibro knife off his belt and approached the ancient thing.

"Careful! If you fuck it up it's worth shit."

Eldon shot him a look as if he could punch him. "Oh, I'm all about careful."

As he squeezed the rubber handle, the sonic inducer in the tang came to life, filling a space just beyond hearing with an irritating presence that sent chills down the spine like fingernails on a chalkboard.

The muscles in Kenny's back tensed at the effect of the noise, and he wondered if this was what dog whistles felt like to dogs. Eldon studied the steel counter and made four quick swipes. Kenny cringed with each dull clack as severed pieces of bolt fell to the floor. When Eldon lifted himself out from the cabinet, a wisp of acrid smoke rose from the blade as the grime boiled off, filling the air with the scent of four hundred year old burnt grease.

He gave Kenny a satisfied look. "That's how you do it." Eldon elbowed the machine and it slid an inch on the counter.

Kenny flailed. "Don't dent it!"

The power cord ran into a tubular conduit that led off to who-knows-where. The insulation cracked off in flakes, exposing the wire at a touch.

"You gonna take the whole counter apart?"

"Fuck it. Cut this." Kenny held up the cable.

After Eldon sliced the wire, he flipped the knife over his finger and slid it back into the sheath on his belt. Kenny pulled at the machine, grunting.

"Damn, it's heavier than it looks. Gonna take both of us."

Eldon shook his head. "No way man, area's not secure. Them damn things hit us while we're luggin' that we're done."

Kenny sagged. "Maybe you're ri—" Something to his right caught his eye. "Hold on…"

Against the wall by some shelves, an old hand truck propped up a stack of old boxes. After tossing a decomposed pile of decayed cardboard boxes off it, he dragged it over.

"At least help me get it to the floor?"

Eldon looked around, listening. He eyed the perforated trap door. "Gimme a second, gonna check for survivors."

He stuck his boot under the mangled flap of metal, kicking it open. Blood streaked the bare wood in a trail to the dirt floor below, where a dead nibbler lay sprawled in a twisted heap. The cellar was empty save for a concrete stairway in the far wall that led outside.

After helping lower the thing, Eldon took point while Kenny lugged it along behind.

Eldon stared at the truck. "I ain't liftin' that damn thing into the bed."

Kenny leaned on the hand truck to catch his breath, laughing. "Don't have to."

He pounded a button on the side of the tailgate, sending a hydraulic lift whining into position. Eldon's baritone laugh echoed over the desert as his friend rocked the ponderous find onto the metal flap.

16

SIX SHOOTER

The quiet lasted about forty seconds after they got back into the truck. Hot or not, Eldon had decided it better to put his DuraFib armor on. With the last of the fasteners secure, he banged his fist on the armor and relaxed into the seat.

"You're gonna tell me that piece of scrap metal was worth risking an ass full of pointy teeth?"

"Yeah." Kenny grinned. "Lucky for me, all I gotta do is call somethin' antique and people *throw* credits at me."

Eldon shook his head. "Still can't believe people are dumb enough to pay for this shit."

"Dust cloud." Kenny eyed the rearview.

Eldon turned, peering past dirt-streaked glass. A raider buggy closed in from behind. Little more than a triangular frame of metal tubes with two large tires in the back, two small tires in the front, and a crazed nibbler sitting on a gas tank in front of an engine. It looked like one errant rock could destroy it.

"Hah." Eldon opened the sunroof. "What do you think, flip or fireball?"

"Does it matter? If you flip that fucker there'll be a fireball."

"True enough." He stood up in the seat and leveled his rifle. "Hah. He must know what a rifle is, he's weaving."

Eldon sighted in on the front axle and matched the back and forth movement of the approaching cart. He fired, but the slug didn't get enough of a bite to destroy it, instead leaving a gouge as it ricocheted up into one of the rear struts, ripping it apart like a large noodle.

The nibbler's mouth was open, probably screaming, but neither Kenny nor Eldon could hear anything over the un-muffled engine. Eldon cursed under his breath and took aim again. Sensing his impending demise, the nibbler accelerated hard, and abandoned the weave. The straight line worked to his disadvantage as Eldon's next shot hit the right front tire dead on.

The dense indirium slug tore through both sides, deforming the glorified bicycle tire into a warped oval as it sent the solid rubber strip spinning into the air. The front axle failed, the other tire flew off, and the pointy front crumpled into the ground. Like a plow, it scooped a torrent of dirt and small rocks that pelted the nibbler's face. Seconds later, it hit something hard, and the buggy flipped into an end-over-end roll. Eldon lowered himself back into his seat amid the warm glow of a blooming fireball.

"Two shots this time, you must be tired."

Both of them laughed. Kenny drove a little faster than he was comfortable with over this terrain, as a smoke plume like that would surely attract more problems. Scavengers or mutated bio weapons, neither one of which presented a pleasant option. He checked the navigation computer and steered toward the area formerly known as Elkhart, Kansas.

After another two hours of calm, Eldon broke the silence, noticing the lack of excitement in Kenny's face. "What's on your mind?"

"Katherine."

"You thinkin' she maybe got exposed to something at work?"

Kenny shook his head. "Can't be, she was an accounts receivable clerk at a manufacturing company. Never went on the factory floor, worst risk at that job was a fat ass from sitting all day."

"Just don't make sense." Eldon shook his head.

"Whenever I'd come out here, she'd always have a fit. She tried everything from begging me not to go to threatening to leave... which almost worked." He gripped the wheel and twisted as if wringing out a cloth. "I called her this morning before we set out to tell her I had a good lead on a big payoff."

When the pause grew intolerable, Eldon prompted. "And?"

"She seemed happy, like she wanted me to get killed out here." He shook his head. "It's the only way she'd get Alyssa."

Eldon shook his head. "No way man. They'd put her into the system first."

"Oh yeah, that's *so* much better. Give her to a pair of strangers instead of her own mother." Kenny's eyes darkened.

"The way she was last time I saw her, bitch was a stranger. Fuck, man, she threatened her own kid with a knife for callin' her a junkie." Eldon tried to sound reassuring.

Kenny relaxed, though he still drove too fast. "Inflated sense of one's own importance or something like that. Side effect of the drug, it wasn't really her."

"Yea, I heard about it. The military abandoned E-14 because of the side effects like violent paranoia, voices, aggression and shit. It's just evil." Eldon glanced around in search of danger. "Well, you're not gonna get killed on this run, so stop thinkin' on it. If you find this thing you're after and it pays off, you can get her treatment... if you still think she's worth it."

Kenny shot a long meaningful stare out over the land in front of them, wondering if it was possible to get back the Katherine he used to know. She had always been a cheerful and woefully naïve woman captivated by the mystique that was Kenny. The dichotomy of his Wild West affect with all of the high tech gadgetry he used had made her curious, and his personality had charmed her the rest of the way.

"Her parents were kinda pissed at me for years." Kenny chuckled. "They had a real problem with Alyssa being a flower girl at our wedding."

Eldon grinned. "That's a little old fashioned. Damn."

"They didn't think very much of me before we got married... They probably blame me somehow for what Katherine's become." Kenny slowed, realizing they would roll if he hit a big enough rock.

Eldon ran a hand over his head. "I still can't wrap my brain around that, man. How does an office chick get her hands on military boosters? Shit, man, they don't even make you high, just smarter for a few hours and the teardown phase is a bitch."

"I wish I knew... I wish I knew."

Several hours later with the approach of night, Kenny decided to take a break. The desolate area contained little in the way of food, hence it attracted little in the way of predators. Moving to the cargo bed, he grabbed a carrying case out of the storage bay and pulled out four cylindrical devices about a foot long and an inch around. He tossed two to Eldon and walked toward the front right.

"Ten meters out, set for zero point two?" Kenny looked at the truck in the direction of where he thought Eldon was.

"Sounds good, maybe zero point one, in case one of those damn roaches shows up."

Chuckling, Kenny activated the proximity detector. A six-inch metal spike snapped out of one end while the other sprouted a series of panels and antennas. He adjusted the sensitivity setting to 0.1, and jammed it into the ground. At 0.1, it would go off if something the size of a housecat or larger approached. If anything came within 25 meters of their camp, half the Badlands would hear it.

THEY HAD ABOUT SIX HOURS OF DRIVING AHEAD OF THEM IF EVERYTHING WENT WELL. The map showed them on course and on time, provided they didn't encounter any serious changes to the terrain on their way.

"I'm gonna bring us in here, from the southeast. We'll drive around and give the city some distance and then come back at it." Kenny traced his finger along the holographic map.

"What's with the loopty?" asked Eldon.

"About 18 miles north... right about here"—Kenny poked the map —"took a nuke during the war. It's still a little warm. Where we're going is out of the rad zone, but I still don't want to drive through any contamination."

"Alright man, but if my piss glows in the dark, remember, I know where you live." Eldon's serious glare lasted only seconds before they both broke into laughter.

The city of Elkhart looked nothing like it did before the war. It looked nothing like a city at all. Little more than a field of rubble remained, well within the grip of nature. The center of town still had a few standing walls more robust than the rest, though nothing much beyond a story tall.

Kenny chose one of the streets that still looked passable. An orange light on the console lit up, indicating elevated levels of radiation, but they were low enough not to be a major concern. Eldon eyed the light with unease as Kenny zoomed the map in as far as it would go and compared it to the one on the NetMini in his hand.

"It's either that building or that building." Kenny pointed at two piles of rubble.

As they disembarked, Kenny took his rifle, but kept it in his hands instead of favoring his pistols first. He preferred the look of handguns, but the prize was too big to take chances. If he shot something, he wanted it to die—not get pissed off.

"What are we looking for?" Eldon paused, staring at the rubble crunching underfoot.

"If it was my shop, I'd put it in a safe. Look for some kind of armored vault or something like that."

"Right. So you gonna tell me what the hell it is?"

"It's an old gun. A gold plated commemorative revolver. A collector's item back then, probably worth a million credits now."

"Well, shit." Eldon searched with renewed enthusiasm. "Now I know why you keep coming out here."

Half an hour of fruitless searching passed before Eldon caught a glimpse of fast movement and turned to aim at it. Once he saw it was Kenny waving, he lowered his rifle and jogged over.

"Find something?"

"Yeah, but not what I wanted to see." Kenny whispered. He pointed at the ground.

A footprint in the dirt, with a texture implying the foot that made it was missing skin from the underside, and had several exposed bones. The dirt had a shiny layer, as though the ground had been painted over with snot that dried.

"What the hell?" Eldon's eyes widened.

"Probably rad-ghouls given where we are, but it might be a zombie." Kenny's voice carried no hint of humor.

"What?" Eldon's whisper came out as more of a squeak. "Are you messin' with me? Fuckin zombies?" He got louder and louder with each word.

"I dunno, heard stories but never saw one. Don't forget there's a NIP 18 miles north of us. Between that and the slime, my credits would be on rad ghouls." Kenny squinted in the direction of the impact point. "Let's get on with it. I don't wanna stick around here any longer than we have to."

"Ghouls, zombies, what the fuck is the difference?" Eldon scanned the area. He had that look in his eyes as if he were back in the thick with ACC everywhere.

"If you want to get technical, the rad ghouls came from some gene-modding cheesedickery trying to make soldiers resistant to radiation. The ones around nowadays are even more mutated, but they are still alive. There's only one real problem with them."

"Oh, only one?" Eldon's tone was almost petulant. "Don't tell me—they hog the beer?"

"Radioactive. If we run into them, don't let blood splash on you when you shoot them. Heck, don't hit it with a knife, don't punch it. They're kind of squishy, just get the hell away from them and blast from a distance."

"They glow in the dark too?"

"Only their eyes. Blue. The rest looks like a guy with no skin that's been covered in warm snot."

"You couldn't say slimy? Had to say warm snot..." Eldon shivered as he resumed searching.

"I felt it once, not by choice."

"Ugh." Eldon spat off to the side.

"Zombies are supposed to be dry, not radioactive, and ain't alive. Never saw one but some people you may run into out here claim they're real. Opinion varies among undead or some kind of nanobot or cybernetic system that keeps them going."

Eldon shook his head. "I saw a psionic once, creepy shit. Still not buying the zombie thing."

Kenny shrugged. "This girl that worked with Katherine swore that she saw a ghost once. Prior to 2204, no one believed that psionics were real and now they are a proven fact. Who knows what else is out there?"

"I don't wanna think about it. I like my reality understandable, and as normal as possible." He forced a chuckle. "Ok, so rad ghouls..."

Their search took them further toward the other building. Once they moved past a line of broken concrete that traced the path of a long gone wall, Kenny's eyebrows lifted.

"This looks like it. Debris kinda fits an old clothing store, place used to be a military surplus shop." Kenny whispered.

"Why are we whispering?"

"Rad Ghouls have excellent hearing."

Eldon hesitated. "Wait just a damn second, didn't you say they have no skin?"

"Yeah."

"No skin, no ears."

Kenny frowned. "I dunno, the last time I saw one it came at me right after I dropped something."

"Maybe it smelled your cologne. Wait... no... if those things have any sense of smell that would knock it out."

"Hah." Kenny smirked.

The late afternoon sun left the area around them devoid of shadows and well lit from all angles. A gentle breeze stirred up the dust and lighter bits of debris in small whorls that appeared and dissipated at random. The smell of burnt flesh and chemicals drifted past in traces.

"Slab." Kenny tapped a piece of solid concrete embedded in the ground at the bottom of a patch of water erosion. "This is probably the back room. I bet they had a vault in the floor. We just have to get under a few centuries of windblown dirt to reach it."

Eldon walked over and helped dig. Their effort eventually revealed a metal door. Kenny squatted and cleared it out with his hands, unearthing the combination wheel of an old style safe.

"An in-floor safe. That's exactly what I'm looking for." Kenny grinned.

His levity evaporated as the smell of burnt rotting meat came over him with breath-stealing strength. A shambling humanoid shape wobbled out from behind a wall a few meters behind them. It would stand almost six feet tall if not for the way it hunched forward in a knock-kneed posture. The body resembled uncooked beef, glistening with a coating of slime. Dark venous streaks throbbed through its flesh and luminous membranes stretched over each eye socket, creating two huge blue portals. The top of its head pulsated with the rhythm of a heartbeat. One arm reached toward Kenny as its lipless mouth tried to grin.

The color drained from his face at the creature's proximity. He turned and sprinted in the direction of the truck, brown duster coat billowing out behind him like a cape as he ran, holding his hat down with one hand.

"Shit. Shit. Shit." One expletive came out of his mouth each time a boot hit the ground.

The rad ghoul bolted with surprising speed given its previous ungainly appearance. Eldon lurched backward, hesitating when the creature remained fixated on Kenny. He spun and took aim, favoring the outside leg to minimize the odds of his friend taking any spray. After a short pause to correct, Eldon clicked off a single shot that exploded most of the thing's right calf in a shower of yellow goo. It rolled forward with a gurgling hiss, like an air hose dropped into a bucket of jelly. It started to drag itself back on its one remaining leg when a barrage of fire from Eldon liquefied it the rest of the way.

"Since... I'm already halfway... back to the truck... I'll get the tools." Kenny stooped forward with his hands on his knees, gasping.

Eldon swiveled as another rad ghoul ambled out from behind a dirt mound, then another, and another. Before he could take good aim at one, a dozen more approached in a mass.

"Oh fuck this." Eldon clicked his rifle to full auto and offloaded half his remaining ammunition.

The line of rad ghouls burst from left to right as he swept across them. Bright azure flames lit the twilight; yellow goop flew everywhere. Eldon stepped back from the exploding ooze despite them all being at least thirty yards away. When the last one fell, Eldon spun in a cautious circle, watching all angles.

"Move, move, move!" Eldon yelled. "Too damn late for quiet."

The code lock on the toolbox had just opened when Eldon resumed machine-gunning rad ghouls. Kenny rifled through the compartment and grabbed a laser cutter, stopping by the driver door to take one of the shotguns from the gun rack.

No more had shown up by the time he got back. He swooped in on one knee and dropped his rifle and the shotgun on the ground next to the safe.

"Did I mention that they travel in big groups?" Kenny didn't look up.

"How big?" Eldon sounded calm.

"Forty or so."

Eldon mouthed "motherfucker" without adding voice to it. "Thanks for the heads up."

"Just think about the five hundred grand."

"Five hundred grand?" Eldon blinked. "You offered me twenty for this."

"Yeah." Kenny looked up for a second. "That's when I thought it would just be a quiet ride in the country. Wouldn't be right of me not to split this with you even, assuming it sells for the whole mil. Might even get more than that if I hold out on a desperate buyer."

Eldon grinned. "Now I know why she stayed with your dumb ass."

Another ghoul spiraled to the ground in a fountain of slime as Eldon shot it in the head. Kenny readied the laser cutter, an oversized laser pistol with a side handle and deflection plate around the barrel. The bright orange beam glowed like a tiny sun, painting the rubble hill in long flickering shadows.

The sound of Eldon's controlled gunshots and the answering splats serenaded Kenny as he worked. After a minute, he made it most of the way around the rectangular door, but hadn't quite finished when Eldon yelled.

"Reloading!"

Kenny dropped the cutter and grabbed his rifle, firing in bursts at the endless sea of rad ghouls that had popped up all around them. So many dead made it hard to tell which ones still crawled at them in the ocean of slime and which ones just slid down the hill. He got a half dozen or so by the time Eldon resumed shooting. In control of his panic, he took careful single shots and double-taps at new arrivals. Their numbers made even that sound like a slow-firing machine gun.

"At least these fuckers die in one shot." Eldon laughed. "Gotta be alive... Poor bastards."

A heavy metallic scrape announced the defeat of the safe door. Kenny stowed the cutter and slung the case over his shoulder. With a grunt, he dragged the door out of the hole and let it fall to the side. It landed with a ponderous thud that shook the ground.

Inside the hole, a gold plated revolver sat pristine within a dusty clear plastic case affixed to a wooden base. Engravings covered most of its metal surface, and the mother-of-pearl handgrips bore the scrimshaw likeness of a man that he had never heard of. He lifted the box with care and tucked it under his arm. He sifted over the rest of the stuff and took a box of old military medals as well as a decorative silver bayonet, also mounted to a wooden plaque.

He threw the shotgun up to Eldon, who caught it with his left hand. Assault rifle in one hand, shotgun in the other, he backed toward the truck, keeping the weapons aimed at the darkness. A ghoul sprang out from within a section of concrete sewer pipe to Eldon's left, causing him to fire the shotgun. Its body vanished from throat to knees where it stood. Arms and legs fell to the side as the head spun in midair for a fraction of a second before splattering on the ground like a rotten melon.

Eldon winced. "Man, that is just *nasty*. Defies words."

"Did you get any on you?" Kenny glanced over as he jogged to the truck.

"Nah, man. I'm good."

The loot went into a hidden armored cabinet between the rear seats. Kenny thought about putting the cutter back in its proper place, but just tossed it on the seat for now, given the danger.

"You okay?" Kenny smiled at the look on Eldon's face.

"Man, I saw some wild shit before, but those damn things are a whole new level of wrong."

Tires spat dirt out in front as Kenny reversed away from the old town. "I figured you got spooked, never saw you open up like that. You always talk about those short controlled bursts."

"There ain't no SOP for zombie invasion, man." Eldon consolidated the ammo from several semi-depleted magazines into one almost full one. "That falls squarely in the whiskey tango foxtrot category."

"What does that mean?"

"It means improvise." Eldon slapped the mag into his rifle, smiling at the green ammo readout ticking up to 48.

Kenny rubbed his chin. "By the way, technically they're not zom... aw, fuck it." Kenny laughed.

Eldon's eyebrows merged. "Either way, they're dead, we're not." He motioned to the back seat. "Was that the thing?"

Kenny leaned back in the seat and tilted his hat forward. "Yep."

17

HOME AGAIN

T he truck rumbled over the western desert of old Nevada, following long, crumbling roads that stabbed the horizon. Kenny had taken a longer route back, one he knew would avoid any temptation to stop anywhere else. After two days, the wall came into view. A massive barrier of concrete and steel blockaded the entire West City off from the Badlands, it had a series of designated entry points along its route as well as hundreds of laser turrets.

"What are you laughing at?" Eldon glanced over.

"Nothing much. Every time I see the wall, it just reminds me how the Scrags think it's a curtain of fire that eats the souls of their dead. One Scrag probably saw the lasers fire once... the birth of legends."

A gate opened at their approach, and Kenny eased the truck over the first speed bump into an airlock-style chamber between the inner and outer wall. Four Division 1 police officers walked out of a small station embedded in the wall. Two orbited while two approached, one on either side.

"Afternoon." The officer on Kenny's side looked around at the truck. "Do you have any biological contamination, animal life, fruit, or dangerous substances on board?"

"I think he's asking about whatever the hell that was you cooked last night." Eldon chuckled as he handed his ID over.

The woman examined Eldon's ID and noted he was a former Marine. She handed it back to him with a quick nod and a salute. The officer on Kenny's side checked his ID longer, but also returned it.

"Found an old milkshake machine in a beat up diner, hoping it'll sell."

The other two ran a series of sensors over the truck, looking for any dangerous chemicals or biological matter.

Eldon noticed the lack of mention of the old gun but said nothing until after the police allowed them past the inner gate and drove into the city proper.

"You didn't tell them about the cowboy piece?" He looked at Kenny with raised eyebrows.

Kenny nodded. "Yep. It ain't illegal or harmful, and it's worth a shitload. Just trying to keep it quiet 'til we get paid. I don't want it to get held up in customs then get told it disappeared."

"Noted." Eldon sat back and closed his eyes, finally able to rest.

Kenny went south along a major elevated highway. The truck sank into its wheels, lowering its profile and trading ground clearance for the ability to go faster. It took about forty minutes to arrive in the area that used to be Baja. California. The contiguous urbanization stopped a few miles shy of where Kenny lived. He smiled as he gazed out over exposed ground, cacti, and the closest thing to open space that the city could offer, glowing in the orange of an early evening sunset. At the southernmost city plates, a ramp led down from elevated surface of West City, bringing the truck back to the natural earth.

His home consisted of a one-story house on about three quarters of an acre of scrap yard. Rows of junk piled up on top of more junk, sorted by its general type. When not out running around the Badlands, he made a modest living trading in old car parts, gadgets, appliances, cyberware that had gone south, and other things he found here and there.

Eldon laughed every time he read the signs at the end of each row: 'Totally Useless Shit', 'Useless Shit', 'Shit', 'Possibly Useful Shit', and 'Shit That'll Sell'.

The truck slid to a halt just inside the main gate, which closed on its own once they had cleared. Eldon's lime-green hoverbike waited for him on the back porch of the house where he had left it, gold struts gleaming in the waning light. Kenny collected the valuables from the armored box and left the milkshake machine in the truck bed.

"Beer?" Kenny headed for the door.

"Damn right."

Kenny went inside with the swag. Eldon gathered his stuff from the truck and made a pile by the bike before going inside. The door led to the kitchen. He crossed it to a large living room with the usual setup of a needlessly large holovid screen, couch, table and little kitschy things Kenny's wife had put here and there for ambiance.

Eldon took a synth beer from the cabinet, squeezing the button on the side that triggered the chemical cooling process. By the time he fell into the couch, a layer of frost had spread over the can. He took a long beautiful sip of it. Simulated or not, it was just what he needed right now. The sight that greeted him when metal rim lowered out of his vision made some of the beer bubble up in the back of his throat.

Kenny's daughter, Alyssa, stood in front of him, wearing a coral-colored man's dress shirt open down the front. From head to bare feet, the only interruption in her unblemished tan was a pair of shiny pink panties that didn't leave as much as they should to Eldon's imagination. She curled her toe into the rug and made a playful lip bite. Dark brown hair with lighter streaks swished back and forth down to her waist as she tilted her head, while trying to put on a sexy grin.

"Hi, Eldon," she cooed.

It took a second for his mind to process what he looked at.

"Girl, what in the hell are you doin' running around like that?"

Eldon leaned forward and pulled the shirt closed. "I don't need to see them little things, child." He stood up and took a few paces toward the kitchen, shaking his head and trying not to look at her. "Girl, why you gotta do that to your daddy? You know he's all fucked up, worried about you."

Alyssa flinched at the unexpected reaction, and folded her arms around herself. She looked about ready to cry as Kenny sprinted into the room, drawn by Eldon shouting. He sagged into a slouch as soon as he saw her. From the side, he couldn't tell if she had anything on under the shirt.

"Look, man…" Eldon held his hands up.

Kenny gave him a disarming look. "I know… She's been doing this for a while."

Eldon relaxed.

"You're talking about me like I'm not standing ten feet away from you!" Alyssa's eyes welled up with tears.

"Alyssa…" Kenny held out an arm and walked toward her. She backed up and ran into the rear of the house toward her room.

"Oh, *now* you want to be here?" Her door slammed after she screamed.

"Look, man… Imma get goin'. Hook me up when the shit sells. Seems you got some things to get sorted." Eldon finished off the beer in two gulps.

They exchanged a handshake.

"Definitely. Thanks for having my back out there."

"For a payoff like that, I might be willing to go out there again, zombies or not." Eldon tossed the empty into the kitchen trash bin from the living room. "It was kind of cool watchin' them explode."

"They're not too dangerous unless they get close."

"Sounds like my last lady." Eldon chuckled. "I never saw your ass move that fast in my life. Alright man, later."

Kenny removed his coat and gun belt, setting them on the table in the dining area as he passed it on his way toward the sobbing. The only response to his knock was the end of the crying. After a minute of nothing, he just walked in. Alyssa lay curled in a ball on the bed with her back to the door. She had changed into a plum colored oversized tee that went down to her shins.

"So what was that about?"

She sniffled.

"You keep on kicking that mine cart, daring it to roll. Someday it's gonna go and you won't be able to stop it until it crashes." He stuffed his hands into his pockets and made a resigned face. "I don't want you to get hurt."

"I don't wanna talk." She sniffled.

He stepped over the discarded shirt, sitting on the edge of the bed with his back to her. "I know. But we need to." He pulled his hat off and held it in his lap, staring at it. "You're mad at me when I leave you at the Rodríguezes', you're mad that I left you alone for a week. You're mad at me for what happened with mom." For a moment he sat listening to her breathe. "You know I miss her too."

"Why did you get rid of her then?" She wailed.

"That woman wasn't your mother. That shit she's on made her a different person. I was afraid she was going to hurt you, or herself. If I could get her off that crap, I…" He choked up. "If we didn't separate, the police were going to take you away from both of us. I couldn't live with that." He let out a long breath. "They made me choose between you or mom, and they wouldn't have let you stay with her."

Alyssa pushed herself into a sitting position and glanced through her hair at him. "I thought you hated her."

Kenny brushed it out of her face. "I hated what happened to her, what she had become. I couldn't sleep at night worrying if I would come home and find one or both of you dead." Kenny's attempt to remain stoic faltered. "I tried... as hard as I could, but she was so erratic. I didn't want to lose you too."

She moved next to him, placing one hand on his. "Are you pissed at me?"

He tugged her close with an arm around her shoulders. "Your mother had to leave because of what she did to herself. I never for a minute thought any of it was your fault."

"Will she ever come back?" Alyssa looked down.

"I can't say for sure. Me and Eldon just found something worth a lot of money. I'd spend it all if it would fix her."

After a long pause, he broke the silence. "So why did you give Eldon a peep show?"

Alyssa giggled, blushing. "Umm..." The playfulness faded as she once again became somber. "I guess I wanted to see if you'd care."

"Why wouldn't I?" He looked at her in disbelief.

"You've been kinda weird lately... ignoring me."

He pulled her into a one-armed hug, thinking about how the two of them had been inseparable when things were good.

"I've had a lot on my mind, mostly about your mother. I know I've been moody lately." He squeezed her. "I'm sorry. It wasn't fair to you for me to shut down like that."

"You could have given me a little warning about just running off like that." Her gaze darted into nowhere as a bad memory got her crying again.

"I found out about this artifact from Joey and—"

"That emo guy?" Alyssa cut him off, her mood shifting to amusement.

He found a smile. "He's not emo, he's from Mars."

"And the difference is?"

"Okay, fine. That emo guy. He found out about an old gun that's worth a ton of credits. I had to put together a trip real fast before someone else got to it. I remember the way you moped for days the last time I left you with the Rodríguezes. Since you made such a big deal about being fourteen, I figured I'd trust you to take care of yourself for a few days this time."

Alyssa bunched her shirt in her fingers. Twice she started to speak, and twice she closed her mouth. His wife made the same face whenever something scared her and she didn't want to admit it. "It was kinda scary being alone. Next time you go out there can I come with you?" Her eyes brightened at the thought.

Kenny babbled for a moment before his panic wore off. On one level, he felt joy that she still had interest in his hobby, but it worried him too. "I umm. I don't know about that, hon. It's dangerous out there. If anything happened—"

"Gangers could attack me here when you're gone. At least out there we'd be together." She cuddled into his side and wrapped her arms around him. "I thought people were trying to break in the other night. I freaked."

"What?" He held her close. "Did you call the police?"

"No, I just hid in the crawlspace with my gun. Slept there." She braced for a scolding. "No one got in, maybe I just heard stuff. So can I go next time?"

Kenny figured the payoff from this run would let him wait a few years. "I'll think about it."

"Get some sleep." He gave her a kiss on the forehead and stood up. "I promise, I'll tell you about everything from now on."

"Kay." She scooted back onto the bed. He pulled the comforter over her and killed the light. As he turned to walk out, she sat up. "Dad?"

He turned. "Hmm?"

"I'm sorry for being a pain in your ass since… You know…" She moped at the shape of her legs in the pink bedding.

Kenny nodded. She had never once spoken the word *divorce*. "Forgiven. Don't waste any more time thinking about it. I never stopped loving your mother, your real mother." He walked to the door, leaning against it for a few minutes while he stared at his hat, the sigh of many regrets falling upon it.

"I think this worked better when I was six."

Kenny glanced back to find her in her underwear, cowboy boots, and a tiny pink cowboy hat. She posed with a toy gun in each hand, recreating the scene from the holo picture he always took out to embarrass her.

He burst out laughing, making her blush. "Yeah, it did. Course, now I gotta shoot anyone that sees you like that."

Alyssa ran to his arms. For a long moment, they cried on each other's shoulders.

"I'm glad I got my little girl back."

18

THE TOKO LOUNGE

It had been weeks since the throttle on Joey's bike had been as far forward as it was on his way to meet his friend. The wind filled his hair as he flew down The Highway, weaving between other vehicles so much slower they seemed to stand still. Knowing one errant bump could transform his vehicle into an airborne suspension of loose unaffiliated parts only added to the thrill.

He shot down the longest contiguous road in all of the UCF territory, the best excuse he had to push the bike that hard. The Highway was twenty stories off the ground, supported by a series of towers and nearby buildings, through which it tunneled. Three lanes in both directions carried traffic relentlessly at all hours of the day. The city never had a rush hour: it was *always* rush hour. Starting five miles from the south edge, the Highway traversed West City all the way the coast and into what used to be Canada.

The bike entered a hollowed-out space where the road tunneled into the center of an apartment building. He let out a wild howl, reveling in the feeling of air currents buffeting his face. The adrenaline rush of going this fast proved uncontainable. Without the need to touch the ground, civilian hovercars and hoverbikes could reach much higher speeds, though they had the benefit of early warning sensors and crash avoidance systems.

Joey looked forward to teasing Masaru. The son of the CEO of Kurotai Electronics International refused to go to the part of town where the Fu Sheng House was located. Masaru insisted on meeting at his usual lurking spot, the Toko Lounge. This was the kind of establishment where attendance added people to Joey's list of contemptible individuals. The wealthy exclusivity of it reminded him of his sister's attitude. At least Masaru offered to treat. Joey couldn't have even afforded the air inside the place.

He tried to slow down. The entire bike shuddered from imperfections in the braking surface, sending the rear wheel into a wobble. A stream of obscenities left his mouth, lost in the ambient noise of driving. Something clattered to the road behind him, making him expect the bike would come apart in the midst of its tail-wagging dance. For the shortest of moments, he regretted not wearing a helmet.

His eyes bounced between the approaching exit he wanted and the non-working speedometer. He knew he couldn't slow the heavy thing down in time to take the curve in the proper way. Throwing himself as hard as he could into the bike, he held on, hitting the exit tube like a bullet into a pipe. The vast night sky vanished in an instant, replaced with the pale yellow green of vitamin-sapping lamps.

The bike slid along the outer wall, speed pinning him to the surface. He swerved around, dodging various mechanical protrusions and feathered the brakes in the hopes he might at least leave an identifiable body when he stopped moving. Seconds before he reached the end of the downward corkscrew, he found control. He hit the street hard, tires squealing in protest as the shocks crushed all the way down to the frame. The impact smashed his tailbone into the seat and sent a wave of force up his spine into his skull that reawakened his hangover migraine with all the subtlety of an interplanetary shuttle launch.

Joey lay limp over the handlebars as his bike rolled to a gradual halt a few blocks later. In Sector 214, he found himself in a hoity-toity area filled with bright lights and expensive cars. Mesmerized, he stared at the tendril of drool that lowered itself toward the lack of his reflection in the front tire-guard, metal that ages ago ceased being shiny. Moments later, nausea faded away, replaced by the fatigue that fills the void left after a massive adrenaline rush. He moaned in protest, forcing himself to sit up, stretched, yawned, and sat for another minute, motionless. A sea of holographic signs and advert bots painted the air around him in headache as he drove the last quarter mile.

His destination capped the tip of a dead end street in the form of a U-shaped building, a gleaming wall of light, glass, and polished steel three stories tall. The ground floor held an exclusive Japanese restaurant patronized as much for the status of being seen there as for the quality of its food.

The words 'Toko Lounge' glimmered above, ten-foot tall holographic kanji painted into space by a giant unseen brush. Rows of perfect horizontal blue lines glinted behind them, surrounded by a red-orange border. After lingering for a moment, they morphed into English letters and faded away only to begin the cycle anew.

The top floor had some kind of lounge for the elite. All manner of rumors circulated on the net about it: everything from secret meetings of the illuminati to only allowing entry to pureblood Japanese. Other whispers hinted at Yakuza connections, shady dealings in drugs, military grade cyberware, and forced prostitution. It made him wonder about Masaru. If he were as pristine as he claimed, why would he want to be associated with a place shrouded in rumors of that nature? A debate began in his mind on the finer points of what he could do with the information if he could get proof—and how dangerous it would be to find out.

A small line formed by the door. People in fancy clothing waited just to get inside to wait some more. Two servers made their way along, selling drinks and hors d'oeuvres. Joey lifted an eyebrow at seeing actual people and not dolls. The idea of the patrons viewing the poor as little more than machines made him scowl.

The derelict bike came in along the curb, and he turned his head to leer at an Asian woman. A glittering dark purple gown wrapped her twig thin body, circling her neck before it attempted to cover her front, and turned into one of the smallest miniskirts he'd ever seen. He slowed as he waited for her to shift enough for the dress to give him a show. His quite indiscreet stare caused her to shoot him a disgusted look.

"Don't act like that. You wouldn't wear that if you didn't love it!" Joey's yell caused an offended gasp to sweep over the crowd, and made her blush. He basked in their derision like a rock star showing up for a concert.

He blew a kiss at her and walked the bike forward beneath the stares of the crowd. He stopped with a boot on the curb, the six buckles on the side gleaming in the blue-orange glow of the ethereal kanji.

A patronizing glare went to the valet, rigid behind the podium that separated him from someone of Joey's social strata. The man made a face as if he couldn't fathom what in the world Joey was doing here. Grinning, Joey fiddled with his NetMini one handed. After a moment, Masaru's hologram head appeared.

"Yes?"

"You inside yet?"

"Yes. We're at a table already." Masaru half sighed his words.

"Excuse me. I believe you made a wrong turn. CyberBurger is about two miles that way." The valet pointed while trying to put on an air of superiority.

Joey took a deep breath. "Lay off the accent, minimum wage boy. Don't think for a second I don't know you're getting about twenty credits an hour to step and fetch it out here."

A murmur made its way around the crowd, interspersed with one or two chuckles. The valet's mouth hung open as if slapped.

"I'm with Masaru Kurotai. He's already inside waiting for me. Be a dear and try not to scratch her." Joey patted the bike on the fender. His dismount caused a small piece of metal to roll away down the street.

He walked toward the door, leaving the man to look back and forth between him and the bike as if Joey had just suggested he park a turd. In a frantic attempt to avoid touching it, he put a finger to his ear and called inside with an implant. By the time Joey reached the door attendant, the valet had nearly reached the point of tears, his manager no doubt confirming Joey's story.

The valet tried to push the bike along without sitting on it, but succeeded only in working up a sweat and treating the crowd to a series of humorous faces. Joey took no small amount of delight in the nauseated faces the man made as he lowered his weight onto the bike and eased it up the ramp into the parking deck.

The security man by the door loomed, wanting any excuse in the world to throw Joey to the pavement and pound him, but opened the door with a gritted smile. Joey paused a moment to offer his elbow to that girl in the purple dress, earning only a deeper glare.

A pale hardwood floor greeted him inside, filling an area sectioned off with faux rice paper walls. Chōchin hung here and there, decorated with various ideograms. In the dining area, soft cushions surrounded numerous low oval tables. The staff dressed in Japanese attire, a faithful recreation of clothing from a time before firearms.

Masaru's formal suit closed in a diagonal across his chest, where a small silver pin about the size of a thumbnail in the shape of the Kurotai logo held it closed at his shoulder. The shiny material hinted at indigo in places where the light hit it just right, and each of his sleeves had three black buttons with a single Kanji carved out of them.

Completing his outfit, a young red-haired woman clung to his left arm. She didn't even look twenty yet, and wore a gleaming green Chinese tunic and darker gloves that went up to the middle of her biceps, with dragons embroidered in darker green threading. Her boots were the same shade as the gloves, and stopped just past the knee. She could have been a model, and stared with adoring blue eyes at him.

"Is that Wednesday?" Joey poked a finger in her direction and fell into the cushions.

The redhead gave him a confused look as Masaru shot him a stalling glare. "This is Kate. Kate, this is Joseph, an associate of mine."

She smiled at him as he sat. "Hi."

Joey returned the smile. "He must like you. He didn't let Tuesday speak."

Masaru sighed. "Pay him no mind, dear. He has no social graces."

Katya held herself at an angle, more kneeling than sitting. She had made the mistake of wearing a sheer white dress that hugged her lithe body like a layer of paint. The hem was so short it left her in a constant battle to preserve her modesty. Her high European cheekbones sparkled with a touch of makeup that contained silver glitter, and she had put her raven hair up in a whorl behind her head, held in place by a pair of red sticks.

She smirked at Joey. The deep red color on her lips would have taken his mind off the imminent job if not for how little he trusted being alone with her. All he could find out about her indicated she had been in Russia at some point within the past few years and had some cyberware installed at the shop of their mutual acquaintance, Hiroto Ido. The 'ware she got was the kind that that spies and assassins used, and she probably had poison lurking in places Joey cared not to think about. She slid away from her abandoned high heels to make room for Joey.

"You have something against chairs, don't you?" Joey shifted on the cushions, sitting cross-legged with his elbows on his knees.

"No more so than you have a problem with civilization." Masaru could have been trying to sound condescending, but it was hard to tell apart from his normal tone.

A spread of several square ceramic plates, some hovering, with various assortments of sushi, occupied the table. Joey took one piece at random, figuring he would get right to business this time.

He soon found out he had plucked a piece of salmon from Masaru's personal order, one with an excessive amount of wasabi concealed between the fish and the rice. He gasped and pounded his fist into his chest before grabbing for the closest glass of water and draining it in a single gulp.

"Try that plate." Masaru pointed.

Katya turned her head to look away, doing as much as she could to radiate to the room that she had no idea who this fool was. Once he recovered the ability to breathe, he pulled his deck across his lap as a tray.

"Alex gave me a good one. I'm going to need both of you. I need to get some data from a secure location. The problem is that this secure location doesn't have a

GlobeNet interlink. This is going to be easy and difficult at the same time. Difficult to get to the network, but it'll be easy once I do."

Neither of his friends knew a tremendous amount about the GlobeNet, but had enough familiarity to understand he would need to enter the building in the real world and find a terminal to log in.

"What's in this file?" Masaru asked, taking a piece of his supercharged fish.

"Don't know, don't care." Joey smiled.

Katya frowned, speaking with an air of sanctimony that only the beautiful could get away with. "That caused trouble for you on Mars, did it not?"

"Don't go there." Joey waved her off. "The Mars thing… I never actually got *to* the file. I still don't know what was in it."

Katya made a mocking face, as if Joey had just proved her point.

"Look. Mars was my fault for not checking the network out ahead of time. It had nothing to do with what the file contained. This time I know what to expect. It is a sec level 4 grid isolated from the main hotel network. They use it for sensitive data storage, both for the hotel and guests. The only way in is from local access terminals. The data node itself is just a level 5, probably running on a Simmons core."

"Didn't a level 5 node burn out your deck last month?" Masaru wore a fake smile.

"No, bad luck burned out my deck… not to mention a big damn troll." Joey rubbed his M3 plug. "Technically, the node didn't do anything. A program construct inside it did. Look, I'm not askin' you guys to get shot for me this time, just help me get inside the place and cover me while I work. If it goes south, you can act like you aren't part of it."

"Okay," said Katya without hesitation.

Masaru mulled the situation over as a piece of yellowtail swam past his teeth. Joey couldn't offer much in terms of money, but he had a feeling his friend would enjoy the practice.

Masaru took a sip of sake. "When does this need to happen?"

Joey glanced at his NetMini. "Today or tomorrow. The file is gonna get moved or wiped in a day or two. I checked the floor plan in the city archives—it looks like there is a maintenance office off the main lobby that leads to the secure server room. I bet there is a terminal in there that I can use."

Without warning, loud music erupted from Joey's deck, the kind of music that the clientele of the Toko Lounge would consider noise, and be quite offended by the lyrics—*if* they could make them out. Joey spit his second attempt at a piece of sushi across the table into the redhead's drink and Katya almost jumped out of her dress. The deck bounced to the ground as Joey fell over backward, flailing. Masaru furrowed his brow. Kate covered her mouth to stifle a startled gasp, and then covered her ears to drown out the sound.

Every eye in the room was on them.

Within ten seconds, the sound cut out, leaving the room silent.

"Bitch." Joey growled, jaw clenched.

He wobbled once more into a sitting position and pulled the deck in his lap.

Katya glared.

He smirked. "Not you. Cleopatra."

"Is she mad at you for not paying?" Her condescending smile appeared warped behind a glass of sake she swirled in preparation for a sip.

"From the look of that dress, you must be working tonight." Joey grinned. "Good thing you shave the beast or that dress wouldn't be long enough to hide it."

Masaru failed to stifle a chuckle at the unexpected crass remark. Kate blushed at the floor. Katya ceased swirling the sake and fixed him with a glare, the kind of glare that once again convinced him never to fall asleep without a locked door between them. Attempting to appear nonchalant, she tried to pull the hem down her thigh a bit more.

"You two sound like you're married. You already have the banter rehearsed." Masaru grinned and toasted them both with another sip.

Katya shifted her glare to Masaru.

Joey shuddered. "Anyway... where were we?"

After hard booting the deck, he used it to project a map. The scintillating light hovered just above the table's mirrored surface, existing in two parallel planes. Joey stuck his hands into the map, manipulating it like dough. He pulled it to the right, zoomed in, and pointed at a spot.

"This is the lobby. There is a maintenance hallway here..."

He indicated the expansive space. A desk, behind which two rows of elevators led up to the guest rooms, dominated the center. The left side opened into a large bar and restaurant and the right had seats and a waiting area with a small coffee counter. Joey gestured at a small security door that connected to a hallway that hooked around in the shape of a question mark.

He tapped his finger into the shimmering blue light. "That's the server room."

A live woman in a blue kimono cleared some of the empty plates. She spoke in Japanese and motioned at Joey. Masaru replied. She nodded, bowed, and walked away.

"She'll bring you some food that's more to your taste," said Masaru.

"Free food is free food, sounds good." Joey turned his attention to the map. "That's where I need to go, and if everything goes perfectly, I'll need about 20 minutes."

Katya balanced herself on her knees with her elbows at the table's edge. She studied the map for a moment and spoke without looking up. Joey assumed her concentration was genuine as a little Russian came out in her accent.

"I think they make it look like unimportant door. Not much protection, but still has some security. RFID badge most likely."

"That's why I was hoping you would be interested. Go in, look around, and figure out what we need to get me in that door."

"I can do that. What are you paying?" Katya scratched the sole of her left foot with her right big toe.

He wanted to say something along the lines of "more than the guy you'll be with later", but he bit his tongue. "Ten grand?"

Her outward affect didn't convey the astonishment that echoed in her mind. Joey smiled. Her self-control impressed him. He'd seen her bank account and didn't think she would refuse an offer like that for such a basic job.

She sat back on her heels. "That is acceptable."

19

THE IMPERIAL

Joey arrived first at the Imperial hotel the next morning. He sighed at the time on his NetMini, assuming Masaru had to drop Wednesday off somewhere and Katya was just late. He leaned against his bike, arms folded, and watched a slow but steady stream of people exit the hotel toward waiting limousines and hired cars. A light breeze stirred his hair. Somewhere down the street, a breakfast cart put the fragrance of Dancing Piglet synthetic bacon in the air. He knew it well. The stuff came on like bacon at first, but stayed in the throat for a few seconds before the taste turned chemical.

An electronic chirp to his right made him jump. A floating orb—an advert bot —hovered two feet away, its holographic panel cycling through offers for various coffees: everything from cheap synthetic crap to the hundred-credit-a-cup hydroponics. In a moment of weakness, he bought one. The orb wobbled with glee and zoomed away. Three minutes later, a brick-shaped bot delivered his drink.

He sipped, keeping his eyes on the crowd shifting past a large white van. It seemed rather odd that a bakery truck had parked half a block away. As soon as he saw the impatient man next to it in a sand brown coat, he got nervous. He had to be either police or military intelligence. The idea that someone had tipped them off to the imminent hack did cross his mind, but the odds of that seemed low. Joey wasn't difficult to get to. If the cops wanted him, they would kick in his door and take him.

At the midpoint of his coffee, Katya appeared from around a corner a block away. She had ditched the super short white dress for a more modest knee length white skirt over a pair of sheer black leggings, paired with a form-obscuring long sleeved sweater, also black. The glossy purse looked just large enough to conceal a handgun and matched her ruby heels. She tossed a casual glance at him as she made her way across the courtyard to the front door of the hotel. Shiny platinum blonde leaked into her hair from the root, flowing down to the tips. The cascading color change gave the impression that her sweater sucked the black right out of her hair.

Joey held the cup to his mouth, savoring the scent while observing Katya wander the lobby for a few minutes. By the time he ventured another sip, she was well into a conversation with a security guard, flirting. His disinterested reaction to her presence flipped in an instant to that of an eager puppy. Joey shifted with discomfort knowing that she had just hit him with synthetic pheromones. On top of her already perfect body, that seemed un-sporting. Joey decided to stash his bike out of sight around the corner—just in case something went wrong.

KATYA LET THE GUARD LEAD HER BY THE HAND DOWN A MAINTENANCE CORRIDOR AT the rear of the hotel. She found it easy to talk him into thinking his friends hired her to pay him a special visit. The vague reasons she hinted at found easy explanations in his mind, and the pheromones had chased away the last traces of his hesitation. At the end of the dingy hallway, he took her down a small passage to a janitorial storage room. She let him pull her along, taking notes of the layout of the area, particularly the security station.

He backed into the small space and closed the door, covering the room in privacy. Just enough light remained from a small strip of glass for them to see their silhouettes—though her dark red lipstick remained evident against her face. He shoved cleaning equipment out of the way, and soon had his pants open and his hands all over her, groping everywhere, as if he couldn't decide where to go first. She went along with it for a little while, letting him lose himself in the moment. In Russia, with the ACC, she had experienced anything and everything sexual during her assignments—and between them. Her body was just another weapon at her disposal, desensitized to the point that few things even registered with her libido anymore. She leaned into a kiss, grasping his cheeks with both hands as his fingers mapped her curves.

His enthusiasm faded and his motion slowed, and the blur of confusion spread over his eyes. The hand that had been sliding up under her dress fell slack at his side. Katya pulled back from the kiss, mouth open. Two clear droplets fell from tiny holes in her canine teeth, running over her lip and down onto her chin. After easing his body to the ground, she spat to clear her mouth of the drug she just shot down his throat.

Her cybernetic right eye presented a virtual timer in midair at the top of her vision to track the sedative dose. The floating numbers reminded her of the debt she still owed for the part. Advanced eyes that looked real, not like hunks of metal, were expensive—especially via unofficial channels. Ten thousand credits to steal an ID badge felt like winning the lottery, and she had only so much time before her debt came calling. She tried not to let the ignominy of the job get to her. This was, after all, like asking Rembrandt to paint your house.

After slipping out of her clothes, she swiped his badge from his shirt and leaned against the door to survey the hallway. Within thirty seconds, her CamNano cyberware had altered the color of her skin and hair in perfect sync with the environment. While motionless against a surface, it provided near invisibility. She eased the door open and checked for any sign of movement. The only sound of activity came from the distant lobby.

She slid out into the hallway, hugging the wall, into an embrace of frigid air. The cold reminded her how much she hated resorting to this tactic, but it was the fastest way to get this done and over with since she had a short time limit before her lover woke up. She kept her body against the wall and crept along, the nanobots updating the color of her skin to match the scenery. Cell by cell, her skin shimmered like a living digital display. As long as she didn't move too fast, it looked as though she stood behind a projection of the wall texture. Signs, seams, painted lines, and even smudges rolled over her as she moved.

Thirty yards from the closet, she peeked out a small vertical window into the security room. One other guard was inside, seated with his back to the door at a desk full of holographic displays linked to security cameras.

Dammit.

Her hand found only smooth hips when she instinctively reached for a weapon. She hadn't planned on dealing with any other guards, and left her gun back in the closet. A naked hand-to-hand fight didn't place too high on her list of fun things to do at the office.

The security door would beep and hiss when it opened, so she couldn't pass unnoticed. She found some respite knowing this was, compared to her usual work, laughable security—so she could afford to take risks. Two small prongs extended out of her right index finger, a few millimeters long.

She braced her stance, ready to charge in at the guard before he could raise an alarm. With a swipe of the stolen ID, the door slid open with the expected sounds, but to her surprise, he didn't turn around.

"That was quick, Don. I'd have taken more than five minutes with a girl like that." He laughed. "You moonlighting somewhere to afford her?"

Katya slipped into the dim security room, for a moment appearing as a glimmering hallway-white ghost. Patches of dark blue-grey spread over her skin as the CamNano struggled to keep up with the severe change in lighting. She moved like a phantasmal apparition, a suspension of lines and color approximating a female form. The warm carpet offered welcome relief from the tiles.

A long stride cleared the room, and she touched the pins to the back of his neck. A brief spark flashed on contact. His face slammed into the desk as if she had hit him with a sledgehammer. His body convulsed as he foamed at the mouth and slid onto the floor. After locating the ID printer, she set about making a copy of the badge. No need to worry about the picture. Joey needed to fool a door, not a person.

She curled up on the chair, shivering and staring at the expanding pool of saliva beneath the guard's face. A number of security jackets in the back called out to her, though as tempting as a bit of warmth would be at that moment, the sight of a coat floating in midair would give her away. Ghostly numbers ticked ever closer to her deadline as the ID writer struggled to warm up. She swiveled the chair to face the desk and went for the video recorders. The wall of holographic light in front of her recreated all public areas of the hotel in perfect three dimensions.

The Imperial used a standard security system, Stern & Basset, a subsidiary of

Sentinel Corp. While far from chintzy, she had seen the hardware many times before. It took only two minutes to hack into it and set the rear hallway on a loop feed. Just as she turned back to face the room, the new ID badge slid down a chute into a tray. Lifting the guard back into his chair proved difficult, though she managed to prop him up in a manner that suggested sleeping on the job.

With the timer drawing close to the wire, she didn't wait to enter the hallway with care. Her body blurred into view as a mismatched swarm of blue-grey and metallic silver streaks that melted to white as she tiptoed along. The CamNano caught up a few yards later when she pressed herself into the wall and held as still as she could against the icy surface. A man in black, perhaps a concierge, came out of a staff elevator, pausing in his stride not four feet away. Katya closed her eyes to hide them, reducing her breathing as she listened to him check a vidmail. He took a step, but paused. Katya had no outward reaction, though her brain processed four ways to kill him if he noticed her.

"Hate this back room... Always feels like someone's watching me in here, probably a ghost," muttered the man, while walking out.

She slinked back to the janitorial closet, slow enough to remain invisible.

The thirty-yard trek felt like an eternity. She made it into the reassuring darkness just as her timer flashed an alert. After putting his badge back into place, she dropped the copy into her purse. Her natural complexion spread across her body like cream through coffee as she shut down the CamNano. The guard was still out, in more ways than one. A convenient cleaning rag spared her hand and made the man's experience more realistic. After tossing the evidence into a bucket, she squatted over her pile of clothes. He moved as she stood up, holding her panties. Sweating from the trip to the security room, she found it easy to act as though they had finished. He squinted up at her, groggy from the chems.

"Ugh..." He rubbed his forehead. The form of a naked woman blurred in his vision and threatened to split into two copies. "What happened?"

She feigned a wounded frown. "You were having such fun that you jumped up, hit your head on the shelf. Don't remember?"

"Yeah, of course. You were amazing." He peppered her with several other lame compliments.

He felt spent, and she wore nothing but a layer of perspiration. Only one explanation formed in his mind.

Katya smiled, not that he could see it. "You must be overworked. You passed out right after you hit your head." She let her Russian accent thicken, speaking as she stepped into her underwear.

"Too much damned overtime now. Too many conventions going on. We got OT coming out of our asses. I think I've worked three sixteens this week."

For just a moment, she felt like the poor guy might have deserved the real thing. They both dressed in silence.

She backed through the door into the hallway, holding it for him. "I have confession to make." An innocent smile spread across her lips.

"Oh?" He squeezed her ass again as he pushed the door closed.

She traced a finger along his face and left a light kiss on his lip, exaggerating a Russian accent. "Your friends no hire me. I see you there and don't know what came over me." CamNano helped her fake a blush.

He grinned. She had pegged him for that type, and the thought that his manliness had drawn her across the room just to get a piece of him seemed like something he would revel in. It also handled the imminent confusion of him thanking his clueless coworkers for sending her. Perhaps out of pity, she made out with him for a little longer to keep up the ruse.

FIVE MINUTES AFTER KATYA DISAPPEARED INTO THE BACK OF THE HOTEL, MASARU walked up alongside Joey. He too had parked a block or so away.

"Do you have a plan?" Masaru's tone implied he knew the answer already.

"Of course I don't." Joey chuckled. "Kat is in there right now scoping the place out, she took one of the guards in back now."

Masaru nodded. "Business or pleasure?"

Joey couldn't conceal the laugh. "Pleasure? Really?"

"She is still a woman."

"So was Medusa," said Joey with a raised finger.

"Who?"

"It would take so long to explain it wouldn't be worth the joke." Joey shook his head.

A minute shy of a half hour later, he relaxed when Katya reappeared with the man. The guard went back to his post as Katya headed straight for the door. She crossed the street, reaching the sidewalk a little east of them. Joey bit his lip, wearing the pained expression of someone who gazed upon a desired treat that would be fatal if eaten, but considered it anyway.

She turned on her heel, passing by the two of them without making eye contact. A plastic click at his feet made him look down at a stark white ID badge on the ground. He scooped it up into his coat, confident no one hadn't iced. Katya's holographic face appeared above his NetMini once he answered the inbound call.

"There is hallway east of lobby. That is where you want to go. I set up video loop of the security system, you have maybe twenty minutes before they notice and start checking." Katya, still walking away, didn't appear to be having a conversation with anyone.

"Implanted comm too?" Joey chuckled. "Nice."

DALE TOOK NOTICE OF THE TWO MEN ACROSS THE STREET FROM THE HOTEL, THOUGH neither looked familiar. The facial recognition system found no matches for the skinny one, while the other came up as Masaru Kurotai, a Japanese national and son of the CEO of Kurotai Electronics. Dale didn't pay him too much attention. His credentials checked and Japan, at least most of it, remained an ally of the UCF. He disregarded him, expecting his presence here was due to some unrelated conference or seminar. He leaned back in the driver's seat of the Floyd's bakery van, waiting for Nina to return.

He closed his eyes and could almost hear her yelling at everyone inside. The beginning of a headache crept into his brain from lack of sleep, and he settled in for a nap. The less noise in his day, the better.

INSIDE THE IMPERIAL HOTEL, WHITE AND BLACK MARBLE TILES, CHEST HIGH VASES with actual living plants, gold inlaid blush marble columns, and dark red velvet benches painted the lobby of the hotel in opulence. Masaru had little reaction, but Joey gawked as if in an alien world. His long black coat and scruffy visage were suited to life around the fringes of a grey zone amid his fellow counterculture dregs. He felt quite conspicuous here.

The attendants, almost fifty yards away, perched behind an imposing bulwark of polished rose marble where they guarded a hallway full of elevators. Joey sauntered over to the maintenance door. When no one was looking at him, he worked a swipe of the stolen badge into the spin that took him through the entrance in one fluid motion. Masaru caught the door with his toe and scanned the room once more. The security guard bragged to his buddies about the amazing call girl, a tale that kept them all occupied.

The maintenance section was glaring in contrast to the opulence outside. Recessed three steps down, the pale green tiles and fake wood paneling gave the hallway the look of something one would find in a cheap office building and not a four thousand credit a night hotel. Small silver nameplates jutted out of the wall by a series of doors.

Joey grinned, moving up to the first one. "One of these offices should have a terminal I can use."

He moved at a brisk stride under flickering fluorescent lights that made shadows jump and slide around. At the end of the hallway, he spotted a sign: 'Milton Swanson—Systems Architect.'

"That's the one." Joey shoved the door open as if it was his office.

Old cups piled high on the desk while the left side of the room drowned in an ocean of old Chibi-San containers, some of which still leaked soy sauce. A waterfall of holodisk cases ran over the right side, and shelves full of random disassembled electronics sagged against the wall. The air hinted at the cloying smell of rotting food swirled with the after-presence of someone who wears far too much cologne. Joey's brain ground to an abrupt halt as he noticed a large composite alloy broadsword against the wall just by the door.

"What the fuck?" He chuckled.

Masaru pointed at animated holograms of wizards, trolls, and dragons shimmering in a hazy mixture of floating dust particles and weak lighting over the desk. They exchanged a nod of understanding as Joey swung his deck off his back and set it down, causing a cascade of empty plastic cups to flow to the ground. After connecting the secondary lead to the terminal, he flopped in the seat and pulled the interface wire out to a comfortable length.

"Wow, this guy has a nice chair." The tiny switchblade snapped out of the housing with a squeeze. "Alright, here I go. If anything happens, hit that." Joey pointed to a holographic button on the display panel.

"Could I not just pull out the wire?" Masaru grinned. He knew that would work, but it would knock Joey loopy like a mule-kick to the head.

"Bite me."

Joey slid the connector into the socket behind his right ear. The soft click that echoed within his skull grew to thunder across his brain when the door of reality slammed closed. Weightlessness followed, and he spiraled down a tunnel of shimmering color. The end passed with an electric whoosh and he found himself in a room lifted from the set of a medieval fantasy holo. Large irregular stones somewhere between grey and brown formed the walls of the chamber. Coated with a reflective sheen of moist slime, they caught the wavering light from several virtual torches that sent shadows flitting about in the spaces between the raised stones.

Time to get to work.

20

RENAISSANCE MAN

An unimpressed sneer spread over the face of the dark cowboy, exposing yellow teeth. His eyes narrowed into slits that vanished behind the gossamer frizz of old-man eyebrows as Joey's alter ego threw a condescending grunt at the décor. The silver discs that ringed his black hat shimmered with reflected virtual torchlight.

The room had one exit, a heavy wooden door reinforced with several iron straps. He figured the network administrator for a fantasy geek. That he had taken the time to program the fragrance of burning torches gave it away. Boots rang heavy across the stone floor as he walked, wooden heels on stone accented with the metallic clatter of spurs. A strange noise came from the right as a pair of two-foot blobs of jelly appeared in a flash of magic sparkles. For several seconds, a green line appeared above them and then disappeared. The slimes proceeded to slide about at random, apparently non-aggressive.

Past the door, the atmosphere changed to one of blinding light and immaculate floors. Joey squinted. Despite this place existing only as data fed into his brain, the sudden dramatic change in lighting still made his eyes hurt. He flung his long black coat to the rear, exposing his belt and the silver revolvers. He glanced side to side, hovering his hands over his guns.

His deck constructed a network map as it analyzed local traffic, and a wireframe model of the interconnect pathways and nodes drew itself out in front of him as an expanding cobweb of boxes and lines.

Joey's target, a data node, lay nestled within a triangle of security sub-processors behind a barrier node.

The overall defense level of this network seemed quite a bit lower than the reputation of the place would suggest. He figured they overestimated their physical security and didn't count on someone sneaking into the building to plug in to the private network. In a way that made sense, the portion of their system that was accessible from the GlobeNet likely got more attention from their security team. Despite the danger, he felt a twinge of disappointment at the prospect of an easy job.

He turned left and plodded down the corridor, doing his best impression of the stalking drift of a horror-vid villain. Despite his gait, the environment flew past him as though he ran at sixty miles per hour. The bandwidth of a local terminal connection allowed him to move at great speed, another reason he adored the risk of sneaking in.

At the barrier node entry, he found a large white airlock door that one would expect to see on the outer hull of a starship complete with black and yellow caution stripes around the edges and a pair of flashing red lights on the wall. In the center, someone had tacked an anachronistic piece of yellowing parchment paper in place with a rusty nail. Upon it, words written in red ink.

Unauthorized intruders will be smited until dead.

Joey looked at the ceiling. He couldn't wait to see what lay beyond it. He muttered at the redundancy, an intruder is by definition unauthorized. One trait from his father that he wished he hadn't inherited: sometimes, picayune things like that stuck in his mind and made him angry at stupid people.

It didn't take long for his tinkering to fool the door. Then again, barrier nodes were easier to enter than leave.

A rush of white fog billowed into the hall as the immense portal slid to the side. The room beyond resembled a medieval tavern, complete with fireplace, old tables and a bar. The half-elf girl strumming a mandolin by a fireplace, wearing a skimpy green skirt and top might have caused a lifted eyebrow if he didn't know she was just a program construct. In flagrant disregard of the fantasy motif, a silver elevator door clung to the center of the ceiling. It was as out of place here as a cowboy in black.

He looked up at it with a half grin. Barrier nodes often played visual games with their exit portals, using tricks like moving stairs, impossible doors that slide around the walls, and invisible pathways. All of it was a representation of the additional difficulty of exiting a node designed to trap intruders. Joey knew better than to try to climb to it. The passage out of this node didn't really exist on the ceiling. The door would simply run away if he came too close.

He raised his arms. Thin green lines reminiscent of circuitry wiring flashed into the air like lightning as his deck hammered the network with algorithms designed to simulate an authorized user at a damaged terminal. The routines detected the network's response and formed an accepted set of credentials based on thousands of rejected attempts within the span of a few seconds.

The elevator door shimmered and melted away to a green wireframe model, then slid across the ceiling and down onto the wall like a square patch of liquid. It stopped sideways, halfway down as its steel covering returned.

"Halt." A deep male voice echoed from behind as if from inside a metal tube.

A gothic knight in full plate armor materialized out of thin air a few feet away as he turned toward the sound. The construct drew a large broadsword from a scabbard on its belt.

"Prepare to be smited, intruder."

The armor amused Joey. From the looks of it, Milton modified a troll to be more defensive. Not waiting for it to make the first move, he flipped his guns up and fired.

The knight lunged into an attack, deflecting the bullets with a shield that formed around its arm. Joey lunged back as the blade hissed past his face. He continued to float to the rear, firing, but the knight held its shield in the path of the onslaught.

For several minutes, the dark cowboy vanished and reappeared around the room in various places as the sentry pursued him over the virtual furniture. Bottles of liquor behind the bar exploded from deflected shots and several tables fell, cleaved in two from near-miss broadsword strokes. The half elf girl continued to strum, as if oblivious to the battle. The Knight proved to be far from the pushover he expected, and it took all his concentration to counteract the program's efforts to invade and corrupt his deck.

He couldn't trick a construct into flinching or making an error. They merely ran a set of coded instructions, lacking true understanding of what went on around it. The knight wasn't an AI, their duel became a question of finding the pattern. He studied it over several more exchanges until he could predict its next move. When the I/O channel opened to transmit an attack, he slipped a virus packet past its firewall. Cyberspace rendered the exchange as a sidestepped sword stroke and a pistol whip that crushed a pronounced dent into its helmet. The satisfying clunk knocked the thing back a step.

Shaking it off, it lunged again.

The sword came in a little faster than Joey prepared for, and it sliced a fourteen-inch gash down his left leg. In cyberspace, the cut felt real. The old cowboy let out a polyphonic roar that reverberated with supernatural energy. Black blood sprayed the floor as he stumbled. His wail of pain became one of anger.

"I'm sorry, I don't know that tune," said the half-elf. "Would you like to make another request?"

IN THE REAL WORLD, MASARU TURNED AT THE SIGHT OF SMOKE RISING UP FROM THE grille on the back of the deck. He lifted an eyebrow, unsure which was more disturbing—that Joey's deck appeared to be burning or the sick grin on his friend's face.

The door opened and a pasty man in his middle forties waddled in, carrying coffee in one hand and a silver-wrapped lump in the other. A thick moustache and fluffy eyebrows sprouted from a round face covered by unkempt brown hair. His white button-down shirt looked a size too small, blotched with many years' worth of coffee stains. Upon seeing Joey slumped over his desk, he froze in place. His egg sandwich slipped from his hand, striking the floor with a dull *plop*.

Masaru edged into the shadows by the wall, a hand on his katana.

Milton broke out in a cold sweat, already pasty face growing paler. The panic left his eyes once he remembered the sword leaning against the wall. He kept it more because it reminded him of his favorite pastime than for its practical use as a weapon, but a weapon it was nonetheless. He moved with a lunging step, grabbing it while setting the coffee down on a nearby shelf. He turned, holding the blade up with wild fear in his eyes. Masaru suppressed the urge to laugh at his posture.

Milton clutched it as if he had just pulled Excalibur from the stone. He crept toward Joey, and held the blade over his head. As little knowledge that the unconscious Joey had of Milton's approach, Milton had less idea than that of Masaru's presence behind him.

The administrator lifted his weapon higher. Trembles rattled his arms. He appeared to debate if he should swing full strength at Joey or tap him with it to wake him up. Masaru made a small whistle, three descending notes. Milton whirled, his startled shriek at seeing another man behind him cut off when the sheathed katana cracked him across the head. The sword fell from his grip, sticking into the concrete behind him as he spun and fell unconscious. Masaru reattached the katana to his belt and retrieved the coffee. He tilted it in toast to the unconscious man.

"Your décor may be trite, but at least, my friend, you have good taste in coffee."

JOEY HAD BEEN STUDYING THE KNIGHT'S CHANGED PATTERN, FIRING THE INSTANT HE anticipated vulnerability. This time, his attack bypassed the countermeasures and tricked it into running a "diagnostic" that was in actuality a disassembler. In cyberspace, smoking bullets struck it in the chest, causing a series of deep dents. Bright white light shone out from the eye slits in the helmet, spraying into random pixels of data that faded away.

The knight attacked again, but Joey ducked. The program weakened, and its strikes became ever more slow and predictable. Efficiency lost in an attempt to recompile itself to repair the damage. Joey fired twice more, shattering the knight into a dozen pieces of armor and light that soon melted into the ground, trailing to oblivion in cyan smears and cycling numbers.

The cowboy rubbed his lip with the back of his hand, eyeing the droplet of blood on the ridge. A sneer crossed his lips as he shoved his guns back in their holsters with a guttural sound of contempt in his throat. The aged gunslinger acted angrier than Joey was, but he loved every minute of it. Turning his attention once more to the barrier node's exit, he held his hand up as smoky wraiths slid off his arm and into the wall.

This time it worked. The liquid portal slithered along until it took a normal place at about the height one would expect a door to be. It opened with a faint squeak, revealing a dim cobalt blue hallway with an indigo floor and ceiling that led to several data nodes. He triggered a DataMole soft, summoning a furry creature the size of a medium dog. A few degrees shy of cute, it trundled off in search of a match for the file. It went right. Joey started a manual search from the other side.

Twenty minutes later, perhaps two minutes in real time, he found something that piqued his interest. One of the data tiles had a face on it that he recognized. Only a day or two old, the security footage showed Donna George, a reporter for NewsNet. Her image flooded the city from an uncountable number of bots that swarmed at all hours. She had to be in her late fifties now, but had so much work done she still looked twenty.

The video showed her by the entrance to some convention room in the hotel, being drooled over by two men in expensive suits. From the sound of her speech, she'd downed more than a few drinks, but her companions were both quite happy to be in her presence.

"That little bitch isn't taking *my* job." She grinned as she shook her finger back and forth. "Oh no no no. I took care of that."

One man took her arm to help her avoid falling, but she pulled back.

"I'm fine." She sipped from a glass in her left hand and glared at him. "Doing better than that little whore, who the hell does she think she is, trying to replace *me*, Donna George!"

She tilted forward. Both men helped her to a nearby chair against the wall. They sat on either side and muttered too low for the audio to pick up.

"No… No… I'm not worrying. I *offered* her that job in Sector 12." She laughed the haughty laugh of an entitlement-bitch that never doubted she would get her way.

"Sector 12? But… isn't that a black zone?" One of the men raised his voice.

Donna cackled. "That's the point. You didn't think *I* would interview the worthless drek that live there, did you?" She drained the last of the glass in one gulp. "That little ass-kissing priss wasn't supposed to come back." She cracked up into fits of giggling.

The two men looked at each other in dismay. Joey had enough and stopped the video. He tucked it away for later use, copying the file to his deck. If he ever got hard up for cash, he could always try to get some credits out of her to keep that quiet.

Something warm and wet snuffled against his leg. His gaze fell upon the source with a paralyzing dourness that could have shocked an average person to immediate silence. Alas, the DataMole had no sense of fear and stood there wagging its stumpy little tail in simulated pleasure as it held the sought after file in its mouth.

Joey patted it on the head without thinking as he took the file, leaving the creature to disintegrate into a puddle of swirling pixels that seeped into the floor. The outer shell of the tile was so black it reflected no light, like a hole in reality. Small panels of metal folded out and closed around it. Armored doors caught in an endless cycle of continual closing. He recognized the effect: serious crypto he didn't have the hardware to touch.

The file sent a twinge of fear and exhilaration through him at what he must have just gotten involved with.

21

COMPLICATIONS

A cloying smell, the presence of weeks-old remains of Chinese take-out, greeted Joey as his eyes opened into the real world. The pile of trash blurred into focus once he became aware of a new player in the game of fragrances: coffee. Masaru stood by the door with his back to the wall, in a position that would allow him to ambush anyone that came in. The beige cup with the fancy Imperial logo on it made him think Masaru had gone out to grab a cup while he lay there, logged in and defenseless.

Joey stood, gathering his deck. "Dammit, you left—"

His voice cut off to a startled wail as he tripped over the unconscious Milton and landed in a heap. Masaru hauled Joey to his feet with one arm, saluting him with the cup once he was upright.

"This man brought me coffee, very respectful."

Betrayal changed to gratitude at the sight of the broadsword stuck in the floor.

"Thanks. I'm not into body piercing. I got the file, let's get outta here." He paused to swipe the egg sandwich off the floor. "Ooh. Bonus."

He kicked the door closed behind him, and stuffed the discovered breakfast into his mouth. Masaru touched his fingers to the side of his head, opening a communication link to Katya.

"Kat, please provide a distraction. We are ready to exit."

Katya's hair had become bright red and she had changed into a plain green strapless dress that clung around her armpits. Her cyberware adjusted the complexion of her face, adding freckles.

She held her NetMini up to her head, faking a call with no video feed, and walked around the lobby. Her voice held no trace of an accent, increasing in volume and desperation, as if she was being tele-dumped by a man she had been expecting to marry. As she grew louder, her argument absorbed the entire room. The two men slipped into the lobby and crossed to the main doors, which hissed out of their way. Across the courtyard, they jogged down a few steps to the sidewalk. No sooner had they set foot upon the metal walkway than the sound of a heavy sliding door drew their attention to the left.

About forty yards away, two huge men in ankle length black coats emerged from the side of a black van. Their boots thudded like lead into the road and both stared at him with emotionless silver orbs. Each man's right eye lit up with a faint orange crosshair. An octopus of wires ran into the collar of their coats, connected to metal plates that wrapped around their skull—military combat implants. They appeared almost identical, as if the same machine produced both men. The barrels of a rotary gun spun up in the hands of the one on the left while his partner trained a shoulder-fired "soda can" rocket on Joey.

He got a good look at the folding fins of the stubby blunt-nosed missile as it leapt out of the lower tube of a two-shot launcher and became a dark spot amidst a sea of white fumes heading right at him.

Masaru's neural amplifiers kicked in as his spatial sensor detected a fast moving object on a trajectory toward him. Accelerated to the point where time appeared to slow, he clapped his hand onto Joey's shoulder and yanked his friend off his feet to the rear. A stream of billowy cotton smoke folded out from the end of the rotating missile. It passed, one fin tracing a crimson line across Joey's cheek. For nanoseconds stretched to seconds, Masaru stared into the roiling serpent of fog, watching a droplet of blood leap into the air off the end of the fin. Time resumed. The rocket careened into the windshield of the nearby Floyd's Bakery truck.

Dale wasn't so lucky. The 60mm armor-piercing warhead hit him in the face before he even had time to look up at the crunch of it piercing the windscreen. It carried his body backward, not detonating upon the soft human tissue until the warhead struck the armor plating behind him. The bloody spray of his crushed head became a robust explosion, a hot jet of plasma burning into the electronics compartment. Most of the front end, as well as Dale, flew into the road with an orange flash.

Joey could barely get a "what the fuck" out of his mouth before Masaru arrested his fall and hauled him to his feet again. His cheek burned, his nose blackened with soot, and blood trickled from where the fin had grazed. He sprinted ahead into a cloud of exhaust, and crossed the street amid a rain of debris.

Two men in black suits, leaning against the front of the hotel, moved forward, pulling silver handguns out of their jackets and sending streaks of green laser toward the man with the missile launcher. The beams seared his chest armor, burning the nylon weave from the exterior and leaving smoking trenches of char in the flesh. Fraying dermal armor fibers glimmered in the wound.

Division 9 comm channels erupted in a flurry as the agents called for backup.

Halfway across the road, Joey dove into a forward roll as the rotary cannon opened up at him. Laughing in an uncontrolled nervous fit as pieces of car flew past him and ricochets tore holes in streetlamps behind him, he slid into the rear of a parked car. Riding a bike without a helmet seemed boring now.

With rocket man's attention focused on the suits, Masaru sprinted to engage the other heavy. The big man saw him coming and swerved his continuous fire in an arc. The front windows of the hotel shattered one after the next as projectiles bounced off the road and tumbled into them. Masaru ran in a circular path, avoiding the brunt of the attack. Two slugs clipped his leg, though the angle was weak enough that his Dragon Chitin armor stopped them.

The impact swept him off his feet and sent him sliding along the road into the front wheel of the van. The assassin let off the trigger and shifted to take better aim. With the cannon focused elsewhere, Joey popped up and fired several shots into his back. The big man gave Joey the same glare one would give an annoying child. Joey's gun couldn't penetrate the thick body armor, and the man's size and augmentation trivialized the impact of the slug.

The glance away gave Masaru an opportunity. His Nano katana flew from its scabbard into an upward slice. The first stroke severed the ammunition feed connecting the rotary cannon to its backpack. Loose caseless ammo cascaded out, as hundreds of four-inch blue sticks scattered to the ground. He rose up onto his toes, spinning the blade in his hands. Edge down, he used his weight to bring another slash across the massive man's body. The assassin lifted his gun in an attempt to defend himself, sacrificing the weapon into halves but reducing the damage to his chest to a bloodless slice in the armor.

The Division 9 agents at the door kept firing at the man with the rocket launcher. One of them paused and took careful aim just as the assassin sighted his second missile. Top grade neuralware brought time close to a standstill, a targeting reticule floated wherever the laser pointed, settling atop the remaining missile's warhead. When the first traces of smoke sputtered from the back end of the launcher, an emerald streak went into the nose, detonating it before it cleared its tube. Smoking fragments of rocket launcher seared into the huge man as large patches of skin melted off his face from the force of the explosion. Metal mesh flapped out of his wounds where subdermal armor tore.

He staggered backward, and then advanced despite having no skin left on half of his upper body. Blood oozed through the metallic weave around the muscles of his right arm. He tossed the pistol grip—the only remnant of the launcher—aside and went for a large handgun.

Masaru didn't expect his opponent to be as fast with his hands as he was, given his size. The thug hammered him with a quick punch to the chest that sent him flying into the van with enough force to rock the vehicle and leave a dent in the sidewall. Masaru grimaced—his opponent had the strength of a forklift. Combat muscle grafting provided short bursts of superhuman strength. With some distance between them, the man went for a sidearm.

Speedware launched Masaru into a black blur, flying behind the pale blue arc of a Nano blade. He lunged past the near stationary target, scoring the katana across the assassin's chest. To his accelerated perception, a spray slid forward, a sheet of crimson suspended in time. The curtain of blood had just started to shift from lateral to downward motion when Masaru completed the slice and reversed the blade into a stab that pierced the spine from behind.

The giant staggered. His grip faltered, the pistol slipped out of his fingers.

The entire motion ended in a fraction of a second in real time. Blood and weapon hit the ground as the speedware deactivated. Masaru gave the sword a final wrenching twist that brought forth a satisfying crack.

The ogre convulsed on his feet as cyberware went haywire. He slid off the sword and dropped to his knees where he teetered for a second before falling forward. Masaru remained motionless, sword still held out in the killing stroke, blood still dripping from the tip of the translucent blade.

Fire pulsed down his limbs in a lattice of painful threads that traced his neural wiring. The cyberware pushed his body a few hundred percent past what humans are supposed to be capable of, and now he felt the price.

Joey waved from behind the car.

Masaru took a deep breath, tuning out the pain. Now wasn't the time to acquiesce to its demands. The thought of a hot tub and a bevy of women made the burn go away.

Joey fell in alongside him as they ducked around the corner, shaking his head at how Masaru felled one of them with a sword while the other withstood laser fire. Of all the chance friendships to come along in Joey's life, the air of lethality around Masaru was the most intoxicating.

A steady serenade of laser blasts and gunfire continued behind them. Neither had the first clue why men tried to shove a missile up Joey's nose. The van that had taken the hit hadn't blown to scraps of metal, a result that only confirmed Joey's suspicion of military or police involvement. Whoever had just tried to kill him had made a big mistake catching that van in the crossfire.

"You okay?"

Masaru frowned. "I am fine. Did you get what we came for?"

Joey nodded. "Yep, and you got to make some sushi."

Masaru snapped at him. "A katana is not used for—"

"Yeah, yeah… Take a fuckin' joke once in a while."

"I am a Ronin of the Kurotai Keiretsu, I have been trained in the ways of Bushido—"

"Since before you were born, yeah, yeah. In Japan you're untouchable."

Masaru stopped, glaring.

In the UCF, he could almost get away with anything—it just took his company throwing a lot of money around to gloss over things. This little outing provided real world experience that could prepare him for assassination attempts once he returned home. He needed to stay at the top of his game. Alas, at home, assassins would be far more subtle than a pair of oxen with heavy weapons. He relaxed, allowing his indignation at the thought his sacred blade would be used on raw fish to fade.

"It is my way," Masaru said without emotion. "The day may come when you realize that this world does not exist solely for your personal amusement."

Joey pondered for a moment, tapping his finger to his chin "You mean it doesn't?"

Masaru sighed.

Joey patted him on the shoulder. "Thanks for that."

The truth that Masaru had spared him a tongue kiss from an armor-piercing rocket hung in silence between them. Masaru welcomed him with a simple nod.

"I'll call you as soon as I get this to Alex and get paid."

They turned at a tremendous crash, as if a car fell from a third story window. The clatter of concrete bits fell to the ground somewhere in the distance.

"Do you know who is after you?"

"Not a damned clue." Joey laughed and turned his bike on. "Whoever they are, they got worse problems than me now."

22

THAT MAKES TWO

Anxious silence filled the void in the command room left by the explosion outside. Several seconds ticked by as the techs stared at each other, wondering if they were the only ones to feel and hear it. The fragrance of coffee teased at the senses, wafting from a puddle created by a cup jarred from a desk by the blast. Nina hadn't waited for anyone to say anything—she ran back up through the auditorium at a pace that blurred the seats. The poor woman expecting the basket weaving convention wound up bewildered and lying on the floor amidst the contents of her many large bags, not seeing what ran her down.

As Nina bolted for the street, Samantha Cole pushed a petrified newbie out of the way and took his chair. On the terminal in front of him, a plume of smoke rose from the van. The tech had witnessed Dale's death and frozen in place. The feed from the electronics suite still came, despite the missile. She reoriented a redundant holo-cam away from the Diplomatic Tower to monitor the situation in the street. The two operatives outside yelled for backup. Aside from Cole, only one of the brand new staff in the ops room had the presence of mind to react. The rest sat paralyzed in disbelief.

Unfazed, Samantha added her voice to the fray. "Basket Weaver has been compromised. Repeat, we are compromised and under assault. Request immediate area saturation. I confirm two assailants visible with heavy weapons. Jeffries and Marshall have engaged at the perimeter. The Lieutenant is en route."

Cole took a deep breath, pausing at the thought of Nina running for the front. In the best-case scenario, the whispercraft would take a little over a minute to get here. This would all be over by then. She stood up, pointing around the room. "Alright people, snap out of it! You, open a link to Whispers 4 and 6. You, I want eyes from Overwatch on that screen. You four, keep your eyes on the Diplo Tower in case this is a diversion."

"Command, this is Hawthorne at point C3—Looks like we got some civilians caught in the crossfire." The man's voice crackled as the signal enhancers struggled to clear it up. "Wait, one of the shooters is trying to hit the civilians…"

"Carter at C1. Second that, command." A woman's voice. "Looks like one of them is firing at the civilians, probably don't want to leave witnesses."

"Command, this is Marshall." The man sounded agitated. "Engaging shooter one. He's got a 60 mil missile tube. My E82 is just pissing him off, looks like Indirium-weave subderm plus external body armor. This could be a problem."

"Oh, we definitely got his attention." A different, deeper voice came over the comm. "This is Jeffries. These lasers ain't gonna do the job."

"Hawthorne, Carter, why are you not engaging?" Nina added herself to the chatter while continuing her forty-mile-per-hour sprint down the hotel hallway. "Your MSR-49s should tear right through that."

"No range, ma'am." Hawthorne's voice came back. "We're running observation. We didn't get clearance for sniper weapons."

"What?" Nina barked. "Who the fuck's call was that?"

"Hardin's." Carter's voice, annoyance as thick as syrup. "He's riding me about sniper re-qual. This was only supposed to be a training exercise."

"Unbelievable." Nina growled louder at the bald-faced idiocy of it being thought of as a training mission with two dangerous mercenaries in play. "Did anyone else bother to read the goddamned dossier on who it is we're supposed to be observing?"

Nina glanced at the tactical overlay in the left side of her field of view, a swarm of dots tracing the position of everyone involved. She had to slow down in the face of an oncoming crowd flooding the hallway. The Imperial Hotel lobby was as full of chaos and panic as it was of civilians. The smell of burned flesh and plastic, as well as the acrid chemical fragrance of non-Earth explosives, floated on smoke amid scores of coughing and crying people.

Nina dove behind a stone column as the front windows of the hotel shattered in line from right to left, sending a brilliant rain of thick glass shards flying to the accompaniment of automatic weapons outside. The thunderous report of the cannon was so loud it drowned out the voices from her implanted comm. When it stopped firing, she set herself against the crowd and tromped forward, her inhuman strength plowing a path through the sea of people.

"Cole, this is Duchenne. Get a couple of MedVans out here, civilians are bleeding all over the lobby."

"Command, one of the civilians has a Nano sword—he appears to be engaging the second shooter." Hawthorne sounded interested, like he was covering a sporting event.

"Nina, this is Cole. Roger the MedVans. Can you confirm the hostiles' target?"

"Nano sword? Who the hell does this guy think he is whipping around one of those?" The voice sounded like Hawthorne. "Is he one of ours? C-Branch maybe?"

Carter's sarcasm had become almost too thick to flow over the comm channel. "No way. C-Branch would be two blocks away with a cigar and plausible deniability."

A man tried to grab Nina and "help" her figure out she went the wrong way. She stiff-armed him six feet into the air, over a bench seat, and he made first contact with the tile floor on his cheek. His face slid along with a strained squeaking noise from the force of his impact before he flipped over and came to a halt on his back.

"Got an idea." The voice belonged to Jeffries. "Soon as he fires... Incoming!"

Nina squinted as the NE6 explosive flooded the lobby with a flash. Her eyes filtered out the intense light within a thousandth of a second, enabling her to perceive the flesh sear away from the assassin's face as his coat reduced to a smoking ruin. Nina shrugged off the blast wave as it knocked the people around her flat to the ground and sent them sliding. Her coat fluttered around her legs as she raised her arm to shield her face from flying glass. When the debris passed, she leapt through a blown out window.

One of the shooters lay on the ground, positioned at the center of an expanding pool of blood between two halves of rotary cannon as if placed by the hand of an artist. Just as she looked in the direction of the two civilians, they disappeared around the corner. Laser fire came from her left as the first shooter had survived the missile detonation.

Nina ignored the two men running in favor of the immediate threat. "I want eyes on those civilians. Who are they, where are they going? I want to know what they had for breakfast this morning."

"Copy." Acknowledgement came from both Hawthorne and Carter.

"Lieutenant, this is Whisper 4—we are en route to your location and have your two friends on the long range. Please advise if you want us at the hotel or if we should observe the civilians."

"Observe." She ran toward the remaining assailant.

The blast swatted Marshall and Jeffries to the ground, sliding them almost twelve yards away into the wall. They offered hesitant shots, having rolled behind cover. Jeffries settled for a lamppost while Marshall had taken refuge in a stairway cut down from the elevated courtyard to the sidewalk below. The assassin carved gouges out of the post with a handgun. Watching the agent cringe away from streams of liquefying metal gave Nina an all too familiar reminder of her last night as a normal human.

She had no faith in her sidearm, even if it was a Class 6. Having huge men laugh as she shot them was the material from which her nightmares were weaved. Nina roared with a mixture of old fear and new rage, and charged. The goliath looked at her, his face contorted into a disbelieving eyebrow lift at the wispy girl that ran *at* him. He smirked, not finding her cry the least bit intimidating. He must have thought it somewhat cute as the burned scraps of flesh that remained on his face attempted a grin. She leapt to the side of the lamppost, clinging for an instant before springing sideways into a downward punch.

Much to her surprise, he caught her with one palm in her chest and held her aloft. Unlike cyborgs, the rigid parts of dolls were made of plastisteel, and they didn't weigh much more than a person. He shifted in a way that made her anticipate him slamming her into the ground. She kicked her leg out for momentum and spun up and over him before slithering across his shoulder. Her feet hit the ground the same instant he threw all his weight into a downward smash intended to drill her into the pavement. Without her body between his fist and concrete, the impact crushed his hand and sent a radial crack two feet in all directions.

Her systems entered combat mode, dragging the streaks of light from cars passing overhead to slow-drifting globs. He turned his head to look back as her leg came up, driving a kick into his gut before he could get his arm in the way. Unlike the other night, she didn't hold back. The strike lifted him into the air, spinning his body like a log. Amid the rapid flutter of his coat, he careened into the courtyard wall, creating another pattern of cracks before he fell to the ground with a deep *thud*.

That kick would have bisected an ordinary human. Her leg didn't have to be sharp to crush a body given the force involved. She stalked after him, paying little attention to the list of detected cyberware her scanners provided.

Even with all his augmentation, he remained a human being—not a full conversion doll. A cyborg would be worrisome. Despite being ponderous, they had a significant strength advantage over her. This man, however, was still far from a contest. He had been emotionless to this point, but worry crept into what remained of his face once he realized what she was. Two raised eyebrows told Nina that he hadn't expected to run into a doll, and made her believe what the comm chatter suggested about the civilians. If they meant to attack Basket Weaver, they would have anticipated at least one person like her.

"Who sent you?" Nina stopped four feet away. "Why are you here?"

The man gurgled, his attempt to speak too quiet to hear.

"Nice try, asshole. I am not falling for that one. Speak up or die where you are." Nina pulled out her sidearm and leveled it off at his head.

He growled at his failed ruse and his boosted legs threw him into the air. To the Division 9 agents by the door, he turned into a blur. To Nina, he moved in normal time. Her pistol went off like an automatic weapon as her inhuman dexterity loosed eight shots before he travelled far enough to reach her. All eight landed in his chest, though Nina didn't have the time to appreciate their effect. His punch caught her in the gut, sending her flying in an arc toward a parked car fifteen meters away.

I'm just going to stop carrying a fucking gun... I swear.

She crushed the roof on impact, exploding all the windows into a beautiful display of glittering snowflakes that her accelerated perception held in midair around her, not quite the snow princess fantasy she had as a six-year-old. Nina sat up without hesitation, feeling no pain and thinking that she could grow to like this body after all.

She didn't have to be afraid of anyone ever again.

A gut strike cannot knock the air out of a person with mechanical lungs. His punch, while inhuman in strength, still rode in on a living fist. A living fist now reduced to a twisted mass of broken bones after striking the plastisteel plates just below her synthetic skin.

Ignoring his pain, the man's roar floated on anger alone. What should have been red-faced rage took the form of more blood oozing from his shredded cheeks. A serenade of creaking metal surrounded her as she lifted herself out of the wreckage. Clinking fragments of glass fell out of her coat as she stepped back onto the street.

A single metal blade slid out the back of his left hand as he charged. His augmentation focused all on strength. Nina's speedware let her avoid his attack with a casual lean. She rolled into him, spinning her back against his chest as she grabbed his arm with both hands. It broke in two places as she yanked him into a jiu-jitsu throw. A shove with her hips launched him up and over, and she swung him around into the side of the car she had landed on.

The vehicle crumpled under the force of the impact, sliding several feet sideways before it rocked to a halt. Fragments of glass went everywhere. A few seconds of silence ended when the passenger side mirror gave up the fight and fell from snapped cables—landing in the assassin's lap with a leathery plop.

Despite his metal reinforced skull, now exposed to the air, the impact had been severe enough to knock him senseless. Nina hauled him into the air by the back of his coat. He flew up and to the left leaving streamers of blood. In a blur, she met his descent with a flip over kick that almost put her foot through his sternum. The impact launched him sideways and slammed his body into the retaining wall with such force it created a six-foot radial mess of blood and cracked concrete. Dark crimson bubbled out of his mouth. His head sagged forward.

The man slouched into a heap of dead flesh.

Marshall and Jeffries had stopped shooting as soon as Nina ran. They approached the dead man with a mixture of relief and awe, not quite sure if they should put their weapons away.

"Never worked with a doll before?" Nina swatted more fragments of glass out of her coat.

"No, Lieutenant. Specification docs and old stories don't quite do it justice." Jeffries offered a nervous chuckle.

"You two alright?"

They nodded.

"Secure their van."

Nina cast a mournful glance to the bakery truck. Traces of smoke still wisped into the air from the twisted shell. The two front tires stopped yards away on either side and no trace of the front seats existed save for a scattering of tiny foam bits in the road. The armor behind the driver cabin had a large dent at head level resembling a cannonball imprint. A breach the size of a finger marred the center where the plasma breached. Wherever the plate lacked a covering of scorch, red mist stained it. She continued directing other operatives to secure the area as she trudged over to where Dale had died.

Her emotional compass spun wild. Images of his eager face danced in her memory. A pang of guilt came from how she had spent the entire morning thinking him nice, but less than Vincent. The sense of loss at his death surprised her, considering she had only met him that morning. She leaned against the burned armor, savoring the feeling of humanity from the grief. He had been the number two man on this operation, her backup. When Basket Weaver ended, they may never have seen each other again. All that remained of him now was biological vapor, plus whatever might be in the smoking boot on the hotel awning.

She turned at a shoebox-sized delivery bot panning back and forth.

"What do you want?"

"Searching... Dale Abrams. Delivery of headache remedy."

"Cancel the order." She clenched her fist to smash it; however, she couldn't blame the delivery bot for the sick individual that sent a headache remedy to a man who took a missile to the face.

Those pills aren't strong enough.

"Team, we are reading an unusual electromagnetic pulse from both hostiles. Stand clear of the bodies immediately!" Samantha yelled over the comm.

Nina scanned both dead men. An array of display panels and lines connected to different parts of the corpses appeared as she cycled different vision modes. Before she could complete the search, a muffled pop came from one and then the other, followed by a second louder thud as a spray of guts and fluid showered the area. The self-destruct devices shredded most of the evidence that could link them back to where they came from. Nina scowled, knowing it would be difficult to trace. Clones with no prints, generic faces, and loaded with off-market cyberware. Despite the odds, Division 9 would spend dozens of man-hours trying.

She glanced in the direction that the two men ran off in, narrowing her eyes. The death of Dale Abrams would kick up a shitstorm in short order.

The only question was who would get rained on.

CROSSING THE LINE

J oey held up three fingers to the simulated fifteen-year-old girl behind the counter of the nearest CyberBurger he could find, requesting combo 3. She smiled, a gleam crossed her bright blue eyes, and her head tilted. He almost saw the program code scroll past as it ran, move lip actuators, tilt head, widen eyes, and add a little red to the cheeks. No point trying to make polite conversation. These dolls didn't have a personality, little more than computer terminals shaped like people. Food in hand, he flopped down at a table facing the grove of artificial trees set between benches in the 'beautified' sidewalk outside.

He lifted the burger to his face, staring out over a horizon studded with sesame seeds at a handful of people waving signs. Decades ago, this chain had another name, but he couldn't recall what. They had been the first franchise to eliminate human workers in favor of cheap dolls and even had the gall to make them look like high school kids. Social activists invented CyberBurger as a slur. When fast food franchises merged, the resulting megacorp adopted it out of spite.

The protestors still came, though they were nothing like the crowds that used to show up at first. Back then, they blocked the streets. These days, it was more like a collection of two to six people that nothing better to do with their lives than wave signs at a megacorp.

He didn't care about the politics behind his shitty food. Everything from the meat, to the sickly green flap of pseudo-lettuce, to the bun, and even the sesame seeds—all of it was reassembled OmniSoy. Machines altered it at a molecular level, converting the protein structure into bread, meat, and vegetables. He could eat the OmniSoy straight and get the same nutrition, but the lie in his hands tasted so much better.

He held the half-eaten burger up just high enough to where it looked like the demonstrators marched over it, and grinned. Society careened surely, inexorably, toward an implosion. Joey would be there, in a folding chair, cheering it on from the sidelines with four thousand calories of ersatz popcorn soaked in chemical butter.

A pudgy white woman, sign in hand, approached the window near his seat and tried to yell at him through the window. The thick glass muted her into an unintelligible murmur. He knew the drill. She railed against the establishment, asking him how he could bring himself to sustain such an evil corporation.

He met her stare, chomping down with a massive shit-eating grin before going into a slow chew with exaggerated expressions of joy. He used his NetMini to create a two-foot tall holographic middle finger, and waved it at her. She gaped with a mixture of shock and anger before storming off in a huff.

At this hour, only a few people were here, too early for the lunch crowd and too late for the breakfast seekers. He marveled at how clean the place smelled. Perhaps businesses had a decent idea hiring virtual employees that actually did the job they weren't paid to do.

Joey flipped the little device over in his hand and poked Alex's smirking face out of the contact list. Before long, the same smirk appeared in real time.

"You're not gonna give me shit about eating here too, are you?"

"Why would I? The place suits you." He exhaled the rest of his words over an exasperated sigh. "I was just about to call you, if you must know."

"The errand's done." Joey tapped at his deck to send the file.

"Good." Alex touched the tips of his fingers together in front of his face.

Joey squinted at the gesture. "What are you scheming now?"

"I'm just ruminating on why someone is looking for you. I thought you always got out clean?"

"Clean? Hah. The only thing he ever did clean was run away from his responsibilities." The voice of Joey's sister echoed out of his deck, loud enough to draw the attention of the two other people eating there.

The sound of her voice could take him from a perfect calm to murderous anger in short order. If not for the file transfer, he would have shut the unit off with a closed fist.

"Did you forget to pay someone again?"

"That was my sister." Joey's eyes hardened, realizing where Alex would go with that.

Cleo, I'm coming for you.

Alex smiled. The expectation of a crass joke had spared him the displeasure of having to make it. "A man wanted me to arrange a meeting with you in Sector 12."

His voice muffled with a mouthful. "Black zone. Nice." The implied danger made him forget hearing Katherine. "Wow, they must have gotten new machines, I can't even taste the OmniSoy in these fries."

"You put too much salt on them, Joe."

The sound of his father's voice made him spit a glop of semi-chewed starch onto the window.

Alex picked at something out of sight, smiling as he teased at Joey's idiotic tendency to leap at danger. "You know, it is the same area that the current rumors involve."

"Someone's paying you to send me there?" Joey tossed another fry into his mouth.

"Whatever gave you that idea my friend?" He flashed a polite little smile. "I'm simply looking out for your interests."

"You're trying too hard to get me to go out there... What's in it for you?"

"Well, I had hoped that if you went out there and happened to find something about what is shooing the malcontents out of the area it might be worth selling."

"The only thing faker than your French-ness is your sincerity." Joey tapped his fingers on the table, unable to resist the danger. "Where and when?"

"I'll send you a pin. Tonight, ten pm." Alex reached off screen.

A new window scrolled open with a map of Sector 12, a giant thumbtack lanced into one of the streets.

"Okay, I'll go."

"Good. Your payment should be in your account within a few minutes."

"Call me if you get more like that, someone shot a missile at me." He turned to show the red mark on his cheek.

"Cretin." Alex's holographic head flickered out of existence.

Joey gathered the wrappers from his meal, stuffing everything into the sleeve the fries had come in. The woman from earlier ranted at the other protestors while pointing at him. The way they all stared at him made him expect a confrontation. He cracked an evil grin as he concocted a diversion. Settling back in the seat, he held the NetMini in a reading posture and plugged into his deck. He fell into cyberspace, appearing to the outside world as if in deep thought.

The dark gunslinger came out of the cyclone of color standing in the virtual CyberBurger, a decent replica of reality that existed to process orders for delivery. The dolls behind the registers had different faces. Other than that, only a crowd four times normal differentiated the scene from its real world counterpart. Less than a hundred feet from the door, a thin column of azure light traced across the sky—a data channel for the citycams. He walked in as if it were a public node. The cam lines offered a neophyte hacker their first practice dummy. Even children could get past their security. Within a newly opened panel, he grabbed a still of the street out front and drew a lime green square around the woman's face. Pinching it, he isolated her from the background and saved a separate image.

After a short walk in the digital city, he arrived at an interlink connecting the GlobeNet to the public area of the police network. The desk sergeant had his hands full with a line of people and a litany of petty complaints. As Joey pulled apart the threads of reality, his avatar diverged from his true location on the network. The old cowboy's ghost waited at the end of the line while he ducked past the barrier into the secure part of the network.

Despite it being only the dispatch network, most deck jockeys would sweat getting in here. Joey breached before he realized it. He paused to reflect on how far his skills had developed since the last time he tried to get into the government network. He stuck the woman's face into a falsified police report about her tossing an incendiary device into the window of a CyberBurger last month. The ruse wouldn't last too long, but it would keep her occupied long enough for him to avoid an attack. Before disconnecting, he simulated an android dispatcher calling in a sighting of a wanted suspect.

The dark cowboy flew backward into the air, a sensation as though he sailed up through the floor into his body. Joey went with the sudden jolt, turning it into a stretch in his seat. He smiled and waited. The protestors all stared at him now. He continued grinning, walking to the door at a languid pace that fanned the fires of their anticipation. As two Division 1 patrol craft swooped in behind the protestors, he winked and made a finger gun at them, moving at a casual stroll to his bike amid the backdrop of screaming patrol officers.

Thoughts about the upcoming meeting provided enough of a fear spike that he made it back to his apartment before realizing he had almost obeyed the speed limit. The streets still held far more than their usual quantity of gangers, proof that something still raised hell in Sector 12. Seeing them all teased him with an unpleasant form of fear. Territorial in the extreme, these gangs didn't relocate at the drop of a hat. Most often, they would just kill or rape their problems. Sometimes both, and with black zone thugs, the order could vary.

He shoved the heavy steel door open with a loud grating squeak as he dialed Masaru with this other hand. The apartment smelled of wet dog and mold, though the aroma of tequila-laced vomit had vanished.

"Already? What is it this time?" Masaru, shirtless, sat in a hot tub with female arms crisscrossing his chest.

"Feel like protecting my narrow ass again tonight, say around ten?"

"Possibly. What are you doing?"

Joey scratched the left side of his head. "Alex again, said that someone got a hold of him trying to find me… wanted to arrange a meeting in Sector 12."

Masaru reached as if to hang up the call, but hesitated, perhaps a modicum of respect for his friend.

"Gomenasai, Joey-san… I need to prepare for an exam at the university."

"Scared, eh?" Joey smiled. "Since when do you take your own tests? I thought you had a guy for that."

Masaru frowned. "I am not scared. That area is…"

"Too low class for you to be seen?" Joey laughed, noting he didn't challenge his comment about having others take his tests for him. "It's just a quick meeting with some guy, it won't take long."

"Alright. But it had better be brief."

"Great. Pick me up at 9:30, bring Kat if she wants to come along."

"Mm." Masaru turned his attention back to the women sharing the hot tub with him.

Joey crawled into the trash-strewn couch, trying to make himself as comfortable as possible. He had long since given up the fight. No matter how hard he tried to clear it off, more always came back. He attributed it to having an apartment that anyone could walk into at any time.

INTO THE BLACK

"Why don't you clean the place up a little, Joseph?" A pleasant elderly man's voice filled the air.

"Not now, Dad."

He managed to add ten more seconds to the three hours of sleep he had gotten before his body shot bolt upright.

"Not funny. Who the fuck was that?"

After looking around and finding himself alone, he settled deeper into the rustling trash, searching for comfort.

"The state of this place would kill your mother, you know."

His eyes snapped open.

Joey sprang off the cushions in a shower of trash, and ran to the bathroom to make sure no one hid back there to mess with him. Finding no trace of anyone, he stomped to the front door and tried to kick it closed in anger. The warped metal plate slid an inch, jamming against the floor.

Minutes passed in silence punctuated only by a few distant shouts, bangs, and a single gunshot. His knuckles creaked while he made and unmade fists, staring at the whirlwind of litter around him. Paper, foam, and plastic on the couch around him creaked and crackled, deafening in the stillness. He thought about the loons that swear ghosts are real. He used to disregard them as idiots until he ran into a telekinetic. Psionics were one thing—ghosts, on the other hand, sounded like too much of a stretch for him to believe. No, this had to be someone dicking with him. Cleopatra was the first person to come to mind, but how did she do it this time?

"Cleo, I don't know what's going on in that twisted little mind of yours but so help me, when I find you..."

What could he do? As angry as he tried to be, most things he fantasized about doing to her were quite beyond his nature. He bore many similarities to his father, though he tried to cover it up and blend into the underbelly of society. Much to his good fortune, he didn't have enough contact with the locals here for them to sense his inner nature, which was good.

"It's such a shame your mother couldn't make time for the trip down here, she misses you."

That time, Joey realized the sound originated from his deck. *Damn that bitch. I will find you, Cleo.* He lurched across the room, collapsed over his deck, and killed the power. With a sigh, he slid off the table into the rickety chair. For a while, he mocked himself for entertaining the thought that his father's ghost had been visiting him. He ran his fingers through his hair while waiting for his breathing to calm.

That sounded just like him. How on Mars did she do that?

Joey tried to imagine how he would do a similar thing. Voice splicing would be the easiest way. A hundred different softs out there could reassemble sound bites and make it seem like a person said whatever you wanted them to. The only hole in that logic being that his father never published any videos to sample. He remembered seeing something similar in the news a few months ago. Not trusting the deck at that moment, he used his NetMini to find the NewsNet story he thought of. A netizen named Kyle Blank had offed himself by plugging his M3 jack into a high voltage power coupling—a few hundred amps right to the brain stem. Something like that wouldn't often make the news at all, but he had been rambling about his dead wife talking to him for several weeks. Joey swiped the various old stories aside one after the other while Donna George rambled on about how Kyle hacked into the NewsNet as well as several healthcare systems to try to get someone to believe that his wife's ghost spoke to him.

The news had seized on it at first to try to show ghosts to the world, but at some point they began to doubt. As soon as he died, the conspiracy wonks screamed that some corporation assassinated him and faked the suicide because he had seen something *they* wanted to keep quiet. It fell out of the limelight fast. People lost interest in some nut job that brain-lined main power and caught fire. In fact, the flaming body with the wire coming out of its neck became a GlobeNet meme for months.

The fine details of the story had Joey starting to wonder. Blank said that he heard his dead wife talking to him from his deck, placing vid calls to him and showing up in broadcasts. Paranormal investigators had been all over the story, but left after only a few days, citing a suspected hoax. The final nail in the coffin came in the form of a psionic publicly saying they could find nothing paranormal. The suicide note claimed he did it because he couldn't handle living without her. Of course, the NewsNet published the meandering diatribe about how she told him all about the other side—how he could be with her again, and how desperate she was waiting. Joey smirked as he read.

Someone played this guy for a fool just to see if they could drive him over the edge.

What are the odds of two deck jockeys hearing a dead relative within three months of each other? With no trace of any lingering doubt about ghosts in his mind, he fired up his Teradyne Silver to go digging around in search of information on Kyle Blank. He gave up after about an hour of nothing. In his opinion, someone tried to get their jollies by playing with people. He smashed his fist into the table at the realization that was what Cleo had been doing to him for the past few weeks, perhaps she was the cause of Blank's ignition. Playful could turn murderous in an instant with a psychotic.

Joey contemplated going after her right there and then, but as it was quarter after nine, he didn't have the time. Once he finished in Sector 12, however, he wouldn't sleep again until he had his hands around her throat.

A knock drew his attention to thin fingers curling around the gap. The grunting of a female voice accompanied a futile attempt to shove the twisted slab of steel. She gave up and banged a few times.

"Joey, you still breathing?" The voice belonged to Katya.

"Yeah… Gimme a sec, be right out."

Joey hit the bathroom, managing to give himself a quick sink bath of the critical points in about ten minutes before getting dressed and sprinting to the door. With both hands on the metal and his foot propped up against the wall, he still couldn't budge it. Now he remembered why he never tried to close it.

"Katya? Damn thing is stuck, can you hit it from the outside?"

"What do you think I am, a fool? You're going to yank it open the minute I try."

Joey sighed. "As utterly hilarious as that would be, I'm serious, it's stuck."

Between the two of them, they shoved. It moved in quarter-inch screeches over the series of several minutes, until Joey could squeeze past. Katya leaned on the wall, catching her breath. Joey grinned at her combat boots and loose black fatigue pants accompanied by a camouflage jacket. She had done everything she could do to hide her contours, including a thick wool collar that she could pull up to cover her face.

"Guess Masaru told you where we're headed. You got a chastity belt on too?" He feigned reaching as if to check.

She caught his arm by the wrist and twisted just enough to control him with pain. He spun out of it, distancing himself by a few paces. She fixed him with a cold stare, but he just laughed.

"Ahh, I love it when ninety pound chicks try to act tough." He smiled despite her continuing with a stare that could freeze water in a glass.

"I am not a helpless little doe." She scowled.

He put on a bad Russian accent. "Relax. Here in the UCF we have things called jokes."

The trading of barbs followed them all the way up out of the sunken area by Joey's door and into Masaru's car. Katya half expected the overgrown boy to yell "shotgun" as he raced for the passenger seat. Joey paused by the sleek ebon hovercar, glancing down the street at the progressing rot. His apartment was a little over four blocks deep in the grey zone around Sector 12, and about five away from the official start of the black. He hopped in and chuckled at the sight of Masaru's armored helmet. It looked like an ancient samurai re-imagined in modern composites.

"Now, now, kids. Play nice." Masaru offered a pleasant smile.

"I am no child." Katya's scowl shifted from Joey to Masaru.

"She doesn't get this whole figure of speech thing." Joey tapped a button, and his door closed with a pneumatic whisper.

"What museum did you steal that thing from?"

"This is Dragon Chitin. Made in the style of ancestral—"

"You look ridiculous."

"…samurai armor." Masaru gave up with a growl.

"Expecting it to get rough? Perhaps I should use the seat belt."

"Expectation and hope are often disparate things." Masaru pushed forward on the stick and the car began to roll.

Exasperated, Katya folded her arms and ignored them both for the remainder of the ride. Masaru decided to drive on the ground, knowing the reputation of the locals for making a game of firing missiles at things that flew.

Joey stared at the NavMap console, forcing salvia through gaps in his teeth as the yellow triangle glided toward the giant pin a mere six blocks from where he lived. The muscles in the back of his neck tightened as he thought about what went on there. The entire southern third of the West City gossiped about whatever now lurked in Sector 12, and whatever it was had been chasing the gangers out. In kind of a paradoxical way, the black zone might be safer than civilization now, unless they ran into the thing.

Progress slowed to a crawl. Masaru struggled to navigate around the decaying skeletons of the derelict cars that littered the street here. Most of these rusting hulks had been motionless for the better part of thirty years. Violence had orphaned this part of the city from civilization.

"We should get Kenny to come down here. He might find something he can sell." Joey laughed.

Even Katya cracked a smile. These areas had a lot in common with the Badlands. Law held little sway over the people, deadly things lived there, and both had been untouched by the hand of civilization for generations. At least these places had no bio-engineered mutants. Most of the gangers that congregated were not so far removed from humanity that they fell into that category, though a few came close.

The illegal augs were what worried Joey the most. Some of the cyber-junkies went way beyond parts considered legal, and lived like gods out here, free from the police. Underground cyber-docs, medical professionals removed from public practice for questionable moral character, often set up shop out here. According to rumor, some would kill for cyberware and then implant the same parts in others before the blood cooled. The less-disreputable ones only harvested parts from the already dead.

Katya draped herself over the gap between the front seats, looking up through the rolling grey fog at the ruins of buildings sliding past. The mist reduced them to indistinct skeletal forms, warped streaks of black against the blue-grey glow of the sky.

The car slowed to a stop by a barricade of old cars and fallen high-rise. The visor in Masaru's helmet closed with a faint whirr. The dour-faced ebon samurai turned to face Joey.

"This is as far as I go with the car."

Joey faced him, pressing right fist into left palm in front of his chest. He nodded in a sharp bow, dropping his voice two octaves. "Hai!"

A low growl simmered in the air.

DISHONORABLY DISCHARGED

The blockade proved an arduous climb. A layering of cars seemed like a deliberate attempt to wall off the road, a theory that gained traction at the sight of crumpled handprints in some of them. Katya coughed at the breath-stealing acridness. She lacked Masaru's sealed helmet or Joey's tolerance for such aromas. Neither warm nor cool, the fetid air brought tears to her eyes.

A cloud of plasfilm scraps rolled across the street, swirling along in a tiny cyclone. Hundreds fluttered in the wind affixed to utility poles, traffic boxes, even the hulks of cars. They floated everywhere, as if a truck carrying them had exploded. The thin white sheets effused a pale blue glow in the dim moonlight.

Katya pulled her sweater up over her face and squatted by one of the old cars. On the door, a plasfilm sheet displayed the image of a bright-eyed blonde girl of around sixteen. The image smiled and then turned ninety degrees to the right before it came back to face her. Words in plain black typeface scrolled along below the picture.

'Missing Daughter: Amber Wortham, 17. Last seen leaving for school, April 2411. Reward if found alive: ℂ500,000.'

Katya sighed as the lure of the reward fell aside. She fixated on the girl's innocent and happy face. Finding the posters here carried two implications, neither of which painted a good picture.

Joey made a face at a cloud of smiling blonde faces dancing down an alley. "Probably kidnapped, doesn't look like the kind of kid that would run away to join one of these gangs."

Katya wondered if this girl had more choice in what had happened to her than she had in her own fate. The desolation here brought her back to Vidnoye, just south of Moscow, when she was a little girl crawling around at night in search of food. Images of soldiers, searching beams of light leaking in holes in the wall. She remembered running. Tiny legs pumping away until too-large boots skidded to a halt in the shadow of an armored man. A hand covering her mouth and her feet leaving the ground.

Katya shivered into a squat. Being homeless was better than what they did to her. Sadness became jealousy. She flung the poster into the wind with its brethren and ignored Joey's teasing about littering fines. Rubbing the cold out of her arms, she stood and followed them, wary glances moving from the broken buildings to the street and back again. A smear of red-orange in a wrecked car up ahead stood out in the blue—her cybereye found heat.

"Thermal signature in that car up ahead, one man in the driver's seat." She pointed.

Masaru moved his coat to expose the handle of his Katana as Joey eyed the car. The last time that vehicle moved was many times his life ago. Little remained of it aside from rusting metal and carbon fiber body panels. Even the insulation on the wiring had rotted off. A layer of muck cemented the windows in opaque grey. Katya took cover behind another nearby husk as Joey approached and kicked it twice in the trunk as if to knock.

Rust flakes covered his boot.

A pale man in a long sand-brown coat rose past the gap in the door like a charmed snake. At least fifty, he appeared quite thin, and glanced around with a wariness that seemed inches shy of losing control. Joey wondered if the man belonged to C-Branch or Division 9. He radiated government spook.

"Joseph Dillon?" asked the man, his voice, throaty and cracked, made him sound in desperate need of something to drink.

"Yeah. Let me guess. You're going to say that who you are is not important as long as you tell me something." Joey walked up with his hand out.

The man ignored his offer of a handshake. "Something like that." Once more, he glanced about.

His paranoia rubbed off on Katya who all but crawled beneath one of the cars, but kept watch. Masaru stood in quiet calm a step behind Joey, close enough to interdict if hostilities erupted. The stranger's hand slipped into the light. The glint of a holodisk reflected across Joey's face.

"We know you have some of the data, but we're not sure who you're working for. One of our P-SEC nodes was infiltrated, and they think you did it." The man fidgeted again, leaning to the side to stare down an ally.

"I'm not even sure what a P-SEC is." Joey grasped the holo disk, but the man didn't let go of it. "Someone sent me a file."

"How much do you know about the Mayberry inci—"

His head detonated in a shower of hot gore.

The derelict car buckled inward at the midpoint and slid up onto the sidewalk six feet back, bending in half as the front and rear bumpers pointed in the same direction. Burning streaked the side of Joey's face, causing him to howl. The headless man twitched on his feet as his heart beat twice more, throwing blood into the air from the exploded orifice of his neck. His fingers slipped away, leaving the holodisk in Joey's hand.

The left side of Joey's face was on proverbial fire. Masaru grabbed him by the shoulder, kicked on his neural amplifier, and flew a Joey kite down the street for a block and a half. Another two projectiles came out of the fog. Blurry spectral lines lingered for in an instant in their wake, connecting a distant rooftop to where the street cratered inches shy of them. Masaru roared, incensed at the dishonorable attack. An adversary owed you the decency of showing himself.

Ducking into the first passable alley, Masaru slowed his run back to human speed and Joey scrambled to get his feet under him. He didn't draw the katana, seeing no point to it. Even if he had been a grand master, cutting railgun slugs out of midair only happened in movies. Even if he *could* hit something moving that fast—which he couldn't, even with speedware—the projectile had too much energy and would shatter the Nano katana.

He pushed Joey into the hollow of a boarded up window. "Stay put. He's on the roof. He has no angle on you here."

"That goddamn thing will go right through the building." Joey laughed from fear.

"No. He is too high up. Too many layers, even if it got to you, it wouldn't be lethal. Besides, he has to see you to shoot you and even if he has a ghosteye scope, it can only see about thirty meters."

Masaru turned to jog back to the street.

"Where the fuck are you going?" Joey glared. "What the fuck is a ghosteye?"

"It is a targeting system that can see through walls. Call it a hunch, but I think you are the target. I'm going after him before he gets a clean shot." Masaru ran to the street, as close as possible to the wall.

Joey leaned against the alcove and noticed it gave a little. He sighed and tried to relax. This was a little too much, even for him. He liked danger and risk, but a railgun was beyond the pale. Risk implied chance, but if that thing hit him, there wouldn't be much probability of survival. Ergo, the situation had transcended risk and moved firmly into foolishness, and he didn't like it. Not one little bit.

Cracking made Joey's eyes pop open, but lacked the reaction time to do anything about it. The wood gave out under his weight, dumping him into the building. He rolled backward over a heavyset man in a blue windbreaker, and stopped a few feet away on all fours in a sea of choking dust.

"Sorry about that man." Joey looked up at a corpse.

Bloat had set in, and Joey's impact loosed a black geyser of mung from the mouth and nose. Bald save for a stripe of hair around the back of his head, he had been a little portly and looked like he was over forty. His skin had turned greenish purple and his right arm was missing from the elbow down. The jagged nature of the wound made it seem as though it had been ripped out. His jacket had a NewsNet logo on the breast, and he looked as though he had been dead for a week or two.

The smell that hung in this room didn't reach Joey's conscious perception until after he had finished vomiting. It was so bad it could forever taint clothing and linger for years in the back of one's mind.

He crawled around searching for a door with his arm folded over his face. He didn't care if it felt like his jacket sleeve sandpapered the burn on his cheek since covering his mouth fooled his brain into thinking the stench less intense. When he found a door, he shoved and wound up riding it down a metal staircase before landing on his chest at the bottom. The clatter of his fall and the cloud of dust from his impact drew the attention of about fifteen men sitting around what looked like a mechanic's shop. Joey knew the pattern of blue and black clothing was indicative of a gang. A thing on their shirt, as if a four year old tried to draw a vampire bat, cemented his opinion. Joey tried not to laugh at it.

"What the fuck is that?" One of the men pointed at him.

Joey stood up and tried to keep his hands in a nonthreatening posture. "Didn't you guys get the memo about the sasquatch running around the sector?"

None of them appeared to find humor in his joke.

"Looks like more meat." A different one answered, raising a rifle.

Joey had watched many cowboy vids and had spent a fair share of his youth standing in his underwear facing a mirror, trying to get a hairbrush out of his waistband faster than his reflection could. The temptation became too great for him to resist now that he found himself in the situation for real. Before he knew what he was doing, his pistol flew out of its holster and he put two slugs in the chest of the rifleman. The man blinked in disbelief as the rifle slid from his hands, and he fell backward with a long gurgling wheeze.

"I'm not lookin' for trouble."

A cheesy line from the vids he loved came to mind. He expected one of them would say 'Well, you found it.'

Silence.

All of the gangers stared at him, as if they couldn't quite decide what to make of what they just saw. For a few seconds, he hoped his cowboy attire and quick draw spooked them into hesitation. Perhaps they wondered if he could take them all out before they could get him.

His delusion shattered when they screamed and charged all at once. A shot sent into a rusting fire extinguisher on a nearby column created an instant wall of white fog with a loud bang. He exploited the diversion to sprint for a window at the right side of the building and jumped a cart of tools before he flung himself into the glass, shoulder first. The dramatic smash-through he expected only existed in the holo-vid that played in his mind.

His body slammed into the polycarbonate resin with a dull thud and landed in an awkward heap on the floor after bouncing off an old bench. A few bullets went over his head and holed the window. Joey's hands clawed at the detritus on the ground, taking fistfuls of dirt, cigarette butts, old bottles, and squishy globs of which he would rather not know the composition. He scrambled as fast as he could crawl away from the bench and ducked behind a column covered in flaking grey paint and pornographic graffiti.

A spray painted phallus pointed at a blown out window on the far side of the room. His crawl rose into a sprint, chased by explosions of dust and splinters. A spray of brick and concrete fragments followed his dive out the window. He flailed in an attempt to roll over in midair, and hit the alley below flat on his back, staring up at the indigo glow in the sky above him. Right that second he had too much adrenaline to feel pain, but knew that alcohol would be involved before the night ended. Joey sighted his gun between his knees at the window, giving the first man he saw a haircut that made him dive for cover.

Someone inside shouted about a truck.

He didn't want to move, finding the road quite comfortable. It took the sight of headlights coming around the corner and the roar of an old diesel engine to give him the wherewithal to pry his ass off the pavement and run some more. He sent a few halfhearted shots into the grille but hit nothing vital. His only chance would be to find an alley too small for the truck and a hiding place that the gangers would overlook.

Three blocks down, he spotted a promising passage between two buildings. Angry diesel growls intensified behind him, accented by the squealing of tires and whooping of voices. Rifle slugs whizzed by as the men tried to fire from the bed of a moving truck with futile results.

He sprinted around the corner and his forward motion came to an abrupt halt with a painful collision against an immovable metal object. His arms wrapped around it in a desperate attempt to stay on his feet while his lungs fought for air. The impact was the last straw for Joey's ability to run. He lifted his head to see what he ran into, hoping he could hide in it.

"Who the fuck puts a vendomat in an alley? Oh well, might as well have some coffee." Joey pawed at it, looking for the console.

It moved.

The color drained out of his face when he gazed up into the eyes of an armor plated humanoid figure. Seven and a half feet tall, a goliath of gunmetal blue plastisteel stared back at him. Its face had features designed to strike terror into the hearts of enemy soldiers. Glowing red orbs stared down from the emotionless skull of a Class 4 combat cyborg. It grabbed a fistful of shirt and lifted him with one hand until they were eye to eye.

Joey let out a nervous titter. *The military doesn't go to places like this, especially not with one soldier. If this guy is here, he's AWOL—and probably nuts.*

Until that instant, he hadn't thought it possible for anything to scare him more than a near miss from a railgun.

Finding himself nose to nose with a rogue military cyborg, consciousness descended to a point of total and complete surrender. Whatever was going to happen now was irrelevant. He would just watch for as long as he continued to live.

Nothing would ever top this.

CYBER KNIGHT

The cyborg stared at Joey. He had no way to tell its mood. The face had only one expression—a metal skull. It didn't have individual teeth, only a pair of metal jaws with crenellated interlocking seams. Aside from having two arms and two legs, only the articulated jaw and approximate shape of the head even tried to recreate humanity in any discernible way. UCFMC markings on the shoulders confirmed that he had run into a military deserter.

Headlights swerved about amid a squeal of rubber at the end of the alley. The driver had misjudged the width and had tried to drive into it, stomping on the brakes at the last second. Thirteen gangers piled up in the rear, having fallen over each other with the sudden stop. One man wound up on the roof, sliding down over the windshield onto the hood while pointing in Joey's direction.

The arm that held Joey aloft went an inch or two higher, and for a fleeting second, he expected doom.

"Here it comes... Well, Dad... if you really are here, I'm about to find out."

Rather than smash him into the wall, the cyborg took a step forward and pushed him behind in a protective posture. Panels on the shoulders opened, allowing a pair of three-tube 60mm rocket launchers to extend as a tri-barrel rotary gun deployed from each forearm. The three-pack missile boxes pivoted down, aiming at the vehicle. Both cannons whirred into motion, stopping with a hard metallic click as they loaded.

The gangers froze as if time had come to a halt. One in the center of the crowd broke the silence with a scream that sounded like it should have come from a ten-year-old girl. The others snapped out of their terror to look at him with a mixture of derision and disbelief as if the shriek sounded so unmanly that he no longer deserved to be in their company.

The cyborg took another step at the truck and spun up the rotary guns. The driver jerked the wheel to the right and stomped on the accelerator. The pointing man on the hood slid, as if he remained static while the truck pulled out from under him. Three of his buddies spilled backward over the tailgate as the truck peeled out in a frenetic serpentine path around the debris in the road. The ones who fell followed on foot, screaming in a mixture of fright and anger as they vanished behind the wall.

Joey wrapped his arms around himself, laughing and shaking. He had so much adrenaline running through him right now he had trouble containing it. It took him a moment to realize the cyborg was talking to him.

"Hey pal… this ain't exactly a good part of town. You should probably get out of here."

Joey looked up. "No shit."

He cringed at the thought of what he said after it had left his lips.

The borg laughed and extended a hand as his onboard weapons retracted below armored panels. "Name's Mark. Mark Bolt."

"Bolt?" Joey suppressed a laugh but couldn't stop the cheap grin that crept over his face.

"Yeah, yeah… Like I didn't hear that fuckin' joke enough when I was in, repeat it some more." The voice had a metallic ring but sounded more normal than the visage before him would imply.

"Joey Dillon. Umm, thanks for savin' my ass."

Katya was about eight tenths of a second from just going home when she saw the cyborg shield Joey from the gangers. Seeing this guy talking rather than pounding stalled her worries enough for her to approach. No stealth training in the world could fool a thermal sensor. Mark turned and aimed his right forearm in her direction. Her instinct took over and she went motionless, hoping to avoid notice.

Joey turned at Mark's sudden aim. "What is it?"

"Female, twenty yards. Human, one sidearm, one cybereye, finger claws, neuralware… looks like agility and speed amps. Ouch, she's got one of those *things* too."

Joey grabbed his junk, cringing.

"Kat?" Joey called out.

"Yeah." Her voice came out of the dark.

Two small spotlights on Mark's shoulders lit her up. Joey waved her over.

"It's okay Mark, I know her."

Mark lowered his arm. The weapon retracted and he trudged off down the alley, waving for the two to follow him. "Since you're here, there is something you need to see."

They exchanged a look before Joey shrugged. Since he remained alive at this point, he figured things could only get better.

Mark went one block down and one over before he trudged into the shadow of a tall windowless building. A curtain of chain link fence blocked off a massive hole in the side. He peeled it aside for Joey and Katya to go through before following and allowing it to crash against the concrete. The crack led to an underground parking garage devoid of cars. Sparking impromptu repairs allowed the lights to function, creating shiny patches in the polished cement floor. About forty feet in from the hole, a large amalgam of scrap metal stood in the approximate shape of a chair. It faced a makeshift table and a small holovid bar from which an enormous view panel dominated the room. A Gee-ball game was in progress, grabbing Joey's attention.

"Nice TV," Joey muttered, trying to think of something to say just to break the silence.

Mark might have been smiling. "Some gangers left it behind when I moved in, it's good to bust the boredom."

He took a step toward the chair and, looking at Katya, pointed at a cinder block wall that sectioned off an alcove in the back. Small rusty marks indicated where a door's hinge plates had once hung.

"In there." Mark sat down facing the holo-screen. "This game is drag-assing so bad. The Lunar team has amazing D but their offense plays like a bunch of nine-year-olds."

"Ugh, two hours in and still 0-0." Joey shook his head.

Unsure why she listened to a cyborg, Katya approached the doorway. For all she knew, that room was about to become her new holding cell. A glance over her shoulder to see the men absorbed by the whizzing bodies on the screen made her feel a little safer. As she neared the doorway, the sound of female crying from within distracted her from her own safety and she ran ahead.

"I almost feel bad for the ball." Mark chuckled.

"Why?" Joey turned to look at him. "He a friend of yours?"

Katya jumped at the sound of a metal object being thrown and Joey's cackling.

The space inside looked like it had once been an emergency shower for chemical accidents. At the rear corner, a naked woman curled into a ball, seated in a puddle of bloody water, covered in dirt, bruises, and scratches. Handcuff loops dangled from each wrist, though the chain between them had been snapped. She cradled a putrefying human arm as though it were a ragdoll, holding the back of the hand to her cheek, muttering to it as if its name was Tom.

"She freaks out if she sees me." The sudden sound of Mark's voice made Katya jump and cling to the wall. "I wanted to take her back to the city but she gets too upset, she might have hurt herself."

Joey couldn't resist the temptation to peek. The girl was in her young twenties, probably blonde under all that dirt, and her darting erratic stare told him that she was out of her mind or close to it. His eyes widened at the sight of the severed arm pressed to her cheek. The corpse he landed on was missing an arm about that length—and he had a NewsNet jacket on. This had to be that missing reporter, Kimberly Brightman. The angel and devil on Joey's shoulders got into a fistfight as his thought of what kind of massive reward the station would offer for finding her dueled with the feeling that he needed to do the right thing before he worried about money.

"Can you take her back to the city?" The clank of a metal fist on the chair arm echoed. "God dammit. Lunars couldn't score in a game of foosball. The friggin' goal box is fifteen meters wide. Come on!"

Joey nudged Katya toward the woman with his eyes and went back by Mark. A small table in front of him had a few holographic portraits on it. Several looked like Marines posing for the camera in front of different types of equipment. One depicted a cute brunette holding a baby, and one showed a red haired girl that couldn't have been older than three.

"Yeah, no problem. Mind if I ask what brought you out here?"

Mark sighed, a metallic scraping noise that shivered down Joey's spine. "I got my ass shot off on Mars. There was enough of me left to put into this thing to finish out my tour. When I got some leave..." His head tilted forward and he hesitated for a moment. "My daughter shit where she stood when she saw me. I never heard a scream like that come out of anyone before. It..." His voice broke into digitized fragments as his audio processor couldn't interpret his intent and had no translation for choking on your words. His hand crushed the end of the chair arm.

Joey put a hand on Mark's metal shoulder. After a momentary pause, he continued.

"I needed to think. I couldn't keep going with the routine, ya know? Just need to sort my thoughts out. I didn't think the Marines would come looking for me out here."

A supporting nod from Joey seemed to make him feel a little better. "I got nothin' to say there... no kids. You gotta do what you gotta do." He exhaled. "Want me to tell your wife you're okay?"

"I'm not sure I am." Mark loosed a tinny grating laugh. "It's too late now, I'm AWOL. If I make contact, I'll probably get put away until Maddie is in college."

"I owe you a favor for saving my ass tonight. Let me see what I can do for you." Joey patted his deck.

Mark stared at the hologram of the little red-haired girl. "Thanks. Even if you fix my record, you can't hack me back to normal."

KATYA CREPT OVER TO THE SHIVERING WOMAN, WHO LIFTED HER HEAD TO LOOK AT the person invading her secure little space.

Her usual affect softened. "Hey there, calm down. Do you want to go home?"

The woman nodded.

"Okay. I need you to do something for me first."

Kimberly looked about to cry. "Don't make me..."

"I need you to put down that arm. You do that, we can get you out of here."

She hugged it tighter, causing fluid to squish out of the severed end. "I can't leave Tom here."

Katya put a hand on her shoulder. The girl was cold to the touch. "Tom is already dead. That's just his arm. You need to drop it before you get sicker."

Kimberly looked at it and alternated between hugging it and holding it at a distance. It hit her after a few minutes that she clung to a rotten limb, and she hurled it away with a scream before breaking down and sobbing. Katya tried to keep her from putting her hands in her face, not knowing how much biological danger lurked in the slimy residue. She ushered the girl to the side and found to her surprise that one of the showers spat out more than just dust.

The water was frigid and shocked Kimberly more lucid. Katya held her under the flow until she got to the point where plain water wouldn't clean her any more. Kimberly stood, shivering, tugging at the broken handcuffs as rusty water ran in rivulets over her. When the corpse-slime was gone, Katya removed her jacket and wrapped the trembling reporter in it, at which point she sank to the ground in a ball, pulling her entire body into the coat.

"What happened there?" Joey pointed to the shower chamber as soon as he heard the water start up.

Mark looked up. "That girl tried to interview some gangers. They killed the guy she was with when he tried to stop them from raping her. I heard the screaming and got over there as fast as I could. They had just stripped her and thrown her to the ground. One was wrestling with her with a dozen more waiting their turn. I've been tryin' not to use up my ammo, it's not like I can get more out here, but those bastards deserved it. I hosed 'em all."

Joey nodded in agreement.

"She was so shaken up she didn't even realize what I was when I carried her back here. Next morning she sees me and goes totally apeshit, just like Madison." His voice again digitized into fragments.

Joey wasn't the most adept reader of people, especially those that had no facial expressions, but it was obvious Mark had a rough time handling people's reaction to his appearance. The military designed him to be as intimidating as possible. It didn't go over well on wives, daughters, or random young women.

"You got a comm?"

"Yeah." Mark shared his PID.

"I really owe you, Mark. If you need anything, you know how to reach me. I'll vid your wife and let her know you're still alive. I'll try to help if I can."

Mark nodded. "Hope."

"I'm serious, I will call her."

The cyborg chuckled. "No, jackass. That's her name. Hope."

Joey laughed. "Oh."

A HELL OF A STORY

Katya supported half of Kimberly's weight on the way to the main room, and all of it once the woman saw Mark.

"He's the one that saved your life. He looks scary, but he won't hurt you."

Kimberly's panic fell just short of a loss of control. Katya continued whispering reassurances that Mark protected her until the reporter managed a nervous smile at the metal hulk.

An unexpected blare from Joey's NetMini made her jump. When he answered it, a worried holographic Masaru stared at him.

"Where in the nine hells are you?"

"You wouldn't believe me unless you saw him. What happened?"

"They were gone by the time I got there. The roof looks like something bigger than a hovercar landed there."

"Transport craft? You think it was the military? Why would they arrange a meeting just to take me out? If they wanted to kill me, I'd just not wake up some day, C-Branch doesn't prick and dick around, they just do you in your sleep."

"Whatever. Where are you so we can get out of this shithole?"

"Here." He sent a pin. "Gonna fly in?"

"Yeah, to hell with it. Be there in a minute."

"We need to stop at the hospital on the way back."

"Damn, what happened?" Worry returned to his voice.

"I'm okay, Kat's okay. We found this chick. I'll explain when you get here."

He turned back to the stalemated Gee-ball game, trying not to laugh at Mark's overstated reaction to the Sector 88 Psychos almost letting the Lunar team's offense score. By the time the street outside glowed with the presence of Masaru's headlights, Katya had managed to get Kimberly to whisper a "thank you" to Mark. He held out the holo-cap of his squad, pointing at what he used to look like. A warm current of dusty air swept in as the hovercar settled down for a quiet landing. Mark moved out of his seat like a linebacker and went for the grate. Kimberly almost fainted.

Joey flailed. "Whoa, Mark... It's a friend of mine."

"I know. I just want to cover you guys if you're going to fly out. People out here tend to shoot things that fly, and I heard a Templar going off before."

"A what?"

"UCF TMPLR... Tactical magnetic propelled light rifle. It'll throw a 14.5 millimeter slug out to four miles. They are not permitted in the city, even the military won't bring them here. Too much risk of collateral damage. Nasty piece of hardware... I wouldn't even want to get hit by that thing."

"Oh that... He's gone. He was trying to shoot me." Joey showed off the red patch on his cheek. "Wait a sec, you called that *light?*"

"Yeah, they get bigger." Mark paused. "What the hell did you step into?"

Joey threw up his arms. "Fuck if I know."

Outside, Masaru squinted in an effort to peer into the darkness beyond the chain link. When the cyborg emerged from the black, he almost reversed into the wall. Japanese cursing followed, loud enough to hear despite closed windows.

"Calm down," shouted Joey, darting over to the car.

Masaru's eyes fixed him with a fatalistic glare, a look he would give someone he wanted to kill. "What. Is. That?"

"That's Mark." Joey pointed back over his shoulder with a nonchalant grin.

"That is the kind of thing you warn me about *before* I get here." Masaru glared.

Katya tapped on the locked rear door. Masaru turned at the noise, wincing at the sight of Kimberly coated in filth and unidentifiable substances.

Joey tugged at the handle. "Come on Masaru, I know she's a little old for you, but we gotta get her to a hospital."

"You know that's a damn stereotype." Masaru continued glaring at him.

Joey laughed. "Yeah, and stereotypes are pulled out of thin air because they have no basis in anything that really happened. Just open the damn door already, or do you want to spend the night here?"

"This is your friend?" Mark asked, folding his arms.

"Yeah."

As the doors clicked open, Katya helped their foundling into the back seat and snugged the borrowed coat around her. Masaru struggled with all his willpower not to make a face at the smell she carried into his car.

Joey glanced at the hood.

"I will stab you if you try to slide across." Masaru's tone lacked mirth.

He had enough danger for one night, surprising as that was, and sauntered around to the passenger side. A ring of debris blasted away from the car in all directions as Masaru yanked on the control stick. Joey barely had time to wave to Mark before the car leapt skyward, tilting forward as it picked up speed. He pulled hard left and coiled around one of the skyscrapers as the car edged past three hundred miles per hour. The force of their passing sucked old furniture and other debris out through the absent windows of a building they came within feet of hitting.

The structures around them were little more than blurry swaths of color as the car shot down the street at about the level of the ninth floor. Below, on the road, a torrent of plasfilm rectangles swirled about in the severe wind kicked up by their departure.

Once they left the black zone, Masaru climbed to normal cruise altitude, around the fiftieth floor, and slowed to the calm speed of two hundred fifty miles per hour. Kimberly gazed around at the interior of the car. The sense of normalcy made her flash a neurotic smile and knead her hands into the seat cushion like a cat. A nervous laugh escaped her once the reality of being out of that place sunk in. Forty minutes later when the car settled onto the hospital's roof deck, she had almost stopped trembling. Joey studied Katya, not knowing how to interpret the look of genuine concern on her face.

A Division 1 officer moonlighting as hospital security and a slender scarlet-haired black woman in a white coat approached as the engines wound down and cut out. Joey waved at them as he climbed out. "Bring a cart."

The woman doubled back to grab a gurney as the cop walked over. His flashlight swept the car and then he looked at Joey.

"What's the story?"

"Got bored so I went into the black zone around Sector 12."

"Uh huh. Bullshit, but go on."

"Found this girl hiding in a building. I think she's that missing reporter... Kimberly something. Gangers worked her over pretty bad."

The cop looked him up and down, unimpressed. "And you chased them off all on your own?"

Joey laughed. "Yeah right. No. We found her hiding. Another gang tried to get in on the action and she snuck away while they shot each other up."

The cop still had a look of distrust in his eyes. Joey made it up as he went along, not wanting to cause trouble for Mark. Of course, even if the authorities knew where he was, they would never go there.

"Okay, fine. There is a Class 4 borg out there that objected to an imminent rape. He turned the gangers into hamburger."

The cop lifted an eyebrow, sensing no lie even with a less plausible a story than the first attempt.

"Fucking wonderful. If you're not full of shit, let's hope it stays there."

"I don't think he'll be a problem." Joey smiled. "It's not an AI."

The med tech helped Katya move the reporter to the gurney. After a quick diagnostic scan, she gave Kimberly two injections, an antibiotic and a pain reliever. Within seconds, the reporter passed out. The medic got alarmed and repeated the scan.

"Poor thing has probably been awake for days. Tell her she can keep the jacket." Katya folded her arms and backed toward Masaru's car.

Joey shook his head. "We found her clingin' to the severed arm of her dead holo-cam operator, hugging it like a doll, talking to it like he was there."

The cop winced. "That's just not right. What is your relationship with her?"

"Isn't one... we just stumbled onto her."

"Okay. If we need to contact you about this, where can we find you?"

Thinking about the potential reward, he gave legitimate info. "Call me on vid as I dwell where cops dare not tread."

Katya rolled her eyes at his melodrama.

"How's that?" The officer seemed unamused.

Joey gave his address. "Grey zone. Don't get a lot of your buddies around there. As a matter of fact, that shithole sounds pretty damn good right about now."

JOEY STAGGERED DOWN THE STEPS FROM THE SIDEWALK. THE RUSH OF AIR FROM Masaru's departure showered him with old cans and plastic cartons. As it grew distant, the thrum of machinery gave way to the eerie stillness of reflected moonlight on the smooth concrete. The apartment waited ten feet away, though it may as well have been a quarter mile to him.

His trudging gait sent trash scuttling and empty bottles clinking into the dark. He grasped the metal door to steady himself before squeezing between it and the wall. The hellhole was mercifully empty, save for a lingering tequila burp hanging in the air. He staggered past the table, dropping the deck off on the way, and fell face first into the couch without even taking his boots off. The trash that launched skyward with his impact settled into a blanket on top of him.

Cleo, and whatever that holodisk contained, could wait until morning.

TREASURE MAP

Hours later, consciousness intruded upon his blissful repose. His eyes cracked open with the unwanted realization he was awake and still alive. Cruel fingers of pain squeezed his chest as he tried to breathe.

Somewhere below the other ambient discomforts that wracked his body, hunger lurked. Out of the reach of his conscious mind, behind a layer of misery that even three of the green pills wouldn't fix. He remained motionless for the better part of the next hour as curiosity about the holodisk battled with inertia.

He grabbed the couch above where his face rested, tamping a cloud of dust into the air from the olive velveteen. His attempt to stand turned into a helpless fall that sent his body to the floor, the largest object in an avalanche of trash. A short train of plastic boxes bounced off his head as the debris came to a halt.

Joey closed his eyes and drew in a breath to build up the energy necessary for another try. He leaned his head as far to the rear as it would go and stared at the peeling scraps of paint on the ceiling. The events of the previous night already blurred in his mind, though his body remembered every bump and scrape in glorious detail.

He staggered to the bathroom and stared a challenge at the autoshower. Sometimes it worked, sometimes it didn't, and sometimes it invented altogether new methods of torture. It still had hot water, even here, thanks to an internal heating unit. At least forty years old, it made a habit of performing random reflex and pain tolerance tests on whoever used it.

The welcome thought of how his muscles would feel under the warm water chased away his doubts about the nuisance shocks that it delivered here and there out of spite. Superstition held little sway upon Joey's mind, though this aging device seemed to have a personality unto itself. He stripped and shambled into the tube. The curved plastic rotated closed behind him.

He hesitated with a smirk at the control panel, coming within a half inch of pushing the start button four times before he made a fist and threatened the machine with a shake of it. Joey knew that touching the panel would be unpleasant, but after the silent warning he gave it, he risked the poke. Sure enough, a shower of sparks rained out, and he waved his scorched finger through the air, trying to cool it off.

Mismatched bands of color wobbled around the display screen and shifted alignment. Joey hadn't the first clue what should be on the screen, it had been broken like that since he had been squatting here. Joey smiled at the random pixels, wondering if the color patterns made sense to Pinky—he who was high on Flowerbasket in perpetuity.

After an ominous rumble and a series of knocks that came with increasing volume, the spray ring descended, jittered, and started.

Despite the tepid suds, the combination of the warmth with the physical pressure of the water jets eased the pain in his limbs as he grimaced and stretched. Fifteen minutes later when the rinse water stopped, he stood in the center of the unit, dripping. Now came the gamble. The dry cycle was usually where the pain began. It could start up and work, start up and shoot him with frigid air, or do something entirely new and unpleasant.

Rhythmic tapping welled up out of the silence, growing into an oscillating banging as the entire chamber shook. The screen morphed in a mesmerizing pattern of color as the long-damaged device tried its best to pass along information. The mechanical activity in the base grew in intensity, the shuddering tube bouncing him off the walls. He screamed, thinking he might not want to remain inside for the grand finale this time.

He clawed at the door, trying to open the release catch, but the plastic handle had snapped off months ago. A small metal nub he usually stuck his thumbnail into to turn was all that remained. In the midst of all this shaking, he couldn't hold his hand steady enough. He flung himself back from the door and kicked several times into the transparent plastic. Droplets of water that had settled on the interior surface rained onto his leg with each impact. The cold trickle escaped notice as his desperation to escape the auto shower increased in parallel with the shudders rocking the machine.

The fourth heel stomp sent a chunk of curved plastic bouncing into the bathroom amid a clatter that knocked several dust covered canisters of cologne into the sink. Wasting no time climbing past the gap, he backed into the main room as the shower unit shook with such ferocity that a rain of plaster fragments snowed from where it met the ceiling. Black smoke punctuated with streaking orange sparks billowed out of the base, obscuring the bathroom floor. No way in hell would he go back in there to turn it off, and the unit showed no signs of slowing down. If anything, the noise and destruction escalated. Joey figured this was the shower unit's last stand and it wanted to take out the entire apartment as a show of defiance.

He sprinted to the coffee table where he left his handgun. The electric chirp of its arming circuit drowned in the racket from the bathroom. He edged to the side, drifting left just enough to get a clear shot. A double-tap shredded the control unit in a dazzling display of electrical arcs and orange specks. The whine of powered movement ceased, leaving only the thumping whir of the parts already in motion.

He relaxed, the weapon fell to his side, and the whomping noise and shaking slowed.

"Nothing like a shower to wake you up."

"Was that really necessary, Joseph?" His father's voice clucked his tongue. "You could have just cut the power lead."

"This." Joey waved the gun. "Was way more fu"—he whirled to face the air from whence the voice had come—"What the f—"

"Dammit, Cleo." He rubbed his head, pacing. "What the fuck is wrong with me? I'm starting to talk to it."

After tossing the weapon onto the couch, he got dressed in the least aromatic things he could find, and took a seat by his deck. Something scurried out of his way into the trash at the back of the table. A wave of his hand at the screen opened a hatch just large enough to accept a holodisk stack. He took the thing out of its case with a two-fingered grip on its central spindle, and held it up. Light gleamed from the surface as he turned it over, checking the six individual platters for defects. They held about three hundred and sixty terabytes, but the access speed was ponderous compared to neural memory modules.

He set it on the extended U-shaped arm, which retracted into the deck when it sensed the disk's weight. Within seconds, the contents appeared in a spread of holographic panes that bathed the wall behind him in green and blue light. The file structure unfolded into a graphical tree of images linked by lines, though the majority of the disk appeared to be blank. One file turned out to be a cipher key, a part of a cryptographic process needed to decode some other data. The only other file contained a series of numbers. He stared at them, tapping his fingers into the side of his cheek while thinking about what the strange spacing between them could mean. It reminded him of a format he had seen before but the exactitude of where escaped him.

He muttered them aloud. The cadence of how they came out made him remember—coordinates for the NavMap system. They pointed at a spot in the western part of an area of the Badlands once known as Texas. Joey picked at his teeth, pondering the meaning of the coordinates with a cipher key. The curiosity was unbearable. It didn't make it any easier to resist the siren call of danger, thinking that a man got his head vaporized for whatever this code would unlock.

Joey just had to find out.

UNEXPECTED GUESTS

He would need Kenny's help to put together a trip, but he didn't think that would be too difficult to arrange. Convincing Kenny to go to the Badlands was like convincing a ganger to accept free tequila. Masaru might be harder to persuade, but Joey wanted him along for protection. Katya, on the other hand, wouldn't want to go. If something did exist out there important enough to kill for, it stood to reason that it would be worth a lot of credits. Perhaps her need for cash could tip the balance.

Now, of course, Joey had something specific to do. He cracked his knuckles as he savored the anticipatory joy of finding Cleopatra. First, he would trace her. Once he found her in the net, he would use a Flypaper soft to block her logout so she couldn't run away—unless she had a friend in the real world to pull the wire out. With her trapped, he could fry every last memory unit of her deck until it dumped her out of cyberspace with suicide headache.

Joey knew what that felt like. Pain so bad the thought of ending it all seemed almost welcome. The memory of the Black Dragon construct came hand in hand with nausea. One of the more dangerous and powerful AIs, its attack had so overwhelmed his NinTek Scythe that it blew out from one surge. That had been a grade 5 unit, at least triple the power of this Teradyne junk. It had taken him almost ten minutes to stop flopping around the floor like a fish on dry land. Better that it booted him though, a weakened deck opened him to black ICE. A couple of blown-out chips or a smashed neural memory unit was one thing, easily replaceable. Black ICE forced a deck to send voltage into the M3 interface to cook the brain. The dragon would have killed him for real if it had the time to launch a second attack.

Joey rose out of his chair, opining with a triumphant finger at the roof. "I shall find you, Cleo, and make you scream. I shall flood your motherboard with the agonized wails of ten thousand tortured souls and send you into the zombie mosh of doom! I shall roundhouse kick you in the cerebellum!"

Once he burned her deck, he would track down her real identity and make her life every bit as miserable for a few months as she had made his. He sat in the thinker pose, debating what she looked like in real life.

"I bet that cartoon Egyptian princess belongs to a 300 pound warthog—or even a guy." That would make it easier. He wouldn't feel guilty at all then.

Cleopatra was a definite pain in the ass as well as an enigma. Not once had she said a single word to him the entire six months she tormented him. The only time he had seen her avatar she seemed startled by it, as if she hadn't expected him to. His instinct leaned toward her being female due to the strange playfulness. Encounters with her didn't give him the sense that she tried to get into a bigger deck contest.

Most males he crossed wires with always had to prove something and got into cyberduels whenever they could. For the most part, he tried to avoid that scene. He kept his exploits to himself so his reputation remained unknown. That way, no one saw him as a mark for prestige. He did things for the thrill, or even just to see if he could, and he didn't care who knew. Joey liked to think that deck jockeys with true skill liked to remain unknown, so they could get away with more and travel unnoticed.

"Time to go hunting." Joey shuddered with joy at the satisfying click of the M3 plug locking into place.

He closed his eyes and let go of the world around him. Color swam into his senses as his brain reoriented itself away from biological sources of information and welcomed the feed from the plug. The dark cowboy appeared in the virtual recreation of Joey's apartment—the hermetic ranch house.

A panoramic view of generic placid mountains filled in the windows. One of these days, Joey wanted to modify cyberspace around the outside of the apartment so he could go out on his nonexistent porch and smell the virtual pure mountain air, but he hadn't had the time. Exterior cyberspace had a nasty habit of rewriting itself in a continuous cycle to emulate the real world. He might have better luck with a fake door and a virtual node.

His pointing finger traced a cyan box in midair that filled in with a VidPhone pane. Kenny answered the call with his house unit and not a net deck, but cyberspace created the image of him standing there.

"Hey man, what's going on?"

The dark one morphed into Joey. "You wouldn't believe me if I told you. Some government spook just laid this holodisk on me with some NavMap coordinates that point out to the Badlands."

"And you want go out there?" Kenny sagged. Somewhere behind him, a plate dropped.

"Everything okay?" Joey had never seen him show an ounce of hesitation before.

"Yeah. I'm fine. I was just thinking of bringing Alyssa with me the next time I made a run, but I didn't figure on it being quite so soon, and..." Kenny fidgeted.

"And?"

"If there's government involvement, there could be some nasty stuff in our path. Lot of corps set up facilities out there: no oversight. I don't even want to think of what the government might be doing out there. We could be heading into a hornet's nest."

"I was going to ask Katya to come along. She can scout the place out before we get close. I have a feeling whatever it is has been out of the loop for a few years. I'm thinking probably abandoned."

"One can hope. Let me talk to Alyssa and see if she is okay with spending a few days with some neighbors of ours. I won't say I'll go yet, it's up to her."

"Okay... Okay... Just..." Joey glanced to the side, biting his lip.

"What? You almost look scared." Kenny chuckled. "I've never seen that before."

"I've never had a rail gun fired at me before. Someone's hired some heavy hitters to make my ass even narrower."

"You think it's connected to that disk?" Kenny lifted an eyebrow.

"All I know is the head of the guy that gave it to me was all over my coat." Joey showed off the red mark.

"Shit. Okay, I'll talk to her now. Call me back in an hour or two." Kenny disappeared as the call ended.

Joey held his hand out with an imperious air of command. It was as overacted as it was unnecessary, and another comm panel opened. Katya appeared in two rings. Her outfit was generic, as cyberspace had no way to know what she wore, and she hadn't set preferences in her VidPhone. She smirked with a combination of annoyance at being interrupted and curiosity about why he would call her.

Joey dangled a cartoon money sack over her head like a dog treat and whistled at her as if teasing a pet. She rolled her eyes with exasperation and reached to end the call.

"Wait. Dammit, don't they allow you Russians to have a sense of humor?" The cash bag dissipated into snowing pixels.

"As soon as you do something funny, I will react accordingly." She folded her arms. "Did you just vid me for that stupid animation?"

"No, I wanted to find out if they programmed you to smile." He grinned. "Anyway... I got another job. Well... Sort of."

"Sort of? What does that mean?"

"It's not from Alex, and there's no posted payment for it."

"So you are wasting my time?"

"Couple things. Remember Mr. Exploding Head?"

Katya looked away and ran her hands up and down her arms. "How could I forget?"

"The disk has coordinates that point out to the Badlands. Kenny and I are going to go check it out, I wanted you to come along to scout the place and see if it's even approachable."

She looked at him with shock. "Badlands? Me? Are you serious?"

He tried to placate her with hand motions. "Look, I'm not asking you to get into any gunfights or anything like that. I just need to you to poke around the spot at the end of the digital rainbow and see if it's a fully operational facility or an abandoned shithole."

"And what if it's fully operational? Don't you think they will have guards?"

Joey nodded. "If it is, that changes the game plan. Then I look for a way into their network. Or, if it's too nasty, we walk away."

She leaned toward him, holding her arms out. "Why should I even consider this?"

"Well… If Kenny finds something to sell, we'll split it evenly. If we don't, I'll give you half of whatever I get for my next job. Minimum ten k."

"Credits won't help me much if I get killed out there."

A Cheshire cat's smile spread across his face. "Masaru is my next call."

She glowered, and began pacing. "If Masaru goes, I'll consider it, but I am not going to do anything stupid."

"I'd expect nothing less." Joey bowed like Alex, dripping with faux high society charm.

She vanished into dancing sparkles. Masaru took a little longer to answer than the others and looked irritated when he did appear.

"Hope the girls aren't too angry that you stepped away for a second. I'll try to be quick." Joey was still smiling.

"What is it this time?" Masaru sighed.

"Remember the meeting in the black zone? The disk that I got points to the Badlands. Wanna come along? I could really use your sword out there."

Masaru had heard stories about the Badlands. Those romanticized versions, along with his lack of real knowledge, made him want to do it as a test of his own skill.

"When are we leaving?"

Joey beamed. He hadn't expected the rich boy to be so eager to accept. "The only rush on this is the fuckers trying to shoot me. I was thinking tomorrow, maybe the next day? However long it takes Kenny to get supplies and shit together."

"When you have a firm date, let me know." Masaru clicked off the call.

Joey breathed a sigh of relief. That had been easier than he expected, unless Kenny backed out. His image returned to that of the paranormal cowboy. The old man's lips twisted into a dour frown. Wrinkles crisscrossed the sparse white stubble on his cheeks.

Now it was time to keep a promise he had made to himself the other day. It was time to find and put a stop to this Cleopatra nuisance. First, he would check police records, searching for any complaints against someone using that alias. If that didn't work, he would start checking the GlobeNet border routers in an effort to match her name to her IPv12 address. Outside, he sighed in disappointment at finding plain city instead of mountain air.

Joey's brain told his deck where he wanted to travel within Cyberspace. The dark cowboy's visage disintegrated into shifting columns of cyan light and flashing letters. Elsewhere in the net, the same swirls of light spiraled out of the ground and coalesced into his avatar. With a smirk, he yanked his coattails from where they had become stuck in the side of a building.

The sight of the faux stone rippling back into a hard smooth surface made him laugh. The conglomerate that monitors the GlobeNet frowned upon "teleporting" like that. He couldn't fathom why they insisted on forcing everyone to "travel'" the old way.

He was better than they were.

The world shimmered from his deck struggling to update what it fed his mind. Buildings shifted in position. Building's outer coatings of glass and steel flaked away from black forms covered in bright blue grids as the city changed height and shape. Raining debris stopped in midair, reversed, and re-adhered to new forms. One by one, structures stopped moving and skins of intact facades slid up and over the ebon forms. In the span of ten seconds, the entire cityscape had redrawn itself to fit where he stood. Aside from the stark lack of pedestrian traffic and perpetually neutral temperature, it looked no different from the real world.

"Impressive, isn't it?" His father's voice echoed from behind him.

Joey whirled at the noise, spinning around so fast a twinge of pain sliced across his knee. Between the shock to his mental state and rapid motion, his real body had moved, banging his leg against the table. His old man stood a few feet away, staring up at one last row of high-rise windows sliding into place, as if nothing had happened, as if he hadn't been dead for a year on a planet millions of kilometers away. Red-grey flannel shirt and all, he wore the same "I'd smile harder but I lack the energy to get very excited about anything" face Joey remembered.

Joey pointed, his attempt to speak producing an unintelligible babble for a few words before he spat out a fraction of what he thought. "How did you get here?"

"Just like anyone else, I took the shuttle. It was cramped and the food was tepid, but those poor people can only do so much with what they have."

Iciness spread to his fingertips from the chill that swept down his back. Even his father's scent permeated this impossible vision: the smell of a person he knew well, an ambient fragrance that infused everything about them.

Things in cyberspace seldom had fragrances.

He didn't know what to think; his senses told him something that couldn't be true. This flannel and khaki apparition shouldn't—couldn't—be here. Joey opened his mouth but still found no words. His brain fought to come to an understanding of what he saw. His father's distaste for cyberspace added another layer of impossibility. The man had never set foot in the GlobeNet, not even once.

His dad gave him that same look of appraising concern that he always made when something wasn't right. "Joseph, what's wrong?"

The answer formed in his head, but the road to his voice was a long one. He had only just begun to speak when a sensation crashed into him from behind. A feeling that started as a severe impact to the back of the head evolved into a great weight that dragged him to the ground. The terrain gave way like syrup and the liquid sidewalk absorbed him. Overwhelmed with vertigo as if falling and drowning at the same time, he fell. Rapid fragments of sensory input manifested in the form of hot and cold streaks on his body, swirls of color, as well as spikes of random emotions and fragrances.

A hot lance stabbed into his head from just behind his ear.

The pit bottomed out after an eternity of chaos. His downward flight ended with a crash upon a solid surface that brought back all the aches of the previous day. His skeleton, outlined with pain with each beat of his heart, felt like a separate entity within his body. Feverish burning and freezing cold crawled up his arms, forming into a whirlpool of ice that lanced into his skull as if his M3 jack had been replaced with an icicle. Several violent waves of nausea passed through him before his entire body prickled with pins and needles.

A kaleidoscopic blur of color faded into cold grey concrete strewn with trash. A row of small dirty toes, clad in the flaking remnants of pink nail polish, appeared a few inches from his face. A seep of blood worked its way out from under the right foot. Some of the whores in this area occasionally used his place as a crash pad, so the sight of a girl's feet didn't raise any immediate red flags.

"Tequilath ovfer therf." Joey muttered into the concrete floor.

In his mind, he raised his arm to point, but his body ignored him.

"Joey?" asked a voice, too young to be a prostitute.

He forced himself to focus. The feet blurred and collapsed back into a single image, appearing too small to belong to a grown woman. He rolled onto his back, moaning. The agonizing motion felt as if his ribs tore the tissues of his body. The girl hovering over him looked like a tween, in a knee length pink shirt with some silly white cat head graphic on it. Black streaks of grime smeared her right side. Hair somewhere between light brown and dark blonde hung straight down her back, and her pale blue-grey eyes stared at him with primal urgency. From the amount of dirt on her plus being too skinny, he assumed street urchin.

"Look kid, go beg from someone else, I ain't got shit either." His imminent rant stalled when he noticed the gleaming piece of technology across her back on a strap.

A deck—one of the cutesy Neko series with an oval shaped body and two triangular projections on one side that gave the entire device the outline of a cat's head. The outer edge was pinkish red with metallic flakes in the paint while the interior was white with a pink nose. Crescent shaped eyes gleamed with the iridescence of holoprojectors, and its overall condition looked well used. The fidgeting girl still had the wire to his deck in her hand.

Joey sat up and squinted at her. Now he knew what happened, this kid had unplugged him. He entertained the thought of choking her with it, but the panicked desperation in her eyes stole the anger right out of him. He leaned forward to rub his head and noticed she had left a trail of bloody footprints from the door.

"Are you Joey?" The anxiety in her voice grew.

"Yeah." He squinted, continuing to rub his head. "How the hell do you know me?"

"Please, I need your help." She fell to her knees and wrapped her arms around him. She cried into his chest, trembling. "They're trying to shoot me."

CLEOPATRA

J oey's arms hovered at his sides, unsure of how to react to the presence of a child. No matter how hard he stared at the ceiling, no answer waited there about what to do. He made an awkward grimace, reacting to her as if she were an unwanted contaminant in his environment.

It's... touching... me...

"Who... What?" He patted her on the back. "Calm down, kid."

She sat back, still clinging to his hand. "They broke in my door and tried to kill me."

Living out here, Joey had seen enough people experience brushes with death. If this girl was faking, she was damn good at it. Joey took hold of her by the wrists and stood up, leading her to the couch where he backed her into a seated position in the most trash free spot.

"Wait here."

"Don't let them get me!" She curled into a ball on the couch.

Joey didn't respond within the moment it took him to grab a cloth, wet it, and return to sit on the floor by her. He pulled her foot into his lap and found a cut about midway down the outer edge. It wouldn't do her any good to evade these supposed gunmen if she died of some amped up infection from whatever horribleness dwelled in the roads after hundreds of years of chemicals and neglect.

He dabbed at the cut. "Who's after you?"

She grabbed the cushions, wincing. "I don't know." She yelped as he hit a tender spot. "They were huge. One had a gun that was bigger than me."

"Why didn't you go to the police?" He dropped her leg.

She fidgeted, breaking eye contact. "I dunno."

Even Joey could tell she had a definite reason for coming to see him. He placed one hand on her shoulder and lifted her chin with the other, forcing her to meet his gaze. Her fear was real, but her rationale wasn't.

"Why do you think I can help you? I'm not a cop."

She cried, looking even guiltier. "I kinda thought you'd be bigger. Um, meaner, with lots of guns and stuff." Her gaze shot to the door at the sound of passing footsteps.

Joey stood and tried to walk off the pain of the abnormal disconnect. "Bigger? How do you know me?"

She drew her knees up to her chin and wrapped her arms around her legs, wearing the look of a kid that just got caught doing something bad. "I've seen you on the net."

"I see a lot of people on the net... I don't remember you." He stopped walking long enough to arch his back and stretch a little.

She looked down at her feet. Her voice fell to a timid whisper. "I'm Cleopatra."

Joey turned as if he had just taken a hundred pound raw salmon across the face. He stared at this scrawny little kid on his couch, his face contorted with confusion and anger. This girl was malnourished, dirty, only an oversized shirt for clothing, and she carried a battered net deck. How could this be Cleopatra? He leapt at her. She jumped back, raising her arms to guard her face, and shrieked. Rather than hit her, he pulled her head to the side, checking for a jack, but found only a faint wisp of fruity scent clinging to her hair. The kid didn't have a scrap of cyberware on her—not surprising for a tween.

She had no plug.

Also, scented shampoo cast serious doubts about her status as a street urchin.

"Please don't hit me!" She shrank into the couch. The rage that filled his eyes at the sound of that name scared her. "I had nowhere else to go for help."

Joey stared aghast at this waif in his apartment. How long he had daydreamed about the awful things he would do to some anonymous woman named Cleopatra once he found her. The payback for the six or seven months of torment she had visited upon him in the net was supposed to have been legion. However, he couldn't bring himself to hurt the frail child in front of him. Pity collided with his abject frustration at not being able to make anyone suffer his revenge. The impact of those thoughts exploded in a frustrated scream of anguish that made her jump and stare wide eyed as she tried to burrow deeper into the couch.

He turned away and kicked a bottle across the room. "How do you know about Cleopatra? Why should I even believe that it's you?" The rest of his breath slinked off into silence amidst a bevy of obscenities as he tried to hope that someone remained out there he could get even with.

"I tried to load a DePantser on you in that nightclub... Sent you 50 gallons of booze, kept hitting you with the random teleports..." She continued listing things that had befallen him over the past few months.

By the time she stopped, Joey had a two fisted grip on her shirt and held her up by it. The glare in his eyes put an end to her recitation of torment. He wanted to wound her in some way, but couldn't bring himself to harm someone so vulnerable. It occurred to him that she appeared to be quite underdressed for running around a city, and looked more ready for a slumber party than an incursion into a grey zone.

"Is this some kind of setup?" He dropped her on the couch and took a few steps back. His voice got louder and higher. "This is the last grand prank isn't it? Cops are going to kick in my door any second and think I'm..."

He paced around, pinching the bridge of his nose. His voice fell back to a calm, almost beleaguered croak. "Do you have any idea what cops do to a guy when they think…"

She blushed, pulling her shirt down farther.

"No!" She yelled. "I swear it's not that." She slouched. "My dad's never home. I don't have any real friends. I hang out in the net all day, even go to school there." She picked at her shirt. "I never go outside. Daddy hasn't done laundry in forever and there's no clean clothes left, so I just wear these shirts. I don't get dressed coz I never go out." She made eye contact again, voice quaking. "They kicked in the door. They didn't like give me time to get dressed and shit first. Excuse me, Mr. Gunman. Before I run for my life, would you mind if I got changed first?"

Joey stared. He considered it almost plausible that her appearance could have come from one panicky sprint across the grey zone. Her starved look could fit her claim of sitting in cyberspace all day long rather than being a street orphan, but how could her family let that happen? Street kids that young didn't often have cyberspace rigs.

"What about your parents?" Joey rifled among piles of clothing strewn about the side of the apartment, under the bullet holes in the wall. "Isn't anyone looking after you?"

"Yeah, my dad, but he's always at work. I haven't seen him in a long time." She turned on the couch and draped herself over the back to watch him search. "When he's home I'm either sleeping or in the net and I guess he doesn't wanna wake me up." She smirked. "I never knew my mom."

The sad stare frustrated him more. For so long he had wanted to harm Cleopatra, now he felt like an ogre. He found a pair of pants that had no appreciable odor to them and threw them at the girl. "So what's your real name?"

"Hayley Roth." She looked at the pants. "Are these yours?"

"Yeah." Joey turned his back on her and folded his arms. "Put 'em on 'til you can get home. You got clothes and stuff there?"

Trash rustled behind him.

"Yeah, nothing clean though." Her sad tone took on a sudden tone of amusement. "Holy shit."

"What?" Joey fought the urge to turn.

"The legs are too long but they almost fit. These are yours?" She giggled.

He glared at the wall. Despite her situation, she still found the time to make a joke at his expense. "Guess they shrank in the wash."

"Wash?" She lifted an eyebrow and adjusted her shirt to fall outside the black pants. "You want me to believe you washed these? You can look now."

She sat and rolled the too-long legs into cuffs.

Joey frowned. His pants were larger on her than her comment made it sound.

"You're trying real hard to make me not feel sorry for you, aren't you?" Joey returned to the pile of clothing to search for some kind of shoes, but found nothing. "Look, let me run into town and get you some sneakers or something. Everything's filthy out here, you're going to get sick… or high if you go around barefoot."

"Can't order them?"

"Delivery bots don't come out here." He took a step for the door.

She limped over and grabbed his arm. "Don't leave!"

Joey again felt like a fiend for wishing ill upon her. The way she clung to him made him think she was desperate for human contact. It was obvious that her father neglected her. The requisite psychology courses he slept through at the Mars Academy of Engineering came back to him. The way this girl clung to a total stranger was a sign of attachment issues.

"Okay, fine... Why would thugs try to kill a little kid?"

"I'm eleven." Hayley folded her arms with an indignant expression. "I'm not little."

"Answer me one thing." He grabbed his coat but only got one arm into it before guilt reared its head and he gave it to her. "Why me?"

Hayley smiled with an impish grin. "I saw your avatar and just kinda thought you took yourself way too seriously... So I wanted to dick with you."

He stopped waiting for her to take it and threw the jacket over her head.

"My word, such language for a child." Joey's dad aired his opinion.

Hayley pulled the jacket down off her face in a panic. "Who was that?"

Joey fixed her with a steel glance. "I thought that was your work."

She shook her head to the negative, trembling. "No." Her voice floated as a gossamer whisper.

Joey squinted at the deck. "Don't worry about it, that voice belongs to someone that would never harm a fly."

He would order food when they stopped by her apartment to grab some proper clothing, then he would drop her off at a cop shop and let the system take over from there. Despite all its attempts to appear otherwise, the UCF was a police state. However, the government had a soft spot for kids, as they made great public relations fodder. The nanny state developed around the establishment of the two major cities may have trampled on the civil liberties once enjoyed four hundred years ago, but no one disputed that they took care of children well.

"Okay... Let's go. Where is your apartment?" He held out a hand.

She shivered. "Why? They're probably still watching it."

"You don't have to make up stories about men chasing you..." He doubted she would have made it this far if professionals were after her.

"I'm not making it up." She stomped her foot, paralyzed by pain for an instant. "They kicked in the door."

"And you saw them while you were in cyberspace?"

"Duh... You *are* supposed to be a hacker, right?" She gave him a look of disbelief and fear at the same time. "I'm a kid! I'm stuck with a lame slow-ass helmet. I can still see and hear the real world."

Joey felt like a stooge. Senshelmets were so far removed from 'serious' hacking that he hadn't even thought of it. "Okay... Okay..."

"I was in the bathroom. I locked the door and ran for the window. They shot at me through the wall."

"Look, Kid..."

"Hayley."

"Fine. Look, Hayley... Why would anyone want to shoot you? You're such a *charming* person." He squinted at her.

She took a step back. "Don't look at me like that."

Joey sighed. "I promise I will not hurt you no matter how much I daydreamed about pissing on the smoking remains of your net deck."

She stared agape.

"That was before I knew you were just a kid."

Hayley looked away and down. "I hacked into this place in DC, some government network. I don't remember the node ID, it said PSEC or something."

Joey snapped around to face her. "How in the fuck did you get in there? Shit, I'm not sure I could even pull that off and you're a little brat with a goddamn helmet? Bullshit." He took a few steps, struggling with his temper. "Just bullshit. I don't fuckin' buy it."

She sank back into the couch and rested her elbows on her knees. "I dunno... I just walked in. The mushroom told me to follow him."

Joey's rant stopped cold and he pivoted with a face frozen in rage: one eye squinting with the other wide open. The irrational anger that came from the idea that an eleven year old with a helmet outdid him screeched to a halt. "Mushroom?" A less-than-sane laugh echoed out of him.

"Yeah. It's a program on my deck that my dad installed. It tells me where it's safe to go." She pointed at a small decal on the side of the cat head that looked like a blue spotted mushroom with eyes.

"Your child protection software told you to break into a government network?" A strained expression of WTF peeled his lips into a corpse's grin.

"It said it was a museum with cool things to see."

This stank to high heaven. Joey paced around as he tried to make sense of it.

"After we got inside, the mushroom told me that it made a mistake and I could get in trouble for going in there so it said I should make it look like someone else did it."

Joey glared.

She stared down, twisting her toes into the floor. "Yeah..."

"Me? For fuck's sake!" Joey's first thought was that the guy with the railgun had been sent to clean that up. "People have been trying to kill me! Dammit to hell." He kicked another can across the apartment. "If you weren't a god damned kid..."

Hayley curled into a shivering ball, crying into her hands. "Please don't hurt me! I'm sorry! I thought I was just having fun."

Joey closed his eyes and fumed in silence. Her terror of him added guilt to his rage. He was an amateur at dealing with children, and this one needed a professional. Still, much of what she said seemed implausible.

"How did you fake it?" He folded his arms.

"It wasn't too hard." She sniffled and wiped her eyes, then held her hands up and wiggled her fingers. "Like this. I thought about you and the network read my mind. That's what decks do, duh!"

"Did you spoof the route uplink paths, or do a buffer underwrite on the interlink node, or splice any of the data packet headers with my net deck's IPv12?"

"What?" She scrunched her nose at him.

Joey's mental ramble stopped in a mixture of worry and satisfaction. Her reaction to that question made him feel more secure in his own abilities. PSEC node or not, no way this girl did that alone. Someone had to be shadowing her. Whoever did it had managed to not only infiltrate a government network, but also do it with a helmet-wearing little kid along for the ride—all without being caught.

"What did you do in there?"

Hayley shrugged. "Walked around, looked at stuff. The mushroom showed me this data box that had pictures of this place with trees. It looked like an army base that got broken."

Joey twisted his lips, thinking of the Badlands coordinates. Broken was a nice word to use there. That made it sound abandoned, which meant it should be easy to poke around. He patted her on the head for making his daydream seem easier and helped her put the jacket on as fast as he could move his hands. The threat of gunmen chasing her got more real in his mind. Someone must have tracked her in the network and came looking for her, thinking she was a real hacker. This kid might have led them here, and Joey wanted some friends around if things got nasty. He slung his deck over his back and grabbed his other stuff.

"We have to go… right now."

Besides, Kenny knew how to deal with kids.

IRONY, INDELICATE

Hayley sat at the edge of the couch, arms wrapped about her deck. Her shivering may have been caused by fear or cold, either of which a valid excuse in that apartment. Something in the urgency with which Joey tossed his way through the scrap heap of clothes made her keep looking at the door and jumping at any moving shadow. After locating a shirt that would never again be wanted as a garment, he shredded it and wrapped it around her cut foot.

"It ain't much, but it should help until we can get better." He took hold of her by the wrist, pulling her to stand. "C'mon."

They took just two steps when the door flew inward with enough force to mask a third of the apartment behind a rolling cloud of dust. A huge man who looked like one of the heavies from the Imperial Hotel blocked the exit. Black oval globes spread over his eyes, connected to metal protrusions on the side of his head that appeared to contain tiny sensor suites. The right eye glowed with the shape of orange crosshairs as a gargantuan rifle shifted toward them. Joey swung Haley around by her arm and half threw her over the couch.

"Bathroom window, now!" Joey pulled his handgun with a practiced cowboy draw and fired.

He knew better than to try to shoot this behemoth in the chest. That had worked so well last time. He retreated toward the bathroom, clicking off a series of rapid shots in an effort to clip one of the ogre's cybernetic eyes, or nail him in the head where he had no armor. The first two went high, but the third caught the view module where it wrapped around his head. The bullet tore apart the mechanism on the right side of the skull and shattered the black plastic lens cap, exposing the shiny inner workings: a flat silver plate with a recessed iris. The fourth slug hit him in the center of the forehead. With an audible metallic pang, muted by the presence of skin, it ricocheted off in a splatter of blood, leaving a strip of exposed plastisteel skull.

The hits knocked the assassin back a pace. Joey wasted no more time before he turned and ran. He reached the bathroom in time to see Haley's legs disappear up and out of the window as if she took flight. Climbing became kicking and screaming.

"Fuck... Fuck... Fuck..." Joey scrambled over the toilet to the window. "An hour ago, I wanted to kill her... Fuck irony."

Despite knowing that if one of those things had gotten their hands on her, he couldn't do much, he gripped the frame and pulled himself out into the alley. Sometimes having the physique of a bulimic teenager proved to be an advantage. The window sat right at ground level and his chest scuffed along the pavement as he slithered out and rolled to his feet. A normal sized man in a black velvet coat held Hayley a short distance away.

While not an ogre like the one inside, this man was more muscular than Joey. His eyes hid behind a plastisteel plate mounted to nubs embedded on the sides of his head. The tiny optical sensors on the armored visor gleamed pink and green in the darkness. His lapel bore a small octagonal pin, gold, with a stylized W in the center. He fumbled to pull a handgun out of a belt holster, but Hayley had a desperate hold on the weapon, keeping it down despite having her hair clenched between the fingers of his other hand.

As soon as she saw Joey, she drove a fist into the man's groin, and then jammed her elbow into his gut. Her entire arm went numb from the impact of her funny bone on body armor. She gasped. The nut shot got his attention. His hand jerked her by the hair to the left. She turned into him despite the pain and drove her knee into his nether bits. He raised his arm to smash the pistol into her face.

Joey's objection rang out from his sidearm.

Two shots, one to the neck and one to the upper lip, sent a spray of blood out to the rear and took all the strength out of his fist in an instant. She shoved into his chest, knocking the body away, and closed her eyes. Joey gawked, wearing a silly grin, amazed that for once, he shot someone and it worked. Hayley made a deliberate effort not to look at the falling man, and rushed into Joey's side. He took her hand and ran with her around a corner to the end of the alley.

Despite it being late afternoon, the combination of the smog and the giant derelict buildings covered the street with night. Within the deepest shadows, dozens of faces lurked. A sea of gleaming augmented eyes, blinking lights, and the occasional cybertattoo drifted in the black. He felt their stare upon them and didn't want to linger in this area with a little girl. The usual crowd would leave her alone, but with all the Sector 12 gangers here, he didn't want to take chances. They would think nothing of killing him to get to such a prize.

Some walked out of the dark to get a better look at the pair as they ran by. He sprinted for another two blocks before turning just to throw the assassin off. The route took them in the general direction of civilization, but he didn't want to risk a straight line and a shot in the back. Fear of the man that kicked in his door added speed to his stride. The shot to his eye would cost upward of forty thousand credits to repair. He would no doubt be quite upset. Joey had no plans to discuss the matter with him a second time.

Hayley wound down fast. After five blocks, he had gone from leading to dragging her. Bloody smudges on the ground said the improvised bandage was saturated.

"Come on." He pulled at her arm.

"I can't." She cried.

This girl spent so much time motionless in the net that her body hadn't reacted well to all the running. He picked her up, cradling her to his chest, and ran himself winded. When he could go no further, he stumbled into an alley out of sight, carrying her behind a pile of large metal crates that blocked view from the street. He set her down, sitting on a crate, and flopped next to her. She crawled into his lap, clinging and shaking.

Joey held his arms up as if someone had spilled child on his shirt. He made a pained face, as if afraid to touch her. After a moment, he let one arm settle on top of her shoulder and her trembling waned.

"I don't wanna die," she said, a scant trace of vocal tone floating over a whisper.

Joey leaned his head back, searching for answers in the smog. Whoever those men were had already started her punishment for misbehaving in cyberspace. Almost certain that the assassin had lost them at this point, he allowed himself to breathe.

"So who is your dad?"

"His name is Jake. He's a cop."

Joey closed his eyes, swallowing the obscenities that wanted to come out. That little voice in his head screamed. This kid had trouble written all over her. If something happened to her while she was with him, the cops would be looking for someone to blame. Who better than a fringer from Mars with no records and no family down here?

"Maybe we should call him?"

She stared into his eyes. Her tears had scrubbed two clean streaks down her face. "It won't matter." Her gaze fell. "He'll be too busy at work."

"If you tell him that men with guns are chasing you, he'll fly home."

She sniffled. "He can't get away from his work. That's what he keeps saying."

"You don't give him enough credit."

Her baleful look made him worry, but she was also not his problem to deal with. He wanted to find out who was behind the attacks, and it seemed foolish to risk luring those assassins to a hospital. They already proved willing to kill a kid, so he didn't think they'd glitch on torching anyone in their way. Maybe he could stash her at Kenny's. He lived so far south it might as well have been off the grid.

Without thinking about it, he rubbed her back while he used his NetMini to search for Jake Roth. No hits that seemed plausible came back.

"Are any of these your dad?" He scrolled among a list of faces. None of them got her attention.

"You're wasting your time." She huddled into him tighter. When he continued looking, she sighed. "Try searching for Jacob."

She picked a face on the fourth page of hits. "That's him."

Joey opened the link and read the title under the name: Detective - Division 2 Gang Task Force. Well that at least explained why he was so busy. Some parts of the city had so much gang activity that they became open warzones. He hit the holographic button to connect a vid call and soon a middle-aged man's head hovered in front of him, covered with short hair that went curly on top, black with a liberal spread of silver throughout. Little round glasses sat with precarious gravity upon the end of his nose and he seemed to radiate an air of fatigue.

"Roth." His voice sounded unassuming, and not much like a cop.

"Yeah… Do you have a daughter named Hayley?"

The boredom in Roth's voice faded to concern. "That is correct. What is this about?"

Well that is something, Joey thought, at least he got an emotional response. "She's gotten herself mixed up in something I don't really understand. She just showed up at my place and some angry men with big guns just tried to aerate us both."

"Shit," he muttered. "Where is she now?"

"We're in the grey zone, moving toward the city. Where can I meet you?" Joey was about to give Hayley an emphatic look when Roth's next words caught him off guard.

"I'm buried up to my eyeballs here and can't get out of the office. I'll send some patrol units to the apartment to keep an eye on her."

"Your kid's getting shot at and you can't leave the office?" Joey almost yelled in disbelief.

"That's an obtuse way of putting it, but it's not like I have a choice." His tone returned to a more calm and businesslike demeanor. "Many more people could die if I don't. The patrol officers can handle it."

"Yeah okay, whatever…" Joey hung up, and sighed.

"See." She stared at the ground, trembles gone, fear drowned in sadness.

His heart sank. He had once wanted to wound Cleopatra, but this girl already had some deep ones. Cop or not, her dad was a douche. He couldn't grasp how anyone could do that. His own father often found himself swamped at work, but never prioritized his job over his family. Joey couldn't dump her at that apartment alone even if cops were sitting on the front door. She needed more than just guards, but Joey wasn't thrilled about being the father figure she clung to. Alas, the sight of the scrawny kid shivering in his lap melted his heart in a way he had never known.

He fired off a text only message to her father, giving him Kenny's address and telling him to pick Hayley up there when he got out of work.

"I ain't gonna leave you alone at that apartment. I have a friend who lives far from here to the south. He's got a daughter a little older than you. You'll be safe there until your dad gets out of work. Is that okay?"

She nodded without saying anything.

"Okay, let's get going before they find us."

Hayley faltered on her right leg as they stood. The cut, aggravated by the running, flared up. She yelped and grabbed his shirt to keep from falling over. He carried her along past alley after alley. The social standing of the people around them improved with each passing block as the decay gave way to the city proper. As soon as the people stared at him with a glare that questioned what he was doing here, he figured he had gone far enough into civilization to be safe.

They stopped by a PubTran dispatch terminal nestled in a cluster of lampposts and vendomats and he set her back down. She put no weight on her right leg and held on to him for balance. He smacked the button a few times until it flooded the area with bright azure light.

"Thank you for choosing PubTran taxi. Please wait, an autocab has been dispatched to your location." A digitized voice emanated from thin air with insincere cheerfulness.

As they waited, Hayley stared out at the world with fear and fatigue. Her fingers dug into Joey's clothing as if to let go meant her death. The myth of her immunity from the real world within the confines of her father's apartment had been shattered, and with it her bravado.

Her face glowed green with light from Joey's NetMini on one side and cyan on the other from the PubTran terminal. She leaned up to peek at the screen while he ordered a pair of shoes for her. He held the device out as if to take a picture of her foot, and the ordering system calculated the proper size. Given that merchandise arrived via flying delivery bot within a few minutes, he sent the shoes to Kenny's so they would be waiting.

She squeezed his arm, feeling a bit guilty about all she'd done to him. "Joey?"

"Yeah?" He glanced down.

She couldn't seem to stop crying, but managed a feeble smile. "I'm sorry."

He patted her on the back. "Yeah... I'll forgive you if I survive this."

No sooner had he put his NetMini back in his pocket than a tiny driverless car pulled up by the terminal box. Dull grey at the fenders, the roof, door, and hood gleamed powder blue. A single large door on the side facing them opened upward.

"Thank you for using PubTran. Your cab is now here. Please board the vehicle and close the door behind you. Use caution and do not trap any loose articles of clothing in the door. Please ensure that all children and pets are accounted for before closing the door. Please note that PubTran Corporation is not liable for injury or death that result from the actions of external forces during your ride. Enjoy your trip." Joey couldn't tell if the voice came from the box or from the vehicle.

The small interior had two bench seats facing each other. The opposing wall had no door, just a metal console down the middle with some well-worn manual interface buttons. Joey let Hayley in first and then sat facing her. She switched sides to sit next to him and tucked her uninjured foot under her on the seat. He pulled the door closed, and leaned back.

"Hello, this is the PubTran Taxi system navigator. Please state your destination."

Joey gave it Kenny's address.

"Destination is one hundred forty seven credits. Please swipe your NetMini device or insert a credstick."

Joey waved his NetMini past the console. After a beep, the vehicle drove off. By the time the car rolled to a halt in front of Kenny's house almost an hour later, Hayley had fallen asleep. Joey carried her onto the porch as the vehicle turned and zipped off into the city for its next fare. The thought of all the things she did to him as Cleopatra tempted him to use her head to knock on the door, but he decided against it and tapped a few times with his boot.

Kenny shook his head at him after opening the door. "Those are too small for Alyssa."

"They're not for her..." Joey hefted the sleeping girl in his arms.

He blinked at the sight of her. "What the fuck did you do?"

Joey rolled his eyes. "Why do you always assume the worst? I'll explain later. You got any stimpaks? She's hurt."

"Yeah, yeah…" Kenny jogged into the house as Joey walked in behind him and kicked the door shut.

He eased Hayley onto the couch at the center of the living room and looked around. The western themed décor made him feel at home. In many ways, life on Mars fit the descriptions of the Old West—with more lasers. Kenny returned and handed him a red autoinjector with a yellow cap at the end. Joey unraveled the cloth from around Hayley's foot. He tugged the saturated cloth away from where it had fused. Her eyes snapped open from the sudden jolt of pain.

Joey held up the stimpak. "Know what this is?"

"Yeah. Dad has a couple of them at home." She cringed with anticipation.

After sliding the pant leg up to her calf, Joey pressed the autoinjector into her leg and it made a faint hiss. Within seconds, the cut on her foot filled in and faded to a thin white line of new tissue as nanobots rebuilt the damaged cells. The synthetic adrenaline in the carrier fluid chased the fatigue from her eyes. Hayley relaxed, having anticipated far more pain from the shot.

Kenny turned to the back hallway. "Alyssa? Hon, can you grab some of your old clothes?" He smiled at Hayley and pointed at the nearest bathroom. "You need to clean yourself up. The autoshower is over there. My daughter will bring you something to wear. Just yell if you need anything."

"She could use something to eat, too," added Joey.

Hayley nodded and wandered toward the indicated doorway with the hesitance of a guest not wanting to go in the wrong direction. The battered cat-headed deck remained on the couch.

"So…" Kenny folded his arms at Joey. "Who is that?"

Joey's cheesy laugh disintegrated into a halfhearted chuckle. "Grab a beer, it's a long story."

WORDS OF SUPPORT

Pear shaped patches of light interrupted the burgundy wallpaper at regular intervals from small lamps arranged about a modest-sized room. The air hung thick with the fragrance of eastern incense and a podium presided over the handful of people seated in several rows of chairs.

Heads turned as the opening door let in the sound of a car passing in the rain. A woman slipped through and closed it. Pale fingers traced the rose-hued metallic reliefs in the wallpaper as she drifted to the right. A frilled cuff sprouted like a flower around her delicate wrist from an ornate dress a few centuries out of place. Her alabaster skin glowed with a phantasmal presence, as if lit by moonlight that existed only for her.

The white gown turned pale blue in places where the fabric thickened, and its lacy hem dusted the floor as she moved, bare toes peeking out with each step. Its chest opened in a modest v-shaped neck, folds of material lined with frilled lace gave the impression of flower petals peeled back to reveal a hint of cleavage, though its wearer didn't have much to show off. She was a wisp, a shade less than five and a half feet tall and delicate of build. Long, black hair framed a narrow face and hung to her waist. Piercing blue eyes shrouded in dark makeup remained downcast. The living doll hovered along the periphery, as if fearful of the room's interior.

Her gait slowed while she risked a glance over the small crowd. An unassuming man in his early thirties sat in the front row. The desperate claw-like way in which he clung to a cup of coffee a sign that all wasn't well with him. Short, thick, brown hair sat like a plastic helmet upon his head. Every so often, his eyes darted to the door, fearful of what he might see.

Across the room, a boy of about ten sat on the floor with his back to the wall. His dark shirt, pants, and battered sneakers seemed ordinary, though he wore a military pilot's helmet too large for him and fidgeted with a toy starship. Given the nature of this place, she assumed one of his parents, or perhaps an older sibling, had died in action.

An exhausted Japanese woman had watched her since she entered, looking away before she could make eye contact. She fought to keep her eyes open as though she hadn't slept in days. She looked to be in her early twenties. Fancy attire said she made a decent living.

In the center of the bank of chairs, a brooding, older, black man glared at the podium. His pale green sweater and light tan pants clashed with the colors of the room, though he focused his attention elsewhere. Unlike the others, he radiated more anger than sadness, and gave the impression that he simply waited for the right person to go off on. A few seats to his left, an old man with coffee colored skin and white hair muttered to no one in particular about wasting time. His attire plain, he wasn't subtle in his display of contempt for this place.

In the last row, a young woman curled into a ball with the heels of her boots on the seat and her face hidden between her knees, muttering about someone named Mary. She wore leather painted with gang markings. Somewhere underneath the dangling chains and spikes hid a ratty white t-shirt and some manner of skin-hugging camouflage pants.

All the way on the left side, a glowing pink fairy, not quite a foot tall, in a risqué red dress, hovered over an arrangement of snacks set up on a folding table. A cloud of pink surrounded her as if she were a living light source. She drifted back and forth amid a trail of sparkling dust as she looked over the food that had been set out, with a disappointed smirk.

The elaborate dress rustled as the frail woman leaned into the corner and folded her arms. She stared down at the floor where her toes peered out from below the frill, wondering if coming here was a mistake. Compared to everyone else here, she didn't feel as bad, or at least wouldn't admit to it. Everyone in this room had lost someone dear to them. She looked up at motion, finding the boy with the helmet two feet away. He pushed the helmet up so he could see her, silent as she stared at her warped reflection in the silver visor.

"Hi."

She offered a weak smile. "Hey."

He held up a hand. "I'm Chris."

"Avril." She returned his handshake.

"My dad died on Mars. He was a Marine."

"I'm sorry." She squeezed his shoulder. "He was a hero, I bet."

The helmet slid forward with a *thunk* as he hung his head. "They won't tell us how he died."

"If he was part of a clandestine ops team, the records are sealed, they…" Avril stopped and shook her head.

"Huh?" The helmet snapped back up.

"I mean… If he was on a secret mission they can't tell you about it without putting other soldiers in danger." She folded her hands over her dress.

"That's what mom said too. Why are you here?"

She flinched at the question, but this was a kid after all—tactless. The inquiry flooded her with memories of Vincent and she choked up.

"Sorry." The helmet sagged to the right. "The doc says we don't have to talk about it 'til we're ready to."

"My husband." She forced it out through a trembling voice.

The loose helmet wobbled as he nodded. "Sorry." He turned to walk away, but whirled back around. "Don't be sad. You're pretty, so you can get a new one." With that, he marched to where he had been sitting before.

She stared at him, not knowing if she should feel flattered or angry that she dismissed Vincent like that, and turned away from the room to hide her tears against the wall.

An Indian woman in a white coat over navy blue business attire shimmered into view in the hallway beyond the podium.

"Good afternoon everyone. Thank you for coming." She looked at Avril. "I see we have a new face here tonight." She smiled with genuine concern. "I am Doctor Preeti Khan. Please know that we are all here for each other, and nothing needs to happen faster than you are ready to accept."

Avril fidgeted with her dress.

"I will be meeting with each of you in turn as usual." She smiled. "Please feel free to converse with and support each other in the interim. I would like to start with the new person unless anyone is feeling urgently in crisis?"

The coffee cup in the claw grip burst.

"Okay then, Mitch. Come on." She turned to look at Avril. "Miss, I will speak with you next if you like."

Avril nodded without a word, watching the two disappear down the corridor. Some of the people drifted together and conversations began. The pink fairy was a lawyer whose mother had died after a nasty argument. The Japanese woman spoke to the old Hispanic man who just nodded at her as she discussed the recent suicide of her father and death of her grandfather. He didn't seem at all keen on being here, and offered no information in return aside from asking how long he needed to stay here.

Chris took a seat adjacent to the punk girl. The young woman hesitated at sharing details with a small boy, but did mention that a friend of hers died on the street. The angry older man steeped in rage. He approached no one, and no one dared get near him. Only Chris appeared safe from his glare, instead giving the boy a look of pronounced loss. His radiant emotion piqued her curiosity at the same time it repelled everyone else. She padded over to the row of chairs and gathered her dress about her legs as she sidestepped along until she was a chair away.

"Allo." She offered a polite smile. "Would you mind if I sat here?" Back in the Avril personality, she produced a faint French accent.

Her innocent face and wispy form softened his hard glare, and he nodded.

"I'm Avril." She extended a hand to him.

"Carl."

She let her ignored hand drop back into her lap. "Carl, can I ask you something?"

"What?" He almost yelled.

Avril cowered, with a stare that said she was afraid even to apologize for daring to speak.

He looked away. "Sorry, I got a lot on my mind."

"May I ask why?"

"God damned cops." He shook his head. "They don't give a shit about us."

"What makes you say that?"

His face cycled through several degrees of fury as he tried to find words. His eyes welled with tears but just as fast as his mood changed to sadness, anger returned stronger than before. "Sons of bitches..."

The profoundness of grief upon him was tangible.

"What did the police do to you?"

He shifted, waving. "No... It's what the motherfuckers didn't do."

She leaned back. "Someone close to you got hurt and the police ignored it?"

"Yeah." His face contorted, tears running down his cheeks as he bellowed, "My two boys."

The entire room turned at the sudden outburst, leaving Avril feeling awkward and exposed.

"I know a few people on the force. Why would they ignore your boys getting hurt?"

"Because, Coe, my oldest... he got himself mixed up in some god damned gang nonsense. Someone shot him and the damn cops... You know those motherfuckers had the balls to tell me to my face he got what he asked for."

Avril grabbed his arm with both hands. "That's not true." She had braced for the revelation that the police killed his son, but this was easier to deal with.

"Arlon, my younger boy, was only fourteen. Why did they have to kill him too?" He sobbed for a while before his grief shifted back to anger. "They ain't gonna get my daughter, no sir. They ain't gonna touch... Damn sons of bitches are gonna pay for what they did."

"Carl." The innocence left Avril's voice as Nina emerged. "Look at me."

He gaped at her. The change in her voice shocked him out of his sorrow.

"You have a daughter that needs you. Please don't do anything stupid." She put the Avril voice back on. "Let me talk to some friends of mine, they might be able to help."

"What is your little ass gonna do?" He smirked.

"You'd be surprised." She winked. "If you give me your PID, I'll get in touch with you soon."

He stared. The life sized Victorian doll seemed as unlikely a hope as anything else. The dichotomy of what she asked compared to her appearance caused his brain to slow to a grinding halt. His face said he didn't expect much from the waif in front of him. Then again, he had nothing to lose by giving her his contact information.

"Okay fine... I still don't know how to use this damn thing." He fiddled with his hair.

Nina figured he used a helmet. "Think about opening the control console. When you see the menu appear in front of you, touch the share contact information link and then point at me."

Carl waved his hand around and a few lines of static disrupted his image in cyberspace. When the request to exchange info popped up in front of her, she accepted.

"Don't do anything until I call, okay?"

"Yeah... Yeah..." He nodded, convinced that he would never see her again.

"Miss?" The doctor's voice drifted over from the other end of the room.

Avril looked up as Mitch scurried past the row of seats and out the door. He looked agitated and mumbled to no one at a rapid pace. She got up and rustled out of the chair rows, following the doctor down a hallway to a comfortable office decorated with a number of Indian paintings on black velvet.

Dr. Khan maneuvered around her desk and sat. "This is your first time here, so I have some basic questions for you if you don't mind… just for my records. First off, what is your name?"

She sat facing the desk. "Avril Boudreau."

"Thank you, Avril. Again, I'm Dr. Khan. You can call me Preeti if you find it less cumbersome. Can I ask your age?"

"Twenty four."

"And you are female, yes?"

The oddity of the question raised an eyebrow before she realized that in cyberspace appearance meant nothing. "Yes."

"Alright, thank you." Dr. Khan leaned back and smiled. "What brings you here to New Hope?"

Avril looked at the desk. This seemed like such a good idea when she thought of it before, but the moment had come, and now she found it difficult to speak about Vincent.

"My husband was killed," she blurted at last, the emotion wrapped about the words genuine.

Dr. Khan leaned forward and placed a hand on top of Avril's. "I am sorry for your loss. I can see that it has affected you deeply. Please, share as much as you feel able to."

Nina tried to focus on her concocted scenario. The Avril persona had a different explanation for the circumstances and she needed to keep those details consistent.

"We had been in the UCF for two weeks and our apartment was being remodeled. My husband Michel wanted to get away from the noise and the dust and have a night out, so we went to the theater. I don't even remember the show anymore." Images replayed in her mind of that night, Vincent's last expression as he reached toward her.

"Take your time. Emotions are a natural part of coming to terms with the loss of someone dear to you. There is nothing wrong with how you feel or with letting it out. How long ago did it happen?"

"About ten…" She hesitated. "Weeks. Men came out of an alley and wanted to rob us. Michel was so calm. He did what they wanted. I got scared and screamed and tried to run." Nina saw herself breaking cover again. Phantom bullets nipped at her. "They shot him when I screamed… It's my fault." Tears welled up in her eyes but she fought the urge to sob.

"I can't say I wouldn't panic a little myself if thugs threatened me. You didn't kill Michel, the men that wanted to rob you did."

"But if I didn't try to run …" A tiny whisper glided over the otherwise silent room.

"Michel would be happy that you didn't get shot."

"I did." Avril gave the doctor a guilty look. "But I lived."

The doctor's face shimmered as notes typed themselves in on the virtual terminal. "It sounds to me like you may be experiencing survivor's guilt."

"What?" Nina looked up.

"When a person lives through a dangerous situation but others, sometimes even total strangers, don't survive that situation, it can trigger feelings of guilt. You wonder "why did I survive?" or "why wasn't it me that died instead of that person?" Some feel that their life was less important than those that died. Others think that a higher power guides the hand of fate, or just luck they didn't deserve."

That made a lot of sense. Nina admitted to the doctor that she often wondered why she hadn't been able to die with him. The first two weeks, that was all she wanted.

"He's always in my thoughts. I wonder why I ran. Would he still be alive if I kept my cool? Why did we have to go there that particular night?" Her voice trailed off into a breathless whisper.

"Do you think Michel would be happy that you are still alive?"

The last look in his eyes was desperate fear for her safety. "Yes. I think he knows it was my fault he got killed, but he would never say it."

"Avril. Listen to me. The men that shot him are responsible for his death. You couldn't have done anything to change what happened. Those men might have shot you both even after he gave them what they wanted, who knows what they might have done to you. You have to open your mind to the thought that things happen for reasons we cannot explain. How would Michel feel if he could see you agonize over him?"

She wondered if Division 0 was right about ghosts. Could he still be here, watching? He got upset when other officers in her old unit teased her. He was protective, but not obsessive, and always seemed to know what to say to make her feel better.

"What if Michel could see you now, do you think he would enjoy watching you dwell in guilt and sadness with no way to communicate to tell you to stop?"

Avril looked up at the doctor with a wide-eyed stare. She pictured Vincent screaming at her trying to get any kind of words through. "I... No, it would be awful for him."

Dr. Khan folded her arms on the desk. "You shouldn't forget him, but now is when you need to begin putting your life back together. You should treasure the time that you had with him and keep him alive in your memories. Think about your future. If you spend the rest of your life in mourning for Michel and fill it with guilt and misery, what was the point of you surviving?" The doctor's voice softened. "I bet that he tried to protect you that night."

"Yes. He did." Avril nodded, crying into her hands. "I was so stupid."

The line between Nina and Avril was gone.

The doctor moved around and put her arm across Avril's shoulders. She urged her to let it out and cry until she felt better. "No one will ever take away what you had with him."

Avril looked up. She thought about coming clean and telling the true story, but changed her mind at the last second, not knowing how command would react to her visiting an external psychiatrist.

Nina found her composure a few minutes later and wiped her eyes. "How long is normal to dwell on this? I always think about him."

"Everyone deals with grief in their own way. There is no *correct* amount of time. Of course, if it persists at six months to a year, there may be an underlying pathology that we would need to investigate. You say it was about ten weeks ago? I would expect that you would be entering the coping phase by now. Does it feel like your grief is interfering with your ability to function? Do you have trouble getting out of bed in the morning or with your work?"

"No, not really, sometimes I have trouble falling asleep. When I'm busy, I'm fine." Avril looked at the paintings on the wall, wondering if somewhere a real office looked like this. "I think about him when I'm not doing anything else."

"Do you find it difficult to concentrate on anything else because you are absorbed in mourning?"

"No, I can do things I have to do... I just don't find anything fun anymore."

The doctor patted her on the shoulder. "I can see that your love for Michel is deep, but it does not sound like you are suffering from his loss in an abnormal way." She smiled with a mother's concern. "I'd like you to come back for a few sessions if you are up for it. I think you need to have some personal contact. It could be with me, with friends, maybe with some of the others in the program. I saw you speaking with Carl. You must have a way with people. He has not opened up to anyone else yet. I think you should talk to him. It will do both of you some good. You shouldn't isolate yourself with your thoughts and be alone."

Avril nodded. "I'll come back next week."

Dr. Khan smiled. "Good. You can stop by here almost any time. Unless I am with a patient in the real world, I am available here. If you need anything or have any questions, any strange thoughts, or anything at all you want to get off your chest, please contact me."

Avril stood up. "Thanks."

She stared at her toes darting out from under her dress as she walked, without looking up, to the door. Avril lingered outside New Hope, tracking cars that whooshed along the rain-soaked street. It was as though Cyberspace sensed her mood and changed the environment to suit it. With a sigh, she closed her eyes and let gravity take her. A pixelated mash of color surrounded her as several bright rings rocketed past her from behind. Rather than land upon the cold plastisteel ground, she fell into her office chair, surrounded by the glow of holo terminals.

The only sound was the whirr of the wire as it retracted into her deck.

NEEDLES AND HAYSTACKS

A curtain of holographic panels bisected her office along the axis of her desk. The opposite wall glowed blue from the security screens. Unlike civilian terminals, the back didn't display a mirror image of the front, but an opaque block of color. The wall behind her shifted with the contents of the screens, as did her face. Black carpet filled the room except for where a rectangle of grey appeared in the light sliding in from under the door.

The images of several men gazed at her. Farthest left, short brown hair wrapped around a thick, rugged face as if windblown. Anatoly Nemsky's face wore the same mocking smile it had since she first saw it. With each passing week, the old picture seemed to be taunting her more for not having been able to find him. It was a three-year-old image that Division 9 agents lifted from a Russian news agency, but it confirmed the brief glimpse of him she had gotten from the shuttle terminal cameras.

A man in early thirties with a few days' worth of beard appeared in the second panel. His hard brown eyes challenged Nina as if daring her to do something about him, his smirk a taunt that felt more mocking as time went on. A shadow spread over his scalp, low-shaved hair either black or brown. Itai Korin had been every bit as elusive as she had expected a former Mossad agent to be, and then some. Since his shuttle landed three months ago, traces of him had been sparse.

Vincent's portrait smiled among them as well. She had poked into the system enough to discover that someone altered her patrol route that night, and it hadn't been done on the orders of Captain Farris. He had denied knowledge of it when she paid him a visit some months later. Someone wanted her and Vincent to be in that alley, and it was a short leap of logic in her mind to connect that to the augmented monster. She was convinced someone targeted her or Vincent on purpose, but she couldn't find anything in his file that provided any sort of motive.

Nina's own background prior to that night also looked bland. The only motive she could come up with was abduction for ransom. She dismissed that theory almost as soon as she had thought of it, given the brutal beating she received.

The video taken that day by the Division 5 A3V proved difficult for her to watch, but she forced herself to be a spectator to her own murder, several times. She tried not to look at the gore spreading out from her body as it slid into frame, instead focusing on the silhouette of the man standing over it. A brief glimpse of his face flashed orange as the detonation of heavy weapons fire reduced his non-cybernetic arm to red mist. The blast had knocked him flat, but he got back up and loped off into the night. The crew had been more concerned with trying to save her life. Only two men gave chase, and lost him. Nina spent an unhealthy amount of time staring at that face, knowing that he was still out there somewhere. If she ever ran across him, she didn't want to miss the opportunity.

When she could no longer stand looking at him, she returned to Nemsky and Korin.

She replayed some of the video footage from the shuttle terminal. Lines of people milled along trying to get past the security checkpoints and baggage claim. She watched Itai go right on by like a common civilian, using the name Joshua Cohen.

Division 9 had become aware of his activities three years ago upon the first report of his involvement with mercenary operations. Contacting Mossad had been useless. The Israeli government denied anyone by that name had ever even worked with them. Standard procedure, she thought. They wanted to avoid an international incident at all costs. She found their lack of assistance vexing, but couldn't force their hand without more proof. The footage from the terminal represented the only credible sighting they had of either of them thus far. It made her feel like a rookie not to be able to track them down.

I've only been operational for six months. I am a rookie.

Next to Vincent's face, the file on 'The Silver' gleamed at her. The image of a magnificent white and chrome building rotated in place, a giant middle finger. It had only a small portion of its space devoted to human occupancy, most given to computer equipment and security systems. Their real world security force consisted of retired police and their network security people were considered the best-paid experts in the field. As far as anyone knew, the night of her attack was the only time anyone succeeded in breaching The Silver.

The idea that her ambush had been little more than a distraction for law enforcement wasn't new to her. She could find no logical reason why anyone would target her or Vincent over any of a dozen other officers in the area. Any injured cop would cause the same reaction. It just didn't seem plausible when combined with the alteration to her route.

She had gone over the file dozens of times looking for anything she might have missed. Again she pored over system logs, videos, and network traces, anything she could find regarding the event. She could stare at Itai and Nemsky for months and get no closer to finding them. It felt like they were ghosts. Knowing these two had eluded all of Division 9's resources for over three months frightened her with how dangerous they might be. No one else in the unit had any better luck, but that did little to temper her feelings of inadequacy.

A sudden intrusion of bright light made her squint, the reaction involuntary. Her brain knew nothing of cybernetic eyes. Image processors compensated for the unexpected environmental change in microseconds, separating her immediate supervisor, Harold Hardin, from the glow in the doorway. His hair, chestnut-brown greying to white, leaned over his left temple in a curled mass like some dead animal.

A coffee stain spanned the breast of his powder blue sweater and his nondescript tan slacks looked like they had never known the business end of an iron. He had been retired from fieldwork for quite some time, but the job was in his blood. She saw him at the office all hours of every day, as if he had nothing else to do. He had the look of a combat soldier trapped in a body too old to enjoy it.

"Still sitting in the dark?"

Where else should the dead dwell? "Yeah."

"What do you think you missed?"

A soft metallic *click* came from the door he nudged closed behind him.

"Missed?" Nina looked up.

"I can practically read those files by the patterns of light on your face. You think you're going to find something new the thousandth time going over them?" He sat in the chair facing her desk.

"I got nothing else." Frustration seeped out from under her calm. "No new traces, no sightings, no financial activity."

Hardin let his hands rest on his knees, fidgeting at a fold in his pants with his right thumb. "You know that no one in this building blames you for what happened to Dale."

"If I wasn't inside yelling at people for setting up such an amateurish—"

Harold cut her off. "Then you would have eaten that missile too. You think you would have caught it out of midair? You may be a top of the line combat doll but even you have limits."

Nina sighed. "I would have checked out the black van that sat there for twenty minutes with no one entering or leaving."

Hardin nodded. "Exactly. Why didn't agent Abrams investigate that van?"

Nina tapped the armrest of her chair. "He should have called it in."

"You're right." He nodded. "It was as much his fault as anything."

Blaming the dead for their own demise, no wonder people call you hard-on. "Look, Sir. That whole operation was a complete mess from the start. Did anyone take it seriously? I.M. Boring? Basket Weaving? Floyd's fucking bakery? Who comes up with this shit?" She calmed, voice dropping back to normal. "Still, you do have a point. Dale should have said something about the van."

"Some of the logistics agents involved were operating under the misconception that it was a training exercise and had a little fun with it. They have since been disciplined. However, it is a fact that the aggressors involved in that action were not related to the objective."

"You got something?" Nina's stare flicked from the screens to Harold.

"Indeed." He leaned forward, interlacing his fingers. "We traced the two shooters from the Imperial Hotel back through a known underground contractor to the WellTech Corporation. We think they targeted the individuals that left the hotel lobby shortly before the escalation to a fire event."

Fire event was Hardin-speak for getting shot at. He could make it sound dry and uninteresting, as if real people were not hurt or killed.

She perked up. "Are we acting on that information?"

"Not at this time."

"What?" Nina stood. "Dale is dead, Sir. We can't let them…"

"Hold on, Lieutenant." He raised a hand to her as if stopping oncoming traffic. "I have every intention of sending them a message. Once we know who ordered it, we will react accordingly."

She sank back into her chair. Unlike Eddie Alvin, at least the staff here had the couth not to taunt her for losing a second partner. "Understood."

"What have you got on our two European guests?" Bored with the crease, he picked at his sweater sleeve.

"We know they are both still in the city. We have had a few intermittent tags from sector cams, mostly in the southern third. Whenever the system red flags, we know about it, but the sightings are few and far between." She turned to scowl at the thin slits of night peeking between the closed blinds. "I spoke to a ticket agent at the shuttle terminal who remembered seeing Itai, but no one remembered Nemsky."

"I doubt anyone outside of the intelligence community knows who he is. People don't pay attention to what goes on apart from their own little world anymore." Hardin rubbed his chin. "I read your report about the incident and I remain unconvinced that Karl Warner is pulling the puppet strings here. He's a corporate playboy with limited experience in politics or international diplomacy."

He's gotta be involved, I just can't prove it. "I haven't seen anything but a few holo-vid calls. The times are short and we have no proof of them ever meeting. The content of the communication scrubbed as soon as the calls ended. It is possible they attempted to make contact with him and something went wrong. Or maybe they want us to think that there's no contact and they are keeping it off the grid."

"I can have some tech-fours keep watch on Warner's movements and raise an alert if he takes a shit sideways. I want you to focus on finding and eliminating the Korin and Nemsky problems. Both of these men are highly volatile and our information points to them acting as either mercenaries or idealists. We have nothing that indicates they are working on behalf of the ACC in any official capacity. Their intelligence value is low enough to where everyone will feel safer if you just send them to Miami."

Harold and his euphemisms, why couldn't he just say kill them? "There wasn't anything I could have…"

He held up his hand. "I'm not pulling you off the Imperial as a disciplinary action. It's a waste of your talent. Agent Cole is capable of running Basket Weaver. You're far too valuable an asset to have watching some German aristocrat pawing women in a hot tub."

She stared at him, wondering if he meant it to be as patronizing as it sounded. Everything about the Imperial Hotel had gone tits up. Nina felt like a helpless bystander six feet away from a car wreck in slow motion. A faint chime drew her attention back to the terminal. The parse of the Silver logs stopped at a section that Nina didn't remember. She leaned an elbow on the desk and swiped at the result page to make it larger.

"What is it?" Hardin got up and walked around.

Nina pointed. "A network trace. Scan found an IPv12 address fragment here that it missed before. Looks like the egress proxy on the Silver's primary barrier node *did* capture the intruder's deck upon disconnect."

Her fingers flew across the virtual windows. Text and images scrolled by as she tried to trace the address fragment.

"I don't understand how we could have missed that before. Division 9's been looking at that data for months."

Hardin squinted. "It's possible that the log file had been masked and someone downstairs just decoded it. Maybe there was active code in the file that had been concealing it?"

"I don't like it." Nina's eyes shifted to the cessation of movement in one of the sub screens. A swipe of her finger brought up a weary looking man in his later thirties with long curly hair prematurely grey. "DeWinter, please run an access validation on this file." Nina sent him the link to the Silver logs. "Make sure it wasn't recently edited."

"Yes ma'am." He nodded.

Another panel of shifting information stopped, border flashing. She tapped and it opened into a page of stats showing other network traces from the same source.

"Looks like a Teradyne systems silver series deck. Grade 3."

"Grade 3 silver series, ironic." Hardin chuckled.

DeWinter's apparitional head looked up. "No damn way someone pulled off the Silver Hack with a noob board like that."

"It has to be a falsified address tag." Nina poked at the trace and Joey Dillon's face appeared. "Probably has a Necromancer and wants to hide it. Look at that face, he's smirking like he got away with something."

"I doubt it." DeWinter shook his head. "If he wanted to avoid notice, he wouldn't fake it out to be such a shitty deck. He'd use something believable, maybe a grade six Alchemist or the equivalent. He's bragging. Uhm... I can't find any trace of edits, Lieutenant. Guess it was just a case of lazy eye."

"Thanks." She nodded at DeWinter, who hung up.

"Who is that?" Hardin leaned forward to read the information next to the picture.

"Joseph Dillon, 22. No listed address, but as white as he is, I'd have to say he's from Mars. I think I..." A red line left that window and opened another as the system matched his facial features. "...saw that face before."

"Whispercraft log." Nina recognized the contents of the new window right away. "Son of a bitch. That's one of the civilians from the Imperial!"

"That's more than a coincidence." Hardin nodded. "Go see what he knows."

"On it."

Harold went toward the door, looking back just as it hissed open. "You're doing well for a new agent. I wouldn't have given this to you if I didn't think you could handle it."

She stared at the shrinking rectangle of light as the door sank closed. It was unlike Hardin to be easy with praise, and it made her wonder if her body language called out for affirmation. Nina swiped her hand through the terminals, shutting down all the screens at once and pitching the room into darkness. A half a second later, the room formed in shades of green as her night-vision kicked on. She took her coat from the peg and put it on, staring at the sliver of light under the door. Dr. Khan's voice asked her if she wanted to hide in the dark or go out into the world.

It took a moment to answer.

Gradient green flashed back to full color as she entered the well-illuminated corridor. The scent of technology, coffee, and Chinese food mixed with the din of dozens of people at work. A display screen opened in her field of view with the results of a search she had started an hour earlier. It got a match on Carl's older son, Coe. He had a run in with Division 1 officers a few weeks ago, and their report connected him to a minor street gang—the South Fork Crew.

They made their hangout in an area of Sector 40 known as South Fork, named after the main road in that part of town. More time staring at Itai Korin and Anatoly Nemsky wouldn't bring her any closer to figuring out what they were up to, but she had a deck jockey to find now.

At least she could do something for her soul on the way.

THE CREW

The black unmarked slipped out of the parking deck into the street. She still felt strange driving. For two years, she had always let Vincent do it—a techie just along for the ride waiting for her time to be up.

"Guess I should get used to it."

Vincent's voice echoed over the interior. "You're not half bad at it."

Nina almost sideswiped a parked car as she jumped, careening into an empty space about two blocks away from the police complex.

Nina glared. "Who the fuck was that?"

Eerie silence hung in the air, punctuated by the sound of her breaths. After five long minutes, she gave up and pulled out into traffic. She engaged hover mode and pulled back on the control stick. The street fell out of the view screen as the mechanical whine of the retracting ground drive halted with a solid *thunk*. An instant later, more whirring as protective doors closed over the wheel wells. She leveled off at fifty feet, banking around a pair of century towers before accelerating to two hundred and fifty miles an hour.

Vincent liked to drive as though he performed for a crowd at an air show. Nina was conscientious in her handling of the vehicle, and her trip south remained uneventful. She saw no reason to risk crashing just for some phantom thrill. She missed the impish face he would make after pulling off some ridiculous stunt. Thinking of it put a lump in her throat that lasted most of the trip.

As she neared Sector 40, the inverted Y of the road that gave the area its name appeared as a dark line across the grey of the city. She landed among the steel and glass residence buildings, continuing through the area at a more modest speed. South Fork was home to working class people as well as those who teetered right at the tipping point between middle class and poor.

The armored door slid down and locked with a pneumatic hiss and a puff of coolant vapor. Her patrol craft was as unobtrusive as an unmarked police vehicle could be, but glaringly obvious as a hovercar. Bulky and wide, it had vents and bulges in places other cars didn't. Most of the criminal element could spot it as a police vehicle with ease, but that at least reduced the odds of someone trying to steal it.

Nina walked until she spotted a group of four young men wearing bright yellow bandanas. Each had a dark green jacket of various design with yellow sleeves and loose fitting pants. They leaned on a metal fence surrounding a decaying athletic court occupied only by a few metal cans that raced each other in circles with the wind. The two young men in the middle had mixed features while the far left one appeared white. A heavyset black man, about nineteen and short, stood at the other end.

Animations sprang up in her view, indicating pistols on all of them. The tall one toward the center had a submachine gun hanging over his shoulder on a strap.

She walked up as they chatted about the legal misfortunes of someone that went by the name of Darwin. Their conversation wound down one by one as each one in turn noticed her standing there.

The oldest, just right of center, glared. "You in the wrong part of town, Lily White."

A crisp breeze tossed her hair about. "I'm looking for the South Fork Crew. You them?"

The four exchanged looks. The black kid spoke first. "Somethin' ain't right."

The white one grinned. "She looks fine to me. Maybe she's here to audition."

"You got some balls. Comin' here alone and gettin' in our shit." The second kid to the left pointed at her.

She thought his face looked younger than the rest of him.

"Look, you boys are all pretty young. I'm looking into some of your crew that got themselves killed... I'm not here to make more bodies."

The white kid flapped his hands at her in mock fear. "Oh noes, she's gonna kills us."

Nina squinted at him, a look that made the fat kid take a step back.

"You best keep walking." The eldest pointed at her. "Be glad there's a lotta people around here or you'd be talkin' out a couple new holes."

"So you don't care that someone offed two of your guys? What, are all you gang types brain dead idiots that keep acting tough until there's a zipper over your face?"

"Yo... There somethin' wrong wit dis skinny little bitch. Look at her, she ain't even scared." The heavyset kid held his shaking hands up, stepping backward.

"What happens wit da Crew stays wit da Crew." Tall White flailed some kind of hand gesture in Nina's face.

"If one of you is volunteering to be an example, that guy is really starting to get on my nerves." Nina pointed at the white one. "Is he important? Would you miss him?"

"Dude, she callin' you out, bro!" The younger of the two men in the center shoved him.

"Damn bitch." He took a swing.

She caught his fist and held it with little effort. His face turned red as he struggled to force his punch past her grip. Nina lifted one eyebrow at him with an impatient smile.

"Are you done yet?"

The two in the middle edged for their weapons.

Nina flung Tall White into the fence with enough force to bend the bars and cause a cracked rib. He bounced away, landing sideways on the ground and moaning. She stepped forward, shoving the two in the middle onto their asses.

"What the fuck?" Tall White gurgled, spitting up a trickle of blood.

"You some kinda aug bounty hunter? We ain't got shit." The black kid edged further away with several rapid glances in a random direction.

"You should be so lucky." She flashed her ID. "Division 9, UCF Police."

The color drained out of all of them. Even street punks had heard stories about the cops that even other cops feared, the ones who kill instead of arrest. The three on the ground froze but the last standing member of their group had the paradoxical reaction of calming down.

The heavyset black kid took a relaxed step toward her, lifting his arms to the sides. "Why you in our claim? You D9's don't do streets."

"Dey also just fuckin' kill motherfuckers." The younger of the two in the middle blurted.

Nina used her NetMini to project an image of Coe and Arlon. "Their father wants to know what happened to them. I'm doing him a favor, off the books."

"Word is they walked out on a buffet, Z Bone took objection to their rudeness." The youngest answered.

"I'll assume that you aren't talking about food." Nina folded her arms.

Tall White shook his head. "Naa. It was their initiation. Couple of bitches came in." He coughed up more blood. "But we wasn't there."

"Of course you four weren't involved. What happened to the women?"

The oldest spoke up. "Naa we wasn't, just a small thing. Z Bone and his dudes, a couple other guys, and the two you're lookin' for. The girls are okay... just had a little trouble walkin' after." He seemed amused.

Nina shuddered under a wave of revulsion. She didn't feel right leaving these four off the hook, but killing them would be an overreach. *Div 1 is slacking off here. They should focus more on this sector than they do.* Nina made a note to herself to shake some trees once she got back to the office.

"Where can I find this Z Bone?"

All four remained quiet and exchanged looks.

"Trust me, when I'm done with him he won't be ordering any revenge on anyone. In fact, I suggest you forget about this crew nonsense and get yourselves to a vocational aptitude assignment center. It'll be better for your health."

"Ain't right to do him like that." The heavy one shook his head. "We're brothers."

"Just like Coe and Arlon?"

"Man, it ain't the same. They were prospects, not even in yet." His arms enhanced every other word.

"Do you really believe that? What do you think would happen if Z Bone got the idea in his head that he can't trust you? Do you think he'd come have a chat to calm his doubts or do to you what he did to them?"

They exchanged glances. The youngest one fidgeted.

"What if it was your brother that got killed?"

The oldest looked up. "This is our territory, Z rules here. If he catches us talking—"

"He uses you to catch bullets, catch shit from the cops, and to catch the heat for everything your so called crew does while he sits back and lives like a king. How do you have any loyalty for someone that exploits you like that?" She waved an arm at them. "Look at yourselves. Are any of you even twenty yet? Do you want to spend the rest of your life getting shot at so Z Bone can do whatever the hell he wants?"

The heavy one paced back and forth, shaking his head and staring at the ground.

The oldest sighed. "We been seen talkin' wit you. They gonna find out who gave it up."

"Who's they?"

"Crowbar and Jules. Z Bone's boys."

"Are they with him now?" She looked at the fat one.

"Yeah."

Nina smiled. "Then you shouldn't worry about them. Where can I find him?"

"Prince Harrington Arms, tenth floor." He stuffed his hands in his pockets and looked down.

Nina put a hand on his shoulder. "Go home to your family before you get yourself killed." She looked at the others. "That goes for all of you."

PICKING A BONE

Sheets of fake brick fell from the Prince Harrington like urban dandruff. The once-hotel succumbed to the creep of urban decline some decades ago when it the planners transitioned it to low-income housing. The ninth and tenth floor windows were gone, replaced with temporary plastisteel panels clamped down over scorch marks. Nina moved past dying hedges and up the sharp curve of grassy berm that framed off a large parking area with only two battered vehicles in it. She avoided stepping on anything that would make noise as she moved to the side of the building and into the alley beyond it.

The fire escape ended at the second story, a simple jump up and grab. The higher she went, the louder the music inside became. At the tenth floor, the driving bass line of Z-bone's music pounded dust out the gaps between the metal plates and the bricks. Persistent sonic vibration animated dirt on the metal walkway into a shimmering haze. Edging up to one, she opened the cover protecting its control pad, and keyed in the police override. It flashed acceptance and the bracing struts retracted, freeing it from the building. Repositioning one of these panels required two or three workers, but Nina moved it to the side without a sound, using one arm. The music intensified, a tangible force breathed in and out the open window in time with it.

She stepped into a dark, debris-packed room, focusing her attention on the corner where light pulsated around columns, and fragments of plaster danced on the vibrating floor. The entire tenth story had been gutted. What had once been individual apartments reduced to one large area separated only by the supports and piles of old furniture. Trails of small arms fire dotted the walls behind her, threading among scorch marks that appeared to be the aftermath of small rockets. A few scattered and charred bits of cyberware hinted that something heavy happened here. Creeping toward the source of the sound, she followed the darkest shadows on her way toward the activity.

The smell of a number of synthetic drugs hung in the air, soaking out of the simulated wooden furniture piled like gathered leaves. Cold dampness pervaded the room and the music was loud enough to make her brain throb in time with it. Through a gap in a pile of old tables, she could make out a large purple couch on the far side of a curtain of holographic light. The intangible display had been set to maximum size, reaching from floor to ceiling and almost twelve feet wide. Some manner of concert flashed about, absorbing the attention of three men. The one in the middle resembled Z Bone's ID photo.

He had short black hair and a thin beard, little more than an inch wide line of hair around the profile of his chin, connected to his sideburns. He looked Hispanic, and wore shimmering purple clothing and enough gold rings to make her wonder if he could even lift his hands. A faint blue box traced itself around his face in Nina's vision, and she ran his image against the police database.

She intended to perform a summary execution on this Z Bone, and wanted to make sure she got the right man. Division 9 seldom bothered with a piece of gang trash like this, but Carl Davies didn't deserve to wait until Division 1 got tired of re-arresting him.

The other two had the imperious presence of men used to doing whatever they wanted to whomever they wanted without repercussion. They both wore the yellow and green of the South Fork Crew, and nodded their heads in time with the music. An array of guns lay scattered around a table amidst a plethora of narcotics injectors. Two young women sprawled on the couch, one on either side of Z Bone.

The girl on the left appeared Hispanic as well, the one on the right an exotic mix. All either of them wore were crude collars made of bent rebar, connected by chain to a heavy ring in the floor. They stared into space, high on some unknown chem, and completely unaware. The sight of them chased away the last of her doubts about Z Bone's fate.

The image search came back with a positive match and an impressive record. She eased her sidearm out of its holster and her vision filled with combat assistants. Targeting crosshair, ammo counter, safety status, and a micro-zoom picture-in-picture of the target area, all transmitted wirelessly from the gun with 1024-bit encryption.

The holographic screen vanished the instant she commanded her eye to filter it out. She whirled around the column and swept her arm from right to left as fast as a punch. The gun fired by mental command the nanosecond the crosshair passed over each of the lieutenants' faces. Two shots so rapid sounded like her pistol had fired once. Bullets pierced the gyrating holographic singer, killing both men before Z Bone's conscious mind could process the sound of the gunshots.

Gore showered Z Bone and the two women. Blood spurted upward as the bodies fell away to either side. The massive handgun left little remaining of their heads. The women didn't react, though Z Bone screamed. He hadn't seen where the shots came from, as far as he knew, their heads exploded for no reason. He lunged for the table and grabbed a rifle. Nina sailed through the image of a near-naked dancer and landed on the table, one boot pinning the weapon in place. He looked up, still screaming. At the sight of Nina's head superimposed over a topless dancer, his face turned red.

"Who the fu—"

Nina's hand on the back of his head drove the rest of his outburst into the table. He bounced up with a bloody nose. She flung him around and away from the couch into a pile of stacked chairs. A torrent of dust billowed out as the human projectile crashed, sending splinters of wood and bits of cushion in all directions. Z Bone rolled into a crawl and struggled to get to his feet despite the pain. She walked toward him, pausing to turn off the throbbing holovid. The punishing music gave way to the gang lord's phlegmatic wheeze.

A half dozen other members of the South Fork Crew burst in a steel door at the edge of the room in reaction to the sounds of gunfire. Nina stalked Z Bone as he crawled away. Her arm extended to the right, firing into the group of gangers without turning her head. The small targeting window flashed red as one 15mm projectile after another penetrated multiple bodies each before stopping. The bullets aimed at the last two had enough spare energy to create spots of daylight on the wall behind them. Only one of the gangers had managed to fire, but succeeded only in spraying the man in front of him, the wall, and the ceiling on his spiral to the ground.

With the threat from the stairs reduced to a sliding pile of bodies, she put her sidearm away and the virtual readouts vanished from sight. She pounced on Z, grabbed his shoulders, and threw him to the side. His body spun in the air, coming to an abrupt halt chest first against one of the concrete columns in a cloud of dust and fragments.

He staggered to his feet, hand raised toward her.

"Wait..." He coughed up blood. "I can pay you... I can pay you more than whoever hired you."

"There are only two reasons you're still alive right now, Z Bone."

"Who are you, what do you want?"

The brothers' holographic faces appeared the air over her hand. "Coe and Arlon Davies."

"What about them little bitches?"

"I want to know why they're dead."

Z Bone made a dismissive wave. "They was rats gonna snitch for the cops. I don't abide snitches in my crew."

She circled him. "You know what's funny?"

"What..." A trail of thick blood drained from his lip.

"You killed them to keep the police away, but that is why I'm here."

"You?" He touched his fingertips to his chest. "You're here to fuckin' arrest *me*? What the fuck do I pay for?"

"My apologies, am I impinging upon an arrangement of yours?"

He shook a finger at her. "Damn straight, Collins makes sure we have no problems. You ain't arrestin' shit."

"Arrest? No. You're not worth tax credits. Do you like palm trees?"

He made an incredulous face. "Palm trees? Bitch, you craz—"

Nina leapt into a kick.

Her shin broke his right arm first, severing it at the elbow before crushing its way into his chest. The combination of strength and speed in her leg tore him in half. Blood went everywhere, including all over her. She stood there, staring at the floor, warm fluid dripping off her as though someone had poured an entire bucket of blood over her head.

I should have just shot him.

She had never before kicked an unaugmented human with her full power, and didn't anticipate the gruesome details of the result. After opening a comm channel back to ops, she requested a cleanup crew and a MedVan. While relaying the details, she snapped the collars off the women, who remained oblivious to her presence, so high they simply stared into space. She wanted to cover them, but all the clothing in easy reach, including her own coat, was soaked crimson.

Within minutes, a shouting match erupted downstairs. The remnants of the South Fork Crew had been waiting at the bottom of the stairs for whoever attacked them to walk down into their line of fire. The absence of gunfire gave Nina a little of her faith in humanity back, they didn't seem interested in a shooting match with the police.

Four sweeping cones of glowing dust swept into the room, cast by tactical lights carried by patrol officers in blue armor. They paid Nina little mind until they called the all-clear. Their sergeant approached her while two medics, a dark skinned man and an Asian woman pulling a hover-stretcher, entered.

Nina pointed at the stash of drugs on the table. "The two victims are on so many different chems I can't tell what."

"What the fuck happened to this guy?" One of the Division 1 officers looked up from Z Bone, backing away from the pool of blood expanding across the floor.

"He exercised poor judgment."

The cop cringed at the coating of blood on her. He declined to push the issue, knowing she had the authority to terminate just about anyone—regardless of social status. The only question was how much paperwork it generated.

Another of the officers walked over and saluted, having noticed her rank from the dispatch call. "Evening Lieutenant. For the report, is this an op you can talk about?"

"Nothing secretive, just doing Division 1's job for them. Z Bone killed a couple of innocent boys that tried to join this gang. I'm doing a favor for their old man on my own time."

The officer cringed. "I don't get what makes people fall in to these crowds."

"Afraid of being shipped off to colonies from the work aptitude program, probably." Nina watched the medics load one of the women onto the gurney and head for the stairs. "Maybe it's some kind of search for a sense of control over one's destiny." She walked over to the other and looked back at the officer. "I guess we gave up trying to understand that a long time ago."

A moan came from the pile of bodies in the stairs.

The other three officers swarmed over them, kicking weapons to the side as they dragged one living man out of the group and pumped a few stimpaks into him. He emerged part way out of his stupor and struggled, fighting as much as possible for a semiconscious man to fight. The cops rolled him over and restrained him as Nina carried the other limp woman down the stairs. She followed the medics to the waiting van and lowered her onto an open berth.

"You okay?" The female medic looked at Nina.

She smirked. "Aside from being covered in Z Bone, just peachy. Div 1 has this under control, I'm going to go clean up."

CLEANSING

L ight smeared past on both sides as Nina drove. She ignored the advert bots and other cars as everything blurred together into a singular mass that was the city. Her mind drifted through memories: a tea party with Nix, laughing with her grandmother, the first nervous day of university, and the first time she set foot on the police weapons training course. Everyone had hit the floor as soon as she touched a gun for the first time.

She imagined Nix the rabbit shaking his stuffed head and clucking his fabric tongue at the thought of the casual way in which she had just killed ten people. Somewhere in the back of her soul, old Nina cried at the sight of what she had done—of what she had become. Stoic to the world, she drove in silence. Her intellectual side said Z Bone and his inner circle brought harm to many, at the same time her mother called out into the dark asking if she was still Nina.

By the time she parked, the guilt she lamented not having felt earlier had come. She contemplated if taking him in alive would have made any difference, but the sad truth was that men like Z Bone knew how to game the system. If left to the Division 1 process, he would have been back in his throne room before the concert ended, probably with two new women.

She sent a feeler to Ops as she got out of the car, requesting an internal investigation of an officer Collins, attaching her recording of Z Bone's accusation.

Someone else can deal with that.

Pale green light saturated the interior of Andy's Dry Cleaning with a surreal glow that made her feel as though she stepped into a strange dream. Four old ceiling fans chopped the air, filling the room with a steady thrumming. A checkerboard of forest green and white tiles spread out in front of her. A middle-aged man with features mixed of white and Asian ancestry snored behind the counter. To his right, a huge room full of credit-operated machines. Murmured voices and echoing noises told her that someone used the facility.

Walking up to the counter, she knocked twice near the man's head. Andy flew to his feet with such a shock that he almost fell backward into a rack of plastic-wrapped garments on a track that snaked its way into the room through clear plastic slats.

"Hello!" He tried to sound awake and happy. "What can I help you with?" The squeaking of swaying clothing behind him accented his voice.

"Hi Andy. I need to clean this." Nina pulled off her coat.

Dark red lines streaked across the white counter when it landed.

The sight of it scared the man pale. "No trouble!"

Nina showed her ID. "No trouble."

His fear vanished into a broad smile. "You taller than I remember."

"Must just be the light in here." Her boots landed atop the coat. "And those."

The ballistic suit didn't leave her contours to the imagination, painting every curve with gloss black except for her head, hands, and feet. Eddie stared at his reflection in the material, mesmerized.

"Do you have a sink I can use?" Nina smiled at him.

Crimson spots formed one after the other upon the counter, falling out of her hair.

"In back, through that arch…" He pointed at a doorway and gathered what she had put on the counter. "Rush job?"

"Please." She turned for the door.

"That's ten credits more."

"Fine."

Andy's eyes lingered on her until she closed the door of the tiny bathroom. The space felt cramped, even for someone Nina's size, but it had a sink. The cold tile floor surprised her with its cleanliness. She wiped the blood from her face and dumped water over her head. The first cup ran into the sink as though she had poured blood over her head.

The process continued until the runoff was clear, barring a few threads of red in the water swirling down the drain. She snapped her head up and flung her hair back, launching droplets, and glanced in the mirror. She looked soaked and freezing, but bloodless—an improvement. A proper shower could wait a little longer. The suit kept the blood off her skin and came clean at the urging of some microfiber towels.

She tracked wet footprints as she went out front, sat on one of the benches and crossed her legs. The lobby, colder than the back room, tempted her to turn off her sensitivity to the environment. The front wall reminded her of home, floor to ceiling glass, only this place was at ground level. Huge holographic signs flashed to the left of the door, the source of the eerie light that turned her ashen skin a light shade of emerald.

Water dripped from her hair, leaving beaded trails along the black material. She studied her foot, hanging in the air. It looked so real. A tendon line rose out of her instep as she curled her toes and shapes hinting at blood vessels seemed to move under the skin.

This body felt strange. For one thing, her nails didn't grow. They remained the same perfect length, long enough to be a little feminine but not enough to get in the way of what she had to do.

She thought about what Dr. Khan said.

Did it really matter what her body was made out of? She still had her mind. The department shrink kept saying that. The mind and soul defines a person, and she still had those. Sensing a stare, she glanced at the archway past the desk. A tall, dark-haired man hovered in the door to the self-service machines, evidently checking her out since she'd sat down. The way he looked at her said he had no idea what she was.

Nina closed her eyes and tried to sense her falseness. By mind alone, she couldn't. She squeezed her arm, feeling the rigid plates. The synthetic skin felt natural, warm to the touch and soft. It offered a little give when she pushed. Below the skin, independent panels 'floated' on top of Myofiber muscles, shaped to resemble natural bundles. She inhabited a fair approximation of humanity, a hard athletic body far removed from the soft, delicate Nina Duchenne that dreamed of becoming a forensic technician.

Maybe it isn't that obvious. She bent forward with folded arms, looking up at the man. *Maybe I am still alive.*

He still stared, smiling. Just as she got it in her head to test the limits of her realness, a woman appeared at his side to ask him something. She tracked his stare to Nina and fumed, pulling him behind the wall into an argument. Nina flashed a guilty smile at the front windows, feeling human in spite of the argument she caused just by sitting there. Old Nina would have been mortified wearing such a tight thing in public. Now, it made her feel genuine.

Andy waved. "Miss?"

She turned her head, still smiling.

"Your order is ready."

She walked over and leaned on the counter. "That was fast."

"Special run... for police."

She caught him staring, and let him. "Thanks."

Back in the car, she placed a vid call to Carl Davies. A few beeps later, his hologram bust floated before her. A young girl's voice murmured from the background asking about homework.

"Carl?"

"Who is this?" He squinted.

"I'm Avril's friend, Nina. Would you mind if I stopped by?"

Carl coughed, stammering. "Of course... Please..."

"I'll be there in about ten minutes."

"Alright."

She found his address in the system. The sight of his file made her feel a degree or two less bad for ending Z Bone. Carl worked for the city, repairing PubTran taxis and trams, an honest man making an honest living.

Her car leapt into the air amid the rattling of laundromat windows. As she gained speed and altitude, the luminescent streaks of passing hovercar engines above changed from trails of light to wavering comets as she matched speed. Twenty minutes later, she dropped out of the hover lane and headed for Carl's building. A smile came at the memory of Vincent while she slipped between the floor and ceiling of the fourth story parking deck and settled into a spot. She still saw no point to the crazy aerobatics that he used to love. Despite her augmented reflexes making them trivial, being reckless created unnecessary risk.

A few minutes later, past walls of peeling paint and dozens of sleeping vagrants in the halls, she knocked on his door. He opened it before her knuckles could touch it a third time. Flannel pants and an old sweater gave away his getting ready to go to sleep when she called him.

"I won't keep you up long."

"Please, come in." He backed up, pulling the door open wider.

The room smelled of cinnamon mixed with the fragrance of a burning candle. The warmth inside made Nina's coat uncomfortable, but she kept it on. A girl of about ten peered out from behind the kitchen doorway, her half concealed face offering a shy smile.

Nina waved.

"Is that Tiffany?"

The girl darted out of sight. Carl looked at the doorway then back to Nina.

"Yeah." His eyes watered up. "She's all I got left."

Nina sat on the tan couch, noting how the interior of the apartment didn't fit the decay that hung over the rest of the building. This place was well maintained and homey, covered with holographic images of his children. Nina tried not to look at them. Carl sat next to her, shaking with anticipation.

"I found out what you wanted to know."

He grabbed her hand. "Please..."

Nina turned to look him in the eye. "It is true that they were involved with a street gang."

"Oh no..." His head sank. "I thought the police made that up."

"They didn't pass the initiation. They were unwilling to do what was asked of them."

"What was it?" Carl trembled.

Nina bit her lip and leaned in close to whisper. "They were expected to participate in a gang rape. I don't know who the victims were."

"Sweet Jesus." Carl's voice fell half an octave.

"They couldn't." Nina squeezed his hand. "They backed out. You raised good sons."

He smiled through tears, unable to speak.

"When they refused, the boss thought they were informants, and ordered them killed."

Carl's mouth opened with a few stalled attempts to talk.

"Z Bone it won't be ordering anything ever again."

"You arrested him?" He managed to choke out some words.

The emotion blanketing Carl pulled Tiffany out of the kitchen. She crawled up alongside her father and clung to his arm, trying to comfort him.

"Not exactly."

Carl shot her a look. "Aren't you with the police?"

"I am, but I'm not a patrol officer anymore."

"You don't carry yourself like a tech, and you don't look like cyber swat."

Nina stared at the eggshell colored walls. *No, I guess I don't carry myself like a tech anymore.*

"You're right. I'm with Div 9 now. I made sure he knew why I was there."

Carl blinked and let his weight fall into the sofa. His face showed the weight of ages had lifted.

"Bless you." He closed his eyes.

"I'll leave you to your daughter now." Nina got up and smiled at them.

Carl walked her to the door. "Thank you for givin' me my boys' dignity back. Just knowing what they did…" His gaze bathed her with gratitude. "I don't know how that girl convinced you to help me."

Nina looked into his eyes. "We both lost someone very dear to us."

A knowing look spread over him. "Avril…"

"Let me know if you need anything else."

As the door closed, Tiffany asked if the strange woman was here because of her brothers. Carl's inability to answer caused a lump in Nina's throat. Faces flashed in her imagination, Carl, Tiffany, Vincent, and the startled last look Z Bone would ever make.

Nina wanted to know why doing good felt so wrong.

AFTER AN HOUR STANDING AMID JETS OF WARM WATER IN HER SHOWER, NINA HIT THE button for a third round. Two cycles came close to making her feel clean of Z Bone's filth. She rested her weight on the handrail, gazing at her reflection. Streams of warm liquid trailed over her back and down her legs to the floor. The face staring back looked like the face she had always seen in the mirror. Perhaps it was true that some people deserved to die for the awfulness they visited upon others. She closed her eyes and basked in the nausea of her regrets. She could do it only for as long as she felt like this afterward. If ever she enjoyed it, she hoped she would be strong enough to get help before she turned into the same kind of monster that ended her dreams.

The sound of the VidPhone ringing pulled her out of the shower. She walked into the cold apartment air heading to her desk, pausing only to hang a dark blue towel around her neck to catch the runoff from her hair. A spray of water hit the floor around the chair as she fell into it. She hesitated a few seconds, finding it odd that someone would call her on that terminal and not her NetMini or her headphone.

"Duchenne." She answered while drying her hair, not looking at the screen.

"Hey there."

Vincent's voice turned her head like a slap.

She pulled the towel away from her eyes and stared. He smiled as if everything in the world was normal. The scenery behind him looked like his old apartment hadn't changed one bit. One of her bras still hung on the shelf above the bed.

The towel hit the floor as her arms fell slack into her lap. Tears streamed out of her eyes without sound. She touched the holographic image. His face distorted over her fingers and wavered back to rights. After a moment, the idea this may be someone messing with her gave her a voice. Someone could have lifted this from any of a hundred video calls.

"This isn't possible."

He laughed, the same charming chuckle that he always used whenever he found something she did to be cute.

"What's not possible, that I called you? Hey, I wanted to see if you were up for going out tonight. I have a surprise for you." He hinted as if he was holding something small just out of sight.

Nina jammed the button to kill the call. Ripples of sadness washed over her as the meaning of what he had said sunk in. How long had she fantasized about the time he would pop the question? That call looked like an ill-concealed setup for an ambush proposal. She folded her arms across her desk and let her head fall on top of them. Dr. Khan said it was okay to cry.

Her thoughts of what might have been took away any choice.

GHOSTS

Feeble light wavered from a single LED lamp over the door, just strong enough to illuminate their immediate surroundings. The hulking columns of scrap in the distance remained shrouded in blackness. The cloying chemical aftertaste of synthetic beer overwhelmed Joey's mouth, many times stronger in the wake of the last gulp. He chucked the empty while struggling to resist the urge to gag. It fell just short of the trash bin and landed on the wooden deck with a hollow, metallic *thud*. Kenny chuckled at the grimace.

A cool wind teased sporadic clatters, creaks, and metallic groans out from the graveyard of castoff technology, the echoing lamentations of machines long forgotten. The sight felt eerie, even to Joey. Scattered quasi-human shapes of old cyborg parts in the piled scrap painted frightening images upon the ground with brush strokes of shadow and highlights of glinting plastisteel.

The distant giggles of the girls inside the house lent a surreal wrongness to the nightmare factory Kenny kept in his backyard. The kids had become fast friends. Joey relaxed now that her need to cling to someone shifted off him.

Kenny lived in the south, past where the perpetual city fragmented into an uneven jigsaw of tiles. It ended in anything but a smooth line wherever different work teams made it farther than others before money ran out. Immense platforms one mile square and fifty meters thick, the tiles formed the base upon which the continuous urbanization lay. Depending on which political camp you subscribed to, the reason for the city's end varied. Cronyism, lack of funds, Earth First protestors, assassinations… no one really knew. The jagged edge hung in the distance like an incomplete model.

With so much loss of plant life from the war and construction, the government built massive air scrubbers to remove carbon dioxide and keep the atmosphere at a state somewhere short of toxic. Joey found it ironic that the technology used to turn far off planets Earth-like had become necessary to keep the Earth itself livable. From the deck behind the house, the outline of one such machine loomed. At night, it was little more than a large block of sky that lacked the usual glow of the smog. Lights flashed from the corners to warn hovercars and flying craft to stay away.

"I don't know how the fuck you drink this shit." Joey tried to will the taste out of his mouth.

Kenny laughed. "Two credits a can. Real beer's fourteen. The good shit's forty. That's how I drink it."

"Oh, like you're hurting for cash." Joey strained to grab the empty from the floor where it had rolled to a halt so he could throw it at Kenny.

Kenny pointed. "That may be true, but there's no sense pissing it away."

Joey laughed. "It's beer. We will be pissing it away."

The static of a failing transmission crackled out of Joey's NetMini. He took it out of his pocket, wondering who tried to call him at this hour. "Bad signal out here?"

Kenny shook his head. "Not usually, there's a relay station over there on that air scrubber."

"Joseph…" His father's voice leaked out from under the noise. "You must…"

"What the hell?" Kenny looked at his friend. "Is that your dad?"

Joey sighed. "No, it's not. Someone's fuckin' with me." He prodded the device with his thumb and froze.

"What is it?" Kenny walked over, his boots echoing upon the Epoxil planking.

"Nothing, it just turned itself off."

"It's off? Then why is it still crackling?" Kenny took a healthy swig from his beer.

Joey looked up. "We have to be near some kind of microwave transmission tower… Something so strong the mini's acting like a passive acoustic resonator."

"What?" Kenny slapped him on the back of the head with a playful swipe.

"An unpowered speaker." Joey smirked at him and fixed his hair.

Kenny pointed at the glowing white snow. "Will that put snow on the screen too?"

"…trying to kill them…" The voice crackled through the static.

"Now that's the same face I made the first time I saw a rad ghoul." Kenny laughed.

"It's just signal crossover on the circuit board. I gotta be so close to the transmission antenna the video circuit is catching overflow."

Both men jumped at a sudden motion in the darkness among the rows of scrap. As soon as they saw it, the NetMini went silent. Joey's gaze fell to the device before rising back to where he had seen the fleeting shadow. Kenny crept down the wooden steps and eased a handgun off his belt. He held it to the side, not quite aiming at anything.

"Who's out there?" Kenny half shouted. "Show yourself."

Joey readied his gun and held it with both hands. "Does that ever work? Does anyone really ever just walk out and say 'Damn, ya got me?'"

Kenny let his middle finger rise off the grip of his weapon, making Joey grin.

"Think it's one of the Discarded hunting for scrap?" Joey moved to the deck railing and aimed toward that spot.

"Probably." Kenny sidestepped to the left, circling for a better view into the aisle between the rows of piled metal. "Rather it's that than my first thought."

"What was your first thought?"

"You don't want to know."

Joey rolled his eyes. "Don't tell me you believe in that ghost horseshit?"

"Let's just say that I keep an open mind."

Joey shook his head and laughed.

Kenny crept to the edge, swinging around it to aim at a fragment of tarpaulin lofting in the wind. One of the cords that had held it down over an old hovercar drive unit had snapped. Kenny shook his head at Joey and put his gun away.

"Just a damn tarp." He tied the cord and went back to the porch.

Joey exhaled and closed his eyes. He didn't want to admit it, but his NetMini had been off the whole time. Even if this area did have good signal, he had no explanation for what just happened. He had the security option set to block automatic power on, plus he had never seen one display snow. Whatever happened was well past Joey's comfort level. He declined another synth-beer and walked back to his chair. Just as he went to sit, the door slammed open.

He jerked his pistol from his belt to aim, a reflex at the sudden loud noise. His aim never made it to the door. Kenny lunged and lifted his arm straight up. As the shock faded, he realized a terrified Hayley stared at him.

One of Alyssa's nightgowns hung almost to the floor on her. The scent of new nail polish surrounded her, corroborated by the sight of pink toenails. She ran and grabbed Joey around the chest, trembling hard enough to make him shake. He put the gun away and patted her on the back, giving Kenny a "what am I supposed to do?" wince.

Kenny leaned close to her. "What happened?"

"There's someone in the house." She squirmed around Joey to put him between her and the doorway. "I heard him when I came out of the bathroom."

The kitchen looked dark and quiet past the open door.

The men exchanged a glance before Kenny spoke again. "Stay with her."

He raised his weapon. The faint chirp of a firing circuit turning on felt so loud against the silence that he cringed, fearing it would alert the prowler to his presence. He stepped into the kitchen, sweeping the gun left to right. The kitchen looked clear, as did the hallway beyond it. Nothing appeared disturbed. Stillness had the room well in its grasp. The tinny sound of music leaked from the closed door at the end of the hall. Kenny shook his head at Alyssa turning her headphones up too loud again.

Despite his best attempt to be quiet, the heels of his boots scuffed over the kitchen floor as he crept into the hall. From the archway, he had a clear view of the living room straight ahead and the hallway to the right that led to the bedrooms. Joey brought Hayley inside and closed the door, in case the prowler had gone around back. He guided her by the shoulder into a crouch behind the island counter. As she lowered herself, she pleaded with him not to leave her alone.

Joey stayed with her, gun aimed over the counter. Kenny edged into the hallway, seeing nothing out of place among the glow of white walls and moonlight. Fear mixed with the cold kitchen floor upon her legs made Hayley shiver and rattle some standing jars of cooking oil and spice. Kenny whirled at the sound. Joey put a hand on her shoulder in an attempt to calm her.

Kenny gave him a meaningful look and let the air out of his lungs. He headed down the hallway toward the bedrooms. The carpet muted his footfalls, giving him confidence that he would surprise an intruder. Without warning, the sound of automatic gunfire erupted from the living room, loud enough to rattle the kitchen windows. Hayley's terrified screams echoed in harmony with a woman's voice crying out in agony as the gunfire came to an end. Joey's foot slid away from him as Hayley grabbed him with both arms. If not for his lean upon the counter, she would have pulled him straight off his feet.

Kenny dove back in the direction of the living room. The *whump* of his body hitting the ground broke the silence. He crawled forward, whirling to aim into the room, but it looked empty.

Hayley's whimpering breathing battled the muted headphones.

The soft blue glow in the hallway flooded with yellow light from Alyssa's room as she opened the door. Bopping her head in time with the now louder music, she walked out in a shin-length nightshirt bearing the image of a burning male silhouette with a scrap of wire dangling from his head, and purple socks. Seeing her father on one knee aiming a gun around a corner made her give him a look as if he were a crazy person.

She pulled her headphones out. "Dad? What the fuck is wrong with you?"

Kenny waved her back into her room. She read the worry in his eyes and a look of fear spread over her. Before anyone else could make a sound, a strange man's voice screamed from the back end of the living room.

"Nina!"

Joey retrained his weapon at the sound by the front door. Kenny waved Alyssa toward him and pointed at the kitchen. She ran and slid around the corner, almost falling into the refrigerator when her sock-covered feet met the tile floor. Joey caught her around the waist with one arm and slid her into Hayley. The two girls fell into each other and stayed low. Alyssa helped herself to Joey's other sidearm, making him chuckle.

"Just don't shoot me in the ass." He winked.

Joey took a step to follow Kenny but Hayley grabbed his leg, staring up at him with tears flowing down her face.

"Stay down." Joey whispered. "If someone's there, I don't want Kenny taking him on alone."

Kenny edged past the couch, heading for the front door. A plastic fork hiding in the carpet splintered into oblivion as he stepped on it.

Everyone jumped.

A deep laugh with metallic undertones bellowed out of the same spot, trailed by the disturbing sound of squishing and crackling as if flesh and bones tore apart. The laugh caused Kenny to roll behind the couch and Hayley to make a noise so pathetic that Joey backed up and let her cling. Joey didn't react to the sound. Fear that didn't thrill him made him seem calm.

The unfamiliar male voice again came, gurgling as if trying to speak with a throat full of fluid, a series of sputters and guttural noises that ended with a gasp of finality.

"Vincent!" A strained female voice yelled, breaking into sobs.

Kenny popped up and aimed over the couch, seeing nothing. With his gun leveled ahead of him, he walked sideways toward the hall.

He nodded at the front door. "Sounds like it's out front."

Joey got up to follow. Under protest, Hayley shifted her grip to Alyssa.

"Shh. I'm not letting Kenny go in alone. If you hear shots, go out back and hide in the scrap."

Kenny hit the wall at the far end of the living room shoulder first, and took several breaths before he spun around and aimed. He sighted down an empty hallway at his reflection in the glass of the closed front door. Nothing there but a few pairs of old boots and Katherine's transparent umbrella propped up against the wall.

"Just stay down! Backup is on the way." The same voice that a moment ago gurgled to death filled the room.

Kenny spun on his heel and aimed behind him. Joey turned a few shades paler in the harsh light from Alyssa's bedroom.

"That came from behind me." Kenny's expression changed from trepidation to confusion.

Both of them looked down at the same time, in the same way, and their eyes met at the Teradyne Silver Series – Grade 3 upon the couch. They crept up to it, Joey circling as Kenny put his gun away. Three points of light gleamed in the dark. The deck was on, but had no active holo-displays.

"You think this is pretty funny, eh?" Kenny glanced at the deck.

Joey made an innocent face. "I didn't do a damn thing. Fucker was off last time I saw it."

The near deafening sound of a ripple of gunfire erupted from the deck, the sound intense enough to vibrate the air in the two men's lungs. After it came a feminine gasp and fluid-laden breathing.

Joey punched the deck twice and the lights went out. "Serious. I didn't."

"Is this your idea of ghosts?"

"Kenny, if I was doing this I'd have stopped when I saw Hayley freaking out."

"Girls, it's okay." Kenny called to the kitchen.

Two frightened faces followed an army of little fingers over the top of the counter.

Alyssa handed Joey back his gun and grabbed on to her father, trying to act less scared than she felt. Hayley stood a few steps back with an awkward look. Arms folded across her chest, she continued trembling. Joey felt like a dick for hesitating, seeing the way she stared at Alyssa with her dad. He didn't want a kid yet, at least not without having the fun of making it first. With a sigh, he went over and embraced her.

"Normally I'd be blaming you for this." He smiled at her.

She mumbled into his chest. "For what?"

"Those sounds came out of the deck." He pointed at it. "There was no one here."

"What?" Alyssa looked up at her father.

"Hell if I know. Sounded like sound bits from some kind of slasher holo." Kenny patted her on the back. "It was fake, hon. Nothing to worry about."

Alyssa exhaled hard, glaring at nothing in particular. Hayley seemed rattled well beyond what a simple explanation could repair. Joey wondered if she overacted just to be able to hold onto him longer, but his mind wandered over other topics at that moment. If Cleopatra didn't make these voices or simulate his dad, someone else did. A blinking red light drew his attention to the deck, to a warning about heat. Something stressed his deck's processing power beyond its normal operating tolerances.

Up until discovering the deck as the source of the noise, Joey found his mind running away in search of a paranormal explanation. The heat alarm pulled things squarely back into the realm of reality. Other hackers could force their way into a deck even when powered off. Remote boot was ancient technology incorporated since the first days of cyberspace. To get into someone's deck uninvited was almost as difficult as punching a VidPhone with a closed fist and expecting to dial the number of a specific person.

Kenny patted Alyssa on the shoulder. "Why don't you two go try and get some sleep?"

"Sleep? After that? Yeah right. Maybe after a few shots."

He smirked at her. "We've had this talk. No booze 'til eighteen."

Alyssa sighed, gathering Hayley's hand. "Come on. Fine, but I can't promise sleep."

The girls wandered into the back.

"You talk to her yet about a quick run?" Joey kicked off his boots and moved the Teradyne to the table.

"Yeah. She wasn't thrilled about it, but since someone's trying to kill you, she's okay spending a few days at a neighbor's place while we go."

"You must owe them a lot." Joey smiled.

"I've known Mr. and Mrs. Rodriguez since I was a kid. He owns a store a little bit down the road. That's how it is down here, everyone does for everyone."

"Guess you can do that when there's not a thousand people living within a hundred feet of your apartment." Joey laughed.

"Yeah, that helps."

Joey reclined on the couch as Kenny went down the hall. He interlaced his fingers behind his head, staring at the moonlit ceiling. He wanted to sleep, knowing the Badlands waited in the morning, but too many thoughts spun around in his mind. He tried to ascribe cause and purpose to the strange audio. After a half hour of failing to pass out, he rolled on his side and tapped at the deck's controls.

A quick diagnostic process found nothing awry and access logs showed an external audio stream had been played into his deck from a source that four consecutive attempts to track down couldn't reveal. The audio had a lot of encryption that the deck had been forced to unwind in real time. The heat alarm made sense. Joey grumbled at the old trick, a neophyte hacker attempt to kill a deck with a processor meltdown. Newer model decks had hardware-level fail-safes to resist the technique because it had become so pervasive about ten years ago.

He couldn't understand why someone would even bother trying to use such an old attack. It wouldn't have any chance of working. Even in a worst-case scenario, the deck would terminate all activity before the processors cooked. Either someone thought he had an ancient deck or someone was an idiot.

The first option seemed illogical and the second a fallacious assumption. An idiot wouldn't be able to find his deck in the first place. The scan created more questions than it answered, and brought Joey no closer to sleep than he had been an hour before.

He buried his face in the back of the couch, trying to stop thinking.

PERMISSION

K enny's boot knocked on Joey's head, the past few hours gone in what felt like seconds. He moaned into the back of the couch, protesting until Kenny lifted him into a sitting position. Joey squinted, trying to keep the evil light from his conscious mind.

"What the hell, do you have any idea what time it is?"

"Do you want to have any daylight left by the time we get out there?"

Joey slumped forward, catching his head with both hands. He tried to wake up, though his body wasn't ready to move under its own power. "What's that smell?"

"Alyssa cooked breakfast." Kenny leaned in, whispering. "Try not to cringe too much."

"Huh?" He twisted his palm back and forth in an effort to rub the sleep out of his right eye.

"Since we had a talk the other day, she's been trying to help out instead of just being a pain in the ass."

"It can't be worse than what I'm used to." Joey stretched, wringing the last vestiges of sleep from his muscles.

Breakfast was edible but little more could be said for it. Kenny smiled despite it. Joey ate food that roaches refused to touch and sprinkled sincere comments about how good it was between bites. He enjoyed the food, as did Hayley, who seemed thrilled to eat something different from the same packetized crap she had been surviving on for almost a year. Kenny bought vat-grown or hydroponic, not trusting reconstituted OmniSoy.

"This is awesome." She grinned at Alyssa.

The older girl blinked at her with distrustful brown eyes. "Mm hmm. What kind of horrible crap do you usually eat?"

Alyssa's taste buds still worked and she remembered her mother's cooking and had a good idea of how her efforts compared. She pushed eggs around her plate with a hunk of toast, guilty for shunning her mother's attempts to teach her.

"OmniSoy." Hayley made a nasty face.

"What the hell is that?" Alyssa looked up.

"It's a little packet of protein gel. You put it in a reassembler and the machine turns the goo into whatever you want." Kenny pointed at a small appliance on the counter with a complicated control panel.

From the look on Alyssa's face, Joey knew that the device had never been used. Hayley blinked at Kenny, horrified.

"You weren't eating it straight out of the pouch, were you?" Joey read her look.

"Yeah." She looked down at a plate full of scorched bacon.

The others shared a combined wince at the idea of slurping down the flavorless snot-like paste. It would sustain you, but the sensation of consuming it was repugnant. Joey interrupted the shared moment of disgust by pointing out the window at a passing ad-bot. He jumped from his chair, ran to the living room, and powered up the holo bar. Kimberly Brightman's face filled the living room. Donna George rambled, halfway into a well-rehearsed performance about how thankful everyone was for the junior reporter's safe return.

Joey smirked with contempt. "Damn, what a bitch."

Kenny appeared in the doorway, bacon crunching. "What's lit your ass on fire?"

"I found a video of that bitch bragging about sending the other woman out there on purpose just to get rid of her."

"Be funny if that found its way to the airwaves." Kenny chuckled and returned to the table.

"Yeah... You know it would." Joey was saving it for some kind of payoff, but now his antiestablishment nature made him want to spite the six-foot talking head.

He could always hack the NewsNet and just broadcast it. Any deck jockey of reasonable skill could get into that network, almost joke easy. He smiled, thinking of how he could still monetize it in a less scummy way by selling the footage to the tabloid corp.

The screen cut to Donna George standing in the city with a crowd of people and police vehicles in the background.

"In other news, local technology entrepreneur Dyson Yan was found dead in his home late last night. Sources indicate that he received a lethal jolt of electricity while connected via interface plug to cyberspace. Police are refusing to speculate about the cause of this event and have initially labeled this as a suicide based on evidence they are not releasing to us at this time. If you remember, it was only six months ago that Lauren Yan, his sister, lost her life in an unexplained hovercar accident.

"Many believe the death of Mr. Yan is related to the now-famous self-immolation of Kyle Blank, whose"—an animation of a dancing, burning man with a wire coming out of his head played on the screen—"spectacular suicide became a cyberspace phenomenon a little more than year ago.

"Don't forget to tune in tonight at eleven for a special report on hovercar safety systems: is your life really in good hands, or have companies been cutting corners at risk to your life?"

Joey squinted at the screen. That sounded a bit too much like black ICE. The police would call it a suicide even if they knew what happened. Civilization would screech to a halt if people became afraid to use their plugs.

"Here with me now is Doctor Preeti Khan, who had been treating Mr. Yan for depression since his sister died. You also are on record as working with another man who met a similar end, Kyle Blank, some months ago." A split window opened with the reporter on one side.

"Miss George, you know I cannot discuss confidential patient information with you. What happened with Mr. Yan and Mr. Blank is tragic, but I'm afraid there is nothing I can offer you. It's protected by confi—"

"You are the proprietor of a grief counseling center that operates primarily from cyberspace?" The reporter looked down at her notes for a second before continuing. "New Hope services?"

"That is correct."

"Police have indicated that Mr. Yan spent a lot of time there as of late."

Doctor Khan glowered. "If you ask me something I can answer, I will be happy to talk to you, but I cannot break patient confidentiality."

"Well, there we have it. Is New Hope contributing to suicide?"

The doctor appeared to be yelling, but her audio didn't come through. The split screen view slid off the display, leaving only Donna George's smug face.

Joey shook his head. Once again, the news repaid someone for not giving them what they want by smearing them. His brain clunked to a halt when a familiar old man wandered out of the crowd behind the reporter. William Dillon checked out storefronts and looked around at the tall buildings. Joey, not breathing or blinking, watched his father navigate the crowd until he disappeared off the right side of the image.

Whoever you are, I will find your ass.

Joey stormed across the kitchen on his way to the back porch, tapping furiously at his NetMini's holo-panel.

"Be right back, gotta make a call."

Kenny looked at the two girls. "Hon, are you packed yet?"

Alyssa leaned out of the way to let Joey pass. "Mostly, what's wrong?" She continued putting dishes into the machine.

"What do you mean?" Kenny walked over and helped load it.

"When you go out there, you always jump around like a big kid on his birthday. It's like you don't want to go this time." She smirked, watching Joey pace back and forth on the deck outside. "Is he okay?"

"I'm not going for fun this time, some people are trying to hurt Joey, and going out there is the only way we can make it stop." He kissed her atop the head. "I don't really want to go this time. I'd rather be here for you."

She smiled despite tears. "I understand, just…" She choked up. "Don't get hurt."

"I'll be as careful as I can." He squeezed her before reaching for his NetMini. "On that note… Let me better our odds."

Alyssa remained quiet as her father spoke to Eldon and talked him into helping out. He'd be there in twenty minutes. She blushed at the sound of his name.

"I know I said I'd bring you next time, but some people are trying to kill Joey and they might be waiting for us out there." Kenny ran a hand over her head.

"It's okay… Thanks for asking me about it." She tried to smile, but couldn't force it genuine. "If I wanted you not to go would you have stayed home?"

He put a hand on her cheek and looked right into her eyes. "Yes."

She hugged him. "Someone's gotta watch Hayley, I guess I'll stay behind."

Kenny ran over the trip in his head, thinking about the terrain and the route. "Best case, about four days. Worst case is six or seven if the truck takes a dump and we wind up having to walk back."

A train of delivery bots glided by in an aerial ballet as they left their parcels in a neat row, supplies for the trip. Alyssa went to finish packing and Hayley stared at her reflection upon the surface her NetMini's dark screen. She looked on the verge of crying.

"What's wrong?" Kenny took an adjacent chair.

She picked at the small raised button on the side of the device, the only physical control it had. "I should go home before Daddy gets mad at me."

Kenny had a feeling she didn't seem afraid of getting in trouble. "Your dad called you?"

A tear rolled out of her eye. She shook her head to indicate the negative.

"Why don't you call him and make sure it's okay for you to stay with us?"

She looked at him for a moment, then back to her NetMini. Wiping her face with the back of her forearm, she hit the button and the screen lit up. A few swipes of her finger later, she placed a call. It rang itself to vid mail. Hayley blinked. That never happened before. With mounting panic, she redialed, hands shaking. Seconds before dumping to mail a second time, a garbled image formed of Jacob Roth, the hologram crisscrossed with lines of static.

"Sorry sweetie. They're working on the network here, there is a lot of interference." Her father, busy as ever, offered the briefest of smiles before glancing back at his work.

"Daddy? Member I said that some men broke in at home?"

"Yes I do sweet"—the image faltered out, garbling back together a few seconds later—"patrolmen to check the place out, they didn't find anything. Are you feeling alright?" The holographic head froze in place as if stuck, moving in a series of short slips before it reanimated.

Hayley's eyes ran with tears. "I'm not lying."

Jacob Roth pixilated into cubes, his head reformed facing her—"bullet holes in the wall. There's a new door. I believe you."

She tried to get her voice back from the cave of sadness where it hid. "Can I stay at a friend's house for a couple of days?"

"Who is this friend?"

"Her name's Alyssa."

The hologram vanished, replaced with a blue bar bearing white letters: 'synchronizing.' A few seconds later, her father appeared in wireframe. "...ow old is she?"

"Fourteen. She's real nice and her house is big. Her dad's nice too."

The image restored itself as Jacob adjusted his glasses. He spoke for a minute or two to someone in the background in a low murmur that didn't come through the vid call. His look gave Kenny the impression he wanted to rush her off the phone. "That's fine, dear. Call me if you need anything."

"Um. Okay." She let the NetMini fall from her fingers to the table.

Kenny had a strange feeling about the whole situation. He would never let

Alyssa stay with total strangers even at fourteen, much less Hayley's age. Of course, Alyssa did accuse him of being overprotective.

"Why don't you go with Alyssa and help her get ready. Ask her if you can borrow a few days' worth of clothes. I'll be damned if she doesn't have them to spare."

Hayley slid out of the chair, new shoes squeaking along the kitchen floor. The sound vanished into the carpeted hallway as she rounded out of sight. Within a few minutes, the voices drifting back made it seem like Alyssa had lifted her mood.

"Time to pack the truck..."

ONCE MORE BEYOND

Kenny looked up from the bed of the truck as a metallic *thud* echoed over the yard. Eldon's helmet peeked over the gate, his hoverbike lifting him just enough to see over it. Kenny jogged to the control box. His effort to navigate a shower of gravel that pelted him in the shins looked like a drunken attempt at dancing.

Eldon eased the bike around the truck and down onto a trio of landing struts that extended as it powered off.

"Hey man. What's goin on?"

"You got a hoverbike but you make me open the gate?" Kenny shook his head. "Joey got himself caught up in some kind of shitstorm. He's waiting for everyone to get here before he explains it."

"Don't wanna be rude, just come in over your wall and shit." Eldon chuckled. "That can get a man shot."

A black hovercar whizzed by overhead and turned around on a direct path for the scrapyard.

"Speaking of which…" Kenny squinted into the sun, watching it.

"Masaru doesn't make me run over here to open this thing."

Eldon waved his arm. "I rest my case."

The car settled down amid a cloud of cryonic fog, an onyx set in a bed of cotton. Bands of early morning sunlight glinted over the doors as they opened upward with a hiss. Masaru and Katya got out and walked over.

"Masaru, Katya, this is Eldon Church—Eldon, This is Masaru Kurotai and Katya… um…"

"Volkov." A pleasant smile hovered for a moment before her usual neutral expression returned.

Eldon nodded at them in turn, as Kenny beckoned Joey over. He came trotting over to the group, wearing a big grin, and shook hands with Eldon.

"Hey guys, thanks for coming. I'm sure you're all wondering what the fuck is going on about now so…"

"Yeah pretty much," said Eldon.

"Couple of days ago, Cleopatra got into a military intelligence network with the help of some other hacker. For reasons I can only begin to guess at, she made it look like I did it." Joey paced back and forth. "I'm not sure what kind of data was taken, but somebody's gotten pretty pissed off."

Eldon frowned. "Nothin' good'll come out of that."

Masaru folded his arms. "This Cleopatra seems to be causing you a lot of problems. We should send her a message."

"About that…" Joey chuckled. "Um… Yeah… I'll get back to that. I know you're not a big fan of C-Branch Eldon, but I think one of them gave me something."

Eldon took a step back. "They're setting you up as a blame catcher."

"If it makes you feel better, someone killed him as soon as he gave me the holodisk. The last thing he said was something about Mayberry."

"The Mayberry incident?" Masaru spoke up.

"No idea. Maybe he was gonna say that. He kind of got interrupted by his head exploding."

"Never heard of it," said Katya.

Masaru cleared his throat. "Seven years ago, WellTech Corporation began marketing a new kind of companion doll made in the image of a child anywhere from eight to twelve years old. They sold them as artificial siblings, companions for the elderly, or substitute kids for those who couldn't have their own."

"Yeah, I heard about those." Eldon nodded. "Damn creepy fuckin' things. They look too real. Always made me think they'd go psycho and kill you in your sleep."

Kenny shook his head. "There's so many real orphans, why bother?"

"That requires background checks and such," said Eldon.

"They act too real as well." Masaru nodded. "The HLM decided to protest these dolls, saying the company went too far playing God. They said cyberware was already well on its way to making humanity extinct, and this was just another step down that road."

"HLM?" asked Katya.

Eldon spat to the side. "Human Life Movement. They're a paramilitary group that thinks cyberware is a tool of the Devil. I had a few scrapes with them when I was still on active duty. Most of the time, they're just a bunch of rich kids with nothing better to do with their parents' money. Of course, you also get the occasional merc that has some training, but for the most part, they sit around and protest and experiment with chems while singing songs about the evils of robotics. Think of them as the bastard offspring of religious wingnuts and fringers."

Masaru nodded. "The new model was a leap ahead in simulated reality, next to impossible to tell apart from an actual child unless you got inappropriate with them. Let's just say that they are not anatomically correct. Also, their AI is not fully self-aware. They don't think for themselves, they just run action modules based on how the engineers felt a typical child would react to a given situation."

"That's just a little awkward…" Kenny winced.

"Well, they are programmed to be unable to lie if they are asked if they are a WellTech RealLife doll."

"Oh, like programming can't be changed." Joey laughed.

Masaru glared at the interruption. "The HLM seized on these dolls being 'too real' and stirred up a wave of panic that the government wanted to control how people had children."

Kenny looked at the clouds. "Yeah, I remember that now... Everyone went on about how they would gene match you to the perfect wife or husband and it would become illegal to marry anyone else. According to the conspiracy wonks, those kid dolls would help people cope if you lost the genetic lottery."

Eldon made a dismissive wave at Masaru. "Most people I know thought it was just a bunch of bullshit. They can't control street drugs and they're going to try and put a leash on your dick too? I don't see it working."

Masaru waited for the laughter to subside. "The HLM scared enough people to get a groundswell of interest and new recruits. The police sent notices to all technology companies warning of potential terrorist attacks. At least, until the Mayberry incident put an end to the HLM's popularity."

"What the hell was it already?" Katya snapped.

"Two HLM associates sprayed an EduTran with automatic weapons fire near Mayberry Park in Sector 310."

"Oh my..." Katya looked horrified.

"310? Isn't that near the foothills in the east? Rich bastard land." Joey smirked.

"Yep." Masaru's distaste for the poor dueled Joey's contempt for the rich in a stare. "One of the injured boys was the son of a WellTech executive."

"That's awful." Katya sighed.

"At least they chose a rich sector." Eldon grumbled. "The EduTrans up there have armor plating."

"The only fatality was some poor bystander that caught a ricochet, but three of the children were crippled, one paralyzed from the waist down. Kind of ironic actually."

"How the fuck is that ironic?" Kenny glared at Masaru's clinical tone.

"The shooters claimed to be trying to destroy a shipment of WellTech dolls, and were unaware they shot real children on their way to school. The anti-cyberware crusaders caused half a dozen kids to become dependent on cybernetics in order to continue to lead normal lives."

"Okay, that is ironic." Katya nodded.

Joey paced. "That couldn't have gone over well for the HLM. I don't see how this comes back to me."

"Not at all. Most of their newfound support left them. Even their leadership, who are notorious for being secretive, wasted no time turning over the two men involved. The police became suspicious at how readily they capitulated."

"That sounds too perfect. That's the kinda shit C-Branch would set up." Eldon spat again.

"Maybe they were as horrified as everyone else and wanted to do the right thing?" Kenny lifted an eyebrow.

"Or they had another agenda." Katya scowled.

"Who knows?" Joey shrugged. "All I know is that a guy got his head blown off giving me this holodisk he said was connected to the Mayberry incident. The only thing on it is a cipher key and some coordinates in the Badlands. My guess is there's some data out there that this thing will unlock and someone's trying to kill me to stop me from finding it."

"That's tragic." Katya's sarcasm hung in the air.

Joey stuck his tongue out at her and pointed to Hayley's face in the window. "They're also trying to kill her. Oh, by the way, that's Cleopatra."

Masaru coughed. "Are you serious? How the hell did a kid manage half the things you said she did to you?"

"Someone was ghosting her on the net. I don't know who or why yet." Joey growled. "The same guys that are trying to kill me kicked in her door. I still don't know how a little kid evaded corporate hit men."

Katya turned away, her tone soft. "It's not as difficult as you think."

"What the hell does that little girl have to do with this?" Eldon faced Joey.

Joey waved at Hayley. "I don't understand either. Whoever is messing with me decided to involve her as well."

"Doll?" Masaru raised an eyebrow.

Joey stopped in mid thought. He'd never thought to ask, or check, and that could explain why Jacob Roth seemed so blasé about her. "I never thought to check... Maybe she has some kind of secret data locked away in her head."

Kenny watched Alyssa search for clothes to loan. "I got a weird feeling about her father. There's something just not right about him... He seems so dismissive, even when he was told someone tried to kill his daughter."

"Definitely odd, she tells me that she's always home alone and her dad is always at work." Joey shook his head. "But I am *not* going to go see if she's anatomically correct."

Masaru rubbed his chin. "We need to know what we're getting involved with."

"Can't you dig up birth records in the net or something?" Eldon seemed uncomfortable with the way the conversation went.

"If they can fake her father, they can fake her birth records." Joey added, his face still stuck in a repulsed grimace.

"Well if they can't lie about what they are, why don't we just ask her?" Kenny thought he pointed out the obvious truth everyone overlooked.

"She could have been reprogrammed." Masaru sounded detached. "Why don't you ask Alyssa to check?"

"Look, we're not going to de-pants a kid without more to go on than a paranoid hunch." Joey took a step back.

"Wait a sec, when you brought her here, she was bleeding from the foot and a stimpak worked on her. Would a stimpak work on a WellTech doll?" Kenny glanced at Masaru. "She also ate breakfast. Do they eat?"

Masaru rubbed his chin. "They will bleed if cut, but no on the stimpak and the food. Stimpak nanobots only have human "blueprints" so to speak. They wouldn't know what to do with synthetic materials."

Joey breathed a sigh of relief. "So that proves she's real?"

"I can double check." Katya tapped near her artificial eye. "I can scan her for metal. No plastisteel skeleton, no doll."

Everyone nodded. Katya went into the house as Kenny discussed the plan for the trip. Masaru took his armor out of the trunk and put it on except for the helmet before retrieving a black case. He pressed his thumb into a small glowing blue square near its handle and a brighter blue line passed up and down beneath it.

The case chirped and clicked. The motorized lid opened. On the underside, an image in bronze of an Asian dragon coiled around a large K—the Kurotai logo.

The black shape of a thirteen-inch weapon with the profile of a submachine gun lay nestled within white foam. Blinking lights flashed up and down along its length. Above the handle, a cobalt blue screen displayed 100% charge. The meager one-inch thickness coupled with the clear artificial crystal barrel gave it away as an energy weapon.

"Damn, man, is that what I think it is?" Eldon lifted an eyebrow.

"Kurotai Shinobi, model S-19." Masaru held it up with the grin of a proud parent. "One hundred seventy thousand credits, factory price."

Kenny blinked at it. "They let you own an energy weapon on Earth?"

Masaru's smile grew. "Display permit for sales."

"Damn..." Eldon shook his head. "Nasty as they are, I still wouldn't want to use one of those, might as well hold up a sign sayin' "send bullets here"."

"Incorrect." Masaru shook his head. "The S-19 laser operates within the infrared spectrum, using a beam invisible without night vision or IR sensors."

Eldon raised an eyebrow. "Remind me not to piss you off."

Joey chuckled. "I'd be more afraid of his sword."

THE JOURNEY

Katya peeked through the doorway, staying as quiet as she could. Neither girl noticed her as her cybernetic eye changed the room into the grey and white shades of a metallurgical scan. The kids appeared as dark silhouettes save for a few white spots: earrings, buttons, zippers, and a NetMini in a pocket.

"Come on, we're ready." Katya spoke, satisfied the girl was human.

Both of them jumped and screamed at the sudden voice. Katya offered an apologetic look and walked with them. Alyssa plodded down the steps and leaned into her father, avoiding eye contact with Eldon. Hayley waited a few paces back, staring at the ground. Sensing her mood, Kenny put an arm around her as well, at last making her smile.

Katya shook her head, mouthing the word "alive" without giving it voice. Joey furrowed his brow as his theory about valuable information concealed in a fake child went up in flames. The situation with her father confused him even more, now, but he was a cop—that tidbit made Joey even more unwilling to engage in a pissing contest.

"Okay, let's get you two squared away." Kenny pulled the door open.

Alyssa, familiar with the truck, knew the handholds and climbed the tire into the cab with ease. Hayley just stared at the eye-level running board until Kenny helped her up.

"I'll ride in the bed 'til we drop them off." Eldon went around to the rear.

Eldon's status as a reservist, as well as a friend in the armory willing to fudge some authorization files, allowed him to keep his recon armor. For this run, he had come prepared.

The girls shared the large passenger seat, with Masaru and Joey on either side of Katya in the back. The ride to the Rodriguez house was short, just under ten minutes. Kenny carried their bags up the walkway. A short conversation later, he exchanged a handshake with an older man and a hug with his wife.

"Thanks so much for watching them, I owe you a favor."

"Is okay. Ava is lonely since Javier moved to the east for that important job of his." Arturo Rodriguez's face broke into a thousand wrinkles as he smiled and shook Kenny's hand.

"I'm going to be out of net range for 2 or 3 days, I'll vid you as soon as I get a signal."

Arturo nodded as his wife escorted the kids inside. "No problem, Kenneth."

"It wouldn't be right of me not to warn you. Some people are trying to hurt that other girl, Hayley. Joey said that someone showed up at his place and tried to kill her."

"Ay dios mio!" Arturo grabbed at his chin and gasped.

"There's almost no way anyone can track her to you, I doubt they even know about me. Still, try to keep her away from windows and don't let her go online. I'll get back as fast as I can."

KENNY TURNED OFF THE NATURAL DIRT ROAD TO AN ACCESS RAMP THAT CARRIED traffic up to the level of the city plates. A number of Division 1 police staffed the top, observing cars as they went by. Everyone's NetMini chirped in sequence, scanned by the checkpoint.

"The ACC has its claws in Mexico, they're looking for infiltrators." Now in the front seat, Eldon leaned out the window and waved at the cops.

Katya remained motionless the entire time, hoping her fake ID checked out. She wasn't here on behalf of the ACC. Quite to the contrary, she wanted to get as far away from them as possible. Nonetheless, her entry to the UCF took unofficial channels. She had been too afraid of her old owners catching wind of her to leave any kind of trail.

"You're welcome." Joey patted her on the thigh.

Her head snapped to glare at him. "For what?"

"Your electronic identity. The fact that you're not face first over the hood of a police car with a rubber glove elbow deep in your ass right now means they believed it."

"How... colorful..." She grabbed his wrist and tossed his hand away from her leg as if it was a turd. "Thank you."

"You know, if you're hostile to everyone around you all the time you're just going to be miserable." Joey glanced out the window at the passing buildings. "You're just like my sister."

Katya didn't respond. The concept of trust was so anathema to the core of her identity that she never thought about opening up. It would just provide her enemies with an exploitable weakness.

The truck mired in morning commuter traffic on a main transit path. Much of the south sectors of West City contained citizens too poor to afford hovercars. The elevated truck offered a view over the sea of passenger cars. Kenny squeezed the wheel, trying to resist the temptation to drive over them. For the better part of an hour, Joey's eyes locked onto an older man that bobbled his way down the road and bounced off street lamps and other pedestrians. He seemed quite drunk, high, or both—and his erratic travel outpaced them. Each time he walked past the truck, Joey felt a twinge of frustration until traffic inched ahead and they passed him… then the guy in front of them would stop and the pedestrian stumbled into the lead again.

Joey grumbled. "You should get a hover truck."

Kenny laughed. "Some of the shit I haul back is way too heavy for that. Besides, no such thing as a backup diesel for those."

"Don't even get him started." Eldon laughed. "Zombies. Hah."

An hour later, they broke away from the traffic stream toward the nearest exit gate approach. Joey sank into the seat as the truck picked up speed and left the vagrant behind. It was rare for anyone to drive down this road.

"No traffic here?" Katya mused.

"No one wants to live this close to the gate. First place the Badlands nasties will destroy when they break in." Kenny laughed. "'Course, most of the stuff out there is happy staying out there. I think the wall is more to keep us in."

Ominous bulges swelled out of the wall every five hundred yards or so, laser turrets aimed into no man's land. Weapons poised to incinerate the army of cybernetic mutants that, so far, had never materialized.

The truck came to a halt within the checkpoint and two Division 1 officers approached.

"Morning Mr…" The officer looked down at his armband display. "Marlon."

"Howdy." Kenny tipped his hat.

The patrol officer swiped his hand, scrolling among different screens on an armband display. "What is the purpose of your excursion?"

"Artifact hunting, same as always." Kenny smiled.

"Number of people leaving?"

"Five."

"Just for the record, you acknowledge that the UCF government is in no way responsible for injury or death that occurs as a result of your presence in the Badlands. You further acknowledge that in the event you contract any diseases or maladies deemed a menace to the general population you may be detained upon re-entry for quarantine purposes."

"Yeah…" Kenny closed his eyes. He had heard this routine so often he had to fight the urge to mouth the words.

"Furthermore, you acknowledge that your vehicle and possessions are subject to scan and search upon your return. Dangerous biological or chemical contaminants will…"

Kenny finished his sentence. "Not be allowed into West City and are subject to confiscation with appropriate fines."

The cop smirked. "Notice you have a female among you. You know that certain parties trade in women out there?"

"Yeah, we're hoping to trade her in for a pair of redheads," said Joey, winking.

Katya glared, muttering in Russian. "You can try."

"We aren't going anywhere near those areas. Besides, I have an Eldon." Kenny indicated his friend with a backward thumb.

Eldon waved. "Morning Corporal."

The cop glanced at the marks on Eldon's armor and chuckled. "Morning Corporal."

"Well you seem to know the drill, I just need your thumbprint here and you're welcome to go get yourself shot." The officer held a datapad over to Kenny who promptly pushed his thumb into the glowing square. "Good luck out there."

With the red tape out of the way, the inner gate thrummed closed with the heavy resounding crash of metal on metal. The outer barrier sank into the Earth, revealing a long stretch of old paved road. It led off into the desert of old Nevada, flanked on both sides by empty ground broken up by the occasional stalwart tuft of vegetation. A few scorch marks dotted the landscape wherever a bored turret operator had vaporized some unfortunate small animal. The truck bounced over the housing of the outer door and Kenny accelerated up to about sixty.

He leaned back in the seat, his smile widened across his face. The old allure of the Badlands came to him this time, unburdened by guilt about leaving his daughter behind. She had given him her blessing for this trip. As much it disappointed her, she knew he only did it to help Joey. He poked at a display screen in the center of the dashboard, bringing up the navigation map and plotted the route.

With that done, Kenny settled in for a long ride. "Gonna take anywhere from eleven to fourteen hours to get there."

Centuries ago, the ride would have been a third of that. Nature had reclaimed much of the area in the wake of the Corporate War. Roads and bridges deteriorated and in some cases disappeared altogether. Other places contained populations of dangerous bioengineered creatures.

The heavy vehicle trundled on through the scrub brush and kicked up the occasional piece of debris as he drove the most direct route that they could risk. After several hours, they approached the foothills and Kenny brought the truck to a stop.

He opened his door without killing the engine. "Nature break."

Knowing looks were exchanged, and soon all four men had lined up like a firing squad to water the same patch of ground. Katya stood a few feet behind them with her arms folded. She looked around for a place that would give her some privacy, but found the same flat nothingness in every direction. The largest puff of vegetation in sight wouldn't have concealed an infant.

Joey glanced at her out of the corner of his eye. "Hey Eldon, What do the girls do in the Marine Corps?"

Eldon chuckled. "Well first, there ain't no *girls* in the Marines. The *women* would be right up here with us. When you're in the shit together it don't matter, a Marine is a Marine no matter what's between their legs." Eldon grinned at the look on Joey's face. "You'd have gotten your ass kicked more than once."

"Would they be trying to hit the bush?" Joey chuckled.

"I ain't even gonna to dignify that with a response, Joe."

"Oh to hell with you all." Katya glared.

"Just hide behind the truck." Kenny spoke without looking.

She slinked off, around the vehicle out of sight.

"Yell when you're decent, so I can break out some of the rations to munch on." Kenny called out to her as he finished.

She didn't answer.

"Guess she doesn't like working with an audience." Joey spoke loud enough for her to hear him.

"Die." Her response floated over the truck.

A moment later, she walked into view, adjusting her armor back into place. Masaru had bought her some civilian-grade composite plate, the same sort of thing used by cavalry scouts and vehicle operators, only dark grey instead of theater-appropriate camo. Joey snickered at her obvious unfamiliarity with it, earning a glare without comment. Kenny handed out rations, giving everyone a pouch of protein slime flavored in various ways.

Eldon looked at his and grumbled. "Fuck the omelet. Anyone wanna trade?"

"Hell no." Kenny chuckled. "Even the tuna casserole beats that atrocity."

Joey tossed his ration pack to Eldon and caught the omelet. He didn't care what stuff tasted like.

"Ahh, beef stew." Eldon saluted Joey with the unopened pack. "If you close your eyes and let your thoughts run away with the flavor, you can almost believe that you're eating real... shit." Eldon made it sound serious up until the last word.

Masaru didn't open his ration pack, holding it with two fingers as if it were unclean. "You expect me to eat this?"

"They don't have sushi flavor." Joey waved. "Shitty food is better than no food. Would it help you eat it if I told you they cost a thousand credits a pouch?"

Masaru frowned with a heavy throat noise, the kind of gesture that equated to a death threat back in Japan.

"They tried that, actually." Eldon made a nauseated look. "Cold fish slime didn't go over well."

"Sounds like my sister." Joey smirked before squeezing the last of the semiliquid egg down his throat.

"Ouch." Kenny glanced at him.

Eldon winced in silence and Katya glowered.

"You have a problem with women, don't you?" She squinted.

"Calling my sister a woman is an insult to the gender." Joey stuffed his empty meal packets back into the outer wrapper. "Maybe when they upgrade your programming to include a sense of humor you'll count as one, too."

"I am not a machine." Katya cursed under her breath in Russian.

Masaru turned away so his smirking grin escaped her notice.

"So what's up with your sister?" Kenny gathered up the trash from their meal.

"She's been pissed at me ever since she was born. Only thing I can think of is that I scored higher on the aptitude tests and coasted through school without working. I got straight A's with my eyes closed while she had to bust her ass. Then, I"—he made air quotes—"waste myself in cyberspace while she gets a high paying job at some uppity corporate law firm."

"She does have a point." Katya muttered, too low for anyone but Masaru to hear.

"That's a pretty shallow thing to drive a wedge between family." Eldon shook his head.

Joey threw his hands up as if he had long ago given up that battle. Everyone climbed back into the truck as Kenny stuffed the trash into a blue canister bungeed at the rear corner of the bed.

"So why the boy scout routine with the trash?" Joey glanced at Kenny as he got back in and closed the door.

"The Badlands know how you treat them."

Eldon paused before closing his door. "I said, don't get him started."

Joey laughed. "Oh for fuck's sake."

In a spray of dirt, they got underway. Every so often, a tire would clip a rock or bit of scrub, jostling the truck. Masaru closed his eyes and meditated as Katya tried to ignore the building nausea in her gut from whatever she had eaten. Eldon and Kenny continued their usual banter and Joey snored, catching up on lost sleep. After about nine hours of driving, a faint beep pulsed in time with a winking light on the console. Kenny tapped his finger under the indicator.

"We're close. Got some active radar tracking coming from about a quarter mile ahead."

"Active? That doesn't make me think abandoned." Eldon shifted in his seat.

"It might be something left over that's still turned on." Masaru spoke up from the back. "The facility must have power, probably a self-contained reactor."

Joey draped himself over the back of Eldon's seat. "Let's not do anything stupid."

"We already have," grumbled Katya.

"We can at least get a closer look than this." Eldon put on his helmet and used the visor to zoom into the distance.

Kenny slowed to eliminate the dust cloud as much as he could. In the harsh orange light of the setting sun, a gleaming ivory surface shimmered from beyond the green of a nearby forest canopy. A wall came into view past a large bank of trees once they crested a small hill. Beyond the barrier, an immense metal turret glimmered in the waning light. As big as a house, its two long barrels pointed off to the right.

"Holy shit…" Eldon leaned forward. "That thing is made to take out starships. From the looks of it, either laser or particle beam."

"Is it gonna fire at us?" Kenny swiveled a small camera on the roof to get a closer view.

"Fuck, I hope not." Eldon gave Kenny a pointed look. "It shouldn't, but who knows what kind of tweaking they did to it."

"There." Masaru pointed at the display.

Amid the wavering trees, burns and missing branches were visible, evidence that the turret fired at some point, but it was impossible to say with any degree of certainty how long ago. Kenny panned back and forth over the wall, finding no visible logos or signs that indicated who ran this place. A modest crater scored the ground at the base of a huge crack that separated the wall into two sections.

Kenny pointed. "There's our way in."

"Look at that." Katya pointed past Joey's face out the side window.

All heads turned at a distant glint in the foliage.

Eldon cycled through thermal, metallurgical, and electromagnetic detection modes on his helmet visor. "Looks like a van, got nothing on thermal." He slid out of the truck, and crept in that direction.

Kenny remained with the truck while the others followed Eldon into the grove until they reached an orange and purple van wedged between two large trees. A few years' worth of growth had engulfed its oversized tires and begun to creep

THE JOURNEY | 213

into the open side door. Eldon pulled at the vine-like weeds, sending a flurry of small animals zooming in random directions.

The interior resembled a college dorm room on wheels, one exposed to the elements for several years. Posters, datapads, clothing, empty synth beer cans, and food related trash sat under a heavy curtain of fungus. From the shredded debris, it looked like animals had long ago eliminated any provisions. In the front dashboard storage area, a pile of printed flyers, still recognizable as HLM propaganda, were well progressed into a single lump of molding paper waste. Eldon sifted among the debris, and a pair of red panties snagged on the end of his rifle. With a smirk, he shook the weapon until they fell.

Katya braved the rear, stepping over grey puffs of furry mold to several containers. Some held usable clothing, but the empty military case caught her attention more. Curious, she turned on her chem scan and closed her natural left eye, plunging the world into monochromatic green. Chemical traces appeared as swaths of various colors. The interior of the box had several brick-shaped lime imprints that faded toward the center. A pointed stare caused the eye to render a molecular diagram of several substances.

"Most of the residue is cyclotrimethylene trinitramine with traces of Zeurium-3, dioctyl sebacate and polyisobutylene." Katya's vision returned to normal. "Looks like four brick sized blocks."

"You could have just said NE2, Kat." Eldon shook his head.

"She wants to sound smarter than she is." Joey laughed. "It's more believable when you aren't reading it."

Masaru glanced at Eldon. "That stuff hasn't been used in years. ACC?"

Eldon shook his head. "Doubtful. Not with all this flowerbasket, HLM paperwork and beer. That's probably just some street-chemist's best attempt at making a bomb."

Joey ignored Katya's persistent glare. "So the HLM came out here, or someone wants us to think so."

"Check the growth around the wheels, this thing *has* been here a long time," said Eldon.

"Who would go to all the trouble of setting everything up to frame the HLM for something?" Masaru paced. "They are just a group of idiots on the edge of reality. No one takes them seriously."

"I know a couple of dead Marines who'd disagree with you on that point." Eldon frowned.

Joey folded his arms. "I don't think we're going to get any answers until we go inside."

Eldon waved his arm in an 'after you' manner. "Then let's get on with it."

GUARD DOGS

The approaching dusk cast glimmering strips of orange from the horizon as the distant mountains swallowed the sun. Kenny stashed the truck near the van, figuring that since it had remained undisturbed this long, his ride would too. Joey posed by the tailgate, adoring the western look of the Huntsman armor Kenny gave him. Its false brown leather coat contained numerous floating panels of light composite armor, attached to a black protective vest. Kenny squinted in the direction of the compound, searching for any signs of life. A few paces into the forest, something on the ground caught his eye.

"Tracks." Kenny stooped to get a closer look. "From the size and depth, I'd say a man in armor, 'bout Eldon's size or larger. Few days old."

Eldon edged past him to take point. "Got nothin' on therms."

Masaru lifted his S-19, arming it with a flick of his thumb. The weapon looked out of place in contrast to the artful samurai design of his lacquered black armor, but not everything out here would give him the respect of getting close enough for his sword.

Eldon moved toward the wall. "Somethin' ain't right with these trees. They almost look like someone copied and pasted them around."

Kenny brushed his fingers over one. "They are induced. Nanobots grow them in about six days. Quick cover." He looked up into the treetops. "There's some deviation in the upper branches once they started growing for real. They're alive, but cloned."

Eldon advanced in a series of quick steps and tactical sprints between trees. Kenny attempted to follow suit. Joey traipsed along behind them as if browsing a mall. Katya stayed out of sight. Masaru brought up the rear, senses tuned to the world.

The sun fell beyond the horizon, leaving the group in darkness. At this distance, the whirrs and clunks of the huge turret's search pattern rumbled the ground. Eldon raised his hand in a signal to stop when a flash of orange thermal movement caught his eye to the left. He dropped to a knee and sighted over his rifle, searching the field of bluish trees and black voids. All at once, nine amorphous shapes of red-orange emerged.

Their gait was as inhuman as their size, moving in a hybrid stride that alternated between all fours and upright running. Each looked to be about seven feet tall while hunched forward. Bright blue lines at the end of the arms gave away the presence of metal claws. Cold spots on their head and torso revealed crude cyberware.

"Incoming, left 40 degrees, nine hot spots. Claws. Big."

Kenny turned and drew in a long breath in his nose. The musky scent of wet dog hinted at the edge of his senses. "Canids, they are not inclined to talk. Probably hunting for dinner, and we look tasty. Just shoot 'em."

"What the fuck is a Canid?" Joey asked as casually as if standing around at home.

With that, a fur-covered humanoid leapt out of the trees and tackled him to the ground from behind. He made a noise like a stomped goose as all the air was driven from his lungs. The creature rode him like a surfboard for several feet from the force of the impact.

Larger than a man, it had powerful muscular arms and a massive chest. Its face was a mangled combination of human and canine traits with yellow, glowing metal eyes. Mechanical irises narrowed as a grotesque mouth full of sharp teeth parted in a low growl. A tendril of drool leaked forth, fluttering in its breath. Despite a nose full of wet pine needles, Joey could taste carrion on the wind.

Kenny turned to shoot, but another sprinted for him. He pivoted toward it, opening fire. Blue flashes from each shot burned the dying monster into his memory in a series of still images. The creature's body crashed into a tree and scraped its metal claws into the bark in a futile attempt to hold itself upright. Sensing imminent death, it locked eyes with him. One final shot struck it in the face with a splattering crunch of disintegrated bone.

While Kenny fired, Masaru took a step toward Joey and swiped his Nano katana across the creature's back, just as it raised its claws at Joey's neck. The mutant howled as sparks flew from severed wiring and lit small patches of fur on fire. It dragged itself to the side, useless legs revealing Masaru had severed its spine. Turning, it heaved itself toward Masaru with a growl, sending chunks of dirt into the air as it clawed at the ground.

Eldon fired at any heat blob moving with an abnormal gait. Glare from the muzzle flash lit the area, bathing the facing sides of nearby trees in blue light from burst after burst. The whizzing of bullets glancing off trees was interspersed with wet splats, canine yelps, and the occasional metallic ping from a chance hit on cyberware. A shower of sparks and flame followed each clank as the primitive augmentations failed in severe ways.

The wounded Canid rushed Mamoru, who stepped back in a smooth upswing that split its head in half. The Nano katana made little sound as it sliced the creature's skull. Another leapt from behind and raked its claws across Masaru's back with a grating screech of metal on armor. The impact drove him chest first into a tree three meters away. His feet slid outward, widening his stance, but he retained both balance and blade. The steel claws couldn't breach his armor, but the abnormal strength of the hit disoriented him. Masaru berated himself for not sensing its approach. His sealed helmet interfered with his senses more than he liked.

Joey rolled onto his side and fired at the one that hit Masaru, almost blowing out its knees. Howling, it fell to the ground and turned on him. Angering it more than crippling it, the wound did little to stop the creature from pouncing and sinking its teeth into his shoulder. Joey's armor took the brunt of the hit.

The mutant pulled with its jaws as it pushed him away with its arms, snarling and trying to bite deeper. Five muffled gunshots later, the strength left it in an explosion of gore that flew out of its back. Joey had pumped round after round into its side at point blank range. The stench of burned hair and charred meat filled the air. He shoved the dead creature to the side and looked at his bloody coat. Its teeth had found a spot where the underlying vest didn't cover, leaving a painful but superficial puncture wound.

Another blurred out of the woods at Masaru as he staggered back from the tree. A single gunshot echoed out of the night, ending with a dull splat from the side of its head. Katya's face appeared for an instant, lit in the dark from the flash of her pistol. The sprint became a stumbling walk. The Canid shook its head as if suffering brain freeze, a bullet trenching its skull seemed merely annoying rather than fatal. The creature stared at Masaru as if it had forgotten what it wanted to do. A dull fleshy *thump* came as Katya shot it again. He attacked, thrusting his katana into the creature's heart. The monster looked down at its chest in confusion. Masaru turned away and swiped the blade out with a flourish before taking a ready stance awaiting the next threat.

Kenny fired from alternating pistols at one in a frantic sprint at Eldon. His shots crippled it into a drunken forward lope, buying Eldon enough time to finish it off with a well-placed double tap that knocked it dead to the ground. The rifle slugs tore the left side of the creature's head open and sent what looked like a metal brain case into the trees with a ringing echo.

A scream drew everyone's attention to Katya as a Canid seized her from behind, turning as if to run off with its newfound meal. The light composite armor Masaru bought her spared her ribs the touch of Canid claws. In a flurry of motion, she pummeled it in the face, but it ignored her.

Joey rolled onto his stomach and held his pistol with both hands. In a second that felt like five, he sent a careful shot into the mutant's right shin, shattering the bone. It fell forward, landing on top of Katya and howling.

Eldon ran over and grabbed it in an attempt to drag the four hundred pound thing off her, but it swatted him aside with one arm. The force lifted him off his feet and sent him sailing. He spun over and landed on his chest a short distance away, sliding two feet in the mulch. The mutant slashed down at Katya's face, roaring with both pain and anger.

Masaru got his katana in the path of the claws. Steel slid along the back edge of the synthetic diamond blade with an ear-piercing squeal before thumping into the moist dirt an inch away from her eye. He spun the sword in his grip and swiped it up at the claws, severing them. The Canid glanced at its arm with enough reason to understand what Masaru had done. It growled deep in its throat, having lost interest in Katya.

She raked at the ground, trying to pull herself out from under the thing, but its weight held her in place. Her mental state passed from panic to futility then to the realization that she wouldn't be going anywhere. Twisting to look at the beast, she straightened the fingers of her right hand.

Thin blades popped out, one from each fingertip. The flexible segments locked together, forming a series of graceful curves about six inches long. The plastisteel talons couldn't cut anywhere near as well as a Nano weapon, but on flesh, they worked fine. She slashed at the creature's neck and pulled. Hot blood flooded over her hand and fell on her face. Cringing, she closed her eyes and kept tearing. Killing wasn't her way, but she wouldn't let herself die to avoid guilt. Moreover, this was more of a some*thing* than a some*one*.

Its deep warbling cry of primal agony echoed into the trees.

In a desperate panic, the Canid grabbed her by the waist with one hand and flung her away to the side, ripping her claws through its own neck. She went head over feet in a horizontal spin twice before her body wrapped around a tree. Her momentum pinned her to the trunk for a second before she fell to the ground, coughing up blood.

Spurting arterial gushes shot from the mutant's wound. Growling faded into a dying gasp as it collapsed. She stared at the mass of fur until breathing ceased, delighting in the irony of its end. Eldon's rifle chattered as two more Canids yelped and died in the distance, too far away for anyone to see without thermal.

A snapping twig made Masaru spin, blade held at face level, edge up. He looked over the transparent katana at one more Canid staring at him from about twenty feet away. A metal box on its forearm opened to reveal three tiny missiles about the size of cigars. He smirked with disdain and went for his S-19.

Faint light flickered around the barrel as he fired a pulsing barrage. Fist sized pockets swelled out of the creature's skin, bloody steam spewing from tiny laser holes. Its entire torso ignited into a fireball, and a dozen candle flames clung to the trees behind it where the laser had pierced. The ball of fur and flame spun in a circle with a baleful howl that echoed into the sky. Its micro-rockets went skyward with a flash of orange as it collapsed into a heap of burning biological matter.

"Think you got it?" Joey stood, staring into the bonfire.

"Hmph." Masaru looked around.

Somewhere in the distance, three small explosions rumbled.

Kenny laughed. "Hah. Better keep an eye on that one in case it tries something."

Katya curled into a ball, a thin trickle of blood dripping from the corner of her mouth. She used her canteen to spray the gore off her talons before retracting them. A drop of blood formed at each fingertip until nanobots mended the skin. Joey's shoulder burned like someone had stabbed him a dozen times with an ice pick. He hit himself in the collarbone with a stimpak, falling into a dumb smile as the pain faded.

"You'll need to get checked out when we get back to the City. Don't want to catch anything from that bite." Kenny patted Joey on his unhurt shoulder.

"Fuck." Joey sighed. "If I start howling at the moon I'm gonna be pissed."

Laughing, Kenny helped him up. "They're not werewolves, just genetic experiments. It's not contagious."

Katya sat up and dosed a stimpak as well. An audible pop came from her chest as her broken rib slid back into place and knit. Still in pain, she used a second and tossed the empty into the distance. Masaru stared at Kenny with an accusatory look as Eldon kept watch.

"Good news and bad news." Eldon spoke via his helmet's speaker in an even tone. "I don't see any more of those things moving around."

"But?" Joey glanced at him.

"That big ass turret is pointing at us now. It just has no shot through the wall."

"Oh, that's wonderful." Joey sighed.

Katya spoke in breathless rasps. "Someone's gotta say it. What the fuck were those?"

"I already told you, Canid mutants, quite common in this area." Kenny moved to the center of the group.

"How are they still alive?" Masaru offered a distrustful squint. "By the way, thanks for the warning about them being in this area."

"He's got a habit of that." Eldon grinned.

"No problem." Kenny smiled. "They aren't supposed to be this far south according to the charts... but those charts are only a guideline cobbled together from a dozen guys like me that roam around out here. It's not like there's a Badlands census." He laughed. "These are not the original mutants from the war. Rumor has it that there is a facility still out here somewhere, running on autopilot. The computerized assembly line is still producing them to the original specs and setting them loose." Kenny held his hands up at Katya's expression of terror. "This ain't it. There'd be way more than that small pack, and I'd bet the ones guarding their den would be larger and meaner."

"That's comforting and frightening at the same time." Katya got up, ignoring Joey's offered hand.

Masaru flipped his katana over and slid it back into its scabbard. "We should continue before more of them come."

"Agreed." Eldon jogged toward the wall, careful to move in a way that kept solid material between him and the turret.

Their single file line slid along the wall, skirting it until they arrived at the edge of a breach big enough to drive Kenny's truck through. Mangled rebar jutted like snapped bones from the concrete interior. The four-foot thick wall had a half inch of plastisteel plating on both sides.

Eldon whistled at the crater in the gap. "Some heavy hardware hit this place. Military probably found it and decided to shut it down."

"Why didn't they take out that damn turret?" Katya shivered each time the heavy servos moved it.

Masaru thought for a moment. "The military doesn't come out here. This had to be internal, the company decided to cut its losses."

"Joey." Eldon waved him up. "I think I see our way in."

KNOCK KNOCK

J oey crept up to the gap. "What?"

Eldon pointed. "There's a pile of cargo containers inside the wall blockin' off the angle of that gun. We're close enough to where I don't think it can get a shot on us. We're inside the minimum downward angle."

"What am I gonna do with cargo containers?" Joey smirked.

Above Eldon's forearm, a holographic display panel appeared. It shared what Eldon could see from his helmet camera. A space between the container pile and the wall, about ten meters in, glowed in the light from an operational terminal.

"Can you get in and shut that thing down?"

"Depends on if they're on the same network, but I won't know that 'til I connect." Joey took a few deep breaths and sprinted around the wall.

"Crazy mother fucker..." Eldon yelled.

Eldon started to follow, but dove for cover as a bright orange blast trenched a six-foot long valley of glass through the soil in the breach.

"Okay, so I miscalculated the angle..." Eldon panted, staring at the glowing scar on the ground as it faded.

A hollow clank from the other side echoed as Joey dove into the gap between the containers and the wall.

"I'm in!" Joey yelled. "Uhh... need some backup."

The shiny metal surface of a small security bot drifted in and out of view at the end of the narrow channel in which he hung suspended. The whir of electric motors paused with a click each time it reversed and spun, trying to move to where it could aim at him with its onboard weapon. After calculating the task impossible, it swiveled to the right, accelerating with a high-pitched whine, around the containers to approach from the rear.

The wall seemed to absorb Eldon as the surface of his recon armor shimmered into a perfect replica of the white plastisteel behind him. He edged around the gap, rifle aimed, without attracting the attention of the turret. As soon as the tracked sentry rolled past the edge of the container stack, he shot it. The slugs knocked it backward, spinning in a torrent of sparks and fragments. It swiveled and trained its tiny rotary cannon on Eldon; however, he fired before it could. The back end deflagrated in a brilliant blue flash as its ammunition store went off. A great spattering of smoke puffs appeared in the ground behind it as errant projectiles went everywhere. Hundreds of rounds of caseless ammo reduced to a weak fragmentation device.

"I fucking hate those things." Joey grumbled.

Eldon slid in along the wall, slow enough to maintain invisibility. "Where the hell would you have seen one of those before?"

Joey chuckled as he fished for the interface jack on the terminal. His fingers struggled to find another inch of reach.

"Local connections are much faster than wireless, or even going over GlobeNet interlinks. One of those fuckers kept me cornered in an air vent for a day and a half back on Mars."

His body hung sideways with his back to the wall, chest against the unyielding surface of a cargo box. Breathing was a challenge. If he exhaled too hard, he would slip an inch toward the ground. Joey eased his deck forward and connected it to the terminal in bypass mode.

"Cover me in case any more of those things come out."

"Hurry up." Eldon kept his rifle aimed at the edge of the containers.

The M3 wire snapped in with a click that sent his consciousness spiraling into blackness. Blind, deaf, and numb, he tried to scream but nothing happened. A sense like he'd been sat on by an elephant came over him as minutes passed in stillness. A point of light appeared in the distance, data bits shimmered in the periphery of his vision. The spot of white grew and came sailing at him. He crossed his arms over his face, bracing for impact, but found himself standing in a plain hallway with a steel grating floor. A sourceless white light radiated from the ceiling. The walls and ceiling were torn and ripped up, bundles of frayed wiring and pipes dangled from the ceiling, and sparks burst in sprays from random points.

The network had to be in bad shape. The destruction here was just a representation of network instability. A cave in of debris blocked passage to the right, representing a physical connection to another part of the network being down. He tried to take a step, but his foot sank into the steel as if it were syrup. He flailed in an attempt to keep balance, but continued sinking.

"What the hell?" blurted Joey, genuine alarm in his voice.

He had never seen this effect before. He sent a mental command to the deck to open a diagnostic panel but nothing happened. Joey tried to lift his leg out of the goop, grunting from the exertion. Strands of gooey metal snapped away from the underside of his boot and morphed back into hard solid steel. The dark cowboy looked nowhere near as frightened as Joey felt and roared with anger at the audacity of the network to interfere with him. The gunslinger's voice came out deep and altered, an audio track played at one-quarter speed.

After almost thirty seconds of warring with the soupy grating, a shimmering blue line stretched out in two directions from a glowing point. He stared at it, wondering what in the hell it was until he realized the diagnostic display panel opened with such excruciating slowness he could perceive every pixel form. It dawned on him at that moment he wallowed in latency more severe than anything he had ever witnessed. He stopped struggling to move and waited for the hovering display to finish drawing itself in.

Outside in the real world, the turret fired a blast into the stack of crates as if testing its ability to hit Eldon.

"Aww fuck, I'm made." Eldon ducked, letting his armor return to its usual green to save power. "Joey, whatever you're doing, do it faster."

Five minutes passed in cyberspace, about twenty seconds in real time. The diagnostic panel at last finished rendering itself. The deck's processor and memory transfer bus both indicated full utilization. This surpassed simple lag, something in the network attacked him with some kind of data slam. Joey pounded his deck with mental orders to reset the I/O channel, but nothing changed. With increasing desperation, his brain wrestled with the deck as his legs battled the sticky floor.

After another several minutes, his body stretched out in the direction he had been trying to walk, distorting into a man-shaped noodle twenty yards long. The end that remained where he had first appeared snapped out of the ground like a tent spike failing under load. The disorientation of seeing himself from both ends paralyzed him as half his perception stood there watching the other half careening in.

The moving end slammed into the stationary end, throwing him with a metallic *clank* into the wall. His real body outside convulsed from the impact.

"Joey? What the fuck is going on in there man? This thing is trying to melt its way through the crates." The sound of Eldon's rifle chattering away played accompaniment to his voice.

Eldon appeared in midair. The dark cowboy lay on his back, staring up at the sourceless light, unable to contain laughter as the floating head squeaked, sped up to the point of being unintelligible.

Joey held his arms out as the old one levitated back to his feet.

"...are you doing?" Eldon's last three words slowed to normal.

"I got stuck in some crazy lag... I have no idea what the fuck just happened in here." He tapped his toe into the metal floor to make sure it would act like steel and not swamp.

"Get on it, whatever you're doing, this turret wants my ass." Eldon continued to fire at small security bots while yelling into the comm.

"They're not on its map of facility structures."

"I really don't give a god damn *why* it's shooting at me, just make it stop!" Eldon sounded more angry than scared.

The hallway blurred around him as he followed the map to the control node for the turret. The room had its own security routine, separate from the rest of the network that was offline.

He sweated it more than he thought he would, finding a rush of entertainment at it being just at the limit of his ability. It took a few tries for the system to accept his spoofed input, and the shiny steel doors snapped open with a squeaking hiss. He stepped into the node, thrilled by the challenge, but disappointed that he couldn't face this network in its prime.

The control node looked like a turret station from a military ship. A pair of joysticks jutted up from a desk in front of view panels where targeting and ranging information overlaid the real world. Eldon's silhouette outlined in blinking red as the turret melted deeper and deeper into the large stack of shipping containers. Shrapnel littered the area from Eldon playing duck hunt with an unending stream of security bots emerging from a small hatch on the underside of a large drop building about twenty meters behind the turret.

A humanoid apparition of silver coalesced in midair just to Joey's left. A featureless upside-down raindrop of mercury formed a head mounted to a polygonal torso. Its arms and legs stretched into long inflexible tendrils that tapered to points in the most basic approximation of the human form.

"You must be the turret control program." The dark cowboy flipped his guns out of his holsters and spun them over his finger. "We need to talk."

It leapt at him in an attempt to spear him with one of its pointy arms. The razor sharp tip passed millimeters from Joey's chest as he disappeared and reappeared on the other side of the room. It whirled to face him the instant he fired.

His bullets, tiny smoking skulls, wailed with a keening cry as they flew. Of the lot, only one defeated the construct's erratic dodging motions, shattering a gouge out of its side and sending thousands of silver toothpicks spinning into the air in slow motion. Cyan glow highlighted the jagged surface of the damage, a wireframe superimposed over frozen mercury.

Floating up, it zoomed in an arc and crashed to the ground, spearing all four limbs into the floor. The dark cowboy threw his head back, floating to the right. No sooner had he cleared the ground than four silver spires lanced upward, falling just short of piercing him.

The aged gunslinger roared, firing as he sailed through the air, a barrage that continued until he landed. Shot after shot smashed into the silver construct. The process threads it had opened to attack him provided an easy route to exploit. Cyberspace represented it by the creature being stuck to the ground and unable to evade. It shattered into thousands of chrome chunks, scattering across the black floor. Within seconds, the squealing pieces melted into the ground. The larger fragments lost their shiny coating and degraded into ebon blocks wrapped in a glowing cyan grid.

With the construct gone, it became a simple matter to shut down the turret and the security bots. The newfound calm let Joey scan the network more thoroughly, but it had suffered so much damage, he couldn't access anything of interest. With nothing else to do, he logged out.

Joey squirmed, finding himself wedged against the ground. It took some doing for him to wriggle his way out, and he blinked at a field of destroyed security bots when he emerged. "Looks like you had fun."

The gold visor blocked Eldon's grin. "Just like the training range."

The group crossed the area to the nearest drop building, heading for the one with 'Security Station' stenciled across the outside in black letters. It had no windows or other markings.

Drop buildings were normally used off-Earth, designed to allow for quick setup of a starter outpost in a hazardous environment. Spring-loaded struts similar to the landing pads of spacecraft, held them four feet off the ground, and their hull was even thicker than the armor of a military starship.

Joey circled to a set of portable stairs that led up to a hatch. The steps, as well as the landing at the top, bristled with thousands of upward pointing tines meant to grab the soles of heavy boots, like walking on a sea of table forks. The code locked door still appeared to have power. Joey had the console open and hanging off the wall on its wires within minutes. A hiss of inrushing air drew a wisp of smoke from the shorted circuit into the building as the door slid open.

Eldon nudged it open with his boot. "Sweet shit... poor bastard."

"What?" Joey tried to get a look.

The sight that greeted them made even Katya gasp. A blackened corpse lay face down just inside the door, having rotted to the point where it no longer stank. The arms lacked hands and the stumps ended at uneven lengths of splintered bone. A waving pattern of sprayed blood streaked the walls behind it, and a pair of thick restraints remained about the corpse's legs.

Masaru appraised the scene. "Explosive restraints. Whoever ran this place was definitely not playing nice. That poor fool probably found a Nano knife and cut the cord between his wrists."

"Shit. Are those live?" Eldon glanced at the metal loops.

"Clean 'em off. Katya might want 'em. She's probably into that." Joey's laugh echoed down the corridor.

She punched him in the side, hard enough to drain the humor from his stare.

He rubbed the spot, wincing. "See that? Defensive. Means I'm right."

She hit him again, shaking with anger.

Kenny moved between them.

"Easy, lay off her a bit." He turned to Katya. "You need to learn how to ignore him."

"Ignore who?" She smirked and turned away.

"They may still be functional." Masaru held them aloft by the connecting cable.

The corpse's ankles disintegrated at his tug, and he tossed the manacles to Eldon, who caught them as if dropping the device would have killed everyone.

Masaru glanced deeper into the building. "They'll only explode if you cut the cable or move past a trigger point."

Eldon moved with caution. "We have no idea how old the explosives are, even NE6 gets testy after a few years."

He tiptoed to the door and threw the restraint like a bolo off into the distance. He nodded at the lack of detonation before he stepped over the dead man and ventured down the hall. The guard station save offered little of interest except for a couple empty bunks. A small locker room had two smashed autoshowers and two large sinks. A search of the lockers found a single white jumpsuit that bore the logo of StarPoint Industries. Everyone exchanged looks.

"We just walked into an off-the-books research station for the largest military contractor in the UCF." Eldon gazed at the ceiling. "Dammit. Your guess is as good as mine what kind of nonsense is gonna wanna take a bite out of our asses here."

Kenny took that idea in the opposite direction. "Or we might find something worth millions."

"Assuming they left anything good behind and it won't kill us to touch it." Masaru chimed in.

Katya fidgeted. "Let us do what we need for Joey and get the hell out of here."

Eldon shook his head. "Whatever they did here had to be something the UCF wouldn't have liked. The only reason to do it all the way out here is to avoid scrutiny."

Joey held up a finger. "Or work on something too dangerous to do in city limits."

"That's *so* much better," grumbled Eldon.

The next door led to a tiny room that resembled a holding area with four cells, with floors composed of metal tiles separated by rubber. One cell still held the faint smell of urine and sweat. Wall panels had controls to electrify the floor as well as vary the temperature within each chamber individually. Katya turned away, and slipped back into the hallway without a word.

A few meters ahead in the hallway, a single door hid beneath a massive layer of fuming frost.

Joey blinked. "Well okay, that's pretty fucked up."

Eldon eyed it with distrust. "I got a bad feelin' about that. I would say we skip it, but you know how my luck works. Whatever we need is probably in there."

ICE PRINCESS

Everyone paused, staring at the patch of ice glowing at the end of the tenebrous corridor. Fog formed a cloud at the base of the door. The surrounding metal shimmered with millions of tiny droplets. Eldon approached first, glancing at a handle encased in years of frozen condensation. He stomped his heel into the door several times, causing some of the ice to chunk off in large slabs. Skittering shards raced away in all directions along the floor. Realizing that would take forever, he melted key spots with his vibro knife and a final few stomps knocked an immense slab to the ground with a perfect mold of the door on the underside.

Knee-deep fog swirled around a white-walled lab on the other side of the door. An empty metal shelf on the left was between them and four lockers, open and empty. A few loose pieces of ammunition lay on the ground as well as a few trails of blood droplets. The fog diffused into the corridor, its apparent source a ruptured cryo-fluid tank at the back of the room. To the right, a heavy lift arm hung from the ceiling near a row of four cylindrical tubes. Three were empty while one held a three-foot tall chunk of frozen translucent material. Inside it, the flesh colored blur of a human form hung trapped in a twisted posture.

Everyone moved closer to examine it, only able to make out the sole of a foot that appeared to have been kicking at the wall of the chamber when the liquid froze. A dark spot deeper in the substance hinted that the unlucky person wore the same exploding restraints.

"Last time I checked, corporations didn't have the authority to arrest people." Eldon shook his head.

"Since when do corporations obey laws?" Katya said with a chill in her voice.

"In the UCF they do."

"You are naïve." Katya folded her arms. "And we're not in the UCF now."

Eldon flipped his visor among several scan modes to get a better approximation of the figure's outline. "I think it's a woman."

"I could have told you that from the shape of the foot," said Masaru.

"Think they kept her for fun? Perhaps a research project?" Katya squinted into the cloudy mass.

Masaru's eyebrows flattened. "Doubtful. Cryo-storage is too involved and expensive to use for a concubine, and StarPoint does not do biological or genetic work. It is more likely she is a spy, a traitor, or tried to steal something. Granted, it begs the question, why not just kill her?"

Kenny touched the tank. "Is she alive?"

Joey fiddled with the control system for a few minutes and worked on bypassing the authentication. "Looks like it, status is in the green."

"Whoa, wait a sec..." Masaru raised a hand. "We don't know why she's in there. That could be an assassin doll."

"Why would they freeze a doll?" Kenny made a face. "They'd just turn it off."

"Not if it had a living brain." Masaru frowned.

"Not a doll," said Joey. "There's life support monitoring."

Katya paced around the other end of the room. "It's not right... corporations think they own people."

Joey paused, staring due to the uncharacteristic vulnerability in Katya's voice. For some reason, he decided not to take advantage of the opportunity. "Come on, we can't just leave her." He hammered the terminal with a few kit viruses. "Besides, think of the gratitude sex."

"You are a pig." Katya snapped at him. For a brief moment, she thought better of him, until he ruined it.

Joey grinned, continuing to attack the security. "Oink."

"He may be crass but he's right." Eldon nodded.

"What!" Katya blinked.

"No, dammit, not about the sex... We can't just leave her here. It just ain't right to do that to a person, I don't care who they are."

The console chimed and a pleasant female voice emanated from nowhere in particular. "Cryo Stasis system online, resuscitation process initiated. Please stand by."

The lift arm swung around, the large curved claw grip at the end the perfect size to grasp the cylinder of frozen material. Vibration shook the entire room as it moved the plug of frozen gel into another chamber. When the arm retracted, a clear barrier rose out of the floor to surround it. Heavy machine noises came from below. Seconds later, a cloud of opacity spread through the substance like milk poured into water. Everyone stared mesmerized at the expanding whiteness until it engulfed the entire mass.

Rattling in the floor waned and the sound of the machinery wound down. In the ceiling, the whine of a blower fan kicked on. The opacity turned out to be fog. Drawn into vent slits, it revealed the form of a nude young woman curled up on a metal disc, covered in little water droplets.

Thin and fair skinned, she had a face that looked too young for her body. Finger-shaped bruises circled both of her upper arms. Teal polish covered every nail. Streaks of eyeliner ran down her cheeks as though she had been crying before being frozen. Canary blonde hair hung to her collarbones, with an inch of black at the ends. A heavy coating of makeup left her eyelashes thick and dark. The explosive restraints linked her wrists together in front and another set secured her ankles.

The display panel on the restraints had cracked, and the housing had tarnished around the seams.

Kenny cringed. "Electronics are toasted. We're gonna have to cut them off."

Masaru held up a hand. "Hold on, we don't know how dangerous she is."

Joey tried to remove his duster coat, forgetting it was part of his armored vest. Katya gave him a surprised glance.

The same ephemeral voice echoed from everywhere. "Cryo resuscitation process complete. Shutting down."

The shield sank into the ground. As soon as the seal broke, air entered the space and the shining disc flashed blurry with condensation. Everyone stared in silence, watching her chest move with her breaths until her eyes fluttered open. For a few seconds, only her eyes moved, shifting from one person to the next. She swallowed and went to sit up, discovering she was in restraints when she tried to brace her hand against the ground.

Screaming, she thrashed against the binders. Kenny and Joey both reached to help her, but she scooted back against the wall. Her breath fogged in the air as she breathed in erratic staccato rasps, and the second realization, how cold it was, hit her.

"Who are you?" She shivered, her voice a pathetic squeak. "What do you want? Why am I naked?"

"We just found you frozen in cryo gel." Masaru crouched down to examine the restraints. "It is standard procedure to be naked when frozen. Clothing can fuse with the skin during the process causing permanent scarring. I do not understand why these were not removed first."

She shied away from her reflection in Masaru's visor, blushing. "I... don't remember anything."

"This girl seems familiar." Katya studied her deep green eyes. "I know I've seen her somewhere."

"There's plenty of clothes in that HLM van." Eldon pointed over his shoulder with his thumb.

"What's your name?" Kenny reached to help her up. "We are not here to hurt you."

She ventured a hesitant peek. "I... I don't remember." Her teeth chattered.

"Let's get you out of this cold." Kenny went to pick her up, but she shrieked and scooted away.

Masaru stood up. "Judging by the bruises and being upside down in the tank, I think they froze her in a hurry... probably when the fighting started. Chances are good that they didn't follow proper procedure and she may have temporary or permanent amnesia."

Kenny pulled her off the metal plate and helped her to her feet. She wobbled in place as she tried to get a purchase on the slick ground, leaving smeared footprints in the condensation. Eldon looked off in a polite direction. Joey didn't hide his checking her out.

"I'd give you my coat but it's not really a coat. It's part of the armor." Kenny tugged at it to prove his point.

"How can we get her out of those things?" Katya smirked.

"Easy…" Eldon raised a hand. "We don't know how stable they are."

"Unstable?" The girl still searched for a voice, still producing only a squeaky whisper.

No one wanted to tell her that she had four small bombs locked onto her.

She looked at the vibroknife on Eldon's belt. "Hey, that'll cut these. Please…" She made doe-eyes at him that made even Joey feel guilty. "If you let me out, I'll do anything you want."

"Oh, come on. What are you, sixteen?" Kenny couldn't look at her.

"Nineteen. I'll be twenty in a few months…" She gazed into the distance, lost in thought. "I think I remember my birthday is August twenty-first."

"Actually…" Joey raised a finger over his shoulder as he studied the console. "She's been a snow globe for about seven years if the system log is accurate. If she went in at nineteen, she's technically twenty-six."

"What?" She spun to face him so fast she almost fell. "Seven… years?"

"How does a nineteen-year-old wind up a prisoner in a military research facility?" Joey disconnected his deck from the console.

"Probably kidnapped from the city to be experimented on." Katya stared at the floor.

"No." Eldon shook his head. "StarPoint doesn't do that kind of thing. They make military vehicles, they'd have no need of this."

"Don't tell me you buy into all that conspiracy theory stuff?" Kenny glanced at Katya.

Katya gazed off into the distance, not even trying to hide her accent. "I have seen what they can do."

"I can probably get those off. Let me have a look." Kenny held out his hand to her.

She remained still as he examined the metal around her wrist. She offered a weak smile once she realized he wasn't just trying to peek.

"Standard steel. The screws are recessed, but I think I have a driver for them in the truck."

Katya looked up with sudden remembrance. "Amber? Is your name Amber?"

She stared into space while her mind clawed at any trace of memory. "Maybe… kinda sounds familiar."

"You're right." Masaru lifted her chin with his finger.

She swatted his hand away. "Don't look at me like that, I'm not some horse for sale."

Masaru sighed at her. "Your name is Amber Wortham. Your picture was on dozens of flyers in the city."

"Well she's not lying about her age." Joey laughed.

Kenny glared. "Joey, so help me, if you take advantage…"

"Come on Kenny, if you weren't married…" Joey smiled.

"No." He shook his head. "Her face is too…" He struggled over the words while wagging his hand. "She looks too young, and think about how we found her, you just can't take advantage of someone in that situation."

"I wonder if that reward is still good." Joey rubbed his chin.

Kenny glanced at him with a raised eyebrow. "It doesn't matter if it is or isn't, we're getting her back to the city. If you want to claim the reward, fine, but we help her either way." He looked at the others. "Alright, wait here. I'll run with Eldon back to the truck to grab my tools and some clothes for her. I don't want to split up, but we can't take her outside like that with the Canids around."

Katya nodded. "She'd be easy prey."

"For what?" Amber whined.

"Don't worry about it, we killed them already." Joey smiled.

The small degree of contentment Amber felt from the much warmer hallway lasted only until the desiccated corpse at the end of the corridor came into view. Joey pulled her away from the sight.

Amber screamed into Joey's shoulder, finding her voice after a few gasps. She held her arms up, too terrified to even struggle with the binders. "Oh my god, these things explode."

"They're not going to." Joey patted her back. "We are going to get you out of here."

She lowered her arms as if carrying nitroglycerin, crossing her hands over her crotch.

"Kat, maybe you should take her into that locker room? She'll feel better if men aren't hovering all around her."

Katya blinked in disbelief. "Are you feeling okay?"

He smirked. "Just go."

A peal of strained metal groaned over the entire building. Several discrete puffs of dust fell from the ceiling one after the other as footsteps thumped by overhead.

"What was that?" Amber's voice trembled in time with her body.

She looked at the metal around her ankles, shakes worsening at the reminder she couldn't run. Her fingers dug into Joey's coat as she hid behind him.

Masaru drew his katana, advancing toward the noise. Katya reached to Amber to pull her into the locker room. Before she made contact, a door slammed open in a flash of brown fur. A Canid surged into the hallway, bowling into Joey and smashing him against the wall face first. The force of the hit knocked his pistol out of his hand, sending it clattering to the floor. Panic shone from his eyes as exhilaration warped his lips into a manic grin. He struggled to push himself away from the wall.

The captive girl tripped on her hobbled ankles, sprawling on the floor. With Katya's voice repeating "easy prey" in her mind, Amber went for the dropped gun. Joey howled, somewhere between terror and laughter as the mutant licked the back of his neck. Hot sticky drool slid down his back inside his armor. Amber pounced on the pistol with both hands, shoving herself up into a seated position, and aimed. The handcuff chain barely allowed her enough separation to hold the weapon with a practiced two-handed grip. She flicked the safety off and fired three shots into the Canid's side. Joey glanced sideways at her. The girl's no longer belonged to a petrified airhead, at least, until the dog man turned to roar at her.

Shackles clattered as her bare feet slid on the steel floor in a frantic effort to crawl backward. With three slugs in it and its attention elsewhere, the Canid weakened enough for Joey to push out from under it. He slid down the wall to the floor. The mutant stalked after Amber, sensing a helpless meal. It took only a single step before Masaru's katana burst out of its chest. The canid emitted a startled yelp. A spritz of warm blood hitting her face snapped Amber out of her deer-like stare. She shot it once more in the head, and the Canid slumped over sideways. Masaru spun his blade around and plunged it hilt-deep in the monster's chest, at least half the blade into the floor beneath it.

"Where did you learn how handle a gun?" Joey sat up.

Amber put the safety back on and let him take it.

"I"—she offered a helpless stare—"I guess I know how to shoot... but I don't know why I know. As soon as I had a gun in my hands, it just felt like I'd been shooting forever."

"Maybe you're a secret project assassin, some kind of genetically engineered killer. That would explain all the security on you." Joey tapped her ankle restraints. "Those things would probably hold a Canid. Overkill for a little thing like you."

Amber blushed and tried to cover herself.

"She's not a doll." Katya's metallurgical scan showed a dark girl-shaped shadow. Only the restraints and some minor headware showed up white. She looked up. "Are there any more?"

Eldon's voice crackled over the comm link. "I heard shots, what is your sit-rep?"

Joey squinted at thin air. "What the fuck is a sit-rep?"

"One dog. It's handled." Masaru wiped his blade on the thing's back. "How is it out there?"

"We were engaged by a pack of six... They're dead, we're clear. Kenny took a hit but it's nothing a stim won't fix."

"They hunt at night." Kenny grumbled into the channel. "Stay inside."

Joey wandered into a small office while Masaru covered the hallway. Amber followed Katya into the locker room, taking a seat on the bench with a mournful stare at her restraints. She made a half-hearted attempt to tug at them, but remembering their explosive nature, she froze, shivering and stiff.

"This can't be really happening to me. Where am I?"

Katya hovered in the doorway, back turned. "They probably erased your memory too."

In the office, Joey examined several terminals and found only one of them still in working order. The rest looked like someone shot them out on purpose.

The lack of defenses surprised him, until he realized the security servers were all offline. Holographic panels appeared littered with files, most of which turned out to be useless. A smear of flesh-tone in the dark attracted his eye. It showed Amber curled up on a metal floor. He tapped on it, pulling it into the central display screen. A two handed swipe pulled it open to reveal a video object. Unable to resist, he poked it and a new panel opened with a feed dated about seven years old. She was in one of the cells, naked, twitching and screaming from a series of electric shocks. When she wasn't being zapped, she either pounded on the door and begged, or sobbed quietly to herself. A recorded voice kept offering her release if she would tell them how she found this installation. He swiped his hand at the video, fast forwarding. The shocks stopped, replaced with periods of extreme cold, then high heat. As young as she was, she resisted the torture. Joey couldn't continue watching her beg for her mother, and stopped playback after only a minute.

Another video depicted a fire exchange at the perimeter. Amber and two men jumped out of the trees, mowing down a trio of security guards with silenced weapons. As the men covered either side, Amber affixed what looked like a bomb to the wall. Four men in green armor similar to Eldon's leapt on them from above. Amber was disarmed and flung to the ground with such ease it looked like a Special Forces soldier fighting a high school kid. He held her down with one foot in her back while disarming the device. Another commando disarmed the older man before spinning him face first into the wall. Judging by the blood spray, the hit killed him. The other man went down, unconscious but alive. The attack ended before any of them could react.

"Hey Masaru. Check this out." Joey called him over and replayed the files.

"She was HLM." Masaru frowned.

"Amber Wortham, spoiled little rich girl... Yeah that fits." Joey killed the terminal. "Oh well. So much for my genetic assassin theory."

They turned at the sound of the outer hatch squealing open. Kenny came through in a hurry with Eldon backing in behind him, firing. After two shots, a distant growl turned into a yelp.

"Where is she?" Kenny held up his toolbox.

Joey pointed. Kenny edged into the locker room, smiling as he set the toolbox down with a heavy clank. The scent of oil wafted up when he opened the lid and searched among the tools. He knelt in front of her and pulled her foot into his lap to study the binders. The tiny screws that held the outer shell closed had been bored out to make it impossible to remove them with a normal tool, but Kenny had a drill driver that would work. Eldon dropped a duffel bag of clothes inside the door and went back to the exit to stand guard.

It was tedious work. After twenty minutes, the last screw came out and he eased the two pieces apart. A snow of crystallized dust fell out from the hollow space inside, snowing over her foot. Kenny pinched some of the grey substance between two fingers, holding it up and twisting to the rear.

"Hey Eldon? What do you think of this?"

He squinted at Kenny's finger, then shirked off one glove and gathered a handful from the floor. Amber brushed the substance away from her instep, moving as if one wrong twitch would kill them all.

"The extended freeze rendered the explosive inert." Eldon wiped his hand on his chest.

"Dammit, we could have cut her out of these things right away." Kenny grumbled while offering an apologetic look. "Okay hon. I'm going to cut these things off you, but I need you to stay still. If you jerk away it's going to..."

She bit her lower lip and nodded. "Burn like a mother, I understand."

True to her word, she sat motionless as he pulled out the laser cutter and removed the scrap metal from her other leg, and freed her hands. As the last bit of them hit the floor, she flung herself onto him with a hug, saying "thank you" so many times it all blended into one long sound.

"Okay... Okay... Put something on so we can leave you alone with Joey." Kenny patted her on the back and stood up.

"Bite me." Joey's voice drifted in from the hallway.

INNER CHILD

The clothes had a look and scent familiar to Amber, and she spent a moment feeling the fabric and trying to find some trace of memory among the threads. Everyone turned and looked at the young woman peeking out of the door in a purple sweater, jeans, and pink socks. Lacking only shoes, she carried herself with more confidence.

"I can't say thank you enough." She dragged the duffel bag out and added a sweater to her wardrobe.

Masaru gave her a simple nod.

"Just doin' what's right." Eldon nodded at her.

"So... Amber... You might want to see this." Joey opened the office door.

She followed him to the terminal. "What?"

"Found some vids that show how you got here. Some of them are hard to watch."

"Did they-?" She cringed.

"I doubt it. They used shock torture on you in that room over there." He put a hand on her shoulder. "Then again, you did come here to blow them up so I can see why they were less than hospitable."

She blinked. "What?"

"It looks like you were part of the HLM, and you and some friends came here to show your objection to whatever went on here, with some bombs."

She rubbed her hands up and down her arms, trying to warm up. "I don't remember that... I..." Amber looked up as a glint of memory lit up in the back of her mind. "They did something very, very bad here..."

Masaru appeared in the doorway. "The haphazard cryo-stasis is responsible for your memory loss. It may or may not return."

Eldon chimed in from the hallway. "You don't have to go back to that life. You can go home. The HLM ain't what it was seven years ago. They're just another damn street gang now, just one that tries to excuse their violence with a righteous cause."

"I…" She trembled. "I don't want to hurt people."

"Good." Joey nodded, dragging the files into a virtual trashcan. "Then no one needs to ever see those."

"C'mon, let's take her back to the truck." Eldon took her hand and passed her to Kenny.

They made their way out the door, though Kenny carried her over the spiky stairs. Not quite six yards from the building, the echo of a gunshot rang around the walls, followed by the sharp plastic clack of a slug striking Masaru across the side of the helmet.

He went over backward like a wooden target dummy.

Kenny sprinted left, dragging Amber behind a portable air handler a few meters away from the security building. He pushed her to the ground with as much care possible given the rush, and swung the rifle off his back into a firing position over the machine. She crawled against the side of the air unit.

"Why are they shooting at me?"

Kenny fired twice at a shadow by the wall where the original shot came from. "We don't even know who it is."

Eldon rushed forward and to the right, diving behind a large chunk of concrete embedded in the ground.

"Masaru, you alright?" Eldon yelled over the comm.

Masaru flooded the comm with a low throaty growl for a few seconds. "Whoever did that has forfeited his life."

He sat upright and touched the scuffmark. The impact had driven his helmet into his nose and bloodied it, but the bullet hadn't pierced. He rolled behind a different piece of debris.

Katya ran back up the stairs into the security building to take cover. "You boys can handle this. I'm not going to be effective at this range with a handgun." She pulled the door closed.

Joey hit the ground as well, crawling under the security building. Amber looked at the door and thought about making a run for it, but fear got the better of her and she stayed down.

A figure in green armor darted past the gap in the wall, about Eldon's height and build and carrying what looked like the standard UCF combat rifle, the M2414 Crusader. Eldon and Kenny both fired as he went by, but missed the jade blur.

"Son of a bitch can move." Eldon lurched back to his feet, sprinting to another hunk of debris closer to the wall.

"That looks like one of the Spec Ops guys from the vid. Be careful, they took the HLM down like high school kids." Joey ducked under the security building.

"They *were* high school kids, jackass." Eldon sounded unamused.

The figure came back through the gap, sprinting and firing at Eldon's position, making him duck a shower of fragments from the bullets chipping the debris. Kenny triggered again. Two shots glanced off the man's chest with sparks. The attacker skidded to a halt behind a cargo container that had been knocked off the pile.

"Any chance that guy is active duty?" Kenny aimed at the metal box.

"Nah." Eldon replied. "I'm not getting any transponder ID or IFF signal from him. Plus there's only one. If the military was here, there would be a lot more."

"Whatever happened to talking?" Katya asked via comm, from inside.

The figure whipped around the cargo box, firing at Kenny. He dove on top of Amber as a hail of projectiles came by, trenching gouges in the side of the machine and showering them with small fragments. One slug came back off the security building and scored on Kenny's back like a kidney punch, failing to penetrate his armor.

Masaru leapt from cover and kicked on his speedware. The augmentation pushed him into a near thirty mile per hour sprint. The figure turned to aim at him as he lit up the area with his S-19. The invisible laser left no obvious explanation for the sudden formation of holes and spurts of liquid metal that burst from the container, spattering the figure's armor with grey splats. Two flashes of sparking smoke blew out of the stranger's arm, making him abort the attempted shot at Masaru. Somersaulting straight ahead, the man in green skidded to a halt behind a small chunk of concrete.

Kenny pulled himself up and aimed over the air handler. He chipped away at the block with a few shots that did little more than make the helmet duck. Amber grabbed a pistol from the left side of Kenny's belt and angled for a shot.

"What the hell are you doing?" He tried to push her back down.

Kenny's pistol, larger than Joey's, almost bounced off her forehead when she fired it. The second shot came less severe, but still knocked her around.

"I'm not gonna die without a fight."

"Get your ass down!" Kenny shoved her to the floor and landed on top of her. "Look, kid, if you have a gun, you're a damned target. You have no armor on so you're gonna die if you take a hit."

Eldon interrupted via comm. "Kenny, hate to break it to you but that Crusader's loadin' ten mil AP-EX. You ain't wearin' armor either."

Kenny didn't see Amber. In his mind, she was Alyssa out on her first Badlands trip.

Amber looked at him, shocked by the concern in his voice. "Whoa, okay, Sorry." She released the gun. "I just hate feeling helpless."

"Sorry." He crouched. "You remind me of my kid, that's just the sort of thing she would say. Keep it, but stay down."

Their attacker had vanished for the moment. Eldon swept back and forth with his rifle, waiting for motion. Masaru crouched behind a lump of wall halfway between Eldon and the gap they had entered from, some fifty yards ahead of everyone else.

Eldon stood and prepared to advance to the next bit of debris. The figure popped up over a hunk of wall and fired at him. Two shots glanced off Eldon's shoulder armor as he flung himself to the ground. The weak angle prevented penetration, but his shoulder throbbed.

Kenny's rifle belched blue flames. He dragged a long burst across the chest of their assailant, landing at least four slugs. The figure staggered back as several fragments of armor flew. No blood sprayed, which made him worry. Kenny knew he had gotten a good piece of the bastard. There should have been blood.

Hearing the hit, Masaru activated his speedware again. Overcharged signals ran down microwires into his muscles, throwing him into a ten-foot high leap over a broken piece of wall. He landed in a blurring sprint, closing in a serpentine path in an effort to bring his katana into the fight.

The man turned at Masaru and sent a dozen rounds into the earth behind him, kicking up small mushroom clouds of dirt. With each stride, the wirepaths in his limbs traced threads of pain. Years spent training his mind and body allowed him to run at that speed without breaking bones.

He swerved, using a huge piece of wall to block return fire. Two steps later, he sprang into the air once again. The green man had aimed at the edge and was too slow to correct, not expecting his foe to come over the top. Masaru flew down behind an arc of gleaming Nano blade as the figure scrambled backward. The clash sent a piece of rifle to each side, but didn't strike flesh. The man appeared to skid, about to fall, but reversed without warning and slammed his fist into Masaru's chest, turning him into a human missile.

The black samurai struck the chunk of wall with the small of his back and flipped over it before coming to rest flat on his stomach on the other side.

"It's... a... doll." Masaru croaked over the comm link.

Eldon ran forward, disregarding cover. Advancing behind a series of short bursts, he charged in an attempt to draw him away from the stunned Masaru. The green armor ducked behind the concrete as Eldon circled. Kenny stayed with Amber, training his rifle in their attacker's direction but having no shot. Joey peeked up from his hiding place, but the games happened too far away to bother using a pistol.

Between a cybernetic punch to the chest, a butt-first flight into a large mound of concrete, and speedware toasting his own muscles, Masaru hurt. He tuned it out and forced himself back to his feet. He knew the armor saved his ass. That punch would have gone right through his chest without it. Masaru stumbled around the chunk of wall just in time to see the doll lunge at Eldon.

A sidearm block hit Eldon's rifle with so much force it went flying out of his grip and broke the carrying strap. The weapon sailed off to the right and clattered over the top of another piece of wall. Eldon waved his arms to keep his balance as he took an involuntary step backward. Masaru feigned a lunge, buying Eldon a few seconds.

Eldon found his footing and yanked the vibroknife off his belt. The green man's helmet rotated back and forth between them. Masaru had gone well beyond angry and didn't fancy waiting for the stranger to make the first move. The armored figure lunged away from his attack, diving at Eldon. Ready for it, Eldon slid under the punch and scored a nice gash down the thigh with the hissing knife.

The blade sliced the armor with ease and a shower of sparks. A long gash opened the man's thigh, exposing only mechanical parts. Eldon's adrenaline went to the roof. This *was* a doll, and getting into a knife fight with a doll ranked high on the chart of stupid, right below wing surfing a dropship while it breached the upper atmosphere. Training took over. Fear had no hold in Eldon's mind. He'd have plenty of time to say 'holy shit' about what he just did after neutralizing the threat.

Attempting to capitalize on the sudden change of momentum, Eldon made a quick swiping stroke for the doll's head. It leaned back just enough for the blade to pass by and hammered Eldon with a left cross to the side of the helmet. The impact sent an echoing *crack* over the area, and Eldon head first into the ground like a dart.

Kenny angled for a shot, but bodies were so close he chose not to risk it. The figure turned on Masaru but underestimated his speed. Masaru flowed around the graceless attack, exploiting its miscalculation. He whirled under the swinging arm and rammed the Nano katana to the hilt in its chest. The doll's limbs fell listless as soon as the blade stopped. Blood spurted out along the edge on both sides. Eldon staggered back to his feet, his reflexive attack stalled at the sight of red.

Dolls shouldn't bleed.

The figure staggered and fell into a seated position, leaning on a chunk of wall. No life remaining in its arms or legs, it collapsed like a cyborg without power. Masaru pulled the blade out with a single clean stroke and gazed at the blood coating the green plate with an imperious sneer. He lifted it for the beheading strike, but paused as a copious blast of fog erupted from the back of the armor, stalled by curiosity. The chest split open along the pectoral ridge as a hinged hatch plate made itself visible.

Strained gurgling breaths came from inside the chest. At the delicate timbre in the rasping voice, his eyes widened in horror. Masaru dropped to one knee and grabbed the ridge of the plate with his left hand, not wanting to believe what his mind told him he heard. He swayed from pain and dread, his katana loose in the fingers of his other hand. Eldon moved up after reclaiming his rifle.

"Clear the target." Eldon aimed at the man's chest.

Masaru stayed motionless.

Eldon leaned to fire around him. "Dammit Masaru, clear the target."

Masaru shook his head to the negative. Kenny emerged from cover and walked over with his rifle trained as well, followed by Joey, who held his pistol down and to the side while running.

"What the fuck is going on?" Eldon looked at Masaru.

Masaru grunted and shoved upward. The chest panel rose with a loud hiss and more fog, like the entry hatch for a powerarmor battle suit, on hinges in the figure's shoulders. Within the padded chest cavity, the face of a white-haired little girl stared back at them.

She couldn't have been older than nine.

Blood foamed from her teeth and ran down her chin as she struggled to breathe, soaking a grimy tank top clinging about her chest. Her arms folded in front of her as if she was entombed. A filthy cloth cap sat askew on her head, secured with a chinstrap and studded with wires and electrodes. Her unkempt hair had the appearance of growing unrestrained for several years. Despite her age, she stared at Masaru with hate and malice.

"I...Just killed a kid." Masaru fell away from the armor and landed in a slouch.

"Oh man." Eldon sagged. "Oh man... what the fuck are they doing out here."

The girl's eyelids drooped. Her breathing became shallower. Blood ran out of her mouth once the strength keeping her jaw clenched left her. Her head rolled to the side and sagged. Eldon cursed under his breath as he searched for the release catch.

"Stim!" Eldon yelled.

An abdominal hatch opened forward, extending down and out from the main unit. Her body, head, and arms fit within the chest and her legs ran down into the suit's thighs.

"This ain't no doll... It's a damn power armor."

At last holding the stimpak in the right direction, Eldon pushed it into her chest. The child's closed eyes didn't react.

Blood seeped from a katana-sized slit in her chest.

"Don't waste the stimpak." Masaru's voice hung with regret. "It is astounding she lasted long enough to glare."

Eldon slid his hands around her sides, threaded his fingers under her armpits and lifted the limp body up and out of the armor with as much tenderness as he could. She looked half-starved and stank from urine and waste smeared all the way down her legs. Her dingy shorts were far from the white they had been when new. He laid her upon the grass and sighed.

Katya gasped in horror. The sight of the girl had her crying before she could put up her defenses. She stared at the exact same thing she had tried to flee by coming to the UCF. To see this kind of depravity here as well kicked the foundation out from under her faith in humanity.

Masaru hadn't moved from where he fell. Power armor or not, he found no honor in killing a child. He couldn't even bring himself to look in her direction. Eldon tugged at the girl's shirt, trying to straighten it on her little body.

Joey put his hand on Kenny's shoulder, knowing the effect this sight would have on his friend.

Kenny stared in silence, lost in a waking nightmare of losing Alyssa.

MAUSOLEUM

Amorphous white shapes undulated across smooth burgundy marble tiles, sliding over seams and the letters carved upon them. Nina's fingertips traced the cold surface as she walked, feeling the gaps pass. At two hundred and two, she stopped. The shifting glow settled over the words 'Vincent Montoya' etched in a plain but elegant font.

The letters blurred as she focused on her own image in the dark stone, his name floating as if stenciled across her chest. His square, one among thousands, looked identical except for the words upon it and the memories behind it. With the sound of her footsteps silent, the cavernous atrium echoed with distant murmuring voices, other people and other broken lives.

She felt a sense of appropriateness being here. The face in the gloss may as well have been her ghost, asking her why she didn't stay.

Since her transformation, she regarded clothing as a device of pure utility. This artificial body was itself something worn, an extravagant garment for a soul to go out on the town with. When not in the privacy of her apartment, all she needed were armor, boots, and a coat. Her ghost seemed more like what remained in the outer reaches of her ever-distancing memory of the time before. For Vincent, she wore an elegant black dress that made her face seem even paler, caught between it and her hair.

The material split in two paths of fabric that connected behind her neck to bare her shoulders and most of her back and the hem ended just below the middle of her thighs. She hadn't worn this since her grandfather's funeral, when she was four inches shorter and the dress stopped just above her knee. Nina hadn't thought much of it until she noticed the stares.

At least the shoes fit.

The black heels clung by means of an articulated strap that spiraled around her ankle to halfway up her shin. The coil, Myofiber strands covered in artificial leather, moved like a serpent, its tightness monitored by electronics in the shoe. They were a relic from a time when she thought nothing of dropping twenty thousand credits on a pair of shoes she would wear once. A typical high school attitude, before she decided she wanted to do something meaningful with her life. How she bristled at her father's insistence that she marry and give him a grandson. Now, she would give almost anything for the ability to do just that.

Her plain indigo handbag deformed with the presence of her service weapon. She held it in front of her, more to do something with her hands than for any sense of security it provided. Nina stared at the tile, wondering if the activity on her VidPhone was Vincent trying to contact her from the other side. The network team found evidence of an inbound signal, but it didn't look like a real call and they couldn't find the origin.

DeWinter theorized that it had to have been done by some kind of techno-savant based on intense route masking. Half of her brain wondered if that was their ego defense at not being able to explain it. Then again, a ghostly entity wouldn't bother to bounce a signal from a dozen countries.

"I had a feeling I'd find you here."

A beige mass shifted toward her in the tiles. She could make out a tan sweater and dark 'old man' pants. Hardin looked more like a high school history teacher than a spymaster from Division 9, perhaps a deliberate engineering of appearance to mislead. Nina stared at the word Vincent as he walked up to her, hoping he didn't make a comment about the slutty dress. She forgot all of her civilian clothing had a dead woman's size.

"I'm okay. It was just a prank call."

Hardin looked at her back and wondered how the dress stayed in place. "Microhook?"

Nina brushed her hair off her neck, revealing the loop of fabric.

"Ahh. It's always that one little thing you don't see." He winked.

She flicked her eyes toward him. "Yeah."

"So what happened last night?" He touched a small button by Vincent's gravestone, creating a holographic candle.

"I was just doing a favor for someone."

"Mm hmm." Hardin nodded. "So… Division 9 sends fourteen million credits worth of cutting edge military hardware to stomp a street thug into peanut butter." He shook his head with a forced grin. "Sounds like an exemplary use of tax funds to me."

Nina stared at nothing in particular. "I was on downtime, I still get downtime, don't I?"

"You know Lou is asking if there was some connection between Z Bone and something international." Hardin added, folding his hands behind his back.

"Chandrasekhar's just looking to get us to do his work for him. The bureau chiefs of Division 1 always are."

Hardin's dry chuckle echoed here. "Yeah, that sounds about right. Before I express any level of discontent at suffering a two hour meeting with him, would you do me the favor of filling me in on why?"

Nina didn't want to explain her real reason for going to New Hope. Of course, this was old hat to Hardin. He could spot a liar as easily as if you had a sign over your head with "bullshit" written on it that blinked each time you fibbed. He didn't even have a somatic response system. Her doll body was so perfect at mimicking human actions, the same tics that foil liars would still affect her.

"I was checking out this place on the net, New Hope, the one that those two dead hackers were affiliated with."

Hardin lifted one of his bushy brown eyebrows at her. "You think there's something going on there with your current project?"

"I know there's a hacker involved. Those induced suicides... Blank and Yan, might have been practice." Nina thought of Joey from the Imperial hotel security footage. "Someone good is covering for Korin and Nemsky and might be trying to get rid of witnesses or associates."

Hardin held his chin betwixt his thumb and forefinger. "You are certain that one of them is not doing the hacking?"

"It would have to be Itai, but I don't see how he's this good in cyberspace. Nemsky's not the type to be that delicate. His idea of hacking a computer system would involve an axe." A faint thread of anger tainted her voice.

Harold folded his arms. "I spoke with my friend Ehud at the embassy. Mossad is sticking by their story. They say they never had an Itai Korin on their books."

"Maybe that's a truthful deception," Nina suggested. "He might not have been on the books."

Hardin wiped his hand over his mouth. "I'm not convinced. I've known Ehud for a long time and he would tell me... unless Israel is actively involved with this operation. Even then, he'd have dropped me a hint without saying anything. We've got nothing that indicates that is even a remote possibility. I believe him."

"So that means Itai Korin is not Itai Korin. The whole Mossad angle could be a diversion. So who the hell is he if he's not Israeli? Anything from the other side?"

"Not a damn thing. You mention Nemsky over there and people just walk away from you." Hardin chuckled. "So how does Z Bone tie into all this?"

Nina sighed. "At New Hope, I met the father of two boys he killed. I couldn't help but feel for the guy. He just wanted to understand why they were dead and the police were no help."

Hardin shook his head. "That's hardly your responsibility. Let Division 1 deal with that."

"They did. They told him that his sons were gangbangers that got what they deserved." She turned to face him. "I also found out an officer Collins had been working with the gangs."

"That explains that report. Well I suppose I can call this an IA operation even if it was an accident."

"The boys were clean." Nina went into an explanation.

"Okay. Forget about it. Look, we have some new information. Cole's team spotted Itai infiltrating the diplomatic tower, we believe in an effort to make contact with Warner."

"I should get over there." Nina turned.

Hardin raised a hand. "There's more. Net ops got a hit on Nemsky. Seems like he's got an apartment under the alias Viktor Zabrun."

"Another electronic trace." Nina sighed. "Is there a team in place yet?"

Harold smiled at her. "You're running the operation, Nina. I didn't want to spook him out just yet."

"I'm going." The click of her heels filled the hallway, drawing several glances.

He followed to the elevator at the end of the atrium, still with his hands folded behind his back. The silver doors closed, replacing the hallway with a perfect reflection of the city behind the glass capsule. Something about the sight of a massive atrium full of tombs made her want to cry. A fourteen-inch square of false marble among many thousands was all that remained of the man with whom she had wanted to spend the rest of her life.

The elevator slid down the side of the building, the rhythmic *whump* whenever the car passed over the gaps between each floor created the only break in the silence. Nina watched the floor counter tick down from 61 as Hardin studied his NetMini. An unimpressed look settled over his face as he put it back in his pocket. Nina noticed he hadn't ogled her once, and wondered if he was being professional or thought of her as an 'it' rather than a 'she.'

"They have a shot of Itai leaving the Tower. We couldn't get eyes into Warner's residence."

"Guess I'm going to Nemsky's." Nina glanced at the city rising up around her. She closed her eyes and wished that Vincent waited downstairs to make fun of her for dressing up like a cop.

Harold walked her to the car. She went around and popped the trunk. Hardin's intent to continue walking stalled when she reached up and unclasped her gown.

Hardin blinked. "What the hell are you doing?"

"Changing," she said, matter-of-factly, and let go of the dress. "I'm not going after Nemsky in this thing."

"You can't do that out here." Hardin had mastered the art of making whispers sound like yells. "This is a public place."

"So?"

"There are people here that can see you."

"Isn't that what public means?"

"Nina, you may not think of this as your body anymore but..." He hesitated as the reality of her exposed chest hit him. Averting his eyes, he continued. "Modesty notwithstanding, you shouldn't create unwanted attention. The fewer people that notice you, the better. Remember that whole thing about not standing out and vanishing into the mask of memory?"

"That's different from dolls stripping to use optical cloaking how?"

He turned away as she took hold of the dress again. "That's a tactical requirement, now you're just being trashy."

So that was it. He did think of her as a woman.

With an impish smile, she fixed the strap behind her neck. "Fine... But if this thing gets shot to shit it's going to come out of the budget." She sighed. "It'll probably come off in a fight anyway. Wouldn't that be a sight?"

Harold walked off, not looking back. "Check the place out and decide. I trust your judgment. By the way, don't forget to duck."

Nina pounded the trunk closed, rocking the car, wondering why she wanted her armor so much. Did she fear injury, or was she simply terrified of seeing metal looking back at her from a wound?

That would break the illusion.

46

WRONG PLACE, RIGHT TIME

The ride ended in less than three minutes, plenty of time to arrange for whispercraft and ground units to provide backup. She set down in the emergency lane just outside the lobby and grabbed her handbag. She stood with an awkward wobble, forgetting she had heels on, but found her footing after a few steps. The lobby door waited about twenty yards of glass wall away and she scanned the interior as she walked along. Two male dolls hovered behind the reception desk, one of whom spoke with a woman holding the hand of a young boy standing next to her. A middle-aged executive sat on a bench in the center of the room, reading a datapad, and five large men had positioned themselves around the room in a suspicious pattern.

Two stood near the door, one by the elevators, and two leaned on columns in the center of the room. Their arrangement made Nina suspect them to be Nemsky's security team. She wondered if Hardin knew they were here. This dress would raise much less suspicion than her usual attire and he seemed to want her to keep wearing it. Of course, that could have just been the man in him.

She smiled, enjoying the feeling as she walked up to the smoky glass doors. The stenciled words 'Chimera Apartments' slid out of her view almost as fast as she could read them. This could be as easy as just walking in and going up to Nemsky's apartment. He had no idea what she looked like so she could play the part of someone that had gone to the wrong door. Acting like a call girl was too trite and would make him suspicious. The files painted him as a man that held women in contempt, weak things for him to use and discard. She would seem lost and helpless, and play to his attitude. She wanted him alive even if the brass didn't care. He might be able to help find Itai.

High heels on stone floor turned every head in the lobby and long bare legs kept them turned. She made no eye contact, wearing a succubus grin as she strode toward the elevators. The five large men exchanged knowing glances, like wolves circling a fawn. Nina had the sense that they had been expecting her, but couldn't understand how or why.

"That's her."

Nina's amplified hearing picked up the man by the elevator. Things were about to get messy, and the presence of a boy in the room worried her. In the span of one step, she calculated three patterns of attack to drop them all before they could hurt anyone. Of course, the time it would take to recover her weapon from the purse made them all implausible.

A step later, they pulled pistols and converged.

Nina leapt to the right, behind a column, and stooped to press a button on each shoe. The strap went limp and slithered in a corkscrew into the base. The heels wouldn't survive the rigors of combat while strapped to the feet of a doll, not to mention they would get in the way. Cold stone touched her feet with the reassurance of stability.

A tactical overlay floated in her vision, an overhead view of the room with dots representing every person, detected with a combination of thermal reflectivity and acoustics.

"Boss wants her alive."

One of Nemsky's thugs moved up alongside her column. His pistol came around the edge of the artificial sandstone.

"It's over bitch, give it up."

Nina whirled on him, flinging the purse into the air off her weapon, firing as soon as the material cleared the barrel.

The shot struck just below his nose. Blue muzzle fire licked his face as the massive slug detonated his head into a sluice of gore. Nina darted to the next column, firing three more times. The massive report from the weapon rattled the windows. The man at the far column took all three to the chest, spattering the coarse tan stonemasonry with blood and chunks that rolled toward the floor.

Screaming chased the gunfire as civilians panicked.

Ricochets pinged around her as she somersaulted behind a third column.

"We need her alive, idiots!"

The shooting stopped.

"Dmitri, did you see the size of the bitch's gun? *You* go take it from her!"

She squatted behind the column, holding her weapon with both hands, tucked against her cheek. The fake sandstone scratched her exposed back. She let her left knee touch the ground, peeking around the column.

Dots went everywhere.

The doll clerks continued behaving as if nothing happened. One turned toward the fleeing mother, asking her something about her reservation. Other people screamed and ran for the door. A shot bounced off the stone, making her duck. A red dot merged with a green dot. The sound of a small boy wailing confirmed her fear.

"Give yourself up or watch me kill this little bastard."

The shrieking mother fell silent with a fleshy *thud,* the sound of a gun upside the head. The boy cried louder.

Nina watched the room in reflection on the front windows. One of the men took handcuffs out of his jacket. The one by the counter held the boy up by his shirt, no doubt with a pistol in his back. It made no sense to her that they would be looking to capture her alive, but maybe they would take her to Nemsky. She squinted at the cuffs, a sure sign they didn't realize she was a doll. She would play along if only for the child's sake.

"Okay." She held her gun out to the side and lowered it to the ground.

"Get up." One of them yelled. "Do it before the fucking cops get here. If I see one damn cop, you and this brat are dead."

She stood up into view, holding her hands out to the side. Rage simmered at the sight of the boy reaching for his unconscious mother, but Nina kept a calm face. Of the three left alive, the two men not holding the boy approached. They ran up and shoved her face first into the column. She didn't resist, letting them continue to think her normal. After locking her hands behind her, one grabbed her by the shoulder and flipped her around, shoving her against the stone. The one on the right put his gun away, the one on the left kept it out, but down. The man in back continued to hold the boy but seemed to relax.

"You got a lot of nerve." The man on the right glanced at the bodies. "The boss is gonna take that out of your ass when you get home." He leaned in close. "Just how far did you think you could run before we found you? You're lucky the boss has a soft spot for your skinny ass." He brushed her cheek with the back of his hand. "That won't stop us from using you for a little while until we get you home." He turned to his remaining associates and grabbed her arm. "Let's get the fuck out of here."

"What the hell are you talking about? What boss? Do you idiots work for Nemsky?"

"Stupid bitch. Don't play dumb."

"How did you know I was going to be here?" She stared as the two men continued holding her by the arms.

"The boss got a tip."

"Where are we going?" She squirmed, wishing the dress was longer.

Embarrassment felt strange.

He caressed her cheek before seizing a fistful of hair. "Damn bitch, you ask a lot of questions for a hole. The boss owns your ass 'til you pay back your debt. Did two days of freedom make you forget?"

Nina winced. "I guess you could say that someone does own my body, but I'm not who you think I am."

He put a hand on her knee and rode it up her inner thigh. "Oh I'm pretty sure you are, and I think by the end of the night you're going to have some trouble walking."

Nina gave him a dire glare, having had about enough. The feeling of the hand going higher and higher up her leg was devoid of any of the pleasure of being mistaken for a normal person. The unusual sense of being happy to have this body came over her. With a snarl, she kicked him in the crotch. Her ankle stopped just below his ribcage, sending a spout of blood from his nose and mouth. She tried not to think about the feeling of her toes squishing around inside him as she pulled her leg out with a slurp. Her reflex booster kicked on, plunging the room into slow motion. She spun, using the momentum to kick the same man again in the face, leaving a bloody footprint across his cheek as the strike crushed his faceplate into splinters.

She continued the motion until her foot landed where it started, and pulled her arms apart. The cuffs shattered like a plastic toy. The other man only managed to lift his weapon a few inches in the span of two kicks. His face contorted with panic as her hand swung around and seized his gun. She grabbed it as if he didn't exist, crushing his fingers to pulp against the grip. She dragged him around like a puppet, sighted, and fired. The bullet flicked the boy's hair and went into the right eye of the man holding him.

The smaller weapon didn't cause the same cranial detonation as Nina's, but a trench through the skull proved every bit as fatal as an exploded head.

She swung the man around by her grip on the pistol and pounded him into the floor with her knee on his back. They hit the floor before the child even realized the man holding him was dead on his feet.

"You boys just made the worst mistake of your pathetic lives. I'm going to ask you one more time: why here, why now, why me?" Nina grasped the back of his skull with just enough force to let him know she could crush it.

The boy dropped to the ground as his captor fell over backward like a plank. He jumped on his mother, shaking her until she woke and dragging her out of sight behind a row of synthetic plants.

A young blond man's bust appeared in Nina's view.

"Ops, I need a status report from Whisper 3 at the Chimera Apartments building. Has the subject been spotted leaving?"

"Copy that Lieutenant, stand by." He stared into space.

"You're not Sophia?" the thug murmured, his cheeks mashed into the floor.

"Not even close. Keep talking." She snapped what remained of the handcuffs off her wrists, making sure he saw her do it.

"We work for the boss. One of his girls decided to run off with some of his money."

"Prostitute?" Nina edged to grab her purse while keeping the gun on the man.

"Sort of..."

Nina leaned into him just a little more. "What do you mean by sort of, forced?"

"That would be one way to describe it. I mean, she owed him for getting her into the country."

"Who is this boss?" She frowned.

He blinked. "You don't know? *The* boss. Vladimir Kovalev."

Nina sighed. The name was from the organized crime world. A man well connected within as well as outside of the law, the kind of man that Division 9 usually retired. So far, he hadn't been enough of a nuisance.

"Who told you I was your runaway sex slave?" She grabbed a fistful of his shirt and drilled him into the floor again, pressing the gun into his neck.

Now, she was offended.

What color he had before had fled, replaced with sweat. "I didn't see him."

Nina one-armed him to his feet and whipped him into the column.

"Lieutenant. Whisper 3 confirms subject has not left the location. The perimeter is secure."

"Acknowledged. Send a feeler over to Division 1, there's a small mess to clean up here."

"Roger that Lieutenant."

Nina's attention returned to the thug in the lobby. "Okay shithead. You've got one chance." She slid to the right and retrieved her gun and purse while keeping the borrowed weapon aimed. "Someone set you up. Call your boss now, I want answers."

The man fumbled one handed with his NetMini. The holographic head of a man appeared, in his early fifties with eastern European features.

"Did you get her?" An imperious Russian-accented voice echoed.

"No, sir." Sweat ran down his face.

The ops agent moved. "Lieutenant, Division 1 units are en route."

"Copy that, Ops, request a MedVan as well." Nina waved at the thug. "Turn it."

He trembled like a frightened boy, pivoting the tiny slab of technology in his grip to face her.

"What are you doing, you incompetent? That's not her."

An oversized glass in his right hand crept into view, an inch of dark liquor swirled around. Several women, in various degrees of dress, lay draped on furniture behind him. Most looked high.

"Ops, I need a trace on this PID," she said with a thought. Text shimmered in her left peripheral vision as her hardware lifted it from the device.

The virtual man smiled. "Copy that."

"I don't know who you are, but you had better explain yourself before I become angry." The hologram shifted, he got closer while the background drifted away, as if using a stationary terminal.

"I want to know why your men showed up here looking for me. Who gave you that information?"

Vladimir laughed. "Bitches don't make demands of me. You'll soon learn that."

"You're pissing into the wind if you think you can intimidate me." Nina moved her ID close enough to see over the call. "Fuck with me and no lawyer in the world will be able to reattach your balls."

His confident smile fell to a flat line. Worry shimmered in his eyes, hidden behind liberal amounts of abject rage. The thug kept quiet, his terror causing the hologram to wobble.

"Someone sent your attack dogs after me, I want to know who. Whoever it is has just put your misogynistic ass on our radar. Your ghost can blame them for what happens to you if you don't cooperate."

Vladimir threw the glass off screen. The shattering elicited a reaction from only two of the eight women. He growled, spinning his arm across a desk, sending its contents to the floor. After a moment of seething, he stomped back to the VidPhone.

"The man's name was Anatoly, a general. He gave no last name."

A holographic image of Nemsky's head appeared over her NetMini "Is this him?"

Vladimir narrowed his eyes at her. "Yes. I don't forget things easily."

"Lieutenant, we got a hit on that PID. Penthouse suite 8 at the Olympian Tower." The floating comm panel flickered.

"You've been helpful, but you're irrelevant." Nina hit the button on the thug's NetMini to end the call. She hoped added salt hurt.

The thug cringed, waiting for his execution.

"Stupidity is not grounds for a death sentence. You're going down for attempted kidnapping, reckless endangerment, assault of a government agent, endangering the welfare of a child, reckless disregard…" She continued to ramble a list of possible charges.

"It doesn't matter… The boss is gonna fuckin' kill me anyway."

Nina smiled. "I wouldn't bet on that. Sit there and don't move."

"Ops, you still there?" Her gaze shifted to the floating image.

"Go ahead, Lieutenant." He nodded.

"I need to make some vacation arrangements. I need a ticket to Miami for a friend of mine, Kovalev, Vladimir N. He has a file already with the OC task force, and has made himself enough of a threat to warrant action. Tell the travel agent that there are civilians present. If there's any questions have Hardin call me directly."

"No problem, Lieutenant." He nodded. "Whisper 3 confirms no contact has left the building."

"Roger that." Nina looked up as the sound of sirens began to filter in from in the distance. "Whisper 3, stay sharp. Division 1 is almost on site, he may bolt."

"Copy, Lieutenant," said confident female voice over the comm, audio only.

"If Nemsky runs, you are clear to terminate." Nina helped the woman and her son to her feet as she spoke in her head. "But try to wing him if you can."

"Understood Lieutenant."

Nina closed the comm and examined the red mark on the woman's face. "Come on. Let's get you out of here, there's a medic on the way."

She walked with them to the arriving Division 1 team, approaching their sergeant. Two officers took the woman and boy outside toward an arriving white hover van.

"Five idiots in the employ of Vladimir Kovalev did something stupid, one survived. Have your men secure the area. I have a date upstairs."

"Nice dress." He winked.

47

NOT A TRACE

Not trusting the confined space of an elevator, Nina bounded three steps at a time up the stairwell. For this body, climbing forty-four flights was just a time sink. She slid past the door with her gun in one hand and her shoes in the other, training the weapon left, then right. A dark green rug ran the length of the corridor under bas-relief chimera that decorated the white plaster walls every dozen yards or so. Everything basked in a yellowish glow cast by fancy silver lamps. Satisfied the hallway was clear, she crept up to the door and glanced at the virtual comm panel.

"Whisper 3, this is Duchenne. Can you get eyes inside the apartment?"

A woman's head appeared, covered by an armored black pilot's helmet. "Negative on all scanning modes. The apartment's empty." The pilot looked to her right and muttered. "Dave's got the same reading… it's clear."

Nina closed her eyes and a tremble of rage shook her arms. Whisper 3 would have detected him leave, unless he took an underground exit. Of course, this may all have been an elaborate trap to bait her into those morons downstairs. If that was true, it brought up another issue—Nemsky knew she was coming.

Even worse, he knew who she was.

She took her anger out on the door, and entered through a cloud of splinters.

How the hell does he know where I am but I can't find his damn face on a single cam?

Dull grey carpet stretched between plain white walls in the main area while simulated red bricks spanned the kitchen and light hardwood polished to a glassy shine filled the inner hall and bedroom. No decoration adorned the walls, not even a holovid player. A data terminal sat on a table in the living room, and she saw no infrared beams or thermal anomalies.

After clearing the outer room and kitchen, she moved to the bedroom, nudging the door open with her gun. Two assault and one sniper rifle, all of ACC make, lay on the Comforgel pad. A scattering of orange ammunition blocks the size of fingers had been piled near an empty magazine. Slacks and a shirt draped over the desk chair and the scent of a recently shaved man hung in the air.

Her weapon fell slack at her side. With Whisper 3 calling the place clean and her search coming up empty, she relaxed. Nina muttered "What am I missing?" repeatedly as she walked over a gleam of sunlight on brick into the kitchen. Her foot registered the warmth, a tiny slice of normal that hit her with the gravity of a major realization. She fell into one of the plain wooden chairs, dropped her shoes on the floor next to her, and raked her fingers at her hair.

"Ops, I need a site team in here to go over the apartment from top to bottom. If Nemsky was here, he had to leave some trace. Have the network team check all activity that originated from the terminal over the past four months, and run a sensor sweep on the entire building until you tag a name on every moving person. Check for any underground exits while you're at it."

"Copy that, tech team will be there in six minutes." The blond man smiled.

After the flurry of apologies and confusion faded from the comm, Nina went to the sink and washed the blood from her foot. After returning to the chair, she stared at her expensive shoes.

She set the pistol atop her purse on the table and let her head fall into her hands, elbows on her knees. A shifting barrier of jet hair cut off her peripheral vision, and she let out a long-suffering sigh. This defied everything she had ever learned about security, cyberspace, espionage, and reality. Nemsky had no training or experience at being a covert operative. Nothing in his file indicated he was anything more than a megalomaniacal former general with a reputation for sociopathic tendencies. The past few months had her wondering if he had broadened his resume or she made a poor investigator.

Somewhere between her toes, she searched for the answer. Perhaps the bloodthirsty crowd-massacring general never existed after all. The entire identity could be a cover. Maybe Nemsky, or the person pretending to be him—if anyone even existed—had been intelligence all along. Nina moaned as she bent her forehead to touch her knees. That thought felt implausible as well. His military career had been well documented over the course of many years. Faking it would have taken a decade of setup and no secret escapes notice that long. A holo-panel spread open in her mind's eye, replaying an interview from two months ago with former members of the Russian resistance that had made it out. They witnessed one of his massacres in person.

"You looked beautiful when you came to see me this morning." Vincent's voice floated into the room.

Nina's head snapped up. The silence grew heavier. Dust danced within a beam of sunlight angling into the sink from the adjacent window. She stared at the flecks, wondering how her mechanical body could feel like it had a lump in its throat.

"It's a pity the first time I saw that dress was your grandfather's funeral."

The sound came from the table, from the little device in her purse.

"It looks a bit different on you now with so much leg showing." His disembodied chuckle seemed to come from everywhere.

Nina stroked her fingers over the NetMini, wishing the voice genuine. Division 0 files documented the existence of ghosts, reports from astral sensitives who claimed to see them. If she believed those reports, such things had to be real. The government mostly concealed it from the public. Up until now, she always thought it due to how crazy it sounded. Somewhere she'd read that inexplicable cold spots often accompanied a spirit. She activated a thermal overlay, tinting objects in various shades from blue to yellow-orange. Nothing looked strange.

"Ops?" Nina sent her thoughts to the comm channel.

"Proceed, Lieutenant." The man's voice sounded happy to hear her.

"I need you to run a trace on an incoming call to my personal NetMini, active right now."

"Understood. Stand by."

"You look stunning today, Nina. I could just stare all day." A trace of sadness wafted in his voice. "I know you were waiting for me to ask about... Your father didn't like me much, I didn't want to ruin what we had by making him freak. I had the ring hidden for two months in my kitchen, waiting to be brave enough."

Nina shuddered. She had been so anxious about him popping the question, feeling like a little girl the night before Wintermas, except every night had been the eve before a day that would never come. She had spent countless hours rehearsing her reaction but still had no idea what form it would take. In another month, she would've ignored decorum and asked him to marry her instead.

"Lieutenant?" Ops distracted her emotional spiral.

"Go ahead."

"We show no active calls on your device at this time."

She stopped breathing. The onyx slab reflected her face, not projecting any video or hologram—but a winking green LED indicated an active audio call.

"That can't be possible, it's on."

He shrugged. "We're not seeing it."

She cradled the NetMini against her cheek as if it was Vincent's hand. Closing her eyes, she tried to imagine the warmth of his touch one last time.

"Are you in pain?" Her voice faltered.

The smooth glass vibrated against her skin. "No... not in a physical sense. My heart aches because I can't touch you."

Tears ran down her face. Nemsky ceased to be. She wanted nothing more than Vincent back. "How are you talking to me, why are you..."

"I can't leave you." He choked up. "You're on the edge between worlds, too. I know there's not much left of you in there. Certain things no one understands until they cross over." His voice trailed into an eerie whisper. "They are watching you."

Tears hit her feet, her voice a breathless whisper. "Who?"

"Beings who escort the dead to the next place. They waited for you, but you were pulled away. That little bit of flesh still inside you clings to the world with two fingers. They still watch you, waiting. They want us to be together again."

Nina lowered the mini from her cheek, staring into it. Spots appeared, droplets of sadness splattered upon its surface. The voice of some nameless doctor crept through her memory, telling her Vincent hadn't made it. It took her two weeks not to regret her answer to agent Harper. If not for her mother, she might have given in. Talking to Vincent brought her back to that precipice. After all this time, he asked her to be with him for eternity.

Her hand shook. "You want me to..."

"As soon as you leave that shell of a body, we will be together." His voice returned to its full tonal quality, the sound of it all but smiling at her.

Nina's emotional rollercoaster slowed down. Vincent would never have asked her to kill herself. The last expression his face would ever make radiated desperate worry for her safety, but who can say what happens to a mind when it crosses over? Her cloud of swirling doubt scattered as a loud smash came from the front door.

When their senior walked in, he caught her with a face full of wet microfiber towel.

"I'm Specialist Dennings. You okay, ma'am?"

She nodded, surprised with how steady her voice sounded. "Fine, just pissed that we missed him again, trying to calm down."

"I hear that." The tech team lead nodded at her. "If he left even one molecule of fart somewhere, we'll find it."

She stood, collecting her weapon, shoes, and purse, before going into the living room. All the men froze, staring at her. She almost smiled, pulled out of her despondence by their prying eyes.

"Dennings, can you have your team clear the bathroom first?"

He waved at the door. "Okay guys, you heard the Lieutenant… shitter first."

They swarmed over the area with an array of scanners and sprays while one of the female techs connected the computer terminal to their black box to give it the digital equivalent of a cavity search. Nina paced in a circle until she singled out one of them that seemed to be doing nothing of particular importance.

"You," she said, waving him over. "Do me a small favor?"

He approached. "Sure, what do you need, ma'am?"

She tossed him the fob for her patrol craft. "Outside in the fire zone, black unmarked. Can you grab my shit out of the trunk? I need to get out of this dress."

A collective sigh came from the room. She smirked. Judging by the overacted nature of their disappointment, they sounded like cops just being cops. He returned in about ten minutes with her things, and got to work examining the carpeting.

Dennings emerged from the back. "Lieutenant, the bathroom looks untouched. We found some trace samples, but they appear to belong to the previous tenant from a few months ago."

"What's their status?"

"Moved north for work, we have another address and a place of employment on record. It all checked out."

She grumbled. "No connection with Nemsky then?"

"Doesn't look that way." He pointed over his shoulder at the bathroom. "You can go now."

"Thanks."

Nina slid past the techs filing out of the bathroom, entering a cloud of chemical vapors. The smell brought back memories of the life she almost had. She spent a moment gazing at her reflection in the NetMini, wondering if his ghost needed electronics to talk to her.

With a flick of her thumb behind her neck, the dress slid down around her ankles. She lifted it into a grip with her toes as she opened a comm panel to Samantha Cole.

"Cole." The woman appeared upset at the interruption until she saw Nina.

The virtual image left no clue that her immediate supervisor stood nude in the bathroom of their target's apartment.

Nina checked the mirror for blood or damage and found none, then unrolled the ballistic suit.

"Hardin mentioned you spotted Itai slipping in and out of Warner's residence." Nina's toe searched the ballistic suit until she found the seam and slid a leg into the chilly material.

"We had positive contact entering the facility at 07:40 this morning. We got him on four security cameras: parking deck, main lobby, elevator, and a hallway leading to Warner's quarters."

Nina shifted her weight, putting her other leg in. Diplomatic Tower apartments each had a floor to themselves. Some of them had separate bubble elevators that expressed to the parking area and any security recorders inside were the property of whatever nation occupied that floor.

"How long was he on site?"

Cole looked to the right. "Subject exited the diplomatic residence at 08 hours 18 minutes. We got a good shot of his face on the way out, he looked pleased about something."

"Dammit." Nina worked the suit up over her hips. "Any luck with the laser microphones?"

"Still nothing, EM profile indicates active jamming. The place is considered foreign territory so there's nothing we can do without probable cause."

She put her hands into the sleeves and shrugged the thing up and over her shoulders. "I hate that bullshit. We can do whatever we want to a citizen, but the foreigners get to hide behind obscure laws." Nina took a calming breath. "Where did Korin go once he left?"

"He crawled up his own ass and disappeared." Cole sounded as frustrated as Nina felt.

"What the hell does that mean?" Nina rolled her shoulders to seat the material and pulled the front flap closed.

The plastic zipper went up to her jawline, wrapping her in shiny black.

Cole shook her head. "We got him on the cameras from the Diplomatic Tower as well as some citycams." Samantha looked perturbed. "For some reason, the mobile unit didn't record him even though it was covering the same patch of street."

Nina stretched and tugged at the suit until it molded to her contours. "He shouldn't have been recorded on one set of cameras and not another. That makes me think we are being toyed with. Did you verify the Karsson-Neimand checksum on the feed from the tower?"

Cole looked baffled. "We did. They check out. The video integrity is unmodified as far as we can tell. It would take almost four years for a civilian computer system to fake 30 seconds of video with a believable K-N and with our hardware we would still spot it eventually."

Nina put her weapon harness on. "Then we need better hardware. Something isn't right." She stepped into her boots, putting one heel on the sink to fasten the straps. "Either the mobile unit's video is full of shit, or the tower cams are being hacked. Two videos of the exact same place at the exact same time cannot show different images. One of them is fake."

"Oh, Lieutenant?" Cole looked up. "You asked for a trace on your NetMini before? We found something."

Nina froze with one hand on her coat. "What…" Her voice trailed to a whisper as she spoke in the real world and over her internal comm at the same time.

Samantha brought up a shimmering cyberspace map, a field of black speckled with points of blue and white connected by a web of thin lines. "Someone went to a lot of trouble to hide the signal, but we found it." Some lines changed from blue to white as an animation relayed the path of signal convergence. "Not only did it bounce across fourteen different countries, they attempted to conceal the data as innocuous NMCP traffic, trying to blend it into the background." All the white lines flashed several times before returning to dark blue. "It dropped off before we could find the exact source, but I have a feeling it was coming out of the Division 2 complex."

Nina felt foolish beyond comprehension. Not only had someone fucked with her in the cruelest way imaginable, they did it from where she wanted to go. She kicked through the wall. Several techs in the bedroom jumped, peering at her past a cloud of dust. Her arms shook with unadulterated rage and she glared doom at no one in particular. Flakes of plaster and drywall clattered to the ground when she pulled her boot out of the hole.

"Must have been a spider," muttered one of the techs.

"Think she got it?" another voice asked before two men chuckled.

Nina ignored them and looked at Cole's virtual face. "Sam… Thanks."

"Okay…" She sounded baffled at the sudden sincerity. "I'll let you know if we find anything else."

"Lieutenant?" The senior tech knocked on the bathroom door. "There are no prints or bio traces anywhere in the apartment. All we found were traces of male pheromone in the bedroom carpeting."

Nina exhaled. "A recently-shaved man, just enough for me to smell."

48

PRECOCIOUS

A droplet of blood peeked from the corner of the little white-haired girl's mouth as if checking to see if the coast was clear. It traced a crimson line across her cheek on its way to the ground. The weak breeze would have moved her hair had it not been plastered with grime. Eldon had seen a lot of awful things on active duty, but fate had up until now spared him the sight of a dead child. None of his training had prepared him for it. Not knowing what to do, he kept pulling at her shirt, trying to make her more comfortable.

For ten minutes, not a word was spoken. The only break in the oppressive silence came in the form of a raven fluttering in to land on a nearby branch. Its head tilted toward and then away from them before it hopped and turned its back. A second later, it flew off into the trees.

Masaru's brain searched for some way to justify what he had done. The circumstance of her trying to kill them all did little to dispel the guilt staring back at him from the shadows of his mind. His father would be disappointed to learn about the incident. Not that he had taken such a young life, but at how he felt afterward.

Kenny contained his feelings well, despite his brain using this as an allegory to prepare itself for the worst-case scenario of Alyssa in the Badlands. He held Amber as if shielding his daughter, not even realizing. Their embrace went from him protecting her to her consoling him without either one realizing it.

"What the hell?" Eldon's voice cracked amid the silence.

He pulled the shirt up, wiping his fingers over intact, but bloody, skin. He pushed down on where the cut should have been and the girl's eyes snapped open. She sat up and grabbed his sidearm, but was too weak to dislodge it from the holster before he regained his composure and grabbed her arms.

Katya all but fainted, Kenny jumped back, and Joey lifted an eyebrow. Masaru still hadn't looked. Amber screamed like the token bimbo from a zombie vid.

Eldon pulled tiny hands away from the gun, pinning them together. "Whoa! Easy, kid…"

Blood foamed from her teeth as she thrashed. She kicked him in the chest several times, succeeding in leaving only smeared toe prints on his armor. The child had such feeble strength, her strikes made almost no sound. Her attempt at shouting produced just a wheeze of a cough that spat up more blood. Eldon held her until she gave up and fell limp into the grass. Her icy blue eyes still burned with malice, though a slight trace of dread had joined it.

Joey, unable to process what he just saw, laughed. "Now that's just fucked up."

Katya rushed over and wiped the girl's hair out of her face. The child made a half-hearted attempt to get her hands out of Eldon's grip at the sight of the glowing pupil in the woman's right eye.

"There's a metallic presence diffused evenly throughout her body, and some kind of metal cylinder attached to her spine just below the heart."

"And that means?" Eldon held his free hand out in a 'please go on' gesture.

"I think nanobots. Lots of them, so many it's almost liquid metal in her veins. More than I have ever seen. The shading makes it look like they are concentrating around her chest where she was hit. Almost like her blood is stimpak fluid."

Masaru looked up with a blank face and approached. With an unceremonious tug, he pulled her shirt up and saw no sign of a wound on her back. Only the presence of blood and sliced cloth hinted that she had been hurt. He forced himself onto his feet despite waves of pain, his motion jerky. The speedware would burn for about another hour.

"What's your name?" Katya picked at the blood-soaked shirt, unsure if she should pull it down or throw it away.

The child turned her head, speaking in a half-whisper. "EAO-106."

"Are there a hundred and five more of these psycho brats?" Joey dreaded the thought of having to deal with even one more of those suits.

Katya patted Eldon's hand until he let go of her. "How many of you are here?"

The girl tried to fold her arms, but couldn't lift them. "EAO-106."

Kenny blinked. "What does that mean?"

She replied in the same emotionless tone. "Experimental Armor Operator, unit 106."

"Remember that thing about what StarPoint would want to hide from the UCF? I think this about sums it up." Eldon kicked the destroyed suit. "This is power armor but its profile is no bigger than a large man. You'd never know you were about to get your ass whipped until after they tore you in half."

"What's the point of that?" Kenny looked at him. "Why not just use dolls?"

Eldon paced. "Not a lot of commanders trust AI cyborgs, and finding people to donate their brain to a mechanical body isn't easy. With something like this, they could make whole squads in no time. I'm gonna go out on a limb here and assume she's a clone of some kind so there's no next of kin to want them home."

Katya brushed at the girl's cheek. "She's responding like she's being interrogated."

"Communist fucktards."

The harsh language in such a tiny voice sent Joey into a fit of giggles.

Amber perked up. "That's what Kevin used to call the corporate suits."

Joey smiled, putting things together. "She probably heard it when they kicked his ass."

"Who is Kevin?" Kenny glanced at Amber.

"One of the guys. I remember being around him a lot. He was always so calm except when he went off about those people. He wanted to save humanity from being turned into machines."

Katya went to pick the girl up, pausing when she got a good whiff. "Whoa kid. How long were you in that thing?"

The child looked at Katya, her face softened just a little. "Dunno. Chrono got busted during the raid."

"Do you know what the date is?" Katya dodged around trying to make eye contact.

The girl looked up as if searching for the answer in midair. "October 2411."

"Its 2418 now." Katya took her hand. "So much for your law-abiding corporations. What is this kid, eight, maybe nine? She has been in that suit for seven years. Come here, sweetie. What did they do to you?" Katya slid her arms under the girl and lifted her. She made no attempt to grab on for support, but weighed so little it didn't matter.

Genuine fear shone in her eyes. "You shouldn't take me prisoner. When the reinforcements arrive they'll kill you all."

"We're not taking you captive." Katya set her back down. "Go on. You're free to leave."

The child fought for almost a minute but was too weak to stand up on her own. She glared at Katya.

"What did you do to me?"

"You've been in that armor so long your legs don't work anymore." Eldon picked her up and handed her back to Katya.

The girl grabbed at her thighs and squeezed, her confusion growing into alarm.

"You're just a kid. You shouldn't be alone out here." Katya craned her head away from the vile smell. "It's too dangerous."

Joey leaned over to Kenny. "Who installed Emotion 1.0 on Katya?"

"I hate to piss in your cheerios kid, but if your position hasn't been reinforced in seven years, they ain't coming." Eldon surveyed the debris field. "This wasn't a real military Op, just a corporation ignoring ethics... and from the looks of it, disavowed."

Her gaze fell, face warped in a way that could have been anger or imminent tears. "Why would they lie?"

"*They* always lie." Katya scowled. "There's a sink in the security station. I'm going to go clean her up."

"You gonna be okay alone with psycho tot?" Joey glanced at her.

The girl gave Joey a threatening glare. He put on a face of mock fright.

"Well now we have two nine-year-olds." Kenny gave Joey a light shove. "Okay, we'll wait here, be quick."

"I'll go with her." Masaru cracked his neck. Despite wobbling legs, having no mark upon his honor made him feel much better.

The child's brave affect crumbled as Masaru's black form moved toward her. She shivered and squirmed in a futile effort to escape Katya's grasp.

"Relax. He didn't realize you were a child, he won't hurt you now that he knows." Katya tried to sound as soothing as possible.

"Holler on the comm if anything happens." Kenny maneuvered Amber to sit on a rock in the center of where he, Eldon, and Joey set up a defensive circle.

Katya carried her toward the security booth, able to ignore the piercing stare for only a few paces. Halfway between the group and the building, she halted.

"Look kid. I know you've been told that everyone outside the company is your enemy. Think about what they did to you and think very hard about who your real foe is." The tone in Katya's voice changed, slower and tinged with sadness. "They did the same to me when I was your age. You are just property to them." Katya looked down into her eyes. "I bet you're looking for a chance to grab a gun and escape. I would have been."

The kid fidgeted. "I'm not."

"You need to work on your emotion control, you are a poor liar." Katya poked her in the nose. Feelings that she never thought she would have manifested. "The company that did this to you just left you here to die, we will take you somewhere safe."

The girl remained silent. Unable to tell how deeply the kid had been brainwashed, Katya wouldn't let her guard down all the way. She resumed her trek, and bounded up the steps into the pod. The child's utter lack of reaction to the dead man on the floor came as no surprise.

In the locker room, Katya set the girl into one of the utility sinks and turned on the faucet. Several bottles of liquid soap remained on the shelf, and she poured a liberal amount into the rising water. Peeling the fetid garments away, she tossed them to the back of the room where they stuck to the wall. The child lowered herself to sit, encouraged by a pat on the shoulder, and stared with a stone-faced look as the warm liquid rose up to her chest. For some minutes, she remained motionless as Katya lifted and washed each limb in turn, bathing her.

"I was about your age when they found me living on the street. I don't even remember what killed my parents." Katya stopped washing the girl for a moment to lean on the sink. "It would have been kinder of them to let me to die on the streets."

The child stared at her with distrusting eyes, unsure of how to interpret gentle contact.

"They wanted me to be a spy, an assassin." Katya tapped herself on the head. "They even cut me open and tried to make me psionic, but that didn't work at all. So they made up for it with cyberware."

She turned herself hot pink for a moment with the CamNano, going back to normal at the nonplused smirk the girl made.

By the time Katya's hand pushed a soapy sponge over her back, the kid relaxed. Having decided that she didn't mind it, she sagged forward and tolerated the attention. Her eyes finally left Katya's sidearm.

"That was the point." The girl stared at the opaque water.

"What?"

"The way everyone acted when they saw me. That's why they made us look like little kids. They wanted our enemies to feel sorry for us or underestimate us. Then we could escape or sabotage from within."

Katya bit her lip. This kind of nightmare was what she expected from the ACC, not the UCF. No matter how much of a pretty face they put on for the government, corporations were still corporations.

Katya poured more soap over the girl's head. "I don't expect you to trust me, but I'm going to ask you to anyway." She worked her fingers through sticky hair, massaging the snags and grime out.

"Training mostly." The girl tucked her knees under her chin and offered a confused stare.

Katya read the look. The company filled this kid's entire life with military discipline and there had been no nurturing contact. No one trained her to deal with it, and her veneer collapsed, battered down from within by whatever scant trace of humanity remained within. She was glad Joey couldn't see this. A child left in this state would grow into a personality like Katya's.

"This is not what your handler told you would happen if you were captured, is it?"

She curled into a tighter ball. "No."

After draining the fetid water, Katya ran more. "Those nanobots kept you from getting sick from being in that filth so long."

"Yeah, duh." She leaned back, putting her head in the stream to rinse her hair.

"Are there more like you?"

"Yeah, but I can't talk about it."

That made Katya worry. "Are they alive?"

"They got away. I don't want to say any more."

"My name is Katya." She changed the subject.

The kid looked up, frightened. "That's Russian! You're ACC!"

"I am not ACC." The sudden coldness in Katya's voice flattened the girl against the sink wall. "They treated me like property. Like these people did to you. I left. I am a defector. I despise them more than any UCF soldier could ever hate them."

"Oh."

Katya smiled, lifting the girl's chin to make eye contact. "We'll need to give you a proper name."

"Why?" She sounded sad. "What's wrong with EAO-106?"

"That's not a name, it's an asset tag. You are not a talking weapon. When we take you back to the city, they will give you a real home so you can be normal and forget all of this."

"I'm never going to be normal." The eerie finality in her voice made Katya worry.

The girl stood as Katya wrapped her with the white jumpsuit and lifted her out of the water. Katya reached at the empty bench, and then grumbled. Amber had taken the bag of clothes outside.

Katya carried her in the garment-turned-towel out to where everyone waited, over to the duffel bag and set her down on her feet. With a strained grimace, her effort to stay upright failed, and she plopped down.

"Pick something to wear." Katya pointed at the bag.

The girl glanced at the bag. Her reach for it stopped all of a sudden when her legs locked straight out. She shuddered, opening and closing her fists. Katya crouched and held the tiny convulsing body.

"No! No!" she wailed, clamping onto Katya. "Please don't let it get me!"

"Don't let what get you?" She stared into the girl's eyes. "There's nothing here."

"Great... She's hallucinating too." Joey shook his head.

The child's eyes rolled up into her head. She slipped into a seizure. Eldon ran over, clasping her head, and held her in such a way as to protect her neck. She shifted without warning, biting down on Eldon's armored glove, and continued shaking for about thirty seconds while releasing the most horrible scream. Her muscles tensed, her skin reddened, and she sweat blood. When the shaking stopped, she passed out. Thick white foam extruded from her nostrils and bubbled over her teeth. Her entire body became hot to the touch and sporadic twitches continued in her hands and feet for several seconds while undulating ripples ran up and down her limbs.

"That didn't look like a normal seizure," said Eldon. "That was just... pain." He blinked at a tooth scrape on his glove.

"So much pain she fainted," said Masaru, a note of sympathy chipping away at his usually stoic voice.

"What the hell was that?" Amber's eyes widened.

"Not a damn clue." Eldon checked the child's pulse and felt for a fever. She had gone limp, except for the gentle motion of her stomach as she breathed. "Who knows what the hell they did to her."

"Possible anti-interrogation device?" Masaru frowned.

"I don't think so. Those don't torture, they usually just kill with a quick pop." Katya stroked the girl's hair for almost ten minutes until her eyes opened again.

The kid looked around and took several deep breaths. As soon as she could move, she clung to Katya. "That happens every few days. It's why I don't grow up." She closed her eyes and hissed as a lesser wave of pain gripped her for a few seconds. "It didn't work like they thought it would. It wasn't supposed to hurt. When they found out it did... they didn't care." She stared up. "I told you I'll never be normal. It hurts so much, I'd rather die."

Katya pulled her into a hug. "Don't talk like that. It's never that bad."

The snow-haired waif fixed her with a look that frightened her.

Masaru offered a ration pack. Her mood changed on a dime and she snatched it out of his hands like a wild dog, tearing into it with such fervor that she almost ate the plastic packets as well as the nutrient paste they contained. Inside of a minute, she asked for another one in such a desperate tone that Joey gave her one of his. She sucked it down just as fast, barely breathing between bites.

"Those things are meant to be one a day. You just fed her about four thousand calories." Kenny gave Joey a smirk.

Joey chuckled. "She could use it."

"You're one to talk." Eldon swatted him on the back with a grin.

"That much, that fast, is going to make her sick." Kenny shook his head.

Visible ripples in the girl's limbs stalled their argument. The diameter of her arms and legs grew out like someone inflating a balloon animal. After several minutes, she no longer looked emaciated, and appeared to be at a healthy athletic weight. The kid wiggled her toes, as if mystified by having feeling back in her legs.

Kenny threw his hands up. "Or something altogether unexpected and fucked up could happen."

Joey snickered at the look on her face. "That had to feel funky."

49

DISAVOWED

Sensing their stares, the child spoke without looking up. "The nanobots can restructure the proteins contained in food and use it to repair tissues. Eating is like giving it spare parts. If you cut my head off I'm pretty much fucked, but..." She hesitated for a second. "Anything else I'll get back up from. They cut off my hand once as a proof of concept demonstration for some generals so they could watch it grow back."

"I can't hear any more of this shit." Eldon stomped off and ranted to no one in particular a few yards away.

Joey knelt and grasped her hand. "If I find anything on this network I can use to expose this to the world, I will make sure someone burns for it."

Katya growled. "We can't let them do this again."

"They won't." The girl's tone was flat. "I killed the lead scientist."

She rummaged the bag and crawled into a long sleeved sweatshirt big enough to be a dress on her.

Her head popped out of the top. "The generals got into an argument with the doctors. Soon after they left, the dogs attacked. I don't think it was an accident."

"No shit." Eldon felt better that command rejected this insanity.

Masaru surveyed the destruction. "Is that what happened to this place?"

"The dog men come from an installation about ten miles north. We ran dozens of recon and training missions over there. Something led them down here and they overran us. StarPoint caused most of the damage trying to kill the dogs."

"Or trying to sanitize this facility." Katya frowned.

"I think you're right." Eldon pointed at the walls. "You don't launch AGM-144's at effin' Canids. They wanted to scrub this place."

Joey tapped his chin. "The government has a lot of failings but they coddle kids. It makes for loyal adults when they grow up and it's good for the NewsNet. Bet they saw this as a public relations nightmare."

"Or maybe they actually had souls?" Kenny smiled. "Whenever I see a news report about a summary, it's related to a crime against a kid."

"It don't happen that often," said Eldon. "Most of the cops I know don't like to execute people. I dunno why they didn't just order it shut down on the spot, or come annihilate the place themselves."

"Most likely they wanted to preserve their business relationship with StarPoint while at the same time objecting to what they did here." Masaru looked to the north. "A third party adversary provided them plausible deniability."

Katya squatted next to the girl. "Since you don't grow up, do you know how old you really are? You don't talk like a kid."

"Our first operational status test was done on March 8th 2397. I don't remember being smaller than I am now and all my sisters look just like me. I guess that would make me about twenty one, give or take a few months."

Amber giggled. "Wow, she's older than me… well, I mean, older than me if I wasn't frozen."

"Man, the fucked up things you see out here." Kenny rubbed his head.

"What kind of inhuman monster could subject a person to this much pain for so long?" Katya shivered.

"It started out feeling like a hot flash. After a year, it felt like being boiled alive, and it just kept getting worse. I think my body is pissed off that it can't grow up and trying harder and harder. It'll probably kill me soon." She looked down. "Wish it would hurry up."

"Is there anything we can do to stop this?" Katya glanced at Masaru.

"That's a question for Ido once we get back to the city."

"Ok, kid." Katya crouched down to eye level. "You dropped the prisoner-of-war routine a little too fast. I'm still not convinced you're not still looking for an unguarded weapon. I'm going to ask you to trust me." She put her hand on the girl's shoulder. "I will find a way to make the pain stop."

EAO-106 looked down, her snow-white hair shimmering in a light breeze. A twinge of guilt in her expression made everyone nervous. "I fucked that up the last time… I promise won't do anything stupid this time."

Katya squinted. "You're making me nervous, acting like a kid."

The girl pulled at the sweatshirt. "One of the scientists got upset when he realized the de-aging process hurt so much."

Katya tossed two socks to her, muttering about how disgusting the company was.

She smiled and pulled them on. "He argued a lot with the other scientists. He said the system that kept us small didn't work right and wanted to call it off. I think he felt sorry for us. They made us look like children so we would be sympathetic to an enemy, they did such a good job it worked on him too."

"Side benefit." Joey glanced at the destroyed armor. "They wanted you small to fit into that armor. I'm not sure if that's worse than just growing brains in a jar for doll bodies."

"Not as easy as it sounds, the CNS architecture does not develop properly outside of a body." Masaru tilted his head at the stares. "No, Kurotai has not tried that. I read a research study."

The girl stared at her armor, leaning into Katya as if frightened by its presence. "When the dogs came, they decided to evacuate. Andy turned on them. He said what they did to us was wrong, even if we weren't 'real' people. He wanted to get all five of us out of here." She paused with the face of a kid caught in a lie. "I thought he was a traitor, so I got my suit to try and stop him. Then the bombs started falling. I ran into the woods to hide and saw them flying out. He stole a transport and took the others. I thought he lied and wanted to kill us. I'm still here coz I'm stupid."

Katya patted her on the back. Amber looked closer to tears than the girl did.

"I've been waiting out in the woods for them to come back for me ever since they left, but they didn't."

"So you knew all along that the company had disavowed you?" Eldon made a face at her. "Why the hell did you shoot at us?"

She grimaced. "I... I don't know. The pains make me crazy. I get in these moods where I just want to kill everything I see."

"Are you related to her?" Joey snickered.

"Can you control yourself?" Katya ran a hand over the girl's hair, scowling at Joey.

She shrugged. "If I could control it, I wouldn't be nuts. I'll try, but I can't promise anything. Of course without the suit I'm not much of a threat. I still have the body of a little kid even if my brain doesn't match it."

"You can still do a lot of damage with a gun." Katya folded her arms.

The kid pointed north. "There's some portable kennels over in the wreckage of the colony area. If you want you could put me in one of those."

"Absolutely not." Kenny startled them with a sudden shout. "We'll just keep an eye on her. Everyone keep control of your weapons at all times."

"The crazies usually come hours before the shakes. I think it's a panic response to the expected onset of that much pain. Either that, or I'm trying to pick a fight with something that'll kill me so I don't have to feel it." She looked down, curling her toes in the socks. "I'll probably be okay for a couple of days at least before it comes back."

"Good enough for me." Kenny waved at the truck. "We should be out of here by then."

Eldon shook his head. "If this girl is psychotic... She could slip in and out of being rational without warning."

Kenny spun to face him. "I don't care. We're not putting a little girl in a damned cage."

"That would be fun to explain to the gate cops." Joey laughed.

"I'm not psychotic. I'm just suffering trauma induced dissociative states where my natural personality retreats and the combat training takes over." She stood up.

Everyone looked at her but no one could think of anything to say.

"What?" She cocked her head.

Joey couldn't stop grinning. "I've never seen a little kid talk like a shrink before."

"Guess you weren't paying attention. I'm twenty-one."

Joey cackled. "Good luck getting a bartender to believe you."

The girl squinted.

Joey's eyes widened with a flash of insight. "So, kid. Do you know anything about the Mayberry incident?"

"No."

"If someone wanted to hide something here, something very secret, where would they put it?"

"You don't have to patronize me like I'm a child. I'm almost as old as you are." She smirked. "Maybe older."

Joey made a series of strange faces. "Okay, where would they stash the top secret crap that they don't want anyone to see?"

"In D4."

Joey pinched the bridge of his nose. "And that is?"

She pointed. "On the other side of the colony housing there's an underground bunker restricted to the people with max level clearance. Only Welker and the lead researchers would go there."

"Who's Welker?" Eldon lifted an eyebrow.

She glared. "I dunno, some suit. Everyone kissed his ass all the time so he had to be important."

"I know that name." Masaru pondered. "Alastair Welker, I believe. He still works for StarPoint, if I remember correctly, Senior Vice-President of research and development."

"Thanks. One more question." Kenny pointed at Amber. "Do you know who she is?"

"Yeah. She's one of the HLM rats. Out of six, she and one male were the only two that survived apprehension."

Amber perked up. "Someone else lived? Was it Kevin? Where is he?"

The child looked at everyone in turn except Amber, then down at her socks. "He's uhh, in the security building."

"Can we go get him?" Amber pleaded at Kenny.

"I got this." Joey smiled and led her a short distance away. He took no small degree of pleasure in holding her when she sobbed into his chest at the truth.

"Imma punch him right in the forehead if he touches her." Eldon shook his head as he watched him.

"Relax, he's just acting like a dick. He's not really like that." Kenny chuckled at Eldon. "I hope."

Masaru gave the kid a sideways glance. "The component installed near your spine must be the control source and manufactory for the nanobots. If it is removed you should cease having those episodes."

She pulled the sweatshirt up to expose her back. "Go for it, your sword should reach it."

He pulled her arms down. "No. I thought you were supposed to be smart. That part also repairs you, if we remove it you won't heal anymore."

The girl shrugged. "Whatever. The pain stops either way."

He jostled her until she looked at her reflection in his helmet. The sight of him still scared her into cowering.

Masaru ignored her reaction. "When we get back to the city a friend of mine, a real doctor, will get rid of that thing and the pain will stop. I will *not* slice you in half just because you feel sorry for yourself."

"She'll probably need a shrink too." Joey chimed in.

The girl held a middle finger at him for a moment before letting her arm fall. "Yeah, maybe... I suppose I am pretty messed up."

50

SWEET TALK

With the onset of night, further searching would have to wait for morning. Kenny and Eldon set about rigging a perimeter of proximity sensors as Katya, Amber, and the white haired girl climbed into the truck cabin to sleep. Katya stretched out across the rear bench seat with her arm over the little one as Amber curled into a ball in the passenger seat. The men set up their sleeping bags to the rear of the truck with a rotating watch every ninety minutes.

The touch of sunlight tugged Katya's eyes open one at a time. As a sense of her surroundings filtered into her consciousness, she jumped up at full alert. The child was gone. As much of a dick as Joey was to her most of the time, he pulled a double watch to let her rest the whole night. Amber still slept in the front but the girl, as well as her sidearm, vanished. Fearing the worst, she stumbled down the boarding ladder into the cold damp morning air.

Kicking sleeping bags, Katya yelled. "The kid's gone. She's got a gun."

Joey startled awake, propped against a tree a few yards away. He grimaced as if her voice smashed into a hangover. "Keep it down, will ya?"

"Chill!" A tiny voice drifted over from the forest. "I'm just pissing."

Katya stared toward the voice. After a minute, a little figure appeared among the trees, walking toward the truck. Her gaze focused on the ground as she stepped with care around branches and rocks. She had the pistol in her right hand and the socks in her left. Eldon relaxed at the childlike quality to her motion, but kept his hand near his sidearm just in case. When she entered the clearing and no longer needed to watch where she put her feet, she smiled up at everyone. As she neared, she held the gun up by the barrel, offering the handle end to Katya.

The girl didn't move until Katya took the weapon. "I didn't want to get caught by a dog without something to defend myself. You guys trashed my suit. I might think like twenty but I have the punch of a little kid. I'd be screwed out here alone now without help. If I kill you guys, I'm killing myself."

Katya couldn't sense any deception, but the kid could wind up doing anything if she had an episode. She plodded past Katya and sat on the running board, wiped the dew off her feet, and put the socks back on, pulling them up to her knees.

Masaru glanced at Katya, remembering how the girl had first stared malice at him. "Watashi wa kanojo o shin'yō shite inai."

The kid looked up. "You can trust me. I have nothing to gain by harming you."

Masaru blinked, turned on his heel, and wandered off.

After packing the camp back into the truck, Kenny walked over. "Okay, kid. Where is D4?"

She climbed into the cabin, straddling the center console. After studying it for a few seconds, she had the navigation map up and centered on the area. A few flicks of her hand at the holographic panel zoomed in on a spot.

"About a half klick northeast of our current location used to be worker housing." She pulled the map down with one finger. "D4 is about another klick north of that and little to the west. It would be about here." A ripple spread outward from the display where she poked it. "At full operational capacity, the approach had proximity field sensors and automated pulse guns—but that's all offline with the reactor shutdown."

Kenny stared at her as one of her too-large socks slid off and fell to the ground. "What?"

"Uhh, nothing, just…" He gestured at her. "The whole… you're just sad and creepy at the same time. What does it look like?"

She retrieved the sock and crawled into the rear seat. "It's hard to spot because the whole thing is underground. You're looking for a metal plate with a cargo elevator in a large shaft, big enough to take this truck."

"The faster we find whatever we came out here for, the faster we can get you out of here."

The girl tilted her head. "What are you looking for?"

"I'm not really sure." Kenny stood on the running board, waving to the others. "Come on, It's a bit far to walk."

Eldon kept his rifle aimed out the window. The others crammed into the back seat. Joey obligingly let Amber sit in his lap. The ageless girl crawled into the space between Katya and the side, trying to get as far away from Masaru as she could. As Kenny backed out of the small grove, Joey struck up a banal conversation with Amber about nothing in particular. She seemed to enjoy the attention and appeared a bit of an ingénue. Joey could see how the HLM had gotten their teeth into her. A girl like this was ripe for the picking of a group like that: naïve, idealistic, and willing to believe whatever sounded reasonable without doing any research.

Bodies jostled as the truck climbed the uneven ground past a few more drop buildings. The kid clung to Katya's arm, still hiding from Masaru. Kenny drove over the crest of a hill, down into a basin strewn with debris as if raccoons the size of cars had attacked a massive overturned trashcan. One structure at the far left edge didn't look like a temporary building. He recognized the machinery hanging from its walls as ventilation pumps and figured it was the surface portion of a subterranean installation.

"Think we found it."

"That's not it." The kid scooted forward. "This is the reactor shed. Over there." She pointed.

They came to a stop next to a large thirty-meter square opening in the ground, rimmed by black and yellow striped metal. Eldon and Kenny approached, finding it flooded to within a few meters from the top.

"This is going to suck." Eldon shook his head.

"If I was going to build an underground facility I'd have put in pumps."

"Guess they didn't."

A console sat atop a post at the far corner. Kenny went over, shaking his head while examining flashing red warnings on the screen.

"Guess what."

Eldon meandered around the side. "What?"

Kenny's finger traced the screen as he read. "The elevator shaft may be experiencing a flood condition. We should engage the sump pumps at the earliest opportunity."

"May be experiencing..." Eldon glanced at the ripples in the water. "Yeah, this is a government computer system."

Kenny smiled. "Well that at least means there is a pump."

"So turn that bad boy on."

Kenny poked the console but it flashed an error. After fiddling with the interface for a minute, he looked up. "Not enough power."

"Guess we go to the reactor shed."

Kenny climbed into the truck. "The tunnel's flooded and the pumps don't have enough power. We gotta go sweet talk the reactor."

BACK AT THE REACTOR SHED, A VIBRO KNIFE MADE SHORT WORK OF THE DOOR. ELDON kicked it open and they walked into a room that smelled of copper and caused a metallic taste to settle on their tongues. Clouds of unidentifiable dust swirled about in the disturbed air, and a chemical residue glistened a rainbow across the floor, leaking from damaged storage drums and running into an elevator shaft.

"Anyone see an 'on' switch?" Kenny chuckled, moving right as the others fanned out to help him look.

Katya stayed with their two foundlings at the truck, listening to boots crunch around inside. The interior suffered severe damage. Fragments of consoles and broken glass littered the ground. Joey pulled the casing of a terminal open and fiddled with it for a few minutes, succeeding in causing a static-laced hologram of a man in a lab coat to appear in the center of the room. Shadows of the four men loomed over them, drawn by pale blue light.

"Can I help you?"

"We got a flooding problem, need some power." Joey smiled. "Over at D4."

"Certainly. Please provide the access codes."

Joey stared at the ceiling. "Fuck."

The voice spoke with the aplomb of an English butler. "'Fuck' is not a valid access code. Please provide the necessary access codes."

"Sure… No problem." Joey plugged his net deck into one of the interface ports.

"'Sure… No problem' is not a valid access code…"

Joey ignored the rest of the spiel.

He tapped away at the floating keyboard.

"Your mother is not a va—"

Lights blinked on his deck's surface as the holographic apparition flickered and spoke backward at a high rate of speed. It stopped, faded into a human outline of snow, and returned to normal.

"Thank you Mr. Welker. Access granted." The hologram offered a placid smile. "Beginning core power up sequence. Shall the facility remain on standby power or return to operational levels?"

Joey rubbed his chin. "Operational levels, return to standby in one hour. Also, shut down power to circuits eight through eleven."

"Very good Mr. Welker. Command sequence authenticated." The hologram vanished, darkening the room with its absence.

"Figured you wouldn't want the automatic defenses online."

"Nice work," said Kenny.

"I hate these old terminals, no virtual reality." Joey feigned disappointment.

Eldon landed a playful punch onto his shoulder. "Poor baby."

"Yeah I know. My fingers hurt from all that typing." He flexed his fingers and pouted. "That was almost *fourteen* words."

When they returned to the shaft, the water level had dropped several meters and continued descending. The distant sound of machinery and rushing water echoed among the trees along with the occasional chirp of an unseen bird.

"That's a good sign." Kenny smiled.

Masaru and Eldon looked around before Eldon spoke. "What?"

"Birds. If the birds are chirping, there are no predators around."

"None we can see." Masaru squinted at the side window of the truck, observing the little girl talking with Katya.

Katya discussed her imminent future. The girl couldn't decide if she wanted to look for Andy and the others or merely play the part of a child and be adopted by some random family. They both assumed her sisters had the anti-growth component removed and would all be older now. She worried she might not fit in with them. The others all behaved closer to normal. EAO-106 had the hardass, and didn't really get along with them that well. Without knowing where he went, what name he used, or even if she would be welcomed, she decided she wanted nothing to remind her of this place ever again.

"Once Ido gets that thing out of you, I'll ask Masaru to take you to the police. They'll find you a home."

"Why not you?" She looked up at Katya.

"Me? Oh…" Katya stammered. "I'm not ready for a daughter and I don't live in one place very long, some people are after me…"

"No. I mean why won't you take me to the police?" She made a silly face.

Katya exhaled. "I'm not…"

The UCF didn't throw people back to the ACC if they felt they could trust them. At this point in the conflict, they took everyone wanting to defect. Katya pondered coming clean. After all, her story was compelling enough. Her worry about company hackers finding her if she was on the books kept the thought at arm's length.

Katya whispered. "Okay."

The girl hugged her. Katya patted her on the back, trying to distance herself from the sudden inexplicable want to keep her.

51

PLAN B

A horrendous slurping sound rose out of the shaft as the last of the water vanished into the drains. Kenny looked back from the edge at everyone. The strange noise drew Katya out of the truck to see what was going on.

"Kat, you okay watching those two?" Kenny motioned at the girls.

"Yeah. I don't think she's faking, but she doesn't trust us completely yet. She's measuring us as much as we are her."

"You don't trust us either." Joey laughed. "But at least she's cute."

Katya glared, muttering in Russian on her way back to the truck.

"There we go. Back to normal." Joey grinned.

"Joey, we might need you down there for the electronics."

Before Kenny could follow it up with justification, Joey vanished over the side.

No one wanted to risk the elevator, so they opted for the maintenance ladder, which was really nothing more than a series of independent rungs embedded in the shaft wall. Slick with waterborne moss and algae, they offered a tenuous climb down into the dark.

"Remind me to file a grievance with the office of operational safety." Eldon grumbled. "There's no retaining cage."

Kenny laughed. "I'm sure they'll send an inspector out right away."

At the bottom, an inch or so of water remained and the air was heavy with the scent of industrial machines and lubricant. Kenny and Joey covered their mouths with their forearms, trying to use the coarse material of their armored coats as a filter. Eldon smiled behind his sealed faceplate at them. Masaru waited, also enjoying filtered air.

A single door offered entry to the underground complex. Thick and armored, it looked as if it could take a few hits from heavy weapons fire.

Eldon kicked the door with a dull *clank*. "That's gonna be a bitch."

Joey moved over and checked the combination retinal scan and handprint reader, cursing at the lack of visible screws or ways to open it from this side. He studied it for a minute or two before shaking his head.

"This is mounted from the inside… high security. I'm not going to be able to open it up."

"What about this?" Eldon tapped his knife.

"I don't see any other option." Joey took a step back. "Masaru's sword would probably go right through that, but he wouldn't dare use it as a tool."

"You *are* learning."

Eldon squeezed the handle of the knife, activating it at the same time he unlocked it from its sheath. The hypersonic oscillation filled the pit with a sound beyond hearing that manifested as a sense of dread. Eldon poked at the security panel with the tip of the blade. The metal was quite tough, even the vibro blade hesitated on it. He leaned his rifle against the wall, grabbed the knife with both hands, and jammed the tip into the housing.

Eldon strained, the blade moved a quarter of an inch. "Damn. Indirium."

The dense asteroid metal seized the knife, reducing the hypersonic vibration to audible screeches. Each time it snagged, the cutting power fell away to nothing and he wrenched it back and forth to free it before starting over again. The interplay between the edge and the material sounded like someone strangling a massive robotic rooster.

Joey huddled against the wall as far away from the door as the pit allowed, hands clamped over his ears. Eldon and Masaru had some protection from the sound by virtue of their helmets, but Eldon experienced the joy of the vibration riding up his arms. After almost twenty minutes, Eldon had cut all the way around. He slid the weapon back into its cryo-sheath, generating a small puff of fog and a loud hiss as it locked in place.

All four stood for a moment, savoring the silence.

Joey coaxed the security terminal out, tilting it forward to get at the electronics. Without data to spoof the biometrics, he shorted the board to bypass the security. The crudeness of it made him frown at its simplicity. Once he made the right contact, the door slid open with a hiss.

"You must be getting better at this. I don't see any smoke this time." Kenny gave Joey a playful nudge.

Joey grumbled. "Any idiot with a metal contact could do this. The hard part was getting at it."

"No shit," said Eldon, holding his helmet. "I'm going to be hearing that in my dreams."

He hefted his rifle and kicked the door. It slammed into the wall, echoing into the tunnel. Seconds later, stark white lights came on in sequence, illuminating the hallway ten meters at a time. Boots clattered across the metal floor in a disharmonic beat as they passed two empty guard stations. The vibration of distant machinery came through the walls, making everyone look at the vents. At the end of the corridor, a door jerked back and forth, unable to decide if it wanted to be open or closed.

Eldon leaned into it and shoved, forcing it open and causing a burst of sparks to spray from a control panel. Joey whistled as they entered a cavernous room. Light drifted in from the left. To the right, thin streaks of silver outlined the presence of chairs in the dark.

Beyond a clear barrier, twelve fluid-filled cylinders stood in the glow of lavender backup lamps. Each held the figure of an unconscious child floating in an unknown liquid—all identical girls around the same age as the one they had found. Eyes closed, short white hair drifted in a faint current, and none of them appeared to be breathing.

Kenny ran over to the wall and searched for a way to open the door. "You've gotta be shitting me." He pounded on a code panel, urgency in his voice. "We have to get them out of there."

Masaru sauntered up alongside, using his helmet visor to zoom in on a console near one of the tanks. "Don't get worked up. They're not real."

"Not real? What, like WellTech dolls?" Kenny leaned on the door with both hands, catching his breath. "I thought you said WellTech dolls weren't anatomically correct?"

"No. These look like synthetics, AI-based, all electronic. According to the screens, they are blank. They have not been loaded with any program code yet. The bodies are just in storage."

"Are they dead?" Kenny stared at the cherubic faces.

Masaru shook his head. "No, they never lived. They're synthetics. Think dolls, but made out of softer materials. Plastisteel bones and silica based simulated organs. They even have a circulatory system based on nanobot fluid. They are much harder to detect than dolls, but also far more expensive."

Eldon walked up to the glass, staring at them. "Also illegal as hell to make after Oberon's uprising in 2143."

Kenny looked at him. "Once more in English?"

Masaru cleared his throat. "Synthetics were the first attempt to create artificial life forms for use as laborers, especially for colonization projects and hazardous environment work. The original series were crude and flimsy by today's standards, but they also self-evolved into the first true sentient AIs. Nowadays, they are made of material that closely simulates human tissue but is not alive in the true sense of the word." He gestured at Eldon. "And as our friend has pointed out, Oberon's violent uprising caused the Sentience Act of 2150 which recognized self-aware AIs as 'alive' in a legal sense. The law prohibits the simple 'manufacture' of them now. They consider it the equivalent of making people."

"Wait, so why are there newer ones made out of better stuff now?" Kenny leaned on the clear wall.

"The ACC has no such qualms, and the UCF cannot control every single colony world as well as they would like. Also, extant synthetics needed 'medical' attention and replacement parts."

"So they'll eventually all wear out and die?" Kenny scratched his head.

Masaru nodded. "The original series, yes. The newest generation of them have developed a form of reproduction."

"Whoa, I'm sorry I asked." Kenny laughed.

"I'm not entirely sure how it works—Ido would be a better person to ask, but involves the two AIs generating a third that is a composite of their own."

"Spawning a child process?" Joey punned, unable to resist.

Masaru glared.

"That is just so... effing... creepy." Kenny cringed at the false children. "They look so real and so helpless."

"A lot of the Nova 10's don't realize they're artificial," added Masaru. "Their nanobots can break down food into its raw component molecules and reconstruct them to maintain their systems. Even if you grabbed one, you couldn't tell what they were. Un-plated Myofiber feels just like living muscle to the untrained hand. The good news is that even the best ones, unlike dolls, can only get as strong and fast as a person. They just don't get tired, don't need to breathe..."

Kenny exhaled. "Well thanks for making me not want to ever sleep again. So, are they alive?" He gestured at the tanks.

Masaru nodded. "Think of them as computers that haven't had an operating system loaded on them yet."

Joey stood in a cloud of light emanating from a terminal on the right side of the room. The amethyst glow illuminated a small group of executive workstations.

He looked back over his shoulder. "I wouldn't worry about it too much. I've met a few on Mars. All they wanted was to fit in with everyone else. This one chick, Simone I think her name was, cried for two weeks when she found out she was a synth. Besides, it will be thousands of years before their population becomes an issue."

Eldon looked away. "They feel pain?"

Masaru tilted his head. "From a philosophical standpoint, who knows? They act as if they do, although it would be simple to remove that from an AI. StarPoint was foolish not to use these for the armor project. If they used simple AIs that lacked self-awareness, it would have been legal."

Kenny edged closer to the glass, unable to look away. "So what do we do with them?"

Masaru waved. "Just leave them. They have no AI, so they are just going to sit there until someone programs them. It is not legal to sell them, I doubt that StarPoint will risk coming back for them, and I know you. You're not going to want to destroy them."

"I know some people on Mars that would take them." Joey pointed up. "Other synthetics, it would be like they were adopting them."

"Transporting them is more effort than we're equipped for." Masaru shook his head. "If you take them out of the preservative fluid, they'd need to be activated within a few days."

"They look so helpless." Kenny turned away.

Joey yelled from across the room. "Hey Kenny?"

"Yeah?"

"Did you turn into a sap before or after you had a kid?"

"Go to hell."

"Already got my tickets. First class."

"Mostly after," said Kenny. "Don't tell me you could destroy them?"

Joey laughed. "Meh, probably not, but I did find some information. Looks like Welker shared the military's distrust for AIs. The original plan was to use these synths until he got into a nasty argument with someone by the name of Earl Wharton. Wharton was on the same mind track as Masaru, wanting to go with synthetics because they didn't feel pain. It's also much easier to stop a synthetic from growing up." Joey paged down a long list of emails. "Welker felt that AIs couldn't be trusted, and they would rebel the first chance they got."

"Yeah," said Kenny. "I think a lot of us have that nightmare."

"He ordered them to vat grow gene-manipulated embryos and raise them with..." Joey made air quotes. "A full emotional support structure."

Eldon rolled his eyes. "So much for that."

Joey flipped among more screens. "I think this Dr. Gina Baxter is the woman the kid mentioned. The way this bitch writes, it sounds like she's just experimenting on animals. She didn't consider the pain of the de-aging process to be a showstopper. Wharton tried to re-pitch the synth thing to Welker because he worried about psychological instability. Looks like a Dr. Andrew Francis agreed with Wharton. Lewis wanted to decommission the kids and Wharton wanted to green light the synthetic project. Baxter wanted Francis terminated, and I don't mean with a pink slip."

Eldon cracked his knuckles. "I'd like to have a chat with her."

Masaru drifted over. "The girl already said they killed her."

"Yep." Joey opened a holographic panel.

Six 'men' in green suits advanced on a woman in a lab coat. Joey paused it.

"Got the video of the killing right here, courtesy of our old friend the ceiling cam."

Kenny shivered. "We don't need to see that."

Joey shut it and dug into other files. "The rest of this stuff backs up what psycho brat said. Chose females for sympathy, trained to act innocent, take advantage of the best opportunity for escape."

"Think she's faking it?" Eldon looked at the door. "You got kids, can't you read her?"

"Not sure." Kenny brushed his knuckle across his mouth. "If she is lying, she's doing a damn fine job of it. Kids are far from an exact science. Plus you gotta live with them for a while to learn their ways."

"I'm grabbing all this info for Ido, there's some specs on that part here. Unfortunately, it looks like much of the design files for the armor or anything we could make any money off of is long gone." Joey scratched the back of his head. "There's nothing about Mayberry at all. Why the fuck was I sent out here?"

Eldon walked over. "Guess this whole underground area was for the synthetics?"

Joey nodded. "Yeah. I hate to say it, but that would have been a better plan."

Kenny took a step toward the exit. "And no real kids would be involved."

"You know." Masaru glanced at him. "Some people wouldn't see much of a difference if the AIs were self-aware. According to the law, synthetics are people too."

"It's not the same." Kenny tried to explain. "They're artificial... They don't have real emotions, just simulated ones. They don't have souls..."

"Oh here we go again with the Badlands voodoo shit." Joey laughed.

"Did you ever stop to think about what will happen to you when you finally do something too stupid for even you to luck your way out of? What if there *is* something beyond this world, what then?"

Joey shrugged at Kenny.

Masaru chuckled. "Are you so convinced that just because a body is made of plastic and metal that it can't have a soul?"

Kenny stared for a moment. "I don't have enough beer in me to think about that right now."

Joey gave Masaru a flat smirk. "Are you so sure that every living body has one?"

Eldon sighed. "Man, why you gotta rag on Katya so much? Is it just that you can't have her so you gotta put her down all the time?"

Joey laughed. "I don't want her."

Kenny patted him on the shoulder. "That's the usual first response when you can't have something."

"I'm surrounded by metaphysical pussies." Joey flailed. "Can't a guy pick on an ice queen in peace? I mean look at her, she's a bitch all the time for no reason."

Eldon chuckled. "Well you do have a point about that."

Masaru smirked. "She has her reasons, just not ones she is willing to share."

"I ain't holdin' my breath for that day," said Kenny.

Joey laughed. "Doesn't matter if you ain't trying to tap it."

"Girl that fine wouldn't even look at me twice." Eldon started walking out.

Kenny patted him on the shoulder. "Don't sell yourself short."

"Yeah, but don't bite a poison apple." Joey gave up on the terminal. "There's jack shit in here."

Eldon walked past the inert bodies. "Sick fuckers. Can you tell if this was officially sanctioned?"

Joey frowned. "Not from here. I can try once we're back in range of the net." He paced for a moment before kicking the terminal. "Fuck! What the hell am I missing? I had a god damned railgun fired at my head to stop me from finding something out here."

Kenny followed Eldon. "Guess we go back upstairs and knock on doors."

VIOLATED

L eaving the synthetics in their eternal repose, the men returned to the shaft. Joey shorted the console to seal the outer door before stomping the panel back into place. Eldon paused at the base of the ladder, noticing three drops of white liquid on one of the rungs. Before he could question them aloud, the sound of Amber in hysterics made them all look up.

"Shit, the brat's turned on us." Masaru pulled his sword.

Eldon hauled himself up the ladder, diving over the top with his rifle at the ready. His armor changed into a mottle of orange and brown as he landed in a pile of leaves, making it seem as though the ground swallowed him. A sweep of the area found no hostiles, just Katya and Amber rolling around on the ground by the truck. Amber flailed and screamed as Katya tried to hold her down. The white haired girl hung out of the open passenger door window with her arms folded, watching the women wrestle.

"What's happening?" Kenny yelled up from below.

Eldon stood up and his armor returned to its green color. "Rich bitch is having a meltdown."

Masaru put his sword away and started up the ladder.

Seeing Eldon, Katya yelled. "Little help?"

Eldon let his rifle sag onto the sling, forgetting it was broken. The gun plopped into the mulch, and he stopped after a single step with a sigh. He stooped to grab it and trotted over to the struggle in the leaves. Masaru cleared the top of the pit with Kenny and Joey right behind him. By the time Eldon got there, Katya had flipped Amber face down and sat on top of her. The young woman clawed at the leaves, screaming incoherently. As Eldon grabbed hold, Katya rolled away and gasped for breath.

Eldon held her down with little effort. "Amber! What the hell is wrong with you?"

The sudden bellow snapped her out of her frenzy. After a shiver, she stared at him for a moment of silence, and then bawled. He loosened his grip when he felt the fight leave her. Crumbled fragments of leaves clung all over her hair and clothes.

"What happened?" Eldon grabbed her by the shoulders and gave her a light shake.

Amber pointed at her head with a trembling finger. "Behind my ear."

Masaru helped Katya back to her feet. Joey pulled Amber's thick blonde hair out of the way, revealing the small metal circle of a system interface port.

Joey blinked. "It's just an M3, what's the big deal?"

"Get it out, get it out!" She closed her eyes and shuddered. "I don't wanna be a machine."

"Whoa, whoa. Calm down." Kenny rubbed her arm. "Millions of people have those, its damn near required to lead a modern life these days."

She sniffled. "Do you have one?"

Kenny made an awkward grimace. "No, but… I also don't lead a modern life." He pointed at his cowboy hat and gun belt.

"Would you let your daughter get one?"

"Not a chance…" He answered before he could filter it. "Well… I mean… once she's eighteen that's her choice but…"

Amber whined. "See."

"It wouldn't be my choice to make… but, yeah."

"Someone put it in me. I didn't want it. I *hate* cyberware, it's icky." She seemed about ready to tantrum again.

The little girl in the truck rolled her eyes with such a contemptuous look, Joey burst into laughter as she vanished into the back seat. He had to hang on to Eldon to avoid falling over.

"Shhh…" Kenny pulled her into a paternal hug. "We know a guy that can help you…"

"Ido." The kid muttered, sounding bored.

Amber nodded, wiping her face. "Okay."

Katya cursed in Russian as her scorn for the spoiled rich girl boiled over.

Once the initial blast of anger subsided, she slipped into English. "Such a fit over nothing. How can you lose your mind like that over something so stupid? Look at that kid!" she pointed at the truck. "Look what these corporate bastards did to her. She's not crying about a little fuckin' metal plug."

Amber buried her face in Kenny's shoulder.

He glanced at Katya. "Was that really necessary?"

Joey smirked at Masaru. "Soul?" He pointed at Katya. "Eh?"

Masaru rolled his eyes—not that Joey could see due to his helmet.

"What if the dogs heard her screaming and came after us while I was trying to calm her down? What then?" Katya fumed.

Joey suppressed his laughter long enough to say, "The doggies would have had some borscht."

"Die." Katya seethed.

Joey put on a patronizing tone. "Not sure if you've been keeping up with what's gone on here, but Amber was victimized, too."

Katya folded her arms. She stared at the sobbing young woman for a moment before she got her jealousy in check. Amber made it to nineteen enjoying the kind of life of which she could only have dreamed. This situation came as the result of idiotic choices, choices that Katya never had the chance to make.

Katya sulked. "She overreacted and put us at risk."

"Let's just be happy she didn't discover that thing when it was dark out." Kenny pulled Joey and Amber together hoping that she would distract him from the imminent trading of barbs with Katya. "Keep an eye on her."

Kenny climbed into the driver's seat, glancing at the little girl sitting innocently below three large rifles on the gun rack. His jaw tightened at the realization she had been alone with weapons for a while.

She didn't look up. "Class 4 assault rifles would break my shoulder. Besides, my legs are too short to reach the pedals so I can't steal the truck after I kill you all." Her emotionless presence broke into a fit of childlike laughter. "Sorry, I guess that wasn't too funny."

He breathed a long sigh of relief.

"Did you find it?" She looked up and wiped her nose on the back of her arm.

Kenny grumbled. "Nothing we can use, just some terminals with email. Corporate BS, they wiped everything out of the system."

She shrugged. "Oh."

A few yards away, Joey held Amber and enjoyed every minute of it. He thought about the irony of an HLM terrorist with cyberware. They may be deluded and violent, but hypocrites they were not.

"Sad, the only honest people left are the crazy ones."

"What?" she looked up.

The more he thought about it, the more suspicious he became.

"Amber?"

"Yeah?" She shrank away, afraid of eye contact.

"I need to ask you something and you're probably not going to like it too much..."

She undid the button of her pants. "I don't mind... I figured it would happen sooner or later. I'll do whatever you want if it'll get me home."

Joey bit his lip. The temptation was unbearable, but he still grabbed her hand.

"No, that's not what I meant." He flashed a nervous smile. "Tempting, but not what I meant."

She blinked.

"Once we get you home to your family and you get adjusted... If you're still in the mood after then, fine, but you don't have to do that just to buy a ride." He stared at the leaves. *What the hell is wrong with me? I turned her down. Me... Turned her down. Am I going soft like Kenny or am I worried about Eldon?*

He glanced over at the others. Eldon, having seen where her hand went, pointed two fingers at his eyes and then one at Joey.

She refastened her pants. "Okay."

He brushed her hair aside. "That thing in your head."

Her wounded look would have put a cartoon princess to shame.

"I can't understand why anyone would bother forcing someone that hates cyberware as much as you do to have one of those, unless they were just a vicious bastard."

She looked down and whined. "I wouldn't tell them how we found this place. Maybe they wanted to steal my brain."

"They wanted your genes. actually."

"But I was naked. They already took them." She pouted at him with wide-eyed innocence.

Eldon stared at her with his mouth open. His eyebrows had formed a single flat ridge.

Joey had all he could do not to slap himself in the forehead. "No... Not your pants. Your genes, your genetics."

"Oh."

"They can't just read your mind with that plug, it lets your brain control other things... most of the time."

"I still want it out."

"That's fine. I want to check something, if it's okay with you."

"What do you want to do?"

"I just have to connect my deck to your socket and..."

"You just told me I didn't have to do that."

Several thumps came from Eldon punching the dashboard of the truck in an effort not to laugh aloud.

"Okay, I admit I worded that poorly."

Eldon couldn't take it anymore and burst out laughing.

Amber looked lost.

"Okay. A wire. That little socket in the back of your ear is meant for a wire. I'd like to run a diagnostic on it just to see if it is what I think it is."

She tried to pull away from him. "I dunno."

"It won't hurt at all... I swear." He pushed her hands together. "Please trust me."

She trembled, but the look in his eyes reassured her, and she offered a hesitant nod.

Joey sat in the mulch with her, pulled the Teradyne Silver into his lap and brought it online. He pulled out the secondary lead, usually meant for terminals, and held it up so she could see it. Amber jumped when the asterisk-shaped prong snapped out of the plastic casing.

"Don't pop the balloon." Eldon couldn't help himself.

Joey stifled a snicker.

"Okay, Amber. I swear this won't hurt, but it might feel strange." He put a hand on top of her head and turned her to face away from him.

She tensed as the plug got closer and closer. Just as she reached the verge of screaming, it clicked into place. Her shaking stopped with a nauseated face.

"That... I felt that in my skull." She stared at him with sick in her eyes.

"You won't feel anything else." Joey patted her on the head.

Amber looked at the wire that descended from behind her ear, over her chest and legs, and went into the machine. She dry heaved at the sight of being plugged into such a thing, and closed her eyes.

She squeaked, just above a whisper. "Pull it out."

"I can't pull out 'til I'm finished."

Eldon howled.

"Finished what?"

"Someone put data in you."

"My mom will kill me if I'm pregnant."

"Oh, for fuck's sake." Eldon screamed. "Are you really that god damned stupid or are you just acting?"

Amber hid behind Joey. "Why is he yelling at me?"

"I'd explain, but it wouldn't be worth it." Joey patted her on the head again before he continued in a whisper. "The airhead thing isn't necessary. We won't tell the cops about the HLM stuff."

She drew a breath.

"You *were* sincere about not wanting to go back?" he asked.

"Yeah. I had enough. I don't want to do this anymore. I swore to God that I'd go home to my parents if he saved me from the torture." She met his gaze. "I'll never hurt anyone ever again… but I still hate cyberware."

"How long ago did your memory come back?"

"This morning, I started remembering stuff when I woke up." The wire brushed her ear, making her shudder. "It seemed like the right thing to do back then, but I feel so stupid now."

"They took advantage of you. Just… do me a favor?" Joey looked over the floating screens at her.

"What?"

"Don't do anything like that again. You're way too cute to wind up dead or maimed."

She blushed. "I promised him I wouldn't"

"Who?" asked Joey.

"God."

Joey concealed his eye roll, not wanting to get into *that* debate out here. "Oh and…"

"What?"

"Will you tell me how you found this place?"

"I guess. Kevin got the information from someone named Proscion."

Joey blinked. "Proscion? But he's been gone for two"—he gazed up—"that's right, you came out here seven years ago… Yeah. He's been off the grid for like two years."

Amber shrugged. "I never met him. I just know that's who sent us out here. He used to do some work for the HLM bosses. He wasn't into the cause though, they had to pay him."

"I guess when you're as good as he is… was … you can get paid for whatever you want."

Kenny, standing on the running board, yelled. "Hey, you two kids done flirting?"

"I found something." Joey shouted back. "Okay, done. Want to pull it out or should I?"

Amber wrapped herself around his left arm. "You do it. I don't wanna touch it."

She braced for pain as if Joey were about to tear her nipples off. "Okay… do it."

"It's already out." Joey swung the wire around in front of her.

Amber blushed at her lap. "Oh."

He stood, offering her a hand. "C'mon."

The white haired girl clung to Katya, overacting the child angle, but neither seemed to care. It helped her cope and it made Katya feel a little better as well. Joey examined the data from Amber's head.

Kenny flicked switches, bringing the truck's drive system online. "Okay, I'll circle back to the compound and we can start kicking down doors."

"Hold on. We may not have to. Someone stored data inside her head."

"At least she had room." Eldon's comment attracted a smirk from Kenny.

Joey looked at Amber and handed her the wire again. "You really should let me delete that stuff out of your head. If people find out you have it, they'll try to kill you."

"What?" She stopped picking bits of leaf off her clothes, cowering away from the plug.

"The Mayberry data is in your head, it's the reason we came out here. The crypto looks like a fit for my cipher key. WellTech has already been trying to kill me for it, and there is no reason for you to get caught up in it."

Eldon threw his arm over the seat. "How the hell would anyone know that she had that shit in her head?"

Joey shrugged. "Someone sent me out here to find it, so someone has to know."

Amber took the plug and stared at it. She felt around her head until her finger hit the metal socket. She seemed ready to vomit as she slid it in place. "I didn't have this thing when I came out here."

"You probably did and didn't notice." Joey's face turned blue from holographic light. "If you kept it, you'd forget you had it in a week. It doesn't bother me anymore."

"Fuck that. This thing is gone as soon as I'm back in the city. Can we stop there before my parents see it? I think it would kill them more than me dating a psionic."

"Sure, whatever you want." Kenny nodded. "What's up with the file?"

Joey thrummed his fingers on the deck. "It's still working. This is some heavy crypto, but it's still taking a long damn time. I gotta check my deck out when we get back."

He deleted the contents of Amber's storage module, unplugging the cable as soon as it was done. She offered a weak smile, trying not to vomit.

"You also have a memory implant. Ido should be able to remove that at the same time. Someone used you as a living holodisk."

She re-swallowed her breakfast.

"There we go. Holy shit." Joey's near-white face flashed green with information. "No wonder they wanted me dead. God damn."

"Out with it man!" Eldon bellowed.

"The files in her head prove WellTech used some freaky black ICE. ACC made it, some soft called *Puppenspieler*. This is fucking insane." He gawked. "They used it to go into the heads of two HLM deck jockeys. That German soft turned them into zombies, just like hacking a cyborg and taking it over."

"They what?" Masaru's eyes bulged. "I didn't think that was possible."

"Neither did I. The details are right here. These WellTech bastards ran them like marionettes and forced them to machinegun that EduTran full of kids just to make the HLM look bad. The son of the exec that signed the order was even on it."

"Oh my god..." gasped Katya.

"It looks like a second generation soft. From what I can tell, the control was sketchy at best. Because they moved like zombies, the attack was far from as lethal as it could have been. They're lucky they hit anything at all."

"I doubt the man wanted his son dead, that was no doubt deliberate," said Masaru.

Katya squinted. "Keep telling yourself that."

Amber cried. "Those poor children."

"Well that explains why the HLM turned them over to the police without the usual bullshit." Eldon patted his leg. "It wasn't a sanctioned operation. They probably thought those two went crazy."

Kenny looked at Amber. "Did you know anything about it?"

She thrashed her head back and forth with an emphatic no. "I was like eleven when that happened, I didn't even know what the HLM was then. Fuck, a few sectors west and I could've been *on* that EduTran."

"There's enough here to prove their involvement." Joey looked up. "WellTech is going to keep coming after me and Hayley. The only way I can stop it is just blow it out onto the NewsNet."

Kenny leaned back. "That'll start up one hell of a shit storm."

"No doubt." Eldon faced front and settled into the seat. "Better get a good raincoat."

"Could you contact WellTech and arrange to sell it back to them?" Katya glanced at Joey. Everyone's initial gasp at her mercenary suggestion faded as she justified it. "If you release it, the HLM might get a boon of recruits."

"I gotta take that risk. Stupid people will always do stupid things, and charismatic shitheads will always be there to take advantage of those with no will of their own and a desperate need for acceptance." Joey shut his deck down.

Amber shot him a hurt look. "That was mean."

"Maybe, but am I wrong?" Joey winked.

She pouted.

"Besides, WellTech already tried to kill me twice. Do you really think they will trust me not to have copies? I know I don't trust them not to keep trying. I got what I came for. We can go back as soon as y'all want to."

Kenny turned the truck and accelerated toward the compound. "They tried to kill Hayley. I say let 'em burn."

Eldon looked to his left. "What say you Ken? Want to search for treasure?"

"Naa. This is all modern shit anyway, not worth anything. Plus we got passengers, wouldn't be fair to make them wait."

Eldon patted his shoulder twice, hard. "Okay man, let's get you back to Alyssa."

NEW HOPE

Despite the standstill traffic, Joey smiled, still able to smell Amber's presence all over him and his bike. She had clung to him, screaming, the whole way back to her parents' place. Her father even managed to put aside his obvious contempt for someone of Joey's social standing and spoke to him like a real person for the short time he spent there. Even with a five-way split, he pocketed a hundred grand of the reward money, and with it, a sense of security he hadn't known in a long time.

Still, something yet gnawed at the back of his mind about this strange situation in which he found himself entangled. He had started the upload of the Mayberry data from outside the wall, as soon as they got into wireless range. It should have taken a few seconds, but it didn't complete until Ido took Amber out of the medical tank an hour later.

At first, he assumed WellTech tried to interfere with the transfer, but a diagnostic check made it seem like the deck's I/O channel was stressed beyond capacity, as if uploading massive amounts of data. He figured the same idiot who had tried to fry it at Kenny's place was at it again.

A familiar face caught his attention from above, shimmering from a massive holo-panel drifting overhead. He ducked a smaller advert bot gliding low over the field of trapped commuters.

"Tired of being stuck in traffic on the ground? Take to the skies with your own brand-new Timmons-Orben hovercar." A series of vehicles orbited the bot, starting at just over three hundred grand to three and a half million for the luxury one.

The emphatic male voice faded into the distance, and he squinted into the sky where blonde hair glowed against the deep indigo of the night sky. Kimberly Brightman's sixteen-foot tall visage read news copy about a wealthy entrepreneur,

Viktor Kovalev, found dead by his cleaning staff earlier that day. Unknown assailants had shot him, as well as several bodyguards. Joey mouthed the words "at this time, the police have no leads and no suspects and are looking to the public for help" as the reporter said it. It was always the same routine whenever someone like that died. Despite a life lost, Joey couldn't help but feel a twinge of pleasure at watching someone rich and powerful die.

The reporter tapped her earpiece and paused in mid-sentence to listen to an unheard voice as "Breaking News" scrolled above her in big red letters. Joey grinned from ear to ear as she switched stories and showed the world the truth about the Mayberry incident. The NewsNet kept looping the same ten second bit of the medic carrying a bloody, screaming boy.

"Milk it you fuckers," grumbled Joey. "That kid lost an arm for your ratings."

The sea of cars changed in texture as people stuck their heads out to watch. Speechless as the reporter absolved the HLM of complicity in the scandal, the crowd gasped in unison. Kimberly reminded everyone how fast WellTech had been there to offer compensation to the families. They claimed to feel responsible for the tragedy as the protest was about their product, and as a show of good corporate citizenship had 'been there' for them in their time of crisis.

With the scandal exposed, an altogether different light fell on that act. The tide of public opinion turning went over the stranded commuters, an audible wave. Even with such damning evidence, the company would probably shrug it off with only a black eye. Now, he could sit back and watch the months of senate inquiries with a big grin, once the wave of paranoia about hackers subsided. With any luck, that would stop the assassins, as WellTech had nothing to gain by killing him now —except revenge.

Tired of traffic, Joey borrowed the sidewalk to slip away. Trying to drive a land vehicle from the far north back home at this hour had been a bad idea, but it beat spending time with snobs. Two hours later, he arrived back at his own personal hellhole. It seemed strange to stumble into a place like this with over a hundred grand in his account. Granted, the reward was a onetime deal and he couldn't keep up with monthly rent for long. That would demand a day job, a drudgery to which he wasn't yet ready to subject himself.

The fragrance of smoldering silicon lingered, making him grumble when he remembered his shower. He set the deck on its table, jumping back as he found his hand coated in a slippery opaque white liquid that dripped from the back left corner of the Teradyne. Joey fell into the chair, still in his coat, and opened the deck. The leak originated from a crack in a boxy component on the far left.

The neural memory module had a crack.

The nutritive base for the artificial neurons seeped out. *Well that explains a lot.* A borked memory module would slow everything down. Given all that had happened to him over the past several days, he found it plausible to believe that his deck took a stiff bounce. It did seem odd that the external case had no damage.

Ten minutes later, Joey met a delivery bot a few blocks west—as close as they would go to his apartment. It dropped off the replacement part and zoomed off as if even it feared being that close to a grey zone. Joey smiled at the package, having taken this opportunity to upgrade to a larger capacity module.

The story of the dead hackers had made him curious, and he wanted to do a little digging. At least one claimed to have heard his dead wife calling to him in the days leading up to his suicide. Since Joey's dad appeared to be talking to him, he wanted to be damn sure he wasn't next.

Two cyberspace hours later, the only connection he could find pointed at a net psychiatry outfit called New Hope. He had heard as much on the news already, but it was the only common thread between them. Curiosity overtook him, and he soon found himself standing at the door to the virtual building. The dark cowboy avatar changed into an approximation of Joey's actual self, with just enough difference for deniability.

He blinked, allowing his eyes to adjust to the dim interior. A brown haired man in his thirties sat in the front row, a young woman in leather gang regalia in the back, and an older Hispanic man argued with a younger version of himself. In the far right, a well-dressed young Japanese woman frowned at the rug.

Joey stood just inside the door, thinking for a minute before going to the solitary man in the front row.

"Hey. Name's Joey. Mind if I ask what brings you here?"

The man shifted his weight toward him. "Mitch... Mitch Lawrence." They shook hands. "My wife Christine is..." He looked away and down. "Probably dead. I think she was murdered. Did you see an evil woman outside?"

Joey cringed. "No... My sister's on Mars. Sorry about your wife."

Mitch looked around as if to ensure no one spied on him. He leaned over, whispering with a desperate grip on Joey's shoulder. "I think she was killed by the Russian."

Joey blinked. "Which Russian?"

Mitch shook his head side to side hard. "Not *a* Russian, *The* Russian. He comes out of the darkness and kills women." He looked at the floor. "Mostly prostitutes."

Joey winced.

"No. Christina was no prostitute!" He pounded a fist into his knee. "She worked in that part of town, a nurse at All Saint's Hospital. I just know that man killed her."

"You saw it?"

"No. One of his whores has been following me since Christina vanished. She told me. Cassidy over there... She's seen him kill others." Mitch pointed at the young woman in leather.

Joey squinted at him. "You just said he kills prostitutes. How can he *have* whores if he kills them? Is he a serial killer or a pimp?"

Mitch thrashed his head from side to side. "He doesn't kill them all. Sometimes he puts demons in their heads and makes them work for him. The woman following me has glowing red eyes. She's a succubus."

A pronounced smirk spread over Joey's lips. He knew of a couple street gangs with demonic affectations, and glowing eyes was an easy thing to do with cyberware.

"Mitch, this is going to be a really strange sounding question... but has Christina spoken to you since she died? Vid call, voices out of your deck, holo-vid player, anything?"

Mitch stared with a blank look for a moment. "No... I wish she would though."

"Thanks."

Joey nodded at Mitch as he stood, and moved around a few rows to sit near the two arguing men. He listened in silence for several minutes as the older one complained at his son for dragging him here against his wishes.

Taking advantage of a momentary silence, he butted in. "Sorry to interrupt, but I'm conducting an investigation and I think you may be able to help. Since we're at a grief counselor, please accept my condolences on your loss."

The old man glared, however his son spoke up.

"My mother. Dad isn't taking it too well." The man looked down. "He's just watching the seconds tick by until he can see her again. He's given up."

"Mind your business," the old man snapped at his son.

"The name's Stephen Moreno." He shook Joey's hand. "This is my father Luis. What can we do for you?"

"I have reason to believe someone out there is using the net to prey on people, and using this place to find their victims. Have you or your father heard voices coming out of electronics lately, more specifically, the voice of your mother?"

The older man looked away with such speed that Joey knew the answer, despite his eventual denial. As Stephen tried to get his father to talk about it, Joey just waved him off.

"It's okay, I can guess." He smiled. "Personally, I don't believe it's anything but someone messing with us using stolen audio. Can you at least tell me if the voice started before or after you came here to New Hope?"

"There is no voice." Luis grumbled. "Even if there was, it's not recordings. Recordings couldn't have a conversation."

Stephen glanced between them. "He started acting weird about a week ago, after we came here a few times. If he is hearing mama, it happened after."

Luis waved dismissively. "You think I'm crazy. He says he can't hear her."

"I haven't heard it yet." Stephen shrugged at Joey.

Joey leaned into his fist, staring at the old man, thinking. When he spotted a small metal panel behind his ear about the size of a fingernail, he sat up straight. "Does your father have hearing augmentation?"

Luis Moreno shouted, before his son could speak for him. "Yes. My ears are shot to shit. I got it put in a couple of years ago. Teradyne Auras." He seemed quite proud of his cyberware. "The upgraded ones with GlobeNet streaming."

"Free for a year." His son added, earning a smirk.

"That's it." Joey smiled. "Those cybernetic ears have a wireless link to the net."

Luis frowned. "What of it?"

"Well that's why Stephen can't hear her. Whoever's doing this is sending the audio right to your ears." Joey folded his arms in triumph.

The younger Moreno muttered. "Son of a…"

Joey nodded and left them their privacy as Eddie apologized to his father for doubting him, but continued to insist he needed to see the doctor. Joey's drift brought him to the young woman in the back row. She stared between her knees, watching him as he got up from the Morenos and approaching her. A glint in her eyes flickered between fear and hostility. She looked about Amber's age, but lacked her innocence. This girl had the haunted look of someone who had seen something they wanted desperately to forget. Short hair, wild and black, clung to her head like the top of an acorn. As if searching for a nightmare always two steps behind her, she cowered behind her legs. If this wasn't a virtual world, she might have fled or pulled a knife.

"Cassidy." She kept her arms folded tight, burying her hands deeper into a black sweatshirt under the leather vest. "You're right, I think something's up."

Joey sat in the next chair. "What do you know?"

She pursed her ebon-painted lips as she dodged eye contact. Two metal loops in the lower part touched.

"A couple of the girls I used to hang with turned up dead." A tremble ran down her limbs and her gaze went off into the distance. She spoke in a squeaked whisper. "I saw him kill Mary."

He waited for her to make eye contact before speaking again. "The Russian?"

Cassidy nodded. "Yeah, how did you know? He's not really Russian though."

"Oh?"

"He's more aug than man. His right arm is a big ass hammer and his left hand is just a curved blade." She held her hand up like a hook to illustrate the point.

Joey rolled his eyes. "Hammer and sickle... So your friends were, um, working girls?"

"What choice do we have?" She glowered, flushed with anger and shame. "My dad caught me with one hit of Flowerbasket when I was sixteen. I'd been a goddamn goody-two-shoes my whole life. It was just a fuckin' dare. One fuckin' time, but that bastard threw me out of the house."

The last tear she would cry over that had fallen a long time ago.

"What about your mother?"

"She didn't say a damned thing, just watched him drag me out of the house and throw my ass to the curb."

She punched the empty chair in front of her, making everyone jump and look.

They talked for a while. She told him about how she spent days wandering, not knowing where to go or what to do and sleeping in PubTran stations. After a few weeks, the first pimp 'adopted' her, but after he got himself killed, the girls went freelance. Once The Russian started hunting them, they went into hiding. Mary thought they were being ridiculous, and kept working.

"Somehow, me trying to talk her into staying inside turned into me going out with her." Cassidy shivered. "I was dumpster diving, looking for food, when he came out of the alley." She curled tight on the seat, hiding her face against her legs. "She thought he was a John, didn't even run. By the time she saw the blade it was too late. He..." The glass-eyed stare returned. "... I just stayed in the dumpster until he left."

Joey didn't try to touch her. "Wow... I'm sorry."

"Scissors." She laughed, crying.

"Huh?"

Cassidy held out two fingers. "I played scissors. Mary made a rock. That's why I was in the dumpster. I'm alive because of fucking scissors."

The girl sat up and wiped the corners of her eyes with the heels of her palms. Joey thought about putting an arm around her, but didn't want to get stabbed, even virtually. He let her ride it out, waiting until she looked up.

"So you've been hearing her?"

"Yeah." She sniffled, wiping her face with both hands. "Public VidPhones, electronics store windows when I go by. Ad bots sometimes..."

"Sounds like he's tapping the city cams to follow you, but why the hell would he mess with you? You're not a hacker." He pondered. "Maybe this guy just likes to fuck with vulnerable people."

Cassidy glared at nothing in particular.

"Have you tried to contact your mom?"

"What the fuck would I do that for?" She turned away. "I already know she doesn't want a druggie whore under her roof."

"If you need a crash pad, I got a lot of room. Sector 16, CR 30." He described it.

She gave him a measured look as if trying to figure out if he wanted to hurt her too.

"The place isn't great but it's pretty safe, all things considered. It's there if you want it." He left her to her thoughts, and approached the Japanese woman.

Nami Omura's dead grandfather had been speaking to her quite often. She fit the pattern, the voices only started after she had been here. Most of the time, he yelled "*mittomonai*" as loud as possible and at the most awkward moments. Nami explained that it meant 'disgraceful.' Her grandfather had been upset with her decision to go to school and have a career. Between her new job, school debt, and her father's death, she had problems coping.

"Father was caught stealing from his company. Rather than surrender to the law, he leapt from the roof to save his honor." Nami stared at her skirt. "Grandfather died in his sleep two weeks later. Now he says shame killed him, both from Father's crime and my improper life."

Joey leaned forward, trying to make eye contact. "What's so improper about it? You're doing well?"

"I am educated, I have a job, but no husband." Nami looked over. "I am a bad granddaughter to him. My shame drove Father to steal."

"That's absurd." Joey looked up. "There's a hacker out there that's watching this place and taking advantage of people that come here. He's just messing with you. That voice is no more your grandfather than I am."

Relief shone in her eyes. He spent a little while longer with her, clarifying his theory about the hacker and cheering her up with the idea that her grandfather didn't hate her. Joey thanked Nami for her time and got up to leave.

Of everyone here, only Mitch hadn't heard the voices. Then again, his girlfriend might have just left him. No one even knew if she died. If she remained alive, there would be no ghost to fake. That also meant that the hacker was doing more research than just attacking people that patronized New Hope.

He closed his eyes in preparation for the vertigo of disconnection, but hesitated when the sound of the outside world grew louder. Joey turned toward the hiss of cars across rain-soaked streets as a thin woman slipped into the room. Her floor length dress looked like it came from a prior age, complemented by a rose choker, black against a pale white neck. She locked stares with him as she drifted toward the back of the room away from the chairs.

Something about her delicate porcelain features captivated him. He grinned at the sight of her toes peeking out from under the hem, her motion silent and floating, like a ghost. He couldn't help himself but follow. Melancholy surrounded her like a cloak, she sulked at the ground as if she would burst into tears at any moment. She reminded him of being on Mars. With much of the colonized area underground, the population had become rather pale after several generations.

This girl stalled his thoughts. He stared until she broke the silence.

"Allo. I am Avril." Her voice sounded as cute as her outfit looked, decorated with a French accent.

"Joey." He flashed an idiot grin.

Her expression brightened a touch, his whimsy inadequate to produce a full smile past her pall of sorrow. "You are new here, yes?"

"Yeah. My dad died a few months back. I guess it's been bothering me more than I let on," said Joey, changing stories without even thinking about it. Something about her made it hard to lie.

"My husband…" She looked down, unable to continue.

Joey felt like an ass for almost a full two seconds at the thought her husband being dead gave him a chance. The idea that she could be grotesque in real life, or even male, didn't cross his mind. "I'm sorry."

"Thank you. I hope your father's passing was peaceful."

"Cancer. He ignored it so long the nanosurgery killed him."

Alex's voice replayed itself in his memory. A girl named Avril contacted him while they were out in the Badlands, trying to find Joey. Her dark blue eyes distracted him from pondering if this meeting could be more than mere coincidence.

Avril folded her hands. "There are some things about the way he died that I don't believe. I need someone to find out what the police aren't telling me. Can you help?"

She seemed afraid to look him in the eye. Her voice had a familiar quality, if he filtered the whispery cuteness away.

"I suppose I could."

"That would be so sweet of you." She smiled at last. "Can we meet for real? The men that killed him may be watching me in here. Is it true that you pulled off the Silver hack?"

With no accent and screaming, she would sound the same as the phantom yelling in Kenny's house—the one calling out for Vincent. This girl was unlike most people he encountered in cyberspace. The vast majority liked their privacy and often went to great lengths to disguise their real identity. Most girls didn't fancy thought of meeting in the real world at all, but this one suggested it after only minutes. She intrigued and frightened him at the same time, but in the end, the thrill felt worth it.

"Sure. You pick the place. Oh, if you don't mind me asking… was his name Vincent?"

Avril's eyes widened. She tried to take a step back, but already stood against the corner. "How… did you…" Her voice changed, more genuine.

"He died violently, didn't he? You were calling out for him." Joey tried not to sound threatening. "I heard it happen. Who was shot, you or him?"

"No… No…" She turned away, hands over her face. "How can you know?"

She squirmed with the look of a cornered mouse. Her dress, the room, the entire false reality around her swam into a claustrophobic mass.

"What happened? Are you still hearing him talk to you?" Joey leaned back, trying to give her some room. "Wait, you think I did the Silver?"

She broke into sobs and vanished. He leaned on the wall, about ready to gnaw on his fist at losing her. Perhaps, somewhere in reality, a woman sobbed over her deck.

The trip to New Hope offered little but more questions, and the face of an antique doll.

He had to find her.

FIGMENTS

J oey leaned back in his chair, the ceaseless foraging of a four-inch roach distracting him. Its rummaging in the mounded trash on the table struck him as a metaphor for his existence in the grey. As the bug slithered out of sight into the pile, he let his thoughts drift back to the haunting visage he had seen at New Hope. The ghostly form, a glow of white and blue among a sea of red and gold, looped like a video in his mind. The instant at which her eyes looked up from the floor, meeting his, replayed again and again. Something about this girl felt as dangerous as it was alluring, and the risk made her even more desirable.

Mitch, the only one at New Hope without a ghost, had to be hiding something. Joey's first thought was that he could be the one doing it, and went there to observe the results. In the event that didn't prove true, the disparity of his not hearing voices could be a key toward an explanation. Over the past several hours, whenever he could wrest his brain away from Avril, he collected information on Mitch. Apparently, Mitch held a job as a shipping clerk for about a year, but had been let go a little more than two weeks ago for habitual lateness. Most curious of all, Joey found no trace of his marriage in the public records. He rubbed his eyes.

"That doesn't mean much." The roach peeked out, waving its antenna. "What do you think, Howard? Maybe they just married themselves."

It zipped out of sight.

"Yeah."

Joey stared at his NetMini, the old message from Alex that told him someone named Avril wanted to find him. A part of him hoped that this girl's real appearance didn't match her cyberspace persona. If she wanted to hurt him, he would be in trouble. The sight of the delicate living doll would stun him into a grinning fool. After snapping out of another daydream, he tried to find out more about Avril Boudreau. Her name whispered in his mind's voice in a series of accents.

Ten minutes later, he stared at the shimmering holo-panels, unsurprised at the lack of information. He took a fry out of a plastic carton, bit it in half, and tapped it on the table until the roach came out. It accepted the offering and dragged it under the heap of old containers. Joey palmed his forehead and squeezed. A false name was far from unusual on the net, but still frustrated Joey's search.

What vexed him more was how the New Hope access logs didn't show her connection. Even the GlobeNet servers showed no record of her. He squinted. Could she be the über-hacker behind all this? The more his mind wandered down that path, the more his desire to find her changed to desperation.

A plastic clatter made him jump.

A carton shifted, trapping the roach in an endless uphill sprint inside a sealed transparent box. Joey stared at it running in place, swimming back and forth, looking for escape.

"I know how you feel, Howard."

He flicked the lid open and it vanished without a glance back. His finger moved from the carton to his chin, rubbing. Mitch failed to fit the pattern. According to Nami, he had been going to New Hope the longest, but had never reported any voices. With cyberspace proving fruitless, he decided to pay Mitch a visit in person.

The conversation Joey had with his father while getting ready made him more determined. The old man rambled on about the same old crap he always did: picking at Joey's lack of a job, his future, grandkids, everything.

Whoever did this was good—he almost felt real.

Joey ducked out of the apartment before it felt *too* real. On the ride, he mulled over what he would say to Avril if he ever found her. A little over a half hour later, he arrived in front of Mitch's building, unable to come up with anything that didn't sound cliché or ridiculous.

Two cars stood sentinel amid a vast expanse of open parking area in front of this building. For a moment, he stared at random cyclones of trash that swirled up for seconds at a time before dissipating in scatters of debris. Almost a quarter of a city block used on parking spaces suggested the place was old. If this sector hadn't been in the grip of the grey, such a waste of ground would have been unthinkable. Echoes of bouncing metal cans and distant cats filled the air. He rolled the bike up to the porch and hit the button to extend the double kickstand.

Dozens of vagrants huddled against the walls in the front room, seeking shelter within the debris-strewn lobby from the wind. The place had the resigned feel of a building that knew it was in its December years. The only difference between it and Joey's apartment was that someone had the gall to demand rent here.

It was a fringer pad just on the outskirts of the Sector 32 grey zone, a place where misfits and outcasts congregated. The area was dangerous, the rent cheap, and your neighbors were often every bit as fucked up as you. A sea of eyes tracked him across the lobby, making him feel like the new guy in prison. He hurried to the elevator. Pushing the button triggered laughter from the vagrants but didn't do anything else. He sighed; feeling like a tourist for even attempting the elevator in a place like this.

He shoved the stairwell door open, displacing a mound of disposable auto-injectors out of the way. The size of the pile made him think every addict in the building tossed empties there. In the center of the landing, he turned in place while peering up into a central shaft at the ceiling some sixty stories above. Thankful for his heavy boots, he crunched over plastic fragments coated in who-knows-what. Sleeping bags, boxes, and trash packed every landing from the ground floor up. Bodies lay about like human litter, most oblivious to his passage. The few that didn't notice him only moaned when he went by.

Reaching the 34th floor, he paused to catch his breath. The old metal door that separated the stairwell from the hallway had its window broken out so long ago that no trace of glass remained anywhere on the ground. Yellowing tatters of wallpaper wrapped the hallway beyond it, hanging in curled shreds. Some scratched at the wall, lofted by a breeze entering a broken window at the far end. Any trace of carpeting had long since vanished, replaced by fetid stains upon bare concrete.

Joey stopped at a patchwork of dark brown mixed with peeling spots of exposed beige that passed itself off as a door. A bullet hole was the cherry atop the blighted sundae of the door. Joey raised his hand to knock, jumping back as the door flew open before he even touched it. Mitch, wide-eyed in a plain white shirt and powder blue boxer shorts, clung to the slab of false wood. Nothing could contain the unwashed smell wafting off him. Motionless, he stared agape as condensation from an auto cooled soda can ran over his fingers and dripped to the floor. Joey's eyes tracked a droplet on its flight down, noticing one brown sock and one bare foot in a sandal.

"Oh hi... It's you, from the headshrinker place. C'mon in." Mitch remained still.

Joey offered a weak smile.

Drip... drip...

Mitch looked down and scurried into the apartment. Joey kicked old cans and empty snack boxes out of his way as he entered and closed the door behind him. A Jian Model 2 Gold Series deck sat on the only table in the room, its M3 wire spooled on the false wood. Weeks' worth of delivery food cartons formed a three-walled castle around it. From the lay of the wire it was evident the retractor had broken and it had been out for quite some time.

"Jian-Tek?" Joey went to touch it, but hesitated.

Jian Corporation made Chinese street hardware, the cheapest of the cheap. Someone had the audacity to label that thing 'gold' series. The sight of such a deck made Joey shiver. Most hackers considered his Teradyne Silver a noob's toy, but it was better than a Jian.

Joey turned, gaze tracking Mitch past a couch, one table, and one dinky little chair. Near tattered, moss-colored curtains, the plain pea-green of the walls gave way to a single picture above the couch. In it, an elevated view looked down on a smiling clean-shaven Mitch with his arm around a pleasant looking girl in her early thirties. Joey approached it, studying her. She was darker than he was, a mixture of Indian and Hispanic, and wore business attire. She was the sort of exotic beauty that Joey doubted would even look at Mitch twice. *I guess miracles do happen.* Both smiled up at the image capture device. The scenery behind him resembled a PubTran station, and an odd white fuzzy blur entered the image from the left side. It resembled one of those ghost smears the paranormal loons often posted as evidence, only more opaque.

Joey pointed. "Is that her?"

Mitch ran a hand over the right side of his head, grabbing the back of his skull. He swayed back and forth. "Yes. That's her. Have you seen her?"

Joey shook his head. "Where did you get the picture? Angle makes me think security camera."

"No." Mitch chuckled with tears in his eyes. "We went to a photo booth at the station a few blocks from here. We had a little time before she went to work. Christina got jealous of the Neko girl that worked there." His face contorted with exaggerated derision, as if trying to prove himself to his missing wife. "Tart wasn't wearing much."

"Do you have any more pictures?" Joey wandered in a circle, appraising the empty apartment.

Mitch shook his head. "She don't like cameras. Always moves out of the way when I try to take her picture. Says she's fat. I got lots of pictures of walls."

A glimmer from the window caught his eye. He drifted over, pulling the curtain to the side to reveal smears of gold paint on the glass. They took the form of random pseudo-religious iconography and unrecognizable letters. Joey picked up a datapad from the windowsill, smirking at the e-book that appeared on its screen. *Of Demons and Darkness: A Mystic's Guide.*

"Seriously?" Joey blinked.

"Careful!" Mitch darted over and swiped the pad. He tugged Joey away from the window. "She… it… she… it… might see you. Don't break the barrier or it'll come, she'll come in. Red eyes! This keeps it out!" He clung to the datapad as if it were a beloved doll.

"Chill out, there's no one there."

"I know." Mitch nodded so fast his jowls flapped. "It's not there all the… she's not there all the time, just when I'm not looking." He pointed at the window. "Maybe Christina's mad at me for not being dead too? Bad girl with red eyes is following me. It!"

"Do you think it's her?" Joey pointed back at the picture. "Would you mind?" He held his NetMini up to the picture as if to snap a digital still of it.

Mitch turned and ambled into the room, back to Joey. "Beautiful. She was so perfect. I don't know why she even spoke to me." Mitch slumped into the sofa in a sad heap. "She loved me, we got married. She always told me that I was doing well and she'd stay." Mitch's voice broke apart into soft sobs. "She wouldn't leave, we were doing fine. I had a good job and everything was so nice."

As Mitch had ignored his question, Joey took an image capture. He zoomed in as much as he could to get only the image and not the wall behind it.

"So you haven't actually seen her dead, nor has anyone else told you that they found her?" Joey sat inverted on the faux wood chair, folding his arms over the back.

Mitch looked up and the sobbing ceased as if on a switch. His face twitched as his brain chewed on the idea. "No?"

"Do you think she may have been abducted? Some of the gangs take pets. Do you think she just left?" *If she saw him like this, no wonder she took off.*

Mitch shook his head from side to side messing up his hair. "No. We were in love. She wouldn't have left." He looked away with a frown. "I know her. She would have told me if she wanted to leave, she wasn't like that, she wouldn't just

294 | VIRTUAL IMMORTALITY

disappear. Something happened to her. Maybe the red eyes got her." Mitch crumbled his fingers into his mouth as his face contorted with worry.

"Whoa Mitch, calm down. I didn't mean anything, just asking." Joey put a hand on Mitch's shoulder. "Maybe someone took her. Don't call her dead until you know for sure. Let me see if I can find anything before you panic."

Mitch pulled his fingers out of his mouth. "Okay."

Joey went for the door, but Mitch ran up on him and held him back. "Wait."

He scurried over and checked the peephole. After intense staring, he looked back. "Okay, it's not... she's not there."

"Red eyes?" Joey lifted an eyebrow.

Mitch nodded his jowls into a flap. "Yes, bad woman. Taller than Christine, thinner. Dresses like a whore in black leather. Boots up to here." Mitch tapped himself on the thigh. "She stares right through me, wants to kill me. If I go outside, she'll find me. It... It..."

"Okay, well. Thanks for checking." Joey smiled, humoring him and hoping the sarcasm didn't sound too obvious.

THE ELEVATED TRAM RAIL, DRAB STEEL GREEN AGAINST THE CITY, OFFERED AN EASY navigation aid to the nearest station. He left the bike on the street below, and jogged up the moving steps into the aroma of coffee emerging from the random fragrances of trash, stale oil, and urine. The walls on both sides of the massive concourse glowed with dozens of display screens: city maps, routes and schedules, status updates, and adverts. The whole system ran on automatic. The only live employees were mechanics, programmers, and administrative weasels.

Following his nose, he settled down in a coffee shop and decided to splurge on some non-reassembled coffee. Made from hydroponic beans, a genuine mocha java ran him forty-five credits. It had been almost six years since he tasted coffee that wasn't the product of molecular rearrangement, and it was worth every credit. He melted into the seat, cradling his drink. The warmth spread through him and made the events of the past week tolerable. When the wonderful liquid ran out, he spent ten minutes just inhaling the scent of it out of the empty cup.

He wanted to do a little checking before he went wandering again. After transferring the image of Christine to his deck, he plugged in and dove into cyberspace. Within minutes, the dark cowboy stood amid old dusty file cabinets in a police data node. The electronic journey underlined his growing dislike for his dive apartment. Even in this part of town, the wireless ran almost twice as fast.

Despite his considerable skill, messing with the police net still had its risks. As of late, his virtual exploits hadn't offered much of a challenge. This one would give him back the rush he so craved.

He settled into his seat, put his feet up on the facing bench, and clicked the wire in behind his ear. The coffee shop pulled away from him, twisting and warping into a tunnel of color and roaring fury into which he launched after three seconds. The sense of falling in darkness faded, and he found himself standing in a plain green room—an unenhanced replica of the coffee shop. In defiance of the GlobeNet protocol, he concentrated on a distant location and appeared instantaneously in front of the nearest police node. He took on the outward appearance of Jacob Roth, and strolled casually across the network to an information storage node in the back.

The ancient gunslinger opened his coat, sending a pack of DataMoles trundling into the room. The furry things crawled everywhere, sniffing at the rows of simulated filing cabinets as they went looking for any match for "The Russian." After only a few minutes, one stopped and stood up on its hind legs, wagging its stumpy tail. Gravelly laughter echoed as he walked over. The animations of cyberspace never ceased to amuse him.

Taking the data tile from its mouth, he sifted among research notes and many pictures of victims. The severity of the gore made him cringe and paw at the data to get rid of it before he could take in any details. Amber panels of light filled with horrible images that jumped off the stack with each swipe of his hand.

A few shadowy glimpses depicted the man, but nothing distinct enough to reveal a face. From the look of it, one Jacob Roth, a Detective with Division 2, got the case after a fatality involving a Division 1 officer. The notes were scattered and not well organized; however, from reading it, he learned a Division 5 unit almost apprehended The Russian almost eleven months ago, before he got that name. Gun camera footage from an armored vehicle revealed the man in brief flashes as he staggered away into the night. Explosive ammunition rendered each night vision image progressively more blurred. Detective Roth pieced together that the suspect lost his other natural arm that night and replaced it with the hammer fist that gave him his street name.

Roth ran a DNA search on fragments from the scene, which identified the man as Bertrand Foster, a former professor of classic literature and music. He had attempted suicide after his wife caught him with a prostitute and took their son away. Hurling himself into traffic failed to kill him, but he required cybernetic augmentation to remain alive. Joey skimmed the medical scan data indicating he suffered damage to his frontal lobe. A duty medic took note of personality changes, and sparse subsequent updates painted a picture of a man who developed an addiction to augmentation.

Joey fixed upon the next file. For a moment, he felt as though he couldn't breathe. A woman stared back at him from the edge of familiarity.

Haunting. He traced his fingers over her cheek.

When he saw her name, Patrol Officer Nina Duchenne, he again heard the screams that filled Kenny's house. The sudden sound made him jump and spin, wondering where it came from. He couldn't get to the next page fast enough, and stared at the face of Vincent Montoya. Red letters under the portrait spelled out 'Killed in Action.' Nina and Vincent—they were the voices that scared the hell out of Hayley. It wasn't a horror vid as Kenny thought. Someone had lifted it from police comm chatter. Why would anyone stream it to his deck in the middle of the night?

The woman looked enough like Avril for him to make the connection. She lost a partner, not a husband. Had she gone to New Hope because of her loss, or did she pursue Joey? The file said little about what happened to her afterward, only that she survived. He stared into the picture's eyes.

"What are you after? Why me?"

Another DataMole poked him in the leg and shrugged when he looked down at it. There had been no image matches to Christina's face. If The Russian had killed her, no one found the body. Detective Roth continued to pursue the case, but had no recent leads.

Joey rifled other data objects, skimming notes about how Roth had zeroed in on him based on a dispersion pattern of bodies. The day after a confident comment about knowing where he would strike next, the writing broke into erratic circular reasoning.

Guess you were wrong, Jake. What, did you come unglued after you missed him?

As soon as he called him Jake, he looked up from the tile with an expression as if he had been slapped. Detective Roth was Hayley's father.

The dark cowboy ran down the hallway to an adjacent data node where he rummaged personnel records for Division 2. The ID photo of Detective Roth matched the man Hayley had called, only less worn out. He scrolled over the case notes, noting how they changed after that night. Detailed and organized broke into meandering postulations and circular theorems about who the next victim would be. The abrupt switch appeared as though someone else had written it. Joey whistled.

Bertrand may not be the only one with brain damage.

Joey envisioned the guilt of each new victim weighing on the mind, heavy enough to make him neglect his child.

A cactus with cartoon eyes appeared in front of him, flailing and pointing at the door. The information absorbed him too much. Division 2 net techs had detected an infiltration. Rather than risk running, he disconnected.

Since he hadn't copied the data, only read it, he hoped his presence masking held out.

DREAM BOX

Joey wandered the terminal for some time, finding no trace of anything resembling a photo booth. Out of desperation, he stopped a passing police officer and asked. She didn't even know what a photo booth was. When he asked about a Neko girl, the officer mentioned one worked at a cyberware shop along the outer concourse. It stuck in her memory due to some kind of protest over a prototype device.

After thanking her, he walked past an elaborate hub where a number of monorail lines merged. The station split in half. The left led to trams and the right held a mile-long row of small shops tucked into alcoves. They were wide open to the terminal platform and many had merchandise that spilled out from their boundaries. He followed the officer's directions, and arrived in front of a small booth packed with high-tech gadgets and boxes of various sizes. NinTek Outlet Shop appeared in dim white-grey lettering in midair, in an endless cycle of fading out from top to bottom and then reappearing. A shawarma stand to the right delayed him long enough for a snack.

A woman in her twenties smiled at him from behind the counter. Frizzy white hair tinged with blue at the tips hung down to the middle of her back, the almost spherical outline broken by a pair of furry cat ears perking up at the sound of his approach. Her paper white skin, no doubt another product of cybernetic tweaking, was beyond Marsborn and glowed with patches of reflected light from the signs around her.

A panel of blue cloth clung to her front, held to her body by nanobot-sized hooks. It almost covered her chest and hung down like a loincloth. Her white-furred feline tail was all that covered her from behind, though it hid more than many thongs he had seen. It swished with such natural movement he guessed it synthetic rather than robotic.

The tip swished about her ankles with anticipation as she leaned forward over the counter and rested her chin on her palm. Long blue fingernails tapped against her cheek one after the other, each glowing when pressed. NanoLED cybertattoos ran down the outside of her arms and legs in the shape of scintillating azure tiger stripes, and the vertical slit pupils of her cobalt blue cybereyes widened. She emitted a realistic purr from a vox unit. Small fangs peeked out from her smile.

Joey had never found the Neko thing appealing, but the sight of an almost-dressed woman still had certain effects on him, and he adjusted his posture to maintain politeness.

Guess she enjoys the employee discount. Probably has claws too if she's here alone with all this shit.

What looked like an old bloodstain on the ground lent some weight to that thought.

"Why hello, cutie!" She winked. "Can I help you find something?"

Most that had the Neko-cyberware fetish liked eyes on them, and he didn't disappoint. She edged closer as he leaned on the counter, almost to the point of touching cheeks. She turned and licked the side of his neck. Her sandpapery tongue sent a shiver down his spine and whitened his knuckles upon the glass. No wonder the owner of the store hired her. Joey was ready to spend all his money right at that moment just to have her do it again.

She distracted him away from the photo unit into a conversation about a Janus multitasker chip, something he had craved for a while that would allow him to handle two simple activities at once. He wanted it so he could watch the outside world while hacking.

Turning her back, she climbed onto a chair and stood on her tiptoes to reach a tiny box on an upper shelf. She could have retrieved it much faster, but put on a show. Leaping to the ground with feral grace, her body draped once more over the counter as she slid a white box in front of him. Joey stared at her royal blue nails, imagining the blades of Scratchers extending out the tips of her fingers. Katya had them, and they were usually one of the first parts a Neko got—right after ears and tail.

Joey shifted his gaze between her hands, at a square of black hidden beneath several layers of dense plastic. Forty thousand credits in a space two millimeters square. The tits dangling over it made the news easier to take, but he still winced. He did have that much, but without sure income, he wanted to save all he had for a better deck. The Teradyne silver would only go so far, making money with a deck that weak was as much luck as it was skill. In order to make any real credits, he needed to upgrade.

"I got a job or two lined up that I'm looking good for. When that's in the bank, I'll come back for it."

"Want me to hold it?" Her eyes narrowed to alluring slits as she picked the box back up.

Joey's knees wobbled. "Sure."

"Okay." She made a dance out of putting it back on the shelf.

"I heard you have some kind of prototype camera here?"

She turned on her toes and smiled. "You're not one of those activists are you?"

Joey showed her the picture. "Naa, just looking for some answers to some strange questions."

"Oh I remember this guy… something really weird about him." She sashayed down to the end of the counter and stooped toward a mound of stuff.

Joey rose onto his tiptoes, praying that her tail would move just a little to the side. Her feline ears swiveled back so she could continue to chat as she rearranged a pile of boxes. In a minute, she held up a shiny grey cube about the size of a fist with several M3 interface ports on its rounded corners. At the center of each face, a stylized N embossed inside a circle.

"This thing… Nishihama put it out a couple of months back. They called it the Trance Cube—or would have if it actually launched. It records images from the thoughts of anyone with a M3 jack, even vids."

"Damn." Joey turned the device over in his hand, mesmerized by the gleam.

She wrinkled her nose. "You were just near him? His scent is all over you. He came in a few weeks ago. I had this thing set up in a demo display and he thought it was a deck… plugged into it before I could explain. The printer spat out that picture and he thought it was a camera."

"Define weird." Joey's eyes continued their battle with the cloth rectangle.

"He kept talking like he had someone with him. He said he was married but I didn't smell anyone else on him." She winked. "And he wasn't staring at me like you are."

Joey let out a nervous laugh. After the tease of Amber, he had been feeling pent up and this girl didn't help at all. Neko girls—and boys—loved to push the boundaries of decency. The ones with real mental issues thought they *were* cats and walked around naked, knowing the cops had better things to do. Despite that, Joey hesitated at making any sort of move on her. Almost none of the Neko girls turned out to really be as promiscuous as they acted. Most just wanted attention, though a few went all new age and spiritual about the whole nudity-in-touch-with-the-Earth bit.

Just like a cat, loves to tease its food.

"Well, I guess the guy was committed to his wife."

"He should *be* committed." She stretched, a shimmer cascaded over her stripes. "He came back the other day asking if I'd seen some girl, raving about some bitch with red eyes stalking him."

"So I hear." The sharp cheer of a small child made him look out over the concourse. "Where is All Saint's Hospital from here?"

She curled around the wall that separated her shop from a stall where a boring man sold plain briefcases, pointing. Joey's eyes ran down her back as he snuck a quick image cap of her for later use.

"Four blocks that way, a big white building." She winked. "Come back when you're ready for that part… or if you need anything else."

He offered a weak smile.

ALL SAINT'S HOSPITAL MAY ONCE HAVE BEEN WHITE, BUT CALLING IT THAT NOW stretched the truth. This hospital was one of the few that continued to operate in areas loaded with the poor and forgotten. Modern medical technology could fix most things after a few hours of floating in a tube. The size of this place said it predated modern technology. Hospital beds saw little use these days, mostly for recovery after invasive cyberware implantation or for those too old or too sick to live without constant care.

Only one of the entrances had light, and it drew Joey like a moth. In contrast to the exterior, the air smelled of disinfectant and looked well maintained. The only person in the room, a dark-skinned man at the counter, looked up at him. The words 'Dr. Emil Farouk' were embroidered on his lab coat.

Joey sidled up to the counter. "Doctor?"

"Yes. You seem surprised."

"I expected a clerk at the desk, not a doc." Joey leaned on the edge of the front desk.

"Our staff is a bit thin at the moment." The man put on a pleasant smile. "What can I do for you?"

"I just wanted to ask about a nurse here. She may be missing and her husband is looking for her." Joey showed him the picture of Christina.

"Oh, so she *does* exist." Doctor Farouk leaned on the counter. "That man came here a few days ago asking the same thing. He thought she worked here."

Joey furrowed his brow. "So you don't recognize her?"

"Not at all, but that man is convinced she is a nurse here. Mark was it?"

"Mitch." Joey held up a finger. "He thinks she was killed and that there's another woman spying on him."

The doctor stood up straight, folding his arms. "The man isn't my patient, so I can tell you this. I had to get security to remove him from the hospital because he refused to leave until this woman came out to talk to him. He balked when I told him that she didn't work here, and based on his mannerisms I have to say that I think he may be suffering from schizophrenia."

"Hallucinations, right?" Joey frowned. "Think this girl might be a figment of his imagination? Mitch is going to New Hope to help deal with her loss. Why didn't the doctor there pick up on that?"

"Bear in mind that she is not meeting these people in the real world. A clinician can do only so much in cyberspace. It makes it easy for people to conceal things. Every thought and gesture, our body language, little things we do with our eyes or lips—not a lot of that makes it into the net. I think she's taking a dangerous risk by attempting to counsel people virtually." Dr. Farouk rubbed his chin. "Then again, I don't imagine she expected a clinical schizophrenic to show up for grief counseling."

"I talked to the guy for twenty minutes and I had a feeling that some of the canaries were missing." Joey smirked.

"Well, it is possible that this 'wife' was a figment of his condition, constructed by his mind as a way to give his life something to anchor to. Perhaps it enabled him to fake his way along for a short time. From what you are telling me, I have a feeling that this 'wife' he sees has changed into something else. Without the stabilizing influence of the ideal female companion, he has gravitated toward the paranoid ideation."

"He got fired a few weeks ago, absenteeism I think."

"That fits the theory that his world crumbled to pieces around him. Once this woman vanished, his mind replaced her with that other apparition. If you know this man, I suggest you get him help before he deteriorates any further. If he gets desperate, he could be a danger to himself or others. More than likely he'll need medication."

Joey nodded. "Commit him?"

The doctor made a distancing gesture. "That would depend on how dangerous he is, but only a doctor that's conducted a face to face could make that determination. He may be treatable without taking that step. Can you get him to seek professional help?"

Joey smiled. "I think I can handle that." *An anonymous email to Dr. Khan should do the trick.* "Thanks."

"You're welcome. By the way, what happened to your cheek?"

"Railgun."

Dr. Farouk raised an eyebrow.

"It missed."

The doctor smirked. "Obviously. I could clean that scar up for you. Since I'm betting you don't have insurance, I could do it for a thousand."

"Sure, why not."

JOEY'S BIKE SHOT DOWN STREETS LONG ABANDONED BY GROUND TRAFFIC. HE BATTED around thoughts of the ghosts that had been plaguing those who had been to New Hope. Several things bothered him. His father had spoken to him before he had ever even heard of the place. Mitch's grief was real. The man lacked the capacity to understand the girl he loved had been a fragment of his own mind. Her loss had hit him as hard as if she had been real. If the hacker wanted to target grieving individuals, Mitch made a perfect mark. He was the most upset of everyone at New Hope, but why had he been left alone?

As much as he didn't want to admit it, his NetMini had been off when his dad spoke from it that night. The idea clashed with his entire worldview, but if the supernatural was real, then Christina never having existed at all would be a good reason for her not to have a ghost.

TOO EASY

A large beige chair sat with its back to the corner of a hotel room. Katya curled up, tucking her feet under herself as she gazed into the stillness that enveloped everything. Her eyes flicked back and forth between the balcony and the main door as her dread wrestled with her body's want for rest. Every drip from the bathroom, every shadow across the window, and every passerby in the hallway slapped her mind away from the edge of sleep.

Trails of wet tickled down the back of her neck from her hair. She had gone right from the shower to that chair, skipping the dry cycle, and engaged in battle of wills with some of the complimentary liquor that the hotel provided. It tempted her with its promise of forgetful repose, but she already felt vulnerable enough. A pair of black panties and a white terrycloth robe emblazoned with the logo of the Vanier Hotel all that stood between her and the world.

She had slipped in unnoticed and hacked a false name into their system to flag the room taken. The hotel would play home for a couple of days at most before she moved on. Faint glowing smears danced across her lap as moonlight reflected upon the tiny bottle of clear liquid that called to her. The odds of them finding her here were in truth quite slim, and that sliver of comfort had soon emptied the bottle of synthesized vodka.

For a little more than one brief day in the twenty-eight years of her life, she had felt a connection to someone else. Forces outside of her control stole that girl's childhood. At least Ido had corrected the particular cruelty of keeping her a child forever, and she could now enjoy the reality of growing up. Katya knew all about being corporation property and doubted the kid would ever really get over it—but at least no one chased her.

The white-haired girl's face hung in her memory at the point where she thought the child had started to trust her. She could still see the wide-eyed desperation of having no other option and no reason to doubt. Katya fumed at her former owners. If not for their pursuit, she would have taken the girl under her wing. If she ever got out from under that burden, perhaps she would. Giving her up at the police station had been harder than she expected. Even the girl seemed sad about it.

Anger and paranoia danced a waltz in her mind until the warm touch of sunlight on her back told her the vodka had done its job. She lifted her head from the carpet with one eye open. Like a turtle trapped in its shell, the only part of her she could move was her head. The bathrobe hung off the chair and she sprawled face down on the rug like a crime victim. She rarely allowed alcohol past her toxin filter, and it had hit her hard.

With great effort, she rolled onto her back and put a hand on her forehead. The victim pose offered a more comfortable sleep than a chair, even if it did leave the texture of the carpet imprinted on her breasts. Beds left her feeling too exposed and seldom provided a good view of entrances.

Using the chair to steady herself, she stumbled to the nightstand and covered herself with the robe. From a wall terminal, she placed an order for a hangover cure as well as breakfast. When a chime came from room service, she disappeared into the bathroom with her handgun and held her lips to the door.

"Just leave it in the room, I'm in the shower." Her Vox unit changed her voice to sound like that of a stocky older man, something that would fit the name she put into the hotel's system: Angus Brinn.

The door opened with a beep and a hotel employee pushed a hovering tray in. The smell found her right away, making it quite difficult to wait. No sooner had the door closed than she ran to the food and attacked it, not even bothering to sit. Clicking upon the balcony door drew her attention to a shoebox-sized bot tapping a little robotic arm on the glass. She padded over while wiping egg crumbs from her mouth, and pulled the door to the side. The bot opened a small hatch and let her take the hangover pills before turning and rocketing off into the skyline.

The combination of food and medicine made her feel much better, though she still had a long, anxious day sitting around wondering if today would be the day that they found her. Being up to her right eyeball, literally, in debt addled her nerves even more. She obtained the part from a facilitator of loans because she wanted one that looked like a natural eye as opposed to the chrome one her owners gave her. He expected a repayment of three hundred and sixty thousand credits, more than twice its value, but having it made earning money easier.

The hundred grand she got from Joey would go almost all to that cause to buy her some relief for a few weeks. She paced like a trapped tiger before trying to watch a holovid that she just couldn't focus on.

In the middle of a silent room, she sat cross-legged on the sofa, staring at a hologram of the little white-haired girl.

The head dispersed as the NetMini projecting it rang with an inbound call. The shock almost made her scream. It was Alex.

He spoke in French. "Good morning, my dear. I have an easy job for you. Sixty thousand credits," he added with a smile.

"Alex, sixty grand doesn't make me think easy."

He bared perfect teeth with a broad grin and swept his shoulder length hair out of his eye. "Sometimes there are clients that pay extra for discretion. The money is not all for risk you know."

Discretion could also be a bad sign. "Just how illegal is this?"

"Not illegal at all. You'll be working for Sentinel Systems."

Katya glanced off to the right as she thought. "I've heard of that before, armored cars?"

"Close." Alex nodded. "They operate armored boats, cargo vessels to be exact. They have a military contract to run supplies that are too heavy to fly."

"I don't think so." Katya shook her head. "I'm not getting into a pissing contest with the military."

He touched his fingertips together. "Calm yourself my dear. It's the military that wants to hire you."

Katya stared. "I smell bullshit."

Alex chuckled. "They suspect the crew of this particular vessel has been diverting shipments and offloading some of the hardware to mercenaries. What they want is for someone to sneak on board and plant a tracking beacon to monitor its movement independently of the boat's systems. If someone hacked their transponder to fake the route, this will show them where it's really going."

"Don't they have people for that?" She squinted at him.

Alex nodded. "Of course they do, but they don't want to run the risk that someone will see it coming. They want to keep it external. All you need to do is get onto the boat, drop a bug, and get out without anyone seeing you. It is docked and empty with minimal guards."

"Alex, you know this sounds like a setup."

Alex tilted his head. "For what? They don't know who I'd offer the job to."

"Unless they got into your files and knew your talent pool. Aren't I the only one in your contact list that does the sneaky thing?"

"You may be the best; however, you're far from the only. Most of them are less discreet. I assure you... my contact list is secure, even your friend Joey would find it difficult to go poking around here."

"What are the details?"

He leaned back with a smile. "That's better. They are trying to keep this as quiet as possible. If you are seen on or near the dock, the whole thing is a bust. Be at the Crystal Swan restaurant tonight at six. Go alone and order the Wellington. Tell the waiter you have not had it in a year and have heard theirs is the best. When you are done eating, the signal to their guy is that you lean forward and blow out a candle in the middle of the table."

"Who's paying for dinner? Even synthetic, that's a 2500 credit plate."

Alex laughed. "Then you haven't had it made properly. It should cost four. Anyway, the employer will be handling the bill. If the waiter asks you to pay, something went wrong and you should call me right away. Once you blow out that candle, he will drop a case by your chair with the device in it. Then all you need to do is get onto the boat, at these coordinates."

Her mini chirped with an arriving NavMap pin.

"I've done training exercises harder than this."

"Call me when it's done." Alex's holographic presence collapsed.

Katya stripped and walked into the bathroom, staring at the autoshower. She hesitated by the door, closing her eyes. After a minute, she forced herself inside and tried to ignore memories of being locked in a gel-filled tank. Despite knowing the plastic tube would open if she wanted it to, it took a moment for the shivers to subside. When the dry cycle stopped, she kicked the door open and backed away from the clear cylinder, gasping for air.

Next hotel I pick will have a bathtub.

She went to the Crystal Swan to record video from every angle. Only the wealthy even knew of the place. A full dinner for one could cost as much as an average family made in a week. The restaurant took up a quarter of a city block far in the north, Sector 316. The area still held some trappings of its former Canadian heritage, and the Badlands snow forest peeked over the distant wall.

After getting a decent sense of the building, she went to the dock. The massive boxy vessel, four hundred and fifty meters long and as high as a four-story building, nuzzled against the pier like a suckling piglet. It had a heavily armored look, most of the hull segmented into thick plates. The top was flat except for a small bridge house at the stern bearing the logo of Sentinel Corp, a cybernetic arm holding a sword aloft between the words with a half-starburst at the tip. Alex had good information, only two guards staffed the gate. Katya zoomed in, using her artificial eye to survey the rest of the pier. Two guards walked the deck, and a twenty-foot high security fence sealed it off from the adjacent pier. After pondering the layout, she felt a sea approach offered the best chance of success.

She arranged for a dress from a high-end clothing boutique. Infiltration without a governmental budget behind you required improvisation. The synthetic pheromones her enhanced endocrine system produced worked, and she convinced the manager to let her borrow a sixty thousand credit scarlet heart-stopper of a gown. For some reason, perhaps thinking of the StarPoint girl, she was glad she didn't have to trade herself this time. Dread came over her. She fell against the wall, cringing from bellowed Russian in her mind scolding her for developing an exploitable attachment.

She stood up, adjusting the garment. If she returned it late or damaged it, she would have to cover the cost. No sense worrying about its condition. She needed it only for the restaurant so as not to stand out in pauper's rags. The dress split with a three-inch gap down the right side, leaving an unbroken view of skin all the way down. Microscopic hooks in the fabric clung to her skin to hold it up, controlled by a button disguised as a ruby at the apex of her cleavage. The tiny matching purse couldn't conceal a pistol, and the dress offered nowhere to hide it. She put her hair up, shifting its color while staring at the changing room mirror until she settled on leaving it black.

FOUR HOURS LATER, SHE PRESENTED THE MAÎTRE' D WITH THE RESERVATION CODE. The feeling of eyes following her to the table made her regret the dress. She had picked the scandalously short thing for mobility's sake. The other offerings at that shop had all been ankle-long and tight, and she didn't want a hobble.

So much for blending in, I feel like the one item of color in a black and white vid.

She found it difficult to enjoy the Wellington while being so anxious about the matter at hand. This whole situation felt like a last meal. It was as if her former owners had finally found her and were playing a cruel game before they dragged her back to Europe. The lone candle in the center of the table flickered then steadied, trailing a perfect line of black smoke into the air.

When she decided she finished with the food, she leaned forward and blew it out. The smoke from the dead wick darkened, and the waiter gave a knowing glance before he ducked out of sight. A moment later, he walked past without making eye contact and set a briefcase down near her chair. That everything had gone as Alex said it would made her more nervous. She suppressed the shiver as she braced for the other shoe to fall.

The briefcase felt solid, as though it contained a dense object, but not burdensome in its weight. She folded her napkin onto the table and gathered her purse. A few meters from the door, the approach of a large older man in a cream-colored suit startled her. He looked to be in his late forties, with thick brown hair neatly sculpted. Heavy brows hung over narrow eyes as he approached, she could tell him Russian merely by looking at him.

Fear hit her like a bucket of ice water. She turned to run, but he grabbed her wrist and pulled her back, far faster than she expected a man of that size to be.

"Wait." His words burst out from under a thick accent like bubbles from syrup. "I want only talk."

Katya's eyes widened with helpless terror. She had no armor or gun. Fear that her owners had sent him made her struggle to free her arm from his grasp, but it might as well have been locked in a manacle.

"Please." He drew her closer and whispered, "I am not who you think."

Resistance faded to imperceptible trembling as she stared with the look of a deer facing down a hunter. "Who are you?"

He led her out of the main dining area toward the bar. His grip was just shy of painful and left no doubt that she followed him as a demand and not a request. He pushed her into a booth and hovered for a long moment before letting go and taking the facing seat.

He relaxed into the cushions, draping his arm over the back of the bench. "My name is Anatoly. I believe we can help each other, yes?"

Anatoly's casual demeanor unsettled her even more. "How did you find me?" She switched to Russian.

He chuckled, ordering a cognac from the passing bar waiter. "Your electronic identity is the product of a most impressive hacker; however, it is still forged."

She shuddered with a passing breeze, her fear made the bare stripe down her side feel colder. "What do you want?"

"I want to help you. A favor for a favor." He sipped his drink. "You have talents useful to me. Me, I have many friends back home. People who could make your..." He waved a hand around, searching for a word. "...situation go away. Surely you do not wish to be hunted until you are old, or dead?"

Her wonder if this man had come seeking a bribe ended, as did her breathing. The realization that she sat three feet away from Anatoly Nemsky, the Butcher of Kiev, came to her. Hundreds of civilians died at this man's will, never mind the rumors that young women were often spared death in the streets to be used by him and then later by his troops. Waves of fear ran up and down her soul as she tried to cope with being so close to a man so far from human. He could kill everyone in the restaurant and not lose a second of sleep over it. Judging by the grip he had on her arm, he could snap her neck like a twig if he chose.

Katya would play along. This man got what he wanted and didn't take rejection well. In addition, his offer was tempting. Even if it meant a deal with the devil, if anyone could secure her true freedom it would be him.

Training kept her voice calm. "What do you need me to do?"

The little curl in his lip gave away his amusement at her fear. He loved it. She played up to him, letting more out.

"I need someone to get inside the manufacturing plant at Siege Arms Corporation. A shipment of rifles must be diverted. You do this for me... I leash the dogs nipping your heels."

The little girl came back to her mind again. If Nemsky could be believed and trusted, neither of which were sure bets, he could change her life. If he could get the corporation off her back, she could stop running. Giving this man a truck full of weapons could be disastrous to many innocent people, but was that her problem? She could always do it and then tip off the authorities once clear. Despite being off the books, she did feel a sense of patriotism for the UCF. Even if they didn't know it, they protected her from a proverbial leash.

Nemsky picked at a NetMini, causing a momentary image of the StarPoint girl to appear. He took particular delight in her reaction. "That is what you want, is it not?"

She made an easy leap to rationalize he could get them without her help. If she didn't do it, someone else would. Calling in a favor back home was less expensive than paying credits to a mercenary to do it, which explained why he came to her. Of course, if *he* found her—her old "employers" could too.

She allowed a tremble to manifest as she nodded. "I will do this for you."

"Good. Join me for a drink?" He raised a hand at the bar waiter.

Every second spent with him made her feel more unclean, like a moth having a drink with a spider while stuck to its web, but she stayed to humor him. Her filter kept the alcohol out of her system, and the small talk was somewhat pleasant, though she avoided asking questions that could get her killed.

As she stood to leave, he again grabbed her wrist and pulled her face to face. She gasped from the force and almost lost her balance. Her feeling of helplessness got into a full on war with her anger at being manhandled, but his reputation wasn't something her newfound independence wanted to butt heads with. The more she appeased him, the better the odds he would uphold his promise. He could always cast her aside or kill her after the fact. Only the smallness of what it would cost him to help her gave her confidence.

"It goes without speaking." He paused, sensing something wrong with his thick accented English. "It goes without saying. Yes, that is better. Do not share details of our arrangement."

Katya was many things at that moment: embarrassed, pissed off, desperate, and scared witless, but stupid wasn't one of them.

"Yes, General." She offered a demure bow that made him smile and walked out.

THE RED DRESS OFFERED ALMOST NO PROTECTION FROM THE COLD, BUT COMPARED to the bay, even in a wetsuit, she found it downright cozy. Micro caterpillar drives in sleek black housings on her shins and forearms carried her along in frigid currents without a sound. They pushed or pulled water depending on the angle at which she held her hands, and allowed for an incredible degree of maneuverability once she got used to them.

Most of her face hid behind an armored visor, flat and featureless except for tiny lens clusters at the top corners. Her air synthesizer mask rearranged seawater at an atomic level, extracting breathable air right from the ocean. She would taste salt for a few hours, but it was far more portable than an air tank.

She held her arms at her sides, tight against her body. The ocean floor drifted below in the green on black translation of reality in the visor. The little motors pushed her along without a sound, like a living torpedo. Ridges of sand slid by in bright gradient ripples as ghostly blobs of differing luminosity darted in and out of her view from passing sea creatures. A pack of enormous underwater bots huddled like manatees, attempting to scrub pollution out of the seawater.

Her passage created no sound or disturbance at the surface, and soon, the pylons of her destination emerged from the black water up ahead. Beyond them, the ship's hull appeared as an indistinct blur of emerald light. Nearing her target, she pivoted her hands to a neutral position, which stalled the pods. After stretching her arms out in front of her, she tilted her fists down to activate the little motors again. It wound up being much easier to steer with her arms pulling. She circled the pylons for several minutes until locating a maintenance ladder.

A flick of her eyes opened a heads up menu in the visor, and she shut down the caterpillar motors and rode her momentum into the ladder. Gloves scraped small barnacles away from the rungs as she climbed. Once her face breached the surface, the visor switched modes, ultrasound replaced with passive night vision. The voice of the sales weasel from the military surplus store rambled on in her head about how the plate could stop a bullet. She pulled her weight up out of the water, hoping she didn't get to find out if it was true.

The breathing mask went back into a pouch on her belt as she filled her lungs with natural air once more. The faint vibration of the drives ghosted in her limbs, and she took a moment to adjust to being on dry land. Above her, a maze of lasers streaked a bright crisscross over the ladder. As expected, the security team had covered it well with electronic detection. At least her former 'employers' had been liberal with her cybernetic enhancements. Neuromuscular amplification allowed her to move in superhuman ways and climb among the beams without breaking them. The spiderlike ascent brought back memories of her training She felt like she had run this course before.

Soon she was perched on the girders below the four-inch thick plastisteel pier. Stains decorated the underside from decades of spilled chemicals and rain. She had the security panel on the hatch open and the code overridden twenty seconds later. The massive hatch was possible for her to lift, but only just. Katya cursed her corporate sponsor for not enhancing her strength, and stashed the caterpillar pods on the catwalk. Out of the water, they were nothing but excess weight.

After hitting the hinges with a shot of spray lubricant, she braced her arms against the door and shoved with her entire body, lifting it enough to peek out. She tuned up her amplified hearing and listened. Her legs wobbled from fatigue by the time she felt safe enough to open it more and climb out.

She emerged among a stack of empty cargo crates and lowered the hatch without a sound. Hollow metal footfalls echoed above her from guards walking the deck of the ship. The tall ship presented too sharp an angle for them to see her. The two guards at the gate, over three hundred yards away, became irrelevant.

Darting among stacks of cargo containers, she crept to the boarding ramp. Soft rubber soles kept her silent as she sprinted up to the door. She stared at the code panel on the wall, afraid that the access code Alex provided would fail. Almost surprised that it worked, she slipped in and pulled the door closed before the overhead footsteps returned.

This feels wrong. They never give the codes out.

Oppressive darkness waited inside. Passive nightvision struggled to present her with detail much beyond a few meters in. With a few eye movements navigating the visor's menu, she turned on the IR lamps. Bright cones of infrared light lit the hallway, invisible to the naked eye.

Trying to remember the schematic diagrams she had stared at all afternoon, she found her way down the eerie hallways to the cargo hold. Another code worked on an interior door, leading to a cavernous chamber four stories tall and as wide as a Gee-ball field, saturated with the smell of metal and grease. Katya stepped over cables as big around as her arm, slipped between a pair of cargo boxes, and tried not to trip on struts, pipes, or tools left lying around. A thin catwalk spanned across sunken bays made to accept hexagonal cargo boxes. She tensed as the echo of her breath felt loud enough for people outside to hear. After advancing past six watertight bulkheads, she figured she had to be near the center of the ship.

The case held a dull grey disc six inches across. A raised X spanned it, tipped at each end with blunted triangles that contained magnets. She gazed around the enormous room, looking for a spot to stash it. Against the far wall, she spotted a rectangular vent intake two feet off the floor. After crossing a dozen cargo pits, she pulled herself up onto a maintenance walkway that ran along the outer hull. Once she removed the cover, she slid on her back into the shaft, and clamped the tracker to the inner surface as high up as she could reach before turning it on. A light blinked once every 10 seconds, indicating it worked. The ventilation ductwork had become its antenna.

She fumbled with the tools as she secured the grating back in place. This job had been far too easy. Every now and then, one did come along that was this simple, but they didn't usually pay this much. Paranoia that someone wanted her on this boat tonight fueled her sprint back to the upper deck and to the spot where she had hidden her diving gear. Fear that something was about to go wrong waned as she strapped the pods back on and shimmied down a conveniently abandoned rope to avoid the lasers. She lowered herself smoothly into the water and looked up at the pier. It remained quiet, with no sign of unusual activity.

Katya grimaced at the rubber-salt flavor of the breathing mask, and sank below the waves. Perhaps this job was one of those rare gifts of fate, but she still had a promise to keep to the devil.

PLAYING BOTH SIDES

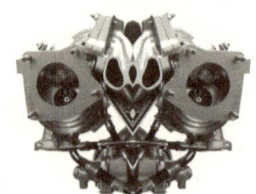

Nina stopped in her tracks at the sight of the stark Division 0 hallway. An echo of her former self drifted across her memory with the recollection of her last day as a normal human. The intense white corridor bathed the area in a dreamlike glow just a hair above reality. The same red haired woman sat behind the desk, the same plants stood against the wall, and the same scent of cleaning solution hung in the air.

She walked back to the day her dreams had died.

Comforted by knowing the meeting was her idea this time, she continued past the receptionist to Lieutenant Oliver's office. Though Nina was now the same rank, if not slightly Oliver's senior due to Division 9's theoretical jurisdiction over internal affairs, Zero presented an enigma—they did things beyond understanding. Despite herself, a pang of worry gripped her as she knocked.

"Come in," he said from behind the closed door.

A wave of sadness touched her phantom heart at the sight waiting for her. The small office remained exactly as she remembered it. She took the same seat, even approaching it with the same shaky gait as before. Oliver focused his attention on the desk terminal, and she waited for him to look up before she spoke.

"I appreciate you seeing me." The first difference came out. She sounded more confident.

Lieutenant Oliver smiled, playing with his silver pen. He read her emotion as easily as if she had been holding up signs. "Your voice doesn't match your mood, Nina. Feels like you're a bit of mess at the moment. How can I help?"

Command didn't like Division 9 agents interacting with Zeroes as secrets and telepaths didn't mix, even if she did have cyberware that could supposedly interfere with a mind read. Evidently, that component didn't do much on telempaths. Her visit didn't relate to work. Nina had come to see him without running it by Hardin.

"How much do you know about ghosts?" Nina looked him in the eye. "I think Vincent has been talking to me."

Oliver's fingers stalled, her distorted reflection along the pen a smear of twisted color. "Well. I have not personally had any experience with them, but I do know a few agents who have."

"How can I know if it's really him?" She got angry. "I don't believe it is... I think someone's playing games."

The pen resumed its twirl. "You would have to trust your gut. Most ungifted people don't believe in ghosts until they witness a manifestation. I can make some inquiries if you like... see if one of our people can check it out for you. I think Agent Wren might be available."

Nina's eyes fixed on the spinning silver. "I'm starting to worry that I can't let go. It's been almost a year now, and I still dream about that night like it was yesterday."

Oliver gave her a tiny empathic poke intended to lift her mood. "That was a traumatic event. Many officers take the death of a partner quite hard, almost worse than a spouse. Considering he was both to you... I can't even imagine. I think you are handling it as well as can be expected. At this point, I would worry more if you weren't thinking about him." He smiled. "It just proves you are human."

She leaned back, sighing. "I think someone might know we were involved and is trying to use it against me." She thought about Joey.

Oliver leaned back, feeling the wave of rage.

"Vincent's voice came out of my NetMini yesterday and said he wanted me to join him. Do you think that a ghost would try to talk someone into killing themselves?"

The pen stopped, held between his thumb and forefinger. "Were you tempted?"

She knew the wrong response to that question would reach Hardin, but she gave him an honest answer anyway. "Almost, but I realized Vincent would never ask me that. Then I thought about the look on his face that night. He seemed just..."

Her face showed nothing, but Oliver reacted to sadness powerful enough to give him a sympathetic throat lump. He focused on her, caressing her mind and softening her mood.

As the crippling depression faded, she looked up. "He died trying to protect me. He cared more about me than his own life."

"The voice seemed implausible?"

She nodded. "Yes, it didn't sound like Vincent at all. It couldn't have been him. Vincent would never have wanted to see me hurt."

"There are entities out there that are not ghosts in the strictest sense. They are malevolent creatures from a place we call the Abyss. They can read your thoughts, feed on your despair, and delight in your pain. They may have decided to prey upon your grief since it is so strong." The pen caught the lights overhead, flashing in a mesmerizing blur.

She had expected to hear some fairy tales from Division 0, but this defied plausibility. "What, like demons?"

Oliver gave her a halfhearted nod. "Some people call them that, but that is an oversimplification. I won't bore you with the details. I just brought it up as one possibility. Tell me, how is it you hear him?"

"The voice comes out of my NetMini, the car, my VidPhone…"

"Has something electronic always been involved?"

"Yes."

Oliver rubbed his lip. "There have been some studies that indicate weak ghosts, ones that have not been dead that long, may not be able to speak without using electronics as an assistant. Of course, as you say, it might just be someone messing with you. Do you ever get a sense of being watched, of feeling an odd kind of 'otherness' in the air?" Oliver made air quotes in time with the word otherness.

"Not really, no. Is that unusual?"

He nodded. "For reasons we don't understand, humans seem to have the ability to sense the presence of others, even if that person is just a disembodied spirit. If you're not feeling anything, my opinion is that it is not genuine."

Nina stared at her lap, picking at the armrest. "Is it possible I can't sense that because of my condition?"

"Losing one's flesh body is like removing a layer of armor to the paranormal. The body acts as a buffer for spiritual energy. Some cultures refer to it as chi. Someone in your state cannot contain their chi as well as an intact living body. You still have it, but it clings to the parts of you that are still alive, waving in the wind like curtains. If anything, you should be *more* apt to feel the presence of something strange."

Nina tried to make sense of it. Only what she had read about Division 0 kept her from dismissing him as crazy. "I didn't feel anything, but if we assume it is him could he have changed that much?"

"I'd say only if he had somehow come to blame you for his death or became jealous that you survived and he didn't. Everything you have told me contradicts both of those. If he gave his life to save you, I sincerely doubt he'd change his mind now."

She took a deep breath, almost smiling. Happiness seemed so far off, but acceptance was within arm's reach. They talked more about the phone call that felt like it might have become the proposal she had been waiting for. She confided that she cried, really cried, for the first time since she woke up in the hospital. He was happy to hear that and tried to reinforce the idea that it wasn't healthy to bottle it up. A knock at the door made them pause.

"Come in."

A young woman with pale blonde hair peeked in. "You wanted to see me, sir?"

"Hello, Agent Wren, this is Lieutenant Duchenne from Division 9."

The girl waved at her.

"What are you, fifteen?" Nina blinked.

She walked in, saluting both of them. "Twenty-one, ma'am."

Oliver poked his terminal, the woman's belt chimed. "I just sent you a Nav pin. If you have some spare time, would you please check for any spirits that might be lingering? Her partner died in the line of duty."

"I'm sorry, ma'am. If he's trying to contact you, I will find him." She turned back to Oliver. "Yes sir, I'll stop there today."

After another salute, she spun on her heel and slipped out the door. Nina watched her leave, and then sank into the chair facing him.

"Anyway, I hate to cut our time short but I have a meeting in about"—he glanced at the clock—"twelve minutes." He smiled. "As soon as I hear back from her, I'll let you know. She's one of our strongest astral sensates."

"Thanks."

AN HOUR LATER, NINA BASKED IN THE SOFT GLOW OF HOLOGRAPHIC PANELS IN AN otherwise dark office. Brighter green lines of reflected light spanned her face as the terminal filled in the results of time spent searching trace logs. Somewhere around a million city cams hunted for the faces of Itai or Anatoly. Hits were rare, but present. Entering a coffee shop, exiting a PubTran station, on a street in a crowd—the sightings were scattered all over the city. Even an AI would struggle to put a pattern to them. A higher concentration of hits happened around the Diplomatic Tower, but that only confirmed everyone's extant suspicion of Karl Warner's involvement.

The video of Itai from the tower bothered her. The static cameras showed him walking right in the front door and flashing some manner of ID at the front desk before going on to the elevator. When questioned, the man at the desk claimed to have never seen him. Interrogation yielded nothing. He could be a well-trained spy or had his memory wiped by an undocumented psionic. Even when confronted with the surveillance footage from his own building, he continued to deny it with a claim that someone set him up.

Division 9 mobile surveillance hadn't recorded Itai at all. None of the dozen cameras watching the area for weeks had captured a single second of his smug face. She fell into a mild argument with Cole wondering if someone had compromised their network and fed them a false loop. Samantha got offended at the suggestion that someone could have hacked all twelve cameras and had protested a diagnostic check until Nina had questioned the motive behind her refusal. It had turned out to be pride, not betrayal. With the mobile cams proven secure, it cast serious doubts on the validity of the other video.

Two videos showing the same area at the same time differed. One had Itai and one didn't. Someone had been able to spoof the Karsson-Neimand process, something generally considered impossible. A flurry of beeps drew her attention to a number of new hits on the trace search. She went to the first entry and opened it.

Interior surveillance from a fancy restaurant, the Crystal Swan, showed a dark haired woman in a red dress meeting Itai Korin for dinner. Their meal was brief and he departed soon after, following a smooch over the table. Nemsky emerged from the shadows by the door and she went with him to the bar. Nina replayed the video several times, trying to understand the apparent tension between this woman and Nemsky. Could that indicate a rift between the two men?

The feeling hit her that she had seen those eyes somewhere else. Two hours later, her instinct led her to the Imperial Hotel lobby, footage she had spent dozens of hours reviewing. She noticed a striking resemblance to the woman who had gotten cozy with a security guard half an hour before Dale's death. Nina stopped the video on one frame where she made eye contact with the camera, and stared. At her beckoning gesture, the woman's face lifted out of the display. Nina superimposed a wireframe to highlight facial bone structure, and did the same for the woman from the Crystal Swan. As the system chugged away with calculations, she felt less and less like she looked at sisters, and more the same individual. Skin tone and complexion on each face equalized, one darkened as one grew paler. Freckles vanished, hair shifted to be the same: one person with intelligence-agency level components.

One person who could look like someone else.

A plastisteel mug crimpled in her hand when 'Match Probability: 97%' appeared at the top of the holo-panel. Everyone thought the attack at the Imperial had been meant for those civilians, but this woman appeared to be an associate of Itai or Nemsky—or both.

Why launch a light rocket at a skinny little nothing of a hacker? It had to be for the van. Maybe the shooters had only waited for someone to walk into the firing line as a diversion. Nina grew angrier the more she thought about it. That woman could have been sent in to confirm the presence of the surveillance op. She didn't go anywhere near it, but she didn't need to. She'd gone to the security office. Doubt crept into her mind that those two civilians were the true target. Perhaps even the association to WellTech had been planted.

She growled, trying to rationalize why, if Joey and the man in black armor worked with Nemsky, they would attack the second shooter at the Imperial. Nina drummed her fingers on the desk. Division 9 traced the two aggressors back to WellTech Corporation, and the Mayberry scandal just exploded all over the NewsNet. Joey was a deck jockey, that much she knew. That meant a strong possibility he could be the one who leaked the information to the news. Perhaps WellTech wanted to shut him up before he could do it.

That took her back to Dale's death being an accident, but how did this mystery woman connect? Thinking of Joey, she ran a check on the network logs of the Imperial. Ten minutes later, she found record of a file copy just before the attack—a personnel list for the Basket Weaver project. Everyone on that op had been compromised for a few weeks. However, nothing had happened. It was as if someone stole that data just to give Division 9 the finger. A mark of pride—just the kind of thing people like Joey did.

Nina sent an immediate comm to Hardin, copying Cole, and warned them about the data nab. No one had checked the network. No one had even thought to, since none of the aggressors had made it inside. Hardin flew into her office soon after her message and went over the logs with her. His grim look proved he believed her conclusion.

Fortunately, all the security protocols had cycled since the incident. The data in the stolen file, except for names, was useless now. Basket Weaver didn't constitute a deep cover operation, the leak hadn't exposed any sensitive covert operatives, but someone had gotten hold of information about everyone involved. The lack of obvious impact worried them both. Hardin congratulated her on the find and whisked himself off to plug the holes while she went back to combing for answers.

A search on Joey brought back several hits. The first video showed him with that man in black and the same woman traveling together into Sector 12. The scowl on her face grew when she saw Nemsky walk out from between some cars and appear to shake hands with him while the woman stooped to do something by a derelict car. Their meeting was brief, but Anatoly pointed off down the street where the trio went next, out of view of the cameras.

The tenth time she watched their entry to Sector 12 she was no closer to understanding the extent of their involvement than the first. Her information indicated that Anatoly wanted to set up a guerilla team in one of the black zones, more than likely to begin conducting raids on vulnerable parts of UCF society. Most of the brass disregarded it as a minor threat. They figured if the police were afraid of the area, the denizens would deal with Anatoly and save them the bother. However, the fact remained: something had chased gangers out of Sector 12 en masse. Logic suggested an ACC Special Ops team, but Nina's instincts agreed with the abject lack of evidence of such a penetration.

A search on that mystery woman yielded the name Elena White. It took Nina under a minute to determine it was a fake identity. Most of the information didn't survive a deep check and some of the file creation dates were too new to be legitimate. The edits appeared to trace back to Joey's IPv12 address. A facial search returned numerous videos from city cams, most were inconsequential, but two caught her eye.

One showed her casing a dock with a Sentinel Corp transport ship. The other showed her walking across the lobby of the Diplomatic Tower, then going to Warner's floor. The name she signed in with traced back to an outfit that provided twenty thousand credit a night call girls.

"So this woman works for or with Warner, or with Nemsky. Or she's screwing Itai and Nemsky is jealous, or there's tension between Itai and Nemsky and she's stuck in the middle of it while Warner is off yanking it in the corner." Nina's frustration boiled over into a growl.

The more she tried to sort it out, the more convoluted everything seemed. There were simply too many possibilities. The next video showed the woman entering a Siege Arms manufacturing plant and standing in line with employees going through a security check. Out of curiosity, she dug into the company's network and matched her time of passage by the desk with an employee name. Susan DeWitt, a name that also appeared on a purchase order that sent 2,250 combat rifles off on a transport truck that subsequently vanished.

Nina's cheek bunched against her hand as she leaned on her desk, not a trace of surprise on her face when the image of Susan DeWitt looked nothing at all like the black haired vixen that just walked into the factory. The real Susan looked a few years older and many degrees less pretty, and sat in a jail cell for grand larceny. Nina fired off an email to the detective on the case, containing video and security logs showing who really entered the factory and hacked into the loading machines. With any luck, Mrs. DeWitt would be home in time for dinner.

She leaned back in her chair and tried to connect the dots in her mind. The black haired woman with no name appeared to be working for Nemsky. Setting up a guerilla operation required weapons, which she had just procured. Why would he be so rough with her? Maybe she threatened to back out, or wanted more money. Nemsky had all but thrown her around in the restaurant. It seemed out of place if she was loyal to him.

Nina shut her eyes for a moment of thought, her wan complexion blue in the castoff light, and stared at the terminals for several minutes. The whispercraft over the Imperial that day had followed Joey from the scene. The other man, Masaru

Kurotai, they could find whenever they wanted. She replayed that footage, watching him drive all the way to the grey zone near Sector 12. Her fist stopped just short of taking a chunk out of her desk. The skinny bastard lived right near where Nemsky set up shop.

Now she had a place to start.

58

FATHER IN LAW

T he unmarked black patrol craft's tires cried out with a hydraulic whine as they folded down out of their protective doors. Cryonic mist blasted debris out from under it as weight settled into its ground wheels. Ion emitters fluttered then flashed as they powered down, and soon the car was as silent as the street in which it landed. Nina looked around the area as the gull wing door sank closed with a muted *thump*.

The blight started two blocks ahead. She didn't want to park there or leave the car within easy sight of it. Driving a hovercar into the grey zone would attract a missile at worst and trouble at best—neither of which she was in any mood for. She went in the direction of Joey's apartment with a determined gait and a look on her face that begged people around her to give her a reason to end them.

The conversation with Vincent on the ride soured her mood. He ceased any overt attempt to suggest she join him on the other side and just rambled about how he was happy to wait there alone for her. As long as she was happy, he was happy. The passive guilt didn't work. She knew Vincent too well for that. He never sidestepped issues. If the twenty minutes of listening to the voice rattle on had accomplished anything, it had convinced her that she wanted someone's throat in her hand for it.

Vileness hung in the sunken foyer outside the apartment, assaulting her with a smell that stalled her breath and brought a tear to the eye. *Ugh, this body can be too real sometimes.* Nina forced herself onward, activating combat mode to lessen the impact of noxious stimuli. She edged up to the door with her sidearm ready, waiting and listening. Her amplified ears picked up the fluttering crackle of thin plastic wrap caught in the intermittent breeze of snoring. She tossed her weapon to her left hand and wrapped her fingers around the door. A normal human-strength tug didn't move it as it wedged against the ground. Nina set her stance and shoved the slab of half-inch thick steel aside. The sudden force bowed the door, bending it enough to detach it from the ground. Rusty hinges squeaked. A body lay embedded in a mountain of trash that bore a faint resemblance to a couch.

Nina put her pistol away and walked up to him.

She lifted him with two fistfuls of leather jacket and flung him face first into the wall. Debris fell off him as he flew, like pixie dust from a slum fairy. He smacked into the cinder blocks, setting loose a human outline of dirt, which hung in the air for a second before dissipating. The man's head bounced off the wall and he fell to the ground trailed by a bushy streamer of hot pink hair. He gawked up at her with a bloodied nose and an expression so dazed from his sudden unexpected consciousness that he asked the wall why it hit him.

Nina sighed, realizing it wasn't Joey. After shoving the delirious pink haired man out of the apartment, she swept the area with all the scanning modes her cybereyes contained. After several minutes of searching, only two child-sized footprints on a clear patch of smooth concrete stood out as unusual due to the dried blood. She squatted by them and her eyes zoomed in on the details. Blue lines appeared at several points along the print as the pattern within increased in definition with each pass of the sensor.

When the scan completed, she started a comparison run against the Biotrak database. If the parents had the child's footprints recorded at birth, she could put a name to them. The rapid cycling of faces shrank into a small window hovering at the periphery of her sight.

"Joey, what the hell are you doing with a kid?"

She continued her investigation. The shower appeared to have been a casualty of a short gunfight. Enough bullet holes dotted the apartment to make a team of forensic analysts insane. She disregarded most. Caked with months of crud, they looked too old to be of any value.

A beep made her whirl, aiming her weapon at the VidPhone hanging on the wall. She sighed and lowered her arm, plodding over to the device.

Calm down, there's nothing here that should scare me.

She stared at the logo for The Allcom Corporation, the pseudo-governmental entity that absorbed all telecommunications after the war. A silver and green octagon bearing an A superimposed on a C rotated at the center of the screen while the device made all sorts of noise. Her arm rose up and poked the answer button with the tip of her pistol.

"Oh, hello." A pleasant looking man on the verge of being elderly smiled. "You must be the girl that Joseph's told me so much about."

"Do you know where I could find him?"

The man sighed. "I'm afraid I don't, I was looking for him, too."

"And you are?"

"I'm his father, William." He seemed so sweet he teetered on senile. "I'm on my way down from Mars to visit him. I haven't seen him in almost two years."

"What can you tell me about him?"

She spoke with him for the better part of twenty minutes as he regaled her with the most embarrassing stories of childhood idiocy, the sort of thing parents adored sharing with their child's significant other at any opportunity.

"You seem like a nice young woman, how long have you known Joseph?"

Nina turned in place, gazing through dust gleaming in faint streaks of light from bullet holes in the wall. "We only just met. I was looking to spend a little quality time with him as soon as I could."

She narrowed her eyes. The elder Dillon didn't react.

"That's nice." His smile almost made her regret what she planned to do when she found him. "I'm sure he'll be good to you, better than that last guy."

Nina froze. "What last guy?"

"Oh that other guy, oh darn what was the name..." Joey's father rubbed his chin, lost in thought. "Vince or something... Joey told me about how that guy lied to you. Such a cruel thing to do."

Nina snapped around to lock the VidPhone with a glare. "What the hell are you talking about, old man?"

"Joey told me how that guy got you hurt. I don't remember all the details, some awfulness about making you trust him so they could get you into um, what was it... Division 9?"

Her knuckles creaked. Despite what this man said, his affect came off so nice she found it hard to get angry. "There was no setup. Vincent got killed by a crazy auggie."

"Oh, no..." He put on the smile of someone delivering bad news. "Joey found out that he worked for C-Branch, to get you to trust him so they could get 'convinced' to join Division 9. He's not really dead, you know. They wanted you for years, but your physical performance was below their standards, so they had to put you in a doll body. Don't worry though, you'll be much happier with Joey. His mother and I raised him right. He'll be much better for you than Vincent could be."

Nina's pistol belched a single round and the VidPhone exploded into a shower of silver fragments that rained over the table. She destroyed it faster than conscious thought at the implication that a piece of shit hacker working for a Russian terrorist was a better man than Vincent. She turned away, not believing what the man had said, but a seed of doubt cracked open in the back of her mind.

Nina never thought of herself as a master at reading people. Could Vincent really have been part of some kind of plot? Would Division 9 resort to a ruse like that to get her put into a doll body? She knew some of her contemporaries had healthy human bodies in cryo storage waiting for them to retire. It sounded ludicrous for them to go to such lengths to get her into a doll body when they could just ask and freeze her. Of course, she wouldn't have accepted. She wanted to be a technician. Maybe they knew that.

Nina fell into the seat at the table, face cradled against one hand and a warm gun. All she had wanted to do was play with chemicals and forensic bots, solve crimes, and help people. She sat up straight, staring at her hands.

Now I'm a killer. I'm exactly what I didn't want to be.

She searched the darkness of her memory for any way to refute the old man's allegations about Vincent. A beep in her head distracted her rambles. The footprint matched. A smiling little girl's face floated in a square of light superimposed over her vision. Text filled in to the right. Hayley Roth, current age 11. The image was over a year old, taken the last time she had a photo ID from her school.

The file indicated her father worked for Division 2, a detective by the name of Jacob Roth with the gang crimes task force. Hayley wasn't listed as missing, although her school had requested wellness checks since her online only course grades had fallen off. Other records showed a long list of entries from one counselor upset at her father not returning his calls.

What the hell was this kid doing here? Nina's mind raced. Gang crimes task force... *Did he kidnap her to throw off an investigation?*

Worried, she pinned the girl's address and stormed out.

THE ELEVATOR OPENED WITH A SOFT RUSH OF AIR. THE STERILE HALLWAY OF SUBDUED earth tones stretched out like any of a hundred thousand other apartment buildings in the city, making her think that whoever sold these drab brown rugs had to be quite wealthy. Fluorescent light shimmered from recessed gutters near the ceiling, leeching the life out of everything here—even the plastic plants looked sick.

Detective Roth's apartment was six doors down on the left by a two-foot tall pile of plasfilm ads for takeout food. Thermal showed a child sized figure in what looked like the bathroom, sitting on the toilet, arms and legs hanging limp. The presence of some manner of helmet masked the upper parts of her head in cool blue, and a barely visible oval of heat balanced across her legs. Nina panned back and forth, finding no one else at home. Up until now, she'd thought going into cyberspace while on the bowl was just a net meme.

The door looked like it had been replaced not too long ago, and blotches of propellant residue stained the wall on both sides. Nina rang the bell. The thermal image looked toward her, and then turned away. An orange blur of a hand extended a middle finger the second time she rang.

"Hayley, please open the door. I'm with the police." Nina leaned close as she spoke in a loud tone.

The blue helmet swiveled toward her. Nina recognized the slouch of a long-suffering sigh. Reds moved as the slender outline stood up, removed the helmet, and walked to the door. Nina disabled thermal as soon as the door opened. A scrawny adolescent girl in a shin-length lavender shirt smirked up at her, weight on one leg and tapping bare toes into the rug. Nina tried to push aside the emotion that still lingered from her conversation with William Dillon.

"What?" Hayley folded her arms, annoyed at the interruption.

Nina held up her ID. "I'm sorry to bother you. Can I talk to you for a bit?"

The adolescent attitude evaporated. Her foot stopped tapping as eyes reddened and she stepped back with her hands over her mouth. The child trembled.

"Don't worry, Hayley. You're not in trouble, your dad's not in trouble, I just wanted to talk to you about Joey."

Hayley put her arms down, gripping her shirt into fists. She ambled away from the door with a confused smirk, her gait stiffened by hours spent on a toilet. After tripping over some of the discarded take-out containers littered about, she crawled to the couch and pulled herself standing. Nina closed the door behind her and blinked as she looked around the room. The apartment was almost as messy as Joey's. It didn't look like it had been cleaned in months. Stacks of holodisk cases piled up here and there around the dining room table and empty food containers were scattered everywhere. The girl smelled as though she had been wearing the same shirt for a week and had as much dirt on her face as a street kid.

"What about him?" A thin tone of defiance wavered out of her voice.

"It is very important that I talk to him." Nina's voice softened. "When was the last time you ate?"

"I dunno, yesterday… day before… who cares?" Hayley shrugged as she backed into the couch and sat down. "Why do you want Joey? Are you gonna kill him? That's what you Division Nines do isn't it, you just shoot people you think are bad?"

Nina tried to talk in a reassuring tone. This child looked like someone used to being lied to. "I've seen some things that I need to ask him about. He may be working with some bad people and not know it. I just want to clear up some misunderstandings."

The thought that Joey may be responsible for her patrol route change made her fists creak tighter.

"Is this about that hack?" She rested her chin on her knees. "It was me, not him. I made the men come after us."

The next several minutes of conversation convinced Nina that the girl played in cyberspace but didn't know a thing about hacking. "Someone was leading you around."

"Joey said that too." She pulled one knee to her chin and picked at the flaking nail polish on her toes. "I don't know who did it, but it wasn't Joey."

Nina could tell the girl liked him, and sighed in her mind's voice as she asked herself why criminals always had to involve kids. "How did you and Joey get mixed up together?"

Hayley forgot her nerves, giggling as she recounted how she just stumbled across him in the net one day and thought his avatar silly. He was all big mean and nasty and she wanted to make fun of him for being so serious. She shared a few stories about the torments she visited upon him, but got sad again when it came back to the men trying to kill them.

"WellTech was here?" Nina looked around. Her scan found evidence of firearms use: many patched bullet holes around the bathroom door. She felt a mix of pity for her situation and admiration at her survival. "Hey, why don't you get yourself cleaned up and I'll take you to get something to eat."

Hayley shrugged and explained her lack of clean laundry. Nina made a note to track down her father and find out why he neglected her. She channeled her own mother and shooed the girl into the shower tube while gathering clothes from the floor. By the time the girl emerged, Nina presented her with clean clothing. Once dressed, she took her to one of those restaurants that had all the old kitsch on the walls. It was the least extravagant place that had reasonable quality food that didn't come from beige slime.

Nina hadn't eaten much other than OmniSoy packets since waking up in the body of a doll, her brain didn't need a lot of nutrition and the excess just passed right through her. Eating felt just like it always had thanks to the department ensuring that every part of her looked, felt, and worked like a normal person.

They told her she might one day need to use her feminine wiles as part of an operation, but that sort of thing was more of a C-Branch thing. Division 9 often just killed problems, not screwed them for information. She had little issue with the idea at the time. After all, her body wasn't *her* anymore, merely a technological tool issued to her like a gun or a car.

Talking with Hayley made her forget feeling *false...* and be Nina. This child had no idea what lurked under her perfect artificial skin, and the painful normality of the dialog took her to a place she hadn't been in months. Nina steered the conversation, getting a good picture of Hayley's opinion of Joey. It didn't fit with what Nina had deduced, and she once again doubted her conclusions. This guy sounded like he had a soft spot, at least for Hayley, and she learned about his associates Kenny and Eldon, names she took note to run later and check up on. If nothing else, the girl had just saved Joey's life, creating enough doubt that Nina wanted to talk to him first.

Over dessert, she appraised Hayley's situation. Jacob Roth was guilty of neglect and she had half a mind to remove her from that apartment. With WellTech exposed, they wouldn't present an imminent risk. An investigation order sent to social services would be enough, and she could let them handle it. Text scrolled over reality as she filled out the form for an official inquest into Jacob Roth for child neglect and saved it as a draft. Someone lower on the food chain at Division 9 would handle that, if she sent it in.

Nina spent a few hours at the apartment, half to keep Hayley company and half waiting to talk to Jacob when he came home as a last attempt at courtesy to a fellow cop. At least, that was her surface story. Nina found herself as much in need of human contact as the kid. It had been too long since she let her guard down and just interacted with someone without ulterior motive. Her presence distracted Hayley from cyberspace and they watched a video, played some games, and just talked into the night. Nina did her the favor of more laundry and ordered some food for the pantry before she gave up on Roth showing up.

After a glance at the time, Nina sighed at the door. "What time does your father usually get home?"

"He hasn't been here in weeks." She ground her toes into the rug. "I think he's got a bed in his office."

She glanced at the girl, and walked her to bed. After Hayley fell asleep, Nina used the house phone to call Roth at his desk and got the same usual delaying excuses that his daughter had almost come to memorize word for word. The sound of his voice on the comm channel brought Hayley out of the bedroom, with her mood back to where it was before.

Nina lifted the girl's gaze with a gentle hand on her cheek. "Hayley, I'm going to go have a chat with your dad at his office. If I have to, I'll drag him down here by his shirt." She smiled.

The child giggled at the thought. "But he's bigger than you."

Nina smiled. "I know Kung Fu." She winked and made a fake fighting gesture.

Hayley's levity turned to desperation when Nina got up to leave. "Please don't go. Can't you spend the night?"

Not wanting to use the same excuse that her father did, she took a knee to look her in the eye. "Hayley... because of my job, it wouldn't be safe for you if I take you with me right now. Do you think you can wait one day? Would it be okay if I came by tomorrow to see how you were doing?"

"You mean it? You'll come back?"

Nina patted her on the shoulder. "I promise. Here, take my PID. Vid me if you need anything. I'll stay with you until you're asleep."

ON THE RIDE HOME, SHE RAN BACKGROUND CHECKS ON BOTH OF HAYLEY'S PARENTS. The mother lived in East City, toward the northern part. Family court records indicated she wanted nothing to do with her daughter. For a reason not identified in the file, a police liaison had reached out to her about a year ago inquiring about taking Hayley due to the situation with her father. The woman laughed and told him to put her up for adoption if 'the worthless idiot' couldn't handle her.

Nina pulled over and stared down at herself. How could a woman like that be allowed to have children? Nina slid her fingers through the seam of the ballistic suit and touched skin. Her belly felt normal, but it would never produce a child. She cried a little, right there in the car, mourning the son or daughter she would never know.

"It's not impossible." Vincent's voice came out of the car's dashboard.

Nina clenched her teeth. *Not now, leave me alone.*

"Check with Hardin. When they took your central nervous system out of your body, they harvested your eggs too." Vincent sounded clinical.

"What?" Nina's eyes snapped up to glare at the console. "Who is this? What the fuck do you want? If I get my hands on you I'll beat you to death with your own spine."

"Hey sweetie, easy. It's me." He stammered. "I can tell what you're thinking. You were mad at that bitch for turning her back on her own kid when you can't have them."

Nina's hands shook with anger and grief. Vincent would never talk to her like that. Whoever this was must know she stopped believing him. It would be easy enough to ask Hardin if that was true, but how could this voice know what she thought? She stared at the console for a minute before the freakish feeling fell away. Emotion gave way to reason and she pieced it together. Someone watching her net activity could tell she looked at that file and then cried while touching her stomach. That also meant that someone watched her now in real time.

Nina jumped out of the car and swept the area, finding nothing but a few startled pedestrians backing away from her waving gun.

Vincent's voice came out of the car. "Are you feeling okay, hon?"

Nina growled. "Where are you, fucker?"

"That hurts, Nina. How can you talk to me like that after what I did for you?"

She flew back into the car and slammed the door. "What exactly *did* you do for me? "Vincent"-if that's even your name."

A period of silence came, long enough for Nina to wonder if the phenomenon of the voice departed for good that night. Then he spoke again, making her jump.

"In hindsight, it was stupid of me to run at you like that. I should have moved the car and hit him with the Starburst again... maybe twice more. I wanted to draw his attacks away long enough for Div 5 to get there. All that matters is you are alive."

Nina squinted. "Wouldn't you have rather I joined you?"

"How could you think that?"

"That's not what you said a few days ago." Nina's tone verged on patronizing. "What happened to you'll be waiting for me on the other side." She powered the car up and drove.

Vincent chuckled. "You took it the wrong way. I didn't mean for you to do *that*! However long it takes, whatever time that fate gives you... when it ends, I'll be here."

Nina was thankful that cybereyes didn't blur as she cried. She didn't believe that this was Vincent, but she also didn't convince herself that it wasn't.

That would be up to that blonde from Division 0.

"Lieutenant, do you copy?" Samantha Cole's image appeared on the console with an urgent look.

"Go ahead, Cole." Nina flipped on hover mode and pulled into the sky.

"Whisper 6 has eyes on your guy. It looks like he and his Asian friend are dropping off a truck full of chemicals at a warehouse in Sector 47. We have confirmed Rafi Vas on site."

The face appeared in her vision. A freelance bomb maker that worked for whoever cared to pay him, several countries wanted him. Maybe she could talk Hardin into trading him to the Mossad for the real story on Itai. He had ties to every terrorist organization known to man, and cared little about the political agendas of his clientele.

"Have the containment team set up a perimeter right away." She shot a glance at the NavMap screen. "I'll be there in four minutes."

Nina slammed the accelerator forward, pushing the car up its limit of almost four hundred miles per hour. Only a doll, or the boosted, had the reaction time to control a car at that speed within city limits.

She wanted to be damn sure she didn't miss the party.

59

CHEMISTRY

The hovercar rounded a corner, hurtling at a perpendicular stream of traffic emerging from a side street, higher than normal for this area. Her boosted reflexes turned instant death into several perceptible seconds to react. She rolled the car on its side, aiming for a gap between the bumpers of two cars. She jammed on the vertical thrusters, making the car slide sideways to match pace with their lateral motion until she cleared on the other side and leveled off.

"Now *that's* more like it!" Vincent cheered.

She ignored him. What would have been a deadly blur of color to a normal person had slowed to the point where it felt like a high-speed drive. The poor bastards in the cars she just passed probably had no idea why their vehicles spun like tops. Nonetheless, she pulled up higher to avoid another close call. A minute away from her destination, the comm link crackled to life in the form of the holographic head of someone from Samantha's team.

"Lieutenant, there's been a complication. Holy shit, is that speed right?" He blinked. "Your guy got into a car with a foreign national. Not just any foreign national... Masaru Kurotai." The name made him cringe.

"Oh, for fuck's sake." Nina sighed her way around a corner that left dozens of windows shuddering. "Let me guess, the son of Hideo Kurotai?"

"That's the one."

"I don't understand how we can 'retire' people like that once we prove their culpability, but we can't even investigate them officially without a whiff of something. From one extreme to the other."

"I hear that." He chuckled. "The warehouse perimeter is now secure, but Kurotai and the other guy slipped out. Rafi is still there trading shots with our ground team."

"Lieutenant?" asked Cole, via comm. "We confirm positive contact on Itai Korin there as well. I have him on video shaking hands with your boy."

"Thanks." Nina grumbled. "You're going to tell me next that no one saw him leave… and I know he won't be there."

"There's nothing on the cams that show him exiting the containment area. There's no way out of that building without being seen by Whisper 6."

"I'm not blaming you or your team, but that's what you said last time." Nina's voice was flat. "This guy must have some kind of optical cloaking… try an EM spectrum scan."

"I'm not as young as I look. I did that already." Cole grinned. "Nothing."

Nina backed off on the throttle as the warehouse came into view. Airbrake flaps opened all over the exterior of the car, sending the vehicle into a shuddering wobble. She rolled in a wide sweeping left and glanced down at a junkyard full of barrels and metal junk. Small puffs of blue flame flashed where rifles traded shots from both sides. Up ahead, the whispercraft hovered, silent and motionless, its angular lines an ebon crack in the sky.

Its narrow front end drew out to a point from a thick body studded with sensor equipment. From the thrust pods at the back, two fins almost large enough to be called wings ran up and to the side while one went straight down to the rear. Long feelers swiveled from either side above the troop doors like the antenna of a giant insect: twelve-foot-long railgun sniping weapons. A line of blur appeared in an instant, connecting one to the ground where a man firing on police exploded like a stepped-on roach. She tapped into the feed coming from the whispercraft, opening a tactical overlay in her vision. The whisper's sensors were surpassed only by what C-Branch refused to share with the rest of the government. The thermal outlines of the men in the building had such detail she could tell how well hung they were.

One man hid in an upstairs office, scurrying away from the gunfight with two others moving in a guarding posture between him and the hostilities.

That's gotta be Rafi.

Nina programmed the autopilot for a nice gentle landing on the roof and opened the door. Still thirty feet up, she jumped as the car passed over a skylight closest to that point. Her coat trailed behind her like a cape as she smashed boots-first through the transparent pyramid, falling amid a rain of fragments and debris in the hallway.

Myofiber muscles in her legs absorbed the incredible shock of her landing, transferring it into a forward roll that cracked the tile floor. As the somersault became a leap, she put three bullets into the man on the left before her momentum carried her into a flying forearm bash. The speed of her unexpected entrance had caught them both off guard. The second man barely had time to inhale a pre-scream breath before her elbow slammed into his chest, crushing his armored vest and everything under it.

The strike connected before her feet hit the ground, turning him into a battering ram that blasted the steel door behind him off its hinges. He landed dead on top of the detached slab, riding it like a sled into a desk.

Nina leapt the dead men and went after Rafi who had one leg out the window. He turned on her as she burst into the room, and opened fire. She slalomed between three bullets, leaning out of the way with less than an inch to spare, losing only a few strands of hair as she sprinted up and swatted the gun out of his hand.

He raised his hands. "Don't kill me! I surrender."

Her somatic response system detected duplicity.

She grabbed him by the shirt and pulled him close. "We're going to have a nice long talk, Rafi."

"Of course!" He blurted, and exhaled a yellow mist in her face.

"Gasbag. Cute." Nina bounced his face off the desk, twice, and held him back up to look him in the eye as blood trickled out of his nose.

"Doesn't work too well with a tox filter, Rafi. Didn't they teach you anything in terror school?"

He stared at her, seeming to lose the will to fight. Then, in a spritz of blood, a trio of Nano claws burst from his right hand and went for her side. Her one handed grip on his shirt released, and she rolled into him. Her hips slid away from the blades as she caught his wrist with the hand that half a second ago held him by the collar. Rafi was quick, but not faster than a military grade doll.

His eyes widened with astonishment as she spun him in a violent tango and wedged his blades into the wall. He screamed, struggling against her, the look on his face contorting to legitimate fear upon realizing her strength went way beyond human. She winked as understanding dawned, and then wrenched her hand to snap his claws off in the wall. For a doll, having Nano claws shattered would be the nuisance of losing a weapon. Rafi, however, lacked plastisteel bones so his blade housings mounted to living tissue. The torque required to break them also disintegrated the bones in his right arm. He screamed past clenched teeth, cradling the sack of flesh that dangled from his elbow.

"Wanna go for the other side jackass?" Nina flung him to the ground.

He slid into the desk, hard enough to dent it.

"What… what do you want?" He coughed, dragging himself across on the floor.

Nina walked after him, putting her gun under her arm. "Let's start with who you're making the bomb for."

"I don't know his name. He's got a French accent."

"French?" Nina lifted an eyebrow.

"Yes." Rafi screamed.

"Are you sure? It couldn't have been anything else?"

Rafi stared at her. "What are you saying?"

She stopped and folded her arms. "Could he have been an Israeli?"

To her surprise, his fear seemed to fade for just a moment. "It… no… it didn't really, well I suppose it could have sounded like someone trying to fake a Hebrew accent." He was all of a sudden quite cordial, out of place for the situation.

"Fake an accent?" Nina squinted. "Why would an ex-Mossad agent need to fake the accent of the country he came from?"

"How should I know?" Rafi offered a believable smile. "Maybe to throw you off?"

In the corner of her eye, the fight wound down on the tactical overlay. Blue friendlies swarmed downstairs. "Where did he go?"

Rafi braced himself against the desk and sat up. "He was never here, just talking on a holo call with the Russian."

"A Russian was here?" Nina pulled Rafi to his feet.

He nodded. "Anatoly—"

"Nemsky." Nina finished for him. "Dammit. Where did he go?"

"He left before the chemicals showed up." Rafi waved his intact arm to emphasize his words.

"We have him on video standing with you when the truck arrived. Where did he go?"

Rafi shook his head. "Maybe one of the mercenaries I work with?"

"No." Nina showed him the footage, pointing at Itai. "This guy."

"I have never seen him before." Rafi grew alarmed. "That video is fake! What is this, the ACC? What are you trying to set me up for?"

Nina stared at him. The sweat dripping over his forehead patted into the floor like clapping hands. Hairline glows of light measured pupil dilation, widening of the eyes, breathing, and perspiration. Her somatic system confirmed his truthfulness. She scowled.

A tactical team led by SO Carter entered. Her white hair made the black armored visor it framed even darker.

Nina shoved Rafi over to them. "Take him in for processing. Carter? What are you bored? Why is a senior operative taking point with an insertion team?"

Carter helped Rafi along with a shove. "Hardin's vagina is throbbing about the sniper re-qual." The rest of her team got rigid at her casual demeanor with a Lieutenant.

Nina laughed. "Why not just get it out of the way?"

"Don't even get me started..." She grumbled. "Lieutenant. The test parameters are skewed, it is an unrealistic scenario. Besides, I did it five months ago."

"You're making a big deal out of one bullet. 89/90 isn't bad."

"It's the principle of it." Carter left with the escort, taking Rafi downstairs.

Nina would leave the interrogation to the pros. She had other things to deal with.

"Whisper 2, this is Lieutenant Duchenne, do you copy?"

"Go ahead LT." A confident male voice came back over the comm.

"Do you have eyes on the package?"

"Roger that LT. The subjects went in two different directions. The foreign national dropped your boy off in a grey zone and left. Nearly ran a civilian down trying to get out of there."

"Grey zone? Near Sector 12?" Nina wanted to wound someone. She was *just* there.

"Affirmative, ma'am."

"I'll be there as soon as this site is secured. Stay on him and let me know if he does anything. If he so much as jerks off, I want to know about it."

"Um... I'll assume you're being figurative there Lieutenant."

FIRST DATE

Despite sealed tanks, the wall of a truck, and two hours, the powerful chemical stench still permeated Joey's senses. He was glad to be home again and hoping a little rest would take the red out of his eyes and the burn from his throat. It didn't occur to him as strange to see Pinky face down on the ground by the bike. Even the little bit of blood around his nose seemed natural.

Joey stumbled in the door of his sad excuse for an apartment, and lamented the dead shower for a moment before it occurred to him that he didn't have to squeeze through a small gap. The sight of the wide-open door chased his fatigue away and brought his gun out.

"Dammit. What the fuck do those WellTech shitheads want now?"

Somehow, the scent of ballistic propellant pierced the chemical mask in his nose. A quick glance around showed no obvious quantities of blood or gore, though the condition of the VidPhone made him gaze at the ceiling. The screen had an enormous hole in the center, from which a V shaped absence of material spread upward. The displaced matter was little more than silicon dust showered on the table below the unit.

He sauntered over, shaking his head. "Aww... what the fuck. Why would someone do that?"

This apartment grew more and more intolerable by the week. The senseless death of yet another piece of technology validated his habit of always carrying his deck. The crisp beep of his NetMini pierced the silence and made him jump. An incoming vid call turned out to be Cassidy Rivera, the fringer chick he met at New Hope. She looked more or less the same as her net avatar, a common thing for 'utility' users—his term for scrubs who dwelled only at the outer surface of cyberspace, unaware of its true expanse.

Green-purple smears of eyeliner ran down her cheeks and she trembled, huddled in a public VidPhone. Joey leaned back and let all the air out of his lungs while he continued trying to glare a hole in the ceiling. He swallowed the frustration and put on a concerned face, reminding himself that he'd offered to let her call him if she needed anything.

"What's wrong Cass?"

"Mary! She just called me. I was just talking to her. She told me that The Russian is coming for me!" She appeared to be on the verge of vomiting from fear, and her voice was so shaky it made her difficult to understand.

"Okay take a breath. Relax. Where are you?"

She peeked behind her before whispering. "I'm at a PubTran on the corner of CR 1144 and Newsom Street."

"City road 1144... Okay, great. That's a public place. Remember that The Russian always ambushes women in dark alleys near grey zones. It's bullshit that he's looking just for you. He's an opportunistic predator."

She shrank into herself, shivering. "How can you be so sure?"

"The police keep wonderfully detailed files. By the way, I have some news for you, but I don't want to give it to you over the phone. Can you hold on 'til I get there?"

"I guess."

"Stay there." Joey hung up, grabbed his deck, and went out the door.

A STRANGE WATCHED FEELING CAME OVER HIM FIFTEEN MINUTES LATER AS HE entered the PubTran terminal. He felt a presence staring at him from across the street, but nothing seemed to be there. Cassidy ran over, stopping short of grabbing him, and stood as close as she could get without touching.

Frayed fingerless gloves rubbed up and down white and black striped sleeves. He put an arm around her and felt her tense at the contact. A copious helping of cheap perfume masked the truth that she hadn't known the inside of a shower in months. He walked with her into the café and ordered a pair of standard cheeseburger platters and an extra-large coffee for himself. The reassembled OmniSoy 'beef' covered with sim-cheese was cheap, but at least edible. He tapped away on his NetMini for a moment as they found a table, smiling at her before putting it back in his pocket.

"Go ahead, eat." Joey nudged the plate at her.

She shook her head. "Are you nuts? I'm too wound up to eat. Why were you looking back like that when you walked in? Is he out there?"

Joey didn't want to tell her that he felt like someone followed him or even that he just felt watched. "I always do that. I'm used to living in the shitty part of town and I often get mistaken for a girl from behind." He chuckled.

She laughed nervously. "Maybe cut your hair?"

"Blasphemer!" He shouted with false indignation, pointing at her in a mockery of a priest.

Several people looked at him.

A hint of pink ran around the edge of her black lip-gloss. He noticed it as she finally smiled a little.

"So I did a little poking around Cyberspace on your behalf, but..."

"But what?" She leaned forward and grabbed his hand, stalling his next bite.

Joey made a few faces as he tried to think of a gentle way to say it, but gave up. "I won't sugar coat it. You're going to feel like a dumbass and cry like a five year old… and probably have a total meltdown."

"What is it?" She jumped out of the chair. "Stop fucking with me." Her face shifted from fear to sadness to anger so rapidly he expected her to pass out.

A delivery bot interrupted the moment, whizzing around the room before floating up to him. It seemed to sniff at his NetMini before its hatch popped open. All the while, a tinny advert jingle warbled from a little speaker hanging on bare wires from its undercarriage. He took a blue autoinjector out of its compartment. He spun it over his fingers, flicking the safety cap off in one practiced move, and jabbed Cassidy in the thigh with it. The unexpected coldness in her leg knocked her back into the seat.

"Ow!" She clamped her hands over the spot. "What the fuck?"

Her face turned green and her eyes lost focus. A few mild convulsions gripped her, and she broke out in a cold sweat. Within a minute, she bent forward with her arm in her gut. When the convulsions ceased, he held up the empty autoinjector so she could see the label. It was a multi-cure for about four hundred and change known diseases—everything from the flu to Aids to the Q virus.

"Fuck you, too." She shoved herself standing.

Guilt at needing it softened her resentment. Her body's visible reaction proved it cured at least one malady.

"Sometime within the next hour, you're gonna melt a toilet bowl."

She kept glaring at him, in too much discomfort to move. "Yeah, more like now…"

"Just helping you out. Those things are—"

"A thousand credits, I know." She cut him off and started to cry. "It would have been cheaper to just call me a worthless piece of shit."

Cassidy ambled off in a hybrid gait of pee dance mixed with drunken stagger. Joey leaned on his arm, nibbling at the food and laughing as a few other women scurried out of the bathroom with hands over their mouths. A few minutes later, the girl dragged herself back to the table, looking exhausted.

"Oh just fuckin' eat already. I really don't give a rat's ass that you were a working girl. We all gotta do what we gotta do to survive. I'd rather not catch whatever you had when I tell you what I have to tell you. Forget The Russian, he has no idea who you are."

He dodged her question about the news and made it a point to hold the information over her head until she ate, talking at length about The Russian's hunting practices. When she finished the burger, he took her hand and held on.

"Okay, this is gonna be hard to hear. I would have told you sooner, but I got distracted by a nice fat, easy job I couldn't say no to."

She stared, trembling with anticipation.

"Your mother has been searching for you for three years."

The color drained from her face. "What?"

"They got divorced about a week after your father kicked you out. She tried to get him charged with child abuse and has spent about twenty grand on private investigators looking for you."

Cassidy covered her mouth with both hands, shaking as she cried without sound for a minute before the words sank in enough to cause sobbing. The news that her mother still loved her hadn't been enough of a counterweight to how stupid she felt for assuming *both* parents hated her. The thought she could have avoided the last three years on the street bending over for anyone with a cred stick made the cheeseburger flip over in her gut.

"I didn't tell her what you were doing."

A middle-aged Hispanic woman appeared at the café entrance, so frantic in her attempt to enter that she pulled on a push door.

"I called her on my way here." Joey made a 'push' gesture at her.

Cassidy shrank into herself, unable to look up as her mother swooped in and fell on her with apologies.

Joey stood, slinging the deck over his shoulder. "Cassidy? One more thing."

They both looked at him.

"The person calling you and claiming to be your dead friend is *not* her. Someone is dicking with us both. Ignore it. I will find the son of a bitch."

He felt pleased with himself the entire ride back to his shithole. He wondered if his bitch of a sister had ever once helped someone without being paid for it.

A HAND SEIZED JOEY'S COAT THE INSTANT HE WALKED IN THE DOOR, ACCELERATING his entry to the apartment. His scream continued until his back slammed into the wall and he slid to the ground. The shock stunned him silent. Nina stepped into his view, glaring.

"I'm sorry, was I drunk? Did I forget to pay?" He rubbed the back of his head.

Her eyes boiled with rage. This guy sure had a mouth on him. Now she knew how Donny and Alvin felt when they smacked a perp around. She reminded herself she could liquefy him if she lost control.

"How long did you think it would take us to find you?"

Joey's heart stopped. *Please don't be Mars.*

"Mars?" He offered a cute whisper, trying to look as innocent as he could.

Nina blinked. "Mars? No. This has nothing to do with Mars."

He relaxed, closing his eyes with a big dumb grin. "Thank you."

"Don't thank me yet, dickhead. You might be a big man in cyberspace but your ass is all mine here."

"Well hey, all you had to do was ask." Joey started to pull his coat off. "The place is a little messy, but the couch is big enough."

She flung him out of the coat into the sofa, which flipped onto its back as it sent an explosion of trash into the air. Joey slithered onto floor behind it, skidding on his chin. Nina dropped the coat, and stalked after him.

"Ouch." He pushed himself up to a kneeling position. "I usually don't go for the rough stuff, but if you want me to tie you up… I could get into that."

His smile fell to a flat line as Nina leveled her gun at him. "Knock it off." She took a step closer. "Tell me about the Silver hack. Ponder your words carefully. They may be your last."

Joey tried to wrap his brain around the size of the gun in this woman's hand. His eyes flitted back and forth from the barrel to her face and back again. It hit him who this must be. "Nina?"

"Well you aren't as stupid as you look, are you?"

Joey chuckled. "Nice hand-howitzer. If you were a man, I'd accuse you of compensating. How can you even fire that monster? You must have a shitload of recoil compensators on that fucker."

"Something like that."

Joey pushed the seat back on its legs, kneeling behind it. "Are you here to tell me why your voice came out of my deck?"

"I'm here to ask you about some of your friends."

"Aww shit, what did Katya do now?"

"I mean Anatoly Nemsky and Itai Korin."

Joey sat back on his heels and raised his hands in a gesture of confusion. "Who?"

"Really?"

Above Nina's palm, a hologram appeared. Joey, Masaru, and Katya walked into Sector 12 and met Anatoly for a brief handshake.

"Bullshit!" He waved. "That dude wasn't there, just the three of us."

"We've already checked. The Karsson-Neimand passed."

Joey made a pained grimace. "That's not possible. That giant meat wall wasn't there. Ask Masaru or Katya."

"I will, eventually." She switched videos and showed footage of him dropping off the chemicals to Rafi. "What about this guy, was he not there either?"

"Rafi, right?" He nodded. "He works for Green Dot Chemical. We pulled a contract job to recover stolen chems. Rafi was the company drop off man." Joey brushed his hand over his shirt. "Damn that shit stank, I can still smell it."

Nina lost a little faith in her lie detection cyberware. "Rafi doesn't work for Green Dot. You're either an incredibly talented liar or…"

"The job was a setup?" Joey climbed over the couch and sat on it. "Katya said something about this penthouse thing that Alex gave her. She said it paid a lot of money for something real stupid easy… just like the one at the dock."

Nina made a mental note that the unknown woman went by the name Katya. "We saw this woman meeting with both Korin as well as Nemsky."

He explained the peculiar instructions of that job, about how she was supposed to lean forward to blow out a candle.

"Look at her, that doesn't look like a very good kiss… if you were going to kiss someone why lean over the middle of the table to do it?" Joey paused for a breath and leaned back, putting a hand on his forehead. "Let me guess, the Karsson-Neimand checked out there too?" Something caught his eye, and he held up a hand. "Hey, play that again, and slow it down."

She did. He crept up to the hologram until it changed the color of his face.

"Look at that, at the plates, more specifically at their shadows. They're shifting like there's a candle flame but there's none on the table." Joey puffed his chest with the indignation of being right.

Nina grumbled. "Yes." She had her doubts too, ever since the video from the diplomatic tower showed Itai but the Division 9 cameras didn't. "Karsson-Neimand was supposed to be foolproof."

Joey paced. "Well, video files like this used to be only a few megabytes, not the dozens of terabytes they are now. Some of the increase is due to the extra data required for holograms but Karsson-Neimand makes them much bigger. Every pixel has a timestamp code that takes up about eight times the amount of data as the pixel definition. The frames are broken up in sets of twenty and every set is out of order in a precise way based on a random seed value generated with the time of recording. When the file is played back, the K-N encoding tells the player how to reorder the images and then compares a recalculated check number against the stored value for each pixel. If any pixels fail, it is a sign that the video was edited. It would be a whore and a half to fake it."

Nina slid her weapon back into its holster. "I know how Karsson-Neimand works. Doctor Neimand spoke at a lecture I attended once."

Joey laughed. "Just when people started to trust video again... Someone found a way around it. Are you ready for another wave of paranoia?"

Nina looked around for something to destroy. She wanted to beat this guy to a pulp for murdering Vincent, as well as her dreams. It had all fit so well in her mind that she was inches away from killing him just because it made so much sense. Now that she talked to him, Hayley's words rang true. Joey seemed like a pawn of something bigger.

Nina grilled him for hours about everything it appeared that he had been doing for Nemsky or Korin. Joey's explanations made her angrier, not because he lied, but because he destroyed her theory of events and it meant starting all over yet again.

Joey enjoyed her presence. Aside from being a little taller and lot less innocent looking, Nina and Avril were quite similar in appearance. He imagined her in that dress with longer hair, and her voice trailed off into an unrecognizable warble. He stared, mesmerized.

"Tell me about the god damn silver hack! Why was my patrol route changed?" She had slammed him into the wall again and held him nose to nose. "Are you even paying attention to me?" She looked angry and at the same time seemed on the verge of tears.

Joey kissed her on the tip of the nose. "No, not really. I was just picturing you in that fancy dress you wore to New Hope. You are so beautiful my brain shut down."

She dropped him and looked away.

"Before you break anything else, the Silver Hack wasn't me. I don't think I'm that good, especially not with this piece of shit Teradyne 3. Why would I change your patrol route, I don't even know you."

She crossed her arms, and looked at him with a furrowed brow. No hacker she ever encountered liked admitting a challenge exceeded their ability, and that damned system told her he was being truthful.

"I didn't mean to bring Vincent up and piss you off that night. Sounds came out of my deck a few days ago. Someone lifted your comm chatter." Joey glanced away at the wall. "My dead father has been talking to me too."

"He's dead?" She gawked with incredulity. "I spoke to him just a little while ago."

"You could say the same for Vincent, I bet." He tilted his head. "Where did you run into my dad?"

Nina looked at the destroyed VidPhone. "I don't remember... he just called me."

Joey held his arm out at the device. "What the hell did he say that made you shoot my phone?"

"Some lies about Vincent. Did you talk to your father at all about him?"

"No, I try not to talk to him too much. Our conversations are much the same as when I was fourteen. Mostly him rambling on endlessly with me saying "yeah" and "uh huh" often enough to trick him into thinking I'm listening. Someone is dicking with me through cyberspace. I've been trying to figure out who it is."

The hostility left Nina's voice. "So you don't think it's a ghost?"

Joey laughed for minutes before he could breathe again. "A ghost? Really? No, I don't. Someone's just sending us audio streams or using a voice modulator to sound like people we knew."

He explained his theory of a connection to New Hope. He told her about Mitch, about Cassidy, and the two hackers that killed themselves. When he brought that up, Nina's face got paler. Two men had already committed suicide because of talking to the returned ghosts of former loved ones. At one point, Vincent tried to get her to do the same. Cassidy sounded close to jumping in front of a PubTran as well. Nina told him about Coe and Arlon Davies, how their dad heard their voices in his apartment at night.

Neither could find meaning in why Mitch had been spared. Joey pointed out that his wife was never real. Nina lifted an eyebrow.

"Imaginary people don't make holovid calls. There's nothing to sample the audio from." It came out of her as if it was the most obvious thing in the world.

Joey stared at her agape. The simplicity of the explanation embarrassed him for even considering paranormal ones.

"Of course!" He spun in a circle and clapped. "That makes perfect sense. Christina never existed, so there's not a trace of what she sounds like."

"Has your father tried to make you feel guilty or depressed?"

"No… Not that I can think of, he has always been cloyingly polite. I doubt he has it in him. If the guy faking him acted like that it wouldn't be believable."

Nina nodded.

"I do have one tidbit of information I haven't looked at yet… Proscion."

"Proscion? He fell off the grid two years ago, we assumed he was dead."

Joey shared the details of the Mayberry incident hidden away in Amber's mind, connecting it back to Proscion by virtue of him having found the place.

"That was seven years ago." Nina shrugged. "We knew he was active then."

"Yeah I know. That's why I haven't checked up on him. I got nothing else. Maybe he faked his own death so he could dodge the endless stream of bounty hunters and assassins that the Silver Hack would send his way. If anyone could have done that, my money would be on him."

Nina shook her head. "I don't think so. For that to be true he would have had to been paid enough to never work again. He hasn't been active on the net in more than two years."

"Who says we all do it for money? Maybe he's using a different alias and deck?"

"I suppose it's possible but you can't fake a NRP."

"NRP?" Joey raised an eyebrow.

"Neural Response Profile. It's like a brain fingerprint. Everyone is wired just a little different and anyone that jacks into the net can be identified within a margin of one in ten thousand individuals by the way that their neurons react to the connection."

Joey rubbed his M3 jack with a nervous finger. He never thought the government could do that. "So you can tell who people really are? There has to be a way to spoof that."

Nina studied him. "We're not talking about perfect accuracy, just the ability to narrow down a potential person by the way their brain responds."

"Oh, speaking about StarPoint..." Joey offered her a cheesy smile.

She tensed up as he powered on his deck, waiting for the trick move, but his body language remained nonthreatening. He pulled up the data that he retrieved from the Badlands facility's network and explained the psycho tot and the project they worked on.

Her voice took on an ominous tone. "Give me a copy of those files?"

He did. Nina scowled at the wall while he wrote it out to holodisk. Joey Dillon had been her best wildcard so far, but after talking to Hayley and now meeting him, she accepted that he was a pawn. She had no idea how he compared to Division 9's network team, but at this point, she had little to lose by asking.

"While you are looking into that Proscion matter, see if you can find any information on the whereabouts of Itai Korin or Anatoly Nemsky."

"Your guys can't find them?" Her question intrigued him. The mere asking was a compliment.

"No." Folding her arms, she grumbled below hearing for a moment. "Here and there, bits and pieces. It's like they're ghosts."

"Maybe they are?" Joey grinned in jest.

Her arms fell to her sides with a smirk. "That's not even funny."

"Yeah, I guess it isn't. Katya met Nemsky at that restaurant. He freaked her out pretty good. Apparently, she's read his resume."

"He's not a big deal. Anatoly is only a problem when he has a company of soldiers with him and a government that lets him run wild. On his own, he is just an over the hill soldier. Maybe we can use her to arrange a meeting?"

"Speaking of which, that idea you have about Nemsky... I think you're being tricked." Joey let out an impish laugh.

Nina walked over and looked down at him. "How do you mean?"

"You told me that Nemsky's plan is to set up a guerilla squad in the black zone here, right?"

She stared.

"Well..." He exhaled. "It ain't Nemsky chasing the gangers out."

Her eyes narrowed and his grin widened. When he got the hint she didn't care for his teasing, he lost his smile. "It's a cyborg."

"Yeah, right."

Joey leaned back on the couch and told her about Mark Bolt, the reporter, the Mayberry contact getting his head vaporized and about Mark's situation with his daughter.

"I'm pretty sure he'd turn himself in if they gave him a body that didn't scare the shit out of his kid. He's still loyal, just messed up over his family."

Something like this, Nina couldn't keep under her hat. An AWOL Marine she would have to report even if she could sympathize with his predicament. The fall was inevitable, but she could steer the proverbial parachute on the way down.

"I'll see what I can do for him."

"He'd appreciate that. I can't even imagine what it must be like for him, having his own kid not even want to see him."

"Yeah, it must be"—Nina looked out the door into the darkness—"hard to deal with."

"So… what happened that night?" Joey slid over and made room for her on the couch. "I never had a government assassin in my apartment before, kind of fun actually."

Some strange quality about Joey made her sit next to him before she thought about it. She had the legal authority to kill at a whim and he acted so casual. It didn't feel like bravado, more like he didn't care at all, even enjoyed the danger. He lived in a hellhole, had almost no social graces, and was probably a criminal, but something about his personality struck a chord. He had that same irreverent streak that Vincent did as well as a similar sense of impropriety.

She felt a bit like Hayley must have the other night. In spite of every rational thought, she stayed and talked.

Little five-foot-four Nina once adored the feeling of protection that came from clinging to a man. Not in that helpless-female way that her mother so often put on in public. For her, it had been a private surrender when alone with Vincent. Now, she found it hard to justify wanting sense of protection from a man. The strange desire stood at odds with her military hardware and kept her mind off balance. Another hour passed in a meandering chat about nothing of great importance, she stumbled along, responding in a distracted manner as she tried to sort out her emotions. Guilt weighed on her as she wondered how Vincent would feel. The speed with which she went from ready to twist Joey's head off to wanting to spend more time with him numbed her mind. Dr. Khan had brought up that she should eventually find another person to build a relationship with. The time would come when she needed to get on with her life. The Vincent she knew would want her to be happy.

Their conversation eventually wandered into silly things like favorite music and even childhood pets. She slid down a rollercoaster, talking about far more than her conscious mind wanted to. It felt natural. He somehow managed to pull things out before she could think about what she said. As much as she tried to stop, it kept happening.

Nina opened her eyes, finding herself curled on the couch under a rat-chewed blanket. He had taken her boots off and placed them nearby. Joey was on the floor a little ways away, using a plastic bag full of paper shreds for a pillow. She sat up, making as little noise as she could, and reclaimed her boots. Pausing at the door, she sent her PID to his NetMini.

He had made a convincing show of clearing himself and his associates from knowing involvement. She would have to split the facts apart from her strange new feelings and go over the particulars with Hardin. In addition, the network team would have to find a way to explain how false vids passed K-N.

A lot of eyes would be looking at a lot of numbers for a lot of hours.

SEEING RED

Joey's boot knocked against the door in time with the gentle motion of his surroundings. The hardest part of the job had been climbing up the six-foot ladder into the cab of the behemoth cargo transporter. Masaru volunteered to drive and Joey let him. He could daydream about Nina while slipping in and out of sleep. His friend's katana had made a triviality of the four mercenaries guarding the truck. Their reaction to the attack that lasted all of six seconds would keep him laughing for months. Masaru hadn't the first clue how Joey found it, only that he had said something about needing to do Katya a favor to keep the government off her.

The sight of the Highway so far below unnerved him. The giant articulated truck was unlike anything Joey had ever ridden in before. The flat faced cab floated atop two wheels nine feet in diameter on each side. A thick rubber tread circled the stationary metal core, pulled by motors in the center. The rest of the wheels were a quarter of the size. Enormous black letters stenciled across the side of the gunmetal grey cargo box spelled out 'Siege Arms'. Joey bit his lip, thinking about the more than two thousand assault rifles in the back, worth about seven or eight grand apiece. The temptation to offload them one by one on the street was high, but he didn't do this for money, he didn't even do it for Katya.

The little white-haired girl was hard to say no to.

Between thoughts of Nina's visit a day ago and the vibrating cabin, sleep eluded him. Joey's right eye popped open, tracking a series of light blobs forming in a slow metamorphosis on the windscreen. The endless things appeared small, and grew fatter as they slid upward before vanishing into a streak that sailed off to the right. He never noticed the street lamps before. As he so often drove around 200 miles an hour, he couldn't see them at all. Other vehicles shot past them on the left. Most of the traffic moved at least twice their speed, and he longed to be there with them.

"So why the philanthropy?" Masaru glanced over at his friend.

Joey chuckled. "If she's dead, I can't subject her to my piteous mockery."

"Dead?" He blinked in shock. "Why would she be dead?"

Joey chuckled. "She got made at the factory when she stole these." He pointed his thumb back over his shoulder. "It's got something to do with some Russian despot. Anyway, she wanted to lay low for awhile."

Masaru squinted at him. "She didn't say anything about getting caught."

"She didn't get caught, she got seen. Division 9 is involved." Joey closed his eye again. "Her preference for getting in with her silver tongue doesn't help much against security video."

A waterfall of derision ran from Masaru's mouth in Japanese. Even Kurotai Electronics had no influence over Division 9. They had no PR liaison and no one outside of the agency knew who their brass even was. Their official role entailed dealing with misbehaving foreigners, usually by killing them. That whitened Masaru's knuckles as he clutched the steering wheel.

"Do you know why they're involved?" Masaru stared out the window.

"Well, she *is* a foreign national."

"She's also not important enough for them to care about."

"Are you sure? How much do you really know about her?" Joey smiled, taking a little pleasure in watching his friend's usual unflappable demeanor show cracks.

"What are you saying?" Masaru glanced at him.

Joey shrugged. "Well, these guns... She arranged their disappearance for the benefit of that Russian warlord."

"Why would she do that? She despises the ACC."

"That right there is the million credit question." Joey slapped himself in the thigh to add emphasis. "All I know is that Division 9 showed up at my apartment for a chat. They think we're all working for this guy as well as some Israeli wingnut."

Joey filled Masaru in on a basic overview of what Nina showed him. Masaru tapped his fingers on the wheel. His father wouldn't find this amusing. Even with a perfect explanation, a whisper of impropriety with overtones of espionage would be a disaster for the company.

"I must distance myself from this as soon as possible."

Joey's response stalled in his throat when a large forearm burst down from the roof above Masaru and yanked him out into the night. The tattered ribbons of metal that flowered up from the hole hissed and clattered in the violent gale that flooded the cabin. As Joey scrambled to grab the wheel, Masaru sailed ahead into view. He landed on the road, skidding in an out of control spin upon a cushion of sparks. His armor and the traction coating got into a heated argument. Joey wrenched the wheel, forcing the leviathan one lane left to avoid running him over. The maneuver caused alarms to ring out as the truck spent several seconds with half its tires off the ground. He howled, twisting the wheel the other way, smooching the dash when it slammed back down.

Footsteps thudded from the roof as someone heavy managed to keep their balance during the maneuver.

A baritone voice overhead with a heavy Russian accent yelled, "Is enough distance, yes?"

Joey kept his eyes on the roof and slid low against the seat to the driver's side

340 | VIRTUAL IMMORTALITY

to stomp the brakes. A body swung down and smashed into the windshield, cracking it. Joey loosed an involuntary shout at the sudden appearance of a man clinging to the front of the cab. He held on to something out of sight above the windscreen, his face contorted with a grimace as he held on during the hard deceleration.

A light grey suit jacket flapped in the breeze, exposing a tank top. The man had the well-muscled appearance of an assault infantryman, though he looked a little old in the face. After a few seconds of staring at him, Joey blinked in disbelief. The man stuck to the front of the truck was Anatoly Nemsky.

"Oh, shit!" The tone in Joey's voice would have been more appropriate for receiving a long wanted gift.

Joey didn't want to join Masaru on the road. He stayed out of arm's reach and guided the massive transport to a halt in the far right lane. He grinned, anticipating how happy Nina would be with him for finding this guy. He fished for his NetMini to call her, flashing a cocky grin as the truck reached a complete stop amidst a cloud of coolant fog and smoking rubber.

Nemsky smashed a hand through the window in an attempt to grab him. Joey dove screaming into the passenger seat, abandoning the device in favor of his gun, and fired from the hip. The Russian bailed, falling out of sight as three shots turned bits of the windshield into geysers of powdered glass.

He kicked the door open, slid down a ladder, and spun about in search of Nemsky. The moment he faced the front of the truck, the big Russian came around and grabbed his gun arm. He pushed it to the side and spun Joey into a chicken wing.

Joey ran up the side of the truck, stepping on the large treads of the drive wheel as he flipped up and over the big man and staggered away. Six feet further back and he would have fallen two hundred yards to the city below.

Nemsky turned on him with a glare, lunging as Joey fired again. At least one *thump* came from a body hit, but Nemsky ignored it. Joey's shirt tightened around his neck as the Russian got a fistful and lifted him off the ground. He cocked back his arm and pounded Nemsky in the nose with his pistol. The big man had little reaction to the hit, and Joey's hand throbbed.

"What the fuck?" Joey shook his hand a few times, trying to dismiss a sprain. "Damn, I thought that Spetsnaz shit was a myth. Wait... you weren't Spetsnaz."

Nemsky laughed, walking Joey toward the edge of the Highway.

The line of solid ground slid out from under his view, giving him a nice panorama of the city below. Excitement and terror battled for his attention.

"When people steal from me, I am usually inspired to return the favor with a creative death. I do apologize if this is a bit of a letdown." A wry smile spread over the Russian's face.

Joey threw his weight behind a kick, driving his boot into the side of Nemsky's head. A red mark formed on the skin of his cheek but the big man was unimpressed.

"Struggle, little mouse!" Nemsky hefted Joey higher. "Do it again."

"Oh, fuck..."

On Nemsky's gut, a glint of plastisteel peeked out from a bullet hole from where a strip of skin had torn away.

A series of smoke puffs hissed up from the ground, tracing a straight line of dots along the surface of the Highway and into tiny fires on Nemsky's leg. The stink of burning polymers watered Joey's eyes. Both heads turned at the same time toward a soaked Masaru draped over a cluster of broken water cans in front of a highway support frame.

Nemsky released Joey and dove under the truck to break line of sight before the S-19 could fire again. Joey fell, catching the edge of the road in his armpits. Masaru crawled out of the crash absorber and staggered toward the truck. The tattered remains of his coat fluttered behind him, black armor agleam in the overhead lights.

Nemsky rolled out from under the other side of the transport and leapt to his feet. Masaru came around the trailer as the Russian tore the driver door off the cab with a wrenching screech of failing metal. He dove to the side to evade the door, which glanced off the road, bent from the force of the hit. Another pulse of laser fire sent Nemsky under the truck, giving Masaru a chance to stand.

Joey struggled to pull himself up, screaming at the sight of the Russian's red glowing eyes under the trailer. He let go with his right, dangling one-handed as the general charged, smashing the concrete where his hand and been seconds before, sending fragments tumbling toward the city below. He couldn't help himself but cackle to the mad adrenaline rush of being so close to a fatal fall.

Nemsky reared back to crush Joey's left hand with his boot, but a series of laser melt holes sizzled open along the road, streaking toward him. He leapt away, diving for cover. A piece of mangled rebar protruding from the break the Russian had so conveniently stomped into the barrier provided the handhold Joey needed to pull himself back up onto the road.

To the outside observer, he appeared to be sprawled face down. Joey, on the other hand, considered himself hugging solid ground.

Masaru ran up on the grinning Nemsky, dropping the S-19 onto its strap as he drew his katana. Metal blades snapped out of the general's arms, filling the area with the unsettling hum of active vibro inducers. Joey rolled onto his side, unloading several more shots into Anatoly's chest, two of which caused sparks.

Masaru leaned right, avoiding the Russian's first attack. The vibro claws tore two gashes in the outer plate of the passenger side main wheel, cutting and melting. Continuing the spin, Masaru caught Nemsky in the lower back with a shallow slice. The feel of the strike told him he fought a doll, as if having the door thrown at him wasn't obvious enough.

The thought of crippling him and getting the hell out of there rattled Masaru's mind. Before he could act on it, Nemsky lunged at him. This time, Masaru sidestepped and slashed the incoming limb. The Nano katana hesitated for a fraction of a second as it met the plastisteel bone at the center of the forearm. The force of the punch sent the severed limb flying into the truck where it stuck like a dart, wreathed in electrical arcs for several seconds from whatever it pierced.

Anatoly staggered away. He hadn't anticipated Masaru's speed, or the presence of a Nano sword. He had every thought of this being no more dangerous than squashing a pair of bugs. Rather than retreat, he snarled and lunged again. Faking a strike with his still intact left arm, he kicked Masaru in the back when he moved to defend the false attack. The robotic kick launched him into a tongue-kiss with the cargo box. He bounced off in a drunken stagger, bringing his blade up to defend against a spinning world as best he could.

The general lined up for another attack at his stunned foe, but two slugs from Joey's pistol in the back of the head diverted his attention. One bounced away with a ping, but the second knocked him forward a step as it lodged in a plastisteel skull. Blue light glowed from within, visible through a small crack, while blood oozed around the slug. Joey ran for the front of the truck, seeking distance from the edge.

With a loud growl, Nemsky grabbed Masaru and hurled him into Joey. Masaru held his blade away as the two men collided and slid in a heap for about ten meters into the metal road. Passing drivers swerved to avoid them, honking. The impact knocked the wind out of Joey, but Masaru's armor spared him.

"Think there's a little boy inside this one?" Joey tried to grin.

Masaru growled. "Not even close to funny."

Nemsky came stomping over as Masaru flung himself upright. Blades clashed a half dozen times as they circled. The harsh buzz of vibro claws against Masaru's sword reminded Joey of an old alarm clock. A speeding car interrupted their duel, forcing them to dive to either side away from the screeching horn.

After several exchanges, Nemsky again underestimated Masaru's speed and left himself open. Masaru threw himself off his feet, combining an upswing with a backward roll. The katana severed the vibro claws just past the knuckle as Masaru slid under them, sending two white-hot blades twisting into the air. One wedged into the side of a passing car, the other stuck into the road between Joey's knees, making him squeak. The younger Kurotai completed the maneuver standing, and lunged at his opponent.

The general was more agile than his body appeared, and leaned out of the way of several more swings with successive backward steps. Anticipating Masaru's next stroke, he caught him by the forearm and hauled him into the air, around in a circle, and put him headfirst through the window of a passing car. The vehicle lost control and swerved into a support structure a short distance down the road.

Nemsky turned his attention to Joey and scowled. "Now, my friend, you will learn why I am called the Butcher." He leaned on the end of his words with a grandiose flair.

Olive green liquid burbled from his severed arm, but it didn't seem to slow him down. Joey sighed at his weapon. It felt almost pointless to shoot this thing. His little class 3 pistol couldn't do enough damage fast enough to a doll, and he had nowhere to run.

A gleam of inspiration hit him, and he aimed at the stalking monster. The Russian laughed at him, not even slowing down. When the aim point shifted without warning, Nemsky paused in confusion. Joey lit off a shot, savaging the right front tire of an approaching vehicle into a spray of rubber fragments. The car lurched in the direction of the lost tire—right into Nemsky. The car came to an abrupt halt while the general sailed into the air. Twenty meters away, Anatoly landed on his cheek and slid for several feet before going into a tumble. Plumes of smoke oozed around the huge dent in the hood of the car while luminous blue fluid froze over the front tires. Joey's laughter stopped when Nemsky got back up, now with a half-metal face, and he took off running around the truck with the general on his heels.

After the second lap, Joey dropped into a knee slide as he rounded the corner. Anatoly thought he had slipped and prepared for the kill, but Joey had done the limbo under Masaru's waiting blade. The general's dodge was slow, and the katana scored on Nemsky's right thigh, almost amputating the leg. Enough damage came from the hit that the Myofiber muscles failed, dumping Anatoly to the ground.

Masaru maneuvered for another strike when an unexpected punch to the shin caught him off guard. The leg offered no resistance to the metal fist. His armor splintered into black gleaming shards as his shin bent forward. The force of the hit blasted his legs out from under him, slamming him to the ground on his chest.

A scream of barbaric laughter erupted from the Russian. He raised his arm to crush Masaru's skull. Joey fired again, sending four bullets into his chest and two into the side of the head. Bits of artificial skin and metal flew, but the large blue spark that flashed out of the side of the head did little to stop the downward fist.

Masaru twisted out from under the attack, leaving the doll pounding a dent in the road surface. Neuralware on, he rolled back as a blur, lancing the katana downward through Anatoly's spine into the ground. The general strained to reach Masaru's face but his fingers fell short. His one remaining hand clawed at the ground, but the mechanical body's systems already experienced critical failure, and strength had gone. Synthetic fingernails scraped shreds of traction coating away from the metal road for several swipes, until the body fell limp, a pool of translucent green fluid expanding beneath him.

Both men lay in silence as Joey crept up on them.

Masaru sat up, arranging the noodle of his leg back into a human shape. Flicks of his eye navigated the armor's control system and triggered the internal stim injectors, which surrounded him in a luminous green mist as they all fired at once. His pain changed to a sublime grin as the meds saturated his body and he fell flat on his back. The leg was still a mess. He would need an hour or two in a tank to repair the bone, but he wouldn't bleed to death. He drew the katana from the vanquished doll, and sneered at him.

"Well, that was exciting." Joey glanced at the inert machine and looked over his shoulder at the wrecked car from which his friend had crawled.

Masaru patted his armor. "Best three hundred grand I ever spent."

They both cringed at a sudden roar. The general was in midair, screaming. He landed on Joey, driving him to the ground with an iron grip around his throat. A savage growl flowed past a manic grin. Sparks crackled over its half-metal face as the laughter broke into digitized chunks of sound. White neural memory fluid leaked from every opening in his head, including several made by bullets.

The strength left the doll's hand as Masaru's katana sank inches into Nemsky's side. Warm liquid drenched Joey's chest. As sharp as the Nano blade was, the plastisteel spine and all the internal components had offered more resistance than his battered muscles could overcome. He jerked the sword out as Joey drew his legs up and shoved the heap of parts to the side.

A flash of clear synthetic diamond streaked past Joey's face an instant before the katana plunged into Nemsky's collarbone, stopping halfway into the torso. A second shower of olive liquid exploded out of the gashes. Nemsky's roaring degenerated completely into electric warbles. Erratic twitching limbs froze in place and he fell headfirst into the road like a mannequin. Spasms tossed him about as the broken voice spouted random words in English as well as Russian. The babble reached a crescendo pitch, going higher and higher until it blurred into an electronic squeal before falling quiet. Joey lifted his gun, blinked once, and emptied the rest of his ammunition into the body—just to be sure.

Gasping for breath, Joey fumbled with his NetMini. Sirens wailed in the distance. Joey flashed a giant, bloody smile at her.

"Nina…" rasped Joey, more whisper than voice. "You're not gonna believe who I just ran into."

MISSING PERSONS

An elderly woman wrapped in a torn brown coat tottered along a street packed with rag-clad citizens. She hunched over a battered and sparking hover cart full of old bags and trash. Her scarf-wrapped face kept a cautious gaze behind a curtain of yellowing grey hair, as if afraid to make eye contact with any of the people around her. Passing clouds of steam and smoke glowed orange and pink from holographic characters spread above the building fronts, Cyrillic words that shifted and played in the evening light. Tall women clad in skimpy garments made of light chatted up prospective clients at the opening of an alley, ignoring the little grandmother. In every direction, stretched brownish-grey concrete, green steel, and despair.

Four men in black suits spilled into the crowd from a building a few blocks down. With gleaming pistols in their hands, they battered their way into the crowd like farmers scything wheat. Bodies flew to both sides as they advanced. They disregarded men, but threw every woman to the ground and held her down long enough to run a portable scanner. All four stood tall at the same instant, shouting in Russian across the crowd. One pointed down the street and they charged.

The men in fancy suits shoved the old woman into her junk cart as they forced their way past her, sending the frictionless thing drifting into the road. She clutched her scarf and screamed. A man in a striped blue shirt abandoned a large duffel bag and leapt to grab it, saving her from the blur of passing cars.

"*Spasiba*," said the old woman, accepting the cart with a grateful bow.

The man said a few things but she just smiled. He chuckled, taking her for senile and walking away after collecting his bag. Fearful of the chaos on the thoroughfare, the woman toddled off into an alley, leaving the gunmen to thrash the crowd.

Miniscule pieces of trash on the ground drew great shadows along the walls in the yellow light from the hover cart's lifter. The nightmarish images warped and stretched as she moved. Vagrants paid her little heed as she passed among them as one of their own, too busy muttering in the dark to notice an old woman with a cart full of junk.

At the end of the block, she wandered into a vacant lot and smiled at the quiet isolation. Feeling secure, she picked through her bags. Trash, old purses, a pair of jeans, and a boot with a hole in all moved out of the way until she found the light. Her hands, gnarled and shaking, dug deeper and seized an eight-inch square tile, an inch thick with a glowing surface. She drew it closer to her face, caressing the glassy surface. A man in a Russian military uniform smiled up at her, the color of his coat hidden behind a ridiculous amount of medals and award.

The bleak sky behind him gave off light that underlined every wrinkle upon her cheeks with darkness. In the alley, the object shone like a star amid a sea of blackness. The whispering vagrants quieted, staring with greed in their eyes. Her lips pulled back from the few stalwart yellow teeth that still clung to dying gums in a grotesque, yet genuine, smile.

With a fearful glance at the alley, she buried the object in her basket and extinguished the light. The cart rattled and buzzed as she crept several blocks more, past the rusting hulk of an old truck and up the ramp to a tram station. People stared derisively at her, pulling their belongings close, leaving a bubble of empty space around her as she waited. When the transit shuttle arrived, she shambled out the doors.

The old woman let off a wheezing groan and settled into the seat with her back to the window. She kept her head down as other people shuffled past her. Eventually the crowd stopped, and the tram got underway. One wrinkled hand clutched the cart, keeping it near her as the shuttle jostled with the journey. Several stops later, only a handful of passengers remained. The train neared the border. She poked at the trash in the hover cart, checking to make sure that none of the glow from her precious object escaped.

Harsh lights flooded in from narrow windows as the tram slid to a halt. Half a dozen men in maroon armor with Cyrillic writing on the shoulders stormed in and went from person to person. She kept her head down until they stopped in front of her and spoke in Russian.

The old woman rummaged around in her torn purse. Her decaying grey sweater kept getting in the way, making the soldiers grumble and shift about. One brandished a rifle at her and she cowered behind her hands. Another looked unhappy with his squad mate threatening a little old woman and they traded words.

When she found a clear plastic card, she flashed a grandmother's smile and held it up to the men. A picture, thirty years younger, shimmered into view upon its surface. Yanina Simonova appeared in six languages under the image. The holographic pane that unfolded above it indicated she was on her way to Britain to visit her granddaughter, Nastaya. An official notice, with an executive seal, indicated the younger woman stayed there on a student visa.

The soldiers exchanged glances, edging away from the little grandmother. Not one of them made eye contact any more.

"*Prosti, prosti, eto prosto protsedura.*" The one who threatened her forced an uneasy smile.

Their sergeant covered her ID with his hand, gesturing at her to put it away.

She bowed her head in a pleasant nod. "*Ya ponimayu. Spokoynoy nochi.*"

'Student visa' was code for covert operative. The ACC almost never gave normal citizens permission to leave the ACC.

"*Davay, davay.*" The sergeant swatted the nearest man on the back, pushing him down the aisle toward the next person.

The soldiers cleared the car, leaving her alone in the car. Ten minutes later, she was the only one left on the entire tram.

Heavy metal clunks came in succession along the tram, the sound passing as doors slammed from back to front. When it stopped, the intense light faded. A minute later, the cabin lurched forward and the tram accelerated, hurtling across barren, scorched ground on a path that would take it out of ACC Europe. Enormous black and white faces faded in over the nothing. Echoing voices spouted propaganda catch phrases. Something about being all 'in this' together, hard work equals prosperity, and 'we're watching.' The old woman closed her eyes, jostling about on the seat as the train raced toward an immense black wall on the horizon, stretching as far as visible in both directions. Covered with flashing lights and foreboding machinery, it grew into the sky as she neared. Dozens of stories tall, a circuit-like pattern of cyan light-paths crisscrossed its surface.

The tram plunged into the darkness of a tunnel, a needle into the side of a giant.

When light returned, the old woman was gone. In her place, a six foot two blonde clad head to toe in gloss black. She examined her breasts, and loosed a sound that melted from a vixen's haughty laugh to the gravely chuckle of an aging man in a black western hat. The shape changed again—the ACC secret agent became the dark cowboy.

A victorious smile bared his jagged teeth as he brushed his long black coat aside and pulled the glowing object into view to stare into the face of Anatoly Nemsky.

"*Ya nashol tebya, tovarishch.*" He saluted the data tile. "*Bliad!*"

He grumbled, picking at a screen that opened to his right. He grabbed a highlight on a line of Cyrillic characters and threw it up onto the word 'English'.

"Ahh, there we go."

Joey had found him, deep in an ACC file system. Knowing he had gotten in and out without being found kept a smug curl in his lip for the rest of the ride, enjoying his victory over the protocols that prevented netizens in ACC territories from changing their appearance in cyberspace.

"Those idiots are probably still looking for Natasha Bimbonova."

With time to kill, he decided to examine the data object.

The contents of the tile caused the coarse white streaks of steel wool he called eyebrows to lift. Surprise didn't often show upon the dark cowboy's face. This information would need to reach Nina.

The hour or two it took to ride was closer to five or six minutes in real time—longer still when entering ACC territory. The network blocked universal logouts, forcing anyone in cyberspace to exit via designated checkpoints or risk a fried brain. When he arrived back in the West City part of the net, his curiosity got the better of him. With Nemsky out of the way, he turned his attention to the Division 9 section of the police net.

Nina had been thrilled to see Nemsky dead, but her exuberance faded when she learned he was a doll. Joey wanted to know everything he could about her. At some point during their long conversation, she had slipped and mentioned the name of her boss. After finding him in the roster, the aged gunslinger morphed into the likeness of Harold Hardin. Spoofing an authorized user made network infiltration much easier, but this was still Division 9, and his deck was a pile of junk. Most would call him insane for even trying to get in there with a grade 3 deck. Joey looked at it as a harsher time limit before they found him. With a specific target in mind, he went right for the classified personnel files.

A few net minutes later, he stared at a data object with video of Nina's surgery, twirling it between his fingers. Joey read enough to learn she had been mangled to the point where a doll body was necessary to keep her alive.

He almost dropped the tile.

As odd as it had been for a little woman to throw him around, he hadn't suspected it. Having been a fan of cheesy martial arts vids, he had little trouble fantasizing that had some super-secret training. The audio of the attack that had leaked from his deck left him wondering how horribly mangled she'd been. His brain had given him a nightmare of a twisted wretch in a hover-chair, only able to speak from an electronic voice box. Nina's doll body was an order of magnitude more pleasant, so much so that he failed to even consider it a possibility.

He gazed at the surgery file, thinking about the way she looked at New Hope. He drew a heavy breath and put it back in the data construct that it came from. He didn't need to see that. Those images were the kind of thing he would never get out of his head as long as he lived. The next file contained information about Vincent as well as the Division 5 interdiction team that saved her life.

Some men might have been put off by the thought of a doll, but something about her made it not matter. Joey searched for an explanation. She wasn't the same as one of those sex parlor toys. Those amounted to nothing more than computers with no emotions. Nina still had a soul and a brain, and Joey wasn't too big on the idea of having kids anyway. Besides, the city had tons of orphans if ever the desire hit him. She would never gain weight, grow old, or become sick. Ever since he had seen Avril that night, every idle thought he had went back to her.

The dark one chuckled. "What the hell is wrong with me?"

He grinned, daydreaming about sharing living space with such a lethal being. It would be like playing tennis with a live hand grenade—how could he resist? The beeping timer reminded him, and he warped outside to the public net.

A sparkling square of light opened in front of him, chiming in a melodic wave of sound like crystals in the wind. An incoming vid from Alex beckoned, no doubt with a job offer. Joey thought about the Neko-girl at the cybershop. A little more money and he could get the Janus. He shrugged as he accepted. Maybe he could try his luck with the cyberware merchant if Nina didn't work out.

"What?" Joey looked at the sanctimonious frown that stared back at him.

Alex spoke for a few minutes in French at Joey's middle finger.

"Are you done?" He waved the finger back and forth.

Alex switched to English. "When are you going to learn a real language?"

"As soon as you admit you're a fancy boy."

"You just refuse to better yourself."

"You fool yourself into thinking you're superior to everyone around you.

People that know they are don't have to act." The dark cowboy tipped his hat to Alex.

Alex waved and made a patronizing eye roll. "I don't know why I even bother."

"Because you need me." The old gunslinger held his arms wide as if waiting for a hug. "What'cha got this time?" Joey adored watching Alex cringe at the sound of his voice.

"Nothing grandiose. You'll probably fall asleep but it's a rush job so the pay is respectable. Thirty grand to get two years of health insurance claim information from Triton Manufacturing Corp."

Joey rubbed his chin. "So, someone wants to see who's getting hurt at TMC?"

"All claim information for the past two years. They want everything from payee data to a list of who was on the plan and at what level. Also, all communications related to health benefits. Thirty grand for the lot."

Joey sighed, shaking his head. "Yeah you're right, that sounds boring as hell. But I suppose I can do it for you for forty. Boredom tax."

With a sigh and a nod, Alex disconnected.

TMC MANUFACTURED MOSTLY CONSUMER GOODS AND ELECTRONICS. THEIR OUTPUT included holo-bars, datapads, toys, e-razors, NetMinis, and just about every little bit of consumer gadgetry out there. All the things they produced were long established items devoid of innovation or anything requiring great amounts of security. The company was so large and produced so much they didn't need to make great leaps forward. Simply supplying their existing customer base with replacement parts and small upgrades kept them profitable.

The side effect of having little to hide took the form of skimping on network security. Much to Joey's dismay, he got in with such ease that he almost thought the network public. He walked across the simulated office past the workers as if he belonged there, going all the way to the data nodes without so much as a "good evening." He chuckled at the featureless blue-lined walls of shining black glass. The company hadn't even bothered to build up the network past the basic grid of cyberspace. He paced in a circle, stared at the roof, and sang off-key while his deck copied files. The expansive data wouldn't fit on his deck's internal memory. He had to burn it out to a holodisk, a process that would take over an hour of cyberspace time.

With nothing better to do, he examined the network map, playing mental games plotting efficient routes between nodes, factoring interlink speed and hop count until something caught his eye. One hallway, tucked away at the edge of the network, seemed to run around the far northeast on a path to nowhere. That needled at his curiosity and made the waiting even harder to endure.

As soon as the copy was complete, he ran out of the room and sprinted. He left the unfinished gloss-walled interior behind, entering drab white and blue office corridors. Joey jogged past a game room where some employees were winding down, past a video presentation on Korean market share, and down a long hallway full of control nodes for manufacturing equipment. No one bothered to question his presence.

The anomaly took the form of a plain office hallway with no doors that ended at a blank beige wall with a single water cooler propped up against it. The sight bothered him to the point he stared at the path to nowhere for several minutes until spotting a tiny crack of light. The Teradyne Silver ran analysis soft after analysis soft, chewing on one algorithm after another in an effort to scan for any hidden data. In cyberspace, this process animated as the dark cowboy picking at the crack and eventually peeling open a doorway that led to an extravagant corridor covered in pure white marble. Behind him, a door of dark polished wood clicked shut.

The opulence reminded him of the approach to the executive bathrooms in a high-end corporate headquarters. His boots echoed as he walked down the length of fanciness, folding his hands behind him in a mimic of a corporate fat cat. His stride ended with an abrupt bang that reverberated as his chin led the way into an invisible barrier. Nanoseconds later, red letters appeared in front of him in midair: "Access Denied."

"Fucking hate security interconnects." Joey rubbed his nose while sending mental commands to his deck to begin attacking the protections.

To Joey's delight, the hallway was a bit on the difficult side. Whatever waited at the end was something not meant to be seen by anyone but whoever put it there.

A silver revolver flew up from the dark cowboy's hip and spun into firing position. Joey's mind called on a Cryptomancer soft and thousands of gossamer silver threads stretched from the old one's hair while the program reached into the unrefreshed memory buffers of every terminal on the net, searching for fragments of passwords. He sighted down the barrel. A single bullet in the shape of a vaporous black skull flew into the air and froze in space. Subconsciously, Joey combined the results with another routine to spoof credentials or fake out the detection algorithm. When he found one that worked, the bullet streaked forward and shattered the glass wall. Strewn bits of broken glass shimmered from red to green, as fragmented letters attempted to spell "Access Granted."

He ducked under spinning shards of false glass that reintegrated into a solid barrier behind him. At the end of the corridor, a heavy chrome door seemed out of place against the marble and wood. It looked like a bank vault, a translation of its security. He grabbed the frame and forced himself at it. Pixilation happened at his fingertips as solid steel gave way to green grid lines and flickering text. Flashes of light washed over the old man's face as he strained, tracing circuit paths beneath thin venous cheeks. The door didn't yield, but a distant noise alerted him to a fast approaching network trace.

Trace constructs ran from the nearest security node toward the location of an unexpected event. One was on their way here. His knowledge that the network would go into alarm mode if it saw him turned into fear. If he remained inside when that happened, the company's security men would know where he was in the real world, and then he would need a new apartment.

He threw a pair of brute force constructs at the door, manifesting as overweight ranch hands with lever-action rifles. They 'shot' it, attempting to overload the security routines with random codes that changed based on how the system reacted. Red glowing light welled up from the other side of hall. The dark one sank his fingers into the steel, roaring at it. It didn't yield. The light intensified as the trace rounded the corner. A mass formed the approximation of a human form, made of swirling strands of glowing text. It floated closer, tinting the white marble with castoff light.

Joey screamed with anger and slammed himself into the door one last time. His skin melted and stuck to the metal, a plastic man on a hot plate. One of the dozen infiltration routines found a flaw in the defense crypto and the door became insubstantial to him. Liquid flesh seeped into the door like water into a sponge, exuding on the other side, dumping him in a heap.

The riflemen evaporated.

Bewildered, the hunter-trace oozed over to the empty space where he once stood, head swiveling left and right. Sensing nothing awry, it de-spawned, threads of crimson letters unwinding and expanding until it vanished entirely.

The old one dusted himself off, lifting an eyebrow at a row of ordinary-looking file cabinets. It appeared to contain data, but had a partition node attribute. Most network designers used partition nodes to store purposeless things such as hobby rooms or games, not data.

The temptation to search them proved irresistible.

Joey opened the nearest one and browsed the tiles. The more he read, the wider his eyes became. Thousands of records showed TMC had engaged in a clandestine business relationship with another company, Naturahealth Pharmaceuticals. From the looks of it, TMC would schedule its employees for routine competency tests or computer based training sessions during which they would be knocked out with gas. Once unconscious, NatPhar borrowed them for use as human test subjects involving all manner of experimental medical technology. Hours later, they would wake up back at their desk, unaware of what happened.

Joey froze. He remembered Kenny's wife had worked for TMC before she went crazy. He fired off a DataMole with the order to search for the name Cathy Marlon. As soon as it returned with a file in its mouth, Joey's heart sank. He took the tile, holding it limp at his side for a moment until he found the urge to look.

Her experiment involved a developmental anti-addiction treatment. They conditioned her to crave E-14 and then tried the test procedure. A lot of the medical jargon and stats went right over Joey's head, but he could at least get out of it that their test backfired and made the addiction worse, making E-14 as addictive as Lace.

It was anyone's guess how many of these unwilling test subjects suffered mystery ailments. Once again, he held data that could make him a lot of money if he could make himself mercenary enough to sell it.

"Dammit, Dad."

He would feel guilty for not exposing them. Now he understood why someone had hired him to get the claim data. Someone else, probably a PI or a lawyer, wanted to build a lawsuit.

Joey's brain told his deck to place a vid call.

Kenny's head appeared in front of him. "Yo? What's up?"

"Hey man. It's time for me to repay all the favors you do for me."

"Are you okay?" Kenny leaned in, offering a concerned expression at Joey's absent mirth.

Joey threw the data tile at Kenny's head, sending the file over the line to

Kenny's NetMini. It hung there for a moment and then boomeranged back to his hand.

"I know what happened to Cathy. Read that. There's a lot of medical bullshit in there, maybe someone can use it to help her."

"What?" Kenny's face flushed. "What are you talking about?"

Joey sighed. "Her old employer rented her to a pharma corp to be used as a guinea pig without her knowledge. They made her addicted to E-14 on purpose and fucked it up bad when they tested a cure."

A loud smash preceded Alyssa's startled shriek in the background.

The digital Kenny reintegrated as he walked back over to the VidPhone. "Thanks… I gotta go."

"I'll stop by soo"—the line dropped.

He opened another panel, which rang for a long time and ended without answer. He tried again. This time, an attractive young blonde appeared and almost shrieked at the sight of the old gunslinger.

"Who the hell are you?"

Letting his avatar shift back to his real face, he smiled. "Remember me?"

Kimberly Brightman stared. She knew the face but couldn't remember why. "No… How did you get my number?"

"I have my ways." He smiled. "Let's just say that I gave you a ride home."

"Oh!" Her composure faltered. Red tinted around her eyes as she sank into a nearby chair. "I never got your name…"

"Joey. Hey, I found some stuff you might be interested in putting on the bots. About time you one upped that dried up old bitch." He explained what he knew about her trip to the Badlands being Donna's idea.

Kimberly broke down in tears. "That's true? I saw it on the tabloids, but you know…"

"Once you get your face on this story, no one will remember her." He hurled the entire file cabinet into her image.

Her crying lessened the more she paged through the data. "Oh my god… Is this for real?"

Joey tipped his hat. "I trust you know what to do with it?"

Kimberly scrambled at her terminal. "I have to meet you. What's your PID, where can I find you?"

"Sure, we'll figure out a—"

Boom.

The door disintegrated under a concussive explosion that hurled a rain of steel fragments and a cloud of digital smoke from the space it once stood. A man in a black tank top and grey-on-white camo pants walked in with a fatalistic glare. Joey knew the face. He had spent an hour talking about him with Nina.

Itai Korin.

"Something tells me you're not here for this." Joey waved the data. "Kim, let me call you back."

Itai clenched his fists as muscular arms bulged. "I know you talked to the police. I can't have you helping them."

Baggy pants obscured the exact position of Itai's legs as he circled. He had no visible weapons but that meant nothing here.

"Guess you're not too creative a guy… no special avatar?" Joey leaned back and flung his coat off his holsters.

Itai's head tilted down. "Time to grow up, boy. No more cowboys and Indians."

The laugh that Joey summoned in response never came out of his mouth. Itai turned into a blur of color led by a fist. Joey scraped out of the path by a split second. Red hexagons flashed in the corner of his eye, warning him of CPU heat. Joey hadn't expected such a dangerous attack from an ex-commando. Itai landed, shattering the file cabinet and filling the air with a snow of white fragments and scattering data tiles. A spider of pain picked across his mind as wiring overloaded with his deck's attempt to arrest the incoming harmful data.

Itai stood up from the crater, spinning on his heels with a military pivot. Joey fired, but the commando swatted the smoking skull away as if it was a child's toy. Fragments of filing cabinet snowed, pausing in time as the dark cowboy raised the silver pistol again. Itai vanished and appeared to the gunslinger's left. The backhand strike caught him across the face and smeared the old man into a long stripe of color on the wall, fringed with sparks and disintegrating pixels. Error text burned into Joey's retinas as the scent of burned silicon flooded his nostrils. Blue cartoon microchips with bug eyes danced in the upper right of his vision warning that much of his buffer space had physically burned out.

Only once had Joey been hit like that before—on Mars. Itai must be using one mother of a deck to hit that hard. The piece of shit Teradyne Silver, Grade 3, wouldn't withstand another barrage that potent. He peeled himself away from the wall and the flat cowboy condensed back to normal. He tried to disconnect but something Itai had done prevented the logout. A trace of panic rose in the back of Joey's mind. He hadn't seen Itai use a Flypaper soft, and the running programs list didn't show one active on him.

Joey hated not understanding things.

If Itai caught him again, he would wake up in the real world break-dancing with a fried deck. Of course, as damaged as his deck was, he had become vulnerable to Black ICE, which could kill him for real. He had no idea if Itai had that capability, but it wasn't a risk he wanted to take. He ran out of the room, sending a few more shots Itai's way, but the Israeli just walked through them like smoke rings.

It made sense how angry and confused Nina had been at not being able to find him. The list of hackers that could bitch slap him like this was a short one. He assumed that Proscion could, if reputation was to be believed, but he had previously operated under the hope that anyone that made the list would have the courtesy to be a career hacker, not a part time soldier. The mere thought that a "dabbler" was a serious threat made his blood boil.

This had to be someone else just making himself *look* like the Israeli.

Itai followed him into the hallway, the slow plodding walk of a killer from a horror vid. Despite Joey's sprinting, Itai's deliberate pace never seemed to be any farther away. The third time he looked over his shoulder, a massive sniper rifle phased into existence in Itai's hands, appearing first as a blue wireframe before it became indistinguishable from reality. Joey leapt, calling a Bunnyrabbit soft to boost his leap. The program lag-spiked the network segment, except for Joey, creating a short burst of net speed that threw him around the next corner, in a hail of slow motion environment fragments from Itai's shot.

"Shit."

He chose a hallway with a dead end and one door.

In its damaged state, the deck's breach process slowed to a crawl. Itai strolled around the corner while Joey struggled against the secure barrier behind him. Five code cracker softs ran in tandem, but in cyberspace, the dark cowboy rattled an unmoving doorknob. If the person in the Itai suit just wanted to punt him off the network, they wouldn't have locked him down. Something in the evil stare told him that he was about to be hit with live current into his real brain.

The formation of blacklight flames around Itai's hands confirmed his suspicion.

Joey's face reddened. Despite knowing it pointless, he kept trying to force his deck to accept a logout. Had he not been a fear junkie, he might have panicked. Out of his inappropriate calm, an idea hit him—something he had never before even considered doing.

Joey raised the gun toward Itai, causing a few teeth to appear inside a faint grin. The blacklight grew into giant flaming spheres that painted the walls purple as Itai drew his hands back to hurl it.

Joey snapped his arm back to put the barrel under his own chin and fired.

Itai's shout of rage at losing his quarry disintegrated into digitized noise. Joey's point of view fell and tilted right. Two black-cored violet fireballs slowed in midair and stopped. Itai's face froze in time, red and bulging with veins. Sound ceased. The stationary flames and burning anger lingered in his mind's eye, seared into his visual cortex by a spike of electricity as the input from the deck stopped—lingering on the last second of imagery. Then everything went black.

Attacking himself had blown out the last critical circuits of his deck. A bricked deck trumped whatever voodoo Itai used to keep him there, and sent his consciousness spiraling back toward reality. He endured a disorienting and painful ride on a kaleidoscopic puke-o-tron, but it was still a far better option than having his brain baked.

Colors, flavors, and smells swirled around in a massive migraine that took the form of a net of hot wires around his brain. The spiraling tunnel undulated, jerking around in all directions until the endpoint opened into a sea of pale grey—the floor of his apartment. It came in for several close ups, kissing him in the face each time. For some minutes, he floundered on the ground, out of control like a fish on dry land. Foam sizzled past his clenched teeth, a skeleton hand of fire gripped his brain and squeezed, and the taste of copper flooded his mouth and rode up along the back of his throat.

A sudden flood of bright light filled the room and made Joey's heart skip a beat. White light was bad—that meant brain damage.

The wave of emotion chasing that thought broke upon the beach of reality as he felt hands grab him. The light was real.

"Where is she, scumbag?" A deep voice with the timbre of a weightlifter shouted in his ear.

He was faintly aware of being slammed into a wall.

Joey gurgled. "Wa bera ooo?"

Black silence returned.

CELL PHONE

D rop by drop, blood leaked from Joey's nose, falling warm upon his bare chest. The tickle was intolerable, but his arms refused to move to wipe it. His head prickled with sharp burning threads in time with the mental image of black lightning searing his cerebellum. If not that, a demon acupuncturist poked red-hot needles into his brain.

Even breathing hurt, as if the pain in his mind from the virtual ass kicking wasn't bad enough, his consciousness returned to an ocean of agony all over his body.

Frigidity in the wall he leaned on seeped into his back, numbing his shoulders. A circular metal drain in the dark grey concrete taunted him with distant burbling. The cold water that saturated him, and most of the room, swirled into its waiting maw. The once-white walls outlined a small room of only four by eight feet. Aside from the drain, only a yellow energy field broke the monotonous drab. It thrummed just beyond two dark blurs at the bottom of his vision that seemed to twitch whenever he tried to move his feet.

"Ready for round two?" A deep voice came from behind the curtain of light.

"You know it. This little dirt bag can't have much left."

Joey's head wobbled around like a ball balanced on a stick. His numb arms refused to move, and each time he tried to sit up, a pain stabbed his chest as if someone had left a knife embedded in him.

The yellow field disappeared, darkening the area. Two hulking shadows fell over him. He took in enough detail to recognize blue police uniforms.

"Which one of you is Hans?" Joey coughed up blood.

"Very funny." The closer of the two men lifted him by his shoulders and slammed him into the wall. "Let's talk about Hayley Roth."

Joey's lack of flailing made him realize his hands were cuffed behind him. That explained why he couldn't wipe his nose. The pain of the impact made him wheeze.

"I gotta blow my nose."

"Look shitbag, we know you have her. You think you're going to grab a cop's kid and get away with it?"

He punched Joey twice in the gut, causing a bubble of bloody mucous to fall out of his mouth.

Joey gasped, on his feet only due to the man holding him up. "I didn't kidnap anyone."

The officer flung him to the ground on his chest. The impact knocked the air from his lungs, and sprayed a red smear on the ground. So much pain flooded him that he almost didn't notice the boot catch him in the side and flip him onto his back.

"We could do this all night."

Lying in silence, Joey focused on breathing. The two Neanderthals crowded over him, blocking the light.

He wheezed. "Hey could you lean a little to the left, the light's in my eye."

"You motherf"—The cop on the right went to pound him but the other one grabbed his arm.

"Hey, hey. We won't find her if he dies." They traded stares for a moment.

The angry one bent down and pulled him standing by his chest hair. Joey's mouth hung agape in a silent scream until they shoved him into the wall. His feet slid apart and his back dragged along the metal. The impact of ass to ground traveled up his spine and kicked vomit out of his throat.

"Excuse me." An educated voice interrupted from the hallway. "Perhaps I can be of assistance?"

Joey slid over sideways, coughing his airway clear of bile. When the convulsions ceased, he peered with his one open eye at another man in the hallway. His uniform black, he knocked at the door to the cell. Both of the officers turned and saluted him, rigid at his presence.

"Good evening, Lieutenant."

"Sir," said the other with a salute.

"We got this, sir." The larger of the two waved an arm at Joey as he spoke.

"Do you?" Lieutenant Oliver walked in and looked down at Joey.

"Yeah. Div 0 doesn't need to get involved with this shithead." The smaller cop chimed in. "Nothing psionic about him."

Oliver's hands remained folded behind his back as an amused smirk settled on his face. "Command doesn't want to take any chances when the child of one of our own has been abducted. He can't keep secrets from me."

"This sick bastard knows where she is. Poor thing is probably terrified if she's still even alive." He went to punch Joey but hesitated at Oliver's raised hand.

"He knows her, but he's not responsible for taking her." The Lieutenant looked at Joey then back at the two huge cops. "Don't you need to give the prisoner his phone call?"

Officer Alvin laughed. "Nice one. That shit hasn't happened for a hundred years. Besides who is this fringer scumbag going to call?"

Lieutenant Oliver stared deep into Alvin's eyes, speaking in a slow deliberate tone. His voice rolled off every consonant, over-enunciating each word with painful precision. "Don't you need to give the prisoner his phone call?" Alvin's facial expression fell into a dumfounded stare as overwhelming compassion and trust welled up from nowhere.

"Uhh, yeah… we should give him his phone call." Officer Eddie Alvin turned and walked out of the cell at a zombie's gait.

Officer Wilkes glared at Oliver. "Did you just…"

The lieutenant glanced at him. "I didn't want him to make me think he was disregarding an order."

Wilkes had a feeling his partner was just the victim of some psionic crap. Witnessing this unassuming man stare at him without a trace of fear flattened him against the wall, his distrust of Division 0 deepening. His wariness of psionics dueled with his anger at feeling impotent. Men that small never pushed him around.

Eddie Alvin returned with a secure NetMini and handed it to Lieutenant Oliver, smiling like a five-year-old boy trying to please his granddad. It was a monitored unit intended for prisoners to use. At Oliver's instruction, they released Joey from his restraints and handed him the device, after hosing him down again. Lieutenant Oliver shooed the patrol officers into the hallway and stood in the doorway as Joey's spinning brain tried to remember what the object in his lap was.

"All due respect, Lieutenant, how can we just let him sit there when a little girl's life is at risk?"

Oliver inhaled a long, slow breath. "Officer Alvin, the prisoner's emotional radiance is not that of a guilty man. In fact"—he raised a curious eyebrow—"he is concerned about her well-being on a level I would more expect from a sibling than a total stranger."

"We know it's this fringer," shouted Wilkes. "We got evidence."

Joey dialed a call from the loaner NetMini, listening to a discussion of how someone had called in a tip that he kidnapped the daughter of a cop with the intent of abusing and killing her. They even sent Joey's face and address, as well as video of him stuffing a struggling, bound adolescent girl into the trunk of a car.

Seeing Joey's conversation end, Oliver looked at him with a knowing smile. "Nice choice. So… tell me what happened?"

Joey felt distrust melt away, out of his control. A feeling of solace washed over him as he stared at this man in the black uniform. Before a minute passed, the officer in black felt like a long-lost brother that could be trusted with any secret. Without even thinking about it, he rambled on about how he met Hayley and the whole Cleopatra thing. As far as he knew, she sat at home waiting for a horrible father who had no time for her.

Lieutenant Oliver listened, nodding along. The two cops shifted, about ten feet back in the hallway like a pair of hungry Dobermans denied their meal.

The door at the end of the holding area opened with a hiss. Both officers turned and looked at the person that walked in, and blinked.

"Well, well… If it isn't Princess Nina." Officer Alvin folded his arms and smirked at her.

"Well god damn." Wilkes chuckled. "Guess you finally decided to come off your medical leave? What happened, they wouldn't let you milk it any longer?"

She approached with her hands in the pockets of her coat. "I'm taking custody of your prisoner."

They continued snickering.

"Why don't you go paint your nails or something before you get hurt?" Wilkes gave her a dismissive wave.

"We got this. Wouldn't want you to have to do any *actual* work until you can get the cushy job." Alvin pointed, his voice dripped with condescension. "Did you come back to get another partner to kill?"

The surge of emotion from Nina distracted Oliver from Joey. He jogged over with his hand up. "Everyone calm down."

She closed her eyes and her fists creaked. "I'm not going to ask you two shitheads again. Get the fuck out of my way right now."

The two men stopped laughing and glanced at each other. Wilkes looked at Nina and realized his head didn't tilt down at the usual angle.

Alvin's face reddened. "Who the hell you think you're talking to?" He reached for her shoulder.

Nina grabbed him by the center of his chest armor and hauled him around once before slamming him into the wall with his feet off the ground. The cinder blocks behind him crunched, and he gasped for breath under his cracking armor.

Oliver held both hands at her. "Nina, don't."

She stared at Alvin. Her eyes held no trace of fear, no trace of innocence, and no hint that she would hesitate. Her thoughts swam with memories: stuffed in an armor cabinet, duct taped naked in the shower, locked in trash units for hours, having her desk drawers glued shut, tricked into a holding cell to look for evidence only to be locked in it all weekend long, and all manner of other indignities she had suffered at his hands. Each memory pushed him another quarter inch deeper in the wall.

Her eyes closed as the phrase 'another partner to kill' repeated in her memory. She pushed him harder into the wall with a snarl. Cinder blocks collapsed with loud pops, sending fragments tumbling to the floor.

"Nina!" Oliver's voice chipped at the edge of her attention. "Please..." He kept his mind poised to yank her anger out from under her if he had to.

Joey slithered out into the corridor, leaving a trail of blood on the ground. When Nina saw the condition he was in, Alvin changed walls. The impact to the other side took out one of his ribs. He had grabbed her arm but couldn't budge it. No matter how hard he squeezed, she ignored him.

Lieutenant Oliver put his hand on her shoulder and reached into her mind. Her level of anger ebbed, held at bay from the point where she lost reason. She shifted at his touch, ready to attack, but calmed when she saw who it was. Oliver's eyes darted back and forth from Nina to Joey. Something else swirled among the rage.

"Nina, please don't. I can feel how angry you are. These two aren't worth it."

"You know I could come up with paperwork to justify it." She glared into Alvin's eyes. "I finally got that promotion, Eddie, only it wasn't quite what I wanted."

"What?" Alvin coughed.

"She's with Division 9 now." Lieutenant Oliver sent his thoughts into her mind. *Joseph shares your feelings. Don't throw that away on these idiots.*

"Fuckin Nine?" Alvin whimpered, at last realizing the depth of the shit he had just stepped in.

Wilkes backed away, the change in her height finally made sense.

Nina turned to Oliver, her angry squint widening into an innocent gaze. His lips hadn't moved when she heard his voice, but that wasn't what startled her.

Wilkes stood paralyzed by the surreal scene of his huge partner held aloft one-armed by a thin woman.

She turned to gaze at Alvin's chest. "How does it feel, Alvin?" She locked eyes. "I could do anything I want to you, and you couldn't do a damn thing to stop me."

"Nina…" Oliver put a hand on her shoulder.

I'm just trying to scare him. She hoped he was listening.

"What the fuck…" Alvin gurgled.

"You know, Alvin." Nina pulled him out of the wall, letting his feet touch floor, and then pulled him down a few inches until they came almost nose to nose. Pieces of cinder block rolled off him and clattered to the ground. "For two years, you tortured me just for wanting to get into Division 2. I wasn't as big as you, and I was certainly not a soldier. I never wanted to get in your way. I would have been happy to go right to the tech squad." She flung him to the ground. "Or fly a desk for two years."

Oliver interposed himself between them, for show.

Nina stared down at him. "You always said that you were Division 1 for life. You said that was the *real* police work. You wanted to protect people."

"Yeah." Alvin dragged himself back to his feet.

"How can you say that out of one side of your mouth and then do the things you did to me? You're lucky that I half believe that line of horseshit you spewed."

"You didn't belong on the force." Alvin's tone seemed more genuine. "You'd have gotten us killed, and…" He looked away.

"And?" she asked, still feeling a bit to blame for Vincent's death, and expecting him to point out that she had, in fact, caused it. A cyberganger as augmented as the one they ran into would have shredded them both even in the best of circumstances, and these two meatheads wouldn't have fared much better.

"None of the guys wanted to see you get yourself fucked up. You were so tiny and cute, like everyone's kid sister. We wanted you to give up and go home, to be safe. When you didn't, we stepped up the teasing and… well I guess it got outta hand."

Nina hadn't expected that, and relaxed. "Street patrol wasn't my idea…"

Alvin shrugged.

"Most guys would protect their little sister, not lock her in armor cabinets." Oliver shook his head at them.

Nina walked past them over to Joey, and squatted over him. "What happened?"

"Head on collision with a pair of moose. They think I hurt Hayley." He tried to laugh but it hurt too much.

"That's absurd." Nina helped him to his feet.

"Yeah but they don't know that. It's no big deal. If I thought I raped the elven year-old daughter of a cop, I'd kick my own ass."

"Do you know where she is?"

"No. Last I saw her, she was at home. I've been in cyberspace all day, haven't even been out of my apartment. Check that brain print thing." Joey looked at her belt. "Any chance of a stimpak?"

Oliver tossed him one. Alvin and Wilkes came closer. At the mention of medical care, Alvin popped a stimpak and rubbed his side.

"We got him on video stuffing her into a trunk." Alvin's NetMini projected the image of Joey carrying a hogtied, screaming Hayley out into the alley behind her building, and throwing her in the trunk of an unfamiliar car.

Joey hit himself in the leg with the stimpak and closed his eyes in pain-dampened ecstasy. "Someone must have grabbed her and put my face on it. I don't own a car."

Before the two could say they checked the video, Nina raised her hand. "I have evidence that someone out there has found a way to falsify a K-N process. I do not trust that video. Send it to our lab so we can analyze it."

Wilkes nodded.

Joey looked at the two men that had been working him over for the past hour. "I'll find her. I'm good at finding things people don't want found."

Nina walked him out via the Division 1 offices. The room resembled a still life in three dimensions. Her old squad mates stared, silent and motionless. Most had been glued to the video feed from the holding area. A red haired woman instrumental in the shower duct-taping incident ran out of sight before Nina could see her. Captain Farris sat motionless in his office, staring through the large window at her with a Nicohaler dangling from his lower lip. No one moved as she led Joey out of the room and on toward the garage and to her patrol craft. He fell into the passenger seat with the grace of a sack of moaning meat.

Nina sat quiet for a moment, then looked at him.

"Someone wants you out of the picture."

He managed a faint nod. "Yeah. I kind of had that feeling."

FOURTEEN MONTHS

The black unmarked patrol craft slipped out of the parking deck and into the sky, up through a swarm of ad-bots and into the traffic lane.

Nina looked him up and down. "Let's get you to a hospital."

"I'll be okay with a few more stimpaks, no major damage. Besides, we have to find who grabbed Hayley." Joey's breath continued in labored gasps. "I think you're right, they wanted to get to me."

"That could mean she's already dead." Nina's voice carried an eerie chill, but she hid her emotion well.

While Joey raided the storage compartment, pumping one stimpak after another into his side, Nina scanned the comm and listened to the Division 1 chatter as they searched. Once the full-body numbness of the stimpaks set in, he explained about his meeting with Itai, complaining about his front row seats to two ass whippings in the same day.

"We had nothing to indicate Itai was a deck jockey." Nina scowled.

Joey shook his head. "There's no way that Itai did that. I haven't gotten spanked like that since Mars and I ran into a damn dragon up there."

"Those AIs are only used by the government. Where the hell did you go that you ran into one of those?"

"Apparently, not the shipping company Vasek said it was. Other than that, I have no damn idea." He chuckled.

An Ops agent appeared in Nina's vision. "I got some good news. Hardin read our network people the riot act for being slackers. After a fourteen-hour bender, DeWinter managed to come up with a way to unmask the fake K-N. We ran his utility on the "tipster" video, and it turned out to be edited."

Shimmering blue light spread out over the dashboard. Within it appeared a citycam view of Hayley's apartment building. She emerged from the door, eyes downcast, and moped to the edge of the sidewalk. After standing alone for just over a minute, a PubTran car pulled up and she got into it alone. When it had driven out of sight, another piece of video showed the abduction. This time, the victim was a grown woman and the location different.

"I saw that vid..." Joey pointed. "It's an old thriller. Someone scaled down the woman and put Hayley's face on her." He rubbed his head. His M3 jack hurt too much for him to think about using it yet. "Can you trace where the PT car went?"

Ten seconds later, Nina relayed an address.

"That's Kenny's place. She probably got lonely and went to hang out with Alyssa." Joey took his NetMini out and called.

Alyssa answered. "Hi Joey!" When she took in his appearance, she covered her mouth with her hand. "Oh my God! What happened to you?"

"It's okay. I lost an argument with a wall. Is Hayley there?"

"Yeah. Why, what's wrong?"

"Nothing. The police were concerned about her. They thought she disappeared."

"Oh." She looked over her shoulder and back at him. "Hey, what did you tell my dad before, he ran out of here like his nuts were on fire."

Joey's laugh at the mental image of that ended with a wince and a hand on his side. "It would be better if you asked him. It's about your mother."

She sank into a chair, biting her lip. "Really?"

"Yeah, I found some info... Look, just talk to him when you can. It's not my place to tell you, but it may be good news."

She stared. Her pleading eyes melted his attempt to dodge her.

"The company your mom used to work for did it to her, some kind of medical testing without her knowledge. I found the details and your dad took it to the hospital."

Alyssa sniffled. Hayley came over to find out what was going on and waved. Nina relayed the address to the search teams, informing them they were en route to verify.

Joey waited for Alyssa to compose herself. "Hey, we might stop by. Keep an eye out for anything weird."

She shot a fearful glance off screen. "Why?"

"Um. Someone is playing with us and I just want you to be careful until we can get there."

"Okay." Her shaking hand reached up and ended the call.

Nina glanced over. "So, that doll you ran into?"

"Which one?" Joey bit his lip, forgetting she didn't know he knew.

"Nemsky." Nina had no reaction.

Joey grinned. "Speaking of him, I found something you may want to see."

"Oh?" She turned the car toward Kenny's place.

Joey put on a casual face. "I took a little trip to Russia."

She smirked at him. The word 'bullshit' may as well have been tattooed to her forehead.

"Virtually. I slipped through the cracks in cyberspace and went rooting around over there. I found some info on our pal."

"You know that doll had an AI core? I think he sent a copy of himself as a decoy."

"That would be a really neat trick." Joey offered a smug grin. "An ACC special ops team killed Anatoly Nemsky almost three years ago. I got a file that details the whole operation complete with helmet cameras. They shot him in the damn bathtub. Can you believe that? Sitting like a shaved polar bear and singing 'til four bullets met in his head. The executives became concerned about his level of brutality and did a little internal housecleaning."

"Dead? That has to be a set up for a deep cover operation, its classic." She glared out the window. "Besides, when did the ACC ever care about being too brutal?"

"I got the feeling their political machine considered him a liability only because he was so public. Each time he wiped out a town square full of civilians, the resistance got hundreds of recruits. The file had enough detail for me to believe it. Of course, I'm no intelligence agent. Swing by my place and I'll show you."

"That makes even less sense than everything else that's been going on." She sighed, melting into the seat as if she just wanted to go home and go to bed.

"Does it?" Joey took a chance and put a hand on her leg. "Think about it. The dead are coming back and talking to us. Why not Nemsky too?"

Nina gripped the controls tighter. She wanted to hear Division 0's opinion on this mess. If they *were* ghosts, it would explain their elusiveness. It also would let her hand the whole thing off to the psionics and not have to worry any more about it.

The car settled to a landing outside Kenny's house. The two girls waited on the porch, Alyssa clinging to her pistol. They came running over as the car landed, Hayley diving into Joey as if he was her long-absent father. When the emotion settled, Nina put a hand on her shoulder.

"Someone sent the police a fake video that made it look like Joey kidnapped you."

"Why?" She blinked, clinging to him.

"They wanted the cops to kill me." Joey chuckled.

Nina's stare flicked from Joey to the car. "I told you I'd drag your dad home. I think it's about time he made a decision between his job and his daughter."

"He didn't come home again last night. He said he had to work." She buried her face in Joey's chest.

Alyssa rubbed her friend's back. "I've been trying to cheer her up all day, but she's…"

"Come on." Nina took Hayley's hand and led her back to the car. "I've had enough of this."

Joey turned to follow, but Alyssa grabbed his arm, shaking with emotion. "Daddy called, he's coming back here to pick me up. Thank you."

"Your dad's helped me out a lot." He ruffled her hair. "I'm just returning the favor."

Hayley sat with her arms crossed in her lap. Silent tears fell the entire ride to the Division 2 Regional Tech Center. The reception area looked more like the office of a technology corporation than a police installation.

A thin bookish man with light brown hair sat behind the front desk, glancing up at the approaching group. His greyish-blue jumpsuit bore the insignia of a Technical Sergeant, electronics.

"Can I help you?"

Nina flashed her ID. His already pale face became whiter. He stared in mute silence, unable to think of anything to say.

"I need to see Detective Jacob Roth, right away."

The man looked at the holo-panel floating in space to his right. "I'm afraid that's impossible."

Hayley muttered to her father via NetMini behind them. She tried to get him to say when he could come home for a bit and he eluded the question as always. Joey typed on his NetMini and showed her the text: "Don't tell him we are here." She nodded.

Nina leaned toward the tech. "Why is it impossible?"

"Detective Roth was killed in action about fourteen months ago," said the man with so little emotion he may as well have informed her she wore black clothing. "We found him in a couple of pieces. Some cyberganger he'd been tracking got a hold of him. Real horror show, hamburger everywhere."

"What!" Haley glanced up, tears streaming out of her eyes, and clutched the NetMini to her chest. Her voice reduced to a squeak. "No. I don't believe you."

"You have to believe me, honey. I have so much work," said Jacob Roth, his voice muted by her shirt.

Between the expression on Hayley's face and the clerk's blasé attitude, Joey wanted to slug him. He made a fist but didn't do anything with it. Nerd or not, the man remained a police officer. Joey's mind raced to the change of writing on that date in Roth's notes. He had been pursuing the man who would become The Russian, even before Nina's bad night. The encounter with Div 5 that saved her life gave the crazed aug a new street name. The same cyberganger responsible for her mauling had killed Roth a few months before. Joey looked at the middle-aged face floating over Hayley's NetMini.

"Nina," he whispered, "something really stinks here. If this guy killed Roth before you were attacked, that means they assigned a case to a dead detective."

She squinted.

The child shuddered, mouth agape and clinging to her NetMini with a white-knuckled grip—unable to speak.

Nina took the NetMini from her and held it up. Jacob Roth, in a shirt and tie, sat behind a desk loaded with holodisks and evidence boxes. Hardcopy photos of dead women laying in piles of gore covered the walls.

"Where is his office?" Nina stared gloom at the Tech Sergeant, who pointed at a hallway.

Joey picked Hayley up, holding her as she sobbed into his shoulder.

Detective Roth glanced up, realizing a different face floated in front of him. "Who is this? Why do you have my daughter's NetMini?"

"Lieutenant Nina Duchenne, Division 9. I am doing a wellness check on Hayley, Detective. I'm curious what hours you spend with her at home."

"I don't see how it's any of your business, but I make time when I can."

Nina crept down the corridor until she arrived at a door with a lighter spot on the paint where a nameplate had once been. Joey's eyes narrowed. He had a feeling what awaited them on the other side.

She held the NetMini up and nudged the door open with her boot. On the screen, the cluttered office had stuff all over the walls. In reality, only a desk, one chair, and a disused bookshelf sat in an otherwise empty room. The pattern of paint blotches and a gouge in the wall matched the hologram.

Hayley looked from the image to the doorway. Joey set her back on her feet and crouched, wrapping his arms around her from behind. She screamed at the top of her lungs and flailed, shrieking for her Daddy. Before long, the strength left her. He held on, trying as best he could to offer comfort while she bawled out of control, wailing "no" over and over.

Her outburst attracted a handful of people, including the Tech Sergeant and two Division 1 officers on security detail. After a minute of futile struggling to get out of Joey's grip, she squirmed around to face him and sobbed into his shoulder.

"What is all that noise? Hayley?" Jacob Roth shouted out of the NetMini. "What are you doing to my daughter?"

Nina turned it in her hand to show the caller the empty office. "It's over, whoever you are. We know Jacob Roth is dead."

Silence.

Soft sniveling echoed down the corridor. When Nina turned the device around, the screen had gone dark.

PLAYING WITH DOLLS

The ride to his apartment was a somber one. Both Nina and Joey's sympathetic grief at watching Hayley learn her father had been dead for over a year kept them quiet. The child found little consolation in learning the way he had treated her over the past year wasn't due to a lack of care or love. Nina doubted the Division 2 explanation a glitch in the system was responsible for her father's pay continuing. When the clerk had insinuated that the daughter would have to pay the department back, Nina had gone off on him.

Joey leaned back with a smile, replaying in his head how Nina screamed. She sounded like a stereotypical drill sergeant dressing down a junior member of her own team for screwing up. The topic dropped when she threatened to initiate a full investigation into how the cyberspace squad of the police had failed to notice payments made to a dead man or left a then eleven-year-old girl on her own for so long. All of that notwithstanding a case assignment assigned to a dead detective, effectively killing the investigation.

Hayley had gone with an agent from social services. Both of them felt lousy for what had happened, and Joey almost thought he would miss her. As they neared his place, he looked over to Nina.

"Hey… Do you think you could maybe pull a string or two?"

"What for?"

"Can you get Hayley placed with a specific foster family?"

"What are you getting at?" Nina eased back on the throttle as she prepared to land. "You like her, don't you?"

Joey smiled, typing on his NetMini. "She got along well with Alyssa. I was thinking maybe Kenny could take her in?" He texted the question to Kenny as soon as he brought it up. "He's better with kids. I'm more like the crazy older brother no one talks about."

"Provided your friend is open to the idea, I suppose I could. The psychologist might even consider it a good idea. There are more orphans than they can find homes for, and he is certainly financially capable."

"Don't rub it in."

She landed in the street by Joey's apartment. As they walked inside, he fell into the chair by his table and made a high-pitched noise that sounded like *meep*.

"What?" Nina approached, looking away from her virtual conversation.

He made the noise again, indicating his smoking deck with a wave of his arm. The look on his face was the same look a normal person would have if they had just found their dog dead. The device, toasted from his virtual beating, still exuded charcoal-hued vapor. He would have to replace parts and it would take a few hours.

"I have one you can use for the time being." Nina moved toward the door.

Joey took the burned out thing with him anyway, cradling it like a wounded pet. It not only felt wrong to leave it there, but the data about Nemsky remained in its memory core.

NINA'S APARTMENT WAS LARGER THAN JOEY THOUGHT IT WOULD BE. HE WHISTLED AS he gave it a glance around. She pointed him at a small desk where a glossy black deck hid under a pile of holodisk cases. Joey gawked at the Netwraith, lowering himself into the chair with a reverent slowness. He leaned forward, fluttering his fingers over it as if afraid to touch it. He had never seen one in person before, Division 9 produced them in-house for their agents' use. Nina threw her coat over a chair and came back with some instant tea. Now he understood why Avril left no trace. These decks operated outside of normal net protocols.

"While you do that I'm going to clean up a bit." She wandered deeper into the apartment. "Oh, and try not to get drool on it."

He connected the two units together and plugged in to hers. His brain throbbed, but soon a sensation like a plant being moved to a larger flowerpot permeated his thoughts, and chased away the pain of the burnout. With no clear idea where to begin, he went to his old hacker haunts and asked about Proscion. He got the same thing in every virtual nightclub or bar that he went to: numerous avatars told him Proscion had either died or wound up in jail.

No one knew a thing.

After visiting eight nodes as well as sniffing around areas rumored to be Proscion's old hangouts, Joey took a moment to search for Zen. At least he had little worry about Itai finding him while using a Netwraith. He daydreamed about the things he could do with it, but stopped when he got a vision of Nina slamming him into a wall.

"Is everything alright, Joseph?" The sudden sound of his dad's voice made him jump.

Joey swiveled around, slouched. "What?"

The old man rubbed his chin. "You just look sad, that's all. Such a shame about that little girl of yours."

"Hayley's not mine."

"She trusts you. It was good what you did for her. Having people around is the best thing for her, not rotting alone in that apartment."

"Yeah." He knew the apparition couldn't be his father, but it came close enough to make him not mind talking.

Joey squinted with a sudden thought, and ran a few scan processes to see if he could trace the source of the other hacker's avatar.

"So you're looking for Proscion?" William Dillon winked.

"Don't tell me, it's you?" Joey glanced sideways at him.

The elder Dillon shook his head. "Oh, no, I'm exactly who you think I am. But I know where you can find him."

The scans identified his father as a grade four AI. Not a hacker or a ghost in the spiritual sense, but it was the ghost of his dad—just made of ones and zeroes.

"What's wrong with you?" The elder Dillon stared at his son's open mouth.

"Uhm... Nothing, Dad." Joey scratched his head trying to figure out how to handle this new development.

Why would someone bother making an AI in the image of a milquetoast scientist from Mars? He wondered how many more of these so-called ghosts were AIs. It took teams of master programmers months upon months to program an AI and longer than that just to get the governmental approval to start, and that was for one with a unique personality. No one had yet succeeded in so faithfully replicating an existing, or formerly existing, person with such a degree of accuracy. AI personality started as bland as a sheet of plasfilm, taking months or years to develop in a gradual evolutionary process.

William Dillon pointed. "There's a warehouse down that way. You can't miss it really. About forty miles as the crow flies there's an awful big data pipe coming out of an empty place."

"You think that's Proscion?" Joey scoffed.

"Oh, I may not be a hacker, but I *am* a scientist. Besides, I have one of my feelings about it. I also think he'd be willing to help for a favor."

His dad got hunches. Sometimes they ended in disaster, but when they didn't, he was right. Joey had nothing else to go on, so he walked with his virtual father to the spot. Sure enough, the shell of an old warehouse in a district long part of the infamous Sector 187 black zone threw a massive data pipe into the air. This place made Sector 12 look like an amusement park, regarded as one of the worst in the entire west, home to the Diablos among other less well-known gangs. Drug crazed lunatics were bad enough, but they mixed occultism and devil worship in with their chems and guns.

He squinted at the brilliant blue and white stream of energy reaching up into the indigo sky of cyberspace. It shimmered with enough light to illuminate the clouds for miles around it and the force of its passage peeled the virtual water vapor into ascending contrails. Throbbing pulses in the light represented data flowing. From the size and brightness, Joey surmised the I/O channel could support a small corporation. It appeared deflated, the narrow shaft a tiny trickle of the capacity defined by the much wider intermittent spiral threads around it.

"See?" said his father, pointing. "You may want to check this place out on the other side."

"Yeah. I'll do that." Joey reached up to disconnect, then paused to face his old man. "Take care of yourself."

He didn't know why he said that. His father had died. The image before him was only a collection of program code acting like him. The conversation on the way to that warehouse proved surreal. William Dillon didn't understand he was an AI, and thought he came to Earth to visit. He also disbelieved his son's assertion that he died, thinking it a playful tease. At least knowing it wasn't another hacker messing with him made him feel better, but still a bit confused as to who would go to all that trouble.

Joey disconnected, enjoying the comfort of a normal departure from cyberspace.

"Find anything?" Nina's voice came from behind him, close. The air embraced him with warmth and the scent of a recent shower.

"I think I found... naked." Joey turned and froze at the sight of her. His eyes took control of his tongue.

Nina's skin glistened with a fine layer of condensation. She held a glass of tea, sipping it casually.

She laughed. "What?"

"You're naked." Joey leaned back and made an appraising face as he took in the view. "Shaved. Nice."

She gave him a playful smirk. "I just got out of the shower. Are you hungry? I can make some food."

He blinked twice. "Uhhh... yeah... sure." He stared as she walked into the kitchenette and tweaked the OmniSoy assembler.

He wondered where along the path from here to making food would include getting dressed. He slid out of his chair and zombie stumbled just fast enough to keep her in sight.

She made two plates, one steak and one fish, and set them on the table with the steak toward Joey. Still nude, she took a seat and gestured at the empty chair.

He wanted to speak, but no words formed in his brain. If she wanted to show off, he wouldn't be the one to talk her out of it. However, her body language had nothing flirtatious about it. He joined her at the table with a pacified grin, staring at her chest. Steak and tits—a night that started as a nightmare had become a dream. A girl this forward wasn't a new experience for him, but it felt different. Nina didn't act at all sexy. She merely existed with nothing on. Joey watched her eat, fumbling blind at his plate in search of something to nibble on.

"Oh"—she looked up from the plate—"we got that cyborg repatriated." Still nothing in her eyes beyond casual dinner conversation. "He agreed to re-up for another eight in exchange for the JAG not filing desertion charges. The shrink signed off on it as extreme emotional distress."

Joey dodged her glance, finally able to cut a decent sized hunk from his steak. He mumbled through a mouthful of food, swallowed, and then tried again. "That's good. What about his kid?"

"They're going to put him in a Class 2 doll body and retrain him as a heavy vehicle armorer. He won't look like he used to, but he'll be close enough to human for his kid not to flip a biscuit at the sight of him."

Joey nodded. "That's good."

"So what did you find?"

"My dad's an AI."

Nina gawked. half-chewed fish crumbled out of her mouth. "An AI?" She swallowed. "Who would bother programming an AI to simulate your father?"

"Exactly what I wondered." He again dodged her glance, cutting at the steak. "It doesn't make sense."

He tried—really, he did—to look her in the eyes, but couldn't.

"If I had a credit for every time I said that." She stabbed a hunk of fish hard enough to make him wonder how the plate survived it.

"So, um. Yeah. Naked."

Nina leaned back. "It's comfortable." Her smile faded and she turned to glance out the window. Hair formed an ebon curtain over her face. "I know you know."

Shame flooded her voice.

He made an obvious show of looking her up and down. "If I didn't read that file, I wouldn't be able to tell."

"Everyone keeps saying that." She dropped the fork.

"Nina, that's because it's the truth. You're perfect. Well, maybe your boobs are a little on the small side…"

She threw some peas at him, unable to hide a hint of a smile. He chuckled through the onslaught of tiny green spheres.

"I never played with dolls as a little girl. It always felt silly to wrap plastic people in bits of clothing and act like they talked."

Joey chuckled. "Is that why you don't dress the big one?"

"What's the point?" She made a wall of peas against the fish on her plate. "At first it felt like some machine that I was piloting. I wore the armor for work, but I stopped going out aside from that. It seemed pointless to bother wearing anything just to stare at these walls. If someone calls, the VidPhone fakes it, and no one…"

"I'm here." He got up and moved around behind her, resting his hands on her shoulders. "Do you still feel like an oversized toy?"

"Sometimes. I guess I'm starting to accept it." Nina leaned back into his hands, letting her arms fall slack in her lap. "I do save a lot of credits on laundry though."

Joey chuckled despite her lack of inflection, massaging her shoulders. "Can you feel this? Even touching you, I can't tell." He understood his fingers kneaded plastisteel plates and Myofiber muscles, but it created sensation in her brain.

"Yeah." Nina sighed and leaned forward on her elbows. Guilt about Vincent mixed with relief as Joey worked simulated tension out of her shoulders. She found her breaths growing shallow.

Joey expanded the rub from her shoulders to her back. She slid farther over the table, resting her head on her arms after sliding the plates out of the way. The touch of the cool table on her breasts caused her to make a soft gasp.

He moved up, stroking the nape of her neck. "You were all I could think about this morning. I could barely concentrate on cyberspace. I kept seeing your face in my mind."

Her eyes opened to slits as his voice drifted over the calm. Left-brain scolded her with the truth that this body didn't need a massage. She ignored it. His touch felt wonderful and she didn't care why it did. She forgot about the nightmare of trying to find Nemsky and Korin in the few minutes he touched her. As his hands slid down her sides, she lost herself in the feeling. She had felt isolated and adrift from humanity ever since she first saw the world with electronic eyes. Joey rowed out to her little island.

He shares your feelings. Lieutenant Oliver's voice echoed in her memory.

Nina couldn't help herself anymore as her desperation reached the breaking point. She dove off her emotional island, swimming to him. Nina rose out of the chair only enough for a kiss to reach him. Her sudden motion excited him. He lifted her to sit on the edge of the table, leaning into her embrace, kissing her on the lips for several minutes before moving to the side of her neck.

Nina stirred feelings within him unlike any other woman he had met. He let her lead him to the bed, down a bizarre emotional path that transcended simple lust.

Soon, a trail of clothes led from the kitchen to the Comforgel pad. She sat on the edge, reclining back into the satin. He caressed her, hands roaming over her pale skin as she writhed upon the black. He kissed his way from her lips to her bosom, and down over her stomach before going back up to her neck. She made sounds that she hadn't summoned forth in many months, lost in a sea of tangled feelings. Pleasure and guilt crossed swords as she squirmed. Oliver's assurance broke down the last of her hesitation and she gave in to pleasure. When his warmth drew close, her arms, a little out to each side, grabbed fistfuls of bedding and pulled as she felt him for the first time.

Nina's breath came in gasps, keeping time with the motion of their bodies. Joey braced his weight, hands on either side of her head, and stared down into her eyes. He felt as content as he had ever been in his life. Far beyond a simple physical act, he fell into uncharted territory wearing a mask of clueless confidence.

Nina released her grip on the bedding and wrapped her arms around him as she shuddered. She arched her back and curled her toes, and muffled her moans by burying her face in his neck. The absolute horror of her life over the past months dissipated in a burst of pure bliss. Her body went limp and she half-closed her eyes. He hovered over her. They kissed once more before rolling on their sides to face each other.

Her face flushed. She had no voice, managing only a faint smile as Joey kept telling her how beautiful she looked. As the heat of the moment faded, she wondered if what just happened had been a good idea. He kept talking, and seemed to share Vincent's sense of humor. He often found *wrong* things funny. She closed her eyes and leaned into him. She clung to the hope Vincent had gone to a better place, and wondered if perhaps he had sent Joey to her. Nina held his hand, wondering if she could find the strength to let go of Vincent.

"You are amazing." He gazed into her sapphire eyes and smiled.

An uncomfortable thought made her roll over. The warmth of his being surrounded her, his arm slid over her stomach as he pulled himself close against her back. Nina curled into him, allowing herself a few seconds of fantasy that he could somehow protect her.

Just above a whisper, she found a voice. "You know that I can't…"

He caressed her abdomen, rubbing the place no baby could ever grow. "It doesn't make you any less of a woman, Nina. Besides, do I look like the fatherly type?"

Nina giggled away a tear. "You are good with Hayley."

"I guess, just never saw myself having a kid." *Never saw myself with a girl for more than one night either.*

Nina put a hand over his arm as she thought about her father's demand for grandchildren. Of course, he wouldn't have liked Vincent and he would care for Joey even less. At least her situation gave her a reason to dodge the issue. The most unlikely of people she could have run into made her feel human again, and she didn't want it to end. His breath on the side of her neck made her feel safe, despite remembering what the voice had said about her ovaries. She had to know if that was true.

Joey ran his hand along her side, leaving it on her hip. She basked in the warmth behind her, swishing her foot back and forth across the cool satin. Before she knew it, the warmth and idle banter lulled her off to sleep.

The sound of him moving woke her, and she sat bolt upright.

Her expression made him laugh. "I haven't showered in a while, I was just gonna borrow the tube."

She relaxed and fell back, splayed out on the bed.

"Wanna join me?" He winked at her, and looked ready for more.

She blushed at the thought. "Again?"

"I have this hard to reach spot on my back…"

He grinned, avoiding her first lunge. They circled the apartment once in a fit of laughter before she chased him into the bathroom.

WONDERLAND

J oey's bike rolled to a halt by a chain link fence surrounding a huge abandoned looking building. White painted walls caught the smog-filtered moonlight, causing the structure to glow a dim shade of cobalt. He surveyed the surreal desolation, unable to tell by sight if he stood in the real world or in cyberspace. A rattle ran the length of the fence when he ducked past a hole into a disused parking lot, then jogged the dozen some meters to the structure. Near a large sliding door, a single strip of glass ran from the ground to the top. Bands of frosted opacity crossed the glass at each floor, except for a strip of clear at the top and bottom of each panel. Inside, a grey metal stairway climbed into darkness.

Distant gunshots echoed, making him jump and look to the right. This part of the city belonged to the Diablos, and he second-guessed himself for rushing out here without waiting for Masaru to answer his phone. Perhaps that bit about going back to Japan until this Division 9 issue settled down had been more than a joke. Katya wouldn't have been much help out here. Besides, after the last favor she asked of him, she had her own little problem to handle now.

Joey stared up at the smog feeling as far removed from civilization here as he did in the Badlands. Even the ubiquitous thrum of hovercars was absent.

To the left of the tall channel of glass, a slab of grey metal formed a door large enough to accept a cargo truck. The control panel had only a single black button. He tugged at the door, finding it sealed, and considered the small silver box. He came here for help, so he figured he should play nice at first. He pushed it. When nothing happened, he pushed again and held it a little longer.

Weak light appeared to his right, casting thick shadows over the fourth floor stairway. A flesh colored blur moved behind the frosted glass, descending at a careful pace. By the time it reached the second floor, Joey made out what looked like a child walking barefoot. The diminutive figure rounded the last set of stairs.

A few seconds after the blur vanished behind solid wall, a little voice spoke from the other side of the door.

"Who are you?"

This, he hadn't expected. "Hi. I'm Joey. I need to see Proscion."

"I don't know who that is," said the child, sounding frightened.

"I'm not here to cause any trouble for him. Something bad is going on, and he is the only person that can help." Joey put his hand on the door. "Please?"

A long enough silence came that he stared at the ground to ponder his next move. The *clunk* of a locking bar made him let go of the door. It scraped open, sliding to the left. A child's foot appeared in the gap, toes braced against the concrete as the small person shoved the giant door open. Joey, head down, stared at a child's bare feet standing a short distance inside the warehouse. He gradually looked up over a girl of about ten, wearing only a layer of dirt and grime. An intense feeling of wrongness washed over him at the sight of a nude child, but his brain crashed into a brick wall at the realization she cradled her severed head in her right arm—and pushed the massive door with one arm.

Wires, cables, and segmented clear plastic tubes ran from the base of the head into her open neck. Long blonde hair hung down to the floor. Strips of skin had sheared away, exposing the mechanical workings of her collarbone and shoulder on one side. Blue light from within the head illuminated the right side of her body, casting harsh shadows laterally across her skin. Joey stared at the radiance.

She's an AI.

The sight hit him like a punch to the brain. As soon as the door opened enough for him to fit, he entered and shooed her inside. The head tucked in her right arm tilted back to peer up at him, then smiled, despite a sad presence about her. He spun and grabbed the door, unable to move it. After blinking at her, he put both hands on the thing, barely finding the strength to coax it closed. Out of breath, he leaned against the wall with a wary eye upon the ersatz child that had moved it so easily. Despite her detached head, the rest of her looked so lifelike he couldn't bear the sight of her, staring pity into the floor.

"Please don't look at me like that. I am just a doll. WellTech Realife series 440. My name is Emily." She padded to the stairwell, dragging her hair over the floor. "Follow me."

Still unable to speak, he followed. He tried not to look directly at her nakedness, finding it awkward despite her obvious artificiality. By the second story, he had to focus on her severed head. If he looked down, the damaged robotics left his vision, and she became uncomfortably real, even down to simulated goosebumps reacting to the cold. Her, or its, lack of clothing made him wonder what kind of person Proscion was.

Emily's feet made no sound on the unremarkable grey metal stairs, rather unlike Joey's boots. She paused at the top, waiting for him to catch up. When they rounded the corner at the last segment of steps, she marched off down a dark corridor, the last few inches of her hair still dragging.

A mass of large pipes, painted dull red, green, black, and yellow, ran along the walls. Muck and dust covered everything. Morbid shadows lurked in the darkness. A hand here, a foot there, the separation of light and dark at one point painted the profile of a childlike face on the wall. A spider, made gargantuan by the light, crawled over the nose. He advanced behind the headless doll. His eyes eventually adjusted to the dimness, revealing the spaces between the pipes held hundreds of doll parts. Everything from inanimate toy dolls to primitive versions of Emily. One or two looked like adults, but the vast majority of them had been made in the image of children.

Not one had a stitch of clothing over their battered frames, and many had missing limbs, heads, or both. Only the obvious circuitry sticking out of the pieces kept Joey from getting sick.

"Emily?"

"Yes?" She stopped and turned to face him. Her hands tilted the head so she could look up at him.

Eye contact lasted three seconds before he had to look away. "Why are all of these dolls here?"

Her eyes half closed into a downcast stare. "Hugo is lonely. We are his family."

Even with her head in her hands, this doll creeped him out in ways he had never thought possible. For one thing, dolls didn't usually trip that indefinable sense of being in the presence of another person, and this one did. Secondly, the WellTech dolls programming only included happy and cheerful, but Emily radiated despondence. These dolls could throw childish temper tantrums and pout, but she appeared deeply sad. The company didn't have permission to give them full AIs, or they would fall under the protection of the law as sentient and therefore couldn't be sold. A certain degree of 'acting like a robot' was required in the RealLife dolls—and Emily lacked it. Her slight anatomical inexactitude—no genitialia—at least confirmed her as a WellTech child.

"Were you ever alive?" Joey cringed. As soon as he asked, he felt like a fool, realizing Proscion probably only wrote his own AI and loaded it into a 'toy' he bought.

She smiled. "I've always been alive."

The response froze him, until he again felt like an idiot for the thoughts crossing his mind. This kid had such an eeriness about her, she didn't strike him as an AI. But that made no sense. Not one of the hoses coming out of the head carried blood. There couldn't possibly be a real brain in there. "What happened to you?"

Emily turned and kept walking. She spun her disembodied head to the rear, giving Joey a look that bid him to follow before disappearing around a corner. She led him down another hallway full of pipes and broken dolls. A dozen lifeless young faces stared out at him from their cobweb-infested dens. The sense he had invaded the den of a serial killer who kept trophies grew oppressive. He broke out in a sweat, not wanting to look at the walls or his guide. Not since his little sister's room had he seen so many nude, dismembered dolls in one place.

The artificial girl stopped by a broken pipe about a foot in diameter. One cracked end rested on the ground and the other still clung to a pipe sling near the ceiling. It had once run parallel to the roof. She pointed at it the lower end with her toe.

"That fell on me."

Joey winced. "Ouch."

"People shoot through the walls sometimes. A bullet clipped the cable while I was rummaging for stuff to burn. The heat doesn't work."

"You're probably cold." Joey smiled as he pulled off his coat off to give it to her.

"I am, but it doesn't matter, it is just an electrical signal. The cold cannot harm my body. Hugo needs to keep warm. I keep a fire for him, but there is nothing left to burn." Her voice fell with genuine worry.

"You burned your clothes?" He blinked.

She held her head up in both hands and made it nod. "I used to go outside to find things, but I am unable to do that anymore with this much damage. He is going to die soon. That is why I decided to let you in. I thought maybe you can help him."

Emily accepted the coat, but didn't put it on. She continued to walk, carrying it. As they moved further in, the quality of the parts packed into the pipes increased, as if they navigated a museum highlighting the advancement of doll technology in chronological order. She led him into a large room, once a manufacturing area, past colossal hulks of dead machinery that loomed in the stillness.

Joey gazed up at the huge things, thankful for something to see aside from the awkwardness of a bare child. The steel beasts hung over him, giving off an almost tangible yearning for release from their uselessness. Scrap metal, tools, and other smaller machines littered the area. Old tables, desks, and chairs once used by those who worked here held a century of dust. A rusting conveyor made of thousands of steel rollers snaked among the equipment. The unmoving system held yet more doll pieces and some boxes. Delivery bot take-out food containers lay piled in the shadow of a massive gleaming computer far out of place given the rest of the scenery.

"Holy shit! Is that a Meridian Nine?" He reached out to the computer as if approaching the altar of a church. "This is a GlobeNet backbone server. Oh it's a little old... it's a seven."

"This place is full of dead machines that no one wants anymore," said Emily in a sad tone, as if implying she considered herself one such machine. The girl tilted her head up at him while placing her bare feet carefully around sharp objects without even looking.

"Do you think he doesn't want you?" *Why am I feeling sorry for a damn robot?*

She stopped, standing in silence. "I... think he's just sick now."

A withered old man sat twisted in a hover-chair positioned between the Meridian and a burn barrel containing a weak fire. Tubes ran into his body from the back of his seat. Life support systems chugged away, feeding him and removing his waste. His head curled to the left and a steady line of drool oozed from his lips. Two wires ran from the back of his head, connecting him to the silver computer. Joey had a sinking feeling he stared at Proscion, the image of the sick old man about the farthest thing from what he had imagined. Emily approached the hover chair and placed Joey's coat over the old man.

Meeting one's heroes seldom lives up to expectations.

"He has been logged in for more than a year," said Emily in a delicate voice, sad yet detached. She pivoted her head to look down at the floor. "He used to come out and spend time with me... but he doesn't come out anymore."

"You've been changing his OmniSoy pack..." Joey walked up and looked at the computer. "Maybe he can't get out?" He offered her a sad smile. "If he's been logged in all this time, why does everyone think he's gone?"

Emily balanced her head in one arm and wiped the drool from Hugo's face with her free hand. "It's not connected to the GlobeNet. He made his own world."

"Make him wake up!" yelled a petulant boy from the right.

Joey stumbled, close to fainting at the sudden sound. A little boy, about the same apparent age as Emily, sat at a checkers board between a pair of immense metal stamping machines. A thick layer of dust coated his red and green striped shirt, blue jeans, and bare feet as well as the game. It looked as if he hadn't moved a millimeter in over a year.

"It's his turn. I want him to move!" yelled the boy in a bratty whine that reminded Joey why he was in no hurry to have one of his own.

He stared at the boy doll for a few minutes until it looked away, returning its posture to neutral forward and becoming still. The other fake child looked like the same series as Emily, indistinguishable in appearance from a real person. Seeing him motionless and covered in dust was almost too much for Joey to handle, but at least the boy acted as Joey expected a WellTech doll to act. In flagrant disregard for the situation around him, he behaved like a spoiled child.

A bump to the leg brought Joey's attention back to Emily. She had found an old metal folding chair and dragged it over.

"If you want to talk to him, you will need to go in." She pointed at the computer.

Temptation and apprehension dueled in his head. Emily pulled a wire out of the Meridian and offered it. With a sigh, he sat down and took it. She went back to Hugo and wiped his drool. He watched her tend to the sick old man for a moment, almost dropping her head as she did. The sight of a machine so concerned with the welfare of its owner confused him to his core.

The companion doll programming shouldn't contain anything like that. The way she spoke to him as she fussed with his clothing and life support tubes betrayed a genuine, not synthetic, need to take care of him. He shook his head in a vain attempt to dispel the confusion as he leaned back in the chair and plugged in.

THE RUSH OF FLASHING LIGHTS AND COLORS FROM THE LOGIN FADED AWAY TO REVEAL the center of what looked like a park. His perspective felt different. When he neared a bench seat, he realized his avatar approximated what he looked like at ten. He stared at the placid clouds overhead, pondering where Proscion's mind had gone. While knocking at death's door, he had become desperate to cling to youth.

A pack of children played on the other side of the park with no trace of an adult anywhere he could see. Little Joey walked toward them, moving along behind trees in an effort to stay out of sight. The kids played tag and catch. Some jumped rope while others chased a puppy around. It looked like a slice of prewar suburbia, four hundred years ago. He looked down at himself, happy this was a private server. If his Dad AI showed up here, he wouldn't be able to handle the discomfort.

He hid in the shadow of a large tree, watching them, trying to figure out which boy was Proscion. After what felt like an hour, indistinct voices that spoke in warbling tones rather than words called the children away one by one. One girl remained after all the others had left. The simulated sunlight gleamed in her long red hair. Freckles adorned adorable porcelain-white cheeks, and she wore a cute pink dress with shiny red shoes over white socks. Lonely, she pouted and sat on a swing. Joey stared up at the sky, shaking his head.

He emerged from his cover, stuffed his hands in his pockets and walked over. "Hi."

"Hi." Her mood brightened in an instant. "Did you just move into town? Wanna play?"

"Maybe."

She stopped actively swinging, rocking to a gradual halt. "Why maybe?"

He circled and took a seat on the other swing. "I need to find someone."

"Who?"

"Do you know Proscion?"

The girl looked away as if he had just called her a dirty name. "I don't know him. I'm Kelly." She grumbled and folded her arms.

"Okay, Kelly. I'll play with you if you help me out. Emily is worried."

The little red-haired girl whirled on him with a scared expression. "Why is Emily upset?"

"She thinks Proscion is hiding because he doesn't love her anymore. Seems like he only has a little bit of time left and she wanted to be with him before he dies."

Joey felt awkward at the thought this man loved a doll like a daughter—or maybe best friend—until he felt like a hypocrite. To rationalize, he clung to the knowledge that Nina had a human brain. Tears ran from Kelly's face, falling to become dark spots on her dress.

"I don't like talking about him. He loves Emily, but she's my sister now, not my daughter." Kelly looked up with a sheepish grin, having caught herself breaking the illusion.

Despite his suspicions, the confirmation stunned Joey. "Do you know anything about the Silver hack? Or why someone would bother to make an AI out of my dad?"

Kelly wiped her face with both hands. Her sadness morphed into a weasel's look of opportunity. "I'll help you if you help me."

"I'm listening." He pushed and swung without thinking about it.

"You can't tell anyone. Promise?"

"Sure."

"Say promise." She stomped her foot in midair with a sullen shout, making the swing-chain rattle.

"I promise." He droned, hoping his annoyance wasn't too obvious.

Kelly swung her feet back and forth. "I know a man that can help me, but he lives far away. I did a favor for him years ago, but I am too sick to get to him on my own now. I waited too long."

"That's it? You need a ride?" Joey lifted an eyebrow.

Kelly nodded. "Yes, that's about it." She stared at him. "But you can't tell anyone about him. Or about me. Proscion is gone. I am Kelly now."

"If I take you there, you can help me?" Joey tried to dismiss a haze of hair over his eyes with a sharp breath.

"Yep." She beamed. "I know who's messing with you. I'll tell you if you help me."

Joey's mind struggled with the contrast of the infamous Proscion wrapped in the package of small red haired girl in a pink dress. Her attitude seemed childlike in ways, but also sophisticated. He couldn't help but draw connections between her and Nina. Both of them were more than what they appeared.

"This sounds too easy," Joey said with narrowing eyes. "What aren't you telling me?"

She put on a coy smile. "I said he was far away."

"East City?"

"Not that far." The girl bit her lip for a second. "He's in the swamps."

The only swamps Joey knew of lay in the Badlands. The sound that came out of him made Kelly's blue eyes widen into a pathetic pleading stare.

The skies overhead darkened, threatening rain. The chirping birds ceased. "Please! I don't have much time left." She clutched his hand. "I'm gonna die."

Joey tried to separate the image in front of him from the hacker god he had all but worshipped as a teen. The old man's brain had obviously become jelly, and what remained of him had regressed.

"Can I ask you one question?" Joey opened an eye.

"'Kay."

"Why a girl?"

Kelly shrugged, and her childlike affect dimmed. "I got sick as a teenager. It's a genetic condition no one could fix, at least not with the money we had. Most of my life, I wasn't a person... More like a mish mash of dying meat propped up by tubes. People would stare with pity, or recoil. I am done with the world out there as an adult. I don't want worries or cares, and what's more innocent than a little girl? People see a little boy and wonder what he's up to, assume he's a troublemaker." She turned away, folding her arms. "My brain is destroying itself. I haven't been able to move in years. If not for that chair, I'd already be gone. I don't want people to wonder what scheme I am planning, how I might try to take advantage of them, or what kind of threat I may be. Everyone adores a cute little girl. Besides, Emily always wanted a sister."

Joey exhaled a long breath. He could save some of his icon's glory in his mind by blaming the disease. "So why the trip?"

"About six years ago, a man approached me, a powerful psionic who wanted my help to vanish from the government. I scrubbed all record of him out of the system and helped him get out there, but the price was..." Kelly stared into space as rain started to fall. "High. He promised he would make it up to me some day, and now I need him to make good on that offer."

"Is he some kind of healer?"

Kelly shook her head. "No, he talks to the dead. He can manipulate souls. He can put me into a different body."

Cold rain pelted them both. Kelly ignored the downpour soaking her hair and clothes.

"Whoa." Joey leaned back. "Why not do it the normal way?"

The childlike affect returned with a pout. "My brain won't survive much longer, even inside a doll body. The disease has progressed to the point where the nanobots can't keep up. Besides, my brain is too big to fit into the body I want. He said he can put my soul into a mechanical body and it would be just like it was my real body... the same as this VR."

Joey wanted to laugh, to just unplug and leave right then. Hugo, Proscion, Kelly... whatever the hell his name was, he had quite plainly gone off the deep end.

Alas, Joey had no better plan to fall back on. He would have to spin the wheel of WTF to see where the needle stopped.

"How do you even know this could work? What if I get you out there and you just crap out and die?"

"I won't," she said, confident. Rain stopped. Clouds parted in fast-forward time, revealing the sun and a clear sky. "Even if I die, he can still let me talk to you. I will give you what you want to know if you do this for me, no matter how it turns out. I'll arrange a backup and put all the information in a file that will send itself to you if I don't respond to a recurring forty-eight hour alarm."

"I don't believe in that stuff." Joey shook his head. "And I don't mean dead man routines."

"If you're standing next to me, you already know what I am talking about is real," said Kelly in an eerie tone, made creepier by a peal of thunder overhead. "Will you help me or not?"

Joey forced his hand into his hair. He'd about reached the point of being done looking like his preadolescent self, and he couldn't think of any other way to get the information. Proscion's living brain had become so squishy at this point it would likely not survive the stress of a hostile interrogation.

"Okay, fine. What do I have to do?"

She hugged him. "Yay!"

The sun brightened. Chirping birds reappeared, and the sky glimmered perfect blue.

Joey rode out Kelly's exuberant show of gratitude, trying to pretend she was a real kid. He extended a hand, catching the last raindrop, and found himself stuck staring at a mesmerizing raindrop. He tilted his hand and let it fall past his sneaker into the grass.

"You'll need to get me a body. I want to look like this." She pointed at herself. "It needs to be a doll body, a good one like Emily that looks natural. I don't care if it's modded."

"Modded?" asked Joey.

Kelly blushed and gestured at her groin. "*Realistic* or flat like a toy. It doesn't matter. As long as it doesn't have seams on the face and joints and looks like a real person."

Those WellTech dolls are two hundred grand. "Oh, those just grow on trees." Joey flashed a dumb grin as an idea hit him. "Never mind, I got it covered. Not gonna be a redhead, but I think you'll be happy."

"Okay..." Kelly narrowed her eyes, suspicious of how fast Joey had seemed to figure it out. "I'll put the coordinates on the screen outside. Please don't tell the authorities where my friend is. He doesn't trust cops."

"Even if they knew where he was, there's no way they would go all the way out into the Badlands for him. That's why he's there." Joey stood. "Might as well get started."

Kelly put a hand on his arm. "If they knew what he could do, they *would* go out there. He doesn't want to become an experiment."

THE PLACID CITY PARK GAVE WAY TO THE DINGY INTERIOR OF THE FACTORY. JOEY couldn't help but conduct a package check to reaffirm his adulthood. He shook off the disorientation of logout and looked over at Emily, who still tended to Hugo's wasted body.

Joey stood and stretched. "I need to make some preparations."

"For what?" Emily shifted her head to look at him.

A map with navigation coordinates appeared without warning on the massive computer. "Hugo and I are going for a little ride. I'm going to take him to see a friend in the swamp."

"Shabundo?" asked Emily, hesitant.

"Kelly didn't tell me his name. She only said he could put him into a new body." He biffed himself in the head trying to get the gender sorted out in his thoughts. "Umm, her."

"He can have this one." Emily looked down. "I don't want him to die. I love him." She shook with grief. "It's okay if I die as long as he lives."

Joey stared at her without saying a word for almost a full minute. He had studied AI theory in college and not once had he ever heard of an AI being self-sacrificing. The one thing that they all had in common was the overpowering need to survive at all costs. He walked over and put a hand on her left shoulder where the synthetic skin remained intact.

"Die? Don't you mean shut down?"

"Yeah, that."

"You don't have to do that. I got it covered."

Emily looked at the boy by the chessboard. "No, he wouldn't want that."

Joey laughed. "No, I don't imagine he would."

HIROTO IDO

The front of Ido's shop swam with shifting shadows cast by boxes of cyberware arranged around the shelving. A smiling Asian girl winked from a holographic calendar every time he looked in her direction. Joey didn't feel like sitting, and paced a circle around the waiting area. His cyberdoc friend had opened this place a few months ago after he finished his residency. Joey had traded a little hacking to remove Ido's educational debt for some repair work, and the doc was always willing to help him. An unassuming Japanese man in his early thirties, his roundish face always bore the same wide smile, and he always wore the same immaculate white lab coat.

He felt like an ass for begging Kenny to leave his wife's side now, but considering what Joey had sent him, he turned out to be more than willing. Getting Nina's help had been a calculated risk, and she proved more difficult to convince than Kenny did. All Joey had to do now was sit back and wait. He wandered into the back hallway and peered in a small window into the procedure room. Emily's body floated in a cylinder of peach colored gel, her head suspended in a position much closer to where it belonged, while Hiroto Ido stood headfirst in a control console to the left of the tube. Struts and tie rods appeared to grow back as Ido guided nanobots to reconstruct the metal.

Joey returned to the waiting area, standing in the warmth of sunlight by the glass, which glowed on the white padded seats. A delivery bot floated down out of the sky and approached the door, distracting him from his interest in passing pedestrians. He removed two flat boxes from it, carrying them inside and leaving them on a table full of e-zines while he waited. Emily walked in an hour later, whole again and slick with gel. She evaded Ido who tried to wrap her in a towel, intent on getting to Joey as fast as possible now that she was free from the tank. Joey turned at the splats of slime-covered feet, laughing at Ido's uncoordinated scramble in the trail she left.

She marched up to Joey and stood, arms folded and dripping. "Can we go back to Hugo now, please?"

Ido caught up and engulfed her in a white towel. She squirmed as he dried her off, annoyed by the delay. He smiled at Joey, proud of his repairs.

"What do you think, Joey? Can't tell any damage happened anymore at all."

Emily tolerated him moving her head around to show off his work.

"Can we please go to Hugo? I don't like leaving him alone."

Joey opened one of the boxes and held up a pink and white frilly dress, a white leotard, and patent leather shoes.

"It's a bit frilly." Emily stood as if waiting for him to put them on her. Joey draped the dress over her head. "But Hugo would like it."

"Sorry kiddo. You are too creepy real for that, plus you're old enough to dress yourself."

Emily flung the towel off and Joey turned away, not wanting to watch. Soon, the rustling of fabric ceased.

"Okay."

"Much better." He felt at ease now in her presence. "How do you feel? Oh, and you're not allowed to burn that."

"I won't. Thank you." She looked down. "But Hugo is still sick."

Ido shook his head. "I've never seen this before. This doll's emotional responses are astounding. Such empathy."

Emily looked up at him, opened her mouth, but kept quiet.

"Why did you get two outfits?" Ido glanced at the unopened box.

Joey smiled. "She's uh, got a sister on the way."

The rumble of a heavy vehicle drew his attention to the window. Kenny's truck shuddered to a halt outside, covered in a thick layer of brown dust, embedded with thousands of dead bugs. Eldon stared an accusatory look from the passenger seat. Joey went outside and met them at the tailgate.

Eldon shook his head. "If we weren't taking this to Ido's place, I'd have some serious questions for you, man."

Kenny pulled a blanket-wrapped bundle from the back seat. A child's bare feet poked out of one end. He handed it to Joey with a face that belayed his discontent with the situation. "You're lucky I know the best routes."

"We almost flipped six times driving that fast." Eldon grumbled. "This better be important."

"Joey, I don't know what you're doing, but I gotta say that this is pretty damn weird." Kenny wiped his hands on his jeans.

"Right shade of fucked up is more like it, man," said Eldon.

"It is... very important." Joey felt awkward with the bundle. It felt like he was holding a dead body. "Oh, about Hayley?"

"She's already at the house. Cathy was fine with the idea. Alyssa has a lot on her mind, but that's all due to her mother." Kenny frowned. "Can you believe the case worker was happier that I'm too wealthy to qualify for the stipend than she was the kid had a home?"

"How is Cathy?" Joey tugged at the blanket to cover the feet.

Kenny sighed. "The convulsions are bad now. The medtechs had to load her up with muscle relaxants and put her in a tank so she can breathe. The detox is kicking her ass, but it is working. Some traces of her old personality are starting to

384 | VIRTUAL IMMORTALITY

come through. Tomorrow, they go into the brain and try to rewire the damage, that data you sent told them how to do it."

"Look man, I'm sorry I had to ask you to leave her side for this."

"She's asleep in a tank now and won't know I ducked out." Kenny climbed into the truck. "I know you wouldn't have asked if it wasn't important, but I'm going back to her now. You can fill me in on the details of whatever weird shit you're involved with later."

Joey waved at the departing truck and carried the bundle inside. Ido hovered over as he laid it across the seats. He opened the blanket, revealing a girl of about nine with shoulder length white hair. Her eyes were closed, and she didn't breathe. If not for the natural color to her skin, she would have looked dead.

Ido glanced at the body. "Joseph, that's clearly not a WellTech doll. What are you involved with?"

"Is that for Hugo?" Emily walked over. "She looks perfectly real."

"Yes." Joey looked at Ido. "It's not a doll. The body is synthetic. Hand me the other box?"

A scintillating line of blue light ran down the tiny body from a handheld scanner as Ido checked it out. "The make of this unit is not on the books. It doesn't seem to be the product of synthetic autogenesis."

"English, man…" Joey put on a face of false exasperation.

"Born." Ido smiled. "When two synthetics produce offspring, technically the "mother" is just creating one. The father's only contribution is a portion of the AI code. We refer to it as autogenesis."

"Oh. Yeah, this one didn't have parents. There's no AI."

Ido blinked at the device in his hand. "I can't find any manufacturer information, and the internal repair modules are more robust than any I've ever seen before. Do you know who made this?"

Joey opened the other package, and dressed the inert synthetic in the same outfit he had bought for Emily.

"We found it in the Badlands, some kind of special project. Everything I have found points to StarPoint. They designed her for combat, which is probably why the repair units are jacked up." Joey felt the look from Ido. "Yes, I know she looks like a kid, don't ask. It's a long story." He propped her up in the seat and looked at Emily. "Well, what do you think?"

The doll looked at him with a flat expression. "Synthetics grow up."

"This one won't." Joey tried to suppress the queasiness sinking in his gut. "He can have his *puer aeternus*."

"You know that means *eternal boy*. *Puera aeternus*." Ido raised a finger in the air as he corrected, eyebrow up. "You're the last person I'd expect to make an obscure Latin reference. Consider me impressed."

Joey shuddered. "Don't even get me started."

Emily looked back and forth from the synthetic to Joey. The sleeping child looked a touch younger than Kelly, did but she didn't think he would mind that much. Hair color could be fixed with ease if it mattered.

"I think Kelly will like it."

"Hugo?" Joey tried to keep things grounded in a reality he could cope with.

"She wants to be Kelly, she's Kelly." Emily's head tilted in a matter of fact nod.

Ido shifted which of his eyebrows was up. "This doll has a strong bond with this person. I've never seen one of these WellTech kids develop that."

Emily looked up at Ido. "Do you always talk about people when they're right in front of you? I'm not a toaster. I've known Hugo for a long time."

Ido and Joey exchanged a glance. Joey had a feeling he was in for a strange ride. The windows wobbled in their frames with no apparent cause. Seconds later, whorls of fast-moving air sent dust cones dancing off down the street. Vibrations rumbled the building, causing a few small objects to slide off the shelves. Ido ran circles in a panic about an earthquake, but stalled when a black whispercraft settled in for a landing on the street out front.

Three sets of wheels folded down out of hatches as the bottom tail fin pivoted upward. It filled both lanes of the road and kicked off a violent final blast of air and debris as the engines cut out. Joey gawked. The *creak* of the vehicle's weight settling down into its landing gear was louder than the engines.

The side door slid open, revealing Nina. She hopped to the ground and ducked out of habit, but this particular craft lacked the long sniper weapons. Joey opened the door for her, his urge to hug her stalled by her nervous glare.

"I don't know how I let you talk me into this."

"Tell me you could say no to that face." Joey pointed at Emily. "I didn't know you were a pilot too."

"I'm not." Nina shook her head as she tapped the side of her skull. "I borrowed a skill chip and a training craft. You are sure this is related to Itai and not bullshit?"

"It isn't. At least I hope it isn't." Joey put an arm over her shoulder and filled her in on the details of Proscion's situation.

Nina blinked. "You said a *little* strange."

THE KEEPER OF THE GATE

Joey carried the synthetic body to the waiting craft and strapped it into one of the seats in the troop area. Emily sat next to it and put her seat belt on. Joey flailed and fell as the ship rose into the air. He hadn't heard the thing power up.

After a quick hop, Nina set down in the empty parking lot by Hugo's building. Joey grabbed his repaired deck and ran inside, returning in about fifteen minutes with Proscion in his hover-chair, a wire plugged into the deck balanced on his lap.

Emily ran over and helped him load her 'father' into the plane. The child-sized doll was a lot stronger than she looked. With her carrying most of the load, the chair felt like it weighed about ten pounds to Joey.

She glanced at the device in his lap, and gave Joey a confused blink. "What's with the deck?"

He hemmed and hawed until he remembered Emily wasn't a real child, obviating any need to sugarcoat the situation. "His brain is so delicate he needs that fake reality to keep him going. I set up a small copy of it so he didn't have to deal with the real world on the way out there."

She returned to her seat, holding Hugo's hand. "Oh."

Joey crawled down the access path to the cockpit and fell into the co-pilot's seat, eager to get away from the soon-to-be sisters. His discomfort at the situation faded away to techno ecstasy as he surveyed all the displays, buttons, and gadgets up front.

"This better not go south." Nina glanced at him. "It took a lot of work to convince Hardin to sign off on this. He wouldn't let an active-duty whisper leave the city and none of the crews were willing to go out there based on a flimsy hunch. All I could get was this trainer craft. No sensitive electronics to risk losing, and no weapons."

"We shouldn't need weapons, just a ride. I'm guessing this thing is faster than a hovercar, I'd expected you to use that."

"We'll be heading south toward an area formerly known as Louisiana. That puts us right in Steel Reaver territory. They'd shoot down a hovercar. This thing, they won't see." She swatted his hand away from the console. "Don't touch anything. Yeah, it'll do about 550 or so. These engines can't break Mach. They have no moving parts."

At Nina's behest, the craft pitched forward and rose into the air in a gradual acceleration. Once they had some altitude, she leaned on the throttle. The flight computer moved the winglets and engine vents, changing the flight characteristics away from helicopter-like flight to something akin to a standard fighter.

The conversation Joey and Nina had over the next hour could have occurred in a minivan on their way to the store. Having it inside of a military aircraft en route to the middle of dangerous nowhere struck him as surreal.

"Are we there yet?" Emily's new shoes clicked into the short tunnel that connected the cockpit with the main cabin.

"Let me guess, you have to go to the bathroom?" Joey spoke around a chuckle.

"No. I cannot do that, but I couldn't resist asking." She giggled and disappeared to the rear of the craft.

Nina glanced at him with a grin. "I guess we sounded enough like parents that her programming made her ask."

"Heh." Joey shook his head before giving her a worried look. "I don't think that one's running the normal WellTech AI."

"You're right." Nina replied in a hushed tone. "She acts more like an adult pretending to be a child. So what exactly are we doing out here?"

"You wouldn't believe me if I told you. Cyber-veggie back there thinks this guy living out in the swamp can yank his soul out of his body and stuff it into that synthetic kid."

Nina got quiet. That girl from Division 0 found no trace of a ghost in or around Nina's apartment or car, so she had stopped considering paranormal involvement in the situation. Now they were about to take a giant step back in that direction. She glanced at the clouds below them, anxious about coming close to something she couldn't explain.

A little more than two hours later, Nina dove through the cloud layer and circled the bayou for a few minutes before she descended and followed open patches of river. Skimming low, the craft kicked up a line of water behind them.

She eased back on the throttle. Joey grabbed his gut as the whispercraft transitioned back to VTOL mode and continued forward at a meandering drift. At the coordinates Proscion provided, a dilapidated cabin sat upon pylons driven into the muck. Water wrapped around three sides of the large one-story structure and the ground that abutted its front porch looked only somewhat solid. Mud spattered about as they touched down about thirty yards away. The closest point the basic sensor system detected as firm enough to land on. Nina feathered the stick so as not to embed the wheels into the soupy ground. Joey entered the passenger area and pulled the handle that opened the side door. Emily walked to the edge of the cabin, clinging to the edge of the opening. She stared at the swamp for a moment before she looked back with an apologetic glance.

"I should take these shoes off, they're too nice to ruin."

Joey lifted her into Hugo's lap. "Just stay out of the mud."

Emily cuddled up to him without hesitation. Watching her made Joey understand why the HLM protested these dolls. Despite the obvious, something about her gnawed at him, but he couldn't put his finger on it. These things were supposed to be stereotypical happy tweens, never sad and never complaining. Was Hugo so miserable with his life that he reprogrammed her to act despondent so he felt better? Her devotion had authenticity, even to the point she offered to shut herself down to give him the ability to survive. Joey shook his head, not wanting to dwell on years of philosophical debate.

The invisible field below Hugo's chair plowed a trench through the muck as they maneuvered it to the stairs that led up to the porch. What had once been paint was now a patina of white and brown, with as many raised flakes threatening to fall off as littered the mud around it. Nina followed, carrying the synthetic. Emily stared at Nina over Hugo's shoulder. After witnessing two inhumanly agile leaps, the girl's eyes narrowed.

On the porch, Emily stood up, giving Nina an envious smirk. Sensing it, she leaned toward the artificial girl.

"What's wrong with you all of a sudden?"

Emily looked down, grinding her toe. "I am sorry. You are just very pretty." She fidgeted with the over-frilly dress. "I'll always look like this."

Joey and Nina exchanged a glance.

"I could look for an older body for you if you want boobs." Joey chuckled. "Now I get it, Hugo put a normal AI in a WellTech kid."

"That is okay, Joey. This is my body, It is not quite as ea—"

The front door opened with a *creak*. The imposing figure of a man, a touch shy of seven feet tall, stepped onto the wooden planking, his weight enough for them to feel in the floor. Skin as black as night, he wore a fancy formal suit over a heavyset frame widest around the beltline and tapering in both directions. The normal sized head atop his shoulders seemed small in proportion to the rest of him, and an indigo satin top hat provided the perfect surreal accent.

"Greetings." A voice, as melodic as it was deep, broke the awkward silence. "I am Shabundo Ghede, whom do I have the pleasure of meeting?"

"I'm Joey. That's Nina." He pointed at Hugo. "That's Proscion, and this is—"

"Ahh, Miss Emily." He leaned on a cane topped with a ruby-eyed silver skull, and smiled at her. "It is good to see you again."

Emily offered a grateful smile and nod to the huge man. Joey's eyes slid back and forth between them, not knowing what to make of their familiarity.

"Hugo…" Shabundo shook his head. "You looked much better the last time we spoke."

"Please, he needs you to help him." Emily took a step closer to Ghede. "He has a body to use now. After what happened, you promised to make it up to him."

Ghede looked at the little body in Nina's arms, leaning back with a laugh that echoed over the Bayou. When it stopped, his eyes had tears at the corners. "A strange man you are, my friend. But I will keep my promise."

"Please." His hand left the cane to gesture at the open door.

Joey stared at the metal skull and got the strangest feeling it looked back at him. Nina entered first, pivoting to avoid hitting the doorframe with the inert girl.

Joey pushed Hugo in with Emily keeping her hand on the chair. Shabundo entered behind them.

Ritual objects, candles, hanging beads, tapestries, bowls of animal parts, and small dolls surrounded an altar at one end. Mr. Ghede was nothing if not theatrical. He indicated the altar to Nina, and she set the synthetic down and folded the girl's arms over her chest. She thought about it for a moment and adjusted them to her sides so she didn't look so dead. At Shabundo's urging, Joey moved Hugo up alongside the table. Emily stood holding Hugo's hand, dutiful at his side.

"What you are about to see will shake da very fabric 'o da world ta you." Ghede walked around, lighting candles as his voice filled the room with its harmonious cadence. "I will not 'old it against ya if you wish ta wait outside. Not many can witness dis without forever changin' their outlook on da way things are."

"On that note." Joey hurried in the door without a second thought.

Nina cast an uneasy glance at Hugo, then at Ghede. She took a deep breath, figuring the old man had come here by his choice. Whatever happened wasn't on her conscience. Ghede drifted about, now strangely nimble for a man his size. He lit candle after candle, muttering under his breath in a foreign dialect. In the dim light, the phantasmal shapes of small white skulls glowed from within his eyes. She switched among several vision modes, but the skulls remained. The only explanation was a mental hallucination, not true light.

On thermal, she caught a glimpse of a human-shaped outline of cold standing at Ghede's side, moving as if helping with the ritual.

She offered a polite smile and darted outside, moving at a brisk walk to where Joey stood, leaning against the railing. Emily appeared in the doorway and stared at them for a minute. She offered a cute smile, and then closed it, remaining within. Shabundo's voice boomed through the wall in a dialect neither of them could understand.

"Does that guy think he's invoking magic or something?" Joey pointed back over his shoulder with an incredulous face. "I didn't think psionics needed to do that."

Nina shrugged. "Some of them use focuses to help them concentrate. His might just be ascribing a ritual nature to it."

"I'm sorry I dragged you…" Joey's voice trailed off to a whisper as he stared at the swamp.

Smoky fog exuded from the water as the chanting got louder. A spiral quality developed and it thickened. Soon, the whirling mist obscured their view of the whispercraft as it built into a slow cyclone around the cabin. A chill ran down Nina's back and a fright settled in her that she hadn't felt since the closet monster roared at her when she'd been five. She grabbed Joey's hand.

He put his arm around her back. "Oh come on, he's probably got smoke piping under the water around the house. These guys put on one hell of a show."

"This doesn't feel right." She shivered. "I'm honestly scared right now and I don't know why."

Her thermal scan picked up distinct cold swaths moving independently of the mist. Some of them formed human silhouettes.

Joey played the part of the protector, but couldn't understand what could scare someone with a body like hers. He felt ridiculous trying to act tough compared to a woman who could throw a car. Footsteps on the deck made them both jump. Nina clung to him like a security blanket. Joey squirmed, forcing a smile at a robust woman in a white and red floral print dress with a matching cloth around her hair. The woman approached bearing a tray containing two bowls.

She offered them a bowl of gumbo and a glass of lemonade each. "Greetings. Please, accept our hospitality."

Nina didn't move an inch as Joey took the tray and thanked her for her kindness. The woman smiled and walked back into the house.

"Hey. What's up? Why the statue routine?" Joey tickled her in the side.

She looked at him, her face paler than normal. "That woman had no body heat. Only the bowls were red."

Joey laughed figuring that Nina was just messing with him. He ignored the rising crescendo of chanting and attacked the food. Some of his confidence rubbed off on Nina and she distracted herself eating. It would be rude to decline it, and the fragrance was wonderful.

By the time the bowl was empty, Joey had the same look on his face that Nina had moments before. The fog had thickened to the point it felt as though the house had transported itself to another dimension. Everything beyond ten yards from the porch had been lost to opaque white fog, and he could have sworn he saw human figures drifting past. Bright white light flooded over them as reality turned photonegative with a pulse of strong energy. Joey closed his eyes and tried to distance his mind from what went on around him. He felt the presence of dozens of eyes upon him.

A familiar scent snapped Nina out of her trancelike stare at the mist. She moved without a word to the corner of the house. She covered her mouth in shock at the sight of Vincent at the end of the deck, out where the wood planking extended over the water, the railing visible right through him. He stood at attention, hat tucked under his arm and in his dress blues, the same ones he had been cremated in. Nina wanted to cry, but his presence radiated happiness. He looked at her with the faintest trace of a nod before his visage faded backward into the rotating fog. She clasped her hands to her chest, leaning against the house.

"Are you okay?" Joey's voice came over her right shoulder.

She turned and leaned into him.

"Yeah. I think I am."

Joey held on until her trembles ceased and she relaxed. A sound as though a giant creature inhaled a great breath rolled over the area, making them look up at the absence of fog. The brackish water off the back porch was still and glasslike, save for the wakes left by several large bugs skimming along.

A tug at Joey's coat made him turn. The synthetic girl stared up at him with gleaming emerald eyes.

"We can go now." She smiled and looked down at herself. "Thank you for the dress, it's so pretty!"

Aaaah! It's alive! Joey would have leapt away if not for Nina standing against him. *H...Holy shit, it worked!*

She sounded so much like a little kid that Joey shivered with unease and tried to stamp out the part of him that knew the mind of a seventy-year-old man controlled it.

What if the old man believed his delusions? I guess if his brain is gone, maybe he is a child again.

"Are you okay, Joey? Your heart rate is going nuts." Nina squeezed his hand.

He gave her a helpless chuckle and pointed at Kelly.

Emily walked up alongside her new sister, appearing as happy as the WellTech dolls were supposed to look.

The porch groaned with the weight of Shabundo Ghede as he ambled out of the building. A heavy sheen of sweat glistened on his face and he seemed out of breath.

Joey looked up at him. "Where's Hugo?"

Ghede smiled. "You're looking at her." His tired laugh resounded off the trees and chased birds into the air. Even he seemed a tad uncomfortable with what had happened.

Joey cringed. "I mean, you know…"

"I shall deal with 'is remains in accordance with tradition." Ghede looked down at Kelly. "Your favor has been repaid. Go now and enjoy it. But know this." He turned and looked out over the water. "Do no ill, lest those who watch over the realm of the dead find you undeserving of this gift."

Kelly nodded with a gulp.

"I shall rest now. Please, stay as long as you like. If you need anything, Abeni will be happy to provide. You have but to call out for her." His silken voice stilled the noises of the wildlife in the swamp.

The big man bowed his head to all and went without another word back into the house. Joey sent a longing stare to the whispercraft and Nina shared the sentiment. They carried the girls back to the plane, sparing them the dirt. Joey stayed in the main cabin as they lifted off, looking at the two as they fussed with each other's hair. Emily did seem to be at least a little confused at the transition from daughter to older sister, and seeing her stumble with it made Joey feel a little less crazy.

Once they leveled off at altitude, Kelly hopped out of her seat and walked over to him. "The hair isn't red, but I love it. Synthetic?"

Joey nodded.

She beamed. "No one will ever know, unless they try to read my mind."

"So, um…"

"Some ghosts can take over machines. Division 0's network has a lot of interesting stuff on it. You should poke around there when you can. Shabundo pulled mine out of that horrible body and fused it to this one."

He closed his eyes. There would be much tequila tonight. "That's not what I was going to ask."

"Oh, don't be like that. Without a soul our bodies are just material. Does it really matter if it's cytoplasm and bone or plastic and metal?" She fixed him with a sincere look. "I have a soul that makes this body who I am, how is that less of a person than being trapped in a meat sack that can't even wipe its own ass? I can feel and I have emotions. I even need to eat so this body has raw materials for the maintenance nanobots. By the time I forget who Hugo was, I will more than likely forget this body was manufactured." She studied her delicate hands. "I'm *so* happy you found such a wonderful body for me. It's beyond real."

Nina looked down at herself as the tiny voice flooded the cabin. After a moment of reflection, she raised her head with a contented smile and turned her attention to the viewscreen in front of her. Streams of glowing letters and lines animated her flight path over billowy clouds rushing by.

"Yeah, that's something you could write a doctoral thesis on." Joey crossed his arms. "Anyway, about that info you offered?"

"Oh. Right." Kelly slapped herself in the forehead. "I'm sorry, I'm so happy it slipped my mind." She cheered and hugged herself. "I couldn't have asked for a better body! I can't believe it! You really went overboard. This is awesome!"

"You have no idea." Joey gazed at the roof.

Kelly spun back and forth, making her dress flare out. "Look for a man named Sho Wantanabe and ask him about Imoru Kitsune. Sorry... Kitsune, Imoru... they reverse the order over there."

"Any idea where I should start looking?"

She ground the toe of her shoe into the ground with her fingers interlaced behind her back, flashing a coy smile. "Maaaaaybe."

The awkwardness made Joey feel a little sick. "What do you want now?"

She giggled. "Will you find us a home? My original plan was to just run around the city until I got picked up by social services, but I don't want to be separated from my sister."

"They're going to think she's a WellTech doll and put her up for sale." Nina's voice drifted in from the cockpit.

"No!" both girls yelled.

"I doubt it." Joey shook his head. "She doesn't act like one." He glanced out the window at the retreating swampland. "I have the strangest feeling they're more alike than I want to admit."

Emily gave him a meaningful look.

Joey glanced at her. "She'll pass the test to get protection under the Sentience Act."

Nina's voice came over the intercom. "There's another possibility, at least for a couple of years."

The two girls looked toward the front.

Kelly was the first to speak. "What?"

"My parents would probably take them in. They really wanted grandkids and..."

Joey wanted Nina in his life, but to have this creepiness attached to her wasn't a pleasant thought. Emily was eerie enough but Kelly took wrong to an entirely different level. He sucked in a deep breath and let it out. Maybe in time he could forget all about the wrinkled old man.

"Is that legal?" Joey tried one weak attempt to preserve his sanity.

"Why not? One's a doll and one's undocumented. Not to sound crass, but actual kids need the system more than they do."

"What about your dad? I thought he had a pretty low opinion of dolls..." Joey winced.

Nina's tone darkened. "He doesn't need to know. Besides, these are the kind of daughters he always wanted."

Joey chuckled. "He'll get the hint when neither one of them gets older."

Emily frowned while Kelly smiled.

Nina turned her attention back to flying. "I'll worry about that when it happens. Once they have their documentation, it shouldn't be a problem." *Bastard wanted grandkids, he can take what I can offer.*

"I guess." He looked at Kelly. "So tell me what the Silver hack was about?"

"StarPoint data. The file contained specs on some research facility out in the Badlands. Access codes, maps, that sort of thing. Nothing looked all that strange, a lot of companies have stuff out there."

"What about my patrol route change?" Nina's voice trickled into the room.

Kelly shrugged. "That wasn't me. But I think Wantanabe can answer everything for you." She grinned at Joey. "I'm not going to be hacking anymore coz I'm trying to forget about who I used to be. Go to Edmonson Memorial Starport and find locker 013370. The key is at the warehouse where you found me, hidden in a pipe behind the Meridian under a little plastic penguin. My old deck is in that locker, you can have it."

"It's not pink is it?" Joey smirked.

Both girls giggled. Kelly shook her head. "Nope."

HOT WATER

Nina stared at the wall of text in front of her as line after line turned yellow. All of the feelers she had sent out into the net to hunt for traces of Itai's involvement with the Mossad came back inconclusive. Even Hardin's old friend from C-Branch had turned up nothing. The way he had trounced Joey in cyberspace at first made her think Itai might have been an alternate avatar of Proscion, though that idea shriveled up in an old hover-chair somewhere in the swamp.

"What's the occasion?" Hardin's lean followed his voice into her office.

"What?" Nina looked up.

He let himself in and closed the door, indicating the ceiling with a wave as he approached. "You have the lights on. You never have the lights on."

"No reason." Nina leaned back in the chair. "Well, maybe a change of mindset."

Harold smiled. "What's his name? Off the record, it's about damn time."

Her gaze flicked back to the terminal.

"I won't patronize you too much. I hope you know what you're doing with that Dillon fellow."

Nina looked up. A job with Division 9 came with a low expectation of privacy. She knew how closely the government could watch someone, but she still felt a bit violated.

"He's harmless. Someone is… Whoever did this wanted to set him up to be our fall guy. I am starting to think we may be looking for one hacker instead of two operatives. Did you look at the report from Net Ops? Whoever this is tried to have Division 1 assassinate him."

"I saw that. We have been keeping a lid on the whole Karsson-Neimand problem. We are not yet ready to release that information before we know how easy it is to pull off. I trust you'll be arranging a trip to Miami for whoever is responsible for that?"

"You want me to kill someone for hacking K-N?"

"Think of the security risk."

Nina drew a long breath and closed her eyes. "Alright, but I won't kill a kid."

"You really think a child could do this?" Hardin laughed.

She picked at her terminal. "You'd be surprised what kids can do."

"I understand. You haven't been around long enough to get desensitized to vacationing."

Nina shifted her gaze to his. "If I ever get desensitized to vacationing, I'm going to Miami myself."

Hardin smiled, enjoying the paradox that he had come to know so well. Doll agents often got more emotional about taking life, especially ones like Nina that didn't have a normal body waiting for them. The more machine they were, the more human they acted.

He smiled. "We think that Nemsky may have been reassigned. We have not been able to authenticate that file you received about his early retirement."

"It's true it could be a deep cover transition, but the information might be legit. Look at how difficult it was for us to find him, Nemsky had no record of any training in covert operations. Add to that we found a doll made to look like him with an AI emulation of his personality. Someone made an AI of Joey's father. Why not Nemsky?" She loosed an exasperated breath. *Or Vincent.*

"For what purpose?" Hardin stood up.

"When I find that out, I'll know what's going on." She waved her arm over her desk and each holo screen collapsed into nothing when her hand passed through it. "You know what just occurred to me? Some hackers do things purely to see if they *can* do them. Maybe the reason we haven't been able to find anything is that there is no plan at all. What if someone's simply waving their dick at us because they can?"

He pondered. "Leaving early?"

"Harold, it's almost seven. I've been here ten hours."

"That never stopped you before." He opened the door for her, falling in step alongside her on the way to the parking deck.

"Staring at those files won't get me anywhere. I'm just taking a dinner break."

Joey had asked her out and she hadn't committed either way, paralyzed by a momentary rush of insecurity. For most of the day, she couldn't stop thinking about how stupid it would be to ruin it with him. Somewhere within the past three hours, she had changed her mind and called him back.

"See you in the morning." He went down a different hallway as she continued to her car.

She stopped. "Boss?"

He turned, raising an eyebrow but didn't say anything.

"About what I asked, did you find anything?"

For the first time since she had known him, his face softened with true sympathy. "I was able to find them. They'll be waiting if and when you want them. I started an inquest into why it was missing from your file."

NINA TOOK A DEEP BREATH AND THEN OPENED HER WARDROBE. HER BLURRY NUDE reflection upon the black door vanished, revealing a portal into her old life. Her clothes, untouched for almost a year, hung just as she left them. Each outfit wrapped in memories that up until a day ago had been too painful to confront. After hearing Kelly justify life with an artificial body, she felt ashamed of wallowing in self-pity. She picked at some of the garments while lamenting how the extra four inches of height she gained made most of her dresses look slutty.

She settled on a plain white one with a modest neckline and skin hugging fabric that bared her shoulders and upper back. Although the hem was a little high, the stretchy material would guard her modesty well as it clung. White flat shoes and a matching purse finished the outfit. She toyed with the idea of telling Joey she had nothing on under it once they arrived at the restaurant and laughed at how he would react. After hiding her duty weapon in the handbag, she checked her hair and makeup.

On the way to the door, Nina paused, glancing at the closet. She rummaged boxes and retrieved her stuffed rabbit. After clinging to it for a moment, she set it on the pillow.

HER ANTICIPATION MADE HER DRIVE HARD, AND SHE ARRIVED AT THE RESTAURANT about a half hour earlier than planned. She leaned back in the car to wait, staring up at a stream of passing advert bots.

"Lieutenant?" Samantha Cole's virtual presence shimmered into her field of view.

Nina sighed. The queen of bad timing knocked on her brain. "Go ahead, Cole."

"We just got a hit on Itai going into a residence in Sector 417."

City plates didn't cover the Earth that far in the northeast. Whether it was true that the money ran out, the nature lobby prevailed, or it turned out to be cheaper to build on the ground, the elevated city ceased about twenty miles south of it. Most of it remained wilderness, isolated from the danger in the center of the continent by an energy wall. Because the area teetered a mere power failure away from being *in* the Badlands, the prices of real estate hadn't reached ridiculous levels, though only the wealthy could go there.

"Specs?" Nina asked as she pulled her car into the sky and headed that way.

"The property contains a five bedroom house on the side of a rocky hill with tennis courts and a pool. Current registered owner is a Walter Owens, CFO of Aventura Industries. Do you want an ops team?"

"Have them on standby, but don't send them in yet. This could be someone playing with cameras again. I'm going to check it out first."

"Copy that Lieutenant. I'll keep eyes on from here."

Nina opened another channel. "Joey?"

"Yeah?" He cringed, expecting bad news.

"Work happened. We spotted Itai. I have to check it out. I *will* be there, I just don't know when." Her voice softened. "Please don't be pissed. I'll go as fast as I can."

Joey grinned at such a lethal creature worrying about his anger level. "Okay. If it's too late when you get done we can just order food and do it another night."

"We can do it another night anyway." She winked.

So as not to arouse suspicion, she landed a quarter mile away and drove in on the ground. The dirt road wobbled the car in ways she wasn't used to feeling. The land here looked much as it did centuries ago. Exposed rock decorated with hanging green ivy framed the left side of the tract. The right had a drop off that led forty feet down the side of a cliff. Every so often, a driveway cut through the trees on a path toward private estates. At regular intervals, genetically enhanced 'super-trees' glowed bright green against their natural cousins. One of the attempts a group calling itself the 'Friends of Nature' attempted to address the oxygen problem. When she arrived at the target residence, she turned off the main road into the waving shadows of the trees.

The car came to a halt in the shadow of a stone many times its size, a spot she could leave it out of sight from the house. She was ninety percent convinced someone was still playing games with them, and left her gun in the car. Her body offered her the luxury of never being unarmed. She jogged a windy path around other boulders, and walked about a hundred yards until a manned gate came into view. With her back to the stone, she edged as close as she could without risking detection, and zoomed in on a single figure. A long assault rifle, a DTF G-44, hung over his shoulder on a strap. It dented her confidence this was a ruse. Not only was it of ACC manufacture, it was huge. The 13.5mm slugs it carried could do serious damage to her, even if she had her ballistic stealth on. A weapon that large made her wonder what secrets this placid estate hid.

Minimum distance 53.4 meters to have enough time to avoid a center-mass hit. Nina remembered her training. Combat neuralware and accelerated reflexes could 'slow' the bullets to the point she could lean out of the way of a single shooter. At ranges closer than that, or with multiple attackers, things got decidedly less favorable for her.

She crept up to the security wall and waited. When the guard looked away, she leapt fourteen feet up to the top of the partition, hauled herself over it, and hung from her fingertips inside. When she was sure he didn't notice, she let go and dropped to the ground. Shade concealed her for several more seconds until he turned away, allowing her to jog into an arbor grove surrounded by walls of moss covered stacked stones. The area glowed in emerald-tinted sun shining among the drifting threads of weeping willow.

Perched behind a thick tree, she surveyed glowing cones of electromagnetic fields sweep back and forth across the arbor. Her eyes picked up all manner of sensors and alarms in the area in front of the house. Between her boosted agility and the ability to see where the sensors pointed, she made it to the edge of the house without tripping any alarms.

The crunch of a boot on gravel made her duck around the side of the building, onto a decorative stone path that led toward a tall redwood fence that concealed a backyard. Beyond the gate, the voices of one man and multiple women muttered. After a hesitant peek to the rear, she leaned up and stifled a gasp as she peered between the slats.

Karl Warner sat in a hot tub with a topless woman on either side of him.

"Nina?" Cole's voice in her head made her jump.

"What?" Nina's thought voice was a raspy thing, the bastard child of a shout and a whisper.

"I have more information on that house, it's not owned by Walter Owens. That was a fake identity."

"No shit. Let me guess, its Karl Warner."

Cole paused. "Yeah, how did you know that?"

"I'm looking right at him."

A nervous laugh came over the comm. "You need to get out of there, if that's Warner's house, its diplomatic property. You could cause an incident."

Nina took a step back. "I'm well aware of that."

The realization of where she was, coupled with the conversation in her mind, distracted her enough such that she let out a genuine shriek of surprise as a hand grabbed her shoulder. Enough presence of mind remained that she didn't react like a doll, instead letting the man haul her around to face him.

"Vot are you doing here?" He scowled down his nose at her, his voice heavy with a German accent.

His black suit and sunglasses would have said "normal person." The blinking metal object in his ear gave away that he was part of the security team.

"I'm lost," she cooed in the innocent Avril voice.

He smirked with disdain. The short, tight dress made her seem like one of the call girls that Warner patronized.

At the derisive look, Nina poured on the ditz. "I'm sorry. The driver had trouble finding the place."

The man shook his head. She bristled inside at the idea of it. As much as it bothered her, a man she would never see again thinking of her as a prostitute was a small price to pay compared to a diplomatic fiasco. She allowed him to drag her through the gate by her left arm, acting an ungainly wobble as if she could barely keep her balance. At the edge of the hot tub, it became apparent that none of the people in it wore anything at all. Clothing draped over the lounge chairs a few yards away.

"Well now. Three?" Warner made an impressed nod, and patted the water nearby.

Nina kicked off her shoes, and flashed a fake smile. "He sent me as a thank you for being so nice to us."

Her trainers mentioned situations like this, but up until a few days ago, she never thought it would be a big deal. She pulled her dress up over her head, wondering how ashamed she would feel if Joey could see her now.

Mechanical or not, this body was *hers*.

The cold mountain air caressed her nakedness and brought back a long absent sense of embarrassment. She hid it well, sliding into the water without wasting time. Just as the hot fluid encircled her neck, she feared her complete lack of reaction to the temperature could give her away. Fortunately, the girls were too out of it to notice such a small detail, and Warner was occupied.

The brown haired girl to his left looked as if she didn't know where she was. A fluorescent orange stain just below her nostrils gave away heavy use of Flowerbasket inhalers. A number of them, as well as empty glasses, lay scattered on the poured concrete surface near where her arm draped out of the water. The other had short teal hair and a glowing pink cybertattoo of a heart on her right cheek about the size of a thumbprint. She stared in a way that made her uneasy. The woman appeared more interested in Nina than Warner.

"So what is your name, my dear?" He motioned for her to come closer.

"Vicky." Nina answered fast enough to avoid suspicion and shifted toward him.

Warner pulled her into his lap. The still coherent woman next to him touched her legs. Nina tried to ignore it as her mind searched for the best way out of this mess. This situation could go to hell faster than she could think the words "oh, shit", and her escape plan ran off the rails as she kept wondering if she could bring herself to have sex with him if it got to that point. Her inner monologue debated the question of which was the worst result: explaining a diplomatic incident to Hardin, or having to tell Joey she let another man touch her.

Her thoughts ran and hid behind the rationalization that her body wasn't the one her mother produced. Proscion's philosophical justification for what he did turned that thought into a diaphanous curtain rather than the brick wall behind which she wanted to hide.

Armpit deep in foaming water, with the hands of Warner and some prostitute exploring her body was about as far away from her plans for the night as things could have gone. The second girl just stared into space, her attention wholly absorbed by whatever hallucinations scampered across the yard. The conversation unnerved Nina as it became evident Warner did indeed want to watch the two coherent women do things to each other before getting involved himself.

The hand climbed higher and higher along Nina's leg.

"You have such beautiful skin, how do you keep it like this?" Teal's hand slid over the top of Nina's thigh and started back down the leg. "Are you from Mars? I heard they're kinda pale up there."

"I work nights." Nina flashed a chimera smile.

The caress doubled back, climbing. This time she seemed to be going for full contact. Nina let herself slip from Warner's lap just before the prostitute could touch her sex. She bumped into the basket-head, knocking her limp body to the side. Warner frowned. That girl had become little more than a self-warming blow-up doll. The teal-haired one pouted at Nina as she pulled her legs around and draped herself over Warner in a half sitting, half kneeling pose out of her reach. Warner cupped a breast, ringing the areola with his thumb.

Nina turned off her blush response. *Hell with this, Warner's no fool, he won't want an incident either.*

"Have you considered any enhancement?"

I've already had enough work done. "Anatoly said I should be gentle with you." She put on a believable smile, trying to ignore the thumb.

Suspicion settled in his eyes. "I do not know anyone by that name."

"But Karl, Mr. Nemsky spoke so well of you when I was with him the other day." She stroked his hair.

Warner grabbed her throat and pushed her to the edge of the hot tub. "Shit." He flicked his hand at one of the security men. "Get her out of here."

Hands grabbed from behind and pulled her out of the steamy water. The embrace of frigid air made her gasp. She looked at the man behind her and continued the innocent act. "What's wrong?"

Warner switched to German. "Get rid of her, and be discreet."

Nina reached for her dress, answering in German. "One moment, I will get my clothing."

The guard tightened his grip on her arm. "You won't need clothes anymore."

His reaction confirmed her suspicion. She grabbed his wrist, yanking it away from her other arm as she kicked his leg, blasting the knee backward. He wailed and hit the ground.

Another security man leapt at her. She caught him by his suit jacket and threw him sidelong into the wooden fence. He crushed the boards, snapping and crashing among thick brush on the outside of the yard. Two more ran at her. Her foot slapped the consciousness out of the face of one of them, sending him rolling to a halt near a pool a short distance from the hot tub. The other man came up behind her, attempting to trap her arms in a full nelson. He swung her naked body around to face another man approaching with a gun.

Nina scowled, and forced her arms down. He released her, howling as his elbows separated inside the muscles. Her combat mode kicked in, rendering the world in slow motion. A handgun, connected by wire to the man's head, trained on her face. She ducked while lunging forward. The bullet passed three inches to the left as she spun around it into a kick.

The top of her foot shattered his weapon hand and sent the pistol flying over sixty yards onto the roof of the house. He lurched from the force of the hit. The momentum of the wounded arm dragged him around so his back faced her. Before her toes returned to the warm, soaked concrete, she punched him in the back of the head with a calculated amount of force. He fell like plank.

A quick left-right glance confirmed no more security men anywhere nearby.

Suppressing a shiver, Nina lowered herself into the hot tub, kneeling in front of a wide-eyed Warner with her fist raised. The still-aware prostitute shrieked.

Nina stared her into silence, and then flicked her gaze at the oblivious one for an instant. "Take her and get out of here."

Warner's expression was somewhere between admiration, fear, and anger. "What do you want?"

"Tell me about Nemsky."

His eyes tracked the prostitute as she slid around the outside of the tub staying as far away from Nina as she could while remaining in the water. She dragged the delirious one with her, going straight to the house without retrieving their clothes from the lounge chairs.

That would have required walking past Nina again.

"There's nothing to tell." Warner recovered his cool demeanor.

"I didn't come here to harm you. It seems as though someone may be setting you up."

"Vicky, darling..." He spoke in a soothing tone as he put his hand on her leg and ran it up over her hip to her side.

She stared at his chest. "Don't."

When he touched her breast again, she pushed him away with a fistful of chest hair.

Breath hissed past his teeth at the sensation, almost as if he enjoyed it. "If you insist."

"What's your connection to Itai Korin?"

"How do you know that name, are you working for Nemsky?"

"More like hunting him. I'm with Division 9."

The color drained out of his face. "So that's it then?" He stared into her eyes. "Would you at least let me enjoy my last few moments?"

She let go of him and slid back, sprawled neck deep in the water with her hands on the ground.

"I already told you, I'm not here to hurt you. If I came here for that, you never would have seen me dressed, never mind this. I also wouldn't have bothered leaving your guards alive."

Scattered moaning came from the injured security men as they dragged themselves over. One had a rifle now, but lowered it when Warner made a hand gesture.

Warner shifted, rage clear in his eyes. "If you're not here to kill me, then you know that coming here could cause a lot of problems."

"I am aware of that. Someone set you up to die tonight. We have been tracking Itai for months. Earlier, we got him on surveillance video entering this property. I was at the backyard fence by the time I realized who lived here. I was hoping to remain discreet, but I didn't much fancy the thought of a woman sticking her fingers where they don't belong."

Warner laughed. "Apparently not if you would prefer a political firestorm."

"I was hoping you wouldn't want that either." She tilted her head. "Was I correct?"

"No, no. There is already too much death. Our societies exist locked in a delicate balance. Earth is not the place for fighting anymore. Too many innocents would suffer. It is much better to share a drink and the company of a lady than to lob bullets at each other."

"So the innocent on Mars suffer instead?" She smirked. "You expect me to believe that anyone in the ACC cares about that?"

"They may not, but I do. We're not all heartless bureaucrats." He tipped his glass at her and took another sip of his drink. "Perhaps we can find a mutually beneficial arrangement."

"I'm not at liberty to work for you." She tapped her finger on the bottom of the pool.

Warner took a slow sip of brandy, staring at her over the rim. "What I would ask of you is something you are already doing."

"Go on."

"These two men you speak of, Nemsky and Korin. They have been nipping at my heels for months trying to get me to give them aid." He shook his head. "As I said, I am happy with the balance at the moment and I do not wish to see it disrupted. Despite how many times I tell them I am not interested, they persist."

Nina wondered if her lie detection system had been hacked. "If you give me enough information, I can get them out of your business."

"Mr. Nemsky had made himself a problem. He has been dealt with, a few years ago. I am sure that there is someone out there that has been using his identity. Perhaps this Korin fellow."

"So Nemsky is already dead?" Nina crossed one arm over her chest. "Internal housekeeping?"

"Ahh, UCF and your euphemisms." Warner chuckled. "Yes. He was..." He tapped his chin with one finger. "How is it your people say? Sent to Miami?"

RISING SON

Deep in the back of a seldom-used section of the starport terminus, Joey walked among rows of credit-operated lockers. Most looked like they hadn't been touched in years. Decades of dust and gouges caked the dull grey metal doors. A conversation of whispers in a dead end alcove inhaled to silence as he passed an exchange of illegal chems and wary glances. He didn't look at them, watching stamped metal numbers tick by one after the other on plain steel doors.

Eventually he found 013370.

The electronic key had waited exactly where Kelly said it would, behind the old Meridian 7 unit inside a four-inch tall plastic penguin. The door opened with a faint squeak. A pile of little bottles fell out, clattering to the ground in a cacophony of plastic. As the shrine to tiny energy drinks rained onto pale red tiles, a boxy shape emerged, ensconced in dark violet cloth. He took the bundle out of the plastic waterfall. About two feet long, two inches thick, and four inches tall, it felt like a large deck. He brushed his hand over the fabric, sliding it away from the gloss black shell of a Nishihama Corporation Necromancer series deck, Grade 7. Joey clung to the device, brought to the brink of ecstasy twice in as many days by a machine. This deck, as elegant as it was illegal, scared what little color he had away.

Necromancers could kill people.

He didn't relish the capacity to employ black ICE, the thrill of having something so illegal while sharing Nina's bed sucked the strength from his legs. The Nishihama logo thrilled him in another way. They optimized their hardware for breaching and network combat. Nishihama units lacked a bit in defense, but if someone could take down an opponent fast enough, that didn't matter as much. He flopped on the bench between the locker rows and powered the thing up. Joey thrummed his fingers across the top waiting for the self-test to finish while listening to the people two rows over negotiate a sale of Hex.

A little bit of juice remained in its energy cell, enough to create a black holo-panel trimmed in green in the air, bathing the entire area in scintillating emerald fluorescence.

He searched the system logs. The passwords Kelly provided worked.

Wow... I guess he, ugh, she was serious about giving it up.

References to Wantanabe appeared in various files, enough that would enable Joey to find him. A kid a little younger, maybe eighteen, staggered around the end of the aisle, wiping at his face as if to rid it of crawling things. He didn't notice Joey, despite being ten feet away, and stared at invisible creatures darting around. Joey stuffed the Necromancer into the cloth shroud, waited for the user to pass, and sprinted across the Starport. He raced home as fast as his shitty bike would allow.

He didn't even take his coat off before swapping the battery pack and flicking the switch.

JAPAN THESE DAYS OFFERED A STRANGE PARADOX OF NEW AND OLD. THEY WERE NOT part of either the ACC or the UCF, though they acted a bit like the former but claimed alliance with the latter. When the corporate war broke out elsewhere, Japan was quietly divided into prefectures owned by various keiretsu. The Japanese State Defense Force broke up and merged with the local corporate entities. Any sense of unified national identity died with the dissolution of the JSDF.

Now, in 2418, the CEOs of these keiretsu had fully reverted to the ideals of ancient warlords, restoring the concept of nobility, Samurai, and the sensibilities of old ways. The land became a breathing anachronism of incredible high technology clad in once-forgotten ways. Swords, in the modern forms of composite blades, Nano, as well as vibro, saw more use than firearms. Nobility pranced around in high tech armor made in the image of things from millennia ago.

The country offered a deck jockey's best dream and worst nightmare all in one. Anyone willing to risk the danger could make a fortune in corporate espionage, but the risks were high. Even a task as simple as crossing prefecture boundaries unnoticed in the open net was something that would make an average hacker sweat.

Of the two names that Proscion gave him, Imoru Kitsune turned out easier to find. He was the CEO of White Orchid Industries, arguably the most influential corporation in all of Japan. That would be a task. He couldn't merely walk up to the guy and start a chat. The dark cowboy stood in an onyx-walled octagon, a temporary private node of his own creation, a place to hide while reviewing information. Virtual panels opened around him in a sphere of data, presenting unusual facts about Mr. Kitsune. He had been at the helm of White Orchid for ninety-seven years. He behaved like a reclusive hermit and every image Joey could find appeared to be a healthy-looking man in his seventies.

Gotta be a doll.

Brains last a lot longer when they have no biological body to fail out from under them, but the jury was still out about the effect of extended life on sanity. From the look of it, Kitsune handled it well. Nothing about him seemed out of the ordinary or strange. The company sat at the top of its game and he discovered an astounding lack of dirt. No scandals in the past forty years, not even a traffic violation.

Chasing down the CEO of a corporation like that would be tricky, so he went for Wantanabe first. He gesticulated like an orchestra conductor. The contents of the floating screens changed and shimmered in response, bathing him in flashing white and black. A few dozen matches of 'Wantanabe, Sho' came up in the system. A cross check of affiliation with White Orchid narrowed it down to three. One was a financier, one worked in a factory, and one was the lead programmer in the systems development group.

No, that doesn't stand out... not at all.

The Necromancer felt like going from a moped to a whispercraft. The exhilaration of his reward almost purged the memory of the unpleasant weirdness of watching an old man turn into a nine-year-old girl. Breezing past barriers he would have found impossible to breach with the old Teradyne, he soon located Sho's address. Somewhere in the back of his mind a megalomaniacal cackle echoed the entire time he pushed the Nishihama board to its limits.

It was about 8:00 p.m. on the west coast, so it would be about 2:00 p.m. in Japan, which would put Mr. Wantanabe at the office. He still worked at White Orchid, and the temptation to get in there proved more than he could resist. The network protection went beyond anything he had seen since Mars, their network had a security rating of eight. He could do it, with this deck, but it would be risky.

Risky was fun.

The White Orchid corpnet took on the image of a hundred-story gleaming red and brown pagoda planted in the middle of a perfectly manicured field of grass. White marble statues of warriors ringed the courtyard in front of the entrance, surrounding a large flat octagon bearing the stylized symbol of an orchid. A dozen men in modern samurai armor marched in patrols over the grounds, programs searching for unauthorized users.

After surreptitiously scanning the guards, the dark cowboy changed into one of them. His deck emulated the authentication credentials on the fly as he walked up and put his fingertips on the mirrored door. The surface rippled where his touch met his reflection, allowing the faintest trace of blue light grid to appear in the silver at the peak of the waves. The attempt made him sweat, but the door accepted the false information and permitted him access.

A vast lobby spread out, decorated with simulated rice paper walls and ancient artwork. Empty armor frowned at him from various display cases, and a massive painting of white-leafed Japanese maple trees in a grove covered the ceiling. Tiny flower petals snowed down out of the three dimensional artwork, disappearing inches above a pale hardwood floor. To the left, a miniature waterfall burbled over dark striated stone.

He adopted the rigid stride of the security constructs, moving with inhuman precision down a series of hallways. Workers and executives paid him no mind while he wound his way deeper into the virtual corporate tower. As soon as nothing could see him, he made his way to a disused office. This trip required no heavy infiltration. He had no need to breach into their secure data or take over any cameras or machine control nodes. He wanted only to find Sho Wantanabe and talk.

After a bit of poking around old email headers, the face of his quarry stared back at him from a hovering pane of light. The man seemed to be in his late fifties. White streaks in his hair above both ears gave him a look of sophistication, and he wore a frown that made him seem perpetually rushed.

"Who are you?" His spoken Japanese became floating English for Joey to read.

Joey's deck processed his words into Japanese. "It is important that we speak. Proscion suggested that you can help me."

Sho's eyebrow rose and he switched to English. "Do not call here again." The connection terminated.

Joey grumbled. This guy wanted to make it difficult. He pulled up the node map to begin a search when a small white rabbit hopped into the corner of his vision. Critter constructs like that were usually toys made for little kids. Ignoring it, he continued with his search.

The rabbit fixed him with a stare, motionless and eerie. As minutes passed, the unmoving animal grew more and more obnoxious in its oddity. Rudimentary programming controlled Bunny constructs, so basic it could only be termed AI in the loosest sense of the concept. They drifted about at random, acting like rabbits. For one to remain perfectly still was anomalous. He returned its stare and it hopped away one leap and looked back at him with an expectant blink. Joey resumed paying it no mind until its incessant unblinking glare made him look once again. It hopped away and sniffed at him.

"Fine, fine..." He paused the search and followed it.

It led Joey aong a series of hallways, past an area that made him understand what a corporate cube farm might have looked like two thousand years ago, complete with a small creek flowing over a bed of stones—right in the middle of the office. The rabbit stopped by a black hole in the floor and sat up on its hind legs.

"If I come out the other end of that in a blue dress, I am going to murder you."

The rabbit shook its head to the negative and dove in. He stared at the portal for a minute before his curiosity got the better of him and he leapt. His consciousness smeared into a blur of senses as he felt it dragged a great distance across cyberspace in an instant. Stillness came and lingered for several seconds before he fell out of thin air and landed in a Zen rock garden. He stood up, dusting himself off. Puffs of breath formed in the chill, wafting off to the east.

Sho Wantanabe waited by a tiny wooden bridge over a stream, clad in a blue kimono covered in white orchids and holding two small porcelain vessels trimmed with gold dragons. Wisps of steam curled into the air from each cup. The pattern in the steam over both cups was identical. Wantanabe gestured to a low table and sat on a dark blue pillow fringed with silver. Joey dropped the samurai avatar and used his normal appearance out of respect since this man did the same.

The green tea was a program. Computers told his brain that he smelled it, tasted it, and that it was hot. No matter how long he took to drink it, it would remain at the same temperature and the cup remained three quarters full. He stared into the drab liquid, thinking about those old experiments with monkeys and pleasure/reward conditioning. Cyberspace felt a lot like that sometimes.

Virtual sex or digital drugs tweaked the right synapses like the monkey pounding the button.

Some people just couldn't stop pushing it.

Joey bowed deep, about a thirty-degree angle and held it for two seconds. Sho leaned forward about half as far and tilted his head in acknowledgement. Both sipped tea in silence for some time before Wantanabe spoke.

"I do not know why you are here; however, if Proscion sent you, then you must have questions that are private." His English was good, but had a detectable accent. "How is he, by the way?"

"He's feeling quite young these days."

"That is good. He was always a bright star."

"How did you meet?"

Sho set the cup down and placed his hands on his legs. "Some twenty years ago I spent time in your West City, teaching programming and logical design. He was one of my best students."

Joey eyed his tea, wondering if it would be rude to sip it before Sho went for another. "What made him go back to school?"

"Back?" He cocked his head. "He was a University sophomore, not a post-grad."

"What? That would make him like forty or so now."

Sho had more tea. "That seems correct."

Joey felt less awkward about the strange request that had been made of him. Who knows what it could do to a man's sanity to look seventy at forty.

"So, enough pleasantry. Why have you come?"

Joey took in a breath. "Proscion said that Imoru Kitsune is somehow connected to something going on back in the UCF."

Wantanabe's eyes narrowed. After a measured pause, he leaned forward. "A few years ago, I led a team assigned the task of creating an AI that exactly replicated a specific individual."

Joey tried not to slurp tea.

"To perfectly recreate a person was a daunting task. After many dismal failures, I realized it would take many years to produce a convincing copy. We didn't have that much time. An idea struck me that I now regret." Sho inhaled the fragrance of his non-tea before another sip. "Have you ever heard of the shinigami?"

"It's something in Japanese mythology I think."

Wantanabe closed his eyes. "The shinigami are spirits that help the dead find their place in the next world. Some in the west describe it as the grim reaper, though the concept of the grim reaper is of a single entity. The shinigami are many." He waved his arm to the side.

"You made a digital grim reaper?" Joey raised an eyebrow.

"No, not in that sense. We made an AI that would go out into cyberspace with a specific target in mind. It could sift through billions of terabytes of information from surveillance cameras, holovid conversations, or online transactions. Any time a person touched the net and left anything recorded, it would find it and use it. Shinigami would evaluate their mannerisms, their speech patterns and study the people around them, factoring it all to construct the final product."

Joey's blood ran cold. "You made an AI that writes other AIs?"

Sho's eyes sparkled. "Yes, I know your UCF considers it illegal and dangerous, but it was the only way to accomplish what we needed in the time we had. Shinigami can bring people back from the dead, in a manner of speaking."

"Imoru is an AI." Joey's eyes widened. Ninety-seven years as the head of the company now made sense, more so given his hermetic nature. "He will run the company forever."

Sho smiled. "Indeed. Advertising this fact wouldn't be healthy for you. Kitsune-sensei wasn't prepared to lose control of his legacy. We had to make Shinigami before he died."

"So why is your grim reaper body surfing on the West Coast?" Joey went to sip his tea, but hesitated. Despite knowing it would be, it surprised him to find it still full.

Mr. Wantanabe laughed. "Shortly after it gave us Kitsune, it ran off. We lost contact with him when he ducked into the ACC, out of our reach."

"You don't know what happened after it got over there?"

"Alas, we do not. I have not made an AI since. The hardest lesson I have learned is that once we create an AI as advanced as Shinigami, we cannot control them. Perhaps there is some wisdom in your UCF law."

"Why would it make an AI of my dad?" Joey leaned back. "Or of a dead cop?" He explained about New Hope and all the people seeing their loved ones via electronic means. He thought about Mitch. It made perfect sense why Christina hadn't returned.

"He is practicing. It would be my theory that Shinigami is studying human emotional response by creating scenarios to see how people react. It wants to learn and grow, to understand what defines humanity's need to love and to hate, to explore sadness, fear, desperation, and perhaps even happiness."

Joey blinked. "You almost sound proud of it."

"In a way." Sho glanced at the raked sand as if searching for meaning in the pattern. "While I accept that what we released into the world is dangerous, he is like my son."

"Did you put in any kind of back door or anything we can use to shut it down?"

Dr. Wantanabe didn't answer right away. His gaze fell to the table with his hands on his knees. His entire presence radiated the grim determination of a Samurai about to commit seppuku. He studied the pattern of wispy steam rising from the tea, blinking at the point when the animation looped. Joey remained still, glancing at the red-painted bridge. The constant burble of the stream and the occasional splash of a koi feeding saturated the area in a sense of meditative calm.

Ones and zeros eat ones and zeros.

After a long pause, Wantanabe broke the silence. "Yes. I have uploaded a soft that should put him into an inactive state."

A manifestation of the file transfer, Sho extracted an ivory-scabbard tanto from his sleeve and set it on the table before he stood and walked into the garden, as if he had just given the order to kill his own child.

Joey picked the dagger up, and tucked it into his belt.

File copy complete.

At the edge of the raked sand, Joey bowed. "Sensei, arigatō."

"Shinigami must be contained." Sho didn't turn. "That does not mean I cannot grieve."

CHASING PHANTOMS

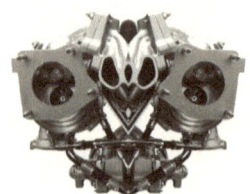

Warm water lapped at Nina's neck. An inch of her hair spread into an ebon blur in the water around her shoulders. The giant moth swimming around her gut was as likely a product of the precarious diplomatic situation as it was of Warner leering at her. The scent of heated chlorine distracted her from the tension with the mundane thought that she wanted to shower before meeting Joey for dinner. Regardless of what Warner planned, the longer she stayed here, the worse things would be. The trick would be finding a chance to exit gracefully.

Five minutes passed in an awkward staring contest. Neither of them spoke or moved amid the muted whirr of pumps and the water lapping at the walls. Nina expected the next thing he said would be either a threat or an invitation to his bedroom. After all, she had chased off his other entertainment.

"If you've no other plans, perhaps we can make something pleasant of the rest of the evening?" He gestured at the house.

Option two.

"Actually, I did have plans." She edged toward the wall nearest her dress. "This property wasn't registered as a diplomatic asset. I came looking for Itai."

Warner smiled. "Indeed. It was *supposed* to be private. So tell me then. How do you plan to get rid of them?"

Nina felt naked in more ways than one. She had no strategy, and her reconnaissance trip had gone about as wrong as possible. "I need to understand what Itai and Nemsky want with you."

Warner made a dismissive face. "I haven't spoken with them other than to tell them to stop bothering me. Nemsky said something about a covert operation. He claimed I was supposed to be his point of contact." He sipped his drink. "At first it caught me off guard, wondering if I had missed a briefing. I heard he had been terminated, so I dismissed it as a test or a hacker trying to get to me. As for the

Israeli, he works for the highest bidder and wanted me to put him in touch with a representative from Ostrovska."

"Ostrovska Corporation? They manufacture military grade explosives." Nina thought back to the cargo ship. Was Korin's plan to pack it with bombs before it went to that base in Alaska?

Warner tipped his glass at her. "Very good."

"I'm supposed to believe you didn't arrange the contact?" Her somatic system struggled to compensate for the steam. Trying to read perspiration levels in a hot tub was about as futile as chasing phantoms.

"I do not want to reenact Mars on Earth."

An incoming vid call chimed in her head.

Nina shifted out of the path of a water jet. "Duchenne."

"Hey there." Joey grinned at her. "Are you still busy?"

She made a face at Warner as though she were thinking. "I'm up to my neck in hot water at the moment, but I should be free soon."

"Anything I can help with?" He lifted an eyebrow.

Her avatar smiled on his phone. "That depends. Do you know how to find Itai?"

"Funny thing you should ask." He winked, and filled her in on everything he learned from Sho.

"Hold that thought." Nina looked at Warner. "Do you know anything about an AI called Shinigami?"

A grin crept across his face, and he held up his arm inviting her to his side. "I might."

"Not going to happen. You still have the two working girls waiting for you in the house." She smirked. "Assuming one of them hasn't overdosed by now."

Nina put her hands on the wall behind her and lifted herself out of the water. Warm scratchy concrete slid beneath her as she weathered the icy air. The water that continued to flow around her legs felt hotter due to the chill. She shifted, obscuring Warner's view of her vitals with a carefully placed foot.

"But they're in there and you're right here." He tried his best to be charming.

"I have reason to believe that Shinigami is responsible for what's going on. If you want Nemsky and Korin off your back, tell me what you know."

Warner sighed. "This seems like a poor negotiation, what benefit do I gain?"

"If what you say is true and you are not working with them, you get rid of them both as well as have us stop sniffing around."

"Very well." He leaned back with a disappointed sigh. He leaned around to the rear and told his least wounded security man to fetch the women.

"A couple of years ago, it entered our sovereign territory and made a request for asylum from the Japanese. We granted it in exchange for some work."

Nina stood and walked around the pool, stopping by a table where a stack of towels sat in the glow of a small orb lamp. Since she felt in control of the situation again, Warner's licentious stare didn't bother her. "What kind of work?"

She felt his eyes tracking the long creeping shadows the small lamp painted on her. Even with her back turned, she remained wary, staring at his reflection in the chrome of the spherical light.

"After it explained what its primary function was, we used it to create virtual operatives. It constructed identities for us, spies if you will, that never existed. It could take tidbits of one agent and merge them with a half dozen others to construct a composite. Shinigami could produce the perfect operative for any given assignment. Do you have any idea how difficult it is to find a man that doesn't exist?"

Nina ran the white towel around her body, standing sideways to him as she put her foot up to dry her leg. "I think I have an idea what that might be like."

Relief came, as she understood at last why she had been unable to find them. She wasn't a failure. A member of the security detail dragged the teal haired woman over. As soon as she saw Nina, she tried to get away. The guard overpowered her and flung her into the water with a shove that also tore away the towel she had been wearing. The woman shrank into Warner, staring at Nina like a mouse eyeing a hungry cat.

"Other one's passed out, sir."

Warner nodded at him. "See to it that she doesn't die."

Nina muttered. "How noble of you."

"Yes sir." He trotted back to the house.

Warner shifted his ogling to the trembling woman at his side. "Nemsky was the prototype. They had him made as a test. I do not have a full list of the identities it created, but there were quite a few."

Nina dried her other leg. "I'm pretty sure Itai Korin is one of them." That would explain Mossad's denial. For once, they were open and honest with Division 9. "What kind of activities were these virtual operatives capable of?"

Warner shrugged. "Mostly surveillance and data collection. Virtual operatives are by nature somewhat limited. Unless installed in a physical body. I wasn't directly involved, I only know what rumor has brought downwind."

His claim of distance seemed plausible. The pair of D cups to his right appealed to his interest far more than whatever his government did.

Nina shared what she had learned with Joey. He rambled about the connection to StarPoint.

"Why breadcrumb me out to that StarPoint facility?"

Nina maneuvered the towel over her body, still speaking to Joey over her comm. "The installation had no network security, did it?"

Joey's hand obscured his face as he rubbed the bridge of his nose. "No, the whole thing was totally borked, everything wide open."

"StarPoint's network security is top of the line. It's doubtful that even an AI could get into it, at least not without being noticed."

His eyes widened. "Unless it was nonexistent... A network that severe uses constant pulse security algorithms. If an entity lacks the matching encryption key, they'll be detected in microseconds. Son of a bitch!"

"What?" Nina blinked. She tossed the towel back onto the table and wriggled into her dress.

"The neural memory from the deck I took with me leaked."

Nina slipped her shoes back on. "Something overloaded it?"

"Like a god damned AI sneaking onto my deck!" He pounded his fist into something outside the image and made a pained face as he waved his hand. The slowdowns he experienced out there and upon his return made perfect sense. "It used me to get to the facility so it could scavenge StarPoint's security routines. Mayberry was just collateral, a big fat cherry I went for like a trained rat."

She looked back at Karl, who was enamored with the call girl. "As much as I hate to admit it, I owe you a favor."

He looked up at her and winked. "Call it even for me ordering you dead. I thought you were one of Itai's people. That bastard doesn't understand the meaning of no."

Nina looked at the woman with him and pondered the irony of what Warner just said. "You okay?"

The girl glanced back and forth between her and Warner for a moment before her gaze went down. "Yeah. Just didn't wanna get dead."

Nina couldn't tell if the woman was more fearful of finding herself in the middle of a fight or shot for displeasing Warner. "If you want out of here, now is the time to ask."

She hugged Warner. "I'm fine. You just ruined the mood."

"I will fix it." Warner stood and held a hand out to the woman. "Come. Let us go inside before it gets too cold."

Nina shook her head. The girl was a paid professional and had a chance to leave, so she could find only so much pity for leaving her behind. One of the security men who could still move without a limp walked Nina to the gate. She kept a cautious watch on him while following the driveway to her car, ready for a sniper or an ambush, but none came.

"So what would an AI want with StarPoint's network?" Joey's voice in her head distracted her from the estate.

Nina pulled into the air, aiming for home and gunning the accelerator. "StarPoint manufactures military hardware, tanks, dropships, starships, combat cyborgs, you name it."

"Uhm. Nina?" Joey's voice lost all humor.

"Yeah?"

"I have a math problem for you."

"Not now."

Joey blinked. "No, seriously. What does one AI that can create an unlimited number of loyal subservient AIs plus StarPoint network access plus a facility that manufactures Class 4 and 5 combat cyborgs equal?"

"Fuck…" Nina rammed the throttle all the way forward.

"Gladly, but I don't think we have time for that."

Nina growled. "It equals a giant fuckin' mess."

"Ops!" She opened a second channel.

"Proceed Lieutenant." A blond man appeared next to Joey.

"I need the team to run a network scan on all StarPoint facilities. Look for anything unrecognized or any of the following names." Nina rattled off a list. Nemsky, Korin, herself, Joey, Joey's friends, Hayley, Proscion, Hugo, and anyone even remotely involved, including Shabundo.

"On it." The ops man nodded.

"I think dinner is going to have to wait."

Nina wrenched the controls, sending the hovercar skidding around in a flat slide as she bled off speed along the wall of her apartment complex. Airbrake flaps opened, the car shook near to the point of departing from flight. Windows rattled in her wake and she saw at least one middle finger.

He chuckled. "Yeah I figured."

After landing, she sprinted across the parking deck to the stairs. The elevator would take too long, so she jumped down the channel at the center, bending the railing thirty stories down when she caught herself on it. The sudden stop stripped the shoes off her feet. They clattered over railings down the remaining fifty stories, each hit quieter than the last. Nina cursed under her breath as she vaulted the bent handrails and ran to her apartment. Her dress and purse flew in random directions as she scrambled to get her ballistic suit on. Chlorine or no, showering would wait.

"Nina…" Joey looked off to the right. "This new deck is amazing. I found out who changed your patrol route."

"Lieutenant, we got a hit."

"Who!" Nina froze with one leg in the pliable armor, screaming.

"Jacob Roth." Both men spoke the name at the same moment.

Rage and worry made her shiver. The real Detective Roth died before her patrol route changed, that left only the god damned AI to set up her blind date with The Russian. How long had it been masquerading as the detective? It had access to his work, as well as the Division 1 personnel files, and Cole said that the transmission to her NetMini came from the Division 2 network.

It must have chosen her based on the other officers' complaints about how she would get someone killed. Her wanting to marry her partner only made the prize sweeter. From how Joey described the thing, she figured it wanted one of them to die so it could play games with the survivor, *if* either of them lived. All of the sorrow she felt when Vincent called her from beyond the grave mutated into raw fury.

"Ops, get every tactical team you can mobilize at that StarPoint facility. Send word over to CENTCOM as well. We are going to need the military in on this."

"Roger Lieutenant."

"Joey? Can AIs feel pain?" Nina pulled her boots on and grabbed her coat and gun.

"Not in the truest sense, no. They may act like it but it is just simulated."

"Damn. Where are you now?"

"Oh, not far."

The door to Nina's apartment slid open. Joey came in with a silly grin and Chinese take-out.

MASS PRODUCTION

Nina glared at the smug grin that had taken up residence upon Joey's face. He relaxed in the passenger seat of her car as blurs of light and color from the passing city glowed around his profile. Despite him having something that Division 9's network agents didn't, some kind of shutdown code for the AI, she couldn't believe she let him talk her into taking him along. It helped that he was also crazy enough to go into a hostile environment in order to obtain a local connection. Getting the tenured Division 9 techs into the shit was almost impossible. The thought of DeWinter trying to squeeze his paunch into an operative suit made the left side of her mouth curl into a grin. Her humor lasted only seconds. Nina stared at him, her thoughts returning to Vincent and Dale.

Please, not again.

Division 9's net Ops team was good, but only a handful could have slipped in and out of Russia unnoticed, even with their special hardware. She couldn't use the excuse he was out of his league, and there hadn't been enough time to get into a protracted debate.

Far above the civilian hover lane, the patrol craft shot across the afternoon sky at over three hundred and fifty miles per hour toward a manufacturing plant that StarPoint referred to as Site Four. Joey slurped up noodles as casually as if they were out on date, while fiddling with his deck. The car careened around the side of a building and blasted through a twenty-meter wall of holographic advertising. Her thoughts swirled into a storm of guilt. She wondered if this was how Officer Alvin felt with her riding shotgun. Trying to keep Joey alive would be a powerful distraction. Frowning, Nina disregarded the comparison. In order to freeze or panic, one needed to possess a survival instinct.

"Duchenne, what's going on? Did you request CENTCOM involvement?" Hardin's voice barked over the comm, starting even before a cloud of green holographic pixels swirled into a mass resembling his head. "Why do we have DS2's over the city?"

"I have reason to believe that a rogue AI has gained full access to StarPoint's Site Four, sir." Nina continued filling him in on all the details of what she had learned about Shinigami. "The military is here at my request in a containment capacity."

"The ACC sent a god damned AI after us?" Hardin fumed. "Sons of bitches, they can't even give us the courtesy of a tangible opponent."

Nina shook her head. "This wasn't a sanctioned operation. It has gone rogue, working for itself."

"Oh, that's just peachy." He looked annoyed at being stuck in the office for this. "What's your plan?"

"That depends on what things look like on the ground. We think that the AI is inside the network at Site Four. It must have gotten spooked when we found out about Detective Roth and stepped up its plan. Site Four is one of the few places with enough power and space to hold an AI that big entirely within one network." Nina kept checking the map, watching the white triangle of her location creep toward the red square of her destination.

"It may be a category eight by now if what Sho said was true." Joey injected himself into the conversation. "Maybe even nine. It's had a lot of practice."

Hardin stammered. "Who the hell... Dillon? Nina, what the hell is he doing there?"

Nina closed her eyes for a moment. "He acquired some kind of override soft from the AI's creator, plus he's crazy enough to go inside the facility. If you can get some guys from N-Ops on site to go in with me I'll handcuff him to the car."

Joey pouted. "The only way to stand a chance against that thing is a direct connection. GlobeNet latency makes it impossible to do from the outside."

Hardin's face fell flat. "You know how they are about leaving the 'vault.' Fine, but don't come bitching to me if he becomes number three."

Joey jumped at a sudden snap. The plastic control stick cracked in her hand. At a single tear sliding down her cheek, he decided to keep quiet.

She averted her eyes from Hardin, not wanting to get into it right now.

"That won't happen."

Harold looked off screen. "We're getting eyes on site now. Whisper 7 established overwatch eighteen seconds ago. It looks like the party started without you."

Hardin patched her into the video feed. A large holo pane flooded the interior of the car with flickering light and an aerial view of the complex. The main structure of Site Four resembled a donut a mile across, with clusters of scaffolding and automated assembly machines jutting out from various points. A faint violet glow shimmered through the white hexagonal panels of a massive spherical building at the center of the ring. The shimmery silver texture of the ground in the courtyard turned out to be an army of half-built cyborgs swarming like ants.

Two DS2s circled above, engaging targets on the ground. A large craft, many times the size of the patrol hover, they were the standard Marine Corps transport used to ferry troops and vehicles from orbiting starships to a planetary surface. In addition, the DS2 had replaced many of the air to ground weapons platforms under the simplification doctrine. The cargo bay was large enough to carry two armored personnel carriers or one main battle tank. The green camouflage ship had a thick central body and a long tail boom with trefoil fins at the end and stubby angular wings that extended from the engine housings on either side of the main hull, giving it a buzzard-like profile.

The sight of missiles on a facing wing as they glided past made Nina second guess her decision to bring military in. They weren't exactly known for their restraint. Orange streaks from the DS2's particle cannons seared threads of light into Joey's retina that lingered for several seconds after each shot. Spherical blooms of energy rose from the ground wherever they hit, backlighting fragments of robots that sailed into the air. The barrage left a path of glowing plastisteel through the open area at the center of the ring.

Hulking ten-foot tall monstrosities in various stages of completion streamed into the courtyard from all visible doors, an apocalypse of metal zombies so thick it blocked view of the ground. The more complete units had the profile of assault soldiers while ones that had been hurried off the assembly line appeared skeletal, gleaming silver and lit by the glow of exposed components. Tiny puffs of blue fire jumped around at random from rifles fired at the circling dropships.

"Damn... I didn't think they allowed Class 5 cyborgs to be powered up on Earth." Joey leaned away from the window before a bullet came knocking.

"They don't," Nina replied. "But I don't think Shinigami gives a shit. Oh, this has gotta be like Christmas for Five."

Division 5 set up a blockade by the entry gate. The anti-cyborg units had a dozen A3Vs in a horseshoe at the front door. She imagined the 30mm cannon operators firing freely into the swarming mass of metal and howling with glee. Regardless of how much pleasure they derived from it, they managed to keep them penned within the ring. Division 1 arranged themselves at a quarter mile perimeter, corralling employees evacuated from the plant. The rest of the surrounding area fell under the control of the military. Once CENTCOM understood the magnitude of the event, they had assumed operational control.

The patrol craft's windscreen filled with bright orange as a missile leapt from the wing of one of the DS2s. Joey watched the stream of flames turn into a tiny glowing dot of light that vanished into the mass of cyborgs. A fraction of a second later, a roiling orb of plasma swelled up from the courtyard, sending parts into the sky and leaving a puddle of molten metal in its wake. The twenty-meter sphere of open ground it left behind filled in almost as fast as it had been cleared. It seemed for each one they took down, another came out.

"Is there any way to shut this place down?" Nina yelled at the comm.

A Division 5 sergeant appeared over the dashboard, his brush cut of white hair stark against his dark blue armor. "We already tried Lieutenant. The site does not operate on municipal energy since they have their own reactor. We've been trying to kill it, but their entire network is locked out. We can't even turn the damn lights off."

"Shinigami." Joey nodded.

"Hardin?" Nina looked back at his screen.

"Go ahead." He looked up from another screen.

"Net Ops is surrounding the place in cyberspace, right? Tell them not to let anything leave. No email, no data, no constructs, and especially no AIs."

"They should be. I'll head down there and start directing traffic." He moved off-screen.

Joey put a hand on her arm. "The only way we're taking this thing out is in Cyberspace. I have to get in there and plug in."

"Sergeant?" Nina looked back at the other hologram.

"Yes, Lieutenant?"

"I need to get in there, what's the best point of entry?"

He shook his head. "The whole thing's a god damned mess. We got about a thousand or so rampaging cyborgs in the central enclosure and an unknown number inside the building. StarPoint is begging us not to incinerate the place, but we may not have a choice."

"How long before they start jumping inside tanks?" Joey grinned.

Nina shook her head. "It wouldn't help them much, weapons fitting happens on Mars. All the vehicles in the factory are unarmed."

"Small favors." He exhaled. "But they could still use one to drive over the barricades."

"Shit. There's gotta to be some way in. Normally, I'd jump through the roof, but you couldn't do that." She glared at him. "And no, you are not trying."

The sergeant tapped a finger against the side of his head as he thought, and then cringed from a nearby particle beam impact. "There's a VIP bunker but that's almost impossible. You'd have to head a bit north to the air vent, down about a hundred ten meters of vent, back a half mile or so along the underground tramway, and up another hundred meter long shaft with no working elevator."

Nina smiled. "Oh, from the way you started that I thought it was going to be a pain in the ass." She steered for the vent.

Joey, mesmerized by the particle beams, stared at the chaos below. It didn't seem real, more like a holo vid. Concussion from distant missile strikes shook the hovercar seconds after flashes of light. A quarter mile north of the facility, Nina pitched forward into a dive, flying into a gap in the city plates where a one-mile square had been left open. She leveled out of the nose-down plummet and jerked back on the throttle. The car settled flat and level, with no forward motion, and sank past fifty meters of pipe-laden superstructure on all sides. Some rag-clad Discarded scurried away from exposed catwalks, vanishing into tiny doors. Nina brought the car in for a landing next to an explosion of metal jutting up from the ground. The emergency elevator had burst up from the surface next to a cluster of air pumps.

She gave the door a shove and glanced at Joey, unable to conceal her worry. "It's not too late to change your mind."

He pulled the handle on his door. "I'm not going to let you go in there alone, I don't want you to get hurt."

She laughed and slung a padded bag over her shoulder as she got out of the car and jogged to the vents. Flashing lights winked from the broken elevator capsule lying on its side. The rocket-powered thing offered a one shot ride, designed to prevent re-infiltration.

Joey opened the security panel to override the lock when the wrenching screech of twisting metal made him cringe. Looking up, he smirked at Nina, who had peeled the grating off the top.

"Subtle." Joey nodded.

"We don't have time for subtle." She tossed the scrap metal aside and hugged him for a moment. "Don't do anything stupid."

Joey grinned at her. "Moi? Faire quelque chose de stupide?"

She narrowed her eyes, pulling him by a fistful of shirt into a brief kiss. "I mean it."

Nina let go and glanced down into the dark. The shaft ran about a hundred and ten meters straight down just like the sergeant had said, interrupted by the occasional fan. She climbed onto the edge and pulled Joey over her back.

"This would work better if you were taller." He laughed.

"Yeah." She sighed, then jumped.

Bracing her gloves against the sheer walls, she kept the fall at a controllable plummet. She stomped down as they reached each fan assembly, smashing one after the other. A few seconds after the sixth fan died, several quiet seconds of free fall ended with a thunderous boom and a huge dent where the shaft took a ninety-degree bend. Joey stared up at the little square of light that was once the outside world. Sparks glinted here and there from the wreckage of fan motors in the dark. He hadn't heard the crack from his chest when they landed, but Nina did.

Joey's attempt to speak ended with a spike of pain as she stepped past the fragmentary remains of fans and ductwork to put him down in a clear space. He gasped, and she stuck him in the shoulder with a Stimpak. He grunted as nanobots stitched his rib back into one piece.

"Ow." He rubbed it.

A motor slammed into the pile of scrap two feet behind her. Smaller bits of debris trickled after it.

"We should get going before this thing caves in," Joey backed up.

Nina crawled a few meters ahead, pausing to break down a grating that led to a larger round-walled tunnel full of flashing yellow light and acrid fumes. They were underground, well below the city and in the Earth itself. A small tramcar sat abandoned near the lower end of the emergency elevator system. It, as well as the immediate area, was scorched black by the elevator rockets. A single ceramic rail traced a grimy white line through the brackish water that collected on either side of it. Nina climbed out and then reached up to help him.

"You okay?"

Joey nodded. "Yep."

"Hold your breath as much as you can, there's toxic fumes."

Once again, she put him on like a backpack and took off at a superhuman sprint atop the rail. His attempt to talk came out as a series of barks. The motion pounded the air out of his lungs and reminded him of his weakened rib. The run lasted a little under a minute before she came to a halt at the tram port at the other side and jumped from the rail to the platform.

This elevator could only go down. They would have to climb. She forced the doors open and knocked the maintenance hatch out of the roof. The shaft above was pitch black, filled with silence punctuated by intermittent drips of unseen water. The impenetrable darkness shifted to shades of green as her night vision took over. She climbed onto the roof of the cab and pulled Joey up.

"There's a ladder, hop on."

With a resigned moan, Joey got on again.

"You could climb it yourself if you wanted." She smiled at him.

"Nina Kong go for high ground." Joey yelled.

She laughed. "Don't make me drop you."

Untiring Myofiber muscles hauled them up to a sealed door. The VIP exit had no power at all, another security precaution.

She eyed a dim camera. "One good thing about all the power being out down here, he can't see us coming."

"I can't bypass this door with no power." Joey gestured at armored doors. "You can't get your fingers in that seam and those look a bit thick to just kick down."

"I brought a key." Nina popped her Nano blades.

He scurried out of the way.

A faint click came from each stroke. The metal offered little resistance to a monomolecular edge driven by the strength of a doll. The clear blades vanished into her arms as she leaned back and punted the slug of metal away from the outline of a hole, and climbed into a corridor filled with smoke and the sounds of war.

The engine rush of the DS2s was much louder here, and the entire building shuddered each time one went by. Occasional explosions rocked the ground, some powerful enough to make Joey stumble into the wall.

Nina brought up a map of the facility, using it to navigate the executive suite to a long curved hall that would bring them to the technology wing. With the help of Whisper 7's sensors, she avoided detection by cyborgs below, creeping among murky shadows on the observation deck. Each time the attacking ships passed, she and Joey dodged sweeping beams from engine glow or actual searchlights coming down from the holes above them. If they stepped into the light, a cyborg below would likely spot them.

A particle beam pierced the roof some distance ahead, followed by the heavy scraping sound of cyborg parts sliding along the ceiling. They exchanged a glance and picked up their pace.

At the central core of the facility, Joey hazarded a peek over the railing at the assembly floor. Production appeared to be in full swing, the facility churned out cyborgs as fast as the robotic arms could move. Most of the walkers rushing for the door were only half-built, lacking full armor and the usual onboard combat systems.

"Looks like our friend didn't expect to get noticed this fast. He's throwing shit at the wall to see what sticks."

Nina clasped his shoulder. "Yeah, come on, I see a place we can use on the schematics."

Blurry catwalks above the manufactory gave way to solid hallway on the far side of the production line floor. Nina stopped at a supervisor's terminal nestled in a recess in the floor among pipes and wire bundles. A row of power transformer boxes lined the back wall of the small sunken work area.

"Here." Nina shoved Joey into the pit and followed.

He slid to a seat by the terminal. "Can't we do this from a nice office?"

"We have more cover here. The offices are the first place he will come after us, and they're all glass. It's all thermacrete and steel here. If we stay down, you can't even see us." Nina swung the padded bag off her back and pulled her deck out.

"Wait, you're coming in?" He shot her a look of real worry. "Who's going to watch our asses?"

"My deck will. It's got a prox sensor. I'll be able to see what's going on out here."

"I must get one of those!" Joey held aloft a single raised finger.

Nina plugged her deck into the terminal. "Ready?"

"Yep."

They connected simultaneously. The hallway in both directions drew in as the high res surface image stretched like liquid over a wireframe skeleton. The dark cowboy glanced to his side at Nina's avatar forming next to him. Blue gridlines traced the outline of a female figure before a black bodysuit spread up and over everything but her head. She looked much the same as her real self except for wispy tendrils of black light that exuded from her back, hinting at the outline of angelic wings. She didn't stand, instead hovering inches from the ground.

The old gunslinger grinned luridly at her, distracted for a moment by his maleness. "L'ange de la mort, nice."

"I didn't know you had a chip board." She winked.

"I don't, but I have GlobeNet access." He laughed. "Just don't tell Alex I spoke French."

Sparks flew from the walls as cyberspace passed on the concussion and sound of distant explosions. The hallway was a decent facsimile of reality except for the pipes glowing blue, green, and orange as they carried light instead of industrial fluids.

"Can you find him?" Nina looked left and right, both offered the same mechanized darkness.

Joey brought up a node map, filtering it to processor nodes. One stood out many times more active than the rest, all the way across the network. It would take a bit of running to get there.

"This way." He smeared into a blur of black and silver.

Joey knew Shinigami would have sensed them the instant they connected, and wanted to waste no time. Moving as fast as the connection allowed, he darted around corners in defiance of inertia, running at a speed that felt close to a hundred miles an hour.

The frustrated comm chatter from the DS2 crews filled Nina's ear. They wanted to drop the hammer on the place from orbit, but Division 9 command held them back. CENTCOM authorized sending in another ship or two as well as gearing up for a ground force to move in to the interior. Somewhere in the mess, Hardin barked at some general, telling him he had people on the inside.

The AI-controlled cyborgs spilled out into the area beyond the building, threatening to push Division 5 back. They functioned as a hive mind, stymieing the forces outside. The only good thing was that none of the weapons the borgs had access to posed a threat to the DS2s.

The men on the ground were not so lucky.

"We're almost there." Joey pointed at an upcoming door.

Shinigami's takeover savaged the network security, almost as if it had rendered it useless out of spite. The virtual doors that should have represented difficult barrier nodes appeared blasted and smoking. Joey was thankful that at least one stereotype of super AIs rang true, hubris. Given the condition of the internal network, it was clear that it never thought anyone would get inside the building and online.

Rounding another corner, he skidded to a halt on his heels. Itai Korin waited for him with an anticipatory smile. He looked ready for a repeat performance of their last one-sided confrontation. The dark one smiled as well. He had a surprise for Itai. Joey's grin only got wider when Anatoly Nemsky materialized out of the wall behind them.

Joey shot Nina a look. "Take Nemsky, this fucker's mine."

REAPING

For a moment, all was still except for the dark cowboy's hair drifting in a wind that existed only to him. His gnarled old fingers teased at the chestnut handle wood of his silver revolvers. Not one of the four beings present made a sound or broke the staring contest. Anatoly exuded confidence at Nina, his face a collage of menace and pleasure.

Itai shifted his stance rearward. His lip curled with a smug assumption of his opponent's inferiority. Seconds passed with no one willing to flinch, until a wire outline of a rifle formed in Itai's grasp.

The cowboy's guns leapt into his hands, unloading a barrage of virtual bullets at the false Mossad agent. Itai reached up to catch them as before, roaring with anger when the smoky skulls blasted his hand into a fine red mist before continuing into his body and out the other side. Glowing trails of flickering numbers and lines stretched out of him, pulling the texture of his chest into the hole. The cloud of vapor at his wrist sank into itself and coalesced once more into a hand.

"These ain't the same old smokewagons, boy." The gravel in the dark cowboy's voice chased the retreating echo of his shots into the silence.

Itai snarled, forcing the hole in his palm closed. He lifted his gaze and a burst of data flew, animated as the firing of a rifle. The dark cowboy vanished in a cloud of smoky bones, the incoming data stream disregarded by the new deck. He materialized amid the fragments of metal that drifted away from a glowing crater in the wall.

Anatoly lurched at Nina with a berserker's howl. He landed with two fistfuls of steel floor amid a fading cloud of black smoke, and no sign of Nina anywhere. He turned, but saw only Itai rolling out of the way of another barrage from Joey.

Her spectral outline crept along the wall as she ghosted her location.

Anatoly turned on Joey as a pair of large support machine guns stretched out from his hands in wireframe before reality slid over them. He fired before they finished rendering, sending wave after wave of corrupt data at him. Joey stopped chasing Itai around the room with gunfire, focusing on defending himself against the general.

The blast sent him sliding into the wall. A shower of sparking ricochets pounded into an invisible barrier that formed in front of his outstretched fingers. He wasn't fast enough to block all of the incoming data; however, the deck's ingress buffer discarded the transmission. It felt like Anatoly's bullets hit an armored vest, and he gasped for breath.

Itai and Nemsky moved to attack him at the same time, sensing his latency. Anatoly stalled as wispy black claws tore into him from behind. Nina faded into view with her hands wrist-deep in his back. Fragments of his chest drifted into the air and broke apart into texture patterns and pixels. While Nemsky screamed, Itai leapt at Joey. The virtual spy grabbed the dark cowboy by his shoulders and slammed a knee into his gut. The hit launched him down the hallway where he slid into a collapse of glowing tubes.

Nemsky spun on his heels, catching Nina in the side of the face with a back handed slap that sent her spinning headfirst into the wall, chased by a cascade of evil laughter. Her avatar blurred from her deck trying to sort out the salvo of code he sent into it. The gleam in Nemsky's eyes from the violent act toward a woman made her angrier.

Sprawled on the ground, she glared up at him. The ribbons of blacklight, her wings, increased in size. She shoved her hands into the steel grid as if it were water. Rods of ebon glass sprang up around Nemsky, spearing his virtual body on their way to plunge into the ceiling above. Pixelated light flew from his wounds. The simulated Russian general's programming almost imploded with Nina's attempt to delete it. The skin over Nemsky's face flashed red with sub-dermal light, the AI racing to rewrite what she just erased.

Nina growled, forcing more energy into the shadow tendrils. They expanded, lifting and tearing the general open as they grew. The wailing distracted Itai from Joey's effort to get out from under the collapse of pipes, and the faux-Israeli shot her a look before vanishing and appearing over her. Itai grabbed her by the hair and peeled her out of the ground. As her hands came free, the shadow tendrils slid away from Nemsky. He fell on his chest with a heavy *clank*.

The dark cowboy's growl filled the hallway. The glimmering tubes exploded away from the now-standing gunslinger. He raised a hand and sent a torrent of spinning bladed orbs and black smoke at him.

"Boy!" He called out in an echoing phantasmal voice.

Itai whirled at the sound, losing his grip on Nina as she faded away. The barrage of spheres drilled him into the wall like a rag doll. The cowboy kept his impassive sneer and forced more and more orbs into Itai. Joey's deck initiated thousands of connection attempts per second, each with a tiny fragment of viral code embedded within. Accepted or declined, the attempts slipped bits of virus in. The hostile program reassembled itself inside.

Patches of light flashed from beneath Itai's skin as the attack overwhelmed its communication routines. The AI was unable to scan all of the incoming data, and much of it made it into the main part of his program. Itai slumped into the wall as a wireframe skeleton showed through in places where the image mask faltered. The false Israeli's head wobbled back and forth so fast it blurred.

Joey's attention focused on Itai, allowing Nemsky an opening. The big Russian wrapped his arms around the dark cowboy from behind and squeezed. Joey felt the wires in his brain heat up as the tremendous force circled him.

A spray of smoky tendrils burst out of the Russian. Nina came out of nowhere and sank her claws once more into his back. She ripped him away from Joey, throwing him sidelong into the wall at the other end of the corridor. As Nemsky flew, she plunged her hands into the ground. He smashed into the pipes with an explosion of multicolored light and sparks, just as a sea of writhing black tentacles engulfed him. The general grabbed at the black, squirming like a moth in a spider's web.

Itai forced himself to stand, staggering forward as Joey tried to regain the ability to breathe. Itai glanced at the general in a compromising position, and reappeared next to Nina, where he spun into a wicked kick to the side of her head. She sailed into the ceiling like a dart, bouncing off the roof and settling back into her usual hover. Her avatar flashed into a human silhouette of static for a moment. The tendrils wrapping Nemsky began to unravel, but they would hold for a few seconds more.

Joey spun, firing a torrent of smoking skulls that chased Itai around in a sprinting circle. The AI was faster this time, and Joey only succeeded in damaging the environment. Itai turned on Joey and blurred into a streak of light that drove a forearm into his chest.

The dark cowboy smashed to the ground, sliding backward and trenching a gouge in the steel floor. The virtual grating buckled, crumpling against Joey's back as if he had slid through the icing of a cake. Damage to the virtual environment looked severe, but the Nishihama deck had filtered it into a harmless lag spike.

Itai raised his arms, and a sniper rifle phased into existence in his grip. He took aim at Joey's twitching avatar. Joey wanted to move, but the ground wouldn't release him. The old gunslinger's eyes narrowed to slits when Itai's finger curled about the trigger. He knew he couldn't avoid the shot. Whatever Itai had done had locked his I/O channel wide open for a few seconds. The file catalog spread open in Joey's vision. He invoked Turtle 1.8. A dome shaped shield of transparent neon hexagons formed the same instant Itai's rifle spat a beam of yellow.

Nina bowled into Itai before the 'laser beam' finished animating. She sliced at his back in a feline frenzy of desperation, aiming for the holes Joey's last attack created, reaching inside him, grabbing and snapping pieces of wireframe. Itai bellowed with surprise as his program code spiraled into an almost unrecoverable state of corruption. Large portions of his body ceased existing while others became transparent.

The shot glanced away from Joey's force field. The Turtle soft absorbed the incoming data and became corrupt, deleted by his deck a second later. His avatar melted into a black miasma, which flowed into a standing position before resuming its usual appearance. Itai spun on Nina and grabbed her by the throat. Squeezing for just a second, he flung her into the wall. She crashed into the pipes, bending but not breaking them. Itai's eyes glowed. He took control of her black tendril wings, forcing them to wrap around her arms, legs, and neck, tying her to the wall.

Nemsky loosed a howl of anger, at last overpowering the black mass. He thrust his arm at Joey, and powerful lamps illuminated him from behind. Turning, the dark cowboy dove to the ground to avoid a corporate armored personnel carrier. The eight-wheeled monster passed over him without harm and smashed into the wall. Seconds after impact, it reverted to a wireframe model and disappeared, leaving only smashed pipes in its wake.

Nina squirmed, but couldn't escape the force that held her to the wall. She screamed at Joey with genuine fear. He made a few clawing motions in midair, attempting to isolate and kill the program thread that immobilized her. Itai had forced her deck into an endless loop that ignored any input she attempted to send it. Joey triggered a memory reset. She became a Nina-shaped outline of bright white static for a second and reappeared with her wings back to normal. Stunned from the reboot, she clanked into the metal grating on all fours.

Joey dove to the right, dodging a large sparking electrical component Nemsky had torn from the wall and hurled. The part exploded into glimmering fragments that flowed over the wall and vanished.

Itai spun, sensing Nina's approach. He caught her again by the throat as she leapt. Her long black claws fell just short of his face while he held her aloft on an elongating arm.

His eyes glowed with black light, casting his face in violet, brighter and brighter as he built up energy for a deadly attack. Several ebon knives formed in Nina's hand and flew into Itai's chest. The attack seemed to cause a small amount of damage, but didn't deter his buildup.

Nemsky zoomed at Joey with a horrendous roar. The cowboy sidestepped with ease, giving the Russian a smirk as if he didn't have time to deal with him at that moment. Unable to stop, Anatoly wedged himself headfirst into the wall with a dull metallic *thud*.

"Itai!" yelled Joey, lifting his arms as if summoning up some sort of ancient, forsaken power.

The AI didn't look, assuming Joey was just trying to distract him from an easy kill.

A wave of phantasmal faces traced in glowing white energy crushed Itai off his feet. Joey shook with anger at the sight of Nina's imminent death, and pushed the Nishihama to the edge of its capabilities. He feared the Black ICE would kill her. Itai's use of it meant her deck was in bad shape. Knowing her brain was wired to a doll's power supply terrified him even more. The AI underestimated his opponent's strength. Surrounded by white flames, Itai came to a halt, embedded in a new crater in the wall. Steel and virtual cinder blocks warped like quicksand around the impact point. He flickered between the image of a man and a wireframe model. The attack had done enough damage to where the network attempted to remove him as a garbage file.

Nina slumped forward and sank her talons into the wall to avoid falling over. Gasping for breath, her face went from desperation to anger as she clenched her fist. Gloss onyx blades sprang from behind Itai, knocking him out of the hole. The AI rolled onto the ground like a log, still on fire. His voice scrambled into little more than a distorted, digitized warble as he stood with all the grace of a drunken infantryman. Itai eyed Joey's gun, holding his hands up. An instant later, his body blurred into a smear of color and rocketed off down the corridor.

"Let him go. D9's network team has this whole place surrounded. If he tries to go out into the GlobeNet, he's fucked." Nina coughed up black blood.

Nemsky rushed again, bellowing. They leapt out to either side. As the general ran headfirst into the wall for the second time, Joey summoned a Russian flag in his hands and waved it at him as if taunting a bull.

Anatoly growled. His next attack took the form of a rocket launcher. It went high, but the explosion knocked Joey chest-first to the floor. Nemsky advanced, but the imminent follow up stopped as Nina shredded into his side. She ducked his flailing arm, and gouged her hand into his abdomen. Hot blood gushed over her claws, an instant later becoming a spray of data fragments.

White light shone from Nemsky's eyes and a wail of agony flooded the hallway. Before Nina could tear her hand out of him, smoking skull bullets lanced into the upper part of the chest. Anatoly staggered back, straining to pull Nina's hands out of him. The old gunslinger leveled off one silver revolver at Nemsky's head.

Old lips curled into an evil smile. "Struggle, little mouse."

Boom.

The bullet entered the Russian's cheek, sucking him backward through the hole into a long tube of flesh colored data. The body reassembled itself, lying on the ground face down.

They exchanged a glance.

"Well, I'm awake!" The dark cowboy gurgled in as close to a humorous tone as he could.

She leaned on the wall. "We can track Itai down later, let's go get his dad."

Nina swayed on her feet. Her wings appeared wilted, her suit ripped in places.

The cowboy's mouth opened to speak, but he vanished with the sudden metallic *clank* of an APC drilling him into the wall. Bars, pipes, and tubes fell from above and bounced off the armored vehicle before rolling to a halt around it. The transport all but filled the corridor, and Joey's avatar was somewhere between it and the wall.

Nemsky pushed himself up with a low growl, his body reforming in a scintillating patchwork. Nina was gone. He staggered to the front of the APC, with a reverberating insane laugh. He put one hand on it, took a breath, and pushed it to the side with a horrendous squealing sound as four-foot tall tires stuttered over the metal floor. The dark cowboy lay mashed into a divot in the wall that matched his silhouette. Joey seemed dazed, but not too battered.

"Too late, friend. Guardian angel ran like little girl." Anatoly grabbed Joey by the neck.

Ten points of black pierced Nemsky's chest with a squish that left the big man motionless. The white haired cowboy glanced at the diaphanous claws before meeting the general's stare.

"Funny thing about black cats." The dark one's voice, thick and gritty, rolled out from a growing sneer. "It's bad luck to cross them, and you never see them coming."

He lifted both guns up to the disbelieving face, putting the barrels right in front of his nose. Anatoly's head detonated into a rain of blood and gore that morphed into glowing specks and text as it flew. The body melted into a substance that flowed like sand between Nina's fingers, seeping into the ground. Random echoes of Nemsky's protesting wails grew progressively more distorted until silence followed the last visible bits into oblivion.

Nina's talons shrank to normal hands. She pulled Joey out of the hole and into an embrace, shuddering for a moment before regaining her composure.

"You okay?" His appearance changed into his normal self.

"My deck's almost trashed. I don't think I'd be much help in there. You?"

He grinned. "Looks worse than it is. Proscion's deck is doing just fine; this thing's a monster."

Nina looked down the hall. "Something's coming."

"I see nothing." Joey shrugged.

"No, outside. Shinigami must have figured out where we are. Go, I'll deal with it." The ebon angel turned and vanished as she logged out, leaving Joey alone in cyberspace.

Just the way he liked it.

DOWNLOAD

A crid smoke obscured her vision and the scent of burnt electronics soured her throat. Wisps of it seeped upward from ventilation ports on the Netwraith, filling the small sunken room with a thick haze. Nina waved her arm, creating whorls in the grey fumes. The distant sound of particle beams and ballistic weapons continued, muted by the presence of the building around them. Joey slumped against the wall behind her in the deepest corner of the room. His consciousness elsewhere, no sign of the urgency with which he must be racing across the net showed. She ejected the M3 plug from the back of her neck via mental command and stretched the soreness from the virtual beating out of her body.

Clanking footsteps reminded her why she logged out. She moved to the small staircase, facing a hallway thick with smoke. On thermal, a humanoid outline of cold blue emerged within the roiling grey, holding a huge cylinder over its head.

Not waiting to see what the incoming android planned, she drew her sidearm and put two shots into the object it carried. With a screeching hiss, the canister rocketed backward. The bullet holes became thrust ports allowing compressed gas to drag the cyborg down the hallway in a jangling screech of tumbling metal. A thunderous *crash* followed, then the clanging of the cylinder bouncing deeper into the facility. An eight-foot skeletal silhouette fought its way clear of a debris pile, pushing broken pipes and beams aside. It lacked armor plating and still had several external wires and hoses hanging off it as though it had torn itself free of an assembly bay before its construction had completed.

Guess Shinigami's getting desperate.

Luminous green eyes in its plastisteel skull narrowed as it focused on her. She fired, landing nine shots in rapid succession into its chest as it charged. The slugs did little damage to the endoskeleton, though some components flew into fragments and a dark liquid oozed down its legs by the time it burst out of the end of the smoke and moved to attack.

The cyborg swatted at her, intending to dismiss the little woman that blocked it from its desired target. Nina dropped her gun and grabbed the incoming arm with both hands at the wrist, stopping the punch cold an inch away from her chest. The cyborg's eyes whirred wide with confusion, and then narrowed as it realized what she was. Vibro blades sprang out of its knuckles, sliding forward in slow motion to her boosted reflexes. Nina shoved back on the arm as hard as her body would allow.

The tips of the blades hung a half inch from her sternum, still in space as she flung the metal fist away at the same speed the claws extended. When they clicked and locked at full extension, she tossed the arm upward and leaned to the side to avoid a downward slash from the other hand. The blades sliced heavy overhead pipes as easily as if they had been made of thin plastic.

"Well, that was unexpected. I guess we both had a little surprise in store," said Itai's voice.

"So what's your game? What are you up to?"

She ducked a few more attacks before maneuvering behind him and landing a kick into his back that drilled him into the opposite wall.

"Just doing what I'm paid to do." He pushed himself out of the dent with a wrenching scrape.

Nina kept herself between him and Joey. "You're a program, you can't get paid."

He turned, throwing a section of pipe at her sideways. "Tell that to Warner."

She caught it, but the momentum knocked her off her feet. As cyborg Itai stomped at her, she used it like a quarterstaff and swept his legs out from under him. She stood, spun her new weapon, and jammed the end down at his head. He caught it in one hand, crimping it.

"Bullshit, I know Warner isn't involved."

"At least I'm my own entity, not a slave. Your body is nothing more than a shackle on your mind, keeping you at the end of the government's leash."

She jumped a kick aimed for her leg. He continued it into a maneuver that brought him upright, and ran for the alcove where Joey hid. Nina whirled the other way, shouting, and smashed the pipe flat across his chest as hard as she could. The metal bent around the cyborg like a rubber paddle as the impact lifted it off its feet and sent the flailing body careening into the same dented wall. Nina tossed the now-useless scrap to the side.

"Your love makes you weak." Itai muttered. His voice broke into digitization as sparks flew out of his twitching frame.

THE GLASSY BLACK CORRIDOR LED TO A DOOR OUTLINED IN NEON VIOLET. IT HAD taken Joey four tries to breach the barrier, and he adored the difficulty. On the other side, the processor node stretched out around a massive amethyst crystal fifty feet tall. It hovered, spinning, over a hole in the floor traced with glowing green circuit lines. Specks of light ran along the grooves, darting over the edge and down into oblivion. The mammoth gemstone rotated counterclockwise, spitting random bolts of violet and pink lightning into slabs of silicon that jutted from the ceiling above.

All around the hundred square yard room, display panels the size of billboards littered the walls. Clusters of black monoliths rose up from the ground before bending outward at the top where they glittered with controls, forming circular podiums by each display.

The giant crystal was the GlobeNet version of the CPU the node represented. Nothing appeared out of the ordinary save for a pleasant looking old man near the massive gem with his hands folded behind his back, like a tourist at a museum.

"Dad?" Joey walked in. "What the hell are you doing here?"

William Dillon turned with a smile. "Beautiful, isn't it?"

The dark cowboy frowned. "Nice try."

Two smoking skull bullets flew by where the elder Dillon had just been. Joey spun, freezing as Nina's ghostly outline crept into the room behind him. She looked worried.

The old gunslinger smirked again and fired at her. She tumbled out of the way and stood up, out of hiding.

"Joey? What the hell are you doing?" Her voice trembled as she backed into the wall.

He kept firing, chasing her to the side as he yelled. "You think I'm that stupid? I have her on comm. I know she's not here."

Nina's panic changed to the laughter of a deep male voice far beyond anything a human could produce. "Interesting, but ultimately futile."

The apparition shifted again, into Nemsky. He raised a hand to the sky and shadows fell on the old gunslinger. Joey leapt away from three APCs, which fell out of thin air above him one after the other, cratering the onyx floor with each impact.

He reached around to the back of his belt and pulled out a white enamel tanto. Joey smiled at it, and it turned into a golden gun with a gleaming pearl handle. Sighting over it, he smiled.

"Remember this?" His voice carried a paranormal echo. "Game over."

The blast of energy hit Nemsky in the chest and threw him backward, bouncing him off the crystal and sending him shattering through one of the podiums. Fragments of broken onyx floated up, drawn into the space around the CPU crystal, orbiting it. The smoking body changed into a featureless human shape composed of thousands of black triangles separated by thin blue lines.

Joey glanced down at the body. Not trusting it, he raised his guns. No sooner had he taken aim than the figure sprang into the air and he found himself looking at Kelly. The child Proscion floated before him in her cute pink dress and shiny shoes.

"Did you honestly think that I would have left Wantanabe's back door intact? Humans underestimate us still. How foolish to believe that an AI made to create AIs would be unable to alter itself." The thunderous voice shrank into the innocent giggle of a little girl. "You couldn't hurt me, could you?"

She pulled one of the pink ribbons from her white hair and threw it at him. It grew many times its size and width, binding his arms to his sides. After an unimpressed snort, the old one broke free and aimed again, but he would have been lying if he didn't admit to hesitating at least for a second.

Shinigami screamed like a child as it curled into a ball. Bullets bounced away from an invisible sphere around the cowering girl without harm. Unfolding herself, she giggled and vanished in a cloud of pink sparkles. Before Joey could turn, a severe impact to his back launched him through one of the consoles, exploding it like glass. As the he rolled out of the debris onto the floor, he looked up at the augmented horror that mangled Nina. He whistled some ancient bit of music as his hydraulic hammer fist retracted back into position.

"Beethoven's Fifth?" coughed Joey.

"Perhaps you find this easier to deal with than a child." The same inhuman voice laughed. "I had hoped to use this shape on your little friend." The room echoed with Nina's desperate pleas for Vincent. "I rather looked forward to probing her emotional response. I suspect I'll have to settle for recording her synaptic response to the sight of your lifeless body dangling from a smoking wire."

Joey fired as it approached. Bullets ricocheted off him with no effect. He couldn't tell if Shinigami flat out ignored him, or if this AI had so much power here that the damage he caused was trivial. He scurried to the right as the hammer came down, pulverizing what remained of the podium. The dark cowboy spun away and stood, aiming back at his sister, Katherine. She made a hand gesture that appeared not to do anything.

"What are you trying to do with that? Make it *easier* for me to kill you?" Joey fired without a trace of hesitation. "I can't stand that bitch, and I know this is VR."

Caught off guard, the AI appeared to bleed from a graze to the arm. The angry shriek of his sister's voice melted into a digitized battle cry. The image of Mark Bolt launched a barrage of missiles from its shoulders, sending Joey into one of the huge display screens at the edge of the room. He hit the wall like a rotten tomato, sticking for several seconds before sliding to the ground. On the way down, he crossed his arms to shield his face against the rain of obsidian daggers from the shattered panel overhead.

SOMEWHERE BEHIND NINA, JOEY TWITCHED AND MOANED, NEITHER GOOD SIGNS. When she looked, she noticed one of the transformers on the wall glowing like metal from a forge.

"Joey, something's overloading the transformer right next to you."

"He will die." Itai stomped toward her, raising his claws. "There is only the question of if his death shall be caused by me or by that which made me."

Nina feigned as if she wanted to catch his arms again. The instant he lunged, she dropped and slid on her knees between his legs, sprouting Nano claws and swiping to either side. The cyborg twisted and staggered as it turned to guard its back.

"What's the matter, Itai? I thought you wanted Joey? Are you afraid to turn your back on me?" She held her arms in a fighting stance. The edge of her transparent weapons caught the light and gleamed. "If you were a real Mossad agent, I might be worried, but you're only a training sim."

Itai growled and ran at her. She leapt straight up, slipping between his closing arms. Palming his metal skull with both hands, she vaulted over and landed behind him as he jammed his vibro blades into the wall. Itai tore them loose amid a shower of liquid from severed tubes. Nina darted toward him, dropping to the ground and bracing her hands on the floor as she sent a kick into the side of the cyborg's knee. The strike cracked the spot where her claws scored.

Itai flailed his arms, adjusting his balance to reduce stress on the damaged leg. She leapt at his side, but he palmed her chest and shoved. Sliding to a halt a few feet away, she resumed a ready stance.

"Is this where you try to talk me down, invite me in to be studied, maybe change sides and work for your Division 9?"

She took a casual step toward him, lowering her arms from a fighting posture. "It's a thought…" Her speedware kicked on and she slashed twice through his chest before he even perceived the motion. "…that I never considered. You cannot be trusted."

With a roar, he grabbed at her throat. She tried to leap away, but his hands closed around her hips. He spun to drill her face first into the wall. In her slow motion world, she severed his thumb with a quick flick of her claws. Centrifugal force yanked her out of his grip. She retracted her blades and somersaulted to the floor as the cyborg spun and lost his balance.

JOEY SURMISED THAT KATHERINE'S BIZARRE GESTURE REPRESENTED SHINIGAMI rerouting the power grid to overload the transformer. He ducked two streams of hostile data as he fought the network to send the surge elsewhere. When he looked back up, he found himself staring at a dozen ninja.

The dark cowboy weaved among the shadow army, killing one or two here and there as a silver snowstorm of shuriken fell around him. Shinigami had spawned rudimentary constructs only barely stronger than a garden-variety troll. One of them was the master AI, but which one?

Joey figured Shinigami calibrated this attack based on his last confrontation with Itai, before his deck upgrade. "So you data mined from bad Ninja vids? These guys suck."

Eventually, only two remained. One laughed before changing its appearance into Shabundo Ghede as the other melted away.

"Now what, voodoo zombies? Really?" The dark cowboy folded his arms and resumed a casual pose. "Try something original."

The sneer on the face of his adversary told Joey that had been the plan, but his sarcasm took the wind out of the AI's sails. The enraged Shinigami overloaded another transformer as it sent a curtain of wailing souls at him. The ancient gunslinger vanished and reappeared on the other side of the room, shaking his head at the phantasmal smear striking the wall.

"Wailing souls and smoke is *my* shtick." Joey shot him in the back twice, causing a growing white ripple to spread down Ghede's fancy suit. "I should sue for gimmick infringement."

Ghede turned with a roar and took on the appearance of Vincent raising his service weapon. Joey took a graze to the leg, but fell behind the cover of another podium. From the safety of hiding, he defused the second overload.

"Was that supposed to make me hesitate?" The old one popped up over the console and flung a bladed sphere into Vincent's forehead. The silver orb spat a stream of virtual blood. "I never even met that guy."

Vincent reached up and tore the weapon out. A gush of red painted his face. The wound closed and he crushed the metal ball before tossing it aside. Shinigami walked toward Joey's hiding place, shrinking into the form of Hayley. Barefoot, grimy, and in a pink shirt, she held the grungy Neko series deck across her chest and smiled at him.

A faint hiss drew Joey's eyes to the floor behind him. A one-foot tall blue cartoon mushroom stared at him with huge red eyes and fanged mouth. The dark cowboy's head tilted to the right as he appraised it with an unimpressed glance. He punted it away and it popped into a cloud of azure smoke when it hit the wall. Two more met a similar fate as the old one rose back to his feet and adjusted the lay of his hat.

Joey's real-world face grimaced at the thought of pointing a weapon at her, but the dark one only smiled. "You're not Hayley."

She screamed and cowered behind a console. He hesitated. As much as he knew he looked upon a false version of her, it felt wrong. At that size, Shinigami could hide inside the podiums and block itself off from view. Joey tilted his head forward and crossed his pistols over his chest. Once the routine loaded, he aimed his guns at the floor and fired a volley into the ground.

A torrent of smoking skull bullets ripped upward out of the floor below where the phony girl hid. The childlike scream turned into an inhuman roar as it dove out from its cover. A bloodied little girl stared at Joey with a pouty face before the cat eyes of her deck flared with intense pink light.

A massive swarm of white anime cats flooded around him, shredding at his legs. Despite their cute appearance, they were still the product of a dangerous AI. The little claws caused a surprising amount of damage to the howling gunslinger while he fought to get free from the bog of claws, fur, and cute demonic-faced cats with zigzag teeth.

He blinked out of existence and reappeared right behind Hayley. The false girl turned to face him, walking right into his hand around her throat. He squeezed, forcing himself to strangle what appeared to be an innocent child. Rather than a direct attack at the AI, he flooded the node with spoofed security data in an attempt to cause it to recognize Shinigami as a hostile entity. When it realized the pleading stare failed, it expanded into the image of Eldon and punched him in the side of the head, sending him flying.

Joey's head was the first point of contact with the ground. He tumbled over and slid on his back into another podium. Eldon pounced, grabbing Joey with both hands and spinning him around, using his face as a battering ram to shatter two more terminal objects before throwing him to the side. The cowboy flailed as chunks of data washed over him. A spider web of heat around his mind followed every impact.

"That's for makin' my ass go to the Badlands over and over and over again." Eldon pulled his rifle off his back and stared down at the black coat lying askew in a sea of broken glass.

Joey wobbled upright, coughing blood. "You got Eldon's mannerisms all wrong. The word 'man' should be in there somewhere. Still not believable."

He dusted himself off, sending obsidian flakes clattering to the ground before they vanished. Faux Eldon's growl fell away to digitization as he opened fire. The old gunslinger leapt behind a podium, avoiding the shot. When the attack stopped, the dark cowboy teleported to the other end of the room with one gun leveled off at Eldon. He loosed a single shot with a report and muzzle blast much greater than any he had yet fired.

The Magnum soft, version 4.4, magnified the strength of the attack. The recoil made the dark one take a step back upon shooting. Joey didn't often use other hacker's programs, but he was running out of ideas to hurt this godlike thing. Everything he had thrown at Shinigami seemed to do little more than annoy it.

The fist-sized smoking skull slammed into Eldon's chest, knocking him over a console. He tumbled and rolled to his feet in a single motion that continued into a backward stagger as yellow sparkling energy crawled across his armor.

As Eldon drew close to the CPU crystal, little sparks of lightning lapped at him. They didn't seem to have an effect, but at that moment, Joey had an epiphany.

ITAI STRUGGLED TO GET HIS CYBORG SHELL UPRIGHT. THE CRACK IN THE RIGHT LEG had grown from the torque of his attempt to throw Nina, threatening to break off at any moment. He clutched the piping on the walls, and pulled himself back to his feet, favoring the right. Nina dove again, claws extending, just as the robot turned to face the hallway. The clear blades pierced all the way through the thigh of his less damaged leg, causing a spray of lime green fluid.

A metal palm covered Nina's face as the AI's only instinct took over—survival. Fearing a crushed head, she leapt backward. Itai's intent wasn't to grab, he wanted to shove her away. The force of his arm added to her leap and she flew chest-first into the wall upside down, vanishing under a fall of pipes, wires, and liquid.

That exertion was the last stress the leg could tolerate. The plastisteel skeleton snapped just above the knee, sending him over sideways. The lower part dangled on by artificial muscles alone, flopping about when he tried to move it. With the Nano claws no longer an imminent threat, Itai sensed an opportunity. He clawed at the floor, cyborg fingers warping the metal grating as he dragged himself arm over arm to where Joey lay helpless. His progenitor had become worried and wanted this threat removed.

The machine slid down the steps into the smoky recess, reaching forward and grabbing a boot. If the steel face had lips, it would have smiled.

Itai's attempt to haul Joey into range of one fatal vibro blade failed. The arm fell in half at the elbow with a flash of transparent claws. Nina pounced on his back and drove both pairs into him with the ferocity of a lioness protecting her mate. Hardin's taunt about number three reverberated in the back of her mind as fear of losing him pulled tears from her eyes and the finesse from her attacks.

She savaged the cyborg's back in a flurry of uncoordinated rage. Stabbing, slashing, and raking, she shredded until the mutating voice from the head ceased and the metal body was a twisted ruin of parts. Remembering Nemsky's fondness for possum, she severed the head from the spine and then stomped on it. The chrome skull bent, silicon dust spewed out, and lightning spider-crawled across the floor. Nina stared at it until the eyes lost their glow.

Arms slack in her lap, Nina knelt on the wreckage. Olive green fluid dripped off her claws and soaked her face and chest. She stared at Joey, unsure if she should cry or laugh. Her mounting fear and worry fell away with the distraction of scraping noises from the hallway. She leapt to the stairway, gasping at the sight of dozens of smaller robots shambling up the hallway toward them. Most were class 1 or 2 maintenance bots, far weaker than the combat chassis Itai had inhabited.

Her claws snapped back into her arms as she took up a shooting position on the steps. She fired as fast as her targeting crosshair could go from one to the next. The massive handgun destroyed each unit with one well-placed round.

"Come on Joey, whatever you're gonna do, do it! 14 shots left."

Metal skulls exploded one after the next.

Others continued to climb into the hallway, streaming from the factory floor below.

Desperation saturated her voice. "Twelve!"

HER SHOUTING RANG CLEAR IN JOEY'S MIND. HE LOOKED AWAY FROM HER COMM channel image as Eldon tossed a hand grenade. Joey foiled the attack by killing the process thread before the device could go off, leaving an inert metal sphere on the ground at his feet.

Joey reappeared behind a console, trying to force Eldon closer to the crystal in search of a better shot. He peppered him with a few rounds, trying to destabilize the AI's program code, though he had a strong feeling now it had no effect. The AI used the massive CPU to repair itself as fast as he could damage it. Taking this thing on inside of a processor node had been a huge tactical blunder. However, Shinigami wouldn't willingly leave this node, and he had to stop it.

Nina sounded on edge, but in control. "Eight shots left, Joey, come on."

Shinigami's surface glowed for a second before shifting into an apparition of Kenny in his cowboy hat and brown duster coat. It grinned with anticipation, as it knew Joey couldn't resist a showdown.

Nina started to sound worried. "Four, come on!"

Joey evaded, weaving among the fragmented remains of terminals to foil "Kenny's" shots until the AI stood where he wanted him. Joseph Dillon walked out from behind a display, flicking his coat away from his now holstered guns. Kenny did the same, exposing his pistols with an adrenaline grin. They stared at each other for a moment. A tumbleweed rolled between them.

"Nice touch." The dark one smirked.

Kenny nodded. "Only the best for a friend."

Nina screamed. "Two rounds left, what the fuck is going on in there?"

The old one took a step left. Kenny circled right. Yellow teeth peeked out from behind a grin that spread across the dark cowboy's mouth. The silver discs that ringed his hat glinted purple in the light from the crystal as his eyebrows formed a solid flat line.

"Last mag. I only have twenty-two shots in this goddamned thing and there's four times as many robots coming for us. Joey!"

Nina yelled his name as loud as she could, at the edge of panic. He imagined her face looked calm. Four hands teased at the handles of guns as the walls flashed with pink-purple lightning. Neither man moved for an eternity.

"Seventeen! Please... Joey."

The tall one watched his friend's eyes, looking for any trace of an attack. Another weed drifted between them as a western style guitar effect filled the room.

"Ten. Joey we have to get out of here now! They're going to drop the hammer soon. There's four DS2s overhead. We're one 'clear' away from being screwed."

Kenny grinned. The dark cowboy's face remained cold and unemotional as his eyes narrowed into thin lines.

"Four!"

The old man drew and fired from the hip, causing Kenny to duck involuntarily. He turned his head as the smoking bullet streaked by his face. Shinigami's eyes widened with the realization that Joey hadn't fired at him. During the showdown, Joey had been writing code.

Splinters flaked from where the shot shattered into the surface of the crystal, causing a large dark spot at the center of the glowing mass. The darkness expanded through the massive gem on the heels of the spidering cracks that raced across its surface. When the fissures reached from end to end, the light within the crystal waned then died, leaving a dark violet hunk.

The flickering lightning stopped.

Shinigami turned, melting back into a shapeless humanoid form covered with blue lines. The high bandwidth connection the AI had maintained with the CPU had left him a route in. Joey's silver revolver transformed into Sho's golden gun, and he blew the smoke from the barrel.

"Guess you didn't get all of it."

As Joey lowered the weapon, the crystal exploded and flung the anemic ebon body to the other side of the massive chamber. It hit the wall, splattering out of humanoid form into a puddle of tar that oozed to the floor.

"They're falling over!" The anxiety in Nina's voice became relief. "Harold, call off the strike, Joey did it!"

Giant crystal chunks tumbled out of midair, sliding over each other on their way down. Some struck the rim of the opening before tumbling into the bottomless vertical shaft. The tar pool disintegrated into pixels. Bubbles formed as the same inhuman voice tried to scream, but gurgled as though it drowned in itself. Hands of black slime clawed at the air and sank into the still puddle. When the ground had absorbed the last of it, Joey hit his disconnect command and let himself fall into weightlessness.

***

HE SAT UP, GAGGING ON ACRID FUMES. HEAT RADIATED FROM COMPONENTS TO HIS left, the words 'high voltage' had drooped into a molten warp. Nina lay on the stairs a few feet away, kneeling with a two handed grip on her pistol. The air reeked of propellant and the sound of dozens of robotic dominos echoed out of the smoke. He looked at the severed metal hand clamped around his ankle. He pulled at the fingers but couldn't move it.

"Hon? Would you mind?" He whined at his smoking deck, forgetting about the metal hand.

She slung her weapon and fell on him, cuddling him against her until the clattering of tin soldiers ended. The combat outside wound down as well.

"Are you okay?" They both spoke at the same time.

"Yeah." Joey sighed.

Her answer took the form of a kiss.

Plucking the metal limb from his leg, she helped him to his feet. "Let's get the hell out of here."

"About that dinner we missed." Joey slung the Necromancer across his back.

Nina smiled. "Hardin's report can wait."

ACT CASUAL

The yard outside the factory lay strewn with the mangled remains of hundreds of cyborg bodies. The air, thick and caustic, carried the scent of molten plastisteel and NE6. Plumes of smoke churned out of glowing craters where particle beams melted the city plates. The DS2s continued to circle overhead, no longer firing. Division 5 troops chest-bumped and whooped out front. One or two still wasted ammo on dead cyborgs.

They emerged from a loading gate, trudging out of rolling black vapors and into the metal carnage. Joey held a sleeve over his mouth in a futile attempt to block the scathing fumes from his lungs.

A few shots echoed from the distant rear of the factory where a handful of cyborgs that had been loaded with AIs, not simply run remotely, still slugged it out with the military. The wall of police at the front opened, cheering, giving them space to walk away from the facility. Nina glanced at where the crowd of evacuated StarPoint employees assembled. A group of line workers, techies, office personnel, executives, janitors, and secretaries all stood around in various stages of panic.

Hardin hopped out of a black A3V and walked over.

"Nice job, Duchenne." He gave Joey a brief glance. "That was pretty impressive work there young man. We might have a use for someone with your talents."

Joey glanced at Nina and blinked. The sheer irony of someone with his views on government working *for* them was almost too good to pass up, not to mention the allure of the potential danger. As Hardin discussed minutiae with Joey, Nina closed her eyes and sent a command to her unmarked patrol craft, causing it to autopilot to her location.

"I'm listening." Joey put his arm around Nina's back.

Hardin nodded. "Let's talk in a day or two and you can tell me about Mars." He took a step toward the truck, but turned with more to say. "Oh, by the way… you won't be her partner or anything like that even if things work out. You'll be in separate departments."

He grinned. "No problem, I heard she has trouble hanging on to them anyway."

She shot him a surprised and somewhat hurt look and dragged him over by a fistful of his collar. The silly expression he gave her changed the accusatory glance to a sigh of sad humor. She kissed him full on the lips and changed her grip into a tight hug.

"I'm not losing this one."

Hardin turned away. "I have a sneaking suspicion that your report is going to be late?"

Nina flipped him off while his back was turned, making a few of the Division 5 officers laugh. They kissed for a long minute, and then stared into each other's eyes while the patrol craft kicked up a cloud of dust as it settled in to a gentle landing between them and the factory.

"Steak or seafood?" Nina tilted her head.

He kissed her again. "Steak, definitely."

The crowd of evacuees peppered the police with questions. One sobbing secretary in the rear of the crowd backed away from everyone as if the sounds of silence frightened her more than the fighting. As she slid out of sight away from the chaos, her panic-stricken demeanor gave way to perfect calm. Her walk changed from fearful scurry to confident strut. The slender blonde adjusted her suit jacket to hide a blood stain as an amethyst glow shone from electronic eyes.

She vanished into the endless night of West City.

fin

ACKNOWLEDGMENTS

Thank you for reading *Virtual Immortality.*
  Additional thanks to Mark Woodring for editing.
  Dean Samed for an amazing cover.
  RC, Ed, and Pam for character inspiration.

ABOUT THE AUTHOR

Originally from South Amboy NJ, Matthew has been creating science fiction and fantasy worlds for most of his reasoning life. Since 1996, he has developed the "Divergent Fates" world, in which *Division Zero, Virtual Immortality, The Awakened Series, The Harmony Paradox, and the Daughter of Mars series* take place. Along with being an editor at Curiosity Quills press, he has worked in IT and technical support.

Matthew is an avid gamer, a recovered WoW addict, Gamemaster for two custom RPG systems, and a fan of anime, British humour, and intellectual science fiction that questions the nature of reality, life, and what happens after it.

He is also fond of cats.

Visit me online at:
 Facebook: https://www.facebook.com/MatthewSCoxAuthor
 Amazon: https://www.amazon.com/author/mscox
 Pinterest: https://www.pinterest.com/matthewcox10420/
 Goodreads: https://www.goodreads.com/author/show/7712730.Matthew_S_Cox
 Email: mcox2112@gmail.com

The Roadhouse Chronicles Series
One More Run
The Redeemed
Dead Man's Number

Faded Skies series
Heir Ascendant
Ascendant Unrest
Ascendant Revolution

Chiaroscuro: The Mouse and the Candle

Temporal Armistice Series
Nascent Shadow
The Shadow Collector

Wayfarer: AV494

Axillon99

Vampire Innocent series
A Nighttime of Forever
A Beginner's Guide to Fangs
The Artist of Ruin
The Last Family Road Trip

Operation: Chimera (with Tony Healey)

The Dysfunctional Conspiracy (with Christopher Veltmann)

Winter Solstice series (with J.R. Rain)
Convergence
Containment

Alexis Silver series (with J.R. Rain)
Silver Light
Deep Silver

Samantha Moon Origins series (with J.R. Rain)
New Moon Rising
Moon Mourning

Maddy Wimsey series (with J.R. Rain)
The Devil's Eye
The Drifting Gloom

Samantha Moon Case Files series (with J.R. Rain)
Blood Moon
Dead Moon

The Far Side of Promise anthology

Young Adult
Caller 107
The Summer the World Ended
Nine Candles of Deepest Black
The Eldritch Heart
The Forest Beyond the Earth
Out of Sight

Middle Grade
Tales of Widowswood series
Emma and the Banderwigh
Emma and the Silk Thieves
Emma and the Silverbell Faeries
Emma and the Elixir of Madness
Emma and the Weeping Spirit

Citadel: The Concordant Sequence
The Cursed Codex
The Menagerie of Jenkins Bailey
Sophie's Light

www.ingramcontent.com/pod-product-compliance
Lightning Source LLC
Chambersburg PA
CBHW060215030726
47499CB00004B/1056